THE MAIAS

The Maia family, rich, noble, cultivated and idealistic, is reduced to a single heir – Carlos Eduardo. On him, after two generations of frustrated ambition and one of tragedy, the patriarch Afonso da Maia pins all his hopes for the revival of the family name.

At first the future of young Carlos seems full of promise. Having received the best possible education, and having moved widely in London and Paris society, his sense of duty and ambition call him home to Lisbon, where, he plans a brilliant career in his chosen profession, medicine, and in the arts and politics, for he is also an aesthete and a reformer. But the lethargy and moral corruption which permeate every level of Lisbon society prove too strong for him.

By an appalling coincidence, Carlos Eduardo falls in love with his own sister, Maria Eduarda, who disappeared from Lisbon as an infant with her runaway mother and has now returned to her birthplace, grown-up, beautiful and quite unaware of her parentage. Their love affair draws to its terrible climax of discovery against the background of a Lisbon peopled with poets, diplomats, politicians and dandies living out the last years of a doomed monarchy.

Eça de Queiroz's characteristic irony and lively satirical sense make this dramatic account of incest and moral collapse modern in both its form and impact.

The MAIAS

EÇA DE QUEIROZ

TRANSLATED BY
Patricia McGowen Pinheiro
AND Ann Stevens

ST. MARTIN'S PRESS, New York

BOOK

1

THE LISBON HOUSE into which the Maias moved in the autumn of 1875 was known in the neighbourhood of Rua de São Francisco de Paula, and throughout the district of Janelas Verdes, as Ramalhete – the House of the Bouquet. Despite the evocative freshness of its name, Ramalhete was a sombre mansion with gloomy walls, a row of narrow iron balconies on the first floor, and above them a line of small windows sheltering under the edge of the roof. It had the mournful look of an ecclesiastical residence, befitting a building constructed in the reign of Her Majesty Dona Maria I; only a bell and a cross on the rooftop were wanting for it to look like a Jesuit college. The house had got its name because there was a square of figured tiles in the form of a panel displaying a big bunch of sunflowers tied with a ribbon, on which letters and a date could be made out, in the place normally set aside for the coat of arms, which had never been put up.

Ramalhete had been empty for very many years. There were cobwebs among the grilles of the little ground-floor windows and the place looked as though it would fall into ruin. In 1858 Monseigneur Buccarini, the papal nuncio, had visited it with the idea of establishing the Papal Embassy there. He had been attracted by the clerical gravity of the edifice and the somnolent peace of the district. The mansion's interior had pleased him too, with its palatial layout, its panelled ceilings, its walls covered with frescoes where the wreaths of roses and the faces of little cupids were already fading. But Monseigneur, who had the tastes of a wealthy Roman prelate, required to be surrounded by the groves and pools of a luxurious garden. And all Ramalhete could boast was a poor, untended yard at the end of a tiled terrace that had been abandoned to weeds, with a cypress, a cedar, a dried-up fountain, a tank filled with rubbish and a marble statue – which Monseigneur at once recognized as the Venus of Cythera – blackening in a corner in the slow damp of the wooded branches. Moreover, the rent asked by old Vilaça, the Maias' steward, seemed to Monseigneur so excessive that he inquired with a smile whether the steward thought the Church was still living in the times of Leo X, to which Vilaça replied that the nobility was no longer living in the time of His Majesty Dom João V either. And Ramalhete had remained uninhabited.

This white elephant – as it was called by Vilaça junior, who had succeeded his father as the Maias' steward – only became useful once more towards the end of 1870 when it was transformed into a storehouse for furniture and crockery from the family mansion at Benfica, an almost historic residence, which had just been bought by a rich Brazilian after being on the market for years. About the same time another property of the Maias, the Tojeira, was also sold; and some of the few people left in Lisbon who could still remember the Maias, and knew that since 1851 they had withdrawn to their country seat at Santa Olávia on the banks of the Douro, had begun to ask Vilaça if the family were in financial difficulties.

'They've still got a crust of bread,' Vilaça had smiled, 'and the butter to spread on it.'

The Maias were an old Beira family. They had never been very numerous. There were few relations and no collateral lines, and they were now reduced to two males: the head of the house, Afonso da Maia, an old man, almost a patriarch, older than the century itself; and his grandson, Carlos, who was studying medicine at Coimbra. When Afonso had retired to Santa Olávia the family income had been more than 50,000 cruzados; but since that time the economies of twenty years in the country-side had accumulated. There had also been an inheritance from a last relation, Sebastião da Maia, who had been living on his own in Naples since 1830 occupying himself with numismatics – and so the steward was certainly in a position to smile with assurance when he talked of the Maias and their crust of bread.

As a matter of fact, Tojeira had been sold on Vilaça's advice, but he had never approved of Afonso's disposing of Benfica simply to be rid of a place whose walls had seen so many family tragedies. Such things, said Vilaça, were common to walls. And so now the Maias, with Ramalhete uninhabitable, no longer had a house in the capital. Although Afonso, at his age, loved the peace of Santa Olávia, his grandson, a young man of taste and fashion who spent his holidays in Paris and London, would not wish to go and bury himself in the Douro hills after he graduated.

8

And in fact some months before Carlos left Coimbra, Afonso astonished Vilaça by announcing that he had decided to come and live in Ramalhete! The steward at once drew up a report listing the inconveniences of the place. The greatest was the need for so much repair-work and expense; then the lack of a garden would be felt keenly by anyone coming from the woods of Santa Olávia; and finally, Vilaça mentioned the legend that the walls of Ramalhete had always been fatal to the Maias – 'Although,' he added carefully, 'I am almost ashamed to mention such trifles in this century of Voltaire, Guisot and other liberal philosophers.'

Afonso laughed heartily at these words, and replied that they were all excellent reasons – but he still wanted to live under a roof that had been in his family for generations; if repairs were required, then they should be made, and without counting the cost; and as far as legends and auguries were concerned all that was needed was to throw open the windows wide and let the sunlight in.

Orders were orders – and as the winter was a dry one, work started at once under the direction of a certain Esteves, architect, politician and kinsman of Vilaça. This artist inspired the steward with a project for a spectacular staircase, flanked by two figures symbolizing the conquests of Guinea and India. He was also planning a china fountain in the dining-room when Carlos unexpectedly appeared in Lisbon accompanied by an interior decorator from London. After hastily looking over a few ideas and the colours of some fabrics with him, he handed the four walls of Ramalhete over to the Englishman, to fashion as he wished a comfortable interior of intelligent and sober luxury.

Vilaça bitterly resented this slight to the national artist and Esteves went to his political club shouting that the country was lost. Afonso, too, lamented the dismissal of Esteves and even insisted that he should be charged at least with the construction of the coach-houses. The artist was about to accept when he was named civil governor.

At the end of a year, during which Carlos often visited Lisbon to assist in the work, 'to add his aesthetic touches', nothing of Ramalhete remained except its mournful façade, and this Afonso would not have changed for, he said, it made the character of the house. Even Vilaça was not slow to admit that Jones Bule –

9

as he called the Englishman – had made a showpiece of Ramalhete, and without undue expenditure and by using the antiques from Benfica.

What immediately took the eye was the patio, once so gloomy and bare, and paved with stones, and now resplendent with a floor of white and red marble squares, decorative plants, Quimper vases and two long antique benches that Carlos had brought from Spain, hand-carved and as solemn as a cathedral choir. In the ante-chamber above, hung like a draper's with oriental stuffs, every footstep was muffled. It was filled with divans covered with Persian rugs, and broad Moorish copper dishes that shone metallically – a harmony of severe tones in which stood forth the immaculate white marble figure of a shivering girl drawing back smiling as she put her little foot in the water. A broad corridor led off this ante-chamber. In it were pieces from Benfica: Gothic chests, large vases from India and old religious paintings. Ramalhete's best rooms opened off this gallery. The drawing-room, rarely used, all in velvet brocades, the colour of autumn moss, contained a fine Constable: the portrait of Afonso's mother-in-law, the Countess de Runa, in a feathered tricorn hat and the scarlet dress of an English huntswoman, against a misty landscape. A smaller room alongside was for music-making. It had an eighteenth-century air about it with its gilt-ornamented furniture and brightly flowered silks. Two faded Gobelin tapestries in grey tones covered the walls with shepherds and woodlands.

In the front was the billiards-room, lined with a modern leather brought by Jones Bule, on which silver storks took flight among a profusion of bottle-green branches. Beside it was the smoking-room, the most comfortable room in Ramalhete. Its ottomans had the soft breadth of couches, and the warm and somewhat sombre cosiness of the scarlet and black fabrics was brightened by the singing colours of old Dutch china.

At the end of the corridor was Afonso's study, hung with red damask like the chamber of some old prelate. The massive table of ebony, low bookshelves of carved oak, the stern luxury of the bindings: everything there had a lofty air of studious peace – further emphasized by the presence of a painting attributed to Rubens; an old family heirloom, of a crucified Christ, his athlete's nakedness outlined against a fiery and troubled sunset.

At the side of the fireplace Carlos had set up a corner for his grandfather with a Japanese screen embroidered in gold, a white bearskin rug, and a venerable armchair whose tapestry still showed the Maia arms in the faded weave of the silk.

Off the second-floor corridor hung with family portraits were Afonso's rooms. Carlos had his own apartment in an angle of the house, with a private entrance and windows on to the garden. There were three rooms opening one on to the other, doorless and unified by the same carpet. The quilted furniture, the silk-covered walls, made Vilaça remark that these were not the rooms of a doctor – but of a chorus-girl!

After it had been put in order the house continued to stand empty while Carlos, who had by now graduated, took a long trip across Europe. It was only on the eve of his return, in that splendid autumn of 1875, that Afonso at last made up his mind to leave Santa Olávia and settle in Ramalhete. It was twenty-five years since he had been in Lisbon; and after a few days he confessed to Vilaça that he was already missing the cool shades of Santa Olávia. But what could he do! He did not want to live too far from his grandson; and Carlos, who had serious projects for an active career, had to live in Lisbon. Not that Afonso disliked Ramalhete, though Carlos, with his passion for the comfort of cold climates, had been rather too lavish with the tapestries, heavy curtains and velvets. He found the neighbourhood very agreeable too – gentle, sleepy and quiet in the sunshine. He even liked the little garden. It was not like the garden at Santa Olávia, of course. But it had a pleasant air, with its tall, straight sunflowers near the terrace steps, the cypress and the cedar growing old together like two sad friends, and the Cytheran Venus, clean and white once again like a statue in a park looking as though it had come from Versailles, straight out of the eighteenth century. And now that water abounded, the little fountain in its niche of shells was delightful, with its three rocks placed like a rustic waterfall, saddening the depth of the sunny garden with the sobbing of a household naiad as it fell drop by drop into a marble bowl.

What had upset Afonso at first had been the loss of the view from the terrace, a view that must at one time have stretched right out to sea. But the houses built round about in recent years had shut off that splendid vista. Now a narrow strip of water and hill, that could be glimpsed between two five-storey buildings separated by the width of the street, was all the landscape in front of Ramalhete. Nevertheless, Afonso ended up by discovering that it had an intimate charm of its own. It was like a seascape, framed in white masonry, hanging from the blue sky before the terrace, in which were pictured, in infinite variations of colour and light, all the fleeting episodes of the quiet life of the river. Sometimes it would be the sail of a boat from Trafaria tacking airily into the wind; at others a three-master with all sails set in a favourable breeze, entering the river slowly in the red of the evening; or perhaps the melancholy of a great packet-boat, coming down, all closed in and ready for the waves, seen for a moment, then gone as though already devoured by the uncertain sea; or sometimes, for days on end, in the dusty gold of the silent afternoon, the dark shape of an English cruiser. And always beyond was the piece of dark-green hill, with a windmill motionless on its summit, and beside the water two white houses, so expressive – sometimes sparkling and throwing off rays from their windows alight with fire; sometimes taking on a pensive air as they became covered in the pale pinks of the sunset at the end of the afternoon, almost like living rosy cheeks; while on rainy days they shuddered sadly, so alone, so white and bare under the rude weather.

Three glass doors opened on to the terrace from the study and it was there in that splendid prelate's chamber that Afonso soon got used to spending his days in the cosy nook his grandson had lovingly made ready for him beside the fireplace. The old man's long years in England had given him a love for restful hours by the fireside. In Santa Olávia the fires had always been kept alight till April; and after that they would be filled with armfuls of flowers like household altars. It was there, beside the hearth in that scented freshness, that he best enjoyed his pipe, his Tacitus or his beloved Rabelais.

But Afonso was still far from being a fireside cat, as he called it. Even at his age, winter or summer, he would be up at daybreak and off out into the grounds immediately after his morning ritual of a good soaking in cold water. He had always had a superstitious love of water; and he would say there was nothing better for man than the taste of water, the sound of water and the sight of water. What he loved most about Santa Olávia was its great wealth of running water: springs, fountains, the tranquil mirror of still pools, the murmur of water irrigating the land. And to this addiction of his he attributed his lifelong good health, without an ache or a pain, in the splendid tradition of his family: tough, resistant to misfortune and time – which passed him by with as little mark as the years and the gales had left on the oaks of Santa Olávia.

Afonso was rather short and thick-set, with strong, square shoulders. His broad face with its aquiline nose, rosy, almost red, complexion, and long, snowy, pointed beard, recalled – Carlos said – a hero of old, a Dom Duarte de Meneses or an Afonso d'Albuquerque. And the old man would laugh as he reminded his grandson jokingly how deceiving appearances were.

No, he was no Meneses, nor an Albuquerque: merely a benevolent patriarch who loved his books, the cosiness of his armchair, and a game of whist beside the fire. He himself would say that he was simply an egoist – but the generous impulses of his heart had never been as deep and wide as now in his old age. A good part of his income poured through his fingers in warm acts of charity. He was growing ever fonder of all that was poor, all that was defenceless. In Santa Olávia the children would run to him from the doorways knowing him to be affectionate and patient. And all living things had a claim on his love: he was a man who would not tread on an ant-heap and who spent pity on the thirst of a plant.

Vilaça said that he reminded him of all that had ever been said of patriarchs when he found Afonso in the chimney corner, in his well-worn velvet jacket, serene, smiling, with a book in his hand and his old cat at his feet. The enormous, heavy Persian, white with golden patches, was now Afonso's faithful companion. He had been born in Santa Olávia and had been named Bonifácio. Then, when he reached the age of love and hunting, he was given the more courtly title of Dom Bonifácio de Calatrava. Now, somnolent and obese, he had finally entered the retirement of an ecclesiastical dignitary and had become the Reverend Bonifácio.

Afonso's existence had not always flowed like a lovely summer river with such limpid and tranquil clarity. This old man, whose eyes now rested tenderly on his roses, and who sat beside the fire relishing his rereading of Guisot, had once been regarded by his father as the most ferocious Jacobin in Portugal! The wretched youth's revolutionary fervour had consisted in reading Rousseau, Volney, Helvetius and the Encyclopedia; in shedding cascades of tears over the Constitution; in sporting the hat and high blue necktie of a liberal; and in reciting abominable odes to the Supreme Architect of the Universe in the Masonic lodges. This had been quite enough to outrage his father, however. Caetano da Maia was an old-fashioned and loyal Portuguese. He crossed himself whenever the name of Robespierre was mentioned, and, in the apathy of a pious and invalid aristocrat, he felt only one sentiment keenly: horror, hatred of the Jacobins to whom he attributed all the ills that beset either his country or himself – from the loss of the colonies to his attacks of gout. To sweep the Jacobins from the land he had given his allegiance to the Infante Dom Miguel, the chosen Messiah and Restorer. And now to have a Jacobin for a son seemed to him a trial comparable only with those of Job!

At first he had hoped that the boy would mend his ways, and he had contented himself with putting on a stern face and addressing him sarcastically as 'Citizen'. But when it reached his ears that his son and heir had been among the mob that had stoned the darkened windows of the Austrian Legate, the envoy of the Holy Alliance, on a night of civic festivity, the boy seemed to him a very Marat, and all his rage exploded. The cruel gout which kept him to his couch did not permit him to flog the Freemason with his Indian walking-stick, in the manner of a good Portuguese father, but he made up his mind to turn him out of his house, penniless and unblessed, disowned like a bastard!

But he was softened by a mother's tears – and above all by the reasoning of a sister-in-law of his wife's who lived with them at Benfica, a highly-educated Irish lady, a respected household Minerva, who had taught English to the boy and adored him as though he were a baby. Caetano da Maia limited himself to exiling his son to the family estate at Santa Olávia. But he continued to lament over the family shame to the priests who frequented his house at Benfica. And those saintly men comforted him, telling him that God, the old God of Portugal, would never permit a Maia to make a compact with Beelzebub and the Revolution! And should God the Father fail to perform a blessed miracle there was always Our Lady of Soledade, the patroness of the house and to whom the boy had been dedicated.

The miracle came to pass. Some months later the Jacobin, the Marat, returned somewhat chastened from Santa Olávia, weary especially of its solitude, where the teas of Brigadier Senna were even more tedious than the prayers of the Cunha cousins. He came and asked for his father's blessing and a few thousand cruzados, so that he could go to England, that land of bright fields and golden heads, of which he had heard his aunt speak so often. With tears in his eyes his father embraced him and agreed fervently to everything, for he had at once perceived the glorious intercession of Our Lady of Soledade! And Father Jeronimo da Conceição himself, his confessor, declared this to be a miracle, in no way inferior to that of Carnaxide.

Afonso departed. It was in springtime, and in England everything was green. England's fashionable parks, its copious comforts, the pervading harmony of all its noble customs, that race so strong and so earnest – all these enchanted him. He quickly forgot his loathing for the surly priests, his fiery hours spent in the café reciting Mirabeau, and the Republic that he had wanted to establish, classical and Voltairean with a triumvirate of talent and festivals in honour of the Supreme Being. During the days of the Aprilist revolt he was at Epsom, at the races, on top of a mail-coach, equipped with a huge false nose and uttering hoarse cheers – quite forgetful of his Masonic brothers, who, at that very hour, were being beaten down by the Infante Dom Miguel on his wiry Arab charger through the alleys of the Bairo Alto.

His father's sudden death obliged him to return to Lisbon. There he became acquainted with Dona Maria Eduarda Runa, daughter of the Count de Runa, a lovely dark-eyed girl, loving and fragile. They were married as soon as he came out of mourning. One son was born and he looked forward to another. He was immediately filled with the grandiose projects of a youthful patriarch: to redecorate the Benfica mansion, plant trees around it, and prepare roofs and shades for his beloved offspring who would later delight his old age.

15

But he could not forget England. It drew him all the more because of what he saw in Dom Miguel's Lisbon, as disorderly as barbarian Tunis: a motley of monks and coachmen filling the taverns and chapels with their shouting; the pious multitude, wild and dirty, surging from church to bullring, and clamouring after the prince who so perfectly personified their own vices and passions.

The spectacle outraged Afonso da Maia, and often on peaceful evenings among friends, with the little boy on his knee, he would vent the indignation of his honest soul. Of course he no longer insisted as he had in his youth on a Lisbon full of great men. He could even accept the idea that an aristocracy had the right to guard its historic privileges; but it must be an intelligent and deserving aristocracy, like the Tory nobility that his love for England led him to romanticize), a nobility that gave moral leadership, informing custom and inspiring literature, living graciously and speaking with taste, a model of high ideals and a mirror for practical exploits. What he could not countenance was the bestial and sordid world of the Queluz Court.

These words had scarcely been uttered than they reached Court. And when the Cortes assembled the police invaded Benfica 'in search of documents and hidden weapons'. Alfonso da Maia, with his son in his arms and his wife trembling at his side, watched the search impassively and without a word – the drawers burst open by rifle-butts, the dirty hands of the informer exploring the mattresses of his bed. The investigating judge could find no case against him – and in the butler's pantry he even accepted a glass of wine and confessed to the major-domo that 'times were rather hard'. After that morning the windows of the mansion were kept sealed and the main gate was opened no more for the lady's coach. A few weeks later Afonso da Maia, accompanied by his wife and son, was on his way to England and to exile.

There he settled in luxury for a long stay on the outskirts of London, near Richmond, at the bottom of a park among the gentle and serene fields of Surrey.

Thanks to the influence of the Count de Runa, a former favourite of Queen Carlota Joaquina, and now a stern counsellor of Dom Miguel, his property had not been sequestrated, and Afonso da Maia was able to live on a lavish scale.

At first he was pestered and tormented by the liberal emigrés. But it was not long before his upright soul revolted against the evidence he saw of class and hierarchial divisions maintained there on foreign soil among defeated supporters of the same ideal: the nobles and judges living in ease and luxury in London while the commoners, the troops, after their tribulations in Galicia, now lay victims of hunger, vermin and fever in the Plymouth camps. Right away he clashed with the Liberal leaders and was accused of being a radical and an idealist. And he ended by disillusionment with Liberalism. And so he cut himself off, although he never shut his purse to them, and alms would be distributed in objective open-handedness. But when the first expedition set off, and little by little the groups of emigrés began to disperse, he breathed at last – and, as he put it, he enjoyed English air for the first time!

Some months later his mother, who had stayed behind at Benfica, died of apoplexy; and his aunt came to Richmond to complete Afonso's happiness with her lucid wisdom, her white curls and her discreet Minerva-like ways. And there he was, living the life he had dreamed of, in a noble English residence, among centuries-old trees, surrounded by vast lawns where well-fed cattle drowsed and grazed; and he felt that everything around him was so salubrious, so sturdy, so free and so solid – just what his heart had wished for.

He entered English society. He studied England's rich and noble literature. He concerned himself, as befitted a nobleman in England, with culture, with horse-breeding and with charitable works. And he looked forward pleasurably to settling down for good to that peaceful and ordered existence.

But Afonso sensed that his wife was unhappy. Pensive and sad, she coughed incessantly through the house. In the evening she sat by the fireside sighing and silent.

Poor woman! Homesickness, longing for her relations and her churches undermined her. A true Lisboan, small and dark, uncomplaining and smiling wanly, since her arrival she had lived in suppressed hatred of that land of heretics and their barbarous language; always shivering and smothered in furs, gazing with horror at the glowering skies or at the snow-laden trees, her heart had never been there, but far away, in Lisbon, in the churchyards, in the streets drenched with sunlight. Her piety – the piety of the Runas – had always been considerable. Now it exalted itself, exacerbated itself in that hostility she sensed all about her against the 'papists'. And it was only at night that she was content, when she went up to the attic to take refuge with the Portuguese maidservants and to say the rosary kneeling on a straw mat, and to enjoy, in that murmur of *Ave Marias* in a Protestant country, the delights of a Catholic conspiracy.

She detested everything that was English and would not agree to her son, Pedrinho, attending school at Richmond. In vain did Afonso assure her that it was a Catholic school. She would not have it. Catholicism without pilgrimages, without fireworks on the feast of São João, without images of Our Lord of Calvary, without monks in the streets – for her this was not religion. She could never surrender Pedrinho's soul to such heresy; and she sent to Lisbon for Father Vasques, chaplain to the Count de Runa, to come and be the boy's tutor.

Vasques taught the boy Latin declensions and, above all, the Catechism. And Afonso da Maia's face filled with sadness as he returned from hunting or from town, from the free world outside, and heard the sleepy, sepulchral voice of the priest in the study questioning the boy:

'How many enemies has the soul?'

And the little boy, sleepier even than his tutor, could be heard murmuring:

'Three. The world, the flesh and the devil.'

Poor Pedrinho! The only enemy his soul had there was the Reverend Vasques, obese and sloppy, belching in the depths of his armchair, with his snuff-box on his knee.

Sometimes Afonso became indignant, entered the room, interrupted the doctrine lessons and grasped Pedrinho by the hand – to take him to run alongside him under the trees by the Thames, there to dissipate in the wide light of the river the gross burden of the Catechism. But Mama would come outside in terror to wrap him in a huge coat – and, besides, the little boy, who was accustomed to cosy nooks and to the laps of the maidservants, was fearful of the wind and the trees. Gradually the two would slow to a disconsolate pace, and silently walk through the dry leaves: the son in dread of the shadows in the living wood; the father with slumped shoulders, thoughtful and saddened by that weakness in his child.

The least attempt to tear the boy from the coddling mother's arms, or from the deadly Catechism of Father Vasques, at once laid the delicate lady low with a bout of fever. And Afonso no longer dared to thwart the poor invalid, who was so virtuous and who loved him so! He would go and pour out his troubles to his aunt; the wise Irishwoman would put her glasses between the pages of her book – a treatise of Addison's or a poem of Pope's – and sadly shrug her shoulders. What could she do?

At last Maria Eduarda's cough worsened – and so did the sadness of her words. She already talked of her last wish, which was to see the sun once again! Why could they not return to Benfica, to their home, now that the Infante was himself exiled and there was peace? But Afonso could not agree. He did not want to see his cupboards burst open again by rifle-butts – and the soldiers of Dom Pedro could give him no greater assurances than had the police of Dom Miguel.

About that time a great sadness came to the house: Aunt Fanny died of a pneumonia in the chills of March; and this further darkened Maria Eduarda's melancholia for she too had loved her very much – because she was Irish and a Catholic.

To distract her thoughts Afonso took her to Italy, to a delightful villa near Rome. There was no lack of sunshine there; punctual and generous, it rose each morning to bathe the terraces all over and gild the laurels and myrtles. And then, down below, among the marbles, was that precious and saintly object – the Pope!

But the wretched lady went on complaining.

What she longed for was Lisbon, with its novenas, the devout saints of her own district, the processions going by in a murmur of lazy penitence through the sunny, dusty afternoons.

She had to be consoled and taken home to Benfica.

Life there was dreary. Maria Eduarda slowly wasted away, paler with every day that passed, lying for weeks motionless on her couch, her transparent hands crossed on the thick furs brought from England. Father Vasques took control of the frightened soul for whom God was a terrible master, and he became the great man of the house. For that matter, Afonso met other canonical figures in the corridors all the time: he recognized Franciscans of former days in cloaks and sandals, or some thin Capuchin who lived off the district. The house smelled like a musty sacristy; and from his wife's room came the constant murmur, doleful and vague, of the litany.

All those saintly men ate, drank and took his port in the pantry. The steward's accounts became overburdened with the pious monthly allowances the lady paid out: a certain Father Patricio had even talked her into two hundred top-quality masses for the soul of an eighteenth-century king.

The atmosphere of bigotry surrounding him threw Afonso into resentful atheism. He wanted to close down churches as well as monasteries; to break up images of saints with an axe; to massacre the priests. When he heard the sound of praying in the house he fled, and went to the bottom of the park under the ivies of the belvedere to read his Voltaire; or else he would go off to confide his woes to his old friend Colonel Sequeira, who lived on an estate at Queluz.

Pedro, meanwhile, was reaching manhood. He remained small and nervous like Maria Eduarda, and showed little of the Maia strength; his lovely, oval face with its warm, dark complexion, two marvellous and irresistible eyes that were ever-ready to melt, made him resemble a beautiful Arab. He developed slowly, without curiosity, indifferent to toys, animals, flowers or books. No strong desire ever seemed to move that half-somnolent and passive soul; but sometimes he would say how much he would like to return to Italy. He was bored by Father Vasques, but he did not dare defy him. He was a weakling in everything, and the continuous dullness of his entire being would culminate at times in crises of black melancholy that kept him silent for days on end, withered, yellow, with deep shadows under his eyes, old before his time. Till now his only lively and intense feeling had been his passion for his mother.

Afonso wanted him to attend the university at Coimbra. But at the idea of parting from her Pedro the poor lady had fallen on her knees before Afonso, stammering and shuddering; and he, naturally, at last gave in before those beseeching hands, those tears that fell drop by drop from the poor waxen face. The boy remained at Benfica where he went for short rides on horseback followed by a uniformed servant and began to stop in for a brandy at the Lisbon taverns. Then he started to show signs of a very amorous nature and at nineteen fathered a natural child.

Afonso da Maia consoled himself with the thought that despite such shameful indulgence, the boy did not lack certain qualities: he was very clever, healthy and, like all the Maias, brave. Not long since, on his own with only a whip in his hand, he had routed three rustics on the high road who were armed with staves and had called him a weed.

When his mother died in the terrible agony of the devout, lingering for days in dread of hell, Pedro's grief excited him almost to madness. He had made the hysterical vow that if she were spared he would sleep for a year on the flag-stones of the patio; and when the coffin had been borne away and the priests had departed, he fell into a gloomy anguish, dull and tearless, from which he showed no desire to emerge, and he lay stretched out face downwards on his bed as obstinately as a penitent. Many months were to pass before this vague sadness left him, and Afonso da Maia began to despair at the sight of that boy, his son and heir, going out every day with a monk's tread, lugubrious in his heavy mourning, to visit the tomb of his Mama.

At last this exaggerated and morbid grief came to an end. It was followed almost immediately by a period of turbulence, dissipation and commonplace extravagances in which Pedro, guided by a run-of-the-mill romanticism, tried to drown his mother's memory in brothels and taverns. But this hectic exuberance, which had developed so suddenly in his unbalanced nature, burned itself out quickly too. At the end of a year's brawling in the Marrare Café, feats in the bullring, hard-ridden horses, hissing at opera stars at the São Carlos, there began to reappear the old crises of nervous melancholia; the days of taciturnity returned, as dreary as deserts, spent in the house yawning through the drawing-rooms, or under some tree in the park stretched out face downwards as though plunged in the depths of bitterness.

During these periods he also devoted himself to religion: he would read the lives of the saints and spent his time in church in the kind of depression that in another age used to lead the weak to the cloisters.

All this tormented Afonso da Maia. He would have preferred to know the boy had returned from Lisbon at dawn, exhausted and drunk, than to see him, a prayer-book under his arm, with an elderly air, on his way to the Benfica church.

Now an obsession began to haunt Afonso da Maia. He had discovered a striking likeness between Pedro and a grandfather of his wife's, one of the Runas, of whom there was a portrait at Benfica. This extraordinary man, whose name was used as a bogey in the family, had gone mad and, believing himself to be Judas, had hanged himself on a fig tree.

But one day the excesses and the crises passed. Pedro da Maia fell in love! It was the love of a Romeo, born suddenly from a fatal and dazzling exchange of glances – one of those passions which take possession of an existence, burst on it like a hurricane, snatch away will-power, reason, human relationships and sweep them all violently into the abyss.

One afternoon in the Marrare Café he had seen a blue chaise stop outside at the door of Madame Levaillant. In it were an old man in a white hat and a blonde lady wrapped in a cashmere shawl.

The old man was short and stocky with an iron-grey beard clipped under his chin, the weather-beaten face of an old seafarer, and an awkward air. He climbed down leaning on a servant as though stiff with rheumatism and dragged his legs as he entered the dressmaker's door opposite; she slowly turned her head and looked for a moment towards the café. Under the rosebuds that ornamented her black hat, her blonde hair, of a tawny gold, waved slightly above her short, classical forehead; her splendid eyes illuminated her entire face; the cold made her marble flesh paler than ever; her grave, sculptured profile, the noble shape of her shoulders and arms under the shawl, all seemed to Pedro at that instant like something immortal and out of this world.

He did not know her. But a tall, sallow young man with a black moustache and dressed in black, who was leaning on the other doorpost in an attitude of boredom, smoking, noticed Pedro's violent interest, his shining and excited gaze as he followed the path of the chaise up the Chiado, and he came over and took his arm. In a thick, slow voice he murmured in his ear:

'D'you want me to tell you her name, my Pedro? Name, origin, dates and principal details? And will you pay your friend Alencar, your thirsty Alencar, with a bottle of champagne?'

The champagne was brought. And after passing his thin fingers through the ringlets of his hair and over the tips of his moustache, Alencar began as he leaned back and gave a tug at his cuffs:

'One golden afternoon in autumn – '

'André,' called Pedro to the waiter, banging the marble table, 'take away the champagne!'

Alencar shouted, in imitation of the actor Epiphanio:

'What! Without satiating the thirst of my lips?'

Well, the champagne might stay, but friend Alencar should kindly forget that he was the author of the *Voices of Dawn* and please explain those people with the blue chaise, in language that was both Christian and practical!

'As you wish, my Pedro! As you wish!'

It had been two years earlier, just about the time that Pedro had lost his mother, that the old man, Papa Monforte, had appeared in the streets of Lisbon and in society with that self-same chaise and that same beautiful daughter at his side. Nobody knew them. They had taken the first floor of the Vargas mansion in Arroios and the girl began to be seen at the São Carlos Opera House where she had created a sensation, sensation enough to cause aneurisms, said Alencar! When she crossed the salon, shoulders drooped in amazement at the aureole that shone from that splendid creature, drawing her court-train with the step of a goddess, always *décolletée* as on a gala night, and resplendent with jewels despite her single state. Papa never gave her his arm. He walked behind her, squeezed into a big white collar like a major-domo, looking more tanned and more of a sailor than ever in the golden light that emanated from his daughter. Shrunken and almost fearful, he carried an eye-glass, a libretto, a bag of bon-bons, a fan and his own umbrella. But it was from the box, when the light fell on her ivory throat and her golden plaits, that she presented truly the incarnation of a Renaissance ideal, a Titian model. The first night he had seen her, Alencar himself had pointed to her and then to the swarthy ladies in the other boxes and had exclaimed:

'My boys, it's like catching sight of a new gold ducat amid the old copper coins of the time of Dom João VI.'

Magalhães, that low pirate, had reprinted the phrase in his newspaper column. But it was his, Alencar's!

Naturally the young men had at once begun to swarm around the mansion in Arroios. But never was a window opened in that house. When questioned, the servants said that their young mistress's name was Maria and that the master was called Manuel. At last one maid-servant who had been bribed with a few coins revealed more: the man was taciturn, trembled before his daughter and slept in a hammock; the lady lived in a nest of dark blue silks and passed her day reading novels. But this did not satisfy Lisbon's eagerness. A methodical, efficient and patient inquiry was begun. He, Alencar, had taken part in it.

Horrors came to light. Papa Monforte was from the Azores; as a very young man a knifing during a brawl and a corpse found at a street-corner had forced him to flee on an American brig. Time passed and a certain Silva, the steward of the Taveira family, who had known him in the Azores, had been in Havana studying the cultivation of tobacco, which the Taveiras wanted to start planting in the islands. There he had met Monforte (whose real name was Forte) hanging around the quayside, in straw-soled slippers, looking for a passage to New Orleans. Here there was a gap in Monforte's history. It seemed he had worked for a time as an overseer on a Virginia plantation. However, when he was heard of again it was as captain of the brig *Nova Linda* that carried cargoes of slaves to Brazil, Havana and New Orleans.

He escaped the English warships and made a fortune out of black skins. Now, rich, respectable and a land-owner, he went to the São Carlos to hear Corelli. However, this terrible chronicle, as Alencar said, was obscure and based on hearsay, and faltered here and there.

'And the daughter?' asked Pedro who had been listening, pale and serious.

But Alencar knew nothing about that. Where had the old man fathered a daughter so fair and lovely? Who had been her mama? Where was she? Who had taught her to wrap herself with such a regal gesture in her cashmere shawl?

'Those, my Pedro, are "mysteries that never unravelled can be and God alone can know!"'

When Lisbon heard the story of blood and slaves however, enthusiasm for the Monforte girl waned. What the devil! This Juno had a murderer's blood in her veins; the Titian beauty was the daughter of a slaver. The ladies, who were delighted at the opportunity of slandering a woman so fair, so lovely, and who possessed so many jewels, at once named her 'the slaver'. And when she appeared in the theatre, Dona Maria da Gama affected to hide her face behind her fan, for she seemed to see on the girl (above all, when she wore her beautiful rubies) the blood of the knife-wounds dealt by her papa! And they calumniated her abominably. So after that first winter spent in Lisbon the Monfortes went away – and at once people eagerly spread it about that they were ruined, that the police were after the old man and a thousand more tales. The worthy Monforte, who suffered from rheumatism, was serenely and prosperously taking the waters in the Pyrenees. It had been there that Melo had become acquainted with them.

'Ah! Does Melo know them?' asked Pedro.

'Yes, Pedro. Melo knows them.'

A moment later Pedro left the Marrare; and that night, before going home, despite the fine cold drizzle, he walked round and round the dark, still Vargas mansion for an hour with his imagination aflame. And when Alencar entered the São Carlos two weeks later at the end of the first act of the *Barber of Seville*, he was astonished to see Pedro da Maia installed in the Monforte box, in front, at Maria's side, with a scarlet camellia in his evening coat – identical with those that lay in a bouquet on the velvet balustrade.

Never had Maria Monforte seemed lovelier. She was wearing one of those opulent and theatrical toilettes that offended Lisbon and made the ladies say that she dressed like 'an actress'. She was wearing corn-coloured silk, with two yellow roses and an ear of wheat in her braids, and opals on her neck and arms. These colours, like a ripe crop beaten by the sun, mingled with the gold of her hair, illuminated her ivory flesh, bathed her statuesque figure and gave her the splendour of a Ceres. Behind her one could glimpse the big blond moustaches of Melo, who was standing up conversing with Papa Monforte, hidden as always in a dark corner of the box.

Alencar went to observe 'the incident' from the Gamas' box. Pedro had returned to his chair and was contemplating Maria with folded arms. For a time she maintained her attitude of an emotionless, insensitive goddess; but after the duet between

25

Rosina and Lindor, she twice rested her deep eyes of blue upon him, gravely and for a long time. Alencar rushed to the Marrare waving his arms in the air and bellowing the news.

It was not long before all of Lisbon started to talk of Pedro da Maia's passion for 'the slaver'. Moreover he wooed her publicly in the old style, standing for hours on the street-corner in front of the Vargas mansion, with his eyes fixed on her window, motionless and pale with ecstasy. He wrote her two letters a day, each on six sheets of paper – disconnected poems that he composed in the Marrare Café. And nobody in the place was unaware of the destination of those pages of criss-crossed lines that accumulated before him on the gin-tray. If a friend came to the door inquiring for Pedro da Maia, the servants now replied as a matter of course:

'Dom Pedro? He's writing to the young lady.'

And he himself, if the friend came up to him, would reach out his hand and exclaim radiantly with that lovely, candid smile of his:

'Wait there a moment, dear chap, I'm writing to Maria.'

Afonso da Maia's old friends who came to play whist with him at Benfica, especially Vilaça the steward, who was a zealous watchdog of the family honour, were not slow in bringing news of Pedrinho's passion. Afonso had already suspected as much: he had noticed a servant leaving the house each day with a great bunch of the best camellias from the garden; he had met Pedro's valet in the corridor on his way to his son's room early each morning, sniffing pleasurably at a scented envelope sealed with golden wax. And the father had not been altogether displeased that some strong and human sentiment should tear his son from his dissipations, from gambling and from the irrational melancholies which led to fits of black depression.

But he did not know the name or even the existence of the Monfortes; and the particulars that his friends revealed to him – the knifing in the Azores, the overseer's whip in Virginia, the brig *Nova Linda,* the whole sinister story of the old man – much displeased Afonso da Maia.

One night when Colonel Sequeira was saying at the whist table that he had seen Maria Monforte and Pedro out riding, 'both of them looking extremely elegant and distinguished', Afonso, after a silence, said with an irritated air:

'Well, all young men have their mistresses. That's the way of things, that's life. And it would be absurd to try to put a stop to it. But a woman with a father like that is a bit too much, even for a mistress.'

Vilaça stopped shuffling the cards. Adjusting his gold-rimmed glasses he exclaimed in astonishment:

'Mistress! But the girl is single, senhor, she's a decent girl.'

Afonso da Maia was filling his pipe; his hands began to tremble; and turning to the steward he spoke in a voice that trembled too.

'Surely you don't suppose, Vilaça, that a son of mine would want to marry that creature – '

The other did not answer, and it was Sequeira who murmured: 'Of course not – not that.'

And play went on for a while in silence.

But Afonso da Maia began to feel troubled. Weeks would go by without Pedro appearing for dinner at Benfica. If Afonso saw him in the morning it would only be for a moment, when Pedro came down at lunch-time, with one glove already on, hurried and radiant, shouting to the servants to know if his horse was saddled; then, still standing, he would drink a gulp of tea, ask hurriedly if Papa had any errands, smooth his moustache before the great Venetian mirror over the fireplace, and he would be off, in a state of exaltation. There were other times when he would not emerge from his room for the whole day; evening would come down, the lights would be lit; and at last the father, disquieted, would go and find him stretched out on the bed with his head buried in his arms.

'What is the trouble?' he would ask.

'A migraine,' he would reply in a dull, hoarse voice.

And Afonso would go downstairs indignant, seeing in all that cowardly anguish some letter that had not arrived, or perhaps some proffered rose that she had not placed in her hair.

Then, occasionally, between two rubbers of whist or as they talked around the tea-tray, his friends made remarks that disturbed him, coming as they did from men who moved in Lisbon society and heard the gossip – while he spent winter and summer there among his books and his roses. It was the excellent Sequeira who inquired why Pedro did not make a long journey to Germany or the East for his education. Or old Luiz Runa,

27

Afonso's cousin, in the middle of talk about commonplace things would break into lamentations for the times when the Intendant of Police could freely expel importunate persons from Lisbon. It was clear that they were alluding to the Monforte girl; it was clear they thought her dangerous.

In the summer Pedro left for Sintra; Afonso learned that the Monfortes had taken a house there. Some days later Vilaça appeared at Benfica in a worried state: Pedro had visited him at his office the day before and had asked for details about his estate, and about means of raising money. Vilaça had told him that in September, when he came of age, he would have his mother's inheritance.

'But I didn't like the sound of it, senhor, I didn't like it at all!'

'And why not, Vilaça? The boy will need money. He'll be wanting to give presents to that creature. Love is an expensive luxury, Vilaça.'

'I hope that's what it is, Senhor, may God help us.'

And Afonso's noble confidence in his son's patrician hauteur, in his family pride, calmed Vilaça.

A few days later Afonso da Maia at last saw Maria Monforte. He had been dining with Sequeira on the Colonel's estate near Queluz and they were both taking coffee in the belvedere, when the blue chaise with its net-covered horses came into view along the narrow road that passed the wall. Maria, sheltered under a scarlet parasol, was wearing a rose-coloured dress whose crinolined skirt, all in flounces, practically covered the knees of Pedro, who was seated beside her. The ribbons of her hat, tied in a great bow that covered her breast, were rose-coloured too, and her face, grave and pure like a Grecian marble, looked quite adorable, illuminated by eyes of dark blue amid those rosy tones. On the seat in front, almost filled up with dressmaker's boxes, huddled Monforte in his big panama hat, nankeen trousers, his daughter's cape on his arm, his sunshade between his knee. They drove in silence and did not see the belvedere; and on that green and fresh roadway the chaise passed swaying slowly under branches that brushed Maria's parasol.

Sequeira sat with his coffee-cup suspended at his lips, his eyes glazed, murmuring: 'By Jove, she's lovely!'

Afonso did not reply. With his head bowed he gazed at that scarlet parasol which now leaned towards Pedro, almost hiding him and seeming to envelop him – like a broad stain of blood covering the chaise under the sad green of the trees.

Autumn passed and winter came. It was very cold. One morning Pedro came into the library where his father was reading beside the fire. He asked his blessing and then looked for a moment at an open newspaper. Suddenly he turned brusquely to his father.

'Father,' he said, making an effort to sound clear and determined. 'I've come to ask your permission to marry a lady called Maria Monforte.'

Afonso put his open book down on his knees and spoke in serious and measured tones:

'You hadn't told me anything about this. I understand she's the daughter of a murderer, a slave-trader, and that she too is called "the slaver"!'

'Father!'

Afonso stood up before him, stern and inexorable, the very personification of family pride.

'What more can you have to say? You make me blush with shame.'

Pedro, who was whiter than the handkerchief he was holding, exclaimed as he trembled and nearly sobbed:

'But you may be sure, Father, that I will marry her!'

He went out, slamming the door furiously. In the corridor he shouted for the footman, very loudly so that his father could hear him give the order for his luggage to be taken to the Hotel da Europa.

Two days later Vilaça arrived at Benfica with tears in his eyes and said that the young man had been married early that morning and, according to what had been said by Sergio, the Monforte's steward, he was leaving with his bride for Italy.

Alfonso, grave and silent, listened to his steward, while he slowly unfolded his table napkin.

'Have you had lunch, Vilaça?'

The steward, amazed at that tranquillity, stammered:

'I've already lunched, senhor.'

Then, pointing to Pedro's place, Afonso said to the footman:

'You can remove those things, Teixeira. From now on there will be only one place at table. Sit down, Vilaça, sit down.'

Teixeira was still new to the house and he cleared away the

young master's things with indifference. Vilaça sat down. Everything around was correct and calm, just as on other mornings when he had lunched at Benfica. The footman's steps made no sound on the thick carpet; the fire blazed merrily, touching the polished silver with gleams of gold; the discreet sun that shone outside in the winter blue made the crystals of frost glisten on the dry boughs of the trees; and in the window the parrot, a radical bird whom Pedro had educated, was snorting insults at the Cabral ministry.

Afonso finally rose and stood gazing abstractedly at the park, at the peacocks on the terrace. Then, as he went out of the room, he took Vilaça's arm and leaned heavily on him, as though he sensed the first tremors of age and in his solitude realized that here was an assured friendship. They went down the corridor in silence. When they got to the library Afonso went to his armchair near the window and began slowly to fill his pipe. Vilaça, with head bowed, was walking the length of the tall shelves on tip-toe, as though in a sick room. A flock of sparrows came to chatter for a moment in the branches of a tall tree that scraped the balcony.

Then there was a hush and Afonso da Maia said: 'So, Vilaça? Saldanha's been dismissed from the Palace after all?'

'True, senhor, true,' responded the other vaguely and mechanically.

And Pedro da Maia was mentioned no more.

2

MEANWHILE PEDRO AND MARIA were travelling blissfully
through Italy from one city to another making stops here and
there on that sacred highway that leads from the plain of Lom-
bardy with its flowers and its crops to Naples, that gentle land
of romance, white under the sky. They planned to spend the
winter there, in that ever-tepid air beside an ever-calm sea,
where the indolence and sweetness of new marriage last longer.
But in Rome one day Maria felt a yearning for Paris. She found
it wearying to travel thus, to the swaying of the coaches, seeing
nothing but *lazzaroni* swallowing strings of macaroni. How much
nicer it would be to live in a cushioned nest on the Champs-
Elysées and enjoy a wonderful winter of love! Paris was safe
now under Prince Louis Napoleon. And anyway, this ancient,
classical Italy was beginning to bore her. So many eternal
marbles, so many madonnas made her poor head ache, she murmured as she hung languidly on Pedro's neck. How she yearned
for the salon of a good dressmaker, for gas-light and the sounds
of the boulevards. Besides, she felt afraid in Italy, where the
whole world seemed to be plotting.

They left for France.

But even Paris at last became distasteful to Maria. The city
was still restless. A vague scent of gunpowder still seemed to
hang about the streets. Each face still held the light of battle. At
night she was awoken by the *Marseillaise*; she thought the
police looked ferocious; everything seemed sad; and the duchesses,
poor angels, still dared not appear in the Bois de Boulogne, for
fear of the workers, that relentless mob! They stayed there, however, until spring – in the nest she had dreamed of, all blue
velvet, facing on to the Champs-Elysées.

Then talk of revolution and *coups d'état* started once more.
Maria's absurd admiration for the new uniforms of the Guard
made Pedro nervous. And when she became pregnant, he wanted
to get her out of that warlike and fascinating Paris and shelter
her in the peace of Lisbon, sleepy under the sun.

But before he left he wrote to his father.

It was at Maria's advice and insistence. Afonso da Maia's refusal had at first plunged her into despair. It was not the rift in the family that troubled her. But her offensive rejection by the puritanical nobleman had branded her doubtful origins very publicly and very brutally! She loathed the old man. And she had hastened the wedding and their triumphant departure for Italy just to show him that genealogies, Gothic ancestors and family pride counted for nothing against her naked arms. Now, however, that she was returning to Lisbon where she would be giving soirées and entertaining, reconciliation had become essential; that father closeted in Benfica, rigid with the pride of other years, constantly reminded her, even among her looking-glasses and her silks, of the brig *Nova Linda* loaded with black men. She wanted to be seen in Lisbon on the arm of that father-in-law with the beard of a viceroy, who was at once so noble and so decorative.

'Tell him I already adore him,' she whispered, as she leaned over the writing-table caressing Pedro's hair. 'Tell your father that if I have a son I'll name him after him. Write him a nice letter, do!'

And Pedro's letter to his father was nice, it was tender. The poor boy loved him. He wrote with emotion of his hopes for a son; misunderstanding would cease around the cradle of that little Maia that was on its way – the heir and bearer of his name. He narrated his happiness with the effusion of an indiscreet lover: tales of Maria's goodness, her grace, her instruction filled two pages – and he vowed that as soon as they arrived he would not delay an hour in going to throw himself at his father's feet.

In fact they had scarcely stepped ashore than he rushed by cab to Benfica. But his father had left two days earlier for Santa Olávia; the affront wounded him to the quick.

A great gulf now divided father and son. When his daughter was born Pedro did not inform him – and told Vilaça dramatically that he 'no longer had a father'. The child was beautiful – very plump, fair and rosy with the lovely dark eyes of the Maias. Defying Pedro's wishes, Maria would not feed it herself; but she adored it ecstatically. She spent days on her knees at the foot of the cradle in worship, running her bejewelled fingers along the tender flesh, bestowing pious kisses on the little

32

feet, on the folds of its little legs, blissfully stammering endearments, already perfuming it and covering it in ribbons.

And in her delirium over her daughter her anger against Afonso da Maia flowed over. She felt outraged on her own behalf, and on behalf of the angel she had borne. She hurled gross insults at the old man, calling him an old idiot, a bearded monster!

One day Pedro overheard her and was scandalized. She answered him harshly. And before those burning cheeks, those blue eyes bathed in tears and black with rage, he was merely able to falter timidly:

'He's my father, Maria!'

His father! And before the whole of Lisbon he had treated her as though she were a concubine! He might be a nobleman, but he had the manners of a serf. He *was* an old idiot, and a bearded monster, too!

She clutched her daughter, and, holding her closely, complained amid sobs:

'Nobody loves us, my angel! Nobody wants you! You've only your mother! They treat you as though you were a bastard!'

The child, shaken in her mother's arms, began to cry. Pedro ran to them and put his arm around them both, now contrite and humble. And it all ended in a long kiss.

And, at last, in his heart he excused the fury of a mother who saw her angel scorned. Moreover, even some of Pedro's friends – Alencar and Dom João da Cunha – who had now begun to frequent Arroios, laughed at the obstinacy of the old-fashioned father sulking in the country, because his daughter-in-law had not got ancestors who had died at Aljubarrota! And where else in Lisbon was there a lady with such *toilettes,* such grace and who received so well? Hang it! the world had changed, and one had emerged long ago from the stiff-necked attitudes of the sixteenth century! Even Vilaça felt moved one day when Pedro took him to look at the tiny girl sleeping among the laces of her cradle, and, as his easy tears rose to his eyes, he declared with a hand on his heart that it was all stubbornness on the part of Senhor Afonso da Maia!

'Well the loss is his! Not wanting to see such an angel!' declared Maria, standing before the glass and making a dainty

33

adjustment to the flowers in her hair. 'And anyway, he is not missed here!'

And he was not missed.

That October, when the little one had her first birthday, a great ball was held in the house in Arroios, the whole of which they now occupied and which had been lavishly redecorated. And the ladies, who had earlier been horrified by 'the slaver' – including Dona Maria da Gama, who had hidden her face behind her fan – all came in their *décolletages*, brimming with amiability, with a ready kiss, to call her 'my dear', to admire the wreaths of camellias that adorned the expensive mirrors, and to appreciate the ices.

A gay and fashionable existence began, which – said Alencar, an intimate of the household and Madame's courtier – 'savoured somewhat of a *distinguée* orgy, like Byron's poems'. They were, indeed, the gayest *soirées* in Lisbon: there were champagne suppers at one in the morning; there was gambling for high stakes till a late hour; there were pantomimes in which Maria displayed her great beauty in the classical robes of Helen, or the sombre luxury and oriental mourning of Judith. At more intimate gatherings she would come and smoke a perfumed cigarette among the gentlemen. Very often, in the billiards-room, there would be great hand-clapping when they saw her beat Dom João da Cunha, the great player of the time, at the French cannon.

And amid all this merrymaking, permeated by the Romantic breath of the Regeneration, one always found Papa Monforte, taciturn and huddled, in his high white cravat, his hands behind his back, lurking in the corners, hiding in the window-bays, showing himself only to save some candle from guttering – and never taking his doting and senile eyes from his daughter.

Never had Maria been so handsome. Maternity had given her a more copious splendour and she indeed dominated and illumined those high Arroios drawing-rooms with her radiant and fair Junoesque figure, diamonds in her braids, the ivory milkiness of her bare throat and the rustle of great silks. And when she wanted to choose a flower for her symbol, like ladies of the Renaissance, she aptly selected the royal tulip, opulent and ardent.

34

Everyone talked about her luxury, her white linen and her lace that was worth a ransom! But she could afford it! Her husband was a rich man, and she would not scruple to ruin him, and her father, Papa Monforte, as well!

Of course all Pedro's friends adored her. Alencar noisily proclaimed himself her 'knight and poet'. He was always at Arroios, and had his own place at table. His resounding periods echoed through the rooms and the sofas were seats for his melancholy poses. He was going to dedicate to Maria (and there was nothing more extraordinary than the languorous and plangent tone, the turbid and fatal eye, with which he pronounced that name – MARIA!) his much-heralded and much-awaited poem, *The Flower of Martyrdom*. And the lines he had written to her, in the singing taste of the time, were often quoted:

'I saw thee on that night, in the splendour of the salons,
With thy golden plaits, wheeling round in madness – '

Alencar's passion was pure; but among the other intimates of the house, more than one, certainly, had already stammered out his declaration in the blue boudoir where she received among her vases of tulips at three o'clock in the afternoon. Nevertheless even the worst of her women friends all vowed that her favours never went beyond some rose bestowed on a window-seat, or some long, sweet look from behind her fan. But Pedro began to pass many a gloomy hour. He did not feel jealous, but he would sometimes suddenly be overcome with the tedium of that life of luxury and pleasure and feel a violent urge to throw them all out of the room – all these men, his friends who crowded so ardently around Maria's bare shoulders.

During all this time Afonso da Maia had not left the shade of Santa Olávia and was as forgotten there as though he were in his tomb. He was no longer spoken of in Arroios. The 'bearded monster' had been left to chew on his stubbornness. Only Pedro sometimes would ask Vilaça how Papa was faring. And the steward's news always infuriated Maria: Papa was splendid; he now had a magnificent French cook; Santa Olávia was filled with guests – Sequeira, André da Ega, Dom Diogo Coutinho.

'The "bearded monster" is treating himself!' she would say ill-temperedly to her father.

And the old slaver would rub his hands, contented to know him thus happy in Santa Olávia; for he had never ceased to shudder at the idea of seeing before him in Arroios that severe nobleman who led such a pure life.

However, when Maria gave birth to a second child, a son, the peace that now reigned in Arroios once more aroused in Pedro's heart the image of his father abandoned amid the sadness of the Douro. He took advantage of her convalescence to speak to Maria hesitantly about a reconciliation. And he was overjoyed when Maria, after a moment's thought, agreed.

'I think I'd be happy to have him here.'

Pedro, excited by her unexpected acquiescence, was for setting out immediately for Santa Olávia. But she had a better plan. Afonso, so Vilaça said, would shortly be returning to Benfica. Well now, she would go there all dressed in black, with the baby boy, and would suddenly throw herself at his feet and ask for his blessing for his grandson! It could not fail! It really could not. And Pedro perceived behind this plan the lofty inspiration of motherhood!

Pedro wanted to name the child after Afonso in order to win his father from the outset. But Maria could not agree to this. She was reading a novel whose hero was the last of the Stuarts – Charles Edward, that prince of romance. Infatuated with him, with his feats and his misfortunes, she wanted to give the name to her son – Carlos Eduardo da Maia! A name like that seemed to bear in its train a whole destiny of love affairs and adventures.

The christening had to be postponed. Maria fell ill with tonsilitis. But it was a mild attack and two weeks later Pedro was already able to go away hunting on his estate at Tojeira, beyond Almeda. He was to be absent two days. The hunt had been arranged in honour of an Italian who had just arrived in Lisbon, a distinguished young man who had been introduced to him by the Secretary of the British Legation, and whom Pedro had liked very much. He said he was a nephew of the princes of Soria; and he had fled from Naples where he had been plotting against the Bourbons and had been condemned to death. Alencar and Dom João Coutinho were also going – and they were to set out at dawn.

That afternoon Maria was dining alone in her room when she heard carriages stopping at the door and a great tumult filling the staircase. Almost at once Pedro appeared, trembling and perturbed –

A grotesque accident! As he was jumping a ditch his gun had gone off and the shot had struck the Neapolitan. It had not been possible to treat him at Tojeira and so they had come back at once to Lisbon. Naturally he could not allow the man he had wounded to go to a hotel, so he had brought him back to Arroios, put him in the green room above, called the doctor and two nurses to look after him, and would himself spend the night at his bedside.

'And he?'

'A hero! He smiles. Says it's nothing. But he's as pale as death. A magnificent fellow! It could only happen to me, by God! And there was Alencar riding beside him – I would rather have wounded Alencar, an intimate friend – we would even have laughed over it! But no – pow! It was the other, the guest of honour!'

At that instant a coach drove into the patio.

'It's the doctor!'

And Pedro went off.

He returned some time later, more tranquil. Doctor Guedes had practically laughed at such a bagatelle: a scratch in the arm and some shot in the back. He promised that within a fortnight the victim would be able to hunt again at Tojeira – and the Prince himself was already smoking a cigar! A fine chap! He seemed to have taken a liking to Papa Monforte.

All that night Maria slept fitfully, in a vague state of excitement at the idea that lying in the room above her was a prince, an idealist, a conspirator, a man who had been condemned to death.

Early the next morning hardly had Pedro gone out himself to supervise the transportation of the Neapolitan's luggage from the hotel, than Maria sent her French maid, a lovely Arlesian girl, upstairs to inquire how His Highness was feeling, and 'to see what he looked like'. The Arlesian came back bright-eyed to tell her lady, with expansive Provençal gestures, that she had never seen such a comely man! He was like a painting of Our Lord! What a neck, what marble whiteness! He was still very pale; he sent his ardent gratitude to Madame Maia; and she had left him reclining on his pillows reading the newspapers.

After that Maria seemed uninterested in the wounded man. It was Pedro who talked constantly about him, full of admiration for the dismal existence of the prince-conspirator; already sharing his hatred of the Bourbons; enchanted with the similarity of tastes they shared: the same love of hunting, horses and arms. Now he went to the Prince's room every morning, in his dressing-gown and with his pipe in his mouth, and would spend hours there in comradeship, making hot grog – permitted by Doctor Guedes. He even took his friends Alencar and Dom João da Cunha along. Maria could hear them laughing upstairs. Sometimes they played the guitar. And old Monforte, infatuated with the hero, never ceased to hover round his bed.

As for the Arlesian, she too appeared there at every moment, bringing lacey towels, a sugar bowl that nobody had asked for or a vase of flowers to brighten the bedside. Maria at last very earnestly inquired of Pedro whether, besides all the friends of the house, two female nurses, two footmen, Papa and Pedro himself, it was also necessary to have her own maid wait on His Highness! It was not. But Pedro laughed a great deal at the idea that the Arlesian had fallen in love with the Prince. Venus had been generous with him, then, for the Neapolitan found her piquante: '*un très joli brin de femme*,' he had said.

Maria's lovely face grew white with anger. She thought all this in very bad taste, gross, impertinent. Pedro had really acted like a madman in thus introducing into the intimacy of Arroios a stranger, a fugitive, an adventurer! And, moreover, all that merry-making upstairs amid hot grogs and guitars, with no consideration for her, still nervous and weak from her convalescence, made her indignant! As soon as His Highness was strong enough to accommodate himself among the cushions in a coach, she wanted him out of there, at an inn.

'What? What are you saying? My God!' said Pedro.

'I've made up my mind.'

And she must certainly have been very severe with the Arlesian too, because that afternoon Pedro found the girl sighing in the corridor and wiping her red eyes with her apron.

A few days later, now convalescent, the Neapolitan wanted to return to his hotel. He had not seen Maria, but in thanks for her hospitality he sent her a splendid bouquet and, as gallantly as any artist-prince of the Renaissance, a sonnet in Italian

among the flowers and as perfumed as they. He compared her
to a noble lady of Syria bestowing a drop of water from her jar
on the Arab knight who lay wounded on the parched highway;
he compared her to Dante's Beatrice.

Everyone thought this extremely elegant, and Alencar said
it was a touch of Byron.

Later, at Carlos Eduardo's christening party given the following week, the Neapolitan appeared and created a sensation. He
was a splendid figure of a man, formed like an Apollo, as pale
as rich marble with a short, curly beard and long, brown hair,
a woman's hair, that waved and shone with golden lights. It
was parted in the middle like the Nazarene's. He did indeed
look like a beautiful Christ, as the Arlesian had said.

He danced only one cotillion with Maria and seemed, actually,
a little taciturn and proud; but everything about him fascinated: his appearance, his mystery, even his name – Tancredo.
Many a female heart throbbed when his velvet gaze roamed
slowly over the room in sombre languor as he leaned heavily
against a door-jamb, with melancholy on his face, exhaling all
the tragic attraction of a condemned man. The Marchioness de
Alvenga, to examine him more closely, begged Pedro's arm and
went up and applied her gold lorgnette to the Neapolitan as to a
museum marble.

'He's delicious!' she cried. 'A picture! And you're friends, are
you, Pedro? You're friends?'

'We are like two comrades-in-arms, Marchioness.'

That same evening Vilaça told Pedro that his father was
expected at Benfica the following day. And as soon as the party
was over Pedro spoke to Maria about going 'to make the great
scene with Papa'. But she refused, giving the most unforeseen
but the most sensible reasons. She had been thinking things
over. And now she realized that one of the reasons for Papa's
stubbornness – of late she had always referred to him as 'Papa' –
had been their extraordinary existence at Arroios.

'But, my dear,' protested Pedro, 'listen to me, it's not as though
we held orgies – a few friends dropping in!'

That was as might be. But she had quite decided to have a
quieter and more domesticated establishment. It would be
better for the babies too. And she wanted Papa to become convinced that a transformation had really taken place so that

39

the peace between them would be both easier and everlasting.

'Let two or three months go by. When he learns that we are living quietly I'll bring him round, you may be sure. It would be a good thing, too, if it were after my father has gone to take the waters in the Pyrenees. For my poor, dear Papa is afraid of your father! Don't you agree, dear?'

'You're an angel,' was Pedro's response as he kissed each of her hands.

And indeed all Maria's ways seemed to have changed. There were no more *soirées*. The evenings were spent peacefully in her blue boudoir with a few intimate friends. She no longer smoked; she gave up billiards; dressed in black, with a flower in her hair, she crocheted beside the lamp. And they all listened to music when old Cazoti came. Alencar, imitating his lady, also entered upon a period of gravity and recited translations of Klopstock. They talked politics earnestly and Maria was very much in favour of the Regenerators.

Tancredo was there every night, handsome and indolent, tracing a flower for her to embroider, or strumming Neapolitan folk-songs on the guitar. Everybody adored him, and nobody more than old Monforte who spent hours buried in his high collar contemplating the Prince tenderly. Then, abruptly, he would rise, cross the room and go and bend over him, touching him, feeling him, sniffing him and murmuring in his seaman's French: '*ça aller bien, hein? Beaucoup bien?* I'm glad!'

And these brusque currents of affection must have communicated themselves for at such moments Maria always either gave Papa one of her dazzling smiles or went and kissed his forehead.

During the day she occupied herself with serious things. She organized a useful charitable association, which had as its aim the distribution of blankets in winter to the needy families; and in the Arroios drawing-room she presided with a bell over meetings to draw up the group's rules. She visited the poor. She also went repeatedly to devotions in church, all dressed in black, on foot, with a thick veil covering her face.

The splendour of her beauty now seemed veiled with a touching shadow of grave tenderness; the goddess had been translated into a Madonna; and she was often heard to sigh all of a sudden without reason.

40

Meanwhile Maria's passion for her daughter had grown. The child was now two years old and really adorable; every night, dressed as luxuriously as a princess, she was allowed for a few moments in the drawing-room. The Prince's exclamations and ecstasies were endless! He drew her portrait in charcoal, in chalk, in watercolour; he knelt down to kiss the little pink hand, as though it belonged to the Holy Child. And, despite Pedro's protests, Maria always slept with the child in her arms.

Early that September old Monforte left for the Pyrenees. Maria wept and clung to the old man's neck as though he were departing anew for the Africas.

But by dinner-time she was already comforted and radiant, and Pedro again spoke of reconciliation with his father, for the time now seemed opportune to go to Benfica and win back for ever that stubborn Papa.

'Not yet,' she said pensively, looking into her glass of Bordeaux. 'Your father is a kind of saint, and we don't yet deserve him – later on, in the winter!'

One gloomy and very rainy December afternoon, Afonso da Maia was reading in his study when the door burst violently open and, lifting his eyes from his book, he saw Pedro before him. He was covered in mud, his clothes were disordered, and on his livid face, under his dishevelled hair, shone the light of madness. The old man got up in terror. And Pedro, without a word, threw himself into his father's arms and sobbed like a lost soul.

'Pedro! My boy! What has happened?'

Perhaps Maria had died! A terrible joy invaded him at the notion of his son, freed forever from the Monfortes, coming back to him, bringing two grandchildren to interrupt his solitude – descendant's whom he could love! And he repeated, trembling too as very lovingly he let go of his son:

'Quietly, my boy! What is it?'

Pedro fell down on the sofa as a dead body falls. Raising a ravaged face to his father he said dully:

'I was away from Lisbon for two days . . . I came back this morning . . . Maria had left the house with the little girl . . . She left with a man, an Italian – and here I am!'

Afonso stood before his son still and mute, like a figure of stone; and his fine face, into which the blood had begun to flow, started gradually to fill with a great rage. In a flash he saw the scandal: the gloating city; the pitying looks; his name dragged in the mud. And it was this son of his, who had scorned his authority, allied himself to that creature, and spoiled the family blood, who had now covered his name in disgrace. There he was! There he lay without a cry, without anger, without any of the brutal fury of the man betrayed! He had come to fling himself on a sofa, weeping wretchedly! This filled Afonso with indignation and he began to pace through the room, erect and harsh, biting his lips to hold in the words of anger and insult, that mounted in his tumultuous breast. But he was a father: there beside him he could hear that painful sobbing; he could see the shuddering of that poor, miserable body that he had once cradled in his arms. He stood beside Pedro and gravely took his head between his hands and kissed him on the forehead, once, then again, as though he were still a child, restoring to him forever all his tenderness.

'You were right, Father, you were right,' Pedro choked between sobs.

There was silence. Outside the rain lashed down on the house and the grounds with a steady din; a great wintry wind shook the trees below the windows.

Afonso broke the silence.

'But where have they gone, Pedro? What do you know, my boy? You can't just weep.'

'I know nothing,' Pedro said with an effort. 'I know she's gone. I went from Lisbon on Monday. That very night she left the house by carriage with a suit-case, her jewel-box, her new Italian maid and the child. She told the governess and the baby's nurse that she was going to join me. They were surprised, but what were they to say? When I came back I found this letter.'

The paper was already soiled. It must have been read many times since the morning, and screwed up in fury. He read it:

'It is destiny. I'm going away forever with the Prince. Forget me for I am not worthy of you, and I am taking Maria because I cannot be parted from her.'

'But the boy, where's the boy?' exclaimed Afonso.

Pedro suddenly seemed to remember.

'He's here with his nurse. I brought him in the carriage.'

The old man left the room at once. A few moments later he came back holding in his arms the little boy, wrapped in a long, white, fringed shawl and a lace bonnet. He was plump, with very black eyes and adorable, fresh, rosy cheeks. He was all chuckles, and gurgled as he shook his silver rattle. The nurse stood at the door sadly with her gaze on the carpet and a little bundle in her hand.

Afonso sat down slowly in his armchair and settled his grandson on his knee. His eyes filled with tenderness; he seemed to forget his son's grief and the family shame; all he was aware of now was that tender little face smiling in his arms.

'What's his name?'

'Carlos Eduardo,' murmured the nurse.

'Carlos Eduardo, eh?'

And he looked at the child a long time as though searching for signs of family likeness. Then he took in his own the two little red hands that clutched the rattle and, very gravely, as though the child could understand, said to him: 'Look at me. I'm your grandfather. You must love your grandfather!'

And at that strong voice the little one did indeed open his lovely eyes wide at him, serious all of a sudden, very steady, fearless of that grey beard; then he started to jump in his arms pulled away his little hand and began to bang him furiously on the head with his rattle.

The old man was filled with smiles at all that lively merriment; he held the child close to his broad chest a very long time. Then, comforted and moved, he placed a long kiss on the baby's face: his first grandfather's kiss. Then with great care, he placed the child in his nurse's arms.

'Go, nurse, away with you now. Gertrudes is already getting the room ready. Go and see what's needed.'

He shut the door after her, and came and sat down beside his son, who had not stirred from the corner of the sofa, nor taken his eyes off the floor.

'Now get it all off your chest, Pedro. Tell me everything. After all, we haven't seen one another for three years, my boy.'

'More than three years,' murmured Pedro. He got up and

looked out through the window where everything was sad under the rain; then, morosely surveying the library, he contemplated for a moment his own portrait, painted in Rome when he was twelve years old, all in blue velvet with a rose in his hand. And he repeated bitterly:

'You were right, Father. You were right.'

Little by little, as he walked up and down sighing, he began to talk of these recent years: the winter spent in Paris, life in Arroios, the intimacy of the Italian in the house, the plans for reconciliation – and at last that infamous letter, shameless, invoking fate, casting in his face the other man's name. When he had first read her letter he had thought of bloody revenge and wanted to hunt them down. But he had kept his sanity. It would have been ridiculous, after all. The flight must certainly have been planned beforehand, and he wasn't going to chase round the inns of Europe in search of his wife – or go and cry to the police to have them arrested! That would have been absurd! Nor would it have prevented her from getting even farther away, sleeping with another man on the journey. All that remained to him was contempt. It was as though he had kept a beautiful mistress for a few years and then she had gone off with another man. Good-bye! He was left with a motherless son who bore a dishonoured name. Never mind! Now what he needed was to forget, go on a long voyage, to America perhaps. His father would see, he would come back consoled and strong.

He said all these reasonable things in a voice that grew calmer as he walked up and down slowly with his burned-out cigar in his fingers. But suddenly he halted in front of his father with a dry laugh and a wild light in his eyes.

'I've always wanted to see America, and this is as good a time as any. It's a splendid opportunity, isn't it? I could even be naturalized – become president – or burst!'

'Yes. Later on we'll talk of these things, my boy,' put in the old man, startled.

At that moment the dinner-gong sounded at the bottom of the corridor.

'You still dine early, eh?' Pedro said. With a slow, tired sigh he added, 'We used to dine at seven.'

He urged his father to go to the table. There was no reason for him to miss his dinner. He himself would go upstairs for a while to his old bachelor quarters. His bed was still **there**, wasn't it? No, he didn't want anything to eat.

'Let Teixeira bring me a glass of gin. Teixeira's still here, good fellow!'

And seeing Afonso still sitting down, he repeated, impatient now: 'Go and dine, Father, go and dine, for God's sake!'

He went out. His father heard his footsteps on the floor above and the sound of windows noisily thrown open. Afonso walked towards the dining-room, where the servants, who must surely have learned of the tragedy from the nurse, were moving round on tip-toe, with that dismal slowness that occurs in a house where there is a death. Afonso sat down to table alone; but Pedro's place was set again; winter roses in a Japan vase shed their petals; and the old parrot, irritated by the rain, fidgeted furiously on his perch.

Afonso took a spoonful of soup, then he pushed his chair over to the hearth; and there he sat, wrapped little by little in that melancholy dusk of December, with his gaze on the fire, listening to the south-west wind on the panes, pondering on all the terrible things that had thus invaded, in sad uproar, his old man's peace. But in the midst of his pain, deep as it was, he sensed a tiny place, a corner of his heart, where something very sweet and very new throbbed with the freshness of rebirth, as though somewhere in his being there was bursting forth and budding a rich sprout of future joys; and his whole face smiled at the merry flame, as he recalled the rosy cheek under the white lace of the bonnet.

Night fell and the lights went on in the house.

Afonso began to feel anxious.

He went upstairs to his son's room. Everything was in darkness, damp and cold as though the rain were falling indoors. A shudder seized the old man and, when he called, Pedro's voice answered from the darkness of the window. There he was, with the window open, sitting outside on the balcony, gazing into the wildness of the night and the gloomy rustle of branches, taking the wind, the water and all that turbulent winter in his face.

'So, here you are, my boy!' exclaimed Afonso. 'The servants will be wanting to get the room ready. Won't you come downstairs for a while? You're all wet, Pedro.'

He felt his knees and his icy hands. Pedro started up impatiently and freed himself from the old man's tender touch.

'Oh, they want to prepare the room, eh? The air does me good, it does me so much good!'

Teixeira brought lamps, and behind him came Pedro's servant, who had arrived that moment from Arroios with a long case covered with oilcloth. The trunks had been left downstairs; and the coachman was there too, as none of the family was at home.

'All right, all right!' interrupted Afonso, 'Senhor Vilaça will go there tomorrow and he will give instructions.'

The servant went on tip-toe to deposit the case on the marble top of the commode where there still stood some old toilet flasks of Pedro's. And the candlesticks on the table lit up the big, bachelor's couch with its mattresses folded in the middle.

Gertrudes had entered busily, her arms filled with bed-clothes; Teixeira gave the bolsters a vigorous beating; the Arroios servant, who had put his hat down in a corner, came to help them, still on tip-toe. Meanwhile Pedro, like a sleep-walker, had gone back to the balcony with his head bared to the rain, fascinated by the darkness of the park as it loomed below with sounds like an angry sea.

Afonso pulled at his arm almost harshly.

'Pedro! Let them get on with the room! Come downstairs for a while!'

He followed his father mechanically down to the library, biting on the unlit cigar that had been in his hand since the afternoon. He sat down far from the light, on the corner of the sofa, and remained there, mute and leaden. For a long time only the slow footfalls of the old man, as he walked beside the tall book-cases, broke the silence that filled the room. The embers gradually died in the hearth and the night seemed to grow more chill. Suddenly there were splashes of water on the window-panes, carried in a squall that brought a deluge clattering down from the roof. Then there was a gloomy silence and far off a whisper of wind fleeing through the trees; in that silence the raindrops fell like a slow dirge; and then a gust of wind approached more fiercely still and swept around the house slamming windows, whirled round and departed again in a desolate howl.

46

'It's like a night in England,' Afonso said as he bent down to poke the fire.

But Pedro got up impetuously at his words. He must have been pierced with the thought of Maria, far away in a strange room, close in another's arms in an adulterous bed. For an instant he clasped his head in his hands, then came up to his father with an unsteady step but a very calm voice.

'I'm really very tired, Father. I think I'll go to bed. Good night. Tomorrow we'll talk about things.'

He kissed his father's hand and went slowly out.

Afonso stayed for a while with a book in his hand. But he did not read it. He was listening for sounds from above. But there was silence everywhere.

The clock struck ten. Before he retired he went to the room that had been given to the nursemaid. Gertrudes, the Arroios servant and Teixeira stood there whispering beside the commode in the shadow cast by a shade placed before the candlestick; they all went off on tip-toe when they heard his footsteps and the nursemaid carried on silently tidying up the drawers. There in the huge bed the child slept like a tired Infant Jesus, his rattle clutched in his hand. Afonso did not dare to kiss him for fear of wakening him with the roughness of his beard; but he touched him on the lace of his nightshirt, tucked in the bedclothes next to the wall, and straightened the curtains, moved to tenderness and feeling all his pain soothed in the shadow of that alcove where his grandson slept.

'Is anything needed, nurse?' he asked, lowering his voice.

'No, senhor.'

And so, without a sound, he went up to Pedro's room. There was a streak of light and he opened the door slightly. His son was writing, by the light of the two candles, with the case open at his side. He seemed startled to see his father, and as he lifted his face, wan and aged, two dark furrows made his eyes seem more prominent and hard.

'I'm writing,' he said. He rubbed his hands as though chilled from the cold of the room and added:

'Tomorrow, early, Vilaça must go to Arroios – the servants are there – I've two of my horses there – many things to be settled. I'm writing to him. His house is number 32, isn't it? Teixeira must know – good night, Papa, good night.'

47

Back in his own room alongside the library, Afonso could not settle down. An oppressive uneasiness made him lift his head from the pillow every now and then to listen; and now, through the silence of the house and the lowering wind, his son's footsteps sounded above him.

Dawn was breaking and Afonso was about to doze off when a shot suddenly resounded through the house. He sprang out of bed, shouting in alarm, and a servant hurried in with a lantern. From Pedro's room, with the door ajar, came the smell of gunpowder. Afonso found his son dead at the foot of the bed, fallen on his face in a pool of blood that was soaking into the carpet, and clutching a pistol in his hand.

Between the two candles, which were fluttering out in livid flickers, he had left a sealed letter with these words on the envelope in a firm hand: 'For Papa'.

Within a few days the house at Benfica was closed up. Afonso da Maia left with his grandson and all the servants for the estate at Santa Olávia.

When Vilaça went there in February to accompany Pedro's remains which were to be deposited in the family mausoleum, he was unable to keep back his tears as he caught sight of that dwelling in which he had passed so very many joyous Christmas days. Black baize covered the coat of arms, and that mourning cloth seemed to have dripped all its darkness over the mute façade and over the chestnuts that decorated the patio; inside, the servants spoke in hushed voices and wore heavy mourning; there was not a flower in the vases; Santa Olávia's particular enchantment – the fresh singing of the live waters from the pools and fountains – now flowed like the sorrowful cadences of a dirge. And Vilaça found Afonso in the library with the shutters closing out the bright winter sun, sunk in an armchair, his face cavernous under his uncut, white hair, and his hands thin and listless on his knees.

The steward went back to Lisbon with the news that the old man would not last out the year.

3

BUT THAT YEAR passed, and others followed.

One morning in April, on the eve of Easter, Vilaça arrived at Santa Olávia after a long absence.

He was not expected so soon; and as it was the first fine day of that rainy spring, the gentlemen were out in the park. The major-domo, Teixeira, who was already turning grey, looked very pleased to see the steward, with whom he sometimes corresponded, and led him into the dining-room where the old housekeeper Gertrudes, taken by surprise, dropped a pile of napkins and threw her arms round his neck.

The three french windows were open on to the terrace that stretched out in the sun with its marble balustrade covered in creepers; and Vilaça, approaching the steps that went down to the garden, could scarcely recognize Afonso da Maia in the old man with a snowy beard, but so robust and so rosy, who was climbing up the drive lined with pomegranate trees, leading his grandson by the hand.

Carlos, who had caught sight of a stranger on the terrace, wearing a tall hat and wrapped in a warm muffler, and had run forward to stare at him inquisitively, found himself gathered up into the arms of the good Vilaça, who let fall his umbrella and covered the boy's hair and face with kisses as he stammered: 'Oh, my little master, my dear little master! How fine you've grown, how big you are – '

'Well, how is it you've come without warning, Vilaça?' exclaimed Afonso da Maia, coming up with open arms. 'We didn't expect you until next week, old man!'

The two old men embraced; then their eyes met for a moment, bright and moist, and they embraced again warmly.

Carlos stood beside them, very grave, very slender, with his hands buried in the pockets of his white flannel breeches, and his cap of the same material on one side over his beautiful black curls. He continued to stare at Vilaça, who, with a trembling lip, had taken off his glove and was wiping his eyes under his spectacles.

'And nobody to meet you, not even a servant, down there by the river!' Afonso was saying. 'But still here we have you, and that's the principal thing. How well you are looking.'

'And you too, senhor!' stammered the steward choking back a sob. 'Not a wrinkle! White-haired, yes, but the face of a boy. I hardly recognized you. When I remember the last time I saw you – and the boy! This lovely boy!'

He was about to kiss Carlos again enthusiastically, but the lad fled with an exuberant laugh, bounding from the terrace, and went to hang from a trapeze set up between the trees, and there he stayed, swinging rhythmically, strong and graceful, calling:

'You are Vilaça!'

Vilaça, his umbrella under his arm, turned and gazed at Carlos in rapture.

'He's a lovely child! A splendid boy! And he takes after his father. The same eyes, the Maia eyes, the curly hair – but he'll be much more of a man!'

'He's healthy and strong,' said the old man smilingly as he stroked his beard. 'And how's Manuel, your own lad? When's the wedding? Come along inside, Vilaça, there's a lot to talk about.'

They had entered the dining-room where the flame of a log in the tiled fireplace flickered in the fine, wide April light; porcelain and silver shone on the sideboards of aloe wood; and the canaries sounded mad with joy.

Gertrudes, who had stayed to watch, approached with her hands folded on her white apron, familiar and affectionate.

'Well, senhor, this is a cause for rejoicing to see this ungrateful creature back at Santa Olávia!'

Then, with a look of fondness on her face, pale and round like an old moon, on which some white whiskers now grew, she added:

'Ah, Senhor Vilaça, things are different now! Even the canaries sing! And I'd be singing too if I could – '

And then she went out, suddenly moved and in need of a good cry.

Teixeira waited, a superior and silent laugh spreading from one point to the other of his turned-up major-domo's collar.

'I believe they've got the blue room ready for Senhor

Vilaça, eh?' asked Afonso. 'The Viscountess occupies your old room now.'

Vilaça hastened to ask after her ladyship, the Viscountess. She was a Runa, a cousin of Afonso's wife, who had once had her praises sung by the poets of the town of Caminha, and had married a minor Galician nobleman, the Viscount d'Urigo de la Sierra, a drunkard and a bully who used to beat her. Now that she was widowed and poor, Afonso had given her shelter, both as a matter of family duty and also to have a lady at Santa Olávia.

'She hasn't been so well lately.' He looked at his watch and interrupted the exchange of news to suggest that Vilaça go and change for dinner.

Surprised, the steward also looked at the clock, then at the table already laid, the six covers, the basket of flowers, the decanters of port.

'So, now you dine in the morning, senhor? I thought it was lunch.'

'I'll explain – Carlos needs a strict schedule. At dawn he is already out in the park; he lunches at seven; and he dines at one. And I, for my part, supervise the boy's manners.'

'And you, senhor,' exclaimed Vilaça, 'you change your habits at your age! What it must be to be a grandfather!'

'Don't be silly! That's not it at all. It does me good. Really, it does me good. But get yourself ready, Vilaça, for Carlos does not like to be kept waiting. Perhaps the Abbé will be here too.'

'Father Custódio? Splendid! Well, if you will excuse me – '

Outside in the corridor Vilaça met Teixeira, the old major-domo, who took his umbrella and wrap.

'Tell me, Senhor Vilaça,' he asked, 'how do you find us all up here?'

'I'm very satisfied, Teixeira, very satisfied indeed. It's a pleasure to come here.' Placing his hand familiarly on the old servant's shoulder, he winked an eye in which there was still the trace of a tear. 'Everything here revolves around the boy. He's brought the old master back to life!'

Teixeira smiled respectfully and agreed that the boy was in fact the joy of the house.

'Hello! Who's that playing the fiddle?' exclaimed Vilaça, stopping on the staircase as the sound of a violin tuning up came down to him.

'That's Senhor Brown, the Englishman, the young master's tutor. Very talented, it's wonderful to hear him; sometimes he plays at night in the drawing-room and the Judge accompanies him on the concertina. This is your room, Senhor Vilaça.'

'Very nice. Yes, indeed.'

The polish on the new furniture shone in the light from the two windows. A beige carpet scattered with tiny blue flowers covered the floor and the cretonne curtains repeated the same blue petals on a light ground. All this fresh country comfort delighted Vilaça. He at once went to finger the cretonnes, rubbed the marble of the commode and tested the solidity of the chairs. So these were the furnishings bought in Oporto, eh? Well, they were elegant. And really they had not been costly. He stood on the tips of his toes examining two English water-colours of pedigree cows, sitting on the grass in the shade of romantic ruins.

Teixeira, with his watch in his hand, urged Vilaça to make haste.

'You've only ten minutes, senhor – the young master doesn't like to be kept waiting.'

Vilaça decided to unwrap his scarf; then he took off his heavy knitted woollen waistcoat; and through his half-open shirt could be glimpsed a scarlet flannel for his rheumatism, and his scapulars of embroidered silk. Teixeira was unfastening the straps of his suit-case; at the end of the corridor the violin had broken into the *Carnival of Venice*; and through the closed windows could be sensed the bright air, the freshness and peace of the fields and all that green April.

Vilaça, now without his glasses, shivered a little as he passed the end of a moistened towel over his neck and behind his ears.

'So our Carlinhos doesn't like to be kept waiting, eh?' he asked. 'It's clear he's the one that rules the roost – I expect he's spoiled beyond words.'

But Teixeira enlightened the steward solemnly and gravely. Spoiled, was it? Poor little fellow. He had been ruled with a rod of iron! He could tell Senhor Vilaça a thing or two. The child was scarcely five years old when he had already been made to sleep by himself in a room without a nightlight. And it was into a bathful of cold water with him every morning, even when it was freezing outside. And plenty of other barbarous cruelties. Were Teixeira not convinced of the grandfather's great love for the child, he should think he wanted to kill him. God forgive him for saying such a thing – no, it wasn't that! It seemed it was the English way! He was allowed to run, fall, climb trees, get wet, get sunburned – like the child of any cottager. And then there was his strict diet! He was allowed to eat only at certain times, and certain foods – and sometimes the child would be wide-eyed and watering at the mouth! It was very, very hard.

'Well, God has willed that he should turn out strong,' Texeira added. 'But neither Gertrudes nor I ever approved of this kind of training.'

Again he looked at his watch, fastened with a black ribbon to his white waistcoat, and took a few slow steps through the room. Then he picked up the steward's frock-coat from the bed and took a brush to its collar, lightly and as a matter of courtesy, while he stood beside the dressing-table where Vilaça was fixing his two long strands of hair across his baldness.

'Do you know, senhor, what the English tutor started by teaching him? Rowing! Rowing, Senhor Vilaça, like a boatman! Not to mention swinging on a trapeze and other clown's tricks. I hardly like to talk about it. For I'd be the first to say that Brown is a good fellow – quiet, clean, an excellent musician. But as I've said to Gertrudes time and again, all that sort of thing may be good enough for the English, but it's not right for a Portuguese nobleman. No indeed! You, senhor, you should hear what Dona Ana Silveira has to say on the subject.'

There was a light knock on the door. Teixeira stopped talking. A footman entered, made a sign to the major-domo, respectfully took from his arm the frock-coat, and then stood with it next to the dressing-table where Vilaça, flushed and hurried, still struggled with his rebellious locks.

Teixeira called from the door with his watch in his hand: 'It's dinner. You have two minutes, senhor!'

Still buttoning up his coat, the steward went downstairs.

Everybody was already in the dining-room. By the fireside where the embers were dying into white ash, Brown was leafing through *The Times*. Carlos sat astride his grandfather's knees and was recounting a long story about boys and fights. Beside them the good Abbé Custódio, his snuff-box forgotten in his hands, listened open-mouthed with a paternal and tender smile.

'Look who's here, Abbé,' said Afonso.

The Abbé turned round and slapped his thigh in astonishment.

'What a surprise! So, it's our good Vilaça! And nobody told me! How are those old bones, man?'

Carlos jogged up and down on his grandfather's knees, delighted at the sight of two old men embracing – one of them with his few remaining hairs plastered across his bald head, the other with a bald crown amid a bush of white hair. And as they continued, hands clasped, to admire each other and study the lines the years had left on each other's faces, Afonso said: 'Vilaça! The Viscountess – '

The steward, however, looked for her in vain with his eyes wide and roaming over the room in search of her. Carlos laughed and clapped his hands – and at last Vilaça discovered her in a corner between the china cabinet and the window, on a low chair, dressed in black, timid and silent, with her fleshy arms resting on her plump waist. Her smooth, flaccid face, as white as paper, the lines on her neck – all were suddenly covered in scarlet as she speechlessly extended a puffy white hand, with one finger wrapped in a piece of black silk, to Vilaça. Then she went on fanning herself with a great sequin-covered fan, her chest heaving, her eyes drooping, as though overcome by the effort.

Two footmen started to ladle out the soup. Teixeira waited, outlined behind the high back of Afonso's chair. But Carlos was still jogging up and down on his grandfather's knees wanting to finish another story. It was Manuel, he had had a stone in his hand . . . First he had thought of making peace . . . but the two boys had started laughing, so he had put the lot of them to flight.

'Were they bigger than you?'

'Three great lads, Grandpapa. You can ask Auntie Pedra. She saw them, for she was on the threshing-floor. One of them was carrying a sickle – '

'Very good, very good, my boy! We're convinced – now dismount for the soup is growing cold.'

And the old man, beaming like a happy patriarch, came and sat at the head of the table.

'He's starting to get heavy – he's too big for my lap.'

But he noticed Brown and, getting up again, presented his steward.

'Senhor Brown, my friend Vilaça – please forgive me, I was careless, it's all due to that gentleman there at the end of the table – Dom Carlos the giant killer!'

The tutor, solidly buttoned up in his long military coat, went the round of the table, stiff and upright, to come and wring Vilaça's arm in a tremendous handshake. Then, without a word, he went back to his place, unfolded his napkin, and smoothed his formidable moustaches; only then did he speak to Vilaça in his strong English accent: 'A very fine day – glorious!'

'A time of roses,' answered Vilaça gallantly. He felt intimidated before that athletic figure.

On that day, naturally, they talked of the journey from Lisbon, the good mail-coach service, the railway that was about to be opened – Vilaça had come on the train as far as Carregado.

'It must be terrifying, eh?' asked the Abbé, suspending the spoon he had been about to lift to his lips.

The worthy man had never left Resende; and all the wide world beyond the shade of his sacristy and the trees of his garden-walk aroused in him the fear of Babel – above all, that iron road about which there was so much talk.

'It does make you shiver a bit,' declared Vilaça with the voice of experience. 'Say what they like, but it does make you shiver!'

The Abbé, however, was most terrified of the inevitable disasters that would occur with those machines!

Vilaça then recalled accidents with the mail-coaches. On the Alcobaça coach, when it had turned upside down, two Sisters of Charity had been crushed to death! In all this sort of thing there were dangers. You could break a leg walking in your bedroom . . .

The Abbé liked progress. He even thought progress was necessary. But it seemed to him that they wanted to do everything in a rush. The country was not ready for such inventions; what it needed were good, safe roads.

'And economy!' said Vilaça, pulling the pimentos towards him.

'Bucelas?' murmured a footman over his shoulder.

The steward raised his glass when it had been filled, admired its rich colour in the light, tasted it with the tip of his tongue and winked an eye at Afonso.

'It's our own!'

'The old one,' said Afonso. 'Ask Brown – eh, Brown, a good nectar?'

'Magnificent!' exclaimed the tutor with fiery energy.

Then Carlos stretched his arm across the table and also demanded Bucelas. His reason was that it was a celebration because Vilaça had come. Grandfather would not consent; the lad could have his glass of Colares, as usual, and one only. Carlos folded his arms on the napkin that hung from his neck, astonished at such injustice! So, not even to toast Vilaça could he have a drop of Bucelas? That was a fine way of receiving guests at the manor! Gertrudes had told him that as the steward had come he would wear his new velvet suit that night for tea. Now they had said it was not a celebration nor even a case for Bucelas. He didn't understand.

Grandfather, who was drinking in his words entranced, suddenly put on a severe face.

'It seems to me, sir, you're talking too much. Only grown-ups may speak at table.'

Carlos immediately drooped over his plate, murmuring very mildly: 'Very well, Grandpapa, don't be cross. I'll wait until I'm big.'

There was a smile round the table. Even the Viscountess was delighted and idly moved her fan; the Abbé, his good face beaming blissfully at the child, clasped his hairy hands against his chest, so witty had these words seemed to him; and Afonso coughed behind his napkin, as though wiping his whiskers – and hiding his smile and the admiration that shone in his eyes.

Such vivacity also surprised Vilaça. He wanted to hear the boy and, putting down his fork, he spoke to him: 'Tell me, Carlinhos, how are your lessons going?'

The lad, without looking at him, leaned back and dug his hands into the waistband of his flannels. He replied in superior tones: 'I can already make Brigida side-step.'

His grandfather was unable to contain himself and burst out laughing.

'That's a good one! He can already make Brigida side-step! And it's true, Vilaça, he already can – ask Brown. Isn't it true, Brown? The little mare's a tiny thing, but clever.'

'Oh, Grandpapa,' cried Carlos, excited now, 'come, tell Vilaça. Isn't it true that I could drive the dog-cart?'

Afonso resumed his severe look.

'I don't deny it – perhaps you could indeed drive it if you were permitted to do so. But, if you please, don't boast of your feats, for a good horseman should be modest – and, above all, don't bury your hands like that under your belly.'

Vilaça meanwhile was cracking his knuckles and preparing to make an observation. There was certainly no better talent than riding on horseback – but what he wanted to know was whether Pedro had already started with his Phaedrus and his Titus Livius.

'Vilaça, Vilaça,' warned the Abbé, with his fork in the air, and the smile of a mischievous saint. 'You're not allowed to talk of Latin here to our noble friend – he won't have it – thinks it's out of date. Out of date it certainly is.'

'Come now, Abbé, help yourself to some of that fricassee,' said Afonso, 'for I know your weaknesses, and leave Latin alone.'

As the Abbé helped himself to some juicy pieces of game, he murmured: 'But you've got to begin with Latin. You've got to begin there – a little Latin's the best foundation!'

'Not at all! Latin will come later!' exclaimed Brown with a forceful gesture. 'Firrrst strrrength! Strrrength and muscles – '

And he repeated the words twice over, waving his formidable fists: 'Firrrst muscles, firrrst muscles!'

Afonso agreed gravely with him. Brown was right. Latin was pedants' luxury. There was nothing more absurd than to start teaching a child in a dead language who Fabius, king of the Sabines, was, or the story of the Gracchi, and other business of an extinct nation, while leaving him in ignorance of the nature of the rain that wets him, or how to make the bread he eats, and all the other affairs of the universe in which he lives.

'But the classics, after all – ' ventured the Abbé timidly.

'To the devil with the classics. The first duty of a man is to live. And for this he must be healthy and strong. All sensible education consists in this: to develop health, strength and the formation of good habits, to concentrate on the development of the animal, and equip him with great physical superiority. Just as though he had no soul. The soul comes later – the soul is another luxury. It's the luxury of grown-ups.'

The Abbé scratched his head and shuddered.

'A little education is necessary,' he said, 'don't you think so, Vilaça? Of course, you, Senhor Afonso da Maia, you've seen more of the world than I – but education, you know – '

'For a child, education is not the recitation of *Tityre, tu patulae recubans*. It's the knowledge of facts, definitions, useful things, practical things – '

He stopped speaking. With shining eyes he signalled to Vilaça to look at his grandson who was chattering away in English to Brown. It must surely have been the tale of feats of prowess, fights with other boys, that he was recounting so animatedly while gesticulating with his fists. The tutor nodded approvingly as he twisted his moustaches. And round the table, the gentlemen with their forks in mid-air, behind them the footmen standing with napkins over their arms – all, in a reverent silence, admired the little boy speaking English.

'A great gift, a great gift,' murmured Vilaça, bending towards the Viscountess.

The excellent lady coloured as she smiled. She seemed fatter thus, all crouched in her chair, silent and continually eating; and at each gulp of Bucelas, she would refresh herself languidly with her great, black, sequin-covered fan.

When Teixeira had served the port Afonso proposed a toast to Vilaça. Glasses were raised in a friendly hubbub. Carlos wanted to cry hurrah! His grandfather silenced him with a gesture. In the contented hush that fell, the little boy declared very earnestly –

'Oh, Grandpapa, I like Vilaça. Vilaça is a great friend.'

'Very much so, and over very many years, sir!' exclaimed the old steward, so moved that he could scarcely raise the glass in his hand.

Dinner was over. Outside, the sun had left the terrace, and the park lay green and sweet in the calm air, under an intense blue sky. In the hearth there were only white ashes; the lilacs in their vases gave off a strong scent, which mingled with the smell of caramel and lemon. The servants in their white waistcoats cleared the table with an occasional tinkle of silver, and all the white damask lay concealed under a profusion of dessert while the golden glint of the port shone among the crystal dishes of conserves. Overcome with the heat, the Viscountess fanned herself. Father Custódio slowly rolled up his napkin and the folds in the sleeves of his cassock shone with wear.

Then, smiling tenderly, Afonso proposed a final toast.

'Long live Dom Carlos, the giant-killer!'

'To Dom Grandpapa!' said the child, drinking the dregs of his glass.

The little head, with its black hair, the old face with its snowy beard, greeted each other from the ends of the table – while everyone smiled, in the fondness of that ceremony.

Then, toothpick in mouth, the Abbé said grace. The Viscountess, shutting her eyes, also joined her hands. And Vilaça, who was a believer, disliked the sight of Carlos taking no notice of grace and jumping up from his chair to throw his arms round his grandfather's neck and whisper in his ear.

'No, no. No, indeed!' said the old man.

But the boy, who hugged him more tightly than ever, argued insistently, more coaxingly than a kiss, and the old man's face softened with indulgence.

'Only because it's a special occasion, then,' he said at last, giving in. 'But mind, now – '

The boy jumped up, clapped his hands, caught Vilaça by the arms, spun him round, and started to chant in a rhythm all his own:

'What a good thing you came, you came, you came – I'm off to fetch Terezinha, inha, inha, inha – '

'That's his sweetheart,' said the grandfather, rising from the table. 'He's already in love She's the Silveira child – We'll take coffee on the terrace, Teixeira.'

Outside the day was inviting and lovely with a smooth blue sky, very pure, very high and without a cloud. In front of the terrace the scarlet geraniums were already out; the sprouts on the shrubs, still tender, as delicate as lace, seemed to tremble at the slightest breath; at times a faint scent of violets mingled with the sweet fragrance of meadow flowers was wafted over; the high fountain sang; on the garden paths bordered with low privet hedges, the fine sand sparkled faintly in the timid sun of that delayed spring which enveloped the green of the park in the distance, and everything drowsed in a fresh, golden light at that siesta hour.

The three men sat down to their coffee. In front of the terrace,

Brown, his Scottish bonnet to one side, and his big pipe in his mouth, pushed the bar of the trapeze high for Carlos to swing on. Then the good Vilaça asked if he might turn his back. He could not bear to watch gymnastics; he knew there was no danger; but even with wooden horses, merry-go-rounds or hoops, he became dizzy; and he was always left with his stomach knotted.

'And I fear it's imprudent just after dinner – '

'Imprudent, indeed! It's only swinging – just look at him!'

But Vilaça did not move and kept his face over his cup.

The Abbé, on the contrary, sat with his lips half open in admiration and his saucer full of coffee forgotten in his hand.

'Look at him, Vilaça,' repeated Afonso. 'It won't do you any harm, man!'

Vilaça turned round with an effort. The little boy, high up in the air, his legs rigid against the bar of the trapeze, his hands on the ropes, was swooping down on the terrace, curving through space with his hair swept in the wind; then up he went serenely, straightening up in the full sunlight; all of him smiled; his blouse and his breeches billowed in the wind; and as he darted by a glimpse could be caught of his bright eyes, very black, very wide.

'I can't help not liking it,' said Vilaça. 'I think it's imprudent.'

Afonso clapped his hands and the Abbé cried bravo, bravo! Vilaça turned back to applaud but Carlos had already vanished; the trapeze swung slowly to a standstill; and Brown, once again picking up *The Times* that he had put aside on the pedestal of a bust, went down the park, wrapped in a cloud of smoke from his pipe.

'A fine thing, gymnastics!' exclaimed Afonso da Maia as he contentedly lit another cigar.

Vilaça had heard they very much weakened the chest. And the Abbé, after taking a sip of coffee and licking his lips, uttered the fine phrase he had arranged like a maxim –

'This education makes athletes, but it doesn't make Christians. I've already said it – '

'You have indeed, Abbé, you have indeed!' cried Afonso gaily. 'You tell me so every week. Do you know, Vilaça, our Custódio is pounding my ears for me to teach the boy the Catechism? The Catechism!'

Custódio sat for a moment looking at Afonso with a disconsolate face and his snuff-box open in his hand; the impiety of that old nobleman, lord of practically the whole parish, was one of his sorrows.

'Yes, the Catechism, senhor, the Catechism, even though you speak of it so scornfully – the Catechism! But it's not only the Catechism. There are other matters. And if I do mention it so often, Senhor Afonso da Maia, it's because of the love I bear the boy!'

And at once the old argument started again. It always came up whenever Custódio dined with Afonso.

The good man found it horrifying that at his age, such a fine boy, the heir to a great house, with future responsibilities in society, should not know his Catechism. He related at length to Vilaça what that virtuous lady, the wife of the clerk of the court, had told him. She had happened to be passing the park gate and had spoken to Carlos. She was affectionate and fond of children and had asked him to recite the Act of Contrition. And what had the child replied? That he had never heard of it! Things like this made one sad. And Senhor Afonso da Maia was merely amused and laughed! Now friend Vilaça could say whether it was a laughing matter or not. No, Senhor Afonso da Maia was very learned and had seen much of the world; but of one thing Abbé Custódio would not be convinced – though he was only a simple priest who had never even been to Oporto – it was that there could be no happiness nor a well-conducted life without the moral training of the Catechism – '

Afonso da Maia interrupted good-humouredly :

'Well now, and what would you teach him, Abbé, if I handed the boy over to you? That one should not steal money from people's pockets; nor lie; nor ill-treat inferiors – because all this is against God's Commandments and leads one to hell, eh? Isn't that it?'

'There's more to it – '

'I know that. But you would teach him not to do any of these things because they're sinful and offend God. However, he already knows he should not do them because they are unworthy of a gentleman and a decent man – '

'But, senhor – '

'Listen, Abbé. There's all the difference here. I want the boy to be virtuous for the love of virtue, and honourable for the love of honour; not for fear of hell's kitchens, nor lured by the bait of heaven.'

Rising, he added with a smile: 'But the real duty of decent men, Abbé, on a day like this, after all these weeks of rain, is to go and take a breath of fresh air in the fields and not to sit here disputing moral theology. So let's be off. And if Vilaça's not too fatigued, let's take a turn round the grounds.'

The Abbé sighed like a saint who sees the black impiety of the times and Beelzebub carrying off the best sheep in his flock; then he looked at his cup and sipped the rest of his coffee with enjoyment.

When Afonso da Maia, the Abbé and Vilaça returned from their walk round the estate night was falling, the house was lit up and there were visitors, the Silveiras, two rich ladies who owned the Lagoaça manor.

Dona Ana Silveira, the elder and the spinster, was known as the talented sister. She was the great authority in those parts on points of doctrine and etiquette. The widow, Dona Eugénia, was content to be known as an excellent and phlegmatic lady, pleasingly plump, dark and long-lashed. She had two children. Terezinha, Carlos's sweetheart, was a thin, lively little girl with hair as black as ink; the son and heir, Eusèbiozinho, was a child prodigy famous throughout the neighbourhood.

Almost since his cradle this remarkable boy had shown an edifying addiction to great tomes and everything connected with learning. While he was still crawling he developed a taste for sitting in a corner on a mat, wrapped in a blanket, leafing through huge volumes, with his little bald sage's pate bent over the pages. When he had grown bigger he had been so well-behaved that he sat for hours motionless in a chair, his legs dangling, picking his nose. He never wanted to play with a drum or a toy gun. Instead he was given exercise books and, to the amazement of Mama and Auntie, the precocious scholar passed his time writing figures, with his little tongue hanging out.

His future had already been mapped out: he was rich so first he would graduate in the law, then he would become a judge. When he came to Santa Olávia, Auntie Ana would at once place him at the table, beside the lamp, to admire the pictures in a huge, rich volume entitled *The Customs of All the Peoples of the Universe.* There he was that night, dressed as usual as a Scot, with a plaid of flaming checks in red and black thrown over his shoulder and caught there by a brooch. In order to keep up this appearance of a noble Stuart, a valiant knight straight out of Walter Scott, he was made to keep on his bonnet on which there heroically waved a shining cock's feather. There was nothing in the world more melancholy than that dull little face, puffy and yellow like butter because of too many threadworms, with its vague and bluish little eyes, without lashes as though they had already been worn away by science, gazing with adult gravity at the Sicilian peasant women or ferocious Montenegran warriors leaning on guns, on the mountain peaks.

Before the sofa where the ladies were sitting, sat that faithful friend, the public prosecutor, a solemn and dignified man, who had been pondering over and meditating marriage with the widowed Silveira sister for five years without being able to make his mind up – contenting himself each year with purchasing another half-dozen sheets, or yet another roll of fine linen to augment her trousseau. These purchases were discussed in the Silveiras' house around the hearth; and the allusions, modest but inevitable, to the two pillow-slips, to the size of the sheets, to warm blankets for cosy Januaries – instead of inflaming the magistrate, disquieted him. On the days that followed he would appear preoccupied, as though the prospect of the sacred consummation of matrimony filled him with the dread of some feat to be undertaken : like having to take a bull by the horns, or swim the rapids of the Douro. And so, for some specious reason or other, he would postpone the wedding to the next St Michael's day. And then, relieved and tranquil, the worthy magistrate would continue to accompany the Silveiras to afternoon teas and church festivals or condolences, dressed in black, affable, helpful, smiling to Dona Eugénia, wanting no greater pleasure than that paternal conviviality.

Hardly had Afonso entered the room than he was informed of misfortunes. The Judge and his lady would not be coming because the Judge was suffering from his pain; and the Branco sisters had sent a message to excuse themselves, poor dears, for it was a sad day for the house as it was the seventeenth anniversary of the day when brother Manuel had died.

'All right,' said Afonso, 'All right! Pain, sadness, brother

Manuel. Let's make up a foursome at ombre – what does our good magistrate say to that?'

The worthy man bowed his bald forehead murmuring that he was 'at your service'.

'To work, to work!' exclaimed the Abbé as he rubbed his hands together in excitement.

The partners went towards the card-room which was divided from the drawing-room by a damask curtain, now drawn back to reveal the green-topped table, and the packs of cards open like fans in the circles of light that fell from the lamps. A moment later the prosecutor returned smiling, saying he had left them to 'indulgence in a threesome for money', and regained his place beside Dona Eugénia, crossing his feet under the chair and his hands on top of his stomach. The ladies were talking about the Judge's pain. He usually had it every three months, and his obstinacy in refusing to consult a physician was reprehensible. The more so as he was very worn out, dried up, yellow – while Dona Augusta, his wife, was fast gaining weight and colour! The Viscountess, burying her corpulence in a corner of the sofa, with her fan open against her breast, recounted that in Spain she had seen a similar case – the man had reached the point of looking like a skeleton, and his wife like a barrel; and at first it had been the other way round; verses had even been composed on the subject.

'Humours!' said the magistrate melancholically.

Then they talked about the Branco sisters; they could remember the death of Manuel Branco, poor boy, in the flower of his youth! And what a perfect-looking boy! What a sensible boy! Dona Ana Silveira had not forgotten – as she never forgot each year – to light a candle for his soul and to say three 'Our Fathers'. The Viscountess seemed very distressed not to have remembered. And she had really intended to!

'Well, I was going to send and tell you!' exclaimed Dona Ana. 'And the Brancos are always so grateful, my dear.'

'There's still time,' murmured the magistrate.

Dona Eugénia made an indolent stitch in her crotchet work, which she was never parted from, and murmured with a sigh: 'Everyone has their dead.'

And in the hush that descended another sigh came from the corner of the sofa, from the Viscountess, who was surely recalling the noble Urigo de la Sierra, and she murmured too: 'Everyone has their dead.'

And, as he passed a hand reflectively across his bald forehead, the worthy magistrate ended by concurring: 'Everyone has their dead.'

The atmosphere grew sleepy. The flames leapt tall and sad from the gilded candlesticks that stood on the consoles. Cautiously and artistically, Eusèbiozinho turned the pages of *The Customs of All the Peoples*. And from the card-room the now blasphemous voice of the Abbé could be heard through the open curtain growling in friendly rage:

'I pass, and that's all I've done the whole blessed evening!'

Suddenly Carlos burst into the drawing-room, dragging his bride, Terezinha, all dishevelled and rosy from play; and at once their prattle enlivened the sleepy sofa.

The bridal pair had just got back from a picturesque and dangerous voyage, and Carlos seemed dissatisfied with his spouse; she had behaved atrociously; when he had been driving the mail-coach, she had wanted to climb up beside him on the driver's box; and ladies did not ride on the driver's seat.

'And he threw me to the ground, Auntie!'

'It's not true! And what's more she's a liar! It was the same thing when we arrived at the inn – she wanted to go to bed and I didn't – when people get to the end of a journey the first thing to be done is to see to the horses – and the horses were soaking!'

Dona Ana's voice interrupted very severely:

'That's enough! That's enough! Stop this nonsense! There's been enough horseplay. Sit down there beside the Viscountess, Tereza. Look at that hair-slide! What a way to behave – '

She always hated to see her neice, a well-brought up miss of ten, playing in this fashion with Carlinhos. The handsome and impetuous boy, untrained in religion or manners, terrified her; and through her old maid's mind there passed a constant train of ideas, suspicions of outrages that he might commit against the little girl. At home, as she wrapped her up before coming to Santa Olávia, she would warn her forcefully against going with Carlos into dark corners! And she must never let him interfere with her clothes! The little girl, who had very languorous eyes, would murmur: 'Yes, Auntie!'

65

But scarcely had they arrived than she would want to play with her little husband. If they were married why shouldn't they play at house, or have a shop and earn their living with kisses? But the violent boy wanted only war, four chairs in a row for a galloping horse, journeys to lands with barbarous names that Brown had taught him. Vexed, seeing her heart misunderstood, she would call him a brute; he would threaten to box her in the English fashion; and they would separate crossly.

But when she nestled beside the Viscountess, a grave little thing with her hands folded on her lap, Carlos at once stretched himself out beside her, half leaning back on the sofa and swinging his legs.

'Come now, boy, your manners!' Dona Ana rebuked him very drily.

'I'm tired. I've been driving four horses,' he answered insolently without looking at her.

But suddenly, in a leap, he threw himself on Eusèbiozinho. He wanted to carry him off to Africa to fight the savages; and he was already pulling him by his beautiful Scottish plaid when Mama ran terrified to the rescue.

'No, you mustn't do that to Eusèbiozinho, child! He's not strong enough for such rough play – Carlinhos, I'll call your grandfather!'

But Eusèbiozinho, who had just been pulled more strongly, rolled to the floor emitting fearful shrieks. Turmoil reigned. Trembling, the mother bent down to him and pulled him up on his soft little legs, wiping away his tears alternately with a handkerchief and with kisses, almost crying too. Dismayed, the magistrate picked up the Scottish bonnet and sadly smoothed the lovely cock's feather. And the Viscountess hugged both her hands to her enormous bosom as though its palpitations might suffocate her.

Eusèbiozinho was then placed solicitously at his aunt's side; and that stern lady, with an angry blush on her thin face, clutching her closed fan like a weapon, made ready to repel Carlinhos who leaped around the sofa with his hands behind his back laughing and snarling ferociously at Eusèbiozinho. But at that instant nine o'clock struck, and the unbending figure of Brown appeared in the doorway.

Hardly had Carlos caught sight of him when he ran for shelter behind the Viscountess shouting:

'It's still very early, Brown. Today's a special occasion. I'm not going to bed!'

It was then that Afonso da Maia, who had not stirred for the piercing howls of the little Silveira, called from the card-table in severe tones:

'Carlos, have the goodness to be off to bed at once.'

'Oh, Grandpapa, it's a special occasion. Vilaça's here!'

Afonso da Maia put down the cards, crossed the drawing-room without a word, took hold of him by the arm and dragged him down the corridor – while the boy, with his heels dug into the floor, resisted and protested desperately.

'It's a special occasion, Grandpapa – it's not fair. Vilaça will be offended – oh, Grandpapa, I'm not sleepy!'

A door closed and the clamour was muffled. The ladies at once fell to censuring such sternness. It was beyond comprehension. His grandfather allowed the boy to perpetrate all sorts of outrages, and then refused to let him share a little of the evening.

'Oh, Senhor Afonso da Maia, why don't you let the child stay?'

'Routine is necessary, routine is necessary,' he answered, coming in all pale from his severity.

At the card-table, as he picked up the cards with trembling hands, he went on repeating:

'One must have routine. At night children must sleep.'

Dona Ana Silveira, turning to Vilaça, who had given up his place to the magistrate and had come to talk to the ladies, twisted her lips in the sceptical smile that she always wore whenever Afonso da Maia talked about routine.

She leaned back in her chair, opened her fan, and declared in a voice heavy with irony that perhaps because her wits were dull she herself had never seen the advantage of routine – it was the English way, so they said; perhaps it worked well in England; but if she was not mistaken Santa Olávia was in the kingdom of Portugal.

And as Vilaça timidly bowed his head, with his snuff-box between his fingers, the clever lady, unburdened herself in a low voice so that Afonso inside could not hear. Senhor Vilaça, of course, did not know, but that education Carlinhos was receiving had never been approved by the friends of the house. To start with, the presence of Brown, a heretic, a Protestant, as tutor in the Maia family, had caused disapprobation in Resende. Above all, when Senhor Afonso could have that saintly man, the Abbé Custódio, who was so esteemed, a man of so much learning – He would not teach the child acrobatic feats; instead he would give him a nobleman's training, prepare him to cut a good figure at Coimbra.

At that instant, the Abbé, suspecting a draught, rose from the card-table to draw the curtain, and now that Afonso could not overhear, Dona Ana raised her voice.

'And you know, Senhor Vilaça, it's a great trial for Custódio. Carlinhos, poor child, doesn't know a word of doctrine . . . But I want to tell you what happened to Macedo's wife.'

Vilaça already knew.

'Ah, you've heard! Do you remember, Viscountess? Macedo's wife and the act of contrition?'

The Viscountess sighed and raised a mute eye to heaven through the ceiling.

'Frightful!' continued Dona Ana. 'The poor woman arrived there at our house overcome. I was very upset. I even dreamed about it three nights running.'

She stopped speaking for a moment. Vilaça, who was embarrassed and uneasy, twisted his snuff-box between his fingers with his eyes fixed on the carpet. A drowsy atmosphere filled the room; Dona Eugénia, her eyelids heavy, made a slow stitch now and then in her crochet; and Carlos's bride, stretched out in the corner of the sofa, had fallen asleep, her little mouth open, her lovely black hair falling down her neck.

Dona Ana yawned slightly and picked up the thread of her talk.

'And not to mention that the child is very backward. Apart from a bit of English he doesn't know anything – no talents at all!'

'But he's very clever, my dear lady,' protested Vilaça.

'Possibly,' drily retorted the intelligent Silveira sister.

Turning to Eusèbiozinho who sat beside her as still as though made of plaster, she said:

'My child, recite those pretty verses you've learned to Senhor Vilaça here. Don't be tongue-tied, come! Come, Eusèbio, there's a good boy!'

But the little boy, limp and dismal, would not move from his aunt's skirts; it was she who had to stand him up and support him so that the tender prodigy should not topple over on his flaccid little legs; and his Mama promised him that if he said the nice verses he would be allowed to sleep with her that night. This decided him. He opened his mouth and a slow and drooling recital began flowing out in a trickle of a voice, as though from a loose tap:

> ' 'Tis night, the nostalgic star,
> Breaks through a leaden sky;
> Its lovely face is shadowed,
> And veiled by the clouds on high.'

He recited it all, motionless, his little hands hanging down, his dull eyes glued on Auntie. Mama marked time with her crochet needle; and the Viscountess, with a weary smile and bathed in the languor of the monotonous rhythm, gradually let her eyelids droop.

'Very good, very good!' exclaimed Vilaça, visibly impressed, when Eusèbiozinho had concluded, covered in sweat. 'What a memory! What a memory! He's a prodigy!'

The servants entered with tea. The partners had finished their game; and Custódio stood with his cup in his hand bitterly complaining of the way in which the other gentlemen had trounced him.

As the next day was Sunday, and there was early mass, the ladies withdrew at nine-thirty. The helpful magistrate gave his arm to Dona Eugénia; a servant from the manor lit them ahead with a lantern; and the Silveiras' servant carried Eusèbiozinho in his arms like a dark bundle, suffocated in wraps with a shawl tied round his head.

After supper, when the guests had departed Vilaça accompanied Afonso to the library where he always took a brandy and soda in the English fashion before retiring.

The room, to which the old ebony shelves gave a sombre air, was drowsing tepidly in the peaceful gloom, with the curtains well-drawn, the remains of a fire in the chimney and the globe of the candelabra shedding its calm light on a table covered

69

with books. Down below the fountains bubbled noisily in the silence of the night.

While the footman wheeled a low table bearing glasses and syphons of soda towards Afonso's armchair, Vilaça stood with his hands in his pockets, pensively gazing into the burning logs as they died among the white ashes. Then he raised his head to murmur absently: 'That little boy is clever.'

'Who? Eusèbiozinho?' asked Afonso, who had been settling himself near the fireplace and cheerfully filling his pipe. 'I tremble when I see him in the house, Vilaça. Carlos doesn't like him, and we had a dreadful business over it. It was some months ago. There was a procession and Eusèbiozinho was dressed as an angel. The Silveiras – excellent women, poor things – sent him here in his angel's garb to show the Viscountess. Well, my dear chap, we were not paying much attention and Carlos, who was hanging about, took possession of him, carried him off to the attic, and, Vilaça – first of all, he was going to kill him because he can't abide angels. But that was not the worst. Imagine our horror when Eusèbiozinho appears screaming for Auntie, all dishevelled, with one wing missing, and the other hanging from a thread and banging against his heels; his crown of roses was around his neck; his golden epaulettes, his tulles, his sequins – the entire celestial raiment in shreds! In short, an angel that had been plucked and drawn! I nearly thrashed Carlos within an inch of his life.'

He drank half his soda and, passing a hand over his beard, he added with deep satisfaction:

'He's a young devil, Vilaça.'

The steward, who had sat down on the edge of a chair, gave a slight chuckle; then he remained silent looking at Afonso, with his hands on his knees, as though forgetful and abstracted. He was about to open his mouth, but he still hesitated and coughed faintly; and he continued to contemplate the sparks that came from the logs.

Afonso da Maia, meanwhile, with his legs stretched out towards the hearth, had again started talking about the Silveira child. He was three or four months older than Carlos, but he was feeble and delicate from an old-fashioned Portuguese upbringing; at his age he still slept in bed with the maids; he was never washed so as not to catch cold; and he was kept wrapped in rolls of flannel. He spent his days hanging on to his Auntie's skirts learning verses off by heart, and entire pages of the *Catechism of Perseverance*. Out of curiosity Afonso had opened this booklet one day and had read there that the sun went round the earth, as was said before Galileo, and that Our Lord gave orders to the sun every morning as to where it should go and where it should rest, and so on and so forth. And thus were they nurturing the mind of a future sage.

Vilaça chuckled again faintly. Then, as though coming to a sudden decision, he cracked his knuckles and spoke:

'Do you know, senhor, that the Monforte woman has appeared again?'

Afonso did not move his head. He leaned back in his armchair and, surrounded by the smoke from his pipe, inquired calmly:

'In Lisbon?'

'No, senhor, in Paris. Alencar, that young man who writes, the one who used to frequent the house in Arroios, saw her there. He even visited her house.'

Neither of them spoke. It had been years since the name of .Maria Monforte had passed between them. At first when Afonso had withdrawn to Santa Olávia his most ardent concern had been to recover the daughter she had taken. But at the time nobody knew where Maria had fled with her prince; neither through the Portuguese embassies abroad, nor even by means of lavish payments to the secret police of Paris, London or Madrid, was he able to discover their 'hideout', as Vilaça called it. The two must certainly have changed their names; and with their Bohemian temperaments who knew if they were not by now roaming across America, India and the most exotic places? Then, little by little, Afonso grew discouraged by these vain endeavours. He was utterly taken up with his grandson, who was growing handsome and strong at his side; his affections were fully engaged; and he began to forget the Monforte woman and his other grandchild, so far away, so vague, whose features he did not know and whose name he scarcely recalled. And now, all of a sudden, the Monforte woman had appeared once again, in Paris! And his poor Pedro was dead! And that child who slept at the end of the corridor had never known his mother.

He rose and paced up and down the library, heavily and

slowly, with his head bent. Near the table, beside the lamp, Vilaça was going through the papers in his wallet one by one.

'And is she with the Italian in Paris?' asked Afonso from the dark depths of the room.

Vilaça raised his head above his wallet and said:

'No, senhor, she's with whoever pays her.'

As Afonso approached the table without a word, Vilaça handed him a folded piece of paper, and went on:

'All these are very serious things, Senhor Afonso da Maia, and I did not want simply to trust to my memory. So I asked Alencar, who's an excellent fellow, to write me a letter setting forth all that he had told me. And so we have a document. I know nothing apart from what is written in it. Read it, senhor . . .'

Afonso unfolded the two sheets of paper. It was a simple enough story, but Alencar, the poet and stylist, had embroidered it with flowers and gilded ornaments like a chapel on a feast-day.

One night on leaving the Maison d'Or he had seen the Monforte woman alighting from a coupé with two men in evening dress; they had recognized each other at once; and, for a moment, they had hesitated, face to face on the pavement under the gaslight. Then she had made up her mind. She had laughed, given her hand to Alencar and asked him to visit her. She gave him her address and the name for which he should ask — Madame de l'Estorade. And the following morning in her boudoir the Monforte had told him much about herself. She had lived for three years in Vienna with the Prince and with her Papa, who had joined them there and who had existed, no doubt, just as he had in Arroios, taking refuge in the corners of the rooms, paying for his daughter's dresses and tenderly patting her lover's shoulder as he had formerly patted her husband's. Later they had gone to Monaco; and there, according to Alencar, 'in a gloomy drama of passion at which she hinted' the Neapolitan was killed in a duel. That same year her father died too, leaving only a slender remnant of his former fortune, and the furnishings of the house in Vienna. The old man had been ruined by his daughter's extravagance, their travels and the Prince's losses at baccarat. She had gone to London for a time, and from there to Paris with a Monsieur de l'Estorade, a gambler and dueller who had ruined her and abandoned her, leaving her only the name of l'Estorade, which was no longer useful to him for he had adopted the more sonorous apellation of Vicomte de Manderville. At last, poor, beautiful, foolish and extravagant, she had embarked on the path of those women of whom, said Alencar, 'the pale Marguérite Gautier, the sweet Lady of the Camellias, is the sublime prototype, the poetic symbol, to whom much is forgiven for having loved much'. And the poet ended – 'She is still in the full bloom of her beauty, but wrinkles will come, and then what will she see around her? The dry and bloodstained roses of her bridal wreath. I emerged from that scented boudoir with my soul lacerated, my dear Vilaça! I was thinking of my poor Pedro, who lies there now under the moon's rays among the cypress roots. And, disillusioned with this cruel life, I went and sought an hour of forgetfulness in absinthe on the boulevard.'

Afonso da Maia tossed the letter aside, less nauseated by the sordid tale than by the lyrical affectations of the writer.

He began to pace up and down again while Vilaça religiously picked up the document, which he had re-read many times, admiring the sentiments, the style and the idealism of its pages.

'And the child?' asked Afonso.

'That I don't know. Alencar was not likely to have spoken of her daughter to her, for he didn't even know she had taken her. Nobody knows this in Lisbon. It was a particular that passed unnoticed amid all the scandal. But as for myself, I believe the child must have died. If not – do you follow my reasoning, senhor – if the little girl were alive, her mother would be in a position to claim the child's legal inheritance. She knows your means; and there must be days, for they are frequent in the lives of such women, when she feels the want of a pound or so. On the pretext of educating the child, or her maintenance, she would already have approached us. She has no scruples. If she hasn't done so it is because her daughter must have died. Don't you agree?'

'Maybe,' answered Afonso. Then he stood in front of Vilaça, who was again staring into the dead embers and cracking his knuckles, and added: 'Maybe – let's suppose they're both dead and speak of this no more.'

It was striking midnight and the two men retired.

In the days that followed the name of Maria Monforte was not mentioned.

73

But on the eve of the steward's departure for Lisbon Afonso went up to Vilaça's room to hand him the Easter present that Carlos was sending to Vilaça junior, a tie-pin with a magnificent sapphire and, while the other, moved, was stammering his thanks, he said:

'But there is something else, Vilaça. I've been thinking. I'm going to write to my cousin, Noronha, who lives in Paris as you know, and ask him to seek that creature out and offer her a few hundred pounds in exchange for handing over her daughter – in the event that she's still alive. And I'd like you to get the woman's address in Paris from that fellow Alencar.'

Vilaça did not reply at once, busy placing among his shirts, well to the bottom of his case, the little box with the tie-pin in it. Then he faced Afonso and scratched his chin reflectively.

'Well, what do you think, Vilaça?'

'It looks risky to me.'

He gave his reasons. The girl would be nearly thirteen. Almost a woman, with her temperament already formed, her character developed, perhaps even her habits – why, she wouldn't even speak Portuguese. She would miss her mother terribly. Senhor Afonso da Maia would be bringing a stranger into his house.

'There's something in what you say, Vilaça. But the mother's a whore, and the child is my own flesh and blood.'

At that moment Carlos, whose voice had been calling in the corridor for his grandfather, burst into the room, dishevelled and red as a pomegranate. Brown had found a little owl! He wanted Grandpapa to come and see it; he had been searching for him all over the house. It made you die of laughter. Very tiny, very ugly, all bald and with two eyes like a grown person's – and he knew where it had its nest!

'Come quickly, Grandpapa! Quickly, because we've got to put it back in its nest or the old owl might get upset. Brown is giving it olive oil. Oh, Vilaça, do come and see! Come along, Grandpapa, for heaven's sake! It's got such a funny face! But be quick, be quick, for the old owl might find out it's not there – '

And impatient at Grandpapa's smiling slowness, such indifference to the disquiet of the old owl, he ran out, slamming the door.

'What a good heart!' cried Vilaça, moved. 'Thinking of the

owl's feelings. And his own mother has none for him! As I always said, she's a wild beast!'

Afonso shrugged his shoulders sadly. They were already in the corridor when he stopped for a moment and lowered his voice.

'I'd forgotten to tell you, Vilaça, Carlos knows that his father killed himself.'

Vilaça's eyes grew round with surprise. It was true. One morning the boy had entered the library and said: 'Oh, Grandpapa, my Papa killed himself with a pistol!'

Some servant must have told him.

'What did you do, senhor?'

'I – What could I do? I said yes. In everything I have observed Pedro's wishes. In the letter he left me he said he wanted to be buried in Santa Olávia, and here he lies. He did not want his son ever to learn of his mother's flight; and certainly he'll never know it from me. He wanted the two portraits of her at Arroios destroyed; as you know they were obtained and destroyed. But he didn't ask me to hide his end from the boy. And so I told the child the truth. I said that his Papa had shot himself in a moment of madness – '

'And he?'

'He,' answered Afonso smiling, 'asked me who had given his Papa a pistol, and he tormented me all the morning to give him a pistol too – and the result of that revelation was that I had to send to Oporto for an air rifle.'

But hearing Carlos downstairs, still shouting for his grandfather, the two of them hurried to admire the little owl.

Next day Vilaça left for Lisbon.

Two weeks later Afonso received a letter from the steward with both the Monforte's address and unforeseen information. Vilaça had gone back to Alencar's house. The poet had recalled other incidents of his visit to Madame de l'Estorade's and had told him that in her boudoir there was the picture of an adorable little girl with black eyes, hair like jet, and a pearly pallor. The portrait had struck him greatly, not only because it was by an illustrious English painter, but also because, hanging from the frame like a funeral tribute, was a splendid wreath of purple and white wax flowers. There was no other picture in the boudoir; and he had asked the Monforte if it was the portrait of a real person or simply imaginary. She had replied that it was the portrait of her daughter who had died in London.

'So all doubts are dissipated,' Vilaça added. 'The poor angel is in a better world. And, for her, it is indeed a very much better one!'

Afonso, however, wrote to André de Noronha. The reply took some time. When Cousin André went to seek Madame de l'Estorade she had already left some weeks earlier for Germany after having sold furniture and horses. And in the Club Imperial to which he belonged, a friend, who knew Madame de l'Estorade well and the *demi-monde* of Paris, told him that the madwoman had run away with a certain Catanni, an acrobat at the Cirque d'Hiver, in the Champs-Elysées, a man with a magnificent figure, a fairground Apollo, whom all the courtesans were wrangling over, and whom the Monforte had captured. Probably she was now travelling around Germany accompanying the circus.

Disgusted, Afonso da Maia forwarded the letter to Vilaça without any comment. And the worthy man replied: 'You are right, sir. It is atrocious; and it would be better to suppose them all dead than to waste more time on such an affair.' Then in a postcript he added: 'It seems sure that the railway is soon to be opened as far as Oporto. In which case, with your permission, I shall come with my boy to beg a few days' hospitality from you.'

This letter was received in Santa Olávia one Sunday at dinnertime. Afonso read the postscript aloud. Everyone was overjoyed at the hope of seeing good Vilaça shortly at the manor; and they even talked of arranging a grand picnic up the river.

But on Tuesday night a telegram arrived from Manuel Vilaça announcing that his father had died that morning of apoplexy; and two days later longer and sadder details reached them. It had been after lunch when, suddenly, Vilaça had felt very stifled and giddy. He had only had the strength to go to his room to inhale a little ether; but when he had returned to the diningroom he was staggering and complained of seeing everything yellow. Then he fell face downwards like a sack onto the sofa. His mind, on the point of being extinguished for ever, still occupied itself at that moment with the family he had served for thirty years. He stammered about the sale of some cork; then he gave a great sigh; and he only opened his eyes again to murmur with his last breath these final words: 'Greetings to Senhor Afonso!'

Afonso da Maia was profoundly affected and, even among the servants, at Santa Olávia Vilaça's death was like a family loss. One afternoon shortly afterwards the old man was sitting sadly in his library with a newspaper forgotten in his hands and his eyes closed when Carlos, who had been at his side drawing ugly faces on a piece of paper, came up and put his arm around his grandfather's neck and, as though reading his thoughts, asked him whether Vilaça would not be coming back to visit them at the manor.

'No, my son, not any more. We shall never see him again.'

Standing between the legs and arms of the old man, the little boy looked down and, as though remembering, murmured sadly:

'Poor old Vilaça. He used to crack his knuckles. Oh, Grandpapa, where did they take him to?'

'To the cemetery, my boy, under the earth.'

Then Carlos slowly loosened himself from his grandfather's embrace and, very gravely, with his eyes upon him, he said: 'Oh, Grandpapa! Why don't you have a nice little chapel made, all in stone, with a statue, like Papa has?'

The old man was moved and pulled the child to his breast and kissed him.

'You're right, child! You have more heart than I.'

And so it happened that the good Vilaça was endowed with his own mausoleum in the Prazeres cemetery – which had been the highest ambition of his modest existence.

More tranquil years passed over Santa Olávia.

Then, one morning in July, Manuel Vilaça, the family steward now since his father's death, climbed the stairs of the Hotel Mondego in Coimbra where Afonso was staying with his grandson. He ran into their sitting-room, red, sweating and shouting:

'He's passed! He's passed!'

Carlos had taken his first examination. And what an examination! Teixeira, who had accompanied the gentlemen from Santa Olávia, ran to the door, and practically in tears, embraced his young master, who was now taller than he, and very handsome in his new gown.

77

Upstairs Manuel Vilaça, still puffing and wiping away beads of sweat, was exclaiming:

'Everybody was amazed, Senhor Afonso da Maia! Even the professors were moved. My God! What talent! He'll be a great man, that's what everybody said – What faculty will he enter, senhor?'

Afonso, who was pacing up and down nervously, replied with a smile: 'I don't know, Vilaça – perhaps he'll take up the law.'

A radiant Carlos appeared in the doorway followed by Teixeira and the other footman, who was bringing in champagne on a salver.

'Come here, you young rogue,' said Afonso, open-armed and very pale. 'So you did well, eh? I – '

But he could not go on – the tears, one after another, were running down his white beard.

4

CARLOS STUDIED MEDICINE. As Dr Trigueiros said, the boy had always shown a vocation for Aesculapius.

The vocation had revealed itself brusquely one day in the attic when he had come across a stained and ancient roll of anatomical illustrations among piles of old books. He had spent days cutting them out and tacking them on the wall of his room – pictures of liver, strings of intestines, heads in profile 'showing all the stuffing'. One night he had even burst into the drawing-room in triumph to show the Silveiras and Eusèbio the horrid lithograph of a six-month-old foetus in its mother's womb. Dona Ana had fallen back with a scream and her fan glued to her face; the public prosecutor, scarlet also, had taken Eusèbio prudently between his knees and had covered his face with his hands. But what had scandalized the ladies had been Afonso's tolerance.

'Well, what's the matter, what's the matter?' he had inquired, smiling.

'What's the matter, Senhor Afonso da Maia?' Dona Ana had exclaimed. 'Why, it's indecent!'

'There's nothing indecent in nature, dear lady. What's indecent is ignorance – Let the boy be! He's curious to know how this poor machine functions. There's nothing more praiseworthy.'

Dona Ana fanned herself. She felt suffocated. To permit such horrors in the hands of a child! Carlos seemed to her a libertine who already 'knew things'; and she would no longer allow Terezinha to play with him alone in the corridors of Santa Olávia.

Serious people, however – the Judge, even the Abbé himself who, to be sure, lamented that there was not more discretion – agreed that the boy showed a remarkable leaning towards medicine.

'If it lasts,' Dr Trigueiros said with a wide, prophetic gesture, 'we have something really big here!'

And it seemed to last.

At Coimbra, as a student at the lyceum, Carlos would aban-

79

don his manuals of rhetoric to occupy himself with anatomy. On one vacation when she was unpacking his bags, his old nurse, Gertrudes, was terrified to find, gleaming white among the folds of a coat, a grinning skull. And if a servant fell ill, there was Carlos studying the case in old medical books from his grandfather's library, never leaving the patient's bedside, and giving a diagnosis that good Dr Trigueiros would listen to respectfully and thoughtfully. The doctor already spoke of the boy to his grandfather as his 'talented colleague'.

This unforeseen future for Carlos – he had always been expected to follow the law – was little approved among the faithful friends of Santa Olávia. The ladies, above all, lamented that a boy who was growing up so handsome, such a gentleman, should waste his life prescribing plasters and soiling his hands with blood-letting. The Judge one day even confessed his disbelief that Senhor Carlos da Maia wanted to be a 'real doctor'.

'What an idea!' exclaimed Afonso. 'And why should he not take medicine seriously? If he chooses a profession it is in order that he may follow it with sincerity and ambition, like everybody else. I'm not educating him to be a vagabond, much less a dilettante; I'm educating him to be of service to his country.'

'Nevertheless,' ventured the Judge with a fastidious smile, 'don't you think there are other things, important too and possibly more appropriate, in which your grandson might be useful – '

'I don't see it that way,' answered Afonso. 'In a country where the general occupation is being ill, the greatest patriotic service is incontestably to know how to cure.'

'Your Excellency has an answer for everything,' murmured the man of laws respectfully.

And what had lured Carlos to medicine was precisely that prospect of a 'serious', practical and useful life – to run upstairs to a patient in the heat of a busy practice, lives to be saved with a flick of the lancet, watchful nights by the sick bed, surrounded by a frightened family, battling against death. Just as the picturesque forms of the viscera had enchanted him when he was a little boy, now the militant and heroic aspects of science attracted him too.

He matriculated with enthusiasm. His grandfather made ready for him a fine house in Cellas for the long years of quiet study.

It was isolated and had the charm of an English cottage, decorated with green shutters, all fresh among the trees. One of Carlos's friends, a certain João da Ega, gave it the name of the Court of Cellas on account of its luxuries, rare at that time in academic circles: a carpet in the drawing-room, armchairs of morocco leather, weapon stands, a liveried footman.

At first this splendour made Carlos the darling of the snobs and distrusted by the democrats; however, when it was known that the owner of these comforts read Proudhon, Auguste Comte, and Herbert Spencer, and also regarded the country as a witches' cauldron, the sternest revolutionaries began to visit the Court of Cellas as familiarly as they did the room of Trovão, the Bohemian poet, the tough socialist, who had only a straw mattress and a Bible for furniture.

At the end of some months Carlos, who was popular with everybody, had conciliated dandies and philosophers. Beside him in his brake rode Serra Torres, a monster who had already been promised a diplomatic post in Berlin and put on evening dress nightly, side by side with Craveiro, wrapped in his Aveiro cloak and his great otter cap, who was composing a work entitled *The Death of Satan*. The Court of Cellas, with its lazy, rustic air, became a hive of activity. In the garden there were scientific gymnastics. An old kitchen was converted into a fencing-hall – for in that group fencing was considered a social imperative. At night in the dining-room serious youths played a serious game of whist. In the drawing-room, under the lustre of crystal, with the *Figaro, The Times* and magazines from Paris and London scattered on the tables, Gamacho at the piano playing Chopin or Mozart, and the learned stretched out on the sofas, there were noisy and fiery debates in which Democracy, Art, Positivism, Realism, the Papacy, Bismarck, Love, Hugo and Evolution, all sparkled in the tobacco smoke, all as light and vague as the smoke itself. And the metaphysical discussions, the revolutionary certainties themselves acquired a sharper savour for the presence of a uniformed servant uncorking the beer or serving croquettes.

Naturally Carlos very soon started to leave his medical textbooks lying on the table with their pages untouched. Literature and Art, in all their forms, absorbed him deliciously. He published some sonnets and an article on the Parthenon. He attempted to paint in oils in an improvised studio. He composed archaeological short stories under the influence of Flaubert's *Salammbô*. And every afternoon he exercised his two horses. He would certainly have failed in his second year had he not been so well-known and so rich. He shuddered at the thought of his grandfather's disappointment, and moderated his intellectual dissipation so as to dedicate himself more to his chosen science. Immediately he began to do well. But the poison of dilettantism flowed in his veins: he was destined, as João da Ega said, to be one of those literary doctors who invent diseases which credulous mankind at once shows itself disposed to die from!

His grandfather sometimes came to spend a fortnight at Cellas. At first his presence was welcomed by the whist players and upset the literary company. The youths scarcely dared to stretch out a hand for a glass of beer and 'Your Excellency' here and 'Your Excellency' there froze the drawing-room. Little by little, however, as they saw him appear in slippers, with a pipe in his mouth, to stretch himself out on the sofa with the amiable air of an elderly Bohemian and to discuss art and literature and tell tales of his time in England and Italy, they began to look on him as a comrade who simply happened to have a white beard. They would talk in front of him of women and revelries. The rich old nobleman who had read Michelet and admired him, even inspired the liking of the democrats. And Afonso enjoyed many happy hours there seeing his Carlos the centre of that circle of studious, idealistic and talented youth.

Carlos spent his long vacations in Lisbon, and sometimes in Paris or London. But at Christmas and Easter he always went to Santa Olávia where his grandfather now made up for his loneliness by busily and lovingly embellishing the old house. The rooms were now filled with Arras tapestries, Rousseau and Daubigny landscapes and luxurious period furniture. From the windows the grounds displayed the noble aspect of an English park: curving, sandy paths separated the smooth lawns; there were statues among the greenery; and plump pedigree sheep drowsed under the chestnuts. But life in this rich atmosphere was no longer as light-hearted as formerly. The Viscountess had grown fatter than ever and fell into long, congested dozes immediately after dinner; Teixeira first, then Gertrudes, had each died of pleurisy, and at carnival time; nor was the benevolent face of the Abbé seen at the table any more, for he lay under a stone cross among the gillyflowers and the perennial roses. The Judge, with his concertina, had been elevated to the Oporto High Court. Dona Ana Silveira, now very ill, never went out; Terezinha had grown into an ugly girl, as yellow as cider; Eusèbiozinho, flaccid and melancholy, with no remnant left of his first passion for figures and learning, was to be married in Régua. Only the public prosecutor, forgotten in that county, remained the same, a little balder perhaps, still affable, still in love with the phlegmatic Eugénia. And nearly every afternoon old Dr Trigueiros would tie up his white mare at the gate to come and gossip with his colleague.

Holidays were really only entertaining for Carlos when he brought home his best friend, the great João da Ega, to whom Afonso da Maia had taken a strong liking – for his own sake, for his originality, and for being the nephew of André da Ega, an old friend of his youth and, in former times, himself often a guest at Santa Olávia.

Ega was studying law, but slowly, cautiously – now failing, now skipping a year. His mother, rich, widowed and devout, had retired to a country estate near Celorico de Basto with a daughter, who was pious, widowed and rich as well, and she only had a vague idea of what Joãozinho was doing all that time in Coimbra. Her chaplain assured her that all must end well; that the boy would end up with a doctorate like his Papa and uncle; and this promise was sufficient for the good lady whose chief concerns were her internal complaints and the comforts of Father Seraphim. She even preferred that her son should remain at Coimbra, or anywhere at all, provided it was far from her home, for he scandalized everyone with his irreverence and his heretical jokes.

João da Ega, in fact, was considered not only at Celorico, but also at the University, which he shocked by his daring and his oratory, as the greatest atheist, the biggest radical that had ever appeared in human society. This flattered him: as a matter of course he exaggerated his hatred for the Divinity, and for all social order; he wanted the massacre of the middle classes; love free from the hypocrisy of matrimony; the distribution of the land; the cult of Satan. His intellectual efforts in this direction ended by influencing his manners and his looks. With his dry, emaciated figure, the hairs of his moustache stiff under his beaky nose, a square of glass fixed in his right eye, he really did look rather rebellious and satanic. After he started at the University he renewed his old Bohemian traditions; rents in his black student gown were sewn up with white cotton; he got drunk on cheap wine; at night on the bridge, with his arms upraised, he hurled insults at God. At heart he was very sentimental, always involved in infatuations with young girls of fifteen – daughters of clerks – with whom he would occasionally spend an evening, taking them little bags of bon-bons. His fame as a rich young noble made him welcome in their family circles.

Carlos poked fun at these town courtships; but he too succumbed to a romantic attachment for the wife of a clerk in the civil government, a little Lisbon girl, who had won him with the grace of her doll-like body, and lovely green eyes. What had turned her head had been his luxury, his groom and his English mare.

They exchanged letters; and he passed weeks bathed in the rough, tumultuous poetry of his first adulterous love.

One day Carlos was driving along taking the air in the market when the Civil Governor's clerk passed close by leading his little son by the hand. It was the first time Carlos had seen his beloved's husband so close. He found him shabby and pale. But the little boy was adorable, very plump, looking more roly-poly than ever that January day covered in his blue woollen wraps, shivering on little legs that were purple with cold, and laughing in the clear light – laughing with all his being, with his eyes, with the dimples in his chin, with his two rosy cheeks. His father held him upright – and the charm, the care with which the young man thus guided the footsteps of his son touched Carlos. He was reading Michelet at the time – and his soul was filled with literary veneration for the sanctity of the family. He felt a wretch sitting up there in his dog-cart coldly planning the dishonour and the tears of that poor father who was so inoffensive in his threadbare jacket! He ceased to answer his beloved's letters, in which she called him her 'ideal man'. The girl, to be sure, revenged herself by slandering him – for the Civil Governor's clerk, from then onwards, began to dart bloodthirsty looks in his direction.

But Carlos 'took a great sentimental tumble', as Ega put it, when he brought back from Lisbon after one vacation a superb

84

Spanish girl and installed her in a house near Cellas. Her name was Encarnacion. Carlos hired a victoria and a white horse by the month especially for her, and Encarnacion dazzled Coimbra like the personification of the Lady of the Camellias, a luxurious flower from a superior civilization. On the Calçada and the Beira road the students would halt, pale with emotion, when she passed by, reclining in her victoria, displaying a satin shoe and a bit of silk stocking, languid and disdainful, with a little white dog on her lap.

The student poets composed verses in which Encarnacion was called the Lily of Israel, the Dove of the Ark, and the Cloud of Morning. A theological student, a rough and greasy fellow from the mountains of the north, wanted to marry her. Against Carlos's advice, Encarnacion refused him; and the theologian began to lurk around Cellas with a huge knife, to 'drink Maia's blood'. Carlos was compelled to take a stick to him.

But the creature's head was turned and she became overbearing. She talked incessantly of other passions that she had inspired in Madrid and in Lisbon, of how much Count So-and-So had given her, or Marquis Such-and-Such, of the high position of her family, related, she said, to the Medina-Coeli. Her green satin slippers were as objectionable as her strident voice. When she attempted to join in the discussions she heard about her she would start calling the Republicans thieves, praising the time of Dona Isabel, her grace and her spirit – for like all prostitutes she was a great conservative. João da Ega loathed her. And Craveiro declared that he would not return to the Cellas Court while that mountain of flesh, priced by the pound like a cow, was still around.

At last, one afternoon, Baptista, Carlos's famous valet, surprised her with a certain Juca who played the part of a lady in the University theatre. Now, finally, there was an excuse! Suitably recompensed, the relative of the Medina-Coeli, the Lily of Israel and admirer of the Bourbons, was dispatched to Lisbon and the Rua St Roque, her natural habitat.

In August, when Carlos graduated, there was a gay party at Cellas. Afonso had come from Santa Olávia and Manuel Vilaça from Lisbon. All afternoon in the garden, among the acacias and the lovely shade, bunches of fireworks were launched into the sky. João da Ega, who had failed once again in his final year, was busy everywhere. In shirtsleeves he hung Venetian lanterns among the branches, on the trapeze and around the well to light up the night. At dinner, attended by professors, Vilaça, nervous and trembling, made a speech. He was about to quote from the current Court poet, when through the window there burst a great tumult of drums and cymbals. It was the University Anthem. It was a serenade. Ega, flushed and with his gown unbuttoned and his monocle dangling down his back, ran in through the french windows declaiming:

'Here we have our Maia, Carolus Eduardus ab Maia, on the threshold of his glorious career, equipped to save sick humanity – or kill it off as the case may be! To what remote part of these dominions has not the fame of his genius already reached? His genius, his dog-cart, the low marks that have stained his past, and this port, contemporary with the heroes of 1820, which I, a man of the Revolution and a drinking man, I, João de Ega, Johannes ab Ega – '

The dark crowd below burst into applause. The orchestra and the other students all invaded the house. Under the trees in the garden, in the drawing-room filled with stacks of plates, servants ran backwards and forwards with salvers of sweetmeats, and the champagne corks went on popping until late into the night. And Vilaça, wiping his forehead, his neck, suffocated with heat, went around saying to all and sundry and to himself as well:

'It's a great thing to have a degree!'

And so Carlos Eduardo set off for his long trip across Europe. A year went by. The autumn of 1875 arrived and his grandfather, at last installed at Ramalhete, awaited him eagerly. Carlos's last letter had come from England, where he was, so he said, studying the admirable organization of children's hospitals. So he was. But he had also been to Brighton, bet on the horses at Goodwood, and made an idyllic journey through the Scottish lakes with a Dutch lady who was separated from her husband, a venerable magistrate at the Hague. Her name was Madame Rughel, a superb creature with tawny gold hair, big and white like one of Rubens's nymphs.

There had begun to arrive at Ramalhete box after box of

86

books, others containing instruments, and apparatus, a complete library and a laboratory – which caused Vilaça to spend entire mornings in a daze in the Customs sheds.

'My lad is coming home with great plans for work,' said Afonso to his friends.

Apart from a photograph sent from Milan, in which everybody had found him thin and sad, it had been fourteen months since he had seen him, 'his lad'. And on that fine autumn morning his heart beat strongly as he stood on the terrace at Ramalhete, binoculars in hand, and saw coming slowly into sight behind the tall building in front of him the big Royal Mail packet that was bearing home his grandson.

That night the friends of the house – old Sequeira, Dom Diogo Coutinho and Vilaça – did not cease to exclaim at 'the good Carlos's trip had done him'. How different he looked from his photograph! How strong and healthy he seemed!

There was no doubt about it. He was a splendidly handsome young man: tall, well-built and broad-shouldered; a marble forehead under black curls; and the Maia eyes – those same irresistible eyes of his father's, as tender and as liquid black, but more serious. He wore a full beard, silky and dark brown, short on the cheeks and pointed at the chin, and a fine moustache arched over the corners of his mouth. He had the air of some distinguished Renaissance knight. His grandfather, beaming, dewy-eyed and overflowing with emotion, swelled with pride as he watched and listened to the young man eloquently describing his travels: lovely days in Rome; his bad temper in Prussia; the singularity of Moscow; the landscape of Holland.

'What now?' asked Sequeira after a moment's silence while Carlos sipped his brandy and soda. 'What plans have you?'

'Now, General?' Carlos answered with a smile as he put down his glass. 'First I want a rest. And after that I'll embark on a career that will be a glory to the nation!'

In fact the very next day Afonso found him pulling out nails and unpacking in his shirtsleeves as he whistled merrily in the billiards-room where his packing cases had been left. Piles of books were strewn about over the floor and the sofas. Among the straw and the unpicked canvas wrappings the light gleamed here and there on a crystal or a varnished surface or else revealed the polished metal of some piece of apparatus. Afonso stared in silent wonder at all that impressive paraphernalia of learning.

'And where are you proposing to house this museum?'

Carlos had thought of setting up an immense laboratory somewhere nearby in the district. It would have ovens for chemical work, a room equipped for anatomical and physiological research, his library, his apparatus; in fact all the instruments for his work would be methodically assembled there.

His grandfather's eyes shone as he listened to these grandiose plans.

'Don't let financial considerations hold you back, Carlos! We've managed to save quite a bit during these recent years in Santa Olávia.'

'Great words, Grandfather! Kindly repeat them to Vilaça.'

The weeks went by filled with these projects. Carlos had indeed come back sincerely resolved to work: science as a mere interior ornament of the mind, less useful to others than the very curtains that draped his room, seemed to him nothing but the luxury of an anchorite. He longed to be of service. But his ambitions wavered and were vague, for all their intensity. At one moment he would decide to build a flourishing practice; at others he would contemplate the massive compilation of an epoch-making book; at still others he would plan experiments in physiology that would be painstaking and rewarding. He discerned within himself, or imagined he discerned, a tumultuous power, but he could not discover a way of applying it. He wanted to accomplish 'something brilliant', as he put it.

For Carlos, in whom the man of fashion was mingled with the man of learning, this could mean a combination of social success and scientific activity: a profound ferment of ideas amid the pampered influences of wealth; the lofty detachment of philosophical study alongside refinements of sport and taste; a Claude Bernard who would be at the same time a Morny. At heart he was a dilettante.

Vilaça was consulted about a suitable site for the laboratory. The steward was very flattered and swore tireless diligence. The first thing he needed to know was whether 'our doctor' intended to establish a practice.

Carlos had not decided to devote himself *exclusively* to medical practice, but he would certainly want to treat patients, even

with no payment, both out of charity and for experience. So
Vilaça suggested that the consulting-rooms should be quite separate from the laboratory.

'There's a good reason for this,' he explained. 'The sight of
medical apparatus, instruments, things, demoralizes sick people.'
'Quite right, Vilaça!' exclaimed Afonso. 'My father always
used to say the ox should be spared the sight of the hammer.'
'Separate, separate, senhor,' repeated the steward solemnly.
Carlos agreed. And for the laboratory Vilaça very quickly discovered an old storehouse that stood, vast and withdrawn, at the
back of a patio near the Necessidades Square.

'And the consulting-rooms, senhor, should not be hereabouts,
but in the Rossio, right in the heart of town.'

This idea of Vilaça's was not totally disinterested. Vilaça
junior was greatly concerned with politics and was a member
of the Progressive Centre. He aspired to become a member of
the City Corporation – and, indeed, on days of particular self-
confidence (for instance when his birthday had been mentioned
in the columns of an illustrious newspaper, or when, amid
applause at the Centre, he had spoken on international affairs) –
it seemed to him that such a variety of talent merited his being
rewarded by his party with a seat in Parliament. A consulting-
room for non-paying patients in the centre of town – a consulting-room with Dr Maia in attendance, 'his Dr Maia' – had at once
occurred to him as something generally favourable towards his
plans. And he so busied himself that within two days he had
taken the whole first floor of a corner building.

Carlos equipped it lavishly. A servant liveried in the French
style stood on duty in a hall lined with leather seats The
patients' waiting-room was gay with green wallpaper patterned
with silver garlands. Plants stood in Rouen vases; there were
vivid paintings on the walls and rich armchairs were grouped
around a *jardinière* covered with collections of the *Charivari*,
stereoscopic pictures and albums of half-naked actresses. And to
banish utterly the dismal atmosphere of a consulting-room there
was even a piano with its white keyboard uncovered.

Carlos's surgery at the side was simpler, almost austere, all
in the darkest green velvet and with shelves of ebony. The
friends Carlos had begun to gather round him – Taveira, his contemporary at Coimbra and now a neighbour near Ramalhete;

89

Cruges; the Marquis of Souzellas with whom he had toured Italy – all of them came to survey these marvels. Cruges ran his fingers up and down the piano keyboard and pronounced it to be abominable. Taveira became absorbed in the pictures of the actresses. The only frank approval came from the Marquis as he stood in the surgery contemplating the divan – truly a piece for a harem: vast, voluptuous and soft. After testing the smoothness of its springs he winked at Carlos and declared: 'Eminently suitable!'

They did not seem to take his preparations seriously. But these were nevertheless sincere. Carlos even had an announcement inserted in the newspapers. But when he saw his name in thick letters between that of a laundress from Boa-Hora and publicity for a boarding-house he asked Vilaça to have the advertisement withdrawn.

He began to devote more of his time to the laboratory, which he had decided to establish in the storehouse at Necessidades. He would visit the site each morning before lunch. The entry was through a large, shady patio, where there was a well and ivy that crept up behind iron clips holding it to the wall. Carlos had already made up his mind to transform this yard into a fresh and dainty English garden. The door of the building captivated him. It was Gothic and noble, all that remained of the frontage of a cloister, and it made an imposing entrance to his shrine of science. But the building-work inside seemed to go on forever. There was always a muffled, desultory tapping in the brown dusty air; always the same baskets of tools lying about in the same layers of wood-shavings! A scruffy sad-looking carpenter seemed to have been there for centuries, tired and listless, smoothing an everlasting plank. The workmen who were enlarging the skylight on the roof went on whistling the strains of a *fado* endlessly through the wintry sunlight.

When Carlos complained to Senhor Vicente, the foreman, he invariably received the assurance that His Excellency would see the difference in a couple of days' time. The foreman was a jolly, middle-aged, soft-spoken, very bewhiskered, very scrubbed-looking man, who lived near Ramalhete and was famous in the quarter as a Republican. Carlos always shook hands with him out of liking for the man as a neighbour. And Senhor Vicente took this to mean that his employer was an 'advanced thinker', a democrat, and accordingly confided his hopes to him. What he longed for, first and foremost, was another 1793, like France.

'What? Bloodshed?' Carlos asked, staring at the fresh, honest plump face of the radical.

'No, senhor, a ship, just a ship . . .'

'A ship?'

'Yes, senhor, a ship chartered at the expense of the nation. And off we'd send the King out of the harbour, together with the Royal Family and the whole gang of ministers, politicians, members of parliament, intriguers and the rest of them.'

Carlos would smile and sometimes argue.

'But are you sure, Senhor Vicente, that if the gang, as you so correctly put it, were to disappear out of the harbour, everything would be solved and all would end happily?'

No, Senhor Vicente was not such a donkey as that. But didn't His Excellency see that once 'the gang' was out of the way, the country would be free – and then men of knowledge and progress could begin to govern the land?

'Do you know what's wrong with us, Your Excellency? It's not that those people are wicked; it's their ignorance. They don't know anything. Anything at all. They're not bad, but they're a stupid lot!'

'You're quite right. But now what about the work, friend Vicente?' Carlos would respond, taking out his watch and bidding him good-bye with a hearty handshake. 'See if you can get on with it for me. I don't ask you in my capacity as the owner, but as a co-thinker.'

'Two days from now and you'll see the difference, Your Excellency,' the foreman would declare, lifting his hat.

The lunch-gong sounded at Ramalhete punctually at midday. Carlos nearly always found his grandfather already in the dining-room finishing off his newspaper beside the fireplace that was filled with hothouse plants instead of a fire, unnecessary in the warm softness of late autumn.

On the carved-oak sideboards around him old silver shone gently in solid and sober luxury. Scenes of legend unfolded across the oval tapestries on the panelled walls: medieval hunters unloosening a falcon; a lady among her pages feeding swans beside a lake; a knight in armour with his visor down riding by a riverside. Contrasting with the dark ceiling of carved chestnut the table was resplendent with flowers among the crystal goblets. The Reverend Bonifacio, who, now that he had become a dignitary of the Church, took his meals with the gentlemen, would already be there, crouched regally over the snowy whiteness of the tablecloth in the shade of some big bunch of flowers. There, amid the scent of roses, the venerable cat liked to lick slowly and stupidly at the bread and milk served to him in a Strasbourg bowl. Then he would nestle down, curl his fluffy plume of a tail round his chest and close his eyes, his whiskers stiff, a round ball enclosed in white fur mottled with gold, as he mildly enjoyed a light doze.

Afonso – as he himself confessed, smiling and abashed – had become a demanding gourmet in his old age. He accepted with a critic's concentration the works of art produced by the French chef they had now: a bad-tempered individual called Monsieur Theodore, a great Bonapartist who bore a close resemblance to the Emperor. Lunch at Ramalhete was always a prolonged and ceremonious affair. Then, at coffee, talk would continue; one o'clock would strike, then half past when, at last, Carlos, with an exclamation, would throw himself at the clock and remember his consulting-room. He would drink down his glass of Chartreuse and hurriedly light a cigar.

'To work, to work!' he would cry.

And slowly filling his pipe his grandfather would envy him his vocation while he had to remain there idling away his mornings.

'When that everlasting laboratory is finished, I may well drop in there myself for a while and get busy with some chemistry.'

'Perhaps you'll be a great chemist. You're quite the type for it, Grandfather.'

The old man would smile.

'This old carcass won't produce anything more now, my boy. It's making ready for eternity.'

'Do you want anything from town?' Carlos would ask, hastily buttoning his riding gloves.

'A good day's work to you.'

'That's hardly likely . . .'

And in the dog-cart drawn by the lovely mare Tunante, or in the phaeton that dazzled all Lisbon, off Carlos would drive in great style for town – to 'work'.

In his consulting-rooms the surgery drowsed with peace and

warmth amid the thick dark velvets in the shade of the drawn green silk blinds. But in the sitting-room three open windows drank in the light; here everything was festive: the easy chairs around the *jardinière* stretched out their arms amiably and invitingly; the white keys of the piano smiled and waited with the *Songs of Gounod* open above them. But no patient ever appeared. And Carlos would light a cigarette, pick up a magazine, and stretch himself out on the divan just like his servant, who dozed, slouching over the *Diário de Noticias* on a seat in the leisure of the hall. But the columns of prose seemed to be permeated with the same morose tedium as the surgery. Soon he would yawn and let the journal fall from his hand.

From the Rossio a clatter of carts, wandering cries of street vendors, the noise of the horse-drawn trams would rise, vibrating the more clearly in the thin November air. A delicate light, wrung gently from the steel-blue sky, gilded the drab housefront, the thin tops of the trees planted by the Corporation and the people idling on the benches. The whole slow murmur of a languid city, the soft air of that southern climate, seemed to steal little by little into the muffled room and slip across the heavy velvets, across the varnished furniture, to wrap Carlos around with indolence and sleep. His head on a cushion, he would lie there smoking in the siesta-like calm, in a fitful daydream, vague and tenuous, like the light, whispy smoke that rises from half-dead embers. Then, with an effort, he would shake off his torpor, pace round the room, open a book here and there among those on the shelves, strum two bars of a waltz on the piano and rouse himself. His eyes on the flowered carpet, he would decide at last that these two hours in the consulting-rooms were an absurd waste of time!

'Is the carriage outside?' he would call to the servant.

He would rapidly light another cigar, put on his gloves, go downstairs, drink in a big draught of light and air, grasp the reins and be off grunting to himself:

'One more day lost!'

On just such a day, lazing thus on the sofa with the *Revista dos Dois Mundos* in his hand, he heard a sound in the vestibule, then a well-known, well-loved voice, calling from behind the arras:

'May one see His Royal Highness?'

'Oh – Ega!' cried Carlos, leaping from the sofa.

And they fell into one another's arms, kissing each other on the face in delight.

'When did you get here?'

'This morning – my God!' exclaimed Ega, groping round his chest and shoulders for the square of glass, then at last fixing it in his eye. 'My God! You seem to have come back quite splendid from London, from those superior civilizations. You've quite a Renaissance air, the air of a Valois. There's nothing quite like a full beard!'

Carlos smiled and embaced him once more.

'And where have you come from? Celorico?'

'Celorico indeed! I've been in Foz. But I'm a sick man, my boy, a sick man. Liver, spleen, a multitude of affected organs. The result of twelve years of wine and brandy.'

They talked of Carlos's travels, of Ramalhete, of how long Ega would be in Lisbon. Ega had come for good. From the coach he had waved a last good-bye to the fields of Celorico.

'You simply can't imagine, my dear Carlos, the delicious thing that's occurred between me and my mother. After Coimbra, of course, I sounded her out about my coming to live in Lisbon, in comfort and with a decent allowance. Not on your life! It didn't work. So I had to stay in the country composing epigrams against Father Seraphim and all the heavenly host. Then came July and an epidemic of sore throats struck the neighbourhood. Horrors! I believe you fellows call it diphtheria. Mama concluded at once that my presence, the presence of an atheist, a radical, who neither fasted nor attended mass, had offended Our Lord and summoned down His punishment. My sister agreed with her. They consulted Father Seraphim. The man had not at all liked seeing me about the house and agreed that it was indeed quite possible that Our Lord had become indignant. So my mother came to me almost on bended knees with an open purse and begged me to leave for Lisbon. I was free to ruin her, she said, but whatever happened I was not to remain there tempting the divine wrath. So off I went the next day to Foz.'

'And the epidemic?'

'It ceased at once,' declared Ega, as he slowly drew a long canary-coloured glove off his thin fingers.

Carlos contemplated those gloves of Ega's; his cashmere spats; his hair worn long with a waved lock drawn across the forehead; the satin tie with an opal horseshoe-pin in it! This was quite a different Ega, a dandified Ega, showy, decked out, artificial and powdered – and Carlos permitted the impatient exclamation that had been trembling on his lips to escape him at last.

'What an extraordinary coat!'

Ega – that former Bohemian in his ragged student gown – was wearing, in that sweet, warm Portuguese autumn sunshine, a pelisse sumptuous enough for the adornment of a Russian prince, a mantle for sleigh and snow, with frogged trimmings like a Brandenburg's; and around his scraggy neck and consumptive's wrists there hung the rich thickness of sables.

'Not bad, eh?' he said at once, drawing himself up, opening out the pelisse and exhibiting its opulent lining. 'I sent for it through Strauss. One of the benefits of the epidemic.'

'How can you stand it?'

'It's a bit heavy, but I've had a cold.'

He leaned back on the sofa stretching out the pointed toe of a patent-leather shoe, and appraised the surgery with a monocled eye.

'And what are you up to? Tell me all about everything. This is splendidly got up!'

Carlos told Ega his plans, his great ideas for work, the preparations for the laboratory.

'Just a moment. How much has all this cost you?' exclaimed Ega, interrupting him and getting up to handle the velvet of the hangings and to examine the woodwork of the ebony desk.

'I don't know. Vilaça looks after all that.'

With his hands buried deep in the vast pockets of his pelisse, Ega was taking stock of the surgery and delivering his judgment.

'The velvet gives an air of sobriety. And dark green is the supreme colour, the aesthetic colour. It has its own meaning, it moves one and makes one reflect. I like this divan. A thing of love.'

He walked slowly towards the patients' waiting-room, with his monocle in his eye, studying the ornaments.

'You're a great Solomon, Carlos! The paper is pretty, and the cretonne's agreeable.'

He handled this too. A begonia in a Rouen vase, its leaves

rusted with silver, occupied him for a moment. He wanted to
know the price of everything. In front of the piano he was
moved to surprise as he caught sight of the open music book –
the *Songs of Gounod*.

'Good heavens, man. Here it is! The "Barcarolle"! Delicious,
eh?'

> "*Dites, la jeune belle,*
> *Où voulez-vous aller?*
> *La voile . . .*"

'I'm a bit hoarse – this was our song at Foz!'

Carlos exclaimed in surprise and, folding his arms in front of
his friend, declared:

'You're behaving extraordinarily, Ega! You're quite a different man. And what's this about Foz, may I ask? Who's this
Madame Cohen? Wasn't she at Foz too? And didn't you write
me letter after letter about her, veritable poems, that followed
me around from Berlin, to the Hague, to London – letters written
with the rapture of the Song of Songs?'

A faint colour rose to Ega's cheeks. Casually he began to clean
his monocle with a white silk handkerchief.

'A Jewess. And so I used biblical lyricism. She's the wife of
Cohen – you must know him – the fellow who's the director of
the National Bank. We went about a lot together. She's very
pleasant. But the husband's a brute. A holiday flirtation. *Voilà
tout.*'

He spoke spasmodically, in snatches, pacing about the room,
sucking on his cigar and still blushing.

'But tell me about yourselves. What goes on in Ramalhete?
How's Grandfather Afonso? Whom do you see?'

At Ramalhete Grandfather played whist with his old-time
partners. One of them was Dom Diogo, that decrepit lion, still
wearing a rose in his buttonhole and twirling his moustaches.
Then there was Sequeira, bulkier than ever, bursting with blood
and waiting for a stroke. The Count Steinbroken was another
visitor.

'I don't know him. Is he a refugee? A Pole?'

'No. The Finnish Minister. He wanted to lease some stabling
from us and so complicated this simple transaction with such
diplomatic courtesies, so many documents, so many papers bear-

ing the Royal Seal of Finland, that poor Vilaça was dumbfounded and sent him to Grandfather. But Grandfather too was overwhelmed, and so he let him have the stables for nothing. Steinbroken regarded this as a service to the King of Finland, to the Finnish Nation, and comes to call on Grandfather in great state, with the Secretary of the legation, the Consul and the Vice-Consul!'

'What a sublime story!'

'Grandfather invited him to dinner. And as the man is very refined, a gentleman and an Anglophile, a great connoisseur of wines, an authority on whist, Grandfather adopted him. He practically lives at Ramalhete.'

'And what about the fellows?'

As for the fellows, there was Taveira, as formal as ever, and now employed in the Treasury Court; a man called Cruges whom Ega did not know, a mad devil, a maestro, a pianist with a touch of genius; and then there was the Marquis of Souzellas.

'No ladies?'

'There isn't anyone to entertain them. It's a den of bachelors. The poor Viscountess – '

'Oh yes, I heard. A fit of apoplexy – '

'Yes, a cerebral haemorrhage. Oh, and of course there's that fellow Silveira. He arrived recently.'

'You mean that cretin from Resende?'

'Exactly, that cretin. He's a widower and is just back from Madeira, still a bit consumptive, all dressed in mourning. A funereal creature!'

Ega had sat down again in the armchair with that air of serenity and solid happiness that Carlos had already noticed. As he slowly pulled at his cuffs he said:

'We must organize ourselves. We need to gather a circle around us. A golden Bohème – winter evenings of art, literature. D'you know Craft?'

'Yes, I believe I've heard of him.'

Ega threw up his hands. It was absolutely essential to know Craft! Craft was quite the best thing that existed in Portugal.

'Isn't he English? Some kind of lunatic?'

Ega shrugged. A lunatic! That was the general opinion in Rua dos Fanqueiros, for the native Lisboan in the presence of an originality as marked as Craft's could explain it only as mad-

97

ness. Craft was an extraordinary chap! He had just come back from Sweden where he had spent three months among the students at Uppsala. He had been at Foz too. He was a personality of the first order!

'Isn't he an Oporto merchant?'

'Oporto merchant be damned!' cried Ega, jumping up and scowling at so much ignorance.

'Craft is the son of a clergyman of the Church of England in Oporto. He had an uncle who was a merchant in Calcutta or Australia – a nabob who left him his fortune. A great fortune! But he doesn't go in for business, or indeed know anything about it. He gives free rein to his Byronic spirit, that's what he does. He's been all over the world; he collects works of art; he fought as a volunteer in Abyssinia and in Morocco; in short – he lives. He lives, in the great, the strong, the heroic sense of the word. You've got to meet Craft. You'll be mad about him. You're right, you know, it is hot.'

He divested himself of his opulent pelisse and appeared in shirt-sleeves.

'What! Didn't you have anything on underneath?' exclaimed Carlos. 'Not even a waistcoat?'

'No. I couldn't have stood it. The coat's for the effect – to impress the natives – but I can't deny it: it's heavy!'

He immediately went back to his theme. No sooner would Craft arrive from Oporto than they were to meet; a circle would be formed: a Decameron of art and dilettantism, fellows and women – three or four women, to sweeten the severity of philosophy with the grace of their *décolletages*.

Carlos laughed at Ega's fancy. Three women of taste and fashion in Lisbon to adorn a literary circle! Those were the lamentable illusions of a man from Celorico! The Marquis of Souzellas had tried once – and once only – to organize something much simpler: a picnic in the countryside in the company of some actressses. It had turned out to be a scandal of the most comic and typical kind. One of them didn't have a maid and wanted to take an aunt and five children to the party; another feared that, if she accepted, the Brazilian who kept her would cut off her allowance; one agreed to come but when her lover heard about it he gave her a beating. One didn't have a dress for the occasion; another insisted on being guaranteed the payment of a pound; yet another was insulted by the invitation and took it is an affront. Then there were their kept men, their favourites, their sweethearts, who all complicated the affair abominably. Some of them demanded to be invited too; others wanted to wreck the party; people took sides; intrigues started. Finally, the dreary business – a dinner with actresses – resulted in a certain comedian's being knifed!

'That's Lisbon for you!'

'Well!' exclaimed Ega. 'If there aren't any women we'll just have to import them. That's the answer to everything in Portugal. Everything is imported in this country: laws, ideas, philosophies, themes, aesthetics, sciences, style, industries, fashions, manners, jokes. Everything reaches us in packing-cases by the mail-boat. Civilization costs us very dear by the time the Customs duty's paid. And then it's second-hand. It's not made for us and so it doesn't fit. We think we're civilized, the same way that the Negroes of São Tomé believe themselves gentlemen, veritable white men, when they put on old tail-coats of their masters over their loincloths. It's a scurvy mob in this country! Where did I put that cigar-case?'

Shorn of the majesty of his pelisse, the old Ega re-emerged. He declaimed with the sharp gestures of a merry Mephistopheles. He threw himself about the room as if about to take flight and soar with his grand phrases. He engaged in a constant struggle with his monocle. It kept dropping from his eye and he would grope for it on his chest and shoulders while he twisted about and contorted, as though tormented by a swarm of insects. Carlos too became animated and the cold room warmed up. They discussed naturalism, Gambeta, nihilism! Then, ferociously, and in perfect accord, they began to flagellate their native land.

But the clock beside them struck four. Ega at once flung himself on his pelisse, wrapped himself in it, twirled his moustaches in the looking-glass, adjusted his expression and, armoured behind his braided frogs, departed with an air that whispered of luxury and adventure.

'John,' called Carlos, who had told him he looked splendid and was about to follow him on to the landing, 'where are you staying?'

'At the sanctuary – the Universal!'

Carlos detested the Universal, and wanted him to come to Ramalhete.

'It wouldn't be convenient for me . . .'

'But at least you'll dine with us tonight and see Grandfather.'

'I can't. I'm committed to that idiot, Cohen. But I'll come to lunch tomorrow.'

He had already reached the stairs. He turned around, fixed his monocle and called up: 'I forgot to tell you – I'm going to publish my book!'

'What? Is it ready?' cried Carlos in astonishment.

'It's sketched out, in general outline.'

Ega's book! It had been in his last two years at Coimbra that he had begun to talk about his book, describing its plan, quoting chapter titles, reciting phrases of great sonority through the cafés. And there was already talk among Ega's friends about Ega's book. By its form and its conception it would initiate a new literary movement. In Lisbon (where he came to spend vacations and gave suppers at Silva's) the book had been announced as an event. Graduates, contemporaries and fellow-students had carried the fame of Ega's book from Coimbra and spread it throughout the provinces and the islands. One way and another the news had reached Brazil! And so, sensing the eager anticipation that surrounded his work, Ega had at last decided to write it.

It was to be a prose epic, he declared, and would describe through a series of symbolic episodes the history of the great periods of the World and of Humanity. It was entitled *Memoirs of an Atom*, and was autobiographical in form. In the first chapter this atom (Ega's Atom, as it was called in all earnestness at Coimbra) was still roaming amid the cloudiness of the primitive nebulae. Then it found itself, a burning spark, in the ball of fire that was later to become the earth. At last it became a part of the first leaf of plant that arose on the globe's still-soft crust. After that, as it voyaged through continual transformations of substance, Ega's atom entered the primitive structure of the orang-outang, the father of humanity, and later it lived on the lips of Plato. It blackened in the coarse sackcloth of the martyrs, gleamed on the swords of heroes, and beat in the heart of poets. In a drop of water in the Sea of Galilee it heard the speech of Jesus at the close of evening as the apostles gathered in their nets; in a knot of wood in the tribune of the Convention it felt the cold hand of Robespierre. It had wandered through the vast rings of Saturn and the dawns of earth had put their dew on it as part of the resplendent petal of a drowsy and languid lily. It was ubiquitous, omniscient. Finding itself at last on the point of Ega's pen, and weary of its journey through Being, it rested as it wrote its *Memoirs*.

Such was the formidable masterpiece.

And when Ega's admirers at Coimbra talked of it pensively and overcome with reverence they said: 'It's a Bible.'

5

ALTHOUGH it was growing late there was still a game of whist going on in Afonso da Maia's study. Beside the fireplace where a flame flickered among the crimson coals, the card-table stood in its usual nook sheltered by the Japanese screen because of Dom Diogo's bronchitis and his horror of draughts.

That old coxcomb, whom ladies of other years had called 'Diogo the beautiful' – an elegant bullfighter who had once shared a royal bed – had just recovered from one of his fits of coughing. They were sepulchral, harsh and painful, and shook him like a ruin. He would try to smother the paroxysm in a handkerchief while his veins swelled and he grew purple to the roots of his hair.

But it had passed and, his hand still trembling, the decrepit lion wiped away the tears that bathed his bloodshot eyes, adjusted the moss-rose in his buttonhole, took a gulp of his weak tea and asked Afonso, his partner, in a voice that was low and hoarse: 'Clubs, eh?'

Once more the cards were laid down on the green baize in one of those hushes that always followed Dom Diogo's coughing fits. All that could be heard was General Sequeira's whistled, almost hissing breath. That night he was a very wretched man, in despair over his partner, Vilaça, and his face was flushed.

A silvery note sounded as, gay and lively, the Louis XV clock struck midnight. Then the tinkling music of its minuet vibrated a moment and died away. Once more there was quiet. Scarlet lace covered the lamps of the two big Carcel chandeliers, and the shaded light that fell on the red damask of the walls and the seats reflected a soft rose colour and a cloudy atmosphere in which the room bathed and drowsed. Only here and there on the sombre oak of the shelves there shone silently the gold of a Sèvres, the pallor of ivory, or some enamelled tint of old majolica.

'What? Still up?' cried Carlos as he drew back the curtain and stepped into the room, bearing with him a distant sound of billiard balls.

Afonso, who was taking up his trick, turned his head and asked anxiously:

'How is she? Resting?'

'She's very much improved!'

Carlos was attending his first serious case – a girl of Alsatian origin married to Marcelino, the baker, and very well known in the quarter for her beautiful hair, which was fair and always worn in loose braids. She had been near to death with pneumonia. Although she was now recovered, as the bakery was close by Carlos still crossed the road sometimes in the evening to go and see her and soothe Marcelino, who sat beside the bed with a cape round his shoulders trying to smother a lover's sobs as he scribbled in his account book.

Afonso had displayed an anxious interest in that pneumonia. And now he was really grateful to Marcelina for having been saved by Carlos. He spoke of her with feeling; praised her dainty looks, her Alsatian cleanliness and the prosperity she had brought to the bakery. He had already even sent her six bottles of Château Margaux for her approaching convalescence.

'So she's out of danger, really out of danger?' asked Vilaça, his fingers on his snuff-box, stressing his solicitude.

'Yes, nearly fit,' answered Carlos as he came up to the hearth shivering and rubbing his hands.

Outside, the night was icy. It had been freezing since dusk and a thin, hard sky gleamed with stars that were like points of sharpened steel. Nobody could remember when the temperature had fallen so low. Then Vilaça recalled a worse January in 1864.

'Shall we call for some punch, eh, General?' cried Carlos gaily slapping Sequeira's massive shoulders.

'I wouldn't say no,' grunted the General as he stared intently and rancorously at the knave of hearts lying on the table.

Carlos still felt chilly, and he stood poking the fire and stirring the coals: a shower of gold fell, a stronger flame leaped and roared, cheering up everything and reddening the bearskin on which the Reverend Bonifácio was stretched out, toasting himself in the warmth and purring contentedly.

'Ega must be pleased,' said Carlos with his feet near the flames. 'At last he's got an excuse for that coat of his. Incidentally, has any of you gentlemen seen anything of Ega these last few days?'

There was no reply: everyone had suddenly again become engrossed in the game. Dom Diogo's long hand slowly gathered up his trick and, still silent, he languidly put down a club.

'Oh, Diogo! Oh, Diogo!' cried Afonso, writhing as though he had been pierced with an iron spike.

But he contained himself. The General, his eyes gleaming, put down his knave; Afonso, now thoroughly wretched, surrendered his king of clubs; Vilaça flung down an ace. They at once fell into a tremendous argument about Dom Diogo's mistake, while Carlos, who was always bored by cards, bent down and scratched the venerable Bonifácio's fluffy belly.

'What were you asking, my boy?' said Afonso at last as he rose, still irritated, to fetch the tobacco for his pipe, that consolation in all his defeats. 'Ega? No, nobody's seen him. He's not appeared since. He's an ungrateful creature that John . . .'

At Ega's name, Vilaça stopped shuffling the pack and raised his head curiously.

'Is it really true that he's about to set up house?'

It was Afonso who answered, smiling as he lit his pipe.

'Setting up house, buying a *coupé*, hiring servants, giving literary evenings, publishing a poem – the devil knows!'

'He was at the office,' Vilaça told them as he started shuffling. 'He came to ask what the consulting-rooms had cost, the velvet furnishings and so on. He was very keen on the green velvet – as he's a friend of the house I gave him the figures and I even showed him the bills.' Then in reply to a question from Sequeira, he added: 'His mother's got money and I believe she gives him enough. It's my notion he'll be going in for politics. He's talented, speaks well and his father was a great Regenerator. He's got his ambitions.'

'There's a woman in the case,' declared Dom Diogo weightily, and he emphasized this pronouncement with a languid caress of the curled points of his white moustache. 'You can read it in his face. You only have to see his face – it's all a question of a woman.'

Carlos smiled, impressed with Dom Diogo's perspicacity, his authentic Balzacian eye; and Sequeira, with all the frankness of an old soldier, at once wanted to know the woman's name. But the old dandy, from the depths of his experience, declared that such matters were never known, and it was better they should remain that way. He passed his thin fingers slowly over his face as, with lofty condescension, he uttered a final judgment.

'I like Ega, he's got presence; above all, he's got assurance . . .'

The cards had been dealt again and there was silence once more around the table. The General emitted a low grunt as he glanced at his hand. He picked up his cigarette from the ashtray and puffed at it furiously.

'You gentlemen are too much like gamblers – I'm off back to the billiards-room,' said Carlos. 'I left Steinbroken in the clutches of the Marquis, who had already taken some 4,000 *reis* from him. D'you want your punch in here?'

But there was no response from the card-table.

Carlos found the same solemn intentness around the billiard-table. The Marquis, who was stretched out across the table with one leg halfway up in the air and his growing bald patch shining in the raw light that fell from the porcelain lamp, was preparing a decisive stroke. Cruges, who was backing him, had abandoned the divan and his Turkish hookah, and had begun to follow the ball restlessly, with his eyes half-closed and his nose up in the air, as he nervously scratched the thick curls that fell in waves down to the collar of his jacket. At the back of the room, silhouetted in his suit of mourning, was Silveirinha, the Eusè-biozinho of Santa Olávia. He too craned his neck, a neck that had been sunk in his widower's cravat of black merino, collarless, gloomy as ever, flabbier than before, with hands buried deep in his pockets – so funereal that everything about him seemed part of his heavy mourning: from his straight black hair to the black of his smoked spectacles. Beside the billiard-table, the Marquis's partner, the Count Steinbroken, waited. And in spite of his fear, in spite of the emotion that gripped this tight-fisted northerner, he conducted himself correctly, leaning against his billiard-cue and smiling. His British appearance was unruffled. He was dressed like an Englishman, an Englishman of the traditional mould: a tight tail-coat and rather short sleeves, broad checked trousers over big, low-heeled shoes.

'Hurrah!' shouted Cruges suddenly. 'Let's have those ten *tostoes*, Silveirinha!'

The Marquis had won the game and was rejoicing too.

'You brought me luck, Carlos!'

Steinbroken had at once laid down his billiard-cue and was

slowly lining up on the cushion, one by one, the four coins he had lost.

But the Marquis, chalk in hand and hungry for Finnish gold, demanded another game.

'No more – you are terrible today!' the diplomat said in his fluent but barbarously pronounced Portuguese.

The Marquis insisted and planted himself before Steinbroken with his billiard-cue across his shoulder like a peasant's staff, dominating him with his massive and elastic presence. He threatened him with a terrible fate, in his powerful voice accustomed to echoing across vast spaces; he was going to ruin Steinbroken at billiards, force him to pawn those splendid rings and reduce him, him – the Minister of Finland and representative of a race of powerful kings – to selling theatre tickets in the Rua dos Condes!

Everybody laughed, including Steinbroken. But his laughter was constrained and uneasy, and he could not take his gaze off the Marquis – that light blue gaze, light and cold, which somewhere underneath its shortsightedness, contained a metallic hardness. In spite of his respect for the illustrious house of Souzella, he found these familiarities, these enormous jokes, incompatible with his dignity and with the dignity of Finland. The Marquis, however, had a heart of gold, and was already warmly hugging him round the waist.

'Well, if you don't want any more billiards, how about a bit of song, Steinbroken, old friend?'

The Minister agreed affably to this proposal and made ready at once, gently stroking his whiskers and passing a hand over his fair curls that were the colour of faded corn.

All the Steinbrokens, from father to son – as he had once told Afonso – were good baritones, and this had brought the family no small social success. His father had captivated with his voice old King Rudolph III, who had put him in charge of his horses and kept him nights on end at the piano in his chambers singing Lutheran psalms, school chants, and sagas of Dalecarlia – while the gloomy monarch smoked his pipe and drank, until, soaked with religious emotion and saturated with black beer, he would fall off the sofa sobbing and drooling. At the piano Steinbroken himself had won much promotion in his career, first as attaché, then as second secretary. But when he was appointed head of a mission he had abstained. It was only after reading repeated praises in *Figaro* for the waltzes of Prince Artoff, the Russian Ambassador in Paris, or for the bass voice of Count Bapst, the Ambassador of Austria in London, that he had decided to emulate these lofty examples and now and then essayed a few Finnish melodies during more intimate soirées. At last he had sung at the Palace. From then onwards he began, with formality and rules, zealously to exercise what Ega called his mission as 'baritone plenipotentiary'. Among gentlemen only, and behind drawn curtains, Steinbroken even dared what he called 'naughty songs': 'Amanda's Lover', or a certain English ballad:

> 'On the Serpentine,
> Oh my Caroline –
> Oh – !'

This final *Oh!* was uttered with a long-drawn-out moan and a barbaric gesture that was both expressive, yet somehow dignified – this, of course, only among the gentlemen and with the blinds drawn.

That night, however, the Marquis, who led him by the arm towards the music-room, wanted to hear one of those Finnish songs, so full of feeling, that did one's soul so much good:

'There's one that has some words I like: *frisk, gluzk – ha ra lá, lá, lá!*'

'The "Spring Song",' said the diplomat with a smile.

But before they entered the music-room, the Marquis let go of Steinbroken's arm, made a sign to Silveirinha to come with him to the end of the corridor, and there, below a sombre panel depicting Mary Magdalen in the desert doing penance and displaying the rich nakedness of a voluptuous nymph, he questioned him in sharpish tones.

'Now I want an answer! Is this thing to be decided or not!'

It was a business affair that had been brewing between them for weeks now, and concerned a pair of mares. Silveirinha cherished a longing to set up a carriage, and the Marquis wanted to sell him his white mares, to which, he said, he had taken a dislike in spite of their being two noble animals. He wanted one and a half *contos* for them. Silveirhina had been advised by

Sequeira, by Travassos, and by others who all understood these matters, that it was a swiz: the Marquis had his own private notions about dealing in livestock and rejoiced in taking in a tyro. But despite these warnings, Eusèbio, seduced by the thick voice of the Marquis, his robust physique and the antiquity of his title, dared not refuse. But he temporized, and that night he gave his usual cautious answer, scratching his chin and gluing himself against the wall.

'I'll have to see, Marquis – a *conto* and a half is a lot of money.'

The Marquis threw up his arms, as menacing as two beams of wood.

'Yes or no, man! What the devil! Two fine animals like that – bah! Yes, or no!'

Eusèbio adjusted his spectacles and muttered.

'I'll have to see – it's a lot of money. A lot of money, you know.'

'Perhaps you thought of paying me with beans? You're beginning to provoke me, you know!'

The piano sounded two full chords under the hands of Cruges, and the Marquis, who was a glutton for music, at once dropped the subject of the mares and tip-toed back. Eusèbiozinho lingered for a while in thought, scratching his chin; at last, when Steinbroken's first notes sounded, he came like a silent shadow and stood between the door-jamb and the curtain.

At a distance from the piano, as was his wont, curved over, with his hair falling down his back, sat Cruges striking out the accompaniment, his eyes fixed on the book of *Finnish Melodies*. At his side, erect, almost official, with a silk handkerchief in his hand, and his hand against his chest, Steinbroken was giving tongue to a festive song in the rhythm of a victorious tarantella amid which, scattered like pebbles, sounded those bits of words so dear to the Marquis: *frisk, slécht, clikst, glukst*. It was the 'Spring Song' – fresh and sylvan; a northern spring in a mountain country, when the entire village dances in chorus under the dark firs; when the snow dissolves in cascades; when a pale sun makes the moss look like velvet; and the breeze bears the aroma of resins. On the full bass notes Steinbroken's cheeks reddened and swelled. On the high notes he reared up on tip-toe as if carried away by the lively rhythm. At that point his hand

you than any of those whipper-snappers you see wandering around and half-rotten. There aren't men like you any more, Dioguinho!'

'There's nothing at all left any more,' agreed the other with gravity, as though he were the last man left alive among the ruins of the world.

But it was late and he had to go and wrap himself up and get home as soon as he had finished his tea. The Marquis still lingered, lazing on the sofa, filling his pipe slowly and letting his eyes wander around this room that entranced him with its Louis XV luxury, its flowered patterns and its gilt, the ceremonial Beauvais armchairs designed for ample panniers, the muted Gobelin tapestries filled with saucy shepherdesses, expanses of parkland, ribands and woolly lambs, shadows of dead idylls, depicted in the woven silk. The drowsiness that weighed heavily at that hour under the soft, hot light of the flickering candles held something of the peaceful air of another age. The Marquis asked Cruges to play a minuet, a gavotte, anything that would recall memories of Versailles, Marie Antoinette, the rhythm of fine manners and the scent of powder. Cruges allowed the vague melody that was melting in sighs die beneath his fingers, and then, stamping on the loud pedal, he attacked the Liberal anthem. The Marquis fled.

Vilaça and Eusèbiozinho were chatting in the corridor seated on one of the low carved-oak chests.

'Talking politics?' inquired the Marquis as he passed them.

They both smiled, and Vilaça replied jokingly: 'Someone's got to save the country.'

Eusèbiozinho too was a member of the Progressive Centre and aspired to electoral influence in the constituency of Resende. There at night in Ramalhete they would both scheme. At that moment, however, they had been talking about the Maias. Vilaça had no hesitation in confiding to Silveirinha – a man of property, a neighbour of Santa Olávia, someone who had practically been brought up with Carlos – certain matters that troubled him in that house, where the authority of his words appeared to be diminishing. For instance he could not approve of Carlos subscribing to a box at the opera.

'Why, I ask you?' exclaimed the worthy steward, 'why, my dear fellow? He never sets foot there. Spends all his evenings here – today, for example, they say it was crowded, but he was here. I know he's been two or three times – and for that he pays out some hundreds of *milréis*. He could do the same thing for a few pounds! This is no way of conducting things. In the end the box is really for Ega, for Taveira, for Cruges – even I don't use it, nor do you. But of course you're in mourning.'

Eusèbio thought spitefully that he could at least have placed himself at the back of the box – had he been invited. Letting a soft laugh escape him, he murmured: 'If things go on this way, they'll end in the workhouse!'

These humiliating words, applied to the Maias, to the house he administered, scandalized Vilaça.

'The workhouse! Whatever next! You misunderstand me – there are unnecessary expenses, of course, but, thank God, the house can afford them! It's true the income is spent up to the hilt; cheques flutter about like dry leaves; and up to now the habit of the house was to put aside, save, lay in stocks. Now the money melts away . . .'

Eusèbio grunted a few words about Carlos's carriages, the nine horses, the English coachman, the grooms . . .

The steward interrupted him: 'No! There you're wrong. A family like this must keep up appearances – have a fine turn out. There are social duties, after all – it's like Senhor Afonso – he spends a lot, yes, he eats money. But not for himself. I've known that coat he's wearing for twenty years. But it's on alms, on pensions, on loans he never sees again.'

'All wasted . . .'

'No, I don't censure him – it's the custom of the house; never from the Maias' gate, as my father used to say, was anyone turned away empty-handed – but an opera-box that nobody uses except Cruges or Taveira!'

He had to stop speaking. Just then Taveira himself appeared at the bottom of the corridor, swathed up to the eyes in the collar of an ulster from which the points of a pale silk scarf peeped out. The footman helped him off with his wrappings; and in his tail-coat and white waistcoat, and wiping his beautiful moustaches that were wet with frost, he came up to shake hands with dear Vilaça and friend Eusèbio, while he consoled himself aloud with the thought that 'the cold was elegant and would be better still with the snow and its *chic*.'

112

'Never, never!' objected Vilaça all smiles. 'Our own Portuguese sunshine is always better!'

Together they went in to the smoking-room, where the voices of Carlos and the Marquis could be heard in one of their prolonged and learned exchanges on the subject of horses and sport.

'Well? What is she like? What did you think of her?' a shower of questions greeted Taveira.

But before he told them about the début of Morelli, the new star, Taveira demanded something hot to drink. Buried in an armchair beside the fire, with his patent-leather shoes stretched out towards the coals, savouring the fragrance of the punch, tasting a cigarette, he at last declared that it had not been altogether a fiasco.

'In my opinion, of course, she's insignificant. She's got nothing – neither voice, nor training. But the poor thing was suffering from such stage-fright that we felt sorry for her. So people were indulgent and there was some clapping. When I went backstage she was all right.'

'Now let's hear about that, Taveira, what's she like?' inquired the Marquis.

'Full,' said Taveira, choosing his words like strokes of a paint-brush; 'tall; very white; good eyes; good teeth . . .'

'And her little foot?' the Marquis's eyes already gleamed as he slowly stroked his bald head.

But Taveira had not noticed her foot. He was not a connoisseur of feet.

'Who was there?' asked Carlos, indolent and yawning.

'Same as usual – by the way, do you know who's taken the box beside yours? The Gouvarinhos. They appeared there to-day.'

Carlos did not know the Gouvarinhos. Explanations came from every side: the Count de Gouvarinho was a peer of the realm, a tall man, with glasses, very affected. And the Countess was an English lady with hair the colour of carrots and very well-made . . . But Carlos did not know them.

Vilaça had met the Count in the Progressive Centre, where he was a pillar of the party. A talented fellow, according to Vilaça. What surprised him was that with all his money problems he could still afford to take a box at the opera. It was scarcely three months since he had had a bill for 800 *milréis* presented in the Commercial Court.

'An ass! A trickster!' declared the Marquis in disgust.

'They have very pleasant Tuesday evenings,' said Taveira, contemplating his silk stockings.

Then there was talk about the duel between Azevedo, the journalist of the *Opinião*, and a former minister of the navy – Sá Nunes – author of *El-Rei Bolacha*, the current fantasy in the Rua dos Condes. They had insulted each other abominably in the newspapers, calling each other rogues and thieves; and ten interminable days had passed since they had challenged each other and an amazed Lisbon had been awaiting blood. Cruges had heard that Sá Nunes did not want to fight because he was in mourning for an aunt; it was said, too, that Azevedo had left hurriedly for the Algarve. But according to Vilaça the truth was that the Minister of the Interior, who was Azevedo's cousin, to prevent the encounter, kept the houses of both worthies barricaded by the police.

'Scum!' cried the Marquis, in one of those brutal pronouncements which swept everything aside.

'The Minister's got right on his side,' observed Vilaça. 'This business of duelling often ends in tragedy.'

There was a brief silence. Carlos, who was dropping with sleep, asked Taveira, with another yawn, if he had seen Ega at the theatre.

'What d'you think! There he was, very well turned-out, on duty, at his post in the Cohens' box.'

'So that business about Ega and Cohen's wife,' said the Marquis, 'seems to be quite clear.'

'Transparent! Diaphanous! Clear as crystal!'

Carlos, who had got up to light a cigarette so as to wake himself up, reminded them of Dom Diogo's great maxim: these things were never known, and it was better they should never be known. On hearing this the Marquis launched into heavy speculations. He was glad that Ega should give chase. It was a question of social reprisals, for Cohen was a Jew and a banker. The Marquis didn't like Jews in general, but nothing was quite so offensive to taste and reason as the banker species. He could understand the footpad lurking in the pine forest; he could accept the communist risking his skin behind the barricades –

but the moneyed men, the So-and-Sos and Co., these made him ill! And he felt that the destruction of their domestic peace was meritorious conduct.

'A quarter past two!' exclaimed Taveira, as he looked at the clock. 'And here am I, a civil servant with duties towards the State tomorrow morning at ten o'clock!'

'What the devil is there to do in the Financial Court?' asked Carlos, 'D'you gamble? D'you talk?'

'You do a bit of everything to kill time – even a bit of work!'

Afonso da Maia had already retired. Sequeira and Steinbroken had gone home and Dom Diogo, in the depths of his old carriage, had gone off too to take his egg-nog and put on his plaster under the solicitous eye of Margarida, his cook and his last love. It was not long before the others left Ramalhete. Taveira, buried once more inide his ulster, walked to his house, a little villa nearby with a lovely garden. The Marquis managed to get Cruges to come home with him in his coupé to make music on the organ until three or four o'clock – religious sad music that made him cry as he thought of his loves and ate cold chicken with slices of salami. And as for Eusèbiozinho the widower, with his teeth chattering, as morose and gloomy as though making for his tomb, he directed his footsteps towards a brothel where there was a girl he fancied.

Carlos's laboratory was ready and very inviting with its new floorings, ovens of fresh tile, a vast marble table, an ample divan of horse-hair for repose after great discoveries, and all around, on top of stands and shelves, the rich gleam of metals and crystals; but the weeks went by and all that fine research equipment lay virgin and idle under the white light of the skylight. Only in the mornings a servant would go and earn his daily *tostão* by making a lazy round with a duster in his hand.

Carlos really had no time to occupy himself with the laboratory and he was disposed to leave to God for a few more weeks the exclusive privilege of knowing the secret of things – as he remarked with a laugh to his grandfather. Early in the morning he had his usual two hours' arms practice with old Randon; then he saw a few patients in the district, where the news of Marcelina's recovery – and the bottles of Bordeaux she had received – had spread like wildfire. He was beginning to win recognition as a doctor. Patients came to the consulting-rooms – usually contemporaries of his student days, who knew he was rich and expected to be treated for nothing. In they came, discouraged and sulky, to tell the old and ill-contrived tale of passions that had left their mark. He saved the daughter of a Brazilian in the Aterro from the croup and thus earned his first pound, the first that any man of his family had ever won by his own labour. Dr Barbedo invited him to assist at an ovariotomy.

At last came the final tribute that Carlos had really not expected so soon: some of his good colleagues who had spoken of 'Maia's talent' when they had seen him spending most of his time driving his English horses, now that they were able to observe the beginnings of a practice began to say that 'Maia was an ass'. Carlos started to consider his career seriously. With laborious stylistic finesse he wrote two articles for the *Gazeta Médica;* and he planned a book of a general nature to be entitled *Medicine Ancient and Modern*. His spare time was always taken up with his horses, his luxury and his bric-à-brac. And in consequence, by virtue of that fatal attraction towards the curious that would cause him to turn his head in the midst of the most absorbing pathological case if he overheard someone talking about a statue or a poet, he felt singularly attracted by Ega's old idea: the founding of a journal that would guide taste, carry weight in politics, regulate society and be the intellectual strength of Lisbon.

But it was useless trying to remind Ega of this great project. He would open a vague eye and answer:

'Oh, yes. The Journal . . . Yes, of course, we must start thinking about it. We must have a talk. I'll drop in . . .'

But he did not drop in, either at Ramalhete or at the consulting-rooms. They merely glimpsed each other occasionally at the opera, where Ega, if he was not in the Cohens' box, would always take refuge in the depths of Carlos's, behind Taveira or Cruges, from which point he could gaze now and again on Rachel Cohen – and there he would stand, silent, with his head leaning on the partition, in repose, as though bathed in happiness.

His days were completely taken up; he was supposed to be searching for a house, looking for furniture. But he was always to be found in the Chiado or the Loreto, wandering around as though seeking something – or else he would be seen in the back of a cab cantering off somewhere in a great, adventurous clatter.

His foppery became more marked than ever; he blossomed, flowering superbly into a Beau Brummel in a tail-coat with yellow buttons over a white satin waistcoat; and Carlos, entering the Universal early one morning, found him white with rage, shrieking at a servant because of some badly polished shoes. His constant companions now were a certain Damaso Salcéde, a friend of Cohen's, and a cousin of Rachel Cohen, a beardless youth with a sly, hard eye, who already had the look of a lender at thirty per cent.

At Ramalhete, but especially in the box at the opera, his friends sometimes discussed Rachel, and opinions differed. Taveira thought her 'delicious!', and said so gnashing his teeth; the Marquis thought that, for the odd occasion, the ripe flesh of a woman of thirty was not unpalatable. Cruges called her a 'pretentious gossip'. In the newspaper features on High Society she was known as 'one of our leaders of fashion'; and all Lisbon knew her, her gold lorgnette on the end of a golden chain, her blue chaise drawn by black horses. She was tall, very pale, especially in the light, delicate of health with a lassitude in her weary eyes, an infinite languor about all her person, an atmosphere of romance and half-withered lilies. Her greatest beauty was her hair, magnificently black, wavy, very heavy, which rebelled against pins, and was allowed to fall artfully in a half-loosened mass on her shoulders, suggesting the negligence of nakedness. It was said that she was well-read and a skillful phrase-maker. Her tired, pale, perpetual smile gave her a vague air. Poor Ega adored her.

He had first seen her in the club at Foz that night when he had been drinking beer with friends, and he had called her a 'honeyed camellia'; some days later he was already dancing attendance on her husband; and now the radical, who had called for the mass slaughter of the middle classes, often flung himself down on his bed and sobbed over her for hours on end.

From the Grémio to the Casa Havaneza in Lisbon there was already talk about Ega's 'cosy little adventure'. But he tried to put his happiness above all human suspicions. There was as much sincerity as there was romantic pleasure in mystery in his complicated precautions, and he would make his furtive way to the most unlikely spots outside town or near the slaughterhouse in order to meet the servant who brought him her letters. But every attitude (even the affected unconcern with which he glanced at the time) revealed the immense vanity surrounding this elegant adultery. Moreover he well knew that his friends were aware of his glorious adventure, and were perfectly acquainted with what was going on — perhaps it was for this very reason that he had never yet mentioned her name before Carlos and the others, nor would he ever permit a sign of excitement to escape him.

One night, however, as he accompanied Carlos to the door of Ramalhete, a night of calm, white moonlight in which they both strolled along silently, Ega, who must have felt some internal wave of passion, uttered a sigh, flung out his arms and declaimed with his eyes on the heavens and a tremor in his voice:

'Oh! *laisse-toi donc aimer; oh! l'amour c'est la vie!*'

The words escaped his lips like the beginning of a confession; Carlos, at his side, said nothing, and blew the smoke of his cigar into the air.

But Ega must have felt ridiculous, for he calmed down and at once took refuge in pure literary talk:

'When all's said and done, my boy, whatever they say, there's nobody like old Hugo . . .'

Carlos silently recalled Ega's naturalist furies, his roaring against Hugo when he had declared him 'a leaking bag of spiritualism', 'an open-mouthed shadow', 'a lyrical grandfather', and worse insults.

But on that night the great coiner of phrases went on:

'Ah! Good old Hugo! Good old Hugo is the heroic champion of eternal truths — a bit of idealism is essential, for heaven's sake! And what's more, the ideal can be real . . .'

And this recantation tore the silence of the Aterro.

In his consulting-rooms days later Carlos had just finished taking leave of a patient — a certain Viegas, who arrived every week to recount the meticulous chronicle of his dyspepsia — when through the waiting-room curtain appeared Ega, in a blue tail-coat and pearl-grey gloves with a roll of paper in his hand.

'Busy, Doctor?'

118

'No, dandy! I was just going out!'

'Good. I'm here to impose on you with prose – a bit of the *Atom*. Sit down and listen!'

He at once seated himself, pushing back papers and books, unrolled the manuscript, flattened it out, pulled at his collar – and Carlos, who had sat down on the edge of the divan, with an astonished expression and his hands on his knees, found himself almost without warning transported from the gurgles of Viega's belly to the murmur of a populace in the Jewish quarter of the old city of Heidelberg.

'But wait a moment!' he exclaimed. 'Let me get my breath. Surely that isn't the beginning of the book? That's not Chaos . . .'

Ega leaned back, unbuttoned his tail coat and also took a breath.

'No, it's not the first episode, it's not Chaos. It's already the fifteenth century – but in a book like this you can start writing at the end. I felt like doing this episode – it's called "The Hebrew Woman".'

'Rachel Cohen!' said Carlos to himself.

Ega opened his collar further and started reading. He became animated, enunciated the words to make them live, loosing great full-voiced vowels at the sonorous ending of periods. After a sombre portrait of a medieval quarter in Heidelberg, the famous Atom – Ega's *Atom* – appeared lodged in the heart of the splendid Prince Franck, poet, knight and bastard of the Emperor Maximilian. And all that hero's heart beat for the Jewess Esther, marvellous pearl of the Orient, daughter of the old rabbi Solomon, a great doctor in law, persecuted by the theological hatred of the vicar-general of the Dominicans.

This was narrated by the Atom in a monologue as sprinkled with imagery as the mantle of the Virgin is studded with stars – and it was a declaration from him, Ega, to the wife of Cohen. Then came a pantheist interval – choruses of flowers and stars burst forth, singing in the language of light or in the eloquence of perfumes, the beauty, the grace, the purity, the celestial soul of Esther – and of Rachel! At last came the dark drama of the persecution – the flight of the Hebrew family across witch-ridden woods and rude feudal villages; the appearance at a crossroads of Prince Franck, who had come with his lance held high, on his great steed, to protect Esther; the footsteps of the fanatical mob rushing to burn the rabbi and his heretical books; the battle, and the prince pierced through with a lance, going to die on Esther's breast, and she dying with him in a kiss. All this was rushed into like a sonorous and tumultuous sob; and it was presented in modern style with a tormented effort swelling the expression, waves of colour thrown everywhere to heighten the tones of life.

At the end, the Atom exclaimed with the vast solemnity of an organ chord:

'Thus that hero's heart I inhabited cooled and stopped; and with the principle of life departed I was now free, and mounted to the stars taking with me the pure essence of that immortal love.'

'Well?' asked Ega, exhausted, almost trembling.

Carlos could only answer: 'It's ardent!'

Then, with seriousness, he praised certain passages – the chorus of the forests; the reading of Ecclesiastes at night among the ruins of the Tower of Othon; and certain other images of great lyrical power.

Ega, who was in a hurry, as usual, rolled up the manuscript, re-buttoned his tail-coat, and, with his hat in his hand, said:

'Well, d'you think it's presentable?'

'Are you going to publish?'

'No, but, well . . .' and he remained reticent while the colour rose in his cheeks.

A few days later, looking through the *Gazeta do Chiado*, Carlos understood everything. There he found a description 'of the reading by our friend João da Ega, at the house of Senhor Jacob Cohen, of one of the most brilliant episodes in his book, *Memoirs of an Atom*.' And, added the journalist, giving his personal impression: 'It is a portrait of the sufferings undergone, in the times of religious intolerance, by those who follow the Law of Israel. What imaginative power! What fluency of style! The effect was extraordinary, and when our friend closed his manuscript at the death of the warrior we saw tears in the eyes of all the numerous and esteemed Hebrew colony!'

Oh, Ega's rage! That evening he burst into the consulting-room, pale and wild:

'Those beasts! Those pigs of journalists. Have you read it? "Tears in the eyes of all the numerous and esteemed Hebrew colony" – it makes everything so ridiculous! And then, "fluency of style". What asses! What idiots!'

Carlos, who was cutting the pages of a book, consoled him. That was the national way of talking about works of art. There was no point in getting worked up.

'No, upon my word! All I want is to smash that hack's face in!'

'Then why don't you?'

'He's a friend of Cohen's.'

And he went on grunting insults against the Press, as he paced like a tiger up and down the surgery. At last, irritated by Carlos's indifference, he said:

'What the devil are you reading there? *Nature parasitaire des accidents de l'impaludisme*. What a joke, medicine is. Tell me something. What the devil is the prickling I feel in my arms as I'm going off to sleep?'

'Fleas, bugs, vermin . . .' muttered Carlos with his eyes on his book.

'Animal!' roared Ega, thrusting on his hat.

'Are you off, John?'

'I'm going. I got things to do!' And beside the curtain, threatening the heavens with his umbrella, he practically wept with rage: 'Those asses of journalists! They're the scourge of society!'

Ten minutes later he brusquely reappeared, with another voice now, speaking in measured tones.

'Listen a minute, I'd forgotten. D'you want to meet the Gouvarinhos?'

'I'm not particularly interested,' answered Carlos raising his eyes from the book after a moment's silence. 'But I've no particular repugnance either.'

'Good,' said Ega. 'They want to meet you. The Countess is particularly insistent. They're intelligent people, it's pleasant there – so? Is it decided? I'll call for you on Tuesday at Ramalhete and we'll go Gouvarinho-ing.'

Carlos remained in thought, considering Ega's proposal and the way he had stressed the Countess's insistence. Now he remembered that she was very intimate with Madame Cohen. Lately, at the opera in the easy neighbourliness of the boxes, he had surprised certain glances from her. According to Taveira she was really setting her cap at him. And Carlos found her enticing, with her red, curly hair, her haughty nose, her dark, very bright eyes, that said a thousand things. She was enchantingly well-made – and she had a very fair skin, fine and sweet to look at, whose satin smoothness could be sensed, even at a distance.

After that rather gloomy, showery day he had decided to spend a good evening working in the corner of the fireside in the comfort of his dressing-gown. But at coffee the eyes of Madame Gouvarinho began to sparkle at him amid the cigar smoke, luring him and placing themselves temptingly between him and his night of study, and sending coursing through his veins the lively warmth of youth – it was all Ega's fault, that Mephistopheles of Celorico!

He dressed and went to the opera. However, as he sat down at the front of the box, in readiness, in his white waistcoat and with a black pearl in his shirt, instead of that curly red hair, he saw the woolly black head of a Negro boy, a Negro about twelve years old, sullen and shiny, wearing a big Eton collar over a jacket with yellow buttons; at his side stood another smaller Negro, in the same school uniform and with one of his fingers, covered in a white leather glove, deep up one of his broad nostrils. Both of them fixed their prominent eyes, the colour of smoky silver, on him. Hidden at the back the person who accompanied them seemed to be suffering abominably from catarrh.

A benefit performance of *Lucia di Lammermoor* was being staged with the main part taken by an understudy. The Cohens had not come – nor had Ega. Several boxes were deserted in all the sadness of their old red paper. The rainy night, with a breeze from the south-west, seemed to penetrate the building, spreading its heaviness, the tepid feeling of its humidity. In the empty stalls sat a solitary woman dressed in light satin; Edgar and Lucia were out of tune; the gaslight drowsed and the bows of the violins on the strings seemed to be going to sleep too.

'This is lugubrious,' said Carlos to his friend Cruges who sat at the back in the dark of the box.

Cruges was plunged in one of his fits of the miseries. With an elbow on the back of the chair, his fingers in his hair, all of him wrapped in gloom, he replied as though from the depths of the tomb: 'A bit dull.'

Out of inertia Carlos remained. He could not take his eyes off that Negro enthroned there on Madame Gouvarinho's green rep chair, his jacket-sleeve on the rail where that lovely arm was used to rest. And, little by little, in spite of himself, his imagination was drawn to her person as he recalled dresses she had worn there. And, now that he could not see it, her red hair had never seemed to be so ravishing, the colour of flames in the light, tightly curled, as though scorched by an internal flame. The Negro's woolly head had a gap cut by scissors in the mass of thick hair instead of a parting. Who could they be? Why were they there? Those Africans with their sullen profiles.

'Have you noticed that extraordinary hair, Cruges?'

The other, who had not altered his funerary monument pose, muttered a dull monosyllable out of the dark box.

Carlos respected his mood.

Suddenly, at a last, harsh, false note from the chorus, Cruges leaped up.

'They ought to be kicked – what a company!' he grumbled, pulling on his overcoat furiously.

Carlos gave him a lift in his coupé to Rua das Flores, where Cruges lived with his mother and a sister. And all the way back to Ramalhete Carlos spent mourning over his lost evening's study.

His servant, Baptista (familiarly known as Tista) was waiting up for him and reading the paper in the comfortable ante-chamber of 'the young master's rooms'. They were lined in cherry-coloured velvet and decorated with pictures of horses and panoplies of old arms, with divans of the same velvet, well-lit at that hour by two globe-shaped lamps placed on oak columns that were covered with carvings of grape vine.

Carlos had been attended by this valet since he was eleven years old, and Baptista had come with Brown to Santa Olávia after having served in Lisbon in the British Legation and accompanied the minister, Sir Hercules Morrison, on several voyages to London. It had been at Coimbra in his student establishment that Baptista had at last become a personality. Afonso wrote to him from Santa Olávia and then he went abroad with Carlos;

together they were seasick on the same packet-boats; together they shared the same sandwiches in station-buffets. Tista became a confidant. Today he was a man of fifty, upright, robust, with a fringe of grey beard under his chin and an excessively gentlemanly air. In the street, very erect in his overcoat, with a pair of yellow gloves gripped in his hand, his Indian walking-cane, his well-polished shoes, he had the considerable air of a high civil servant. But he remained as refined and as sophisticated as he had been in London when he had learned to waltz and to box in the rude tumult of the dance-halls, or as later, during the Coimbra vacations, when he had accompanied Carlos to Lamego and helped him over the wall into the garden of the excise clerk – the one who had such a pretty wife.

Carlos went to get a book from his study, came back into the bedroom, and stretched himself out, tired, in an armchair. In the opaline light from the globes, his turned-back bedclothes under the silk of the hangings displayed an almost feminine luxury of Breton lace and embroidery.

'What's in the evening paper?' he asked, yawning, while Baptista helped him off with his shoes.

'I've read it all through, senhor, and it doesn't look to me as if anything's happened. It's still quiet in France – but one never knows, for these Portuguese papers always misprint foreign names.'

'They're a lot of animals! Senhor Ega was furious with them today . . .'

Then, as Baptista deftly prepared a hot grog, Carlos, who had already got into bed, nestled down and lazily opened the book, turned over two pages, shut it, picked up a cigarette and lay smoking with his eyes closed in profound bliss. Through the heavy curtains he could hear the southwest wind lashing the trees, and the water beating against the windows.

'D'you know the Count de Gouvarinho, Tista?'

'I know Pimenta, senhor, who is the Count's valet – valet and footman.'

'And what does he have to say for himself, this Tormenta?' asked Carlos in an indolent voice, after a moment's silence.

'Pimenta, senhor. Manuel Pimenta. Senhor Gouvarinho calls him Romão, because he used to have another servant called Romão. And that is not really nice, because every man has a right to his own name. Manuel is Pimenta. And Pimenta does not like . . .'

Baptista placed the salver with the grog, the sugar-bowl and the cigarettes on it, near the pillow. Then he relayed Pimenta's revelations. The Count, apart from being very demanding and very fussy, was not what you would call a gentleman. He had given a suit of light cheviot to Romão (that is to say Pimenta), but it was so worn and so full of inkstains, from wiping his pen on his leg and his shoulder, that Pimenta had thrown the gift away. The Count and his lady did not get on together. On one occasion since Pimenta had been with them they had quarrelled at table in such a fashion that she had picked up a glass and a plate and broken them on the floor. And any other woman would have done the same, because when he started to nag and complain the Count was not to be tolerated. The arguments were always over money. Old Tompson was tired of opening his purse . . .

'And who's old Tompson, who makes his appearance at this late hour?' asked Carlos, interested in spite of himself.

'Old Tompson is the Countess's father. The Countess was a Miss Tompson of the Oporto Tompsons. Lately, Mr Tompson has not wanted to lend one more penny to his son-in-law; and so, once – since Pimenta's time – the Count in fury told the lady that she and her father should remember they were in trade and it had been he who had made her a Countess; and, begging your pardon, senhor, the Countess told the Count there at the table that he could take his title to the devil – this sort of thing does not suit Pimenta.'

Carlos drank a mouthful of grog. A question danced on his lips, but he hesitated. Then he reflected on the puerility of such severe scruples in connection with people who in a footman's presence at dinner smashed porcelain and sent their ancestors' titles to the devil. And so he asked the question.

'What does Pimenta have to say about the Countess, Baptista? Does she seek her own amusements?'

'I believe not, senhor. But her maid, that Scots girl, that one's well known. And it doesn't look good for the Countess to be so familiar with her.'

There was silence in the room, and the rain sang more loudly against the window-panes.

'On another topic, Baptista. Let's see, how long is it since I wrote to Madame Rughel?'

Baptista took out a notebook from an inner pocket of his coat, went up to the light, adjusted his spectacles on his nose, and methodically confirmed the dates.

'January 1: Telegram sent with New Year's greetings to Madame Rughel, Hotel d'Albe, Champs-Elysées, Paris. January 3: Telegram received from Madame Rughel returning the compliment, expressing friendship and announcing her departure for Hamburg. January 15: Letter posted to Madame Rughel, Wilhelmstrasse, Hamburg, Germany. After that there's nothing more. So Master Carlos can see that five weeks have passed without writing to Madame Rughel.'

'I must write to her tomorrow,' said Carlos.

Baptista made a note of this

Then, puffing languidly, Carlos's voice spoke again in the drowsy peace of the room.

'Madame Rughel was very pretty, don't you think, Baptista? Isn't she the prettiest woman you've ever set eyes on?'

The old servant put his notebook back in the pocket of his coat and replied without hesitation, very sure of himself.

'Madame Rughel was a very attractive-looking woman. But the most beautiful woman I've ever seen, if my young master will permit me, was that lady, the wife of the colonel of hussars, who used to come to the hotel room in Vienna.'

Carlos flung his cigarette on to the salver and, sliding down under the bedclothes, wholly invaded by a wave of pleasurable memories, he exclaimed from the depth of his well-being, in the joking, emphatic tones of his student days:

'You've no taste at all, Baptista! Madame Rughel was a Rubens nymph, sir! Madame Rughel was as splendid as a Renaissance goddess, sir! Madame Rughel ought to have slept in the bed of Charles V – get out, sir!'

Baptista tucked in the coverlet, cast a solicitous glance over the room and, satisfied with the order in which everything slept, went out taking the lamp with him. But Carlos could not sleep; and it was neither the hussar colonel's wife nor Madame Rughel who occupied his thoughts. The figure he saw in the shadows of the curtains, reflected in the gold of her loosened hair, was Madame Gouvarinho – Gouvarinho who was neither a splendid

Renaissance goddess like Madame Rughel, nor the most beautiful woman Baptista had ever set eyes on, like the colonel's wife. But, with her haughty nose and large mouth, she shone more brightly now than anyone else in Carlos's mind – because he had waited for her that night and she had not come.

On the promised Tuesday, Ega failed to fetch Carlos to visit the Gouvarinhos. And some days later Carlos, pretending to enter the Universal quite accidentally, asked Ega with a smile: 'Well, when are we going Gouvarinho-ing?'

At the opera that night, during an interval in the performance of *The Huguenots*, in the corridor behind the boxes, Ega presented him to the Count de Gouvarinho. The Count was most amiable and at once recalled that he had more than once already had the pleasure of passing the gates of Santa Olávia when he had been on his way to visit his old friends, the Tedins, at Entre-Rios – also a beautiful place. And they talked of the Douro and Beira and contrasted the scenery. For the Count's part there was nothing in all our Portugal to be compared with the fields of the Mondego; but his partiality could be forgiven for he had been born and reared in those fertile fields. And for a moment he spoke of Formozelha, where he had a house and where his mother, the Dowager Countess, lived, elderly and ill.

Ega, who was affecting to drink the Count's words in, started an argument by propounding the superior beauty of the Minho, that idyllic paradise, as though it were a matter of religious dogma. The Count smiled. As he observed to Carlos, patting Ega amiably on the shoulder, he could perceive here the rivalry between two provinces. For that matter, it was a fertile rivalry in his view.

'For example,' he said, 'there's the jealousy between Lisbon and Oporto. A veritable duality like that between Hungary and Austria. That's what people complain of, at least. Well, now, were I in power, I would encourage it, and, if you gentlemen will permit the expression, exacerbate it. In this battle between the two great cities of the realm, others may see mean spite. I see elements of progress. I see civilization.'

He let fall these judgments as though from the height of a pedestal, far above ordinary men, letting them drop prodigally from the treasure-house of his mind like priceless gifts. His voice was slow and rotund; the glasses in his gold frames scintillated brilliantly; and in his waxed moustache, his short goatee, there was at once something of the teacher and something of the fop.

Carlos said: 'How right you are Count!'

Ega said: 'You see these things from the heights, Gouvarinho!'

He crossed his hands under the tails of his coat, and all three stood looking very grave.

Then the Count opened the door of his box and Ega disappeared. And a moment later Carlos, introduced as a 'neighbour of the opera', received a hearty handshake from the Countess accompanied by the tinkling of an infinity of silver bracelets and Indian bangles over her black glove with its twelve buttons.

The Countess, a little flushed, a little nervous, reminded Carlos right away that she had seen him the previous summer in Paris in the salon of the Café Anglais. For that matter, there had been an abominable old man there that night with two empty bottles in front of him, recounting horrifying stories about Monsieur Gambetta in a loud voice. Somebody beside him had protested; but he had taken no notice. It had been the old Duke of Grammont. The Count, with an expression close to anguish, passed slow fingers across his forehead; he could recall none of this! He at once began bitterly to complain about his lack of memory. Memory was something quite indispensable for one who takes part in public affairs! But unhappily he did not possess an atom of memory! For example, he had read – as all men should – the twenty volumes of the *Universal History of César Cantu;* he had read them attentively, shut up in his study, absorbing himself in the work. Well, gentlemen, he could remember none of it – and there he was, ignorant of history!

'Have you a good memory, Senhor Maia?'

'I've a reasonable memory.'

'You enjoy an inestimable advantage.'

The Countess turned towards the pit and covered herself with her fan, looking constrained, as though these puerile words of her husband's diminished and tarnished her. Carlos then spoke of the opera. What a fine Huguenot page Pandolli made! The Countess could not abide Corcelli, the tenor, with his harsh notes and that obesity which made him grotesque. But where could you find tenors today, Carlos reminded her. That great

race of Marios, men of beauty and inspiration, who had played
the great lyrical parts, had passed away. Already Nicolini was
degenerating. This reminded them of Patti. The Countess adored
her and her fairy grace, her voice like a rain of gold.

Her eyes sparkled with a thousand messages; in certain attitudes her tightly curled hair took on tones of red gold; and around
her there hung, in the heat of the gas and the crowded house, an
exaggerated fragrance of verbena. She was dressed in black, and
in the Valois fashion a choker of black lace covered her neck
where two scarlet roses were pinned. Her entire person had
something of an air of provocation and attack. Standing silent
and serious, the Count tapped his thigh with his closed clapper.

The fourth act opened. Carlos rose; and his eyes fell directly
on Ega in the Cohen's box, with opera-glasses, observing him,
looking at the Countess and talking to Rachel, who smiled and
moved her fan with a vague and lazy expression.

'We are at home on Tuesdays,' said the Countess to Carlos –
and the rest of her words were lost in a murmur and a smile.

The Count saw him out into the corridor.

'It is always an honour for me,' he said, walking at Carlos's
side, 'to make the acquaintance of persons who are of some
consequence in this country – you are among this number, so
unhappily few.'

Smiling, Carlos protested. But the other continued in his slow,
rotund voice.

'I'm not flattering you. I never go in for flattery – but I can
say these things to you because you belong to the élite. Portugal's misfortune is that it hasn't got people. This is a country
without personnel. You want a bishop? There isn't a bishop to
be had! You want an economist? There aren't any economists!
It's always the way. You can even see it in trade. You need
a good upholsterer? There aren't any upholsterers . . .'

A burst of instruments and voices, in tones sublime, broke
through the half-open door of the box and cut off his final remarks regarding the insufficiency of photographers. He listened
with a hand raised in the air.

'It's the "Dagger Chorus", isn't it? Ah! Let's listen to it – it
always does one good to listen to. There is philosophy in this
music – it's a pity that it so vividly recalls the times of religious
intolerance, but it's certainly got philosophy!'

———————

6

THAT MORNING Carlos was about to pay a surprise visit to Ega's house, the famous Villa Balzac, which the coiner of phrases had been planning and dreaming about ever since his arrival in Lisbon, and where he had installed himself at last.

Ega had given it this literary name for the same reasons that he had chosen a distant suburb, Penha de França – so that the name of Balzac, his patron, the country silence, the clean air and everything else should encourage study, hours dedicated to art and ideals. For he was going to closet himself there as in a cloister of learning to complete his *Memoirs of an Atom*. Only on account of the distance he had hired a coupé by the month.

Carlos had some difficulty in finding the Villa Balzac. It was not, as Ega had told him at Ramalhete, just immediately beyond the Largo da Graça, nor was it a little chalet that lay withdrawn, shaded and smiling among the trees.

First you had to pass the Cruz dos Quatro Caminhos; then you came into a broad lane between gardens, descending the slope of a hill but accessible to carriages, and there in a corner, surrounded by walls, you at last came upon a ramshackle structure with two stone steps in front of a door fitted with scarlet glass.

In vain, however, did Carlos that morning pull desperately at the bell, hammer at the door-knocker and shout the name of Ega at the top of his voice over the garden wall and the treetops. The Villa Balzac remained mute, as though deserted in its rustic retirement. But it had certainly seemed to Carlos that just a moment before he had knocked he had caught the sound of popping champagne corks.

When Ega was told of this visit, he was indignant with the servants who had thus abandoned the house and given it the suspicious air of some wizard's den.

'Come tomorrow. If nobody answers, climb in through a window and set fire to the building as though it were the Tuileries.'

But when Carlos arrived the next day the Villa Balzac was waiting for him all festive. At the door stood a 'page', a boy with horribly vicious features wearing a blue jacket with metal buttons and a very white, very stiff tie. The two open windows above, disclosing the green rep of the hangings, drank in wide all the country air and winter sunshine. At the top of the narrow stairway, carpeted in red, Ega in a prodigious dressing-gown of some eighteenth-century damask material – the court dress of one of his grandmothers – bowed his head to the ground and cried:

'Welcome, my prince, to this philosopher's humble hovel!'

With an expansive gesture he raised a curtain of green rep, a green that was ugly and sad, and introduced the 'prince' into the drawing-room where everything was green too: the rep that covered the walnut furniture, the beamed ceiling, the vertical stripes on the wallpaper, the fringed table-cloth, and the reflection from a round mirror above the sofa.

There was not a picture, a flower, an ornament or a book – only on the *jardinière* stood a statue of Napoeon I balanced on the globe in that characteristic pose in which the hero, with a well-fed and fatal look, hides one of his hands behind his back and buries the other in the depths of his waistcoat. Beside the statue a bottle of champagne capped in gilded paper waited between two tall glasses.

'What have you got Napoleon here for, John?'

'As a scapegoat,' said Ega. 'I practise talking about tyrants to him.'

He rubbed his hands joyfully. This morning he was bright and cheerful. And he immediately wanted to show Carlos his bedroom. A profusion of cretonne patterned with pale garlands on red ground reigned there; and the bed filled and dominated it all. It seemed to be the *raison d'être*, the nodal point, of the Villa Balzac, and it had exhausted all Ega's artistic imagination.

It was made of wood, and as low as a divan, had high boards, a valance of lace, a luxury of scarlet hair rugs on either side and a broad curtain of red Indian silk enveloping it around like a tabernacle. Inside, on the headboard, as though in some bordello, there shone a looking-glass.

Very gravely, Carlos counselled Ega to remove the mirror. Ega regarded the entire bed with a sweet, silent gaze and, passing the tip of his tongue over his lip, said: 'It has its *chic* . . .'

On the bed-table lay a mound of books: Spencer's *Education* beside Baudelaire; Stuart Mill's *Logic* on top of the *Knight of the Red House*. On the marble-topped dresser there was another bottle of champagne between two glasses; the dressing-table, somewhat disordered, displayed an enormous box of face-powder amid shirt-fronts and white ties belonging to Ega, and a mass of hair-pins beside some curling tongs.

'And where do you work, Ega? Where is the great artistic work produced?'

'There!' cried Ega gaily, pointing to the bed.

But without more ado he showed Carlos his study corner, formed by a screen beside the window, all taken up by a three-legged table, where a startled Carlos found a *Dictionary of Rhymes* among Ega's beautiful notepaper.

The tour of the house proceeded.

In the nearly bare dining-room, distempered in yellow, a glass-fronted cupboard of pinewood melancholically sheltered a new, cheap china service; and from the window-fastening there hung a red garment that looked like a woman's.

'It's sober and plain,' cried Ega, 'as befits one who is nourished on a crust of Ideals and two forkfuls of Philosophy. Now, for the kitchen . . .'

He opened a door. The freshness of fields came in through the open windows; and there was a glimpse of trees from the garden, the green of empty fields, and at the bottom the white of houses shining in the sun. A very plump, very freckled girl shook a cat off her lap, and rose with the *Journal de Noticias* in her hand. Ega introduced her in jocular tones.

'Senhora Josefa, unmarried, of sanguine temperament, the culinary artist of the Villa Balzac and, as you may see from the paper in her grasp, a great reader!'

The girl smiled, without embarrassment, and seemed accustomed to this jocular mode of address.

'I shall not be dining here today, Senhora Josefa,' Ega went on in the same voice. 'This handsome youth you see beside me, Duke of Ramalhete, Prince of Santa Olávia, is going to provide his philosopher-friend with today's rations – and when I return, as perhaps you, Senhora Josefa, will have already abandoned yourself to the sleep of the innocent, or to the vigil of libertinage, I hereby instruct you to have two fine partridges ready for my lunch tomorrow.' Then suddenly, in a different tone, he added with a meaningful look: 'Two nice partridges, well roasted and golden. Cold, of course – as usual.'

He took Carlos's arm and they returned to the parlour.

'Frankly, Carlos, what do you think of the Villa Balzac?'

Carlos gave the same answer as he had after the episode of the 'Hebrew Woman': 'It's ardent!'

But he praised the cleanliness, the view from the house and the freshness of the cretonnes. And besides, for a bachelor, for a place to work . . .

'I,' began Ega, pacing across the parlour with his hands deep in the pockets of his prodigious dressing-gown, 'I can't stand ornaments, bric-à-brac, antique chairs, art furniture – what the devil? Furnishings should harmonize with the ideas and feelings of the man who uses them! I don't think or feel like a knight of the sixteenth century, so why should I surround myelf with sixteenth-century objects? Nothing makes me more melancholy than to see a venerable cabinet of the period of Francis I in a drawing-room receiving conversation about elections and investments full in its face. It has the same effect on me as it would to view a fine hero in steel armour, his visor down and profound faith in his heart, sitting at a table playing cards. Each century has its own spirit, its own attitude. The nineteenth century conceived democracy and here is its attitude . . .' He suddenly sat down in an easy chair and stuck out thin legs in the air. 'Now this position is impossible on a stool built in the period of the early Portuguese kings. Let's drink up our champagne, dear boy!'

As Carlos regarded the bottle with suspicion, Ega added: 'It's excellent, you know! It comes directly from the best house in Epernay. Jacob procured it for me!'

'Who's Jacob?'

'Jacob Cohen, Jacob . . .'

He was about to cut the string around the cork when he recollected something all of a sudden and, putting the bottle down again and fixing his monocle in his eye, he said:

'Ah, yes! What was it like the other day at the Gouvarinhos'? Unfortunately I couldn't go.'

Carlos described the soirée. There had been ten people scattered around the two salons, in a drowsy hum in the half light of candelabras. The Count had bored him indiscreetly with politics, idiotic admiration for a great orator, a deputy for Mesão-Frio, and endless explanations about educational reform. The Countess, who had had a bad cold, horrified him by voicing opinions about England that were, despite the fact that she was English, the opinions of Oporto's Rua de Cadofeita. She held that England was a country without poets, without artists, without ideals, occupied only in heaping up pounds . . . In short, he had been bored.

'Hell!' muttered Ega in tones of real disappointment.

The cork popped and he filled the glasses in silence. With an unspoken toast the two friends drank the champagne – which Jacob had procured for Ega, for Ega to enjoy with Rachel.

Then, standing up, with his gaze on the carpet, slowly agitating the newly refilled glass in which the foam was dying, Ega went on murmuring, in that sad tone of unexpected disappointment: 'What a pity . . .' And after a moment: 'You see, dear boy, I thought you liked the Gouvarinho woman.'

Carlos confessed that at first, when Ega had spoken of her to him, he had been somewhat attracted, drawn by that brass-coloured hair: 'But now that I've met her the attraction has fled.'

Ega sat down with his glass in his hand, and after contemplating his stockings of scarlet silk like a prelate's for a short space, he let fall these words, very gravely:

'She's a delicious woman, Carlinhos.'

And as Carlos shrugged his shoulders, Ega persisted. Madame Gouvarinho was a lady of intelligence and taste; she had originality; she had audacity and a touch of romanticism that was very alluring.

'And as for her figure – there's nothing better between here and Badajoz!'

'Get thee to hell, Mephistophles of Celorico!'

Ega was amused and started to carol:

> '*Je suis Mephisto,*
> *Je suis Mephisto . . . !*'

Carlos, meanwhile, was smoking lazily and talking about the Gouvarinho woman and about the sudden satiety that had overcome him after he had exchanged scarcely three words with her in the drawing-room. And it was not the first time he had experienced these false surges of desire, that invaded him almost like love and threatened, at least for a time, to engulf his entire being – only to culminate in tedium, in 'drought'. They were like trails of gunpowder on a stone – a spark enlivened them and in an instant they turned into a vehement blaze that seemed to be about to consume the Universe. But in the end they only made a black mark that soiled the stone. Could it be that his was indeed one of those frail, limp, flabby hearts that could not conserve a feeling and allowed it to flee, to slip away through the loose weave of cheap cloth?

'I'm dried out!' he said, smiling. 'I'm sentimentally impotent like Satan. According to the Fathers of the Church, the great torture of Satan is that he is unable to love.'

'What a way to talk, dear boy!' muttered Ega.

Talk, indeed! It was a frightening reality! He had wasted his life seeing his passions fail him in his hands like spent matches. For instance, there had been the wife of the colonel of hussars in Vienna! When she did not keep their first rendezvous he had wept handfuls of tears with his head buried in the pillow, and kicking the bedclothes. Two weeks later he was posting Baptista in the window of the hotel so that he himself could make a getaway if the poor woman rounded the corner! And it had been still worse with Madame Rughel, the Dutch lady. In the first few days he had been mad with love – he had wanted to settle forever in Holland, marry her (as soon as she was divorced), and other lunacies. Soon the arms she threw around his neck – and what lovely arms they had been – seemed as heavy as lead.

'Get away with you, pedant! And you still write to her!' shrieked Ega.

'That's another matter. We are still friends – a purely spiritual relationship. Madame Rughel is a woman of very high intellect. She wrote a novel, one of those intimate and delicate studies, like Miss Broughton's, called *Withered Roses*. I've never read it – it's in Dutch.'

'*Withered Roses!* In Dutch!' exclaimed Ega clutching his hands to his head.

He came and planted himself before Carlos and, with his monocle in his eye, he said:

135

'You're an extraordinary chap . . . ! But your case is plain. It's the case of a Don Juan. Don Juan too had these alternations of flame and ashes. He was in search of his ideal, *his woman*, seeking her principally and as though of right among the wives of others. And then, *après avoir couché*, he would declare he had made a mistake and that she was not the one after all. He would beg pardon and retire from the scene. Thus in Spain he tried one thousand and three. You are like him – simply a debauchee; and like him you'll end in some infernal tragedy!'

He drank another glass of champagne and paced about the room.

'Carlinhos of my heart, it's useless for a man to go round searching for *his woman*. She'll come. Each man has *his woman*. You may be here in the Cruz dos Quatro Caminhos, and she may be in Peking, but you, who sit there scraping my rep with your patent-leather shoes, and she, praying in a Confucian temple, are each unconsciously, irresistibly, fatally, making towards one another! I'm very eloquent today, and we've said some idiotic things. I must get dressed. And while I'm adorning my carcass you can compose some phrases to Satan!'

Carlos stayed and finished his cigar in the green parlour while, inside, Ega slammed drawers and hummed Gounod's 'Barcarolle' in a rough and completely tuneless voice. When he came back he was wearing a tail-coat and white tie and was putting on his overcoat while his eyes sparkled from the champagne.

They went downstairs. Before the door the page stood on guard beside Carlos's waiting coupé. His blue livery with its yellow buttons, the gleaming live satin of the magnificent pair of bays, the silver of the harness, the majesty of the blond coachman with a flower in his lapel – all of these, there beside the Villa Balzac, painted a splendid picture which enchanted Ega.

'Life is good,' he said.

The coupé drove off and was about to enter Graça Square when an open cab met them coming the other way at a swift trot. Inside it an individual in a low flat hat was reading a large newspaper.

'It's Craft!' bellowed Ega, leaning out the window.

The coupé drew up. Ega was on the pavement in a bound, running and shouting.

'Craft! Craft!'

Carlos too alighted from the coupé a moment later when he heard two voices approaching; he found himself facing a short, fair man with a fresh, rosy complexion and a chilly appearance. Under his impeccable dress-coat one could discern the build of an athlete.

'Carlos, Craft!' shouted Ega throwing down this introduction with classic simplicity.

The two men smiled and shook hands. Ega insisted they should all go back to the Villa Balzac, drink the remaining bottle of champagne and celebrate the 'Coming of the Just'! Craft excused himself in his calm, placid way: he had arrived the night before from Oporto and had now greeted the noble Ega; so he would make the most of this journey to such a distant suburb in order to visit old Shlegan, a German who lived in Penha de França.

'Another time, then!' exclaimed Ega. 'We must have a talk and you two must get to know one another better – why don't both of you come and dine with me tomorrow at the Hotel Central? Agreed? Perfect! At six!'

Hardly had the coupé set off again than Ega broke into the usual eulogies of Craft, delighted at this meeting that had added yet one more luminous touch to his happiness. What fascinated him about Craft was that imperturbable and unfailingly gentlemanly air with which he played a game of billiards, went into battle, made approaches to a woman, or set off for Patagonia.

'He's one of the best things in Lisbon. You'll be crazy about him. And what a house he has in Olivais, what marvellous furnishings!'

Suddenly he paused and with a troubled look and a frown on his brow he said:

'How the devil did he know about the Villa Balzac?'

'You don't make a secret of it, do you?'

'No – but neither do I advertise it. And Craft only arrived yesterday and hasn't seen anyone I know yet – curious!'

'In Lisbon everything gets about!'

'Devil of a town!' muttered Ega.

The dinner at the Central was postponed, for Ega had

gradually expanded the idea until now it was transformed into a ceremony in honour of Cohen.

'I dine there often,' he said to Carlos. 'I'm there every evening; one must repay hospitality – a dinner at the Central will be just the thing. And, for the moral effect, I'll place the Marquis and that animal, Steinbroken, at the table beside him. Cohen likes that sort of person.'

But the project had to be further altered: the Marquis departed for Gollegã, and poor Steinbroken was suffering from colic. Ega thought of Cruges and Taveira, but he feared Cruges's untidy hair and those attacks he had of bitter depression which were liable to ruin a dinner-party. So he ended by inviting two of Cohen's intimates – which meant he had to cut out Taveira because he was on bad terms with one of these gentlemen on account of words that had been exchanged in the house of 'Fat Lola'.

Once the guests were decided upon and the date of the dinner fixed for a Monday, Ega held a conference with the Central's *maître d'hôtel*, advising many flowers and two pineapples to decorate the table, and insisted that one of the courses, whatever it might be, should be *à la Cohen* – he himself had thought of *tomates farcies à la Cohen*!

That evening at six o'clock, on going down the Rua do Alecrim towards the Hotel Central, Carlos caught sight of Craft inside Uncle Abrahão's antique shop.

He went in. The old Jew, who had been showing Craft a spurious *faïence* from Rato, at once removed his dirty cap with its pom-pom from his head and bowed down low before Carlos with his two hands over his heart.

Then in an exotic idiom in which some English was mingled he asked the good Senhor Carlos da Maia, such a dignified gentleman, such a beautiful gentleman, to be good enough to examine a real little marvel that he had kept by for him; and his most generous gentleman had only to turn his eyes and there was the little marvel on a chair. It was the portrait of a Spanish woman done in strong brushwork on a bold background of withered rose-colour: a face of spent beauty, blemished with pock-marks, white as chalk, exuding vice, and bearing a bestial leer that promised everything.

Carlos serenely offered him ten *tostões*. Craft protested at such prodigality; and the good Abrahão, with a soundless laugh that disclosed a great mouth, in which was a solitary tooth, hidden in his grey beard, greatly enjoyed 'his dear gentlemen's little joke'. Ten *tostões* indeed! If that portrait had the dear name of Fortuny under it, it would fetch ten *contos*! But it did not bear that blessed name – even so it was worth ten good notes of twenty *milreis*!

'Ten ropes to hang you with, you soulless Hebrew!' exclaimed Carlos.

And out they went, leaving the old fraud in the doorway, bowed double with his hands on his heart, wishing a thousand good fortunes to his generous noblemen.

'He hasn't a single decent thing, that old Abrahão,' said Carlos.

'He has his daughter,' said Craft.

Carlos thought her pretty, but horribly dirty. Then, *à propos* of Abrahão, he spoke to Craft of those fine collections at Olivais which Ega had described as sublime in spite of all the disdain that he affected for antiques and art furniture.

Craft shrugged.

'Ega doesn't understand these matters at all. You can't call what I have a collection, even in Lisbon. It's a haphazard lot of stuff, and, for that matter, I want to get rid of it.'

This surprised Carlos. He had understood from Ega that it was a collection that had been built up with love, over the laborious passage of the years – the pride and care of a lifetime.

Craft smiled at this myth. The fact was that he had begun to interest himself in antiquities only in 1872; he had just come back from South America at the time; and everything he bought, things discovered here and there, had accumulated there in Olivais, a house that had been rented on a whim because the barn of a place, with its bit of garden around it, had seemed to him one morning to have a picturesque air in the April sunshine. But if he could get rid of it now, he would dedicate himself to building a homogeneous and compact collection of eighteenth-century art.

'Here in Olivais?'

'No, at the manor I have near Oporto, right by the river.'

They were entering the courtyard of the Hotel Central, and at that very moment a hired coupé, arriving at a smart trot from Rua do Arsenal, pulled up at the door.

A splendid, grey-headed Negro, in tail-coat and knee-breeches, at once hastened up to the window; inside the coupé a very thin young man, with a very black beard, passed into his arms a delightful little terrier bitch with straggling hair that was as fine as silk and the colour of silver. Then the young man stepped down, indolent and affected, and gave his hand to a tall, fair lady who wore a half veil that was very tight and very dark and heightened the splendour of her ivory-white complexion. Craft and Carlos drew to one side. She passed them by, with the regal carriage of a goddess; she was marvellously well-proportioned and shed behind her, like light, a reflection of golden hair and a fragrance in the air. She wore a fitted coat of white Genoa velvet, and for an instant there shone on the stones of the court-yard the patent-leather of her shoes. The young man beside her, like a stick in his suit of English checks, was negligently tearing open a telegram. The Negro followed with the tiny dog in his arms.

Craft's voice murmured in the silence: '*Très chic!*'

In the room above to which a servant led them, Ega waited, seated on a Morocco leather divan in conversation with a short, fat young man with hair as wavy as a rustic bride-groom's, a camellia in his buttonhole and a shirtfront of azure. Craft knew him; Ega presented Senhor Damaso Salcêde to Carlos and then ordered vermouth to be served as, he said, it was getting late for such a literary and satanic refinement as absinthe.

It had been a fine, clear winter's day; the two windows were still open. In the wide sky over the river the afternoon was dying without a breath of wind, in an elysian peace of high, small clouds that hung motionless, brushed with rose colour; on the farthest bank the meadows were sinking now in a vel-vety, purplish mist; the water lay smooth and glistening like a thin sheet of new steel; throughout the vast anchorage slept great cargo ships, long, foreign packet-boats and two English cruisers, their masts at rest, as though taken by laziness and abandoned to the lure of that sweet climate.

'We have just seen downstairs,' said Craft as he went to sit on the divan, 'a splendid woman with a splendid terrier bitch, attended by a splendid Negro!'

Senhor Damaso Salcêde, who was unable to take his eyes off Carlos, at once interposed:

'I know them – Castro Gomes and his wife. I know them well. I came from Bordeaux with them. Very *chic* people who live in Paris.'

Carlos turned to look at him more closely and asked, affable and curious:

'Have you just arrived from Bordeaux?'

These words appeared to entrance Damaso as though they were some celestial favour; he rose at once and came up to Maia wreathed in smiles:

'I came back on the *Orinoco* a fortnight ago. From Paris – for that's where I go whenever I can! I got to know these people in Bordeaux – or rather, I really met them on board. But we were all at the Hotel de Nantes . . . very *chic* people . . . a valet, an English governess for the little girl, a chambermaid, more than twenty trunks – really *chic*! It seems incredible that they're Brazilians . . . but she hasn't the slightest trace of an accent . . . speaks like us in fact. But, as for him, he's different, a strong accent – but elegant too, don't you think?'

'Vermouth?' asked the waiter, offering him a tray.

'Yes, a drop for the appetite. Won't you take some, Senhor Maia? Now me, the minute I can, I'm off to Paris! There's a place for you! This is a pigsty. For my part, if I don't get away each year, believe me, I begin to feel ill. Those boulevards, eh? Oh, I really enjoy it. And I know how to enjoy myself, let me tell you, for I know Paris like the back of my hand! Why, I've even an uncle there!'

'And what an uncle!' cried Ega, coming up to them. 'An intimate of Gambetta's. He practically governs France! D'you hear me? Damasco's uncle governs France, dear boy!'

Damaso was scarlet and swelling with delight.

'Ah, yes, he's got influence all right! An intimate of Gambetta's – they're on very familiar terms. Why, they practically live together. And it's not just Gambetta – it's MacMahon, Rochefort, the other fellow whose name I forget, all the Republicans in fact. He can get anything he wants. Don't you know him, Senhor Maia? A man with a white beard – my mother's brother! His name's Guimarães. But in Paris they call him Monsieur de Guimaran.'

At that instant the glass door burst open and Ega exlaimed: 'All hail the poet!'

A very tall person appeared, all buttoned up in a black frock-coat, with a hollow face, sunken eyes and long, thin, romantic grey moustaches under his aquiline nose; he was already quite bald in front but fluffy ringlets of very dry, coarse hair fell in inspired fashion on his collar. About all his person there was something archaic, bogus and mournful.

He silently held out two fingers to Damaso; opened slow arms towards Craft; and then declaimed in a drawling, cavernous, theatrical voice: 'So, it's you, my dear Craft! When did you get here, my lad? Let me feel those honourable bones, honourable Englishman!'

He did not even cast a glance towards Carlos. Ega came up and introduced them: 'I don't know if you've met. Carlos da Maia – Tomas d'Alencar, our poet.'

It was he! The illustrious bard of *Voices of Dawn*, the stylist of *Elvira*, the dramatist of *The Knight's Secret*. He took two slow paces towards Carlos and stood clasping his hand a long time in silence . . . And then, filled with emotion, he spoke, more cavernously than ever:

'Sir, as indeed social custom requires me to address you thus, scarcely do you know whose hand you have just clasped . . .'

'I know your name very well,' Carlos murmured in surprise.

But with vacant eye and trembling lip the other proceeded: 'The comrade, the inseparable, the intimate of Pedro da Maia, my poor, my valiant Pedro!'

'Well, what the deuce! Embrace each other!' shouted Ega. 'Embrace each other with sobs, according to the rules.'

Alencar had already clutched Carlos to his chest, and when he let him go he gripped his hands once again, shook them and exclaimed with noisy tenderness:

'So let's drop the "sirs"! For I saw you born, my lad! I held you oft upon my lap! Many a trouser of mine did you wet! Hang it! Here, embrace me once more!'

Craft looked on at this touching reunion impassively; Damaso seemed moved; Ega presented a glass of vermouth to the poet:

'What a great sight, Alencar! Good God! You must drink up to recover your feelings!'

Alencar swallowed his vermouth at one draught. He declared to the company that this was not the first time he had seen Carlos. Many times already he had admired him in his phaeton with his beautiful English horses. But he had not wished to intrude himself. Never had he thrown himself into anyone's arms, except a woman's. He went and filled another glass with vermouth and, holding it in his hand, he planted himself in front of Carlos and began in tones of pathos:

'The first time I caught sight of you, my lad, was in the Pote das Almas! There was I in Rodrigues's bookshop, looking through some of that old literature that is nowadays so despised. I even recall that it was a volume of our delightful Rodrigues Lobo's *Eclogues* – that true poet of nature, that Portuguese nightingale – who is today, of course, laid aside since Satanism, Naturalism and all those other stinking isms have appeared upon the scene. At that moment you passed by. I was told who you were and the book fell from my hand. For an hour I stood there, believe me, meditating and reliving the past.'

He tossed the vermouth down his throat. Ega was impatiently regarding the clock. A waiter came in and lit the gas. As the shadows dispersed the table could be seen with crystal and china gleaming upon it and a profusion of camellias in bunches.

Meanwhile, Alencar (who seemed more tarnished and older than ever in the light) had begun a lengthy narrative – how he had been the first to see Carlos after his birth; how it had been he who had given him his name.

'Your father, my Pedro,' he said, 'wanted to call you by Afonso's name, after that saint, that knight of other years – Afonso da Maia! But your mother, who had her own ideas, insisted that you should be Carlos. And it was precisely because of a novel I had lent her. In those days you could still lend novels to ladies – there were as yet neither pustules nor pus! It was a romance about the last of the Stuarts, that fine fellow, Prince Charles Edward, whom all of you, my lads, know well, and who in Scotland at the time of Louis XIV – well, never mind! Your mother, I must say, knew literature, and the best. She consulted me; she always consulted me; in those days I was *somebody*. And I remember having answered – I remember, despite there having passed five and twenty years; what am I saying? Twenty-seven! Just think, my lads, twenty-seven years! Well now, I turned to your mother and said exactly these words: "Give him the name of Carlos Eduardo, my dear lady, Carlos Eduardo.

That is a name truly worthy of the title page of a poem, of the fame of heroism, or of the lips of a woman!"'

Damaso, who had continued to stare at Carlos, uttered thundering 'bravos'; Craft tapped his fingers lightly; and Ega, who was standing nervously by the door, his watch in his hand, emitted an indifferent 'Very good'.

Alencar, who was delighted with the effect he had produced, strewed smiles about him that displayed his rotten teeth. Once again he embraced Carlos, flung a hand on his heart and cried: 'God, my lads, I feel alight inside!'

The door opened and Cohen entered in haste, with immediate apologies for his lateness, while Ega, who had hurried up to him, helped him off with his coat. Then he introduced him to Carlos, the only person there with whom Cohen was not on intimate terms. Then, pressing the electric bell-button, Ega said:

'The Marquis couldn't come, dear boy, and old Steinbroken, poor devil, has his gout, his diplomat's, his lord's, his banker's gout – that gout that is destined for you too, dear boy!'

Cohen was a man of short stature, elegant, with beautiful eyes, and whiskers so black and shining they seemed to be soaked in varnish. He smiled as he removed his gloves and said that according to the English there was also a poor man's gout, which was evidently the sort that he would get.

Ega, meanwhile, had taken his arm and placed him carefully at the table on his right hand; then he presented him with a camellia-bud from one of the bouquets: Alencar too affixed a flower on himself, and the waiters served the oysters.

Immediately talk turned on a recent crime in the Mouraria, a drama of *fado*-singers that had outraged all Lisbon: a girl had been slashed in the belly with a knife by a woman companion and had gone into the street to die in her night-dress; two pimps had knifed one another. A whole alley had been bathed in blood – a real 'punch-up', said Cohen, smiling and sipping his Bucellas.

Damaso had the satisfaction of being in a position to provide details. He had known the girl, the one who had administered the knifing, when she was the mistress of the Viscount da Ermidinha. Was she pretty? Very pretty! The hands of a duchess – and how the pretty thing could sing *fado*! The worst of it was that even in the Viscount's time, when she had the height of *chic,* she already had a taste for drinking. To his credit the Viscount had never stopped being friends with her; he respected her; he had promised her that if she wanted to give up her life among the *fado*-singers, he would set her up with a confectioner's shop near the cathedral. But she would not hear of it. She liked the life, the Bairro Alto, the cheap cafés, the pimps.

That world of *fado*-singers and their men seemed to Carlos to be worthy subect of study, a novel even. At once the talk turned to Zola's *L'Assomoir* and realism in literature. Wiping the drops of soup from his moustache, Alencar immediately begged them not to discuss that literature of the latrine at dinner. Here everyone was a clean person, a person who might enter a drawing-room, were they not? So there was no point in mentioning *excrement*!

Poor Alencar! Naturalism – those powerful and vigorous works published in thousands of copies; those harsh analyses that had taken Church, Royalty, Bureaucracy, Finance and all the sancrosanct subjects, brutally dissected them and displayed their diseased organs like corpses in an amphitheatre; those new styles that were so precise and malleable and caught the very beat of life in the act, the line, the colour – all this, which in his muddled mind he entitled the 'New Idea', had fallen upon him suddenly and had shattered the romantic chathedral at whose altar he had for so many years served and officiated. It had all disoriented poor Alencar and had become the literary tragedy of his old age. At first he had fought back. 'To erect an impassable dike against the horrid tide', as he had said to the assembled Academy, he had written two cruel pamphlets. Nobody read them. The 'horrid tide' surged forward, deeper, wider. And so Alencar took refuge in morality as on a solid rock. Was not naturalism, with its alluvial obscenity, threatening to corrupt social decency? Well then he, Alencar, would be the paladin of morals, the gendarme of good habits! And thus the poet of *Voices of Dawn,* who for twenty years in song and ode had proposed erotic commerce with all the ladies of the capital; thus the author of *Elvira* who, in novel and drama, had propagated illicit love and represented conjugal duties as mountains of tedium and given all husbands fat and bestial forms and all lovers the comeliness, the splendour and the genius of Apollos of antiquity – he, Tomas d'Alencar, who (were one to credit his autobiographical confessions in *The*

145

Flower of Martyrdom) had himself experienced a deplorable life of adulteries, voluptuousness and orgies amid the velvets and wines of Cyprus, now turned austere and incorruptible, all of him a monument of prudery. Meticulously he began to scrutinize newspapers, books and plays, and scarcely did he discern nascent symptoms of realism in a kiss that smacked too loudly or in the whiteness of a skirt gathered up too high, then there was Alencar, ringing throughout the land a great peal of alarm. He flew to his pen, and his imprecations (as far as the easily-satisfied Academicians were concerned) recalled the roaring of an Isaiah. But one day Alencar was subjected to one of those revelations that prostrate the sturdiest of mortals: the more he denounced a book as immoral, the more it sold! The world became a dreadful place, and the author of *Elvira* was overwhelmed.

From that time forward he reduced the expression of his rancour to a minimum, to that curt phrase uttered in disgust: 'Lads, don't mention *excrement*!'

But on that night he had the good fortune to encounter allies. Craft also could not tolerate naturalism, the ugly reality of things and society stripped bare in a book. Surely Art was an idealization? Good! Then it ought to depict superior types of perfected humanity, the most beautiful forms of living and feeling. Ega was horrified and clutched his head in his hands. On the other side Carlos declared that the most insupportable thing about realism was its great scientific airs, its pretentious aesthetics deduced from an alien philosophy, and the invocation of Claude Bernard, experimentalism, positivism, Stuart Mill and Darwin, when it was simply a matter of describing a washerwoman sleeping with a carpenter!

Thus caught between two fires, Ega thundered back. It was precisely the weakness of realism that it was still insufficiently scientific and invented plots, created dramas and gave itself up to literary fantasy! The pure form of naturalist art should be the monograph, the dry study of a human type, a vice, a passion, just as it was dealt with in a pathological case, without picturesqueness, without style.

'That's absurd!' said Carlos. 'Characters can only be depicted through action . . .'

'And the work of art,' added Craft, 'only exists through its form . . .'

Alencar interrupted them, exclaiming that so much philosophy was unnecessary.

'You're whipping a dead horse, my lads. Realism is to be criticized in this way – hand on nose! When I see one of those books, I rub myself at once in *eau de cologne*. Let us not discuss *excrement*!'

'*Sole normande?*' asked a waiter, coming to his side with a platter.

Ega was about to fulminate against Alencar, but he noticed Cohen's weary and superior smile at this literary talk and he controlled himself. He dedicated his attentions to this guest alone, asked him what he thought of the St Emilion and, when he saw him conveniently served with *sole normande*, he questioned him with a great display of interest.

'Well, now, Cohen, tell us all about it. Is the loan to be issued or not?'

And he aroused everyone's interest by turning from side to side and saying that this question of the loan was serious. A tremendous operation, a really historic event . . .

Cohen placed a pinch of salt on the side of his plate and replied authoritatively that the loan had *absolutely* to be realized. Loans in Portugal nowadays constituted one of the sources of revenue, as regular, as indispensable, as well-known as taxation. The only occupation for the ministries, as a matter of fact, was this – gathering in the taxes and issuing loans. And that was how it must go on.

Carlos did not understand finance, but it seemed to him that the country would in this manner proceed gaily and prettily towards bankruptcy.

'At a nice gallop, very surely and very directly,' agreed Cohen, smiling. 'Oh, on that score nobody has any illusions, my dear sir. Not even the ministers of finance themselves. Bankruptcy is inevitable – like the answer to a sum!'

Ega looked impressed.

'What a state of affairs, eh?'

And everybody listened to Cohen. Ega, after filling Cohen's glass anew, put his elbows on the table the better to drink in Cohen's words.

'Bankruptcy is so sure, things are so disposed for it,' continued Cohen, 'that it would even be possible for someone, in a matter of two or three years, to force the country into depression . . .'

Greedily Ega demanded the recipe. It was simply this: the maintenance of constant revolutionary agitation; the organization of a couple of hundred sturdy rogues to start a scuffle on the eve of issuing a loan and to pull down lamp-posts amid hurrahs for the Republic; then to telegraph this news in big headlines to the Paris, London and Rio de Janeiro newspapers; the markets would be frightened, the Brazilians would be terrified – and bankruptcy would be on the way. The only objection was that this course was not convenient to anybody.

Ega protested vehemently. Why was it not convenient to anybody? What a thing to say! It was just what would suit everybody! Bankruptcy would be followed by revolution, for sure! A people that lives from the product of loans that are not paid takes up the cudgel; and for this reason, or even merely for revenge, their first concern is to sweep away the monarchy that heads the swindle, and with it all those crass personages who represent contitutionalim. And then, when the crisis was over, Portugal would be free of the old debt, the old people, that grotesque collection of animals.

Ega's voice hissed. But seeing those men of order, who cause banks to prosper, assailed as grotesques, as animals, Cohen placed a hand on his friend's arm and appealed to his good sense. Of course he would be the first to admit that among all those gentry who had been prominent since 1846 there had been mediocrities and idiots – but there had been men of worth, too!

'There's talent, there's knowledge,' he declared in tones of experience. 'You ought to acknowledge it, Ega. You are very precipitate! No, sir, there's talent and there's knowledge!'

Recollecting that some of those animals were Cohen's friends, Ega granted them talent and knowledge. Alencar however, sombrely curled his moustache. He had tended latterly towards radical ideas, towards that humanitarian democracy of 1848; with romanticism discredited in letters, he was by instinct taking refuge now in political romanticism. He wanted a republic governed by genius, the brotherhood of nations – the United States of Europe – and he had, moreover, long complaints to lodge about the politicians, the people in power today who had once been his colleagues in the editorial room, at the café and at the gambling-table.

'Talent! Knowledge!' he sneered, 'Fairy tales! I know those fellows, my dear Cohen!'

Cohen interrupted him.

'No, indeed, Alencar, no indeed! You're another of these chaps – it doesn't become you to say such things. It's an exaggeration. No, indeed! There's talent, there's knowledge!'

And faced with this assertion of Cohen's the respected director of the National Bank, the husband of the divine Rachel, the owner of that hospitable house in Rua de Ferregial where one dined so well – in the face of all this, Alencar contained his disgust and admitted that, after all, there was some talent and some learning.

And then, having thus recalled those rebellious spirits to respect for Parliamentarians and veneration for Order by means of the influence of his bank, the beautiful eyes of his wife and the excellence of his cook, Cohen condescended to say in his smoothest tone of voice that the country was in need of reforms.

But on that night Ega was incorrigible, and now he uttered another enormity.

'Portugal doesn't need reform, Cohen! What Portugal needs is a Spanish invasion!'

Alencar, who was an old-fashioned patriot, became indignant. Cohen smiled the indulgent smile of a superior man, displaying his fine teeth, and perceived merely one more of 'our Ega's paradoxes' in the remark.

But Ega was speaking in earnestness and was full of reason. Obviously, he said, invasion would not involve absolute loss of independence. Such a stupid fear was worthy only of a circle so stupid as that of the members of the *Primeiro de Dezembro* club. There was no example of a country of six million inhabitants being swallowed up in a single gulp by a country that had only fifteen million. And who would permit this beautiful Portuguese coastline to fall into the hands of Spain, a military and maritime nation? Not to mention our alliances in exchange for the colonies – those colonies we only use, as ruined heirs do the family plate, to go and pawn in case of crisis. There was no danger! What would happen, if there were an invasion during the course of a European war, would be that we would get a tremendous beating; we would have to pay a big compensation; we would lose one or two provinces – and perhaps see Galicia extending to the Douro river.

'*Poulet aux champignons*,' murmured the waiter, presenting him with a platter.

And while he helped himself, everyone showered him with questions – how would the salvation of the country result from a catastrophe of such dimensions, a catastrophe that would make a Spanish settlement out of Celorico de Basto, noble Celorico, cradle of heroes, cradle of the Egas?

'In this: in the revival of public spirit and the Portuguese genius! Beaten, humiliated, downtrodden, destroyed, we would have to make a desperate effort in order to survive. And what a splendid position we'd find ourselves in. No monarchy; that pack of politicians gone; that mushroom of the public debt ended! For everything would vanish; we would be brand new, clean, polished like a piece of cutlery that's never been used. And a new history could begin, a different Portugal – a Portugal that would be serious and intelligent, strong and decent, studious, thoughtful, contributing towards civilization as in earlier times! Nothing regenerates a nation like a terrible drubbing! Oh, God of Ourique, send us the Castillian! And you, Cohen, pass me the St Emilion!'

Everybody became animated now as they discussed the invasion. Ah, what a splendid resistance could be organized! Cohen would advance the money! Arms and artillery could be purchased in America – and Craft immediately volunteered his collection of sixteenth-century swords. But what about generals? These could be hired! For example, there was MacMahon! He must be going cheap.

'Craft and I will organize a guerrilla,' shouted Ega.

'At your service, Colonel.'

'Alencar,' Ega went on, 'is charged with rousing the provinces to patriotism with songs and odes.'

At this the poet put down his glass and made the motion of a lion shaking his mane:

'This carcass may be old, my lad, but it's still fit for better than odes! It can still shoulder a gun! The aim's still true and it'll bring down a couple of Galicians yet. But my God! Just to think of such things makes my heart sink! How can you all talk like this and laugh when it's the country that's at stake, this land that gave us birth? Hang it! It may be bad, I agree, but dear God, it's the only one we have – we have no other! Here we must live, and it is here we must die. No, let's talk about something else – let's talk about women!'

He had pushed back his plate and his eyes were moist with patriotic fervour.

In the silence that fell Damaso, who had not said a word since the information he had imparted about the *fado*-singer, and had been occupied in gazing reverently at Carlos, slowly raised his voice and said, with a mixture of common sense and cunning:

'If things came to such a pass, if they looked that ugly – as for me, I'd take the precaution of going off to Paris.'

Ega screamed with triumph and leaped gleefully in his chair.

There you had it – on Damaso's synthetic lip – the spontaneous and genuine cry of Portuguese valour! To make off, get out – that was the way the whole of Lisbon society reasoned, from top to bottom, the whole Constitutional crowd from El Rei, our Lord the King, down to cretinous clerks.

'My dear boys – at the first breath of a single Spanish soldier on the frontier the country will take to its heels and run like hares! It will be the greatest rout of history!'

There was indignant protest.

'Down with the traitor,' cried Alencar.

Cohen intervened with the declaration that the Portuguese soldier was valiant, in the Turkish fashion – undisciplined but sturdy.

Even Carlos put in very gravely: 'No, sir! Nobody will fly – and they will die honourably!'

Ega roared. For whose benefit were they putting on this heroic pose? Were they ignorant of the fact that this race, after fifty years of Constitutionalism, bred in the slums down town, taught in the scurvy high schools, eaten with syphilis, rotting in mouldy offices, taken out for an airing only on Saturdays on the dusty pavements – this race had lost its muscles as it had lost its character? It was the feeblest, most cowardly breed in Europe.

'Those are the people of Lisbon,' pointed out Craft.

'Lisbon is Portugal,' cried the other. 'Outside Lisbon there's nothing. The entire country lies between the Arcade with its ministries and São Bento with its so-called parliament. It's the most wretched breed in Europe!'

He went ranting on – and what an army! After a two-day march a regiment was fit for nothing but admission to hospital. With his own eyes he had seen a Swedish sailor on the day the Cortes opened – a sturdy northern fellow – disposing with punches of an entire company of Portuguese soldiers. The soldiers had literally taken to their heels with their cartridge-cases banging against their hips; and their terror-stricken officer had hidden in a doorway to vomit.

Everyone protested. No, no, such things were not possible! Hell! He had seen it for himself. Perhaps he had, but it must have been with the mistaken eyes of imagination.

'I swear it on my mother's health!' shouted Ega furiously.

But he fell silent. Cohen had touched his arm. Cohen was about to speak.

Cohen wished to say that the future lay with God. However, that the Spaniards were contemplating invasion seemed to him beyond doubt – especially if they were to lose Cuba, as seemed likely. In Madrid that was what everyone had said to him. Negotiations for supplies had already opened.

'Spanish tricks! Galician tricks!' snorted Alencar between his teeth as he twisted his moustache gloomily.

'In the Hotel de Paris,' Cohen continued, 'in Madrid, I met a magistrate who told me with an air of conviction that he had not lost all hope of coming to establish himself for good in Lisbon; Lisbon had greatly pleased him when he had been here at the seaside. And as for myself, I believe there are many Spaniards who await this augmentation of territory in order to acquire posts for themselves!'

At this point Ega fell into ecstasies and clasped his hands to his breast. What a splendid report! What admirable observation!

'This Cohen,' he exclaimed to everybody, 'how closely he notices things! What exquisite appreciation! Eh, Craft? Eh, Carlos? Delightful!'

Everyone courteously admired Cohen's finesse. He thanked them with a look of emotion as he caressed his whiskers with a hand on which a diamond gleamed. And at that instant the waiters presented a dish of peas in white sauce, murmuring:

'*Petits pois à la Cohen.*'

152

A la Cohen? Each of then scrutinized his menu attentively. And there it was – the vegetable dish: *petits pois à la Cohen!* Damaso enthusiastically declared this to be 'fantastically chic!' And now the champagne was opened and the first toast was drunk to Cohen.

Bankruptcy, invasion, the homeland – all were forgotten, and the dinner ended merrily. Other toasts were exchanged, ardent and eloquent. Cohen himself, smiling like one who gives in to the caprices of a child, drank to the Revolution and to Anarchy, a complicated toast proposed by Ega, whose eye was by this time very bright. The dessert lay strewn about in disorder on the tablecloth, and on Alencar's plate cigarette butts were mixed with bits of chewed pineapple. Damaso bowed double beside Carlos, eulogizing Maia's pair of English horses and that phaeton that was the loveliest thing that drove around in Lisbon. Then, following hard upon his Radical's toast, and for no reason at all, Ega set about Craft – he insulted England; he wanted her excluded from the community of thinking nations; he threatened her with a social revolution that would soak her in blood. The others responded with nods of the head as Craft sat cracking nuts imperturbably.

The waiters served coffee. And as the guests had already sat three long hours at table everybody got up, finishing off their cigars and talking animatedly with the liveliness imparted by the champagne. The room, with its low ceiling and its five gaslights burning brightly, was hot and heavy and permeated now with the strong aroma of the chartreuse and liqueur amid the smoke's milky mist.

Carlos and Craft both felt suffocated and went out for a breath of air on the balcony. A community of tastes had begun to unite them, and they resumed the conversation they had begun in the Rua do Alecrim about the beautiful collection at Olivais. Craft proffered some details: the one rich and rare thing he possessed was a Dutch sixteenth-century cabinet; for the rest, a few bronzes, *faiences* and some good weapons.

But they both turned round as their ears caught the sound of raised voices among the other group near the table. It seemed as if a quarrel was starting. Alencar was shaking his locks and cursing 'philosophical forage'; facing him with a glass of cognac in his hand stood Ega, pale but affecting a superior air of calm as he declared himself in favour of police intervention against the publication of 'all that lyrical verbiage'.

'They're at it again,' said Damaso to Carlos, coming out on to the balcony; 'It's because of Craveiro. Really, they're too delicious!'

The altercation had indeed arisen over modern poetry, over Simão Craveiro, and his poem – 'The Death of Satan'. Ega had been enthusiastically reciting from the episode of 'The Death', where the huge symbolic skeleton walks in bright sunlight down the boulevard dressed like a harlot and dragging rustling silk:

> 'And betwixt two ribs, at the neckline,
> A bouquet of roses lay . . .'

Then Alencar, who loathed Craveiro the man of the 'New Idea', the paladin of realism, had exulted and laughed as he at once denounced in that simple stanza two grammatical errors, an incorrect scansion, and imagery robbed from Baudelaire!

Ega, who had drunk two glasses of cognac one after the other, became very provocative and very personal

'I know why you're talking this way, Alencar,' he proclaimed, 'and the motive is not a noble one! It's because of the epigram he made about you:

> "Alencar from Alenquer
> With his roving eye."

Hasn't any of your heard it?' he went on, turning and calling to the others. 'It's marvellous – one of the best things Craveiro's done. Haven't you heard it, Carlos? It's delightful, especially this stanza:

> "Alencar from Alenquer
> Passes not his hours
> Roaming through the country
> Gathering meadow-flowers.
>
> No, our airy poet,
> What he's seeking there,
> In the fresh, sweet woodland
> Is a maiden fair!"

I don't recall the rest, but it ends with a note of common sense, which is the only response to all that cheap lyricism:

> "But, Alencar from Alenquer,
> Hush those lover's moans,
> For the maiden's sweetheart
> Has sworn to break your bones!" '

Alencar passed a hand across his livid forehead, fixed a hollow eye on Ega and spoke in a harsh, slow voice:

'Look here, João da Ega, let me tell you something, my lad! All those epigrams, all this stupid jeering from that weed and his admirers – all this flows beneath my feet like water in a gutter. All I do is tuck up my trouser leg! I tuck up my trousers – just that, Ega! I tuck up my trousers!'

And he actually did tuck them up, displaying his underwear in a sudden, delirious gesture.

'Well, when you come upon a gutter like that one,' cried Ega, 'kneel down and drink from it! It'll put some blood and strength into your lyricism!'

But Alencar was not listening to him; his shouts to the others rent the air:

'Were that Craveiro creature less of a weed, perhaps I'd amuse myself by kicking him all the way down the Chiado, him and his verses – all that pretentious ordure with which he has bored Satan to death! And after I'd smeared him all over with filth, I'd smash in his skull!'

'Skulls are not smashed in that easily!' said Ega in a cold, leering tone.

Alencar turned a terrible face towards him. Rage and brandy had fired his gaze. He trembled all over:

'I'd smash his skull, yes! I'd break it, João da Ega! I'd break it, like this, look, just like this!' And he began stamping on the floor so that the room shook and glasses and china jumped. 'But I don't choose to, lads! For inside that skull there's only excrement, vomit, pus, green matter – and if I crushed it, for crush it I could, lads, all that rotting brain would run out and infect the city; the cholera would be upon us! Worse, by God – we'd have the plague!'

Seeing him thus excited, Carlos took his arm and tried to calm him: 'Come Alencar! What foolishness! Is it really worth it?'

The other tore himself loose, panting, and unbuttoned his frockcoat to fire this last salvo:

'Of course it's not worth anyone's getting angry on account of that notorious Craveiro and his New Idea – that fraud, who forgets that his slut of a sister is a tuppenny whore in Marco de Canavezes!'

'This is really too much, you swine!' roared Ega, squaring up to him with his fists clenched.

Frightened now, Cohen and Damaso caught hold of him; Carlos immediately pulled Alencar over to the window as, his eyes blazing, he struggled to loosen his tie. A chair had fallen to the floor; the formal room with its morocco leather divans, its bouquets of camellias, was filled with cigarette smoke and had taken on the air of a tavern occupied by brawling ruffians. Damaso, who was very pale and almost voiceless, went from one to another pleading:

'My dear fellows, here in the Hotel Central! God! Here in the Hotel Central!'

And Ega was shouting hoarsely from Cohen's arms:

'That swine! That coward! Let me go, Cohen! No – I'll hit him for this! Dona Ana Craveiro, a saint! What a calumniating beast! No! I'll choke him for this!'

During all this, Craft was impassively sipping his chartreuse. He had frequently had occasion to witness rival schools of literature assailing one another, rolling on the floor, howling imprecations – and Alencar's low jibe about the other poet's sister was part and parcel of the armoury of criticism in Portugal. It all left him unmoved, smiling disdainfully. Besides, he knew that a reconciliation, warm with embraces, would not be far off.

He was right. Alencar emerged from the window-bay behind Carlos, buttoning up his frock-coat and looking grave and repentant. In a corner of the room Cohen was addressing Ega in authoritative tones, as severe as a father's; then he turned, lifted his hand, raised his voice and declared that everybody there was a gentleman – and as befitted men of talent and noble heart they should embrace.

'Come Ega, shake hands, for my sake! Come, Alencar – I'm asking you as a personal favour!'

The author of *Elvira* stepped forward; the author of the *Mem-*

oirs of an Atom extended a hand; but the first clasp was gauche and flabby. Then Alencar, generous and open-hearted, exclaimed that between him and Ega *not even a cloud should remain!* He had exceeded himself. It was his wretched temper – that hot-bloodedness that had been the bane of his life! And he was ready to declare there and then, so that all could hear, that Dona Ana Craveiro was a saint! He had met her in Marco de Cana-vezes, in the Peixotos' house – as a wife and a mother, Ana Craveiro was above reproach! And, from the depths of his soul, he recognized that Craveiro had a wealth of talent.

He filled a glass of champagne and raised it aloft before Ega, like a chalice before the altar:

'Your health, João!'

Generous too, Ega responded:

'Your health, Tomas!'

They embraced. Alencar swore that only the previous evening, in the house of Dona Joana Coutinho, he had said he knew nobody more scintillating than Ega! Ega at once affirmed that nowhere but in the poems of Alencar could be found such a fine lyrical vein. They embraced again with pats on the shoulder. They called each other *brothers in art,* they called each other *geniuses!*

'They're quite remarkable!' murmured Craft to Carlos in a low voice as he looked for his hat. 'They unhinge me! I must get some air.'

The night was advancing. It was eleven o'clock. But more brandy was drunk. Then Cohen went out leading Ega with him. Damaso and Alencar went down with Carlos, who was returning on foot through the Aterro.

At the door the poet solemnly halted.

'My lads?' he exclaimed, taking off his hat and liberally refreshing his forehead, 'Well? It seems to me that I behaved like a gentleman!'

Carlos agreed and praised his generosity.

'I appreciate that, my boy, because you, of all people, know what it means to be a gentleman! And now let's be off up the Aterro – but let me go over there a moment first to buy a packet of tobacco.'

'What a fellow!' exclaimed Damaso as soon as Alencar was out of hearing; 'And things were beginning to look ugly!'

Then, at once, without a pause, he launched into praise of

Carlos. Senhor Maia had no idea how long he had been wanting to make his acquaintance!

'But, senhor – '

'Believe me, sir, I'm not one for flattery – you can ask Ega how many times I have said that you, sir, were the best thing in Lisbon!'

Carlos lowered his head, biting back a laugh. Damaso was repeating from the depths of his heart:

'This is sincere, Senhor Maia! Believe me, this is from the heart!'

It really was sincere. Ever since Carlos had come to live in Lisbon he had unknowingly inspired in that fat, plump-cheeked youth a worship that was mute and profound; the very patent-leather of his shoes or the colour of his gloves was motive for Damaso's veneration and as important as principles. He considered Carlos the very epitome of *chic* – his beloved *chic* – a Beau Brummel, a d'Orsay, a Morny – one 'of those things you only see abroad', as he would put it, rolling his eyes. That afternoon, knowing he was to dine in Maia's company, that he was at last to meet Maia, he had spent two hours before his looking-glass trying on ties; he had perfumed himself as though for a woman's arms; and on account of Carlos he had ordered the coupé for ten o'clock, driven by a coachman with a nosegay in his buttonhole.

'So that Brazilian lady lives here?' asked Carlos, who had walked ahead and was looking up at a lighted window on the second floor.

Damaso followed his gaze.

'She lives on the other side. They've been here a fortnight. *Chic* people – and she's very appetizing, as you may have observed. On board ship I was after her – and she talked to me. But I've been very busy since I arrived – dinners here, soirées there, some little adventures. I haven't been able to visit them, and I've only left cards; but I'm keeping my eye on her, for she's going to stay here. Perhaps I'll call tomorrow. I'm already beginning to tingle. And if I catch myself alone with her – ha! – I'll plant a kiss on her right away! As far as I'm concerned – I don't know if it goes for you too – but for my part, as far as women are concerned, this is my theory: you have to grab them when you can!'

At that moment Alencar returned from the tobacconist, a cigar in his mouth. Damaso took his leave, shouting the address of Morelli, the second lady of the São Carlos Opera, in a loud voice to the coachman so that Carlos could hear.

'A good lad, that Damaso,' said Alencar, taking Carlos's arm as they both walked up the Aterro. 'A constant companion of the Cohens. Very well thought of in Society. A lad with a fortune, son of old Silva, the moneylender, who fleeced your father – and me too. But he signs himself Salcêde; perhaps it's his mother's name. Or maybe he invented it. A good lad – the father was a swine! I can almost hear Pedro saying to him with that aristocratic air of his: "Silva, you Jew, I want money and plenty of it!" Ah, those were different times, my Carlos, great times. A man's times!'

All along the sad and gloomy Aterro, its gaslights flickering low like a funeral procession, Alencar continued to recall those 'great times' when he had been young with Pedro; and behind his poetic language Carlos sensed the old fragrance of a world that was dead. It had been a time when the young men had still felt traces of the heat of the civil wars, and they would let off steam by going about in bands to turn taverns upside down or to half-kill old coach-horses in wild gallops to Cintra. In those days Cintra had been a trysting-place, and beneath its romantic foliage noble ladies had surrendered to the arms of poets. They had been the Elviras and the Antonys. There had been no shortage of money; the Court had been gay; the gallant literary Regeneration had ennobled the country, made it the beautiful garden of Europe; graduates came down from Coimbra swelling with eloquence; ministers of the Crown gave piano recitals; the same poetic breath filled both odes and legislative enactments.

'Lisbon was certainly more amusing,' said Carlos.

'It was a different place, my Carlos! One lived! There was no place for all these scientific airs, all this philosophical scrabbling, all these positivist nonsenses. But there was heart, boy! There were sparks! Even in politics. But look at the pigsty we have now, that gang of rogues we have! In those days you could walk into the Parliament building and you sensed the inspiration, you felt the flashes of wit! There was some illumination in those heads – and then, my boy, there were wonderful women!'

His shoulders slouched in his nostalgia for that lost world. And he looked very sorrowful with his poet's mane falling out from under the broad brim of his old hat and his worn, badly-made frock-coat pitifully pinching his waist.

For a while they strolled along in silence. Then in Janellas Verdes, Alencar expressed the wish to 'refresh' himself. They entered a small booth where the yellow light of an oil-lamp glowed in the subterranean shadow, lighting up the damp zinc of the counter, the bottles on the shelves and the sad bulk of the proprietress who had a kerchief tied around her chin.

Alencar seemed an intimate of the establishment – for scarcely had he learned that Senhora Candida had toothache than he began to advise remedies, familiar now and down from the clouds, with his elbows on the counter. When Carlos wanted to pay for the white rum he got angry; he threw his two *tostões* down on the polished zinc and exclaimed loftily:

'In the taverns, my dear Carlos, I am host! In palaces, it is others who pay – but here in the tavern I pay!'

At the door he took Carlos's arm. After a few slow paces in the silence of the street he halted again, and murmured in a vague and contemplative voice that sounded as if it had been soaked in the vast solemnity of the night:

'That Rachel Cohen is divinely lovely, my boy! D'you know her?'

'By sight.'

'Doesn't she put you in mind of a Biblical heroine? I don't mean those viragos Judith and Delilah, but one of those poetic lilies of the Bible – she's angelic!'

Rachel was now Alencar's platonic passion, his lady, his Beatrice.

'Did you see the lines I wrote to her in the *Diário Nacional?*

> "April has come! Be mine,
> Said the wind to the rose."

Not too bad! "April has come! Be mine" – there's a subtle hint there – but it's at once followed by "said the wind to the rose"! D'you get it? The effect was quite good. But you must not imagine there's anything in it, or that I'm wooing her – she's the wife of Cohen, a friend, a brother. And Rachel, poor little thing, is like my own sister. But she's divine. Those eyes, my lad, like liquid velvet!'

He took off his hat and cooled his vast forehead. Then he spoke in another tone, as though it cost him an effort.

'That Ega has a great deal of talent. He's often at the Cohens' – Rachel finds him amusing.'

Carlos had stopped. They had reached Ramalhete. Alencar glanced at the severe convent-like walls that slept without a light visible.

'It has good looks, your house – well, go in, my boy, for I'm off up there to my lair. And whenever you feel like it, lad, you'll find me there in Rua do Carvalho, number 52, third floor. I started by living on the ground floor, for the building's mine, but I've been moving upwards – the only thing I've climbed up in fact, Carlos, is storeys.'

He made a gesture of scorn for these tribulations.

'You must come and dine with me. I can't offer you a banquet, but you'll get soup and a roast. My Matheus, a Negro but a friend, has been with me many a year and when there is anything to cook he knows how! Many a dinner he made for your father, my poor Pedro. Ah, in those days it was a merry house, my boy! There I gave bed, board and pocket-money to many a fellow who today belongs to that pack who trot by in hired coupés with a runner at the back – but when they catch sight of me nowadays they turn their snouts in the other direction.'

'That's your imagination,' said Carlos consolingly.

'No it's not, Carlos,' replied the poet, very earnest and very bitter. 'It's not. You don't know my life-story. I've suffered a lot of rejection, my lad. And I have not deserved it! On my honour, I have not deserved it.'

He grasped Carlos's arm and went on with a choking voice:

'Look now! Those men who are important today used to get drunk with me; I lent them much cash and gave them many a supper – and today they're ministers, they're ambassadors, they're personalities and I don't know what else! Well now, have they offered you a little of that cake that they've got their hands on now? No! Nor to me! This is hard, Carlos, this is very hard, my Carlos. Hell, I don't ask them to make me a count, or give me an embassy! Just something somewhere in an office – but not a crumb! Well, I've still enough left for a bit of bread and half an ounce of tobacco. But this ingratitude has turned my hair grey. Well, I don't wish to bore you any more, and may God make you as happy as you deserve to be, my Carlos.'

'Won't you come inside for a while, Alencar?'

Such openness moved the poet.

'Thanks, my boy,' he said, embracing Carlos. 'And I'm grateful, for I know it comes from the heart – all of you have heart. Your father had, as wide and big as a lion's! And now I want you to know something: you have a friend here. This is not just talk, it comes from within . . . Well, good-bye, my lad. D'you want a cigar?'

Carlos accepted it as though it were a gift from heaven.

'Well, here's a cigar for you, lad!' exclaimed Alencar enthusiastically.

And that cigar given to such a rich man, to the owner of Ramalhete, took him back for a moment to the times when he would hand around a full cigar-case there in the Café Marrare with his grand air of a sad Manfred. So he became involved in that cigar. He lit it himself with a match. He checked to see if it was well lit. And what was it like? A decent cigar? Carlos found it an excellent cigar.

'Well, it was a *good* thing I gave you a *good* cigar!'

He embraced him again; and it was striking one when he at last went off with a lighter step, more contented with himself now, humming a snatch of a *fado*.

Up in his room Carlos stretched himself out on the chaise-longue and finished Alencar's abominable cigar while Baptista made him a cup of tea before he went to bed; and he went over the strange past that the old romantic had evoked for him.

He wasn't a bad fellow, poor Alencar! What exaggerated care he had taken in speaking of Pedro, of Arroios, of the friends and loves of those years, to avoid even pronouncing the name of Maria Monforte! More than once, along the Aterro, he had been about to say to him: 'You may speak of Mama, Alencar, my friend – I know perfectly well that she ran away with an Italian.'

And then his thoughts began to return to the way in which that lamentable history had been revealed to him at Coimbra –

almost grotesquely, on a night of merry-making. For his grandfather, in obedience to Pedro's last wishes, had told him a decent myth: a marriage of passion; temperamental incompatibilities; a courteous separation; Mama's withdrawl with her daughter to France where they both had died. That was all! The death of his father had always been presented to him as the abrupt climax to a long drawn-out depression.

But Ega had learned the true story from his uncle. And one night after they had supped together and Ega had become very drunk, he had launched upon a tremendous paradox in one of his flights of idealism, denouncing chastity in women as the origin of a race's decadence. In support of his argument Ega declared that natural sons were invariably intelligent, brave and glorious! He, Ega, would have been proud had his mother, his own mother, instead of being the saintly bourgeoise who told her beads by the fireside, been like Carlos's mother, a passionate creature who for love of an exile had abandoned fortune, respectability, honour and life! On hearing this Carlos had stood stock-still in their path across the bridge in the calm moonlight. But Ega was in no condition to be questioned further. He was already stammering, unintelligible and sick; and in a moment he began ignobly to vomit in Carlos's arms. Carlos had had to drag him to the Seixas's house, undress him and bear with his kisses and drunken affection until he left him hugging his pillow and drooling and sobbing that he 'wanted to be a bastard and have a harlot for a mama.'

But that night Carlos had been unable to sleep with the thought of his mother, so different from the story he had been told, fleeing in the arms of an exile – perhaps even a Pole! Early the following day he had entered Ega's room to demand in the name of their great friendship the unvarnished truth.

Poor Ega! He was sick; he was as white as the cloth tied round his head with towels soaked in soothing lotions; and the poor fellow was speechless! Carlos sat on the side of his bed, as he always did during their night-long arguments, and soothed him. He had not come out of a sense of injury, but out of curiosity! He had been given an intimation of a remarkable story that concerned his own family. He wanted to know what lay behind it. There was romance here. Let him hear that romance!

And so Ega gained courage and at last stammered out the

tale – or what he knew of it from his uncle: Maria's passion for a prince, her flight, the long silence of the years that had fallen around her name.

The holidays were upon them. Scarcely had Carlos reached Santa Olávia than he told his grandfather about Ega's drunken bout, his crazy speeches and that revelation made amid hiccoughs. Poor Grandfather! For a moment he had been unable to speak – and then his voice had come so faint and desolate that it seemed his heart was failing. But he told Carlos, detail by detail, the whole ugly story up to the night when Pedro had come to him livid and covered in mud to fall into his arms and sob out his pain with the helplessness of a child. And the end of that guilty love, added the grandfather, had been the death of the mother in Vienna and the death of the little girl she had taken, his granddaughter whom he had never seen. And that was all. Now the family shame lay buried there in the mausoleum at Santa Olávia and in two far-off graves in a foreign land.

Carlos remembered quite distinctly that on that very evening after his melancholy conversation with his grandfather he had tried out the English mare; and at dinner they had talked only of the mare, whose name was Sultana. As it turned out, within a few days Mama had been forgotten. Nor was it possible for him to feel more than a vague, somewhat literary interest in that tragedy. The whole thing had happened more than twenty-odd years before in a society that had practically vanished. It was like some historical episode in an old family chronicle – an ancestor dying at Alcácer-Quibir, or one of his grandmothers sleeping in a royal bed! It had caused him not a single tear nor had it brought a blush to his cheek. Naturally he would have preferred to have been proud of his mother, like a rare and noble flower of honour – but he was not prepared to spend the rest of his life embittered by her errors. And in any case, why should he? His own honour did not depend on the false or base impulses that may have throbbed in her heart. She had sinned, she had died, there was end of it. Still – there was the picture of his father, dying in a pool of blood, in despair over that betrayal. But he had never known his father; all he had of him and of his memory to cherish was a cold, expressionless painting that hung in his dressing-room and portrayed a dark youth with great eyes, yellow suede gloves and a whip in his hand. Of his mother there was not even a daguerreotype or a pencil sketch. Grandfather had said she was blonde. He knew no more. He had known neither of them; he had not slept in their arms; he had never received the warmth of their tenderness. Father and mother were for him mere symbols of a conventional cult. Papa, Mama, those beloved beings – they were both embodied in the person of his grandfather.

Baptista brought the tea and Alencar's cigar was finished. He lay in the chaise-longue, softened by these memories and succumbing now, half drowsy, to the fatigue of that long dinner-party. And then, little by little, before his closed lids, a vision rose, took on colour and filled the room. Above the river the evening died in Elysian peace. The courtyard of the Hotel Central stretched before him, still in daylight. A grey-haired Negro came with a little bitch in his arms; a woman passed, tall, ivory-fleshed, lovely as a goddess, in a coat of white Genoa velvet. Craft at his side was saying: *'Très chic!'* And he smiled under the spell of these images that had taken on the relief, the outline, the colouration of live creatures.

It was three o'clock by the time he went to bed. And hardly had he fallen asleep in the darkness of the silk curtains than once again a beautiful winter's day was dying without a breeze, bathed in rose colour; the commonplace courtyard of the hotel opened out, still light in the afternoon; the black groom returned with the little bitch in his arms; a woman passed with a coat of white Genoa velvet, taller than any human woman, walking on clouds, with the magnificent air of a Juno climbing Mount Olympus; the toes of her patent-leather shoes burned with the azure light; and behind her, her skirts billowed in the wind. And she went on passing and re-passing; Craft went on saying *'Très chic!'* Then everything became muddled and it was only Alencar, a colossal Alencar filling all the sky, hiding the brightness of the stars with his black, badly-made frock-coat, his moustaches waving in the tempest of passions, raising his arms and clamouring through space: 'April has come, be mine.'

7

LUNCH WAS OVER at Ramalhete and the three windows of the study were open wide, drinking in the tepid light of the fine March day. Afonso da Maia and Craft played at chess in the chimney-corner, where there was no fire now but piles of plants, fresh and festive as some domestic altar. In a slanting sunbeam on the carpet the Reverend Bonifácio, enormous and fluffy, lay taking a light siesta.

Craft had in the space of a few weeks become an intimate of Ramalhete. Carlos and he with their community of tastes and ideas – the same passion for collecting, the fervent pursuit of fencing, an equal dilettantism of spirit – had taken to each other immediately in a relationship that was superficial, easy and amiable. Afonso, for his part, had at once taken a great liking to this gentleman of good English stock, with everything he most appreciated about it – cultivated and sturdy, with grave manners, strict habits, fine feelings and straightforward thoughts.

They had discovered a common enthusiasm for Tacitus, Macauley, Burke and even the Lake poets; Craft was an expert at chess; his character had gained the rich solidity of bronze in the course of his long and arduous travels. As Afonso da Maia said, Craft was a 'real man'. Craft, who rose at dawn, would leave Olivais early on horseback and sometimes come thus by surprise to the Maias for lunch; Afonso would have liked him to dine there always; but at any rate he invariably spent the night at Ramalhete, having at last, as he said, found a corner of Lisbon where you could talk in comfort surrounded both by ideas and good manners.

Carlos seldom went out. He was at work on his book. The flock of patients that had given him reason to hope for a full, active, busy career had dispersed; only three patients were left to him in the neighbourhood; and now he felt that his carriages, his horses, Ramalhete, his luxurious habits – all condemned him irrevocably to dilettantism. The clever Doctor Theodosio had told him frankly one day: 'You are too elegant for a doctor. Your female patients are bound to flirt with you! You terrify their menfolk!' Even the laboratory was a damaging factor. His colleagues declared that Maia, who was rich, intelligent and in favour of innovations and new-fangled ideas, performed fatal experiments on his patients. They had mocked at his theory, presented in the *Gazeta Médica*, of preventing epidemics by means of inoculation with viruses. They considered him a visionary. And so he took refuge in that book on medicine ancient and modern, *his book*, elaborated with the delays of the rich man of letters, a work that would give him a year or two's intellectual occupation.

That morning, while the chess game was proceeding inside in gravity and silence, Carlos was stretched out on the terrace in a vast Indian bamboo chair in the shade of the awning, finishing his cigar as he scanned through an English magazine, bathed by the tepid caress of a spring breeze which softened the air and inspired a desire for trees and lawns.

At his side on another bamboo chair, also with cigar in mouth, Senhor Damaso Salcêde was looking through *Figaro*. With his legs outstretched in intimate indolence, his friend Carlos at his side, Afonso's roses beside him on the rose-trees next to the terrace, behind him through the open windows the rich and noble interior of Ramalhete, the moneylender's son was savouring one of those delicious hours that had been his to enjoy since his admission to the Maias' intimacy.

The morning following upon the dinner at the Central, Senhor Salcêde had called at Ramalhete to leave his cards. These were complex and showy objects that bore, on a simulated fold in the corner, a small photograph of himself. A helmet with plumes stood above his name: Damaso Candido de Salcêde; underneath this was his decoration: Commendador de Cristo; at the bottom was his address: Rua de São Domingos, à Lapa. But this latter indication was crossed out and beside it in blue ink was a more impressive one: *Grand Hôtel, boulevard des Capucines, Paris, Chambre No. 103*. Thereafter he had sought Carlos in his consulting-rooms and left a card with the servant. At last, one afternoon in the Aterro, seeing Carlos passing on foot, he ran up to him, attached himself and succeeded in accompanying him to Ramalhete.

From the moment they reached the door he had bubbled with ecstatic admiration as though inside a museum; and carpets, china and pictures all elicited the utterance of that great phrase of his: *Chic, chic* as can be!' Carlos took him to the smoking-room, where Damaso accepted a cigar; and there, with one leg crossed over the other, he began to expound his opinions and tastes. He considered Lisbon vulgar, and only felt at ease in Paris – above all, on account of 'the genus female for which one starved in Lisbon'; although, on that point, Providence was not treating him unkindly at the moment. He liked antiques too; but you could pick up a lot of rubbish, and old chairs, for example, did not seem to him comfortable things for people to sit on. Reading entertained him, and he was never without books on his bed-table; lately he had been attempting to get into Daudet, who he had heard was very *chic*, but he found him a bit confusing. As a youth he had always stayed up at night until four or five in the morning merry-making! But now he was changed and tranquil; of course he would not go so far as to say that at times he did not surrender to a little excess, but only on holidays. And his questions were terrible. Did Senhor Maia think it was *chic* to have an English carriage? Which was the more elegant place for a man of the world who wanted to spend the summer abroad, Nice or Trouville? Then, with an intensely serious, almost emotional air, as he took his departure, he asked Senhor Maia (if Senhor Maia did not make a secret of it) to tell him the name of his tailor.

And from that day forth he never left his side. If Carlos appeared at the theatre Damaso immediately sprang from his seat, even if it was in the middle of some lovely aria, and, treading on gentlemen's toes, crushing ladies' dresses, he would suddenly rush away and come and install himself in the box at Carlos's side, with his cheeks aflame, a camellia in his lapel and displaying his cuff-links shaped like two enormous balls. Once or twice when Carlos had casually entered the Grémio, Damaso had immediately stopped playing, indifferent to the indignation of his partners, in order to come and attach himself to Maia's side and offer him maraschino and cigars and to follow him from salon to salon like a dog. On one such occasion when Carlos had uttered some trivial joke, there was Damaso bursting into guffaws of laughter, rolling around on the sofas, his hands on his ribs, shouting that his sides were splitting! Members gathered round; suffocated with laughter, Damaso repeated the joke – and Carlos fled in vexation. He had begun to hate Damaso; answered him in monosyllables; made dangerous turns in his dog-cart if he caught sight of that plump cheek, that roly-poly thigh in the distance. In vain: Damaso Candido de Salcêde had laid hold on him and was not going to let him go.

Then, one day, Taveira appeared at Ramalhete with an extraordinary tale. The previous evening in the Grémio (he had the story at second-hand, for he himself had not been present) a fellow called Gomes was among a group that had been talking about the Maias, and he had raised his voice to exclaim that Carlos was an ass! Damaso, who was near by, absorbed in a magazine, rose, very pale, and declared that as he had the honour of being a friend of Senhor Carlos da Maia, he would smash in Senhor Gomes' face with his stick if he dared to insult that gentleman again. And Senhor Gomes had swallowed the affront with his eyes on the floor, for he was a born weed – and also because he was a tenant of Damaso's and very much behind with the rent. Afonso da Maia thought this a brilliant feat – and it was on his account that Carlos had brought Senhor Salcêde to dine one evening at Ramalhete.

That day was as glorious for Damaso as though it had been woven of blue and gold. But better still was the morning when Carlos, who was somewhat indisposed and still in bed, had received him in his bedroom as though he were an intimate. Their familiarity had dated from that occasion and now Damaso began to address him less formally too. Then, that week, he revealed useful talents. As Vilaça was away in the Alentejo, he went to clear a box of clothes through the customs for Carlos. He called at a moment when Carlos was copying out an article for the *Gazeta Médica* and he offered his own splendid handwriting, a prodigious script of lithographic loveliness; and from that instant he was to spend hours at Carlos's table, flushed and concentrated, with the tip of his tongue sticking out, his eye very round, copying notes, extracts from reviews and material for the book. Such devotion merited the most familiar form of address, and Carlos permitted it.

Meanwhile Damaso was meticulously imitating Maia in everything, from the beard he had just started to grow to the style of his shoes. He began collecting. His coupé was always full of antique rubbish, old iron-work, bits of tile, the broken handle of a teapot. And if he met an acquaintance he would stop, open the window and exhibit his treasure —

'What d'you think? Very *chic*! I'm going to show it to Maia. Look at this, eh? Pure Middle Ages, the reign of Louis XIV. Carlos will be green with envy!'

All the same, Damaso passed some dreary hours in this bed of roses. It was not amusing to be present in silence, in the depths of an armchair, during the endless discussions that went on between Carlos and Craft on the subjects of art and science. And, as he confessed later, he had been somewhat overwhelmed when they took him to the laboratory in order to perform electrical experiments on his body. 'They were like two devils clutching on to me,' he said to the Countess de Gouvarinho, 'me, who can't stand spiritualism!'

But all this was royally compensated when at night, on a sofa in the Grémio, or at tea in the house of friends, he could say as he ran his fingers through his hair:

'Today I spent a divine day with Maia. We fenced a bit, looked over some antiques and talked. A *chic* day! Tomorrow I'm to spend the morning working with Maia — we're choosing bedspreads.'

And it was that very Sunday they were supposed to buy bedspreads at Lumiar. Carlos had conceived the idea of a dressing-room all decorated in antique satin bedspreads, embroidered in two special tones of pearl and gold. Uncle Abrahão was looking out for them all over Lisbon and its suburbs; and that morning he had come to announce to Carlos the existence of two such gems, so beautiful, oh! so lovely! in the house of some ladies called Medeiros who would expect Senhor Maia at two o'clock.

Damaso had already coughed three times and looked at the clock, but as he saw Carlos comfortably absorbed in the *Revista* he too fell back into his fashionable indolence and continued investigating *Figaro*. At last the Louis XV clock inside chimed out two o'clock in silvery tones.

'That's a good one!' cried Damaso at the same instant, slapping his thigh. 'Look who's here! Suzanne! My Suzanne!'

Carlos did not lift his eyes from the page.

'Oh, Carlos,' he continued. 'Please! Listen! Listen, this is a good one. This Suzanne is a girl I knew in Paris — a romance! She fell in love with me and wanted to poison herself. Well, it says here in *Figaro* that she's made her début at the Folies Bergères. They write about her – isn't that amazing? And she was a stylish little thing. And *Figaro* says she's had adventures, so naturally they must know about me – everybody in Paris knew. Fancy Suzanne! She had pretty legs. And it was difficult to get rid of her!'

'Women!' muttered Carlos, taking refuge in the depths of his magazine.

Damaso was interminable, torrential, inundating when he started to talk about 'his conquests', in the solid satisfaction he felt that all women, poor dears, were irresistibly fascinated by his person and by his toilette. And, as a matter of fact, in Lisbon this was true. As he was rich, esteemed in Society, and had a coupé and pair, all the girls had soft looks for him. And in the *demi-monde* he had, as he put it, 'real prestige'. He had been celebrated in the capital since boyhood for the Spanish women he kept; he had even given one a hired carriage; and this exceptional generosity had rapidly made him the King Dom João V of the bawdy-houses. Another cause for fame had been his liaison with the Viscountess da Gafanha, whose carcass was as lank as a greyhound's, painted, plastered, worn out by all the virile men in the kingdom; and who was nearly fifty when Damaso's turn came! And although it was not what one might call a delight to hold that creaking and lascivious skeleton in one's arms, it was said that in her youth she had slept in a royal bed and that august moustaches had tickled her – such *cachet* fascinated Damaso. He attached himself to her skirts with such a spaniel's fidelity that the decrepit creature, soon fed-up and annoyed, had to shake him off with force and insults. After that he had savoured the delight of tragedy; an actress at the Principe Real theatre, a mountain of flesh, became infatuated with him and on a night of jealousy and gin swallowed some phosphorous; she recovered within a few hours, of course, having vomited abominably over Damaso's waistcoat as he wept at her bedside. After that this great lover considered himself irresistible! As he pointed out to Carlos, after suffering so much tragedy in his life he now literally almost trembled to look at a woman.

'There were such scenes with Suzanne!' he murmured after a lull during which he had been picking skin off his lips.

With a sigh he went back to *Figaro*. Again there was silence on the terrace. Inside the chess game continued. Outside, beyond the shade of the awning, the sun was now becoming hot, striking the stone and the vases of white pottery, in a pale golden reflection where the wings of the first butterflies fluttered as they hovered about the carnation plants not yet in bloom. Below, the garden was green and still, without a branch moving, refreshed by the song from the water spout, by the liquid brightness of the water in the pond, livened up here and there by the red or yellow of the roses, by the pink of the last camellias. The patch of river which could be seen between the buildings was deep blue like the sky; and between the river and the sky the hill raised a great bar of dark green, nearly black in the resplendence of day, with the two windmills on the top, the two little houses glowing white down below, so luminous and plangent they seemed alive. A sleepy Sunday peace reigned over the district; and very high, through the air, there rang out the clear peal of a bell.

'The Duke of Norfolk has just arrived in Paris,' said Damaso in a meaning tone as he crossed his legs. 'The Duke of Norfolk is *chic*, don't you think, Carlos?'

Without raising his eyes Carlos flung a gesture towards the sky intended to convey the ultimate in *chic*!

Damaso dropped *Figaro* in order to place a cigar in his holder; then he undid the last buttons on his waistcoat, gave a tug at his shirt in order the better to display the monogram there – an enormous 'S' under a count's coronet; and with his eyelids closed, his lower lip protruding, he gravely sucked on his cigar-holder.

'You look very splendid today, Damaso,' said Carlos to him as he too dropped his newspaper and regarded his companion with melancholy.

Salcêde blushed with pleasure. His gaze slid to the patent-leather of his shoes, to his flesh-coloured socks and then he returned his bulging blue orbs to Carlos.

'I'm very well – but very *blasé*.'

And it was indeed with a *blasé* air about him that he rose and went to the garden at the side to fetch the *Gazeta Ilustrada* from a table on which there lay newspapers and cigars, 'in order to see what was going on in the kingdom'. Scarcely had he glanced at it when a cry escaped him.

'Someone else?' asked Carlos.

'No! It's that beast, Castro Gomes!'

The *Gazeta Ilustrada* announced that 'Senhor Castro Gomes, the Brazilian gentleman who was a victim of his dedication on the occasion of an accident in the Praça Nova, Oporto (of which our correspondent J.T. has given us such a full and vivid account), is now recovered and is expected today at the Hotel Central. Our congratulations to that fearless gentleman!'

'So, His Excellency has recovered, has he?' snarled Damaso, throwing the paper aside. 'Well, well! Now's the time for me to tell him to his face what I think of him, the swine!'

'You exaggerate,' murmured Carlos, who had taken brisk possession of the paper and was re-reading the report.

'Come now!' exclaimed Damaso, riding. 'Come now! I would like to see what would have happened had you been involved. He's a brute, a savage!'

And once again he repeated to Carlos the story that pained him so. Since Damaso's arrival from Bordeaux, as soon as Castro Gomes had installed himself in the Hotel Central, he had twice left cards – the last time on the morning following Ega's dinner. Well, now, the presumptuous fellow had not even deigned to acknowledge the visit! Then they had left for Oporto; and there, walking alone in the Praça Nova, Castro Gomes had seen two horses drawing a chaise breaking their harness, and two ladies screaming. He had grasped the horses by the bit, been thrust against the railings and dislocated an arm. He had been obliged to remain in Oporto at the hotel for five weeks. And Damaso (ever with an eye on his wife) had immediately dispatched two telegrams: one of sentiment lamenting the event; another of inquiry asking for news. Neither to the one nor the other had the beast replied.

'It's the limit!' exclaimed Salcêde, pacing round the terrace and recalling these insults. 'I'll show him! I'm not quite sure how yet. But I'll make him pay dearly for it. When it comes to snubs, I'll take them from nobody – nobody!'

His eyes bulged menacingly. Since his feat in the Grémio when the frightened weed had been struck dumb in front of him, Damaso had turned ferocious. On the slightest pretext now he would talk of 'smashing in faces'.

'Nobody!' he repeated tugging at his waistcoat. 'Snubs from nobody!'

At the moment the brisk voice of Ega was to be heard from

the study – and almost at once he appeared with a hurried, perturbed air.

'Hallo, Damaso, dear boy – Carlos, can I have a word with you outside?'

They descended the terrace, entered the garden and walked up to two Judas-trees in flower.

'Have you any money?' was Ega's immediate, anxious question.

And he related his terrible problem. He had a bill due the next day for ninety pounds. Besides that, he owed twenty-five pounds to Eusèbiozinho, and the latter had now demanded it in a rude letter; this was what had made Ega desperate.

'I want to pay that scoundrel, and when I see him I'll stick his letter on his face with spittle. And then, there's the bill! To pay all this, all I've got is a few *tostões*.'

'Eusèbiozinho is a man . . . Well, d'you want a hundred and fifteen pounds?' said Carlos.

Ega hesitated, flushing. Already he owed Carlos money. He was always making calls on their friendship, as though it were a bottomless treasure-chest.

'No, eighty will do. I'll pawn my watch and the pelisse. It's not cold now . . .

Carlos grinned and at once went up to his room to write a cheque while Ega carefully sought a dainty rosebud to decorate his coat. Carlos was not long away and when he returned he bore the cheque in his hand – he had made it out for one hundred and twenty pounds so that Ega could be 'armed'.

'God bless you, dear boy!' said Ega, putting the cheque in his pocket with a sigh of relief.

And there and then he commenced to thunder against that villain, Eusèbiozinho! But he had already planned his revenge. He would return the entire sum in copper, in a coal-sack with a dead rat inside, accompanied by a note that would start something like this: 'Scurvy worm, filthy reptile! I now throw in your snout, etc. etc.'

'I don't know how you can permit him to come here and use your furniture, breathe your air – that repulsive being!'

But it was indecent even to mention Eusèbiozinho! He wanted to know about Carlos's work, about his great book. He spoke too of his *Atom*. At last, in a different voice, and scrutinizing Carlos through his monocle:

'Tell me something else. Why haven't you been back to the Gouvarinhos'?'

Carlos had one reason only: he did not enjoy himself there.

Ega shrugged his shoulders. This seemed childish.

'You simply don't get the point!' he exclaimed. 'That woman is infatuated with you – it's enough to pronounce your name and the blood rushes to her face.'

And when Carlos laughed incredulously, Ega gave his word of honour in all earnestness. Only the previous evening Carlos's name had come up and he had watched her. He did not have to be a Balzac, or a water-diviner; his sight was perfect; and in her face, in her eyes, he had observed every sign of a sincere emotion.

'I'm not romancing, dear boy – she likes you, on my honour! You can have her whenever you feel like it.'

Carlos answered that he was entranced by that satanic naturalness with which Ega tempted him to break an infinity of religious, moral, social and domestic laws.

'Ah, well,' cried Ega, 'if you're going to prate of the catechism and the moral code, let's talk no more about it! If you've caught the itch of virtue, with scruples about any little thing, then it's my turn to say: "There was once a man . . . !" Go and join the Trappists and read Ecclesiastes!'

'No,' said Carlos sitting down on a bench under the trees, still feeling the laziness of the terrace. 'My motive is not so noble. The reason I don't go there is because I find Gouvarinho a bore.'

Ega smiled to himself.

'Ah! If one fled from women who have boring husbands . . .'

He sat down beside Carlos and began to draw silently on the sandy soil. Without raising his eyes, and letting the words fall sadly one by one, he said:

'The day before yesterday, all night, without stirring, from ten to one, I listened to the story of the lawsuit against the National Bank.'

It was almost a confession, an outburst against all those secret tediums that enveloped his artistic temperament in that world of Cohens. Carlos was moved to tenderness.

'My poor Ega! The whole lawsuit?'

'The whole thing! And a reading of the report of the General

Assembly. And I showed interest! And I had views to express!
. . . Life is hell.'

They went up to the terrace. Damaso had gained his bamboo
chair and was grooming his nails with a little mother-of-pearl
penknife.

'Is it decided?' he asked Ega at once.

'It was decided yesterday! There'll be no cotillion!'

They were referring to the great masked ball the Cohens were
going to give for Rachel's birthday. The idea of this function
had been suggested by Ega, and at first it had been planned on
the great scale of an artistic gala, a historical resurrection of a
festival of Dom Manuel's time. Then it became clear that such
a celebration was unrealizable in Lisbon, and the plans descended to a more sober level: a simply fancy-dress ball, but well
organized.

'Carlos, have you decided on your costume?'

'Domino – a severe black domino, as becomes a man of science!'

'Well!' cried Ega, 'if it's a question of science, go in a frock-
coat and cloth slippers! Science is practised in the house in
slippers. When did anyone discover universal laws inside a
domino? What a tasteless thing, a domino!'

In fact the very thing that Senhora Dona Rachel wanted to
prevent at her ball was an endless series of dominoes. And for
Carlos there was no excuse. He was not tied by a question of a
mere twenty or thirty pounds. With his splendid Renaissance
appearance it was his duty to grace the room as a superb Francis
I at least.

'This,' Ega added with fire, 'is the beauty of a masked ball!
Don't you agree, Damaso? Everyone should exploit his particular type of looks – for instance Madame Gouvarinho will be
just right. She had an inspiration: with that red hair, short nose,
and high cheekbones, she's a perfect Margaret of Navarre – '

'What's this about Margaret of Navarre?' asked Afonso da
Maia, coming out on to the terrace with Craft.

'Margaret, Duchess of Angoulême, the sister of Francis I, the
Margaret of Margarets, the pearl of Valois, the patron of the
Renaissance, the Countess de Gouvarinho . . .'

He laughed a great deal and went up to embrace Afonso and
explain that they were talking about the Cohens' ball. He immediately demanded Afonso's opinion, and Craft's too, about

176

Carlos's abominable domino. Wasn't this great fellow, with his airs of a knight-at-arms, made especially for a superb Francis I, in all the glory of Marignan?

The old man threw a tender look at his grandson.

'I'll tell you, John, perhaps you're right, but Francis I, King of France, cannot get out of a cab and come into a drawing-room alone. He needs a count, heralds, nobleman, ladies, jesters, poets – all that presents difficulties!'

Ega bowed. Yes, indeed! He agreed! There, now, was an intelligent way of understanding the Cohens' ball!

'And you, how are you going?' asked Afonso.

It was a secret. He had the theory that on such occasions surprise was one of the delights – for example two fellows dine together in evening dress at the Bragança, and then they meet later, one in the imperial purple of Charles V, the other with the gun of a Calabrian bandit.

'As for me, I'm making no secret of it,' said Damaso noisily. 'I'm going as a savage!'

'Naked?'

'No. As Nelusko in *L'Africaine*. Senhor Afonso da Maia, what d'you think? D'you think it'll be *chic*?'

'Perhaps *chic* is not quite the expression,' said Afonso, smiling, 'but impressive, certainly.'

Then everybody wanted to know Craft's plans. Craft was not going as anything at all; Craft would be staying at Olivais in his dressing-gown.

Ega shrugged his shoulders, weary and almost vexed. Such indifference to the Cohens' ball wounded him like a personal affront. He was devoting much of his time to this function – studies in the library, an exhausting exercise of the imagination – and it was gradually taking on in his eyes the importance of an artistic festival that would demonstrate the genius of a city. The 'dominoes', the abstentions, all these seemed to him testimony to an inferiority of spirit. He then cited the example of Gouvarinho: there was a busy man for you, with a public position, a man about to become a minister, who was not only going to the ball, but had thought about his costume. He had studied it and he had made a very good choice – he was going as the Marquis of Pombal!

'An advertisement for his forthcoming ministry!' cried Carlos.

'Not necessary,' said Ega. 'He has all the qualifications for a minister: he's got a sonorous voice, he's read Maurice Block, he's in debt, and he's an ass!' But amid the general mirth, he felt suddenly repentant at having thus demolished a fellow who was supporting the Cohens' ball, and he added quickly: 'But he's a very good fellow, and doesn't give himself any airs at all. He's an angel, really.'

Afonso rebuked him, smiling and paternal:

'Now, John, you who respect nothing – '

'Irreverence is the condition for progress, Senhor Afonso da Maia. Anyone who's respectful falls. One begins by admiring Gouvarinho and then, unawares, one finds oneself revering the monarch, and when one least expects it one has descended to venerating the Almighty! One must be cautious . . .'

'Get away, John! Get away! You're anti-Christ himself.'

Ega was about to reply exuberantly and in good vein, but the silvery bell of the Louis XV clock indoors silenced him with its gentle minuet.

'What, four o'clock?'

He was horrified, looked at his own watch, shook hands rapidly and silently all round and disappeared like the breeze.

The others too were astonished at the lateness of the hour. It was too late now to go to Lumiar to see the antique bed-spreads of the Medeiros ladies.

'Would you like half an hour with the foil, Craft?' asked Carlos.

'That's an idea. And Damaso must have his lesson.'

'That's true, the lesson . . .' muttered Damaso, without enthusiasm and trying to smile.

The fencing-hall was a room on the ground floor under Carlos's quarters. It had barred windows on to the garden through which a greenish light shone from the trees. On misty days the four gas lights had to be lit. Damaso followed the other two with the slowness of a suspicious ox.

Those lessons that he had urged because of his love of *chic* had now become odious to him. And that afternoon, as always, scarcely had he padded himself with the leather breast-plate and covered his face with the wire mask, than he began to sweat and turn pale. Craft, facing him, with his foil in his hand, seemed cruel and bestial, with those shoulders of his like a serene

178

Hercules, and his clear, cold look. The two steels scraped. Damaso trembled all over.

'Stand firm,' shouted Carlos to him.

The wretched fellow balanced himself on his plump leg; Craft's foil vibrated, scintillated and flew above him; Damaso drew back, suffocated, wobbling and his arm flabby.

'Stand firm,' Carlos called again.

Damaso, exhausted, lowered his weapon.

'Well, what d'you expect? It's nerves! It's because it's just play – if it were the real thing, you'd see!'

The lesson always ended this way; and afterwards he would crouch, cowed, on a leather stool, fanning himself with a handkerchief, as white as the whitewashed walls.

'I'll be getting home,' he said a little while later, tired now of so much clanging metal. 'Is there anything you'd like, Carlinhos?'

'I want you to come here to dinner tomorrow. The Marquis will be here.'

'How *chic*! I shall certainly come!'

But he did not come. And as all that week he did not appear at Ramalhete, Carlos became sincerely disquieted thinking him dying, and went one morning to his house at Lapa. But the servant – a sad, uncouth Galician whom Damaso had insisted on squeezing into a tailcoat and mortally crippling in patent-leather shoes ever since his acquaintance with the Maias – declared that Senhor Damaso was in good health and had in fact gone out on horseback. So Carlos went to see Uncle Abrahão. Uncle Abrahão also had not for some days seen the good Senhor Salcêde, that beautiful gentleman! Carlos's curiosity took him to the Grémio – there none of the servants had seen Senhor Salcêde lately. 'He must be enjoying a honeymoon somewhere with some Andalusian beauty', thought Carlos.

He had reached the end of the Rua do Alecrim when he saw Count Steinbroken walking towards the Aterro followed by his victoria. It was the second time the diplomat had taken exercise since his wretched attack of colic. But there were no longer any traces of his illness; he was all rosy and fair, very solid in his frock-coat and wearing a lovely tea-rose in his buttonhole. He even declared to Carlos that he was 'strrronger'. Nor did he regret his sufferings, for they had provided him an opportunity

179

to appreciate the number of friends he had in Lisbon. He was very moved. Above all, the concern of His Majesty, the august concern of His Majesty, had done him more good than 'all the drugs in a chemist's shop'. Really, never had relations between those two close allies, Portugal and Finland, been 'more firm, so to speak, more intimate', than during his intestinal disorders.

Then, taking Carlos's arm, he alluded with emotion to the offer of Afonso da Maia who had put Santa Olávia at his disposition for a convalescence in the strong, clean Douro air. Oh, how that invitation touched him *au plus profond de son coeur*! But unfortunately Santa Olávia was far, so far! He would have to content himself with Cintra, from where he could come once or twice each week to keep an eye on the Legation. *C'était ennuyeux mais* – Europe was going through one of those times of crisis when statesmen and diplomats could not withdraw to enjoy even the smallest repose. Their presence was essential, on the spot, observing, reporting.

'*C'est très grave*,' he murmured and paused with a vague fear in his blue eyes – *c'est excessivement grave!*'

He asked Carlos to look around him at Europe. Everywhere there was confusion and disorder. There was the Eastern question; there was socialism; and then there was the Pope on top of it, who complicated everything. '*Oh, très grave!* Take France for example – there was Gambetta. Oh, of course, one cannot deny that he's strong – he's remarkably strong – but . . . *Voilà c'est très grave.*'

Then there were the radicals, '*les nouvelles couches*' – it was all excessively grave.

'And I'll tell you something else, just between ourselves!'

But now Carlos neither smiled nor listened to him. A lady was approaching quickly from the end of the Aterro. He recognized her at once by that walk of hers that had seemed like a goddess's walking on earth, by the little silvery bitch that trotted beside her skirts, by that marvellous form vibrating with a warm, flowing, nervous grace under those rich lines of old marble. She wore a dark costume, a very simple dress of serge that was like a natural complement to her person; it was very well-fitting and its correct formality gave her a chaste, strong air. In her hand she carried an English umbrella as tight and slender as a cane. And as she thus approached along that dismal pier of the old city in the clear light of the afternoon, her entire person had an air of foreign distinction, the expensive refinement of superior civilizations. That day no veil hid her face. But Carlos could not distinguish her features; all he could perceive amid the marble splendour of her flesh was the profound blackness of two eyes that fixed themselves on his. Insensibly he took a step after her. Steinbroken at his side had seen nothing and was now finding Bismarck terrifying. As she moved away she seemed to him taller and more beautiful; and that false, literary image of a goddess treading the earth gripped his imagination. Steinbroken had been aghast at the Chancellor's speech in the *Reichstag*. Yes, she was certainly a goddess. Her hair in a rolled braid under her hat looked brown, almost blonde in the light; the little dog trotted by her side with its ears erect –

'Of course,' said Carlos, 'Bismarck is disquieting.'

However, Steinbroken had now abandoned Bismarck. Steinbroken was now attacking Lord Beaconsfield.

'*Il est très fort . . . Oui, je vous l'accorde, il est excessivement fort – mais, voilà – où va-t-il?*'

Carlos looked towards the Cais de Sodré. But everywhere seemed deserted. Steinbroken had said just that, before his illness, to the Minister of Foreign Affairs – Lord Beaconsfield was very strong, but where was he going? What did he want? And His Excellency had shrugged his shoulders, His Excellency did not know . . .

'Yes, indeed! Beaconsfield is very strong – have you read his speech before the Lord Mayor? Startling, my dear fellow, startling! But – *voilà*, where is he going?'

'You know, Steinbroken, I do not think it very prudent for you to stand here and catch a chill on the Aterro – '

'Indeed?' exclaimed the diplomat, passing his hand rapidly over his stomach and his abdomen. He would not delay another minute! As Carlos was going home too, he offered him a seat in his victoria to Ramalhete.

'Then come and dine with us, Steinbroken!'

'*Charmé , mon cher, charmé . . .*'

The victoria set off. And the diplomat wrapped his legs and his stomach in a great Scottish plaid and said:

'Well, Maia, we had a delightful outing – but one cannot really call the Aterro an entertaining place!'

So, the Aterro was not entertaining! On that afternoon Carlos had found it to be the most delicious place on earth!

He returned earlier the next day; and he had scarcely taken a few paces among the trees than he at once caught sight of her. But she was not alone; at her side her husband, dapper, elegant, wearing an off-white cashmere jacket, a diamond horseshoe pin in his black satin tie, smoked indolently and languidly as he carried the little dog under his arm. He threw a surprised glance at Carlos as he passed – as though he had at last discovered a being of civilized mien in those barbaric surroundings, and he spoke a few words to his companion in a low voice.

Carlos's eyes again met hers, deep and serious; but she did not seem to him so beautiful now; she was wearing a different dress, less simple, in two colours, grey and cream, and on her hat, which was wide-brimmed in the English style, there was something red – a flower, perhaps, or a feather. That afternoon she was no goddess descending from the golden clouds that rolled by over the sea; she was simply a pretty foreign woman walking back to her hotel.

Three times more he returned to the Aterro but he failed to see her; and then he began to feel shame and humiliation at that romantic curiosity that had thus led him to sniff round the Aterro with the restlessness of a stray dog, from Santos Ramp to the Caís de Sodré, in wait for a pair of black eyes and blonde hair on a visit to Lisbon, which would be borne away any morning on a Royal Mail packet-boat.

To think that all that week he had left his work abandoned on the table! And that every afternoon he had tarried in front of the mirror before going out in order to study his tie! Oh, wretched, wretched nature.

At the end of that week Carlos was in his consulting-rooms making ready to leave and already putting on his gloves when his servant drew back the curtain and murmured excitedly:

'A lady!'

A very pallid little boy appeared with fair curls and dressed in black velvet – and behind him came a woman, all in black, wearing a veil as tight and thick as a mask.

'I'm afraid I've come late, Senhor Carlos da Maia,' she said, hesitating near the door. 'You were just leaving . . .'

Carlos recognized the Countess de Gouvarinho.

'Ah! Countess!'

Immediately he removed the pile of newspapers and brochures from the divan. She stared for a moment, indecisive, at that ample couch, soft enough for a seraglio; then she sat down lightly on the edge with the child beside her.

'I bring you a patient,' she said without removing her veil, and speaking as though from the depths of that black toilette that disguised her. 'I did not send for you to come, because as a matter of fact it's really nothing serious, and I had to pass by here in any case today. Besides, my little boy is very nervous; if he see the doctor coming in he thinks he's going to die. This way it's like paying a visit – you're not frightened, are you, Charlie?'

The child did not answer; he stood quietly by his Mama's side, delicate and frail under the angelic curls that fell to his shoulders, and devoured Carlos with big, sad eyes.

In tones that were almost tender Carlos asked:

'What's wrong with him?'

A few days ago some rough skin had appeared on his neck. And also there was something hard, like a swollen gland, behind his ear. This worried her. She was strong, of good stock that had produced athletes and men who had reached a great age. But there was hereditary anaemia in her husband's family, in all the Gouvarinhos. The Count himself, behind all that appearance of solidity, was a valetudinarian. She feared that the debilitating influence of Lisbon did not suit Charlie and had vague plans to send him to spend some time in the country at Formoselha in his grandmother's house.

Carlos drew his chair a little nearer and stretched out his arms to Charlie:

'Well now, come over here, my good little friend, and let us have a look. What lovely hair he has, Countess.'

She smiled. And Charlie, all serious and well-trained, with none of that fear of the doctor mentioned by his Mama, came at once, delicately unfastened his big collar, and stood between Carlos's knees, bending his neck that was smooth and white as a lily.

Carlos could find nothing but a small, fading pink mark; as for the lump, there was not a sign of it; and then a light flush rose to his cheeks, and quickly he sought the Countess's eyes as

183

if he had understood everything and wanted to see the confession of that sentiment that had brought her there on a childish pretext, enveloped in that black dress and those concealing veils.

But she continued to sit impassively on the edge of the divan with her hands crossed, attentive as though hanging on his words, with all a mother's vague terror.

Carlos buttoned up the little boy's collar and said:

'It's absolutely nothing, Countess.'

Nevertheless he put a doctor's usual questions about Charlie's regimen and constitution. The Countess complained in a heavy voice that the child's upbringing was not to her liking – she would have him stronger, more manly – but his father opposed what he called 'English aberrations' like cold water, open-air exercise and gymnastics.

'Cold water and gymnastics,' said Carlos with a smile, 'have a better reputation than they merit. Is he your only child, Countess?'

'Yes, and he's spoiled on account of it,' she said as she stroked the child's fair hair.

Carlos assured her that for all his nervous and delicate appearance Charlie should not give her cause for anxiety; nor need he be exiled to the airs of Formoselha. Then they sat in silence for a moment.

'You cannot imagine how you have set my mind at rest,' she said as she rose and adjusted her veil. 'And especially as it is such a pleasure to come and consult you – why, there's not the slightest atmosphere here of illness or medicines. This is really very beautifully arranged,' she added, glancing slowly around at the velvets of the surgery.

'That is precisely its defect,' explained Carlos, laughing. 'It inspires no respect at all for my learning. I'm considering altering everything – putting in a stuffed crocodile, owls, test-tubes, a skeleton, piles of folios!'

'The cell of Faust!'

'Precisely! The cell of Faust!'

'Mephistopheles would be missing,' she said gaily, with a shining look under her veil.

'No! It would be Marguerite I'd miss!'

The Countess shrugged her shoulders with a graceful movement, as though discreetly doubting. Then, with Charlie's hand in hers, she took a slow step towards the door, once again adjusting her veil.

'As you have shown such an interest in the rooms,' said Carlos, wanting to detain her, 'let me show you the rest.'

He drew the curtain. She approached and murmured a few words, approving the freshness of the cretonnes and the harmony of pale tones. Then the piano made her smile.

'Do your patients dance quadrilles?'

'My patients, Countess,' replied Carlos, 'are not sufficiently numerous to form a quadrille. It is rare indeed for me even to have two for a waltz . . . The piano is merely there to provoke happy thoughts. It is a sort of tacit promise of health, of future soirées, of lovely arias from *Il Trovatore* in family gatherings . . .'

'How clever,' she said, taking a few steps familiarly through the room with Charlie glued to her skirts.

Carlos walked by her side.

'You have no idea how clever I am, Countess!'

'You said that the other day – how did you put it? Ah yes: that you are very inventive when you hate.'

'Much more so when I love,' he laughed.

But she did not answer; she stopped beside the piano, fingered the scattered music sheets for a moment and struck two notes on the keyboard.

'It's like a cattle-bell!'

'Oh, Countess!'

She continued her examination and scrutinized an oil-painting copied from Landseer – the head of a St Bernard dog, massive and benevolent, asleep on its paws. As he practically brushed against her dress, Carlos could smell the fine verbena scent she always used to excess; and in contrast to her dark clothes, her skin seemed lighter, sweeter to the eye, and as alluring as satin.

'This is a horror,' she murmured as she turned round, 'but Ega tells me there are lovely pictures at Ramalhete. He particularly mentioned a Greuze and a Rubens. It's a pity I cannot see these marvels.'

Carlos also lamented that a bachelor life prevented him and his grandfather from receiving ladies. Ramalhete was assuming the doleful air of a monastery. If it continued for very much longer without the warmth of a dress, the fragrance of a woman there, grass would begin to grow on the carpets.

'That's the reason,' he added very gravely, 'that I'm going to insist that Grandfather remarry.'

The Countess laughed and her pretty little teeth brightened the dark of her veil.

'I like your light-heartedness!' she said.

'It's a matter of regimen. Are you not light-hearted, Countess?'

She shrugged her shoulders; she did not know. Then, as she tapped with the point of her parasol on her patent-leather shoe shining against the pale carpet, she murmured with lowered eyes, letting the words flow in tones of intimacy and confidence:

'They say not. They say I'm sad, that I'm melancholy . . .'

Carlos's look followed hers and rested on her shoe, delicately fitted over a fine, long foot. Charlie was entertaining himself by touching the piano keyboard – and he lowered his voice to say to her:

'It's because you follow a bad regimen, Countess. You must have treatment; come back here; come and consult me. I may, perhaps, have a great deal to say to you! – '

She raised her eyes to his, and a look of tenderness and triumph escaped from them as she interrupted him quickly –

'You could, instead, come to me and say it! Why not come and take tea with me, one of these days at five o'clock . . . Charlie!'

The child came at once and clung to her arm.

Carlos accompanied her down the street, lamenting the ugliness of his stone staircase.

'But I shall order it all to be carpeted by the time you return to honour me by requesting a consultation.'

She replied, merry and smiling:

'Ah, no! You have promised us all health – and naturally you don't expect me to be the one to come here and take tea with you.'

'Ah, Countess, when I start building hopes, there are no limits at all to my expectations . . .'

She stopped, the child's hand in hers, and looked at him as though astonished and delighted at such grandiose self-assurance.

'So you take things that far?'

'I take things that far, Countess!'

They were on the last step, facing the light and noise of the street.

'Call a coupé for me!'

At Carlos's signal a driver immediately drew up his cab.

'And now,' she said with a smile, 'ask it to go to the Graça church.'

'Are you going to make the Stations of the Cross, Countess?'

She coloured a little and murmured:

'I'm making my devotions . . .'

Then she sprang lightly into the coupé, leaving Charlie to be picked up in Carlos's arms and placed paternally at her side.

'May God be with you and watch over you, Countess!'

She thanked him with a look and a movement of her head – both as sweet as caresses.

Carlos went back up the steps. Without removing his hat, he stayed and rolled a cigarette as he paced round that room that was usually so bare and deserted and where there was now some of the warmth and fragrance she had left behind her.

Really, that audacity of hers charmed him – just imagine coming to the consulting-rooms like that, all disguised, practically masked, in a fashionable black dress and inventing a lump in Charlie's healthy little neck, just so that she could see him, so that she might tie a sudden and closer knot in that frail thread of acquaintance that he had so negligently let fall and break.

For once Ega had not been romanticizing; that lovely body offered itself as surely as though it had disrobed. Ah! If only she had flighty and easy sentiments – what a fine bloom to gather, savour and afterwards cast aside! But no! If Baptista was right, the Countess had never indulged in light diversions. And he did not want to find himself involved in a jealous passion, one of those stormy attachments, an affair with a woman of thirty, from which it was afterwards difficult to extricate oneself. His heart would remain mute in her arms – and as soon as his first curiosity was satisfied, the tedium of kisses that were not desired would set in, the unspeakable boredom of cold pleasure. Moreover, he would be compelled to become an intimate of the house, receive the Count's pats on his shoulder, listen to that morose voice distilling doctrine . . . All this horrified him – and yet, he had liked her audacity! There was a touch of romanticism there that was quite unusual and piquant, and she must be deliciously well-formed. His imagination undressed her, and became involved in the satin of those curves that concealed something that was at

187

once mature and virginal. And again, just as on those first nights at the São Carlos, those curls, so red, so crisp, so hot, began to tempt him.

He went out. And scarcely had he taken a few steps up the street when he caught sight of Damaso in a coupé, going at a great trot, with his face at the window, red and radiant, calling to him, telling the driver to stop.

'I haven't been able to come to see you,' he cried, taking possession of Carlos's hand and squeezing it with enthusiasm the moment he came up. 'I've been in a great commotion. But I'll tell you about it later. A divine romance. I'll tell you all about it! Careful with the wheel! Off we go, Calção!'

The coupé drove off; he was still leaning out of the window, waving his hand and shouting through the noisty street:

'A divine romance – really *chic*!'

A few days later, in the billiards-room at Ramalhete, Craft, who had just beaten the Marquis, put down his cue, lit a pipe and inquired: 'Any news of our Damaso? Has that regrettable disappearance been explained yet?'

Carlos told them how he had encountered him, rosy and triumphant, throwing the news to him of a 'divine romance' out the window of the coupé, in the middle of the Rua Nova do Almada.'

'I know about it,' said Taveira.

'How d'you know?' exclaimed Carlos.

Taveira had seen him the night before in a great hired landau in the company of a splendid, very elegant woman, who looked like a foreigner.

'Good God!' cried Carlos. 'With a little Scottish bitch?'

'Exactly, a Scottish bitch – a silvery one! Who are they?'

'And a thin young man, with a very black beard and an Anglicized air?'

'That's it – exactly, a sporting air. Who are they?'

'Brazilians, I think.'

They were certainly the Castro Gomeses! This seemed extraordinary. Only two weeks had passed since Damaso had inveighed on the terrace, with fists clenched, against Castro Gomes and his 'snubs'! Carlos was about to ask Taveira for more details, but the Marquis's voice came from the depths of the armchair in which he was stretched out, wanting to know Carlos's opinion on the great news in that day's *Gazeta Ilustrada*. In the *Gazeta Ilustrada*? Carlos didn't know; that morning he had not seen any newspapers.

'Then don't tell him,' cried the Marquis. 'Let's give him a surprise! Where's the *Gazeta*? Find the *Gazeta*!'

Taveira tugged the bell-pull; and when the footman brought the paper he took possession of it, and made ready to deliver a solemn reading.

'Let him see the picture first,' shouted the Marquis, getting up.

'No! Find the article!' cried Taveira, hiding the paper behind his back.

But he gave in and held the paper opened wide like an unfolded handkerchief before Carlos's eyes. Carlos recognized Cohen's photograph at once – and the prose spread out around it, framing the dark face with its black side-whiskers, was a work of six columns, in a curlicued, lyrical style, praising to the skies Cohen's domestic virtues, Cohen's financial genius, Cohen's witty sayings, the furniture in Cohen's drawing-rooms. There was even a paragraph that referred to the approaching party, the Cohens' great masked ball! And all this was signed J. da E. – the initials of João da Ega!

'What nonsense!' Carlos exclaimed wearily, throwing the paper on top of the billiard-table.

'Worse than nonsense,' observed Craft, 'it's an absence of moral sense!'

The Marquis remonstrated. He liked the article. He thought it was brilliant and malicious – and anyway who cared about moral sense in Lisbon?

'You don't know Lisbon, Craft! Everybody thinks this sort of thing quite natural. He's an intimate of the house and sings the praises of its owners. He's the wife's admirer and so he flatters the husband. This is in the logic of the country. You'll see what a success this article will be. And as for its elegance, there's no doubt of that!'

He picked up the paper from the billiard-table and read an extract aloud. It was about the pink boudoir of Madame Cohen ' – where there is a breath of something perfumed, intimate and chaste, as though all that rose colour exhaled the fragrance of the rose itself'!

'Hang it!' exclaimed the Marquis. 'This is beautiful by any standards. He's very talented, that devil! What wouldn't I give to be as talented as he!'

'None of that,' insisted Craft, smoking quietly, 'prevents it from displaying an extraordinary lack of moral sense.'

'It's insanity, pure and simple,' declared Cruges, uncoiling himself from the corner of the sofa in order to drop the syllables of this weighty opinion.

The Marquis took him up.

'What d'you understand of such things, maestro? This article is sublime! And d'you want to know another thing – it's crafty too!'

The maestro felt too lazy to argue and went to coil himself up again in silence at the other end of the sofa.

Then, standing up and waving his arms, the Marquis appealed to Carlos, and demanded to know what principles Craft understood by 'moral sense'.

Carlos, who was impatiently pacing the room, did not answer. He took Taveira's arm and led him out into the corridor.

'Tell me something – where did you see Damaso with those people? Which way were they going?'

'They were going down the Chiado – the day before yesterday at two o'clock. I'm convinced they were off to Cintra. They were carrying a small trunk in the landau, and a maid followed behind in a coupé with a larger trunk. It all looked very much like a trip to Cintra. And the woman's divine! What a toilette, what an air, what *chic*! She's a Venus, my boy! How did he get to know her?'

'In Bordeaux, or on the boat – I don't know!'

'What I liked were the airs he gave himself as he went down the Chiado! He nodded to the right, nodded to the left, bowed to the woman, speaking to her in a very low voice and with a tender eye, boasting, showing off his conquest.'

'What a swine!' cried Carlos, tapping the carpet with his foot.

'You may well call him a swine!' said Taveira. 'A civilized and decent-looking woman arrives by chance in Lisbon, and it's he that becomes acquainted with her, it's he that accompanies her to Cintra! You may well call him a swine . . . Come on, let's have a game of dominoes.'

Taveira had latterly introduced dominoes to Ramalhete, and

there were often fierce battles now, expecially when the Marquis appeared. For it was Taveira's passion to beat the Marquis.

But the Marquis was still waving his arms and inflicting his arguments on Craft, while the Englishman, with his pipe in his hand, replied in sleepy monosyllables from the depths of the armchair. They were still on the subject of Ega's article and a definition of 'moral sense'. The Marquis had already invoked God, Garibaldi and even his celebrated pointer, Finório. Now he was defining conscience: according to him it was nothing but fear of the police. Had friend Craft ever yet seen anyone suffering from remorse? Of course not! Only in the theatre, in melo-dramas!

'Believe me, Craft,' he concluded, giving in to Taveira, who was pulling him towards the table, 'this business of conscience is a matter of education. It is acquired in the same way as good manners: to suffer in silence for having betrayed a friend is learned exactly as one learns not to put one's fingers in one's nose. It's a question of training. But with most people it's simply fear of jail, or the stick. Ah! So you want to take an-other beating at dominoes like last Saturday? Delighted, I'm all yours.'

Carlos, who had been looking over Ega's article once again, came up to the table too. And they were all seated shuffling the pieces, when Count Steinbroken appeared at the door in evening-dress and decorations, his Grand Cross over his white waistcoat, as fair as wheat, all dapper and resplendent. He had dined at the palace and had come to Ramalhete to finish off his evening on an intimate note.

The Marquis, who had not seen him since his famous attack of colic, abandoned the dominoes and hastened up to embrace him noisily. Without letting him sit down, or extend his hand to the others, he at once beseeched him to sing one of his beautiful Finnish songs, just one, one of those that did so much good to his soul!

'Only the "Ballad", Steinbroken. I can't be too long, the game's here waiting. Only the "Ballad"! Go on, Cruges, go inside to the piano!'

The diplomat smiled, said he was tired, having already made delicious music at the palace with His Majesty. But he could never resist the Marquis's 'playful' air – and off they went to the music-room arm in arm, followed by Cruges, who took an eternity to unwind himself from the corner of the sofa. And a moment later, through the half-drawn curtains, the beautiful baritone voice of the diplomat projected through the rooms, amid the sighs of the piano, the swaying melancholy of the 'Ballad' with its lyrics that the Marquis adored, translated into French, that spoke of sad, northern mists, cold lakes and blonde fairies.

Meanwhile Taveira and Carlos had started a game of dominoes at a *tostão* a point. But Carlos could not rouse any interest that night, and he played distractedly, as he hummed sad bits of 'Ballad' under his breath. Then, when Taveira already had only one piece in front of him, and he was interminably buying the remainder, he turned to Craft and asked if the Hotel Lawrence in Cintra was open all the year round.

'Damaso's trip to Cintra has got under your skin,' grunted Taveira impatiently. 'Come on, play!'

Carlos slackly put down a piece without replying.

'Domino', shouted Taveira.

And triumphantly bounding up he himself counted the sixty-eight points that Carlos had lost.

Just then the Marquis came in and Taveira's victory made him indignant.

'Now, us!' he exclaimed vigorously drawing over a chair. 'Oh, Carlos, let me give this robber a thrashing. Then we'll play a threesome. How d'you want it, vile Taviera? Two *tostões* a point? Ah, just a *tostão*! Very good. I'll teach you. Come on, surrender that double six right away, wretch . . .'

Carlos stayed for a moment watching the game, a burned-out cigarette in his fingers, and with the same distracted air. He seemed suddenly to come to a decision, crossed the corridor, and went into the music-room. Steinbroken had gone to the library to see Afonso da Maia and the game of whist. Cruges was alone, between the two candles on the piano, his eyes wandering over the ceiling while he improvised for himself melancholically.

'Tell me, Cruges,' asked Carlos, 'would you like to come with me to Cintra tomorrow?'

The keyboard fell silent and the maestro looked at him in astonishment, but Carlos did not even give him time to answer.

'Of course you would. It can do you nothing but good to come to Cintra. I'll be at the door tomorrow with the brake. Put an extra shirt in your bag, for we might spend the night there. Punctually at eight, eh? And don't say anything about it inside!'

Carlos returned to the room and stood watching the game of dominoes. Now everything was quiet. The Marquis and Taveira slowly and wordlessly moved the pieces with expressions of mute rancour. On the green baize of the billiard-table the white balls slept side by side under the light that fell from the porcelain lampshades. The sound of the piano, doleful and vague, could be heard now and again, and Craft, with his arm hanging down from the armchair, was dozing blissfully.

8

PUNCTUALLY AT EIGHT the following morning Carlos's brake pulled up in the Rua dos Flores in front of the well-known gate of Cruges's house. But the footman he sent upstairs to ring the third-floor bell returned with the curious news that Senhor Cruges no longer lived there. Then where the devil did Senhor Cruges live? The maid had said that Senhor Cruges now lived in Rua de S. Francisco, four doors beyond the Grémio. For a moment Carlos felt desperate and thought of setting off for Cintra alone. Then away he drove again for Rua de S. Francisco, cursing the maestro, who had moved house without letting him know, vague and imponderable as ever! He was like that in everything. Carlos knew nothing of his past, his character, his affections or his habits. The Marquis had brought him one night to Ramalhete and whispered in Carlos's ear that here was a genius. And there and then he had entranced them all with the modesty of his manners and his marvellous skill at the piano; and everybody at Ramalhete began to address Cruges as maestro, to speak of Cruges as a genius, and to say that even Chopin had never produced the equal of Cruges's 'Autumn Meditation'. And no more than that was known about him. It had been through Damaso that Carlos had known Cruges's house and learned that he lived there with his mother, a still youthful widowed lady who owned property in the town.

Carlos had to wait a quarter of an hour at the gate in Rua de S. Francisco. First a maid appeared furtively at the bottom of the stairs, with her head uncovered, to peep at the brake and the liveried servants and then flee up the steps. Then a manservant came in shirt-sleeves carrying his master's valise and a travelling-rug. At last the maestro descended at a run, nearly tripping, bearing a silk muffler in his hand, his umbrella under his arm, and clumsily buttoning up his coat.

As he bounded down the last steps a shrill female voice called from upstairs:

'See you don't forget the cheese-cakes!'

Cruges climbed quickly onto the box by Carlos's side growling that he had scarcely slept a wink with the worry of waking so early.

'But what the devil's the idea of moving house without letting anyone know, man?' exclaimed Carlos throwing a piece of the tartan rug that wrapped him round the maestro's knees, for Cruges seemed to be shivering.

'This house is ours too,' stated Cruges simply.

'Clearly that's as good a reason as any!' murmured Carlos, laughing and shrugging his shoulders.

They set off.

It was a very fresh and cloudless morning, all blue and white with a lovely sun that gave no warmth but shed gay patches of golden light on the street and the façades of the houses. Lisbon was gradually waking up: vegetable women were still going from door to door with their baskets of greens; the fronts of the shops were being slowly swept out; the note of a far-off church bell for mass died away in the soft air.

Cruges finished adjusting his muffler and buttoning his gloves, and cast a glance at the splendid pair of bays that shone like satin under the silver sparkle of their harness, at the servants with their nosegays on their liveries, at all that formal luxury swaying along rhythmically — and his own coat seemed like a blemish. But what impressed him most was the resplendent aspect of Carlos — his burning eye, his fine colour, his beautiful smile, a touch of something vibrant and luminous under his simple jacket with its small brown check, as he sat thus on that bourgeois cushion of the break — something that gave him the impetuous look of a happy warrior driving his war chariot. Cruges suspected an amorous adventure, and the question that had hovered on his lips since the previous night sprang out:

'Frankly, just between ourselves, what's the idea of going to Cintra?'

Carlos responded jokingly. Could the maestro swear to keep a secret, on the melodious heart of Mozart and the fugues of Bach? Well then, the idea was to go to Cintra, breathe the air of Cintra, pass the day at Cintra. But for heaven's sake this should not be revealed to anybody. And he added, laughing:

'Never mind, you won't regret it!'

No, Cruges did not regret it. He even thought the outing a delightful idea, for he always liked Cintra very much. However, he had no clear recollection of it – simply a vague notion of great rocks and springs of running water. And finally he confessed that he had not been to Cintra since he was nine years old.

What! Did the maestro not know Cintra? Well then, they must stay there, make all the classical pilgrimages, climb to Pena, go and drink water from the Fonte dos Amores and roam through the meadows by the river.

'What I'm looking forward to is Seteais and the fresh butter!'

'Yes, lots of butter,' said Carlos, 'and donkeys, lots of donkeys, a rustic ramble, in fact!'

The brake drove along the Benfica road. They passed the flowered walls of old manor-houses, great sad buildings with broken windowpanes, little taverns with a packet of cigarettes hanging from a string in the doorway – and the meanest tree, any bit of greensward with poppies on it, a fleeting glimpse of a green hill in the distance, all enchanted Cruges. How long it had been since he had seen the countryside!

Gradually the sun came up. The maestro shed his great scarf. Then, stifled with heat, he threw off his coat and declared that he was perishing with hunger.

Fortunately they were nearing Porcalhota.

He would most have liked to eat the famous braised rabbit of the place – but as it was early for that delicacy, he decided after much thought in favour of a consoling dish of scrambled eggs and sausage. That was something, now, that he had not tasted for years, and it would give him the feeling that he was really in the country! When the landlord, pompously and as though performing a favour, placed the enormous platter containing this dainty on the bare wood of the table, Cruges rubbed his hands and said it was all charmingly rustic.

'We ruin our health in Lisbon!' he declared as he dragged a mountain of egg and sausage on to his plate. 'Aren't you having anything?'

Carlos accepted a cup of coffee to keep him company.

Cruges proceeded to devour the food and a moment later exclaimed, with his mouth full:

'The Rhine must be magnificent too!'

Carlos looked at him in amazement and chuckled. What on earth had made him think of the Rhine? It was because the maestro had been filled with thoughts of travel and scenery from the moment they had left the town behind them; he would like to see great mountains where there was snow, and rivers famous in history. His dream was to visit Germany and journey with a knapsack on foot through that sacred land of his gods – Beethoven, Mozart, Wagner . . .

'Wouldn't you sooner go to Italy?' asked Carlos lighting a cigar.

The maestro gestured in disdain and uttered one of his sibylline judgments: 'Nothing there but country dances!'

Then Carlos spoke of his plans to go to Italy with Ega in the winter. For Ega, going to Italy was an act of intellectual hygiene: he needed to calm that stormy, nervous, peninsular imagination amid the placid majesty of marble.

'What he needs more than anything else is a thrashing!' growled Cruges.

And he returned to the theme of the previous evening and the famous article in the *Gazeta*. He repeated his view that it was pure and simple nonsense, and an indecorous piece of bootlicking. What troubled him most was that all that talent and scorching verve of Ega's should be so wasted.

'Everybody is wasted,' said Carlos, rousing himself. 'Take yourself, now. What do you do?'

After a pause Cruges growled and shrugged his shoulders: 'If I wrote a good opera who would peform it for me?'

'And if Ega were to write a fine book, who would read it?'

'This is an impossible country . . . I think I'll have a cup of coffee too,' the maestro said, ending the matter.

The horses had rested, Cruges paid the bill, and they left. Soon they came to the heath and it seemed interminable. On either side as far as the eye could see the ground was dark and sad; and above stretched an endless blue that seemed sad as well in that solitude. The steady trot of the horses beat monotonously on the road; no other sound could be heard. Occasionally a bird cut the air in brusque flight as it fled from that aggressive wilderness. Inside the brake one of the servants had fallen asleep; Cruges felt heavy from his egg and sausage and gazed vacantly and dolefully at the shiny rumps of the horses.

Meanwhile Carlos was reflecting on the motive that brought him to Cintra. He really did not quite know why he was going. But two weeks had passed since he had seen that form with a step like a goddess treading the earth, since he had met the deep black of two eyes that had fixed themselves on his. And now that he supposed her to be in Cintra, there he was hastening to Cintra. He hoped for nothing, he desired nothing. He did not even know if he would see her; perhaps she had already left. But he was on his way – and already it was delicious to dream of her like this all along the highway, and with that sweetness in his heart to penetrate under Cintra's lovely woods. And the possibility existed that in a little while, at the old Lawrence, he would suddenly pass her in a corridor, brush against her dress perhaps, maybe hear her voice. And should she be there, she would certainly dine in the dining-room, that dining-room he knew so well, that he looked forward to so much, with its cheap muslin curtains, artless bunches of flowers on the tables and great chandeliers of old brass. She would enter that room with her beautiful golden look like a blonde Diana; the good Damaso would present his friend Maia; and those black eyes that he had seen passing from afar like two stars would rest for longer on his; and very simply, in the English fashion, she would extend her hand to him . . .

'Well, here we are at last!' cried Cruges with a sigh of relief and breathing more freely.

They had reached Cintra's first houses, there was greenery now on the roadside, and the first strong, fresh breath from the mountain beat in their faces.

The brake drove into the woods of Ramalhão at a trot. The peace of those shadowy trees enveloped them gradually in a slow, all-embracing rustle of branches like the diffused and vague murmur of running waters. The walls were covered with ivy and moss and long sunbeams slanted through the foliage. Around them the air was subtle and velvety, redolent of new verdure; here and there among the darkest boughs there was the shrill piping of a bird; and that simple stretch of road, all dappled with patches of sunshine, already announcing the religious solemnity of thick forests, the distant freshness of living springs, the sadness falling from rocky peaks and the lordly repose of summer mansions. Cruges drank in deep voluptuous breaths.

'Where's the Lawrence? On the mountain?' he asked, suddenly thinking he would like to stay a month in that paradise.

'We're not going to the Lawrence,' said Carlos, brusquely

breaking his silence and urging on the horses. 'We're going to the Nunes; we'll be much better off there.'

It was an idea that had come to him suddenly, as soon as they had begun to pass the first houses in São Pedro, and the brake had entered roads where he might come upon her at any moment. He felt overcome with a shyness that was mingled with a trace of pride – the touchy fear of committing an indiscretion in thus following her to Cintra, even though she would not recognize him . . . going to install himself under the same roof . . . taking a place at the same table. And at the same time the idea of being presented to her by Damaso was repulsive to him. Already he could see him, plump-cheeked and dressed for the country, displaying 'his friend Maia' with a ceremonious gesture, addressing him intimately, affecting familiarity with her, gazing at her with a tender eye. It would be intolerable.

'We'll go to the Nunes. The food's better there.'

Cruges did not reply; he was speechless, carried away, imbibing religiously all that sombre wooded splendour, the high mountain peaks seen for an instant up there amid the clouds, the fragrance absorbed with delight, and the sweet whisper of water dropping down into the vales.

It was only when the palace came into sight that he opened his lips.

'Ah! Yes! It's got style!'

And it was what pleased him most – this massive, silent palace, without fleurons or towers, seated patriarchially among the houses of the town, with those lovely windows that give it a noble and royal look, with the valley at its feet, leafy, dense and fresh, and on high its two colossal chimneys, disparate, summing up everything as though that residence was all a kitchen built on a scale to suit the gluttony of a king who daily devours an entire kingdom.

And scarcely had the brake driven up to the Nunes than Cruges went to look timidly at the palace from a distance, as though in fear of a rough word from the sentry.

Carlos meanwhile sprang down from the box without delay and took the hotel servant who had come to collect their luggage to one side.

'Do you know Senhor Damaso Salcêde? Do you know if he's in Cintra?'

The servant knew Senhor Damaso Salcêde very well. Only yesterday morning he had seen him coming into the billiards-room opposite with a black-bearded gentleman. But he must be staying at the Lawrence because Senhor Damaso Salcêde only came to the Nunes when he was on outings with ladies.

'Quick, then! Two rooms!' cried Carlos with boyish glee, certain now that *she* was in Cintra. 'And a private dining-room just for us, for lunch!'

Cruges, who had joined them, protested against lunching alone. He preferred a round table. At a round table you usually met people –

'Very well,' exclaimed Carlos, laughing and rubbing his hands, 'serve lunch in the dining-room. You can even serve it in the square, if you like – and lots of fresh butter for Senhor Cruges!'

The coachman drove the brake away and the servant carried in the valises. Cruges in his enthusiasm for Cintra bounded up the stairs whistling – keeping his travelling-rug around his shoulders for he would not be separated from it as it had been lent to him by his Mama. No sooner had he reached the door of the dining-room than he stopped dead, raised his arms and cried:

'Oh, Eusèbiozinho!'

Carlos hurried up and stared too – it was indeed the widower, in the process of finishing his lunch, accompanied by two Spanish girls.

He sat, as though presiding, at the head of the table facing the remains of pudding and plates of fruit, looking yellowish and uncombed and still in his heavy mourning, the broad ribbon of his black eye-glasses behind his ear, and a wafer of black taffeta on his neck covering some burst pimple.

One of the *espanholas* was a big, swarthy woman with a pock-marked face; the other was a slender little thing with soft eyes and a feverish colour that her powder was unable to disguise. Both of them wore black satin and smoked cigarettes. In the light and freshness that shone in through the window, they looked even more ravaged and limper, clammy still from the warm sloth of the blankets, and exuding the must of bedrooms. There was another person in the party – a fat, short, neckless man with his back to the door and his head bent over his plate, sucking at half an orange.

For a moment Eusèbiozinho sat frozen with his fork in the air. Then up he got, napkin in hand, and came to shake his friends' fingers, all the while muttering an involved excuse that the doctors had ordered a change of air and that his companion had insisted on bringing the girls. Never had he looked so mean, as now grunting hypocritically and shrinking in Carlos's shadow.

'You were very wise, Eusèbiozinho,' said Carlos at last, patting him on the shoulder. 'Lisbon is a dreadful place, and love is sweet.'

But the other persisted in his excuses. And then the little thin *espanhola* who sat and smoked, with her chair pulled back from the table and one leg crossed over the other, butted in to ask Cruges whether he was going to speak to her or not. The maestro looked at her for a moment and then hastened forward with open arms to greet his friend Lola. And there, at the corner of the table, hearty handshakes followed, and a warm exchange of salutations in Spanish. Then Lola, assuming a portentous countenance, introduced the big woman – Señorita Concha. On seeing this the obese individual, who had hardly raised his head for an instant from the plate, became impressed with so much familiarity and decided to examine these friends of Eusèbio's more attentively. He crossed his knife and fork, wiped his mouth, his forehead and his neck with his napkin, laboriously placed a pair of large spectacles with thick lenses on his nose, raised a broad puffy face the colour of cider, and stared at Cruges, and then at Carlos, with calm insolence.

Eusèbiozinho presented his friend Palma; and his friend Palma, hearing the well-known name of Carlos da Maia, at once wished to demonstrate in the presence of a gentleman that he too was a gentleman. He threw aside his napkin, pulled back his chair, stood up, extended limp fingers with bitten nails to Carlos and, gesturing towards the remains of the dessert, cried:

'Won't you join us, senhor? No standing on ceremony! We come to Cintra to sharpen our appetites and do our bellies good!'

Carlos thanked him and was about to withdraw. But Cruges had become livelier now and was joking with Lola; and he too made his introductions from the other side of the table.

'Carlos, I would like to you to meet the lovely Lola, an old friend of mine. And this is Señorita Concha, whom I've just had the pleasure – '

Carlos greeted the ladies respectfully.

But Concha snorted a dry 'Buenos dias.' She seemed in a bad humour, heavy with eating, drowsy and taciturn, her elbows glued to the table, her heavily lashed eyelids drooping, smoking and picking her teeth. But Lola was amiable, put on a ladylike air and rose to reach out a sweaty little hand to Carlos. Then she picked up her cigarette once again, tugged at her gold bracelets and declared with a flutter of her eyelids that Carlos's name had long been known to her:

'No ha estado usted con Encarnación?'

Yes, Carlos had had the honour of Encarnación's company – and what had become of her, the beautiful Encarnación?

Lola smiled slyly and touched the maestro's elbow. She could not believe that Carlos was ignorant of what had become of Encarnación – at last she admitted that Encarnación was now with Saldanha.

'Not to be confused with the Duke of Saldanha!' exclaimed Palma, who was still on his feet, his tobacco pouch open on the table, and was rolling a big cigarette.

Lola replied drily that Saldanha might not be a duke, but he was a very decent fellow.

'Look,' said Palma slowly as he placed his cigarette in his mouth and took a flint from his pocket, 'I gave him two good smacks in the face not three weeks ago – ask Gaspar, Gaspar was there! It was in the Café Montanha – two smacks that made his hat fly into the middle of the street. Senhor Maia, you must surely know Saldanha – yes, you must know him, for he's got a little horse and buggy too!'

Carlos indicated silently that he did not; and once again he took his leave, bowing to the ladies. But Cruges called him back yet again, wanting to retain him a little longer while he satisfied his curiosity – he wanted to know which of the young ladies was friend Eusèbio's 'wife'.

Thus interrogated, the widower stiffened and, without raising his spectacles from the orange he was peeling, snorted in morose tones that he was there on an outing, that he had no wife and that both the young ladies were attached to friend Palma.

He was still chewing the last words when Concha, who had been sitting digesting her meal with her legs outstretched, suddenly straightened up as though about to spring, banged the edge of the table, and, with flaming eyes, challenged Eusèbio to repeat what he had just said. She wanted to hear him say that he was ashamed of her and of admitting that he had brought her to Cintra. Eusèbio was uneasy now, and tried to joke and to caress her. At this she lost her temper and, banging the table all the while, called him frightful names in a fury that distorted her mouth and caused two red patches to rise on her swarthy face. Lola was embarrassed and pulled at her arm, but her friend pushed her aside. She became more and more excited by the loudness of her own voice and she vomited out all her resentment, called him a pig and a skinflint, and generally wiped the floor with him.

Palma bent across the table in distress and cried anxiously: 'Oh, Concha, listen – Listen here! Concha, let me explain – '

Suddenly she got up, the chair fell to one side, and the big woman flounced out of the dining-room, her great satin train furiously lashing the floor, and a door could be heard slamming. A bit of lace mantilla lay on the floor.

The waiter, who had entered on the other side with the coffee-pot, paused and his inquisitive eye gleamed as he took in the scandal; then, quietly and drily, he served coffee to everyone.

For a moment there was a hush. The waiter had no sooner withdrawn, however, than an indignant Lola and Palma both attacked Eusèbiozinho in lowered voices. He had conducted himself atrociously! He had not behaved like a gentleman! Having brought the girl to Cintra he should respect her; he ought not to have thus disclaimed her, brutally, before everybody –

'You can't do that sort of thing!' declared Lola, standing up and gesticulating, her eyes sparkling as she turned towards Carlos. 'It was very nasty!'

Cruges smilingly regretted having been the involuntary cause of the disaster, and she lowered her voice to tell him what a fury Concha was, how she had come unwillingly to Cintra and how since morning she had been in a very bad mood – but Silveira had played her a very dirty trick.

The wretched man sat with his head sunk and his ears burning as he desolately stirred his coffee. His eyes were invisible behind the thick dark glasses, but a great sob could be heard rising in his throat. And then Palma put down his cup, licked his lips, stood up in the middle of the room with his face shiny, his waistcoat unbuttoned, and summed up the scene in precise tones:

'It all stems from one cause, begging your pardon, Silveira, for saying it – but you don't know how to deal with Spanish women.'

At these cruel words the widower succumbed. The spoon fell from his fingers. He rose, hastened towards Carlos and Cruges, as though to shelter beside them and seek comfort in the warmth of their friendship, and vented his feelings with these anguished words:

'Can you credit it! We came here to a place like this in order to enjoy a little poetry and then a thing like this has to happen – '

Carlos patted him sadly on the shoulder: 'That's life Eusè-biozinho.'

Cruges stroked his back: 'You can't hope for pleasure, Silveir-inha.'

But Palma, who was more practical, said it was essential to patch things up. One did not come to Cintra for scenes and sulks, indeed not! On outings like this one wanted harmony, gaiety and enjoyment. Not brawls. One might as well stay in Lisbon. It would be cheaper.

He went up to Lola and stroked her face lovingly with his finger:

'Come, Lola! Go inside to Concha and tell her not to make a fool of herself and to come and have coffee – come! You know how to persuade her. Tell her that *I* ask her.'

Lola delayed for a moment, selecting two good oranges, then she went and patted her hair in front of the mirror, gathered up her train – and out she went, throwing a look and a little smile at Carlos as she left the room.

No sooner were they alone than Palma turned to Eusèbio and proceeded to lecture him very seriously on the way to deal with *espanholas*! They had to be persuaded with good manners; it was for this reason that they took up with Portuguese, because, there in Spain, they were accustomed to ill-usage. Of course, he was not saying that in certain cases a couple of smart blows, even a couple of beatings, might not come in handy. – Did they know, for instance, when one ought to beat a woman? When she didn't like one and played hard to get! Then, certainly! Then, slap, take that! And then she would be all over one. – But afterwards there should be moments of gentleness and courtesy, just as with French women.

'You can believe me, Silveira! I've got experience, you know. And Senhor Maia will tell you whether I'm right or not, for he's got experience and knows how to get on with *espanholas*.'

This was said with such warmth, such respect, that Cruges burst out laughing and this made Carlos laugh too.

Somewhat taken aback, Senhor Palma adjusted his spectacles and looked at them:

'You may laugh, gentlemen! Do you think I'm joking? Let me tell you, I began going with Spanish girls when I was fifteen years of age! No, Don't laugh. On this point nobody can get the better of me. As far as knowing how to deal with *espanholas* is concerned, I'm the man! And let's admit that it's no easy matter. You've got to have a certain flair. Herculano may be able to write beautiful articles in a fine style, but let him try his hand at *espanholas* and we'll see! It won't work.'

Meanwhile Eusèbiozinho had twice been to the door to listen. A great silence had fallen on the entire hotel and Lola had not returned. Palma now counselled a decisive step.

'Go inside, Silveira; enter the room and then, without more ado, approach her – '

'And beat her?' inquired Cruges with great earnestness, enjoying himself at Palma's expense.

'Beat her be damned! Kneel down and ask forgiveness – this is a case for begging her pardon. And, Silveira, take the coffee in to her yourself!'

Eusèbiozinho looked at his friends questioningly with a mute, anxious regard. But his mind was already made up. And a moment later, the piece of mantilla in one hand, and the cup of coffee in the other, off he went with slow steps, embarrassed and emotional, to beg Concha's pardon.

Carlos and Cruges left the room after him without taking leave of Senhor Palma, who, for that matter, was indifferent too, and had already settled himself at the table where he was preparing his grog.

It was two o'clock by the time the two friends finally left the hotel for Seteais, which destination had been beckoning the maestro since the moment they had left Lisbon. In the square before the unpeopled, silent shops, stray dogs were sleeping in the sun; through the bars of the jail prisoners were begging alms. Filthy, ragged children played in corners; and the best houses still kept their windows shuttered, continuing their winter sleep among the now green trees. Now and again there was a glimpse of the mountain with its wall of battlements running above the crags, or the castle of Pena could be seen alone there on the heights. And everywhere the luminous April air scattered its velvet mildness.

Carlos slowed his pace before the Hotel Lawrence and pointed it out to Cruges.

'It looks more agreeable,' said the maestro. 'But it was worth going to the Nunes, if only to witness that scene – so, Senhor Carlos da Maia has experience with *espanholas*?'

Carlos did not answer; he was unable to take his eyes off that commonplace façade in which there was only one window open, where a pair of plimsolls lay drying in the air. At the door two young Englishmen, each in knickerbockers, stood silently smoking pipes; and in front, sitting on a stone bench, two muleteers beside their donkeys kept their eyes fixed on them, smiled at them and tempted them as though they were prey.

Carlos was about to walk on when he thought he heard, far off and melancholy, from the depths of the silent hotel, the vague sound of a flute; and he stood expectantly, searching his memory, almost certain that Damaso had told him that Castro Gomes had played the flute on board.

'This is sublime,' exclaimed Cruges at his side, moved.

He paused before the railing that overlooked the valley. And there he gazed down in wonder at the immense wealth of dense trees, only the round tops of which could be seen, clothing one slope of the mountain the way lichen covers a wall, and at that distance seeming in the brilliant light as soft and smooth as a blanket of dark-green moss. And amid the thick, dusky green the glimpse of a house stood out and caught his eye, shining white, hidden in the foliage with an air of noble repose under the age-old shadows. For a moment he was overcome by an artist's dream: he longed to live in that house with a woman, a piano and a Newfoundland dog.

But what enchanted him was the air. He flung his arms wide and inhaled it in delicious gulps.

'What air! This is really healthy, my boy! This brings one to life!'

To enjoy it more fully, he seated himself on a piece of low wall that faced a raised terrace, with rails where old trees cast their shade over garden benches and cast the freshness of their foliage across the road, full of the chirping of birds. Carlos pointed to his watch and told him that the hours were slipping by if they wanted to see the palace, Pena and the other sights of Cintra, but the maestro declared he would sooner stay there listening to the running water than gaze at dull monuments.

'Cintra is neither old stones nor Gothic ruins. This is Cintra – water, a bit of moss. This is paradise!'

His feeling of content made him talkative and he repeated his jest: 'And Your Excellency should know, for you've had experience with *espanholas*!'

'Spare me! Have some respect for nature,' murmured Carlos as he pensively poked the earth with his walking stick.

They fell silent. Cruges was now admiring the garden beneath the wall where they sat. It was a thick nest of greenery, shrubs, flowers and trees, choked with the prodigality of a sylvan grove, with space only for a round pond, where the still and icy water, on which two or three water-lilies lay, shone green under the shade of that profuse verdure. Here and there, among the lovely wilderness of foliage, arrangements in bourgeois taste could be distinguished: a curve in the path as narrow as a ribbon glittering in the sun, or the banal paleness of a plaster statuette. In some corners of that rich man's garden open to public view, there were pretentious hothouse touches: aloes and cacti; the umbrella-like arms of Chilean pines rising up among the black needles of the wild pine-trees; the blades of palms, with their sad look of plants in exile, rubbed against the light and scented branch of the rose-coloured, flowering Judas-trees. Here and there, graceful and discreet, gleamed the whiteness of a big bunch of ox-eye daisies; around a rose, solitary on its stem, fluttered pairs of butterflies.

'What a pity this doesn't belong to an artist!' murmured the maestro. 'Only an artist knows how to love these flowers, these trees, these sounds . . .'

Carlos smiled. Artists, he declared, love only the effects of line and colour in nature; to interest oneself in the welfare of a

tulip, to make sure a carnation does not suffer from thirst, to feel
grief when frost has bitten the first acacia buds – this only the
bourgeois would do, the bourgeois who goes down his garden
each morning with a watering-can and an old hat and sees in
his trees and plants a mute family that needs his care.

Cruges, who was not really listening, exclaimed:

'Good God! I mustn't forget the cheese-cakes!'

A sound of wheels interrupted them and an open chaise approached at a trot from the direction of Seteais. Carlos rose at
once, certain it was *she*, and that he would see her lovely eyes
shining and sparkling like two stars. The chaise passed, bearing
an old man with a patriarchal beard and an elderly Englishwoman with her lap full of flowers and a blue veil floating behind
her. And immediately in their wake, practically in the dust raised
by their wheels, appeared a tall man strolling pensively,
hands behind his back, all in black, with a big panama hat over
his eyes. It was Cruges who recognized those long romantic
moustaches and shouted:

'Look! It's Alencar! Oh! Great Alencar – '

For a moment the poet stood transfixed with outstretched arms,
in the middle of the road. Then with the same noisy effusion
he held Carlos tight against his heart, kissed Cruges on the
cheek – for he had known Cruges since his infancy, Cruges was
like his own son. Bless him! This was a surprise that he would
not have exchanged for a duke's coronet! What a supreme joy
it was to meet them here! How the devil did they happen to
be here?

Without waiting for their reply he at once launched into his
own tale. He had had one of his throat attacks accompanied by
a spot of fever; and Melo, the good Melo, had recommended him
a change of air. Now as far as he was concerned that could only
mean Cintra, for here not only one's lungs breathed deeply, but
also one's heart, my lads! And so he had come, the day before,
by omnibus.

'And where are you staying, Alencar?' asked Carlos at once.

'Now where d'you think I'd stay, my lad? There I am at my
old Lawrence. Poor old place! It's getting on in years! But for
me it is ever a friend, almost a sister – and what of you? Where
are you off to with those flowers in your lapels?'

'To Seteais – I'm going to show Seteais to the maestro.'

Well now, he would turn back to Seteais too! He had nothing to do except inhale the fresh air and meditate – all morning he had wandered there, vaguely hanging dreams on the branches of trees. But now he could not leave them; indeed, it was a duty to go himself and do the honours for Seteais to the maestro.

'It's a place very dear to my heart, you know, my lads! There's not a tree there that doesn't know me . . . I don't want to start right away imposing verses on you, but you may in fact remember something I composed in Seteais and that was rather like:

> What moon-drenched nights I've seen there!
> What sweet April morns!
> A thousand sighs I've breathed there
> In those dewy dawns!

And so you see, my lads, I have reason to know Seteais.'

The poet sighed emptily and for a time all three walked along in silence.

'Tell me something, Alencar,' said Carlos in a low voice, stopping and touching the poet's arm. 'Is Damaso at the Lawrence?'

Not as far as he knew. The truth was that the night before he had no sooner arrived than he had retired weary to bed; and that morning he had breakfasted in the solitary company of two young Englishmen. The only animal he had seen had been a lovely little pet dog barking in the corridor.

'And where are you staying?'

'At the Nunes.'

The poet stopped again, regarding Carlos benevolently.

'You did very well to drag the maestro here, my boy. How many times haven't I told that devil to get into an omnibus and come and spend a couple of days in Cintra! But no one can get him away from hammering at the piano. And, mark you, even for music, for composing, for understanding Mozart or Chopin, one ought to see this, hear these sounds, the melody of these branches.'

He lowered his voice and pointed to the maestro who strolled blissfully ahead of them.

'He's got a lot of talent, a lot of melodic ideas . . . you know,

I've carried him on my shoulders – and his mother, my lad, was a very fine woman!'

'Look at this, you two,' cried Cruges, who had stopped and was waiting for them, 'this is sublime!'

It was only a little bit of road, squeezed between two old walls covered with ivy, screened by great interwoven trees that made a roof of foliage open to the light like lace; on the ground patches of sunlight quivered; and, in the freshness and the silence, somewhere unseen waters coursed and sang.

'If you want the sublime, Cruges,' exclaimed Alencar, 'then you must climb the mountain. There you'll find space, cloud, art.'

'I don't know. Perhaps I like this better,' murmured the maestro.

His timid nature certainly preferred these humble corners framed with a little fresh greenery and a bit of mossy wall, quiet shady spots where the indolent could dream and shelter with more comfort.

'As a matter of fact, my lad,' continued Alencar, 'everything in Cintra is divine. There is not a nook or cranny that is not a poem. Look, take this lovely blue flower, for instance,' and tenderly he picked it.

'Let's get on, let's get on!' muttered Carlos impatiently, more certain than ever, now that the poet had mentioned the pet dog, that she was saying at the Lawrence, and that he was soon to see her.

But when they arrived at Seteais, Cruges became disillusioned in face of that vast courtyard covered with grass, with its mansion at the bottom – dirty, broken-windowed and its great coat of arms rising pompously in the sky above the archway. He had preserved an idea from childhood that Seteais was a picturesque, rocky hill, dominating the depths of a valley; and to this he had vaguely added a memory of moonlight and guitars. But what he saw there now was a disappointment.

'Life consists of disappointments,' said Carlos. 'Come!'

And he hastened his step across the courtyard while the maestro, who grew livelier each moment, shouted to him the joke of the day:

'And you should know, Senhor Maia, because you know how to deal with *espanholas*!'

Alencar, who had lingered behind to light a cigarette, cocked a curious ear and wanted to know what was this about *espan-holas*. The maestro related the meeting at the Nunes and the fury of Concha.

They were walking along one of the side paths, green and fresh, as religiously peaceful as a leafy cloister. The garden was neglected; the lawn that stretched over it grew untended, all starred with white daisies and buds of gold that gleamed in the sun. Not a leaf stirred. The sun cast its sheaves of golden rays through the latticed branches. The blue sky seemed to have retreated to an infinite distance, soaked in luminous silence; and all that could be heard was the monotonous, sleepy voice of a cuckoo now and again in the chestnut trees.

All that habitation, with its rusty railings lining the road, its rosettes of stone worn by the rain, the heavy rococo coat of arms, the windows filled with cobwebs, seemed to be dying of its own accord in the green solitude – disappointed with life since the last graces of tricorn and sword and the last panniered dresses that had swept those lawns had vanished for ever. Cruges was now describing Eusèbiozinho's expression when, coffee-cup in hand, he had gone off to beg for Concha's pardon; and all the while the poet, with his great panama hat, kept bending down to gather small wild flowers.

When they came to the archway they found Carlos sitting on a bench pensively smoking a cigarette. The mansion cast the sad shadow of its walls over that part of the terrace; a freshness and a clear air rose from the valley; and, somewhere below, a fountain could be heard sobbing. The poet sat down beside his friend and spoke about Eusèbiozinho in disgusted tones. That was really a vile trick of which nobody could accuse him – bringing harlots to Cintra! Neither to Cintra nor to any other place! But least of all to Cintra! He had always held that everyone should come here to worship these trees and reverence these green shades.

'As for that Palma,' he added, 'he's a low rascal! I know him; he had some sort of newspaper, and many a beating I've given him in the Rua do Alecrim . . . It's a curious tale . . . I'll tell you about it, Carlos . . . What a swine! When I think of it! That vile little lump of rotting flesh – that little sausageful of pus!'

He got up twisting his moustache nervously, excited now by the recollection of that old dispute, fulminating against Palma with fierce names, all in one of those conflagrations of the blood that had been his downfall.

Cruges, meanwhile, leaned on the parapet and contemplated the great field that stretched out below, rich and well-worked, divided in squares of light green and dark green that reminded him of a patch-work cloth just like the one he had on the table in his room. White strips of road coiled down its centre; here and there a house shone white among the trees; and, now and again, on that abundantly watered soil a row of little willows disclosed some fresh stream, running and glistening in the grass. The sea lay far off, joined to the sky in a line that was smudged in the diffused tenuousness of the bluish mist; overhead curved the great lustrous sky like some lovely enamel with only a little patch of mist that hung there, high up, forgotten and sleeping, ragged and still in the light.

'I was sickened,' cried Alencar as he fierily ended his tale. 'Upon my word, I was sickened! I threw my stick at his feet, folded my arms and said to him: "There's the stick, you coward, all I need are my hands!"'

'Hang it!' murmured Cruges to himself as he drew away from the parapet; 'I mustn't forget those cheese-cakes!'

Carlos rose too, looking at his watch. But before they left Seteais, Cruges wanted to explore the other terrace, and he had no sooner reached the top of the two old stone steps than he uttered a joyous cry:

'I was right! Here they are – and you said they did not exist!'

They came upon him triumphant, facing a pile of rocks polished by use, already wearing the vague shape of seats, left there long ago fancifully to adorn the terrace with the savage grace of the wild woodland. Well, hadn't he said so? He had been quite right about there being rocks in Seteais.

'I remembered them perfectly. The Rocks of Memory! Isn't that what they're called, Alencar?'

But no reply came from the poet. He stood before those stones, his arms folded, smiling mournfully; motionless and gloomy in his black suit, with his panama hat pulled down over his forehead, he took in all that scene with a slow, sad gaze.

Then his voice rose, nostalgic and doleful in the silence:

'D'you remember *The Flower of Martyrdom*, lads? One of the best things in it is called "The Sixth of August", in free rhyme.

Perhaps you don't recall it. Well, I'll recite it for you, lads ...'

Mechanically he took a white handkerchief from his pocket. He drew Carlos towards him, called Cruges to his other side and, the handkerchief waving in his hand, he lowered his voice as though for a solemn confidence, and began to recite with muffled ardour, biting the syllables, tremulous, in all the ephemeral passion of his nervous temperament:

> 'You came! I held you to my breast.
> The night was dark around;
> No pillow had we for our rest,
> Only the rocky ground,
> No bridal couch or lace-trimmed sheet,
> Only a mantle of stars,
> But our restless passion's heat
> Warmed that couch of ours.
> And there we lay till break of day
> Silenced the distant guitars.'

He stood a moment, his eyes resting on the white stones where the sun beat down, and gestured sadly towards them, murmuring:

'It was on that very spot!'

And he moved away, slouched under his big panama hat, his white handkerchief in his hand. Cruges, who was always affected by this sort of romanticism, stood staring at the rocks as at a historic place. Carlos could not help grinning. And when they had both left that corner of the terrace the poet, bent double near the archway, was tying up the leg-band of his underwear.

He straightened up immediately; all his emotion had left him and he displayed his bad teeth in a friendly smile and exclaimed, pointing to the archway:

'Now Cruges, my lad, look at that sublime canvas!'

The maestro was speechless. Through the archway, as though framed heavily in stone, a magnificent landscape shone in the rich afternoon light, almost fantastic in composition, like an illustration of some splendid legend of chivalry and love. In the foreground was the garden, deserted and green, all speckled with yellow buds; farther off the thick row of old trees with ivy on their trunks made a fence of shining foliage all along the railing; and emerging abruptly from that bushy line of sun-drenched timber, in the full splendour of the day, outlined vigorously in sharp relief against the background of the light-blue sky, rose the peak of the mountain, all dark-violet colour, crowned with the castle of Pena, romantic and solitary on the heights, with its gloomy park at its feet, its slender tower vanishing in the air and its cupolas shining in the sun as though made of gold.

Cruges found that picture worthy of Gustave Doré; Alencar had ready a fine phrase about the Arab imagination; Carlos impatiently urged them to make haste.

But now Cruges was impressed and filled with a desire to climb to Pena. Alencar for his part would accompany them with pleasure. For him Pena was yet another nest of memories! Nest? Rather he should say cemetery.

Carlos hesitated and paused close to the railing. Might she not be on Pena? And he looked at the road, the trees, as though he might divine from the prints in the dust, or from the rustling in the leaves, which direction her steps had taken. At last an idea struck him:

'Let's first go to the Lawrence. And then if we want to go to Pena we can hire donkeys there.'

Nor would he even listen to Alencar who had also had an idea and had begun to talk about Colares and a visit to his friend Carvalhosa. He speeded up his pace towards the Lawrence while the poet again fixed the leg-band of his underpants and the maestro ornamented his hat with ivy leaves in a fit of bucolic enthusiasm.

In front of the Lawrence, the two donkey-men, having been unsuccessful in capturing the Englishmen, were lazing in the sun with cigarettes in their mouths.

'Do you know if a family staying here at the hotel has gone to Pena?' Carlos asked them.

One of the men thought a moment and then exclaimed at once, taking off his beret:

'Yes, senhor. They went a while ago, and here's a donkey for you also, senhor!'

But the other man, more honest, denied it. No, sir, the people who had gone to Pena were at the Nunes:

'The family you are talking of, senhor, has just gone towards the palace – '

'A tall lady?'

'Yes, senhor.'

'And a fellow with a black beard?'

'Yes, senhor.'

'And a little bitch-dog?'

'Yes, senhor.'

'Do you know Senhor Damaso Salcêde?'

'No, senhor – is he the one who takes photographs?'

'No, he doesn't take photographs – here, take this.'

He gave them a coin and turned to the others, declaring that really it was late to climb up Pena.

'Now, what you ought to see, Cruges, is the palace. That's what has originality and *cachet*! Isn't that so, Alencar?'

'I'll tell you, my lads,' began the author of *Elvira*, 'historically speaking – '

'And I must buy those cheese-cakes,' muttered Cruges.

'Precisely!' exclaimed Carlos. 'You've still got to buy the cheese-cakes; we must lose no time; let's get on!'

He left the others undecided, made towards the palace and in four broad strides he had reached it. And there in the square he at once caught sight of that famous family with the pet dog who were installed at the Lawrence, already leaving the gate, passing close to the sentinel. It was indeed a fellow with a black beard, and shoes of white canvas; and at his side was an enormous matron wearing a silk cape and gold things hanging on her breast and neck, and carrying a furry dog in her arms. They came past bad-humouredly growling something to one another in Spanish.

Carlos stood looking at the pair, with the dismal mien of someone contemplating the broken fragments of some lovely marble. He did not wait any longer for the others; he did not want to see them. He hastened back to the Lawrence by a different route, avid only for certainty; and there the waiter who attended him told him that Senhor Salcêde and the Castro Gomes couple had left the previous day for Mafra.

'And from there?'

The waiter had heard Senhor Damaso saying that from there they were returning to Lisbon.

'Good!' said Carlos, flinging his hat on the table. 'Bring me a glass of cognac and some fresh water.'

Suddenly Cintra seemed intolerably deserted and sad. He had

no heart to return to the palace, nor did he wish to go out again. Tearing off his gloves, pacing around the dining-table, where yesterday's flowers stood withering, he felt a desperate longing to gallop back to Lisbon, rush to the Hotel Central, invade her room, see her, and feast his eyes upon her. For he was becoming irritated now with his inability, in the smallness of Lisbon where everyone ran into everyone else, to encounter this woman he sought so eagerly. For two weeks he had wandered the Aterro like a stray dog; he had made ridiculous pilgrimages from theatre to theatre; one Sunday morning he had gone to every mass! And he had not seen her again. Now he had learned she was in Cintra and to Cintra he had flown, and he had not seen her here either. She had passed him on the Aterro one afternoon, lovely as a roving goddess, and had disappeared. She had evaporated, as though she had really returned to the heavens, henceforth invisible and supernatural; and he had remained behind with that glance in his heart, perturbing all his being, silently orienting all his thoughts, desires, curiosities, all his inward life, towards an adorable unknown, of whom he knew nothing except that she was tall, fair and had a little Scottish bitch-dog.

So it was with stars that cross in the sky! They are not in essence any different, nor do they contain more light than others; but for the very reason that they pass fugitively and vanish, they seem to give off a more divine radiance, and the dazzle they leave in the eyes is more perturbing and lasts longer. He had not seen her again. Others had seen her: Taveira had seen her; in the Grémio he had heard an ensign of lancers speaking of her, asking who she was, for he saw her every day; the ensign saw her every day! He did not see her, and he could not rest.

The waiter brought the cognac. Then Carlos conversed with him as he slowly prepared his refreshment, spoke for a moment of the two English youths, then of the obese Spanish lady. Finally, dominating his feeling of shyness, almost blushing, and with long pauses, he put some questions about the Castro Gomeses. And each reply seemed a precious acquisition. The lady was a great one for early rising, said the waiter: by seven o'clock she had taken her bath, was dressed, up and off out alone. Senhor Castro Gomes, who slept in a separate room, never stirred before midday; and at night he would remain for an eternity at table, smoking cigarettes and wetting his lips with glasses of cognac and water. He and Senhor Damaso played dominoes. The lady had mountains of flowers in her room; and they had intended to stay until Sunday but it had been she who had hastened their departure.

'Ah!' said Carlos after a silence, 'it was the lady who hastened their departure?'

'Yes, sir, she was concerned about her little girl who had stayed behind in Lisbon . . . Will you have more cognac, sir?'

Carlos declined with a gesture and went to sit on the terrace. The evening was falling, calm, radiant, without a rustle of leaves, full of golden light, in a deep serenity that pierced the soul. He would have met her thus, there on that terrace, also watching the evening fall, had she not been impatient to return and see her daughter, some fair babe who had been left alone with her nurse. So the bright goddess was also a good mother. This gave her an even deeper charm; he liked her even more like that, with human tenderness warming her marble beauty. She was in Lisbon by now; and he imagined her in the laces of her peignoir, with her hair coiled in haste, tall and white, holding the baby in the air in her splendid Junoesque arms, and talking to it with a golden laugh. He thought her adorable thus, and all his heart flew to her. Ah, to have the right to be close to her, in those intimate hours, very close, smelling the fragrance of her skin and smiling at a baby. And little by little, there began to arise in his soul a romantic idyll that was radiant and absurd: a breath of passion, stronger than human laws, would toss them violently and join his destiny to hers; then, what a sublime existence, hidden in a nest of flowers and sun, far away in some corner of Italy. Every sort of idea of love, absolute devotion, sacrifice, invaded him deliciously – while his eyes forgot themselves, lost themselves, carried away with the religious solemnity of that lovely sunset.

From the direction of the sea there rose a marvellous pale golden colour, which mounted high up to dissolve the blue and give it an indecisive and opaline white, a sweet, swooning tone; and the trees clad themselves in golden hues, delicate and sleeping. Every sound took on the gentleness of a lost sigh. Everything was still, as though motionless in ecstasy. And here and there the windows of houses that faced towards the west were aflame; the round tops of the trees clung together, descending the mountainside in a thick sweep to the valley; everything seemed to be still, in grave and melancholy withdrawal, as he watched the departure of the sun which slowly sank into the sea . . .

'Carlos! Are you there?'

It was the thick voice of Alencar calling him. Carlos appeared on the terrace.

'What the devil are you doing there, my lad?' exclaimed Alencar, gaily waving his panama. 'We've been waiting in that royal den. We went to the Nunes. We were just off to look for you in the jail.'

The poet laughed heartily at his joke, while Cruges stood beside him with his hands behind his back, and his face raised to the terrace yawning disconsolately.

'I came for refreshment, as you call it, to have some cognac; I was thirsty.'

Cognac? It was the very thing that he, poor Alencar, had been longing for all afternoon since Seteais. He at once bounded up the stairs of the terrace, after shouting inside, into the depths of 'his dear old Lawrence', for some brandy to be brought out to him.

'So you saw the palace, eh, Cruges?' Carlos asked the maestro when he appeared with dragging footsteps. 'Then it seems to me that all that remains is for us to have dinner and be off.'

Cruges agreed. He had returned from the palace looking jaded, weary of that vast historic house, the monotonous voice of the guide showing them the bed of His Majesty the King, the curtains of Her Majesty the Queen ('better than those at Mafra') and the bootjack of His Highness. He now brought back with him some of that melancholy peculiar to the atmosphere of royal dwellings. Cintra's natural beauties at dusk, he said, had begun to sadden him.

And so they decided to stay and dine at the Lawrence and thus avoid the sordid spectacle of Palma and the two ladies; they would order the brake to come to the door and be ready to leave as soon as the moon rose. Alencar would take advantage of Carlos's carriage to return with them to Lisbon.

'And to crown our excursion,' he cried as he wiped the cognac from his moustaches, 'while you go to the Nunes to pay the bill and give orders for the brake. I shall go downstairs to the kitchen and have prepared for you Cod à l'Alencar, my own recipe –

and you'll see what a cod dish is really like! And you will see, my lads, that although others may perhaps make better verses nobody can make better cod!'

As they crossed the square Cruges begged God that they would not see Eusèbiozinho again. But as soon as they set foot on the first steps of the Nunes the voices of that band of merrymakers could be heard above them. All quite reconciled now, and Concha contented, they sat in the ante-chamber installed at two corners of a table playing cards. Palma, armed with a bottle of gin, was gambling with Eusèbio; and the ladies, cigarettes between their lips, were lazily playing cribbage.

The widower was pale and losing. In the bank, that had started miserably with two crowns, gold already gleamed. Palma was rejoicing, joking, and planting smacking kisses on his sweetheart. But he was also playing the gentleman, talked of giving the other a chance to recoup: he was willing to stay there till morning if necessary.

'Well, aren't you gentlemen tempted? We're just passing the time – in Cintra anything will do . . . Jack! You've lost another crumb with that king! Another fifteen *tostões*, Silveira!'

Carlos, followed by the servant, passed them without answering. Eusèbiozinho, who was now angry and suspicious, demanded there and then to check whether all the kings were there, his dark glasses almost touching the pack.

Palma placidly and without any sign of annoyance laid out the cards. Hell, between friends anything was admissible! But his *espanhola* for her part was scandalized and defended her man's honour: Palma was not the sort to have hidden the king! Concha, zealously guarding her widower's wealth, exclaimed that the king might have been lost. But the kings were all present.

Palma tossed a glassful of gin down his gullet and majestically started to reshuffle.

'Well, aren't you tempted, sir?' he asked again, addressing the maestro.

Cruges had in fact paused and was now sidling round the table, his eye on the cards and the gold in the bank, already weak-willed and jingling the change in his pockets. An ace suddenly decided him, and he slipped a pound under it with a nervous hand and bet five *tostões*. He lost right away. When Carlos came back from the room, accompanied by the servant who was bringing the luggage down, the maestro was already deep in vice, with his pound at stake, his eyes bright and a dishevelled look.

'What are you up to?' exclaimed Carlos, severely.

'I'm coming at once,' growled the maestro.

And he went hastily on with the game in a tern against the king. A sickening hand, Palma declared, starting to put down his cards with emotion and squeezing them out one by one in deadly slowness. A card made him curse. But it was only a deuce, and Eusèbiozinho lost another coin. Palma gave a sigh of relief; and covering the pack with both his hands he raised his steaming spectacles to the maestro:

'Well, d'you want to go on with the whole pound?'

'All of it!'

Palma sighed anxiously; and, paler now, he turned over the cards abruptly.

'King!' he shouted, dragging the gold towards him.

It was the king of clubs; and his *espanhola* clapped her hands as the maestro stalked off in fury.

Dinner at the Lawrence went on till eight o'clock and the lights had long been lit. Alencar talked the whole time. All life's disillusionments, all his literary rancours, were forgotten and he was in excellent vein that day. There were stories of Cintra in the old days, recollections of his celebrated journey to Paris, spicy tales about women, bits of intimate chronicles of the Regeneration – and all of it in strident tones, 'lads this!' and 'lads that!', great gestures that made the candle-flames flutter, and large glassfuls of Colares downed in one draught. The two Englishmen on the other side of the table, formal in their black evening-dress and with white carnations in their buttonholes, sat amazed, embarrassed and somewhat disdainful at all this disorderly Latin exuberance.

The cod, when it reached the table, was a triumph, and the satisfaction of the poet so great that he even wished, 'by God, lads!', that Ega could be there!

'I'd like him to have tried this cod! As he doesn't appreciate my verses at least he would appreciate my cooking, for this is the cod of an artist in any part of the world! I made it the other day at the house of my beloved Cohens; and Rachel, the dear, came up to me and kissed me. For the poetic and culinary arts, my lads, are sisters! Just look at Alexandre Dumas. Perhaps you think Dumas *père* was not a poet – but what of d'Artagnan? D'Artagnan is a poem – he's a spark, a fantasy, an inspiration, a dream, a passion! So, by God, you can see he's a poet . . . Well, one of these days you must come and dine with me, and Ega shall come too, and you will have partridges *à l'espagnole* that will make castanets grow on your finger-tips. Believe me, I like Ega! And as for all those questions about realism and romanticism – fiddlesticks. A lily is as natural as a bed-bug – some people like the stink of the gutter. Good! Then let the public sewers flow! For my part I prefer scented powder on a white breast; I prefer the breast. Here's to your health! What's wanted is heart! And that Ega has. And he's got sparkle too; he's got a stroke of genius; he's got style. Well, there you are and here's to Ega's health!'

He put down his glass, passed his hand over his moustache and growled in a more subdued voice:

'And if those Englishmen go on staring at me, they'll get a glassful in their faces, and there'll be a storm here that will teach Great Britain what Portuguese poets are made of.'

But there was no storm; Great Britain persisted in ignorance of what makes Portuguese poets, and the dinner ended serenely with coffee. It was nine o'clock and the moon had risen when Carlos took the reins.

Alencar was wrapped in a cloak, an authentic country priest's cloak and in his hand he carried a bunch of roses. His panama was now stowed away in his case and he wore an otter cap. The maestro, heavy from dinner and low-spirited, huddled mutely in a corner of the brake, buried inside the collar of his coat with Mama's rug over his knees. They set off. Cintra lay sleeping in the moonlight.

For a time the brake wheeled along in silence in the beauty of the night. At times the road seemed bathed in a hot, sparkling light. The housefronts loomed up still and pale, amid the trees, looking romantic and melancholy. The murmur of water was lost in the shadow; and near the branch-covered walls the air was filled with fragrance. Alencar lit his pipe and gazed at the moon.

But after they had passed the houses of São Pedro and had entered the sad, silent highway, Cruges stirred, coughed and gazed at the moon too, murmuring from inside his wraps:

'Oh, Alencar, recite something for us.'

The poet at once deigned to do so, despite the fact that one of the servants was with them there inside the brake. But what could he recite under the spell of that brilliant night? Heard under the moon all verse sounded frail! Well then, he would narrate a story that was true enough and sad enough. Swathed in his great cloak, he went and sat beside Cruges, emptied his pipe, stroked his moustaches for a moment and then began in intimate, everyday tones:

> 'In an old-fashioned country garden,
> As simple and sweet as May,
> With lavender bushes and roses
> And the scent of – '

'Blast it!' roared Cruges suddenly leaping out of his rug with a bellow that dumbfounded the poet, caused Carlos to turn in his seat and frightened the coachman.

The brake stopped and they all stared at him in consternation; and in the immense silence of the heath under the peaceful moonlight, Cruges shouted despairingly:

'The cheese-cakes! I've forgotten the cheese-cakes!'

9

AT THE END of that fine, sunny week the eagerly awaited day of the Cohens' ball dawned foggy and dismal. When Carlos opened his window on to the garden early in the morning he looked out on a glowering sky that seemed made out of dirty cotton-wool. The trees shivered and dripped; the river was turbid in the distance; and the warm breath of the south-west wind could be felt wandering in the heavy air. He decided to stay indoors, and from nine o'clock onwards he sat at his desk wrapped in his vast blue velvet dressing-gown that made him look like a fine Renaissance prince, and did his best to work – but that morning two cups of coffee and endless cigarettes could not shake off the fog that drowned his brain just like the sky outside. It was one of his terrible days; he felt stupid; and the quantity of torn, crumpled paper that piled up on the carpet by his feet made him feel a total wreck.

In fact it was a relief, a respite from that battle of rebellious ideas, when Baptista announced Vilaça, who had come to speak to him about the sale of some property in the Alentejo that was part of his inheritance.

'A little business matter,' said the administrator, placing his hat on a corner of the table and putting a roll of papers inside it, 'that will bring you in over two *contos*. Not a bad present, early in the morning!'

Carlos folded his hands firmly behind his head and stretched himself:

'Well now, Vilaça, I don't mind having two *contos*, but I should prefer you to bring me some lightness of spirit. I'm very stupid today!'

Vilaça looked at him for a moment wickedly.

'D'you mean to tell me that you would rather write a page of elegant prose than receive nearly five hundred pounds?! Well, it's all a matter of taste, senhor, a matter of taste! It isn't a bad thing to turn out to be a Herculano or a Jarret, but two *contos* are two *contos*. They're well worth an entire pamphlet. Well now, to get down to business . . .'

He would not sit down and explained hurriedly, while Carlos sat with his arms folded, thinking what an abominable tie-pin Vilaça was wearing – a large coral monkey eating a golden pear – and understanding hazily through his mental fog that the affair concerned the Viscount de Torral and some pigs. When Vilaça presented him with the papers he signed them with a lifeless expression.

'Well, won't you stay for lunch, Vilaça?' he said, seeing the steward putting the roll of papers under his arm.

'I'm much obliged but I must meet our friend Eusèbio. We're going to the Ministry of the Interior together – he's got some expectations there. He wants the Order of the Conception – but his government is displeased with him.'

'Ah!' murmured Carlos with respect as he stifled a yawn, 'so the government is not satisfied with Eusèbio?'

'He did not conduct himself well in the elections. Just a few days ago the Minister of the Interior said to me confidentially that Eusèbio is a worthy fellow, but difficult ... Cruges told me you met him in Cintra the other day?'

'Yes, he was there earning the award of the Order of the Conception.'

After Vilaça had left, Carlos picked his pen up slowly and hesitated with his eyes on the half-written page as he scratched his beard, feeling discouraged and barren. But almost at once Afonso da Maia entered the room, still wearing his hat, having just returned from his morning stroll around the district. He held a letter for Carlos in his hand that he had found in his study mixed up with his own post. Besides, he had expected to find Vilaça there.

'He was here, but he hurried off to go and arrange a decoration for Eusèbiozinho,' said Carlos, opening the envelope.

To his surprise the paper inside – smelling of verbena like the Countess de Gouvarinho – contained an invitation from the Count to dine the following Saturday, written in terms of cordiality so choice as to be almost lyrical; there was even a phrase about friendship and a mention of the atomic theory of Descartes! Carlos burst out laughing and told his grandfather that a peer of the realm had invited him to dinner with references to Descartes.

'They're capable of anything,' murmued the old man. He

cast a cheerful eye over the manuscripts scattered on the desk:
'So, work is proceeding, I see?'

Carlos shrugged his shoulders:

'If you can call it work – look at the floor. Look at all that wastepaper. When it's simply a matter of making notes, collecting documents, assembling material, I can manage. But when it comes to presenting ideas and observations in a tasteful and harmonious form, giving them colour, pointing them up – then that's another matter altogether!'

'A peninsular preoccupation, my boy!' said Afonso sitting down near the table and holding his hat with its turned-down brim in his hand. 'You must shake it off! That was just what I was saying the other day to Craft, and he agreed – the Portuguese can never be a man of ideas because he is too concerned with form. He has a mania for the brilliance and music of the fine phrase. If he has to falsify an idea or leave it incomplete, or exaggerate it so that his phrase can gain in beauty, the wretched fellow does not hesitate. Thought can go by the board, but the fine phrase must be salvaged.'

'It's a question of temperament,' said Carlos. 'There are inferior beings for whom the sonority of an adjective is more important than the exactitude of a system – I am one of these monsters!'

'Hang it! Then you're a rhetorician!'

'Who isn't? And in the last analysis it isn't certain whether style isn't a discipline of the mind. In verse, you know, Grandfather, it is often the requirement of a rhyme that produces the originality of an image – and how much oftener is it not the effort to round off the cadence of a sentence that brings about new and unexpected developments of an idea. Long live the fine phrase!'

'Senhor Ega,' announced Baptista, drawing back the curtain just as the lunch-gong began to strike.

'You were speaking of phrases – ' said Afonso, laughing.

'Eh? What phrase? What is it?' cried Ega, bursting into the room with a distracted air, the collar of his coat turned up and still unshaved. 'Oh, you here at this hour, Senhor Afonso da Maia! How are you, sir? Tell me, Carlos, can you help me out of a difficulty – have you possibly got a sword that will fit me?' Carlos stared at him thunderstruck, and he went on impatiently:

'Yes, man, a sword! It's not for fighting with – I'm at peace with the whole human race – it's for tonight, for the fancy-dress ball!'

That animal, Matos, had only delivered his costume the previous evening, and what had been his horror to discover that instead of an artistic sword he had provided a sabre from the municipal guard! He had felt like sticking it in his guts. He had rushed to Uncle Abrahâo, but he only had court swords, as common and cheap as the Court itself! Then he had remembered Craft and his collection; that was where he had just come from, but all he had were some iron swords, blades that weighed hundreds of pounds – the great broadswords of the brutes who had conquered India. Nothing that would suit him. It was then he had remembered the ancient armoury at Ramalhete –

'You must have one. I want a long, slender sword, with its hand-guard made of steel filigree, lined with scarlet velvet. And no cross, above all no cross!'

Afonso at once took a paternal interest in this difficulty of John's and remembered that in the corridor upstairs there were some Spanish swords –

'Upstairs, in the corridor?' cried Ega, his hand already on the curtain.

There was no use rushing off like that, John would not be able to find them. They were not on display but were still kept in the boxes that had come from Benfica.

'I'll go, man of destiny, I'll go and see!' said Carlos getting up in resignation. 'But they've no scabbards you know.'

Ega looked defeated. And it was Afonso who again came to his rescue.

'Have a plain black velvet scabbard made; it'll take about an hour. And tell them to sew bands of scarlet velvet along the length.'

'Splendid,' cried Ega, 'what a thing it is to have taste!'

And no sooner had Carlos gone out then he started inveighing against Matos.

'Just imagine, sir, a sabre of the municipal guard! And he's the fellow who makes all the costumes for all the theatres! What an idiot! Everything's like that in this ridiculous country!'

'My dear Ega, surely you don't wish to make all Portugal, the State and seven million souls responsible for Matos's behaviour?'

'Yes, indeed, sir!' exclaimed Ega walking around the study

226

with his hands buried in the pockets of his coat. 'Yes, sir, it's all of a piece. The costumier sends a sabre of the municipal guard with a fourteenth-century garment; the minister recites the *Meditations* of Lamartine in connection with taxes; and the man of letters, that supreme beast – '

But he stopped speaking the moment he saw the sword that Carlos brought in his hand – a sixteenth-century blade, highly tempered, slender and vibrant, with its hand-guard worked in filigree; and engraved on the steel was the illustrious name of the swordmaker, Francisco Ruy de Toledo.

He at once wrapped it up in a newspaper, hurriedly declined the lunch he was offered, gave two lively hand-clasps, threw his hat on his head, and was about to rush off when Afonso's voice detained him –

'Listen, John,' said the old man jovially, 'this is an ancestral sword and, I believe, has never been drawn ingloriously – mind how you use it!'

Ega turned back from the curtain and exclaimed, holding the weapon wrapped in the *Jornal do Comercio* against the breast of his coat:

'I shall not draw it without cause, nor stain it without honour! *Au revoir.*'

'What vitality, what youth!' murmured Afonso. 'He's a happy fellow, is John . . . Well, get yourself dressed, my boy, it's already rung once for lunch!'

Carlos still lingered a little while to re-read with a grin the affected letter he had received from Gouvarinho; and at last he was just about to call Baptista to come and dress him, when the electric bell started to vibrate violently from the private entrance downstairs. An anxious step sounded in the hall and Damaso appeared, puffing, eyes glaring and face burning. Without giving Carlos time to express his surprise at seeing him at long last at Ramalhete he flung his arms in the air and shouted:

'Thank God you're here! I want you to come with me, and see a patient . . . I'll explain everything . . . It's those Brazilians. But for heaven's sake come quickly, dear fellow!'

Carlos rose, turning pale.

'Is it she?'

'No, it's the child; practically dying . . . But dress yourself Carlinhos, dress yourself . . . I'm responsible.'

'It's a baby, isn't it?'

'Baby, indeed! She's a big child, six years old – come along!'

Carlos, in his shirt-sleeves by now, was stretching out his foot to Baptista, who knelt on the floor and, hurrying too, had almost torn the buttons off Carlos's boot. Damaso, who had his hat on, was getting agitated, exaggerating his impatience and bursting with importance.

'The things one gets involved in! What a responsibility! I went to visit them as I do sometimes in the morning – and, if you please, they'd gone off to Queluz!'

Carlos turned round, still putting on his frock-coat:

'What on earth?'

'Listen, man! They'd gone to Queluz, but the child had remained behind with the governess. After lunch she felt a pain. The governess wanted an English doctor as she only speaks English. They sent from the hotel for Smith, but he didn't come – and the child there dying! Fortunately I arrived in the meantime and at once remembered you – what luck to find you, eh?'

Casting a glance at the garden, he added:

'Imagine going to Queluz on a day like this! They'll enjoy themselves all right! . . . Are you ready – The coupé's waiting . . . Don't bother with gloves; you're fine without gloves.'

'Tell Grandfather not to expect me for lunch,' Carlos called to Baptista as he reached the bottom of the stairs.

Inside the coupé there was a huge bunch of flowers practically filling the seat.

'It was for her,' said Damaso putting it on his knees. 'She's mad about flowers.'

As soon as they were on their way Carlos shut the window and asked the question that had been on his lips from the moment Damaso had appeared:

'Now, who wanted to smash in the face of that Castro Gomes?'

Damaso at once narrated everything triumphantly. It had all been a misunderstanding! Castro Gomes's explanations had been those of a gentleman. If not he'd certainly have smashed his face in! For he was not taking snubs from anyone, not from anyone! But it had been this way: the cards he had left had still had the address of the Grand Hôtel, Paris. And Castro Gomes, thinking he lived there, had sent his cards there in obedience to that indication! Curious, eh? A stupid thing to do, really! And the lack of response to his telegrams had been due to Madame's negligence at that time of affliction, her husband with an injured arm . . . Ah yes, they had apologized to him humbly, and now they were close friends; he spent almost all his time with them.

'In fact, my boy, it's a romance – but I'll tell you about that later!'

The coupé drew up at the door of the Hotel Central. Damaso jumped out and ran up to the doorman.

'Did you send the telegram, António?'

'It's on its way – '

'You understand,' he said to Carlos as they climbed the stairs, 'I sent them off a telegram at once to the hotel at Queluz. I can't carry this responsibility indefinitely!'

A servant with a napkin under his arm passed them in the corridor in front of the office.

'How's the little girl?' called Damaso.

The servant shrugged his shoulders not understanding.

But Damaso was already hurrying up the next flight of stairs, panting and shouting:

'This way, Carlos. I know this place like the back of my hand. Number 26!'

Noisily he opened the door of number 26. A maid who was at the window turned round.

'*Oh, bonjour, Melanie*,' cried Damaso in his extraordinary French – was the child better? The doctor had come.

Melanie, a thin, freckled girl, said that Mademoiselle was quieter now, and she would go and advise Miss Sarah, the governess. She passed her duster over the marble top of a console, straightened the books on the table, and went out, darting a look as lively as a spark at Carlos.

The room was spacious, furnished in blue rep, and a great mirror hung over the gilded console between the two windows; the table was covered with newspapers, boxes of cigars and novels of Cappendu; on a chair at the side a piece of embroidery lay folded up.

'This Melanie, the slut,' muttered Damaso, shutting the window with an effort over the difficult bolt. 'Leaving everything open like this! Good Lord, what people!'

'This chap's a Bonapartist,' declared Carlos, seeing copies of *Pays* lying on the table.

229

'Oh – we have terrible arguments,' exclaimed Damaso. 'I always wipe the floor with him. He's a good fellow, but not much depth.'

Melanie came back and asked *Monsieur le docteur* to come into the dressing-room for a moment. And there, after picking up a fallen cloth and darting another petulant glance at Carlos, she said that Miss Sarah was coming at once, and withdrew on the tips of her toes. Outside in the drawing-room the voice of Damaso could be heard talking to Melanie about *sa responsabilité et qu'il était très affligé.*

Carlos was alone in the intimacy of that boudoir that had not yet been tidied that morning. Two trunks stood open. They certainly belonged to Madame – enormous, magnificent, with fastenings and corners of polished steel; within one could be seen a rich train of heavy wine-coloured silk; and in the other a delicate froth of white garments, all a secret and rare luxury of embroidery and lace, as white as snow, soft from use and sweet-scented. On a chair lay a heap of silk stockings of all shades, plain, embroidered, lace-worked, and so light that a breeze would have carried them away; and, on the floor, was a row of little patent-leather shoes, all in the same long, low-heeled style, with big ribbons to tie them with. There was a basket uphostered in pink satin in a corner, surely for the little dog to travel in.

But Carlos's gaze rested longest on a sofa where there lay at full length, its two sleeves open like outstretched arms, the white coat of embossed Genoa velvet that she had been wearing the first time he had seen her as she entered the door of the hotel. There was not the slightest padding in the lining of white satin, so perfect must be the body it covered; and there, lying on the sofa, in that lifelike attitude, unbuttoned as in semi-nudity, the material shaped to receive the fullness of breasts, arms wide open surrendering themselves utterly, that cloth seemed to exhale a human warmth, and took on the shape of a loving body, swooning in the silence of the boudoir. Carlos could hear his own heart beat. An indefinite but strong scent of jasmin and tanglewood emanated from all those intimate things and brushed his face like a soft caressing breath.

Then he looked away and approached the window that looked out on the shabby front of the Hotel Shneid.

When he turned round Miss Sarah stood before him dressed in black and very highly coloured. She was pleasant-looking, plump and small, a well-fed turtle-dove with sentimental eyes and a virginal forehead under her straight fair hair. She murmured a few words in French among which Carlos only caught the word *docteur*.

'Yes, I am the doctor,' he said to her in English.

Her face lighted up. Oh, how wonderful it was at last to have someone that she could understand! The little girl was much better! Oh, the doctor's coming was such a relief! She drew back the curtain and led him into a room where the windows were all shuttered and he could just manage to make out the shape of a big bed and the gleam of crystal on the dressing-table. He asked the reason for such darkness.

Miss Sarah thought that the dark would do the child good and help her to sleep. And she had brought her there to her Mama's room because it was larger and airier. Carlos made her open the windows, and when the bright light came in and he saw the child in the bed under the open curtains he was unable to contain his admiration.

'What a lovely child!'

He stood an instant looking at her with an artist's rapture as he reflected that the most delicate, the loveliest shade of white under the most skilful combination of light could not equal the marble paleness of that wonderful skin – that adorable whiteness which was enhanced by intensely black, strong hair that shone under her lace cap. Her two big, deep, liquid blue eyes seemed larger at that moment as they looked at him wide with solemnity. She was lying back against a big pillow, quite motionless and still frightened from the pain, lost in that great bed, and clasping in her arms an enormous dressed-up doll with curled hair, whose eyes were also blue and wide open.

Carlos picked up her little hand and kissed it and asked if the doll was sick too.

'Cricri had a pain as well,' she answered very seriously, without taking her magnificent eyes off him. 'But my pain's all gone!'

She was in fact as fresh as a flower, her little tongue was very pink and she already felt like having her lunch.

231

Carlos reassured Miss Sarah. Oh, she could see that Mademoiselle was all right. What had frightened her was finding herself alone that morning, with such a responsibility. That was why she had put her to bed. Oh, if she were an English child she would have gone out with her into the fresh air. But these little foreign girls were so frail and delicate – And the full lip of the Englishwoman betrayed a pitying scorn for these inferior and degenerate races.

'But her Mama is not sickly?'

Oh, no, Madame was very strong. The Senhor, now, he seemed frailer –

'And what is your name, my dear little friend?' asked Carlos sitting at the head of the bed.

'This is Cricri,' said the little one, showing him her doll again. 'I am Rosa, but Papa calls me Rosicler.'

'Rosicler? Really?' said Carlos, smiling at that name from a book of chivalry, redolent of tourneys and fairy woods.

And then, as if simply collecting the usual doctor's information, he asked Miss Sarah if the child had felt the change of climate. They normally lived in Paris, didn't they?

Yes, they lived in Paris in the winter, in the Parc Monceaux; in summer they went to their country house in Touraine, right near Tours, where they stayed until the beginning of the hunting-season; and they always spent a month in Dieppe. Or at least it had been this way for the last three years since she had been with Madame.

While the Englishwoman spoke, Rosa, with her doll in her arms, never ceased to stare at Carlos in grave astonishment. Now and then he smiled at her or stroked her little hand. Her mother's eyes were black; her father's jet black and small; from whom could she have inherited those marvellous eyes that were such a rich blue, liquid and sweet?

But his professional visit had ended, and he rose to prescribe a sedative. While the Englishwoman very carefully got out writing-paper and was trying a pen, he examined the room for a moment. In that commonplace hotel room certain touches of delicate elegance revealed a woman of taste and luxury: there were big bunches of flowers on the commode and the table; the pillow-slip and sheets were not the hotel's, but her own, in fine Breton linen with lace and large monograms embroidered in two colours.

On her easy-chair a Tarnah cashmere disguised the abominable faded rep.

Then, while he was writing out the prescription, Carlos noticed on the table a few richly-bound books — novels and English poets among which there stood out, strangely, a singular pamphlet: a manual for the interpretation of dreams. And on the dressing-table alongside it, among the ivory of the brushes, the crystal of the flasks and the fine tortoise-shell, was another extravagant object, an enormous powder box, all in gilded silver, with a magnificent sapphire set in the lid inside a circle of tiny brilliants, an exaggerated and tawdry bauble that introduced a bold, dissonant note of rough elegance.

Carlos went back to the bedside and asked for a kiss from Rosicler; she immediately offered a little mouth as fresh as a rosebud; he hesitated to kiss her thus in her mother's big bed and simply brushed her forehead.

'When are you coming again?' she asked him, clutching the sleeve of his coat.

'It won't be necessary to come again, my dear. You're all right, and so is Cricri.'

'But I want my lunch. Tell Sarah I can have my lunch — and Cricri too!'

'Yes, both of you can nibble something — '

He gave some advice to the governess and then took the little girl's hand.

'And now, good-bye, my pretty Rosicler, as that's what you're called . . .'

And not wanting to be less amiable with the doll he also shook its hand.

This seemed to captivate Rosa even more. The Englishwoman beside them smiled with two dimples in her cheeks.

It was not necessary, advised Carlos, to keep the child in bed, or to inflict exaggerated precautions on her.

'Oh no, sir!'

And if the pain reappeared, be it ever so mildly, she should send for him at once.

'Oh yes, sir!'

And he left her his card with the address on it.

'Oh thank you, sir!'

When he returned to the drawing-room Damaso, who had been

glancing through the paper, leaped from the sofa like a wild animal whose cage is opened.

'My God, I imagined you were going to stay there all your life! What have you been doing? What a to-do!'

Carlos began to put on his gloves and smiled without answering.

'Well, is it anything serious?'

'There's nothing wrong. She has lovely eyes – and an extraordinary name.'

'Ah, Rosicler!' murmured Damaso, clutching his hat bad-temperedly: 'Quite ridiculous, don't you think?'

The French maid appeared again to open the drawing-room door, darting at Carlos the same hot, lively look. Damaso urged her repeatedly to tell her master and mistress that he had come at once with a doctor; and he said he would return that evening to give them a surprise and to see how they had liked Queluz.

Then, as they passed in front of the office, he poked his head inside to tell the book-keeper that the little girl was all right, and that everything was quiet.

The book-keeper smiled and nodded.

'D'you want me to take you home?' he asked Carlos, when they were outside, as he opened the door of the coupé still looking slightly bad-tempered.

Carlos preferred to go on foot.

'And you can keep me company, Damaso. You haven't anything to do at the moment.'

Damaso hesitated and looked at the harsh sky, the clouds heavy with rain. But Carlos had taken his arm and was impelling him along, joking amiably.

'And now that I've got you, you old devil, I want to hear about this romance of yours – you said you were having a romance. I shan't let you go! You're mine! Let's hear about this romance. I know how successful you always are. I want to hear about this romance!'

At last Damaso smiled and his cheeks began to glow with satisfaction.

'Life goes on – ' he said, bursting with pride.

'You were all at Cintra?'

'Yes, we were, but that was not at all entertaining . . . the romance is a different matter!'

234

He released himself from Carlos's arm, made a sign to the coachman to follow them, and all along the Aterro he regaled himself by recounting his romance.

'The whole point is this – the husband's off to Brazil in a few days' time. He's got business there. And she's staying behind! She's remaining here with the servants and the little girl to wait for him, for two or three months. He says that they've even been looking over furnished houses, because she does not wish to stay in a hotel – and, as an intimate, the only person she knows, I shall be in on the inside. Now d'you see?'

'Clearly!' said Carlos, flinging his cigar away nervously. 'And of course the wretched creature is already fascinated! You've already given her the customary ardent kiss behind the door! And doubtless she's already preparing to do away with herself when you abandon her!'

Damaso was embarrassed.

'Now don't you start with your wit and scoffing. I haven't given her any kisses yet, because I haven't had the opportunity. But I can assure you the woman's mine!'

'Well, it was high time,' exclaimed Carlos, unable to contain a brusque movement and spitting out the words like whiplashes. 'It was high time! There you were, mixed up with thoroughly bad company, the scum of the brothels. Now at least you've made some progress. I like to see my friends leading an ordered, decent love-life. But take care! Don't get up to your usual performance. Don't go bragging about it round the Grémio and the Casa Havanesa!'

Damaso stood stock-still, nearly choking, astonished at his companion's manner – at so much sourness. At last he muttered, very pale:

'You may know a lot about medicine and antiques, but you can't give me any lessons as far as women are concerned and how to handle things!'

Carlos looked at him with a brutal desire to give him a thrashing. Then, suddenly, Damaso looked so inoffensive, so insignificant, so puffy and plump-cheeked, that he felt ashamed of the dull scorn that had overcome him, took his arm and spoke more amiably:

'Damaso, you don't understand me. I do not want to vex you – it's for your own good! What I'm afraid of is that, in your imprudent, impetuous, passionate way, you will lose this wonderful adventure all because of an indiscretion.'

Damaso recovered his equanimity right away, smiling now and surrendering his arm to his friend, sure now that Maia was anxious only for him to have a *chic* mistress. No, he had not been annoyed, he never got annoyed with a close friend. He knew perfectly well that Carlos had spoken as a well-wisher.

'But sometimes, you know, there's something you've picked up from Ega – you like your bit of irony.'

And he proceeded to reassure Carlos. No, he was not going to let imprudence risk 'the thing slipping through his fingers'. Everything was proceeding according to the rules. He had more than enough experience to see that. Mélanie was already eating out of his hand – he had already given her a couple of pounds.

'And what's more, this is a serious affair: she knows my uncle, she's been a close friend of his since her childhood and they are on intimate terms – '

'What uncle?'

'My Uncle Joaquim – Joaquim Guimarães. Monsieur de Guimaran, who lives in Paris, the friend of Gambetta . . .'

'Ah, yes! The communist . . .'

'Communist indeed! Why, he even has a carriage.'

Suddenly he remembered another matter – a point of dress on which he wished to have Carlos's advice.

'Tomorrow I'm to dine with them, and there will be two other Brazilians there, friends of his who arrived here some days ago, and who are leaving on the same boat. One of them is *chic*, from the Brazilian Legation in London. So it's a formal dinner. Castro Gomes didn't say anything but – what d'you think? Should I wear evening-dress?'

'Yes, give them evening-dress, and a nice rose in the lapel!'

Damaso looked at him pensively.

'Actually, I'd thought myself of wearing the Order of Christ.'

'The Order of Christ! Yes, put the Order of Christ round your neck, and stick a rose in your buttonhole!'

'But wouldn't that perhaps be too much, Carlos?'

'No, it suits your type!'

Damaso signalled to the coupé, that had continued beside them, to draw up. He shook Carlos's hand and asked:

'Are you still going to the Cohens' in a domino? My savage's costume has turned out marvellously. I'm going to show it off tonight to the Brazilian woman. I intend to enter the hotel wrapped in a cloak, and then I'll suddenly appear in the drawing-room as a savage, as Nelusko, singing:

> *Alerta, marinari,*
> *Il vento cangi.*

Terribly *chic*! Good-bye!'

At ten o'clock Carlos began to dress for the Cohens' ball. Outside, the night was very gloomy, with squalls of wind and torrents of water that lashed continually and aggressively down on the garden. His dressing-room was filled with the faint scent of soap and good cigars. The lighted candles in the raised arms of the two branched candelabra of old bronze, that stood on top of the ivory-inlaid ebony commodes, cast soft shadows on the chestnut silk of the walls. Beside the tall pier-glass on an armchair lay the domino costume of black satin with its big pale-blue bow.

Baptista, with Carlos's tail-coat in his hand, waited for his master, who stood in shirt-sleeves and white tie, to finish the cup of Indian tea that he was drinking in gulps. Suddenly the electric bell at the private entrance throbbed hurriedly and violently.

'Perhaps it's another surprise,' murmured Carlos. 'Today is the day for surprises.'

Baptista grinned and was just about to lay down the tail-coat to go and open the door when another brutal ring, frenetic and impatient, sounded from below.

Carlos became curious and went out into the hall. As the door opened, letting in a harsh breath of night, there suddenly appeared in the dim half-light of the Carcel lamps, dimmed by the cherry-coloured velvets, a lanky, scarlet-clad figure, emitting a confused rattle of iron. The cock's feathers waved on the staircase; a scarlet cloak billowed – and Ega stood before him, his face painted, dressed as Mephistopheles!

Ega's aspect so dumbfounded Carlos that he was hardly able to say 'bravo'. Despite the make-up that rendered him almost unrecognizable – devil's eyebrows and ferociously exaggerated handle-bar moustaches – it was easy to discern Ega's disturbed state. His eyes bulged and he was terribly pale. He gestured to Carlos and hurried into the study. Baptista at once discreetly withdrew, drawing the curtain behind him.

They were alone. Then Ega, clasping his hands together desperately, spoke in a voice that was harsh with anguish:

'Do you know what's happened to me, Carlos?'

But, choking and trembling all over, he was unable to go on and Carlos stood facing him, devouring him with his eyes, overwhelmed and trembling too.

'I arrived at the Cohens' house,' continued Ega at last making an effort and almost stammering, 'earlier, as we had arranged. When I entered the drawing-room there were already two or three people there . . . He came straight up to me and said: "You, you infamous scoundrel, get out of here . . . immediately . . . out of here, or else, right here in front of these people, I'll kick you out!" And I, Carlos – '

But again anger choked his voice. And he stood a moment biting his lips, holding back the sobs, his eyes brimming with tears.

When words came back to him, they came in a savage expression:

'I'll fight a duel with that swine, at five paces, and I'll put a bullet through his heart!'

Strangulated sounds escaped from his throat; he stamped his foot furiously, beat the air and went on and on shouting as though saturating himself with the stridency of his own voice:

'I'll kill him! I'll kill him! I'll kill him!'

Then, without seeing Carlos, he began to pace round the room like a man in a trance: stamping his feet, his cloak thrown back, his sword, insecurely buckled, banging against his scarlet shins.

'So he's found out about everything,' murmured Carlos.

'Of course he's found out everything!' cried Ega, throwing his arms in the air in his wild march. 'How he found out I don't know. That is what I do know, and it's enough: he put me out! I'll put a bullet through him! By the soul of my father I'll shoot him through the heart! I want you and Craft to go there first thing in the morning – and these are the conditions: pistols at fifteen paces!'

Carlos, who had now regained his calm, finished his cup of tea. Then, very quietly, he spoke:

'My dear Ega, you cannot challenge Cohen!'

The other halted abruptly, his eyes flashing with an anger to which the dreadful crêpe eyebrows, the two cock's feathers waving in his cap, gave a theatrical and comical ferocity.

'What? I cannot challenge him?'

'No.'

'You mean to say he can put me out of his house!'

'He was within his rights – '

'Within his rights? There in front of everybody – '

'And weren't you his wife's lover in front of everybody?'

Ega stood gazing at Carlos for a moment like one stunned. Then he made a sweeping gesture:

'It's got nothing to do with his wife – his wife wasn't mentioned! For me it's a question of honour. I'm going to challenge him and I shall kill him.'

Carlos shrugged his shoulders:

'You're not in your right mind! You've only one course: stay at home tomorrow and see if he challenges you – '

'What? Cohen?' cried Ega. 'He's a coward. He's a swine – either I'll kill him or I'll slash his face with a whip. Challenge me! He! You're mad!'

And again he began his rapid pacing from the mirror to the window, panting and grinding his teeth, pushing back his cloak with movements that made the tall candle-flames flutter in their holders.

Carlos stood beside the table slowly refilling his cup and said nothing. The whole affair began to look scarcely serious, scarcely dignified: threats of kicks from the husband, Ega's melodramatic furies – and it was difficult to repress a grin before that lanky Mephistopheles who strode around the room scattering the scarlet gleam of his velvet cloak and shouting furiously about honour and death, with false eyebrows and a leather purse at his waist.

'Let's go and speak to Craft!' exclaimed Ega suddenly, stopping with abrupt determination. 'I want to see what Craft has to say. I've got a cab downstairs, we'll be there in a moment!'

'Go to Olivais at this time of night?' said Carlos, as he looked at the clock.

'If you are my friend, Carlos!'

Without calling Baptista, Carlos immediately finished dressing.

Meanwhile Ega was preparing a cup of tea and pouring rum into it, still so nervous that he could scarcely hold the bottle. Then, with a deep sigh, he lit a cigarette. Carlos went into the bathroom adjoining, lit by a strong jet of gas that whistled. Outside the rain poured down, constant and monotonous, and the water from the eaves splashed down on to the soft soil of the garden.

'Do you think the cab will stand it?' asked Carlos from within.

'It'll stand it, it's Canhôto's,' said Ega.

Then he noticed the domino, went to pick it up, examined its rich satin and the beautiful blue bow. Then, catching himself before the big pier-glass, he fixed his monocle in his eye, drew back a pace, looked himself over from head to foot; and finished by putting a hand on his belt and resting the other, gallantly, on the hand-guard of his sword.

'I didn't look bad, eh, Carlos?'

'You were splendid!' replied the other from inside the alcove. 'It was a pity to spoil everything – how was she dressed?'

'She was dressed as Marguerite.'

'And he?'

'That animal? As a Bedouin!'

And he continued to stand before the glass, admiring his slim figure, the plumes in his cap, the pointed velvet shoes and the flaming tip of the sword that lifted his cloak at the back in a chevaleresque fold.

'But listen!' said Carlos, as he appeared drying his hands, 'have you any idea what took place, what he'd said to his wife, the scandal – '

'I've no idea at all,' said Ega, now calmer. 'I went into the first drawing-room and there he was, dressed as a Bedouin; there was another individual dressed as a bear, and a lady dressed as I don't know what – a Tyrolean I think. He came up to me and said: "Get out!" I know nothing else – and I can't understand! The swine – if he has found out he's naturally said nothing to Rachel, so as not to spoil the party. The trouble will come later.'

He raised his hands to heaven and muttered: 'It's horrible!'

He took another turn about the room and then spoke in a different voice, creasing his forehead:

'I don't know what the devil that Godefroy gave me to glue on these eyebrows with. They itch like the devil!'

'Take them off!'

As he stood facing the glass Ega hesitated to dismantle his ferocious Satanic figure. But at last he tore them off, and the tightly-fitting plumed cap that was making his head burn. And then Carlos suggested that he should get rid of the cloak and sword and wrap himself up warmly in one of his overcoats for the journey to Craft's. Ega again gazed long and silently at his flaming infernal raiment and then, giving a deep sigh, he unbuckled his sword-belt. The coat, however, was very big and wide, and he had to turn the sleeves up. Carlos made him put on a deerstalker. Thus garbed, with his scarlet devil's stockings showing under the overcoat, the red Charles IX ruff emerging from above the collar, the old travelling-hat on his head, poor Ega wore the sorrowful look of an indigent Satan, clothed in the charity of a gentleman's cast-off suit.

Baptista, grave and discreet, lit their way, and as he passed him Ega murmured:

'Things are very bad, Baptista, things are very bad!'

The old servant made a sad motion with his shoulders, as though to signify that nothing in the world went well.

In the dark street the quiet horses dropped their heads in the rain. When Canhôto heard about the reward of a pound he started off with whiplashes, making a thunderous din, and the old cab went on its way at a gallop, dripping water and rumbling along the roadway.

Occasionally a private coupé passed them with the rubber coats of the grooms shining in the light of the lanterns. Then the vision of the party that must now be reaching its height – Marguerite, ignorant of anything amiss, waltzing in the arms of others and awaiting him anxiously; the supper later; champagne; the brilliant things he would have said – all these lost delights smote poor Ega's heart and drew hoarse imprecations from him. Carlos smoked in silence, his thoughts in the Hotel Central.

After Santa Apolonia the highway opened out, endless, unsheltered, swept by the fierce wind from the river. Neither said a word, each in his corner, shivering in the cold that came in through chinks in the framework of the cab. Carlos could not stop thinking of the white velvet coat with its two sleeves open, like two outstretched arms . . .

It was after one o'clock when they reached Olivais. The bell at the gate, pulled by the drenched coachman, echoed dolefully in the dark silence of the countryside. A dog barked furiously; other barks far off answered; and they had to wait a long time before a sleepy servant grumblingly appeared with a lantern. An acacia avenue led to the house and Ega cursed as he sank his beautiful velvet shoes in the muddy ground.

Disturbed by the uproar, Craft came to meet them in the corridor in his dressing-gown, with the *Revista dos dois mundos* under his arm. He realized immediately there had been a disaster and led them silently to his study, where a welcoming coal fire warmed and enlivened the room, all gay in light cretonnes. Both of them went straight up to the fire.

Ega embarked at once on an account of his case, while Craft, imperturbably and silently proceeded with the methodical preparation of three cognac-and-lemon grogs. Carlos sat by the fireplace warming his feet; Craft came and sat down in his armchair on the other side of the chimney, his pipe in his mouth, and heard Ega out.

'So,' cried Ega, standing up and folding his arms, 'what do you advise me to do now?'

'There is only one thing for you to do,' said Craft, 'and that is to wait at home tomorrow until he sends you his seconds – which I'm sure he won't do – and then, if you do fight, you must allow yourself to be wounded or killed.'

'Precisely what I said,' murmured Carlos, sipping his grog.

Ega looked from one to the other of them, thunderstruck. And then, in an outburst of disordered words, he complained that he had no friends. There he was, in this crisis, the most serious crisis of his life – and instead of encountering support, solidarity, loyalty *à tort et à travers* in his companions of childhood and Coimbra, they abandoned him, appeared to want to bury him and expose him to greater ridicule than ever. He began to be worked up; his eyes reddened behind the tears and when either of them tried to put in a sensible word, he stamped his foot and persisted in his obstinacy – a duel, the death of Cohen, revenge! He had been insulted. Nothing else mattered! Nothing had been said about the wife. It was he who should first send seconds and avenge his honour. There had been company in that drawing-room when the other had insulted him. There had been a bear and a Tyrolean woman . . . And as for permitting himself to be hit by a bullet – no, indeed! He had more right to live than Cohen who was a bourgeois and a usurer – while he, Ega, was a man of letters and the arts! In his head he had books, ideas, great things! He owed himself to his country, to civilization; if he went to the duelling-ground, it would be to take aim and slaughter Cohen, there and then, like a noxious animal . . .

'But the trouble is, I have no friends!' he cried at last, exhausted, dropping on to a corner of the sofa.

Craft drank his cognac in draughts silently. It was Carlos who finally rose, serious and harsh. Ega had no right to doubt their friendship. When had he ever failed him? But it was necessary not to be childish or theatrical. The fact was simply that Cohen had discovered that Ega had been making love to his wife. And for this reason Cohen was entitled to kill him, to hand him over to the courts or to belabour him with kicks in his drawing-room.

'Or, worse still,' interrupted Craft, 'he could send you the lady with a note saying: "Keep her"!'

'Even that!' continued Carlos. 'However, he will limit himself to forbidding you the house, a little sharply perhaps, but it's by the way of indication that having done as much, he wants nothing more violent, or more dramatic. He has therefore acted in moderation. And you want to challenge him for that?'

But Ega was in revolt once more. He bounded up and strode around the room, without his coat now, dishevelled, looking more fantastic than ever in that simple scarlet-sleeved tunic with his muddied velvet shoes, and his long stork's legs covered in knitted red silk. And he persisted that they were missing the point. It was not a question of the wife! That was a different matter.

Carlos began to get angry:

'What the devil did he evict you from his house for, then? Don't be absurd, man! We are telling you what a man of sense would do. And it's a sad thing that it costs you so much to understand what good sense commands. You have betrayed a friendship – let's get that quite clear! You shouted your friendship with Cohen from the rooftops. You betrayed him, and you must abide by the rules – if he wants to kill you, you must die. If he doesn't want to do anything, you'll just have to keep your arms folded. If he wants to shout after you in the street that

243

you're a scoundrel, you'll have to lower your head and recognize your infamy.'

'So – I've got to swallow the affront?'

The two friends explained to him that his Satan's costume must have disturbed his capacity to judge the situation by earthly criteria and that it was descending to baseness for him, Ega, to talk of *affronts*.

Ega collapsed once more on the sofa, his courage lost, and for a moment he held his head in his hands.

'I no longer know what to do!' he said at last. 'You two must be right – I'm beginning to feel an idiot . . . Well, let's see, what must I do?'

'Have you got the cab waiting?' asked Craft tranquilly.

Carlos had ordered it to be unharnessed and the soaked horses looked after.

'Splendid! Well, my dear Ega, there's one other thing you can do before your possible death tomorrow, and that is to sup tonight. I was about to have supper, and for reasons which would take too long to explain, there happens to be a cold turkey in the house. And there ought to be a bottle of burgundy.'

Not long afterwards they were seated round the table in Craft's beautiful dining-room that always delighted Carlos with its oval tapestries depicting lonely woodland scenes, severe Persian *faiences*, and its unusual chimney flanked by two black Nubian figures with gleaming crystal eyes. Carlos, who declared he was starving, was already carving the turkey, while Craft reverently uncorked two bottles of his old Chambertin for the consolation of Mephistopheles.

But Mephistopheles, gloomy and red-eyed, rejected his plate and at first pushed away the glass, though he then condescended to try the Chambertin.

'Now,' said Craft, holding his fork, 'when you arrived I was reading an interesting article on the decadence of Protestantism in England – '

'What's that over there in that tin?' asked Ega in a lifeless voice.

It was *paté de foie gras*. Wearily Mephistopheles selected a truffle.

'Very good, this Chambertin of yours,' he said with a sigh.

'Come on, eat an honest meal!' cried Craft. 'Stop dramatizing yourself. You're hungry. All your ideas tonight are the consequence of inanition!'

Ega then confessed that he must be weak. With all the excitement of getting costumed as Satan he had not dined, and he had counted on having a good supper at the other fellow's . . . Yes, certainly he had an appetite! Excellent *foie gras*! And in a little while he was devouring everything: slices of turkey, an immense portion of Oxford tongue, two helpings of York ham – all those good English things there always were in Craft's house. And he drank practically an entire bottle of Chambertin on his own.

The footmen had gone to prepare the coffee; and meanwhile a discussion was proceeding of all the hypotheses and the probable attitude of Cohen towards his wife. What would he do? Perhaps he might forgive her! Ega said not: Cohen was vain, and bore long-standing grudges. And as she was a Jewess he could not shut her up in a convent.

'Perhaps he'll kill her,' said Craft in all seriousness.

Ega declared tragically, his eyes already shining from the burgundy, that in that event he would enter a monastery. The other two joked pitilessly. What monastery did he think of entering? None existed suitable for Ega. He was too thin for a Dominican, too lascivious for a Trappist, too talkative for a Jesuit, and too ignorant for a Benedictine. It would be necessary to found an order especially for him. And Craft suggested it should be called the Order of Saint Humbug!

'You two have no heart!' exclaimed Ega, pouring out another big glassful. 'You have no idea how I adored that woman!'

And then he embarked on the subject of Rachel. Perhaps those moments were the best he had of all that passion – for now, without scruple, he could allow his lover's halo to shine brightly and bathe himself in the milk-bath of vainglorious confession. He began by recounting his meeting with her at Foz – while Craft, not missing a word, like one instructing himself, rose to open a bottle of champagne. Then he told of the outings in Cantareira; the notes, still hesitant and platonic, exchanged between the pages of borrowed books, in which she signed herself *Parma Violet*; the first kiss, the best, snatched behind a door while the husband had run upstairs to get Ega some special cigars; several meetings in Oporto, in the Cemetery of Repose; the ardent hand-clasps in the shadow of cypresses and voluptuous projects made among the grave-stones . . .

'Remarkable!' said Craft.

But Ega had to keep silent, for the servant was coming in with coffee. While the cups were being filled and Craft had gone to fetch a box of cigars, he finished off the bottle of champagne, pale now and his nose more pinched.

The servant went out, closing the tapestry-hanging behind him; and Ega, with a glass of cognac beside him, at once took up the thread of his confidences, describing his return to Lisbon, the Villa Balzac, the delicious mornings spent there with her in the warmth of that love-nest –

But now he interrupted his narrative, his eyes misty and vacant, as he buried his head in his hands for a moment. Then out came further details: the lascivious names she had given him, a certain coverlet of black silk where she shone like a jasper. Two tears bathed his eyes, and he vowed he wanted only to die . . .

'If you two only knew what a body she had!' he cried suddenly. 'Oh, my lads, what a body – imagine a breast – '

'We do not wish to know,' said Carlos. 'Shut up, you wretch, you're drunk!'

Ega got up, straightening his legs, and hanging on to the edge of the table –

Drunk? He? What an idea! Something he never could manage was to get drunk. He had done everything possible, drunk everything, even essence of turpentine – but it had been no good, he simply could not get drunk.

'Look here! I'll drink that whole bottle and you'll see – I simply remain cold; I remain impassive! Discussing philosophy. D'you want me to tell you what I think of Darwin? He's an animal! That's what I think. Give me the bottle!'

But Craft refused, and Ega stood tottering for a moment as he stared at him with a livid face.

'You either give me the bottle – you either give me the bottle, or I'll put a bullet through your heart . . . No, you're not even worth a bullet – I'll hit you!'

Suddenly his eyelids closed; he dropped back in his chair; and then on to the floor like a sack.

'He's out!' said Craft serenely.

He rang the bell; the footmen entered and they gathered up

João da Ega. And while they carried him to the guest-room and stripped him of his Satan's suit, he never ceased to whine and place wet kisses on Carlos's hands as he stammered all the while:

'Little Rachel! Rachel, my little Rachelkin! D'you love your little Egakin?'

When Carlos set off in the cab for Lisbon it was no longer raining, a cold wind swept the sky and dawn was brightening.

The next day at ten o'clock, Carlos returned to Olivais. He found Craft asleep and went up to Ega's room. The windows had been left open and a broad sunbeam gilded the bed; he was still snoring, bathed by that golden ray, as he lay on his side, with his knees drawn up against his belly and his nose under the sheets.

When Carlos shook him, poor John opened one sad eye and abruptly raised himself on his elbow, surprised by the room, the curtains of green damask, the portrait of a powdered lady that smiled at him from her gilt frame. Then memories of the previous evening must have swept over him because he buried himself again within the sheets right up to his chin; and his green, withered face expressed reluctance to part from those soft mattresses and the comfortable peace of the manor and to have to go to Lisbon to face every kind of bitterness.

'Is it cold outside?' he asked dolefully.

'No, it's a wonderful day. But get up quickly! If anyone goes to your house on Cohen's behalf, they'll think you've run away!'

Ega sprang out of bed at once and, stupefied and dishevelled, he searched for his clothes while his thin, naked legs bumped against the furniture. He could only find Satan's tunic. They called a servant, who brought a pair of Craft's trousers. Ega quickly donned them and then, without washing and still unshaven, the collar of his overcoat turned up, he thrust his head at last into the deerstalker, turned to Carlos, and said with a tragic air:

'Let's get on with it!'

Craft had risen and he accompanied them to the gate where Carlos's coupé was waiting. In the avenue of acacias that had been so sinister yesterday under the rain, birds were now singing. The park, fresh and washed, glistened green in the sunshine. Craft's great Newfoundland bounded around them.

'Have you got a headache, Ega?' asked Craft.

'No,' the other replied as he finished buttoning his coat. 'I wasn't drunk yesterday. I was just weak.'

But as he got into the coupé he observed with a profound and philosophical air:

'What a thing it is to drink good wine – I feel as though nothing had happened!'

Craft suggested he send a telegram if there was any news, then he shut the door of the coupé and they set off.

No telegram reached the manor during the morning and when Craft appeared at the Villa Balzac, where one of Carlos's carriages waited outside the door, it was already getting dark and two candles burned in the dismal green parlour. Carlos lay stretched out on the sofa, dozing with an open book on his stomach; and Ega paced up and down, all dressed in black, pale and with a rose in his buttonhole. He had been in the parlour waiting in that tedium all day for a word from Cohen.

'What did I tell you? Nothing is going to happen, and nothing can happen,' murmured Craft.

But Ega was now troubled by black thoughts and feared Cohen might have murdered his wife! Craft's sceptical smile made him indignant. Who knew Cohen better than he? Under that bourgeois appearance a monster was hidden. He had seen him kill a cat just for the whim of seeing bloodshed.

'I have a presentiment of disaster,' he stammered in terror.

And at that very moment the bell rang. Ega woke Carlos precipately and pushed the two friends into the bedroom. Craft still had time to say that at that hour it could not be friends of Cohen's. But Ega wanted to be alone in the parlour; and there he waited, paler, more rigid, very buttoned up in his frock-coat, with his eyes riveted on the door.

'How tiresome,' said Carlos in the bedroom as he groped in the dark. Craft found the remains of a candle standing on the dressing-table and lit it. A sad light glowed and revealed everything in disorder – a night-shirt lay in the middle of the floor; in a corner was the bath, filled with soapy water; and in the centre the enormous bed, surrounded by its red silk curtains, had the majesty of a shrine.

For a moment they were silent. Craft methodically and studiously examined the dressing-table where there was a packet of hairpins, a garter with its clasp broken and a bunch of withered violets. Then he went and looked at the marble top of the commode: a plate with chicken bones had been left there; and beside it lay half a sheet of paper written on in pencil, and all corrected – part of some literary work of Ega's. He found all this quite remarkable.

From the parlour there could meanwhile be heard the subtle and intimate whisper of voices. Carlos, who was listening, thought he could make out the muffled voice of a woman and impatiently he went to the kitchen. The maid was sitting at the table with a hand in her hair, doing nothing and staring at the light; the page was slouched on a chair sucking at a cigarette.

'Who came in?' asked Carlos.

'It was Senhor Cohen's servant,' answered the urchin as he hid his cigarette behind his back.

Carlos returned to the bedroom announcing:

'It's the confidante. Things have ended happily.'

'And how did you think they would end?' said Craft. 'Cohen has his bank, his business affairs, his bills to honour, his credit, his respectability, all that arrangement of things that a scandal disturbs – this is what calms husbands down. And besides, he has already satisfied his honour; he has already threatened Ega with kicks!'

At that moment there was a noise in the parlour and Ega violently threw open the door.

'Nothing is going to happen,' he exclaimed. 'He gave her a beating, and they are leaving tomorrow for England.'

Carlos looked at Craft, who was nodding his head like one who sees all his forecasts fulfilled and thoroughly approves.

'A beating!' said Ega, with his eyes aflame and in a sibilant voice. 'And then they made it up – it'll be a model *ménage* yet! A stick purifies everything – what scum!'

He was furious. At that moment he hated Rachel – unable to forgive his idol for having succumbed before a beating. Then he remembered Cohen's walking-stick, an Indian bamboo with the head of a greyhound for a handle. And that object had thrashed the flesh that he had clasped with passion! That object had imposed purple bruises where his lips had left pink marks! And they had *made things up*! And thus had ended, vulgar and rowdy, the greatest romance of his life! He would have preferred her dead than known her beaten. But no! She had taken her beating and then lain down with her husband, and he, Cohen, would certainly have been penitent, have called her sweet names, and, dressed in his underwear, would have helped her to apply tincture of arnica to her bruises! It had all ended in tincture of arnica!

'Come in here, Senhora Adélia,' he called into the parlour, 'come through! These are my friends. The secret is out; prudery is finished with! These are friends! We are three but we are one! Before you stands the great mystery of the Most Holy Trinity. Sit down, Senhora Adélia, don't stand on ceremony – and you can tell them, for, my dear fellows, Senhora Adélia here saw everything; she saw the beating!'

Senhora Adélia, a fat and short little female, with pretty eyes and a hat trimmed with red flowers, immediately came in from the parlour to correct Ega's narrative. No, she had not seen it . . . Senhor Ega had misunderstood her . . . She had only heard . . .

'This was how it was, sirs! I was up, of course, until the ball had ended, and I could hardly keep myself awake. It was already as light as day when my master, still dressed as a Moor, shut himself up in the bedroom with my mistress. I stayed in the kitchen with Domingos waiting for them to ring the bell. Then we suddenly heard screams – I was very frightened and even thought it might be burglars. We ran up, me and Domingos, but the door to the bedroom was locked with the two of them inside, right inside the alcove. I even put my eye to the keyhole, but I could see nothing . . . But the sound of punches, and falls and the stick – ah! yes! these could be heard plainly, and the screams. I said to Domingos at once: "Oh, it's a fight! Oh, it's all over with her!" But suddenly there was complete silence! We went back to the kitchen; and a little later Senhor Cohen came in, all dishevelled, in his shirt-sleeves, to tell us we could go to bed, that they did not need us for anything, and that tomorrow we would have a talk. And there they were all night, and by morning they seemed to have become very friendly. I didn't set eyes on my mistress. Only Senhor Cohen got up, came into the kitchen, settled up with me and dismissed me – he was very bad-mannered and even threatened me with the police. It was through Domingos that I learned just now, when I returned for my box with a porter, that Senhor Cohen was going to England. Well, it

was quite a dust-up . . . I've had my stomach upset all day.'
And with a sigh Senhora Adélia fell silent and dropped her gaze.
Ega stood with his arms folded, looking bitterly towards his
friends. What did they think of that? A beating! As though a
coward like that did not deserve a bullet through his heart! And
as for her, allowing herself to be knocked about without trying to
escape, and then consenting to sleep with him! What scum!

'And hasn't Senhora Adélia any idea,' asked Craft, 'how he
found out – ?'

'That's the extraordinary thing!' cried Ega, clasping his hands
to his head.

Yes, extraordinary! It had not been an intercepted letter: they
did not write to each other. He could not have surprised any of
the visits to the Villa Balzac: things were arranged very subtly
and were absolutely undiscoverable. To come there she had never
committed the indiscretion of using her own carriage. Never had
she entered directly through the door. His servants had never
seen her and did not know who the lady was that visited him. So
many precautions had been taken, and all destroyed!

'Strange! Strange!' murmured Craft.

There was silence. Senhora Adélia ended by depositing herself
familiarly in a chair, her little bundle on her lap.

'Well now, Senhor Ega,' she said, after reflection, 'you can believe me – it was in dreams. It's happened before – my mistress
talked in her sleep about you and revealed everything. Senhor
Cohen overheard her, became suspicious, spied on her and discovered her game – and I know that she talks in her sleep.'

Ega stood in front of Senhora Adélia and stared at her from
head to foot – from the flowers in her hat to the hem of her skirt,
his eyes flashing.

'How could he possibly overhear her? They had separate
rooms – I know they had!'

Senhora Adélia lowered her eyelids and fingered the little round
bundle on her lap with her black-gloved fingers and spoke in
a lowered voice:

'Oh, no they didn't, sir. No indeed! My mistress wouldn't
hear of such an arrangement. My mistress is very fond of her
husband and she's very jealous of him.'

There was an embarrassed and unpleasant silence. On the

dressing-table the remains of the candle were fluttering out in the gloomy light. And Ega, who affected to smile, and shrugged his shoulders, now walked around the room with slow, leaden steps, twiddling his moustache with a tremulous hand.

Then Carlos, disgusted and weary of this interlude that had lasted since the day before and was like churning mud, declared that it was time to stop this business! It was eight o'clock and he wanted his dinner.

'Yes, let us all go and dine,' murmured Ega looking confused and stunned.

Then, abruptly, he made a sign to Senhora Adélia, led her back into the parlour and shut himself up there again.

'Aren't you becoming weary of this, Craft?' exclaimed Carlos in desperation.

'No. I find it an interesting study.'

They waited another ten minutes. Suddenly the candle went out. Carlos shouted furiously for the page. And the urchin was just entering with a filthy oil lamp when Ega came back from the parlour, more composed now. Everything was over; Senhora Adélia had gone.

'Let's go and have dinner,' he said. 'But where can we go at this hour?'

It was he himself who suggested the André in the Chiado. Outside, Carlos's coupé and Craft's cab stood waiting. The two carriages set off. The Villa Balzac lay in darkness, dumb, from henceforth useless.

They had to wait a long time at the André in a dismal room with paper covered in little golden stars, little curtains of cheap muslin under drapes of blue rep, and two hissing gas-jets. Ega, who looked exhausted, sank down into a sofa that had loose, worn-out springs, and he closed his eyes; Carlos contemplated the engravings on the walls – all depicting Spanish women: one emerging from church; another leaping over a small pool of water; another, her eyes cast down, listening to the counsels of a priest. Craft, already at table with his head resting on his hands, sat looking through the *Diário da Manhã,* which the waiter had handed him.

Suddenly Ega banged the sofa and it creaked deplorably.

'What I can't understand,' he shouted, 'is how that devil found out.'

252

'Senhora Adélia's hypothesis,' said Craft, looking up from his paper, 'seems a likely one. Either dreaming or waking the poor lady revealed herself. Perhaps it was an anonymous denunciation; perhaps it was an accident. The fact remains: he was suspicious, spied on her and caught her.'

Ega stood up.

'I didn't want to tell you in front of Adélia, who was not completely in on the secret. But you know the house in front of mine, the other side of the lane – a house with a big garden? An aunt of the Countess Gouvarinho lives there – Dona Maria Lima, very respectable. Rachel went there from time to time. They are intimate friends – Dona Maria Lima is intimate friends with everybody. Then she would go out by a little gate in the garden, cross the lane, and be at the door of my house, the side door, the door to the stairs that lead to the bathroom. So you can see – the servants couldn't even see her. When she lunched, the lunch was already served in my room and the doors were closed. Even if anyone did see her, it was simply a lady in a black veil who came from the Lima house . . . How could the man catch her? And besides, in the Lima house, she used to change her hat and put on a waterproof.'

Craft complimented him.

'Brilliant!'

'And so,' said Carlos smiling, 'that respectable noblewoman – '

'Dona Maria, poor thing . . . I tell you, she's an excellent old lady, received everywhere. But she's poor and she does people favours – sometimes even in her own house.'

'Does she charge much for these services?' asked Craft calmly. Throughout this affair he had been seeking to instruct himself.

'No, the poor thing,' said Ega. 'People give her five pounds once in a while.'

The servant came in with a platter of shrimps, and the three sat down in silence at the table.

After dinner they retired to Ramalhete. Ega was going there to sleep, as his nerves were so excited that he feared the solitude of the Villa Balzac. They set off with cigars alight in an open chaise under a sweet, starry sky.

Fortunately, nobody was at home when they reached Ramalhete. Ega, who was tired out, was able to retire at once to his room, a guest-chamber on the second floor, where there was a beautiful antique ebony bed. As soon as the servant had left him Ega went up to the mirror where the lights burned and drew out a gold locket that hung around his neck beneath his shirt. It had a photograph of Rachel inside that he now intended to burn, consigning the ashes of that passion to the slop-pail. But when he opened the locket that pretty smiling face under the oval glass seemed to look out at him with sadness in the velvet of those languid eyes. The photograph showed only the head, with an opening in the neckline of her dress; but in his memory Ega once again unfastened that dress; once again he looked on that form, the extraordinary satin of her skin, the little mole on her left breast. The taste of her kisses once more came to his lips, and again in his imagination he felt the echo of the tired sighs she had given in his arms. And now she was going away. He would *never* see her again! The desolate bitterness of that *never* overcame him utterly – and the poor radical, the great phrase-maker, buried his face in his pillow and sobbed for a long time in the secret of the night.

That whole week was painful for Ega. The very next day Damaso appeared at Ramalhete and brought all the Lisbon gossip. Every-where – in the Grémio, in the Chiado – it was already known that he had been evicted from the Cohens' house. The bear and the Tyrolean shepherdess who had witnessed the episode had re-counted it eagerly. It was even said that Cohen had actually kicked him. For their part, Cohen's friends, especially Alencar, swore fervently to Dona Rachel's innocence. Alencar stated pub-licly that Ega, an inexperienced provincial and a Don Juan from Celorico, had taken his hostess's smiles of friendship as tokens of passion, had written an almost obscene letter to Dona Rachel; and she, the poor little thing, had gone all in tears to show it to her husband.

'So, they're running me down, eh, Damaso?' murmured Ega as he sat huddled in an armchair in Carlos's dressing-room wrapped in an old ulster and listening to these things with a sick, weary expression.

Damaso admitted that in society they were indeed running him down.

Ah, he could well imagine it! He knew he had enemies in Lisbon. Nobody had yet forgiven him his pelisse. His sarcastic wit offended people. And many found it an unpleasant thing that a man so dangerous and fiery had a rich mother and was independent.

Then when Carlos returned from his dinner at the Gouvarinhos' the following Saturday – a dinner that had been excellent – he related his conversation with the Countess. The Countess had spoken to him very freely, like a man, of Ega's disaster. She had been most distressed, not only for Rachel, poor dear, who was her friend, but for Ega, whose talents she so appreciated – he was so interesting, so brilliant – and who had come out of it so soiled! Cohen had told everyone (he had told Count Gouvarinho) that he had threatened Ega with kicks because the latter had written a lewd letter to his wife. Those who knew nothing, like the Count, believed and held up their hands in horror; and those who knew the truth, those who had been grinning about Ega's intimacy with the Cohens for the past six months, affected to believe too and clenched their fists in indignation. Ega was hated! And all that little Lisbon that lives between the Grémio and the Casa Havanesa enjoyed itself 'burying' Ega.

Ega, indeed, felt 'buried'. And that night he declared to Carlos that he had decided to retire to his mother's estate and spend a year there finishing the *Memoirs of an Atom,* and he would reappear in triumph in Lisbon when his book was published to crush all these mediocrities. Carlos did not attempt to shatter this radiant illusion.

But just before his departure, when Ega went to examine his business affairs concerning the house and his financial situation, he found himself faced with an abominable development. He owed everybody – from the upholsterer to the baker; he had three bills to meet; and all these debts, if he left them unpaid, would be added to the public scandal over the Cohen business. Then, besides being the lover threatened with kicks, he would also be the penniless victim of creditors! What alternative had he than to turn to Carlos? And, to settle everything, Carlos lent him two *contos.*

Then, after he had dismissed the Villa Balzac servants, other complications arose. The page's mother came to Ramalhete a few days later, very insolent, shouting that her son had disappeared! Which was, in fact, true: the celebrated page, perverted by the cook, had gone off with her to the alleys of the Mouraria and there had embarked upon the interesting career of a *souteneur.*

Ega refused to listen to the mother's complaints. What the devil had such sordidness to do with him?

But the creature's lover intervened with threats. He was a policeman, an arm of the law; and he let it be understood that he could easily prove that the Villa Balzac had been the scene of 'unnatural practices', and that the page was not there simply to serve at table. Sick to death, Ega surrendered to this blackmail and gave five pounds to the policeman. When, on that last night, a sad, watery night, Carlos and Craft accompanied Ega to Santa Apolónia Station, he spoke a few words to them in the carriage, the dismal summary of that great romance:

'I feel as though my soul had fallen into a latrine! I need a bath inside!'

When Afonso da Maia had learned of Ega's disaster, he had said sadly to Carlos:

'A bad beginning, my boy! An extremely bad beginning!'

And that night when he got home from Santa Apolónia, Carlos meditated on these words and repeated them to himself.

'An extremely bad beginning!' For not only Ega had made a bad beginning – so had he. And perhaps because that was just what his grandfather had been thinking his words had been so sad. Extremely bad beginnings! Six months had passed since Ega's arrival from Celorico, wrapped up in his big pelisse, ready to astound Lisbon with the *Memoirs of an Atom*, dominate it with a journal, become a beacon, a power, a thousand and one other things . . . And now, debt-ridden and ridiculed, he had returned to Celorico like a hunted man. An extremely bad beginning! For his part, Carlos had arrived in Lisbon with colossal plans for work and armed like a warrior; there were the consulting-rooms; the laboratory; a first book; a thousand geat ideas – and what had he achieved? Two articles in a journal, a dozen prescriptions, and that melancholy chapter on 'Medicine Among the Greeks'. An extremely bad beginning!

No, life did not seem promising to him at that moment, as he paced around the billiards-room with his hands in his pockets while his friends conversed around him and the south-west wind howled outside. Poor Ega, how miserable he would be feeling huddled there into the corner of his wagon-lit! But his companions here were no merrier. Craft and the Marquis had begun one of those discussions about life, gloomy and despondent. What was the use of living at all, said Craft, if one were not a Livingstone or a Bismarck? And the Marquis declared with a philosophical air that the world was becoming stupid. Then Taveira arrived with a horrible tale about a colleague of his whose son had fallen downstairs and been smashed to pieces the same instant that his wife was dying of pleurisy. Cruges growled something or other about suicide, and the words drew themselves out dismally. Carlos moved about restlessly turning up the lamps.

But everything became cheerful again a few moments later when Damaso appeared to tell him that Castro Gomes was unwell and in bed.

'Naturally,' added Damaso, 'they will be sending for you, as you have already visited the child.'

The following day Carlos did not leave the house, waiting for a message and bristling with impatience. No message came. And two afternoons later, going down to the Aterro, the first person he saw in Janellas Verdes was Castro Gomes in an open chaise with his wife at his side and the little dog in his lap.

She passed by without seeing him. And there and then Carlos resolved to end this torture and ask Damaso very simply to present him to Castro Gomes before he left for Brazil. He could not stand it any longer, he needed to hear her voice, to see what her eyes had to say when they were questioned from near at hand.

But all that week he found himself constantly and unaccountably in the company of the Gouvarinhos. It began by a meeting with the Count, who had caught his arm to draw him into the Rua de S. Marçal, put him in an armchair in his office, and read him an article destined for the *Jornal do Comércio* about the position of political parties in Portugal; then he had invited him to dinner. The following afternoon they had a croquet party. Carlos went. And, there at the window, open on to the garden, he had a moment of intimacy with the Countess and told her, laughing, how her hair had bewitched him the first time he had seen her. That night she spoke of a book of Tennyson's she had not read; Carlos offered to lend it to her and took it round to her the very next morning. He found her alone, all dressed in white; and they were laughing with lowered voices, their two chairs close together, when the footman announced Senhora Dona

Maria da Cunha. It was an extraordinary occurrence! Dona Maria da Cunha at that hour! Carlos, however, was very fond of Dona Maria da Cunha, a pretty old lady, all goodness, full of tolerance for all sins – indeed she had herself been very much a sinner when she had been the lovely young Madame Cunha. Dona Maria was a great talker and seemed to have something private to communicate to the Countess; so Carlos left them, promising to return one afternoon to take tea and talk about Tennyson.

On the afternoon he was dressing to go there, Damaso appeared in his bedroom to bring Carlos news that filled the plump-cheeked youth with disgust and rage. That idiot of a Castro Gomes had changed his mind, and was no longer going to Brazil! He was going to stay there, at the Central, until the middle of the summer! And how all his plans were ruined.

The idea at once occurred to Carlos of speaking to him about an introduction to Castro Gomes. But unaccountably – just as when he had been in Cintra – repugnance overcame him at the thought of meeting her through Damaso's offices. And so he went on dressing in silence.

Meanwhile Damaso was cursing his luck.

'And I'd really have had that woman! I'd have had her, if there'd only been the opportunity – But what the devil can you do, things being as they are?'

Then he began to complain against Castro Gomes. To put it briefly, he was an idiot. And the man's life was a mystery – what the devil was he up to in Lisbon? There were money difficulties involved. They didn't get on well either. Yesterday there had certainly been a quarrel. When he had called on them her eyes had been red and she seemed embarrassed; and he had been pacing nervously round the drawing-room pulling at his beard. Both of them had looked uncomfortable, uttering only a word each quarter of an hour.

'D'you know what?' exclaimed Damaso. 'I'm thinking of sending them both to the devil!'

He complained about her too. Above all she was very uneven-tempered: sometimes friendly, sometimes icy. And occasionally, when he said something perfectly normal, the sort of thing one says in society, she would start to laugh. It was enough to put one off, eh! In fact they were very queer people.

'Where are you going?' he asked with a sigh of boredom, when he saw Carlos putting on his hat.

He was going to take tea with Countess Gouvarinho.

'Well, look, I'll come with you – I'm bored stiff!'

Carlos hesitated for a moment; finally he agreed.

'Come along – you will even be doing me a favour!'

The afternoon was lovely and Carlos drove the dog-cart.

'What a long time it's been since we've been out together like this,' said Damaso.

'Well, if you will get mixed up with foreigners . . .'

Damaso sighed again and said no more. Then at the door of the Gouvarinhos', when he learned that the Countess was receiving, he suddenly resolved not to go in. No, no, he would not come in. He felt very stupid, unable to find a word to say.

'And another thing I've just remembered!' he exclaimed, delaying Carlos still before the door. 'Castro Gomes asked me yesterday what he ought to send you for visiting the child. I said you'd gone as a favour, as my friend. And he said he'd have to call on you and leave his card. Therefore it's likely you'll get to know them.'

So it was not going to be necessary for Damaso to present him after all!

'Come and see us one night, Damasozinho; come to dinner tomorrow!' cried Carlos, suddenly radiant and clasping his friend's hand ardently.

When he entered the drawing-room a footman had just finished serving tea. The room was lined with a severe green and gold wallpaper on which hung family portraits in heavy frames, and it opened through two balconies above the foliage of the garden. Baskets of flowers stood on the tables. On the sofa, two ladies in hats, and both in black, were conversing, cup in hand. The Countess, on extending her fingers to Carlos, became as rosy as the quilted silk of the chair on which she leaned back, beside a candlestick of aloe wood.

She immediately observed Carlos's happy expression and asked smilingly what good thing had happened to him. Carlos smiled too and asked how anyone could possibly enter her drawing-rom with any other expression. Then he inquired after the Count.

The Count had not yet appeared; he must certainly be delayed

259

in the House of Peers where they were discussing a draft law on the Reform of Public Education.

One of the ladies in black hoped that the curriculum would be lightened. The poor children really suffered with all that they had to get off by heart; her little boy, Joãozinho, was so pale and so pinched that sometimes she felt like allowing him to remain in perpetual ignorance. The other lady put down her plate and, touching her lips with the lace of her handkerchief, complained above all of the examiners. It was scandalous the demands and difficulties they made, just in order to make the pupils fail. Her child had been put the most stupid, the most vulgar questions: for example, what was soap, why did soap wash?

The other lady and the Countess clasped their hands on their bosoms in consternation. And Carlos very amiably agreed that it was an abomination. Her husband, went on the second lady, had become so desperate that when he met the examiner in the Chiado, he had threatened to give him a thrashing. An imprudence, certainly; but the man had in fact been disagreeable. There was really only one thing worth studying – foreign languages. It was nonsense to torture a child with botany, astronomy, physics. What for? Things that were quite useless in society. For example, her little boy was now having chemistry lessons – how absurd! As his father said, what was the use if he was not going to be a chemist?

After a silence the two ladies rose at the same time; and there was a murmur of kisses and the rustle of silks.

Carlos stayed with the Countess, who sat down again in her rose-coloured chair.

At once she asked for Ega.

'Poor fellow – he is up there at Celorico.'

She protested with a lovely smile at that ugly phrase – 'he is up there at Celorico!' No, she would not have it – Poor Ega! He deserved a better obituary than that. Celorico was a horrible end to a romance.

'You're right!' exclaimed Carlos, laughing too. 'It would be nicer to say: "He is in Jerusalem"!'

At that moment the servant announced a name and Teles da Gama, a close friend of the house, appeared. When he learned that the Count must still be battling over the Education Reform, he lifted his hands to his head as though lamenting such an ugly waste of time, and he would not stay. No, not even the Countess's excellent tea could tempt him. The truth was that the grace of God had so deserted him, he had so lost his feeling for beautiful things, that he had in fact called not to see the Countess but merely in order to speak to the Count. She pouted prettily at this, like an offended princess, and asked Carlos if such rude and craggy sincerity did not make one nostalgic for the polished manners of olden days. With a smile that displayed his magnificent teeth, and swaying to and fro on his heels, Teles da Gama declared that he was a democrat and a nature-lover. Then, as he left, he shook Maia's hand and asked when the Prince of Santa Olávia would finally condescend to do him the honour of dining with him. The Countess affected to become indignant. No, this was really too much! To extend invitations in her drawing-room, in her presence – a man who had talked so much about his German cook and had not so much as even offered her a plate of *chou-croûte*.

Still laughing, Teles da Gama went on swaying and vowed that he was in the course of making ready his dining-room in order to give a party for the Countess, a party that would go down in history! But as far as Maia was concerned, it was a different matter; they would both dine in the kitchen with their plates on their knees. And off he went, swaying all the while, still laughing in the doorway and displaying his magnificent teeth.

'He's a merry fellow that Gama, don't you think?' asked the Countess.

'Very merry,' agreed Carlos.

Then she looked at the clock. It was half past five and there would be no more callers; at last they could talk for a moment like good friends. A slow silence followed and their eyes met. Then Carlos asked after Charlie, his pretty patient. He was not well, he had a slight cough that he had caught on the promenade at Estrela. That child never ceased to cause her concern! She fell silent, gazing abstractedly at the carpet and fanning herself languidly. She was rather over-dressed that afternoon in heavy silk the colour of autumn gold that rustled like dry leaves at the slightest movement.

'What wonderful weather there has been!' she declared suddenly, as though rousing herself.

'Wonderful,' agreed Carlos. 'I was at Cintra a few days ago and you cannot imagine – it was idyllic.'

And then he at once regretted having spoken – he felt uncomfortable at mentioning his Cintra trip in that drawing-room.

But the Countess hardly heard him. She had risen and was talking about some songs she had received that morning from England – the latest novelties of the season. Then she sat down at the piano and ran her fingers over the keyboard and asked Carlos if he knew the tune – 'The Pale Star'. No, Carlos did not know it. But all those English songs were the same, always the same doleful tones, romanesque and very maidenly. And always there was a melancholic park, a running brook and a kiss under the chestnuts.

Then the Countess read the words of 'The Pale Star' aloud. And it was indeed the same as ever: a little star of love throbbing in the dusk, a pale lake, a timid kiss under the trees.

'It's always the same,' said Carlos, 'and it's always delightful.'

But the Countess threw the paper aside and declared it stupid. She began nervously to sort through the music sheets with a frowning look. Carlos, in order to break the silence, praised her lovely flowers.

'Ah! I've been meaning to give you a rose,' she cried at once, leaving the music.

But the flower she wanted to give him was in her boudoir, the adjoining room. Carlos followed her long train, from which there flowed the golden reflection of autumn foliage beaten by the sun. It was a room lined in blue, with a beautiful Louis XV mirror on a tripod and, on a heavy oak pedestal, a heavy terracotta bust of the Count wearing his orator's look, his forehead raised, his tie undone, his lip roaring.

The Countess selected a bud with two leaves and came up herself to pin it to his frock-coat. The warm scent of verbena rising from her heaving breast assailed Carlos's senses. She took a long time pinning the flower; her fingers were tremulous and slow, and seemed to linger and sleep on the cloth of his coat.

'*Voilà*,' she murmured at last in a low voice. 'You look like my fine knight of the Red Rose – and you mustn't thank me!'

Without knowing how it happened, irresistibly, Carlos found himself with his lips on hers. The silk of her dress rasped against his suit with a soft rustle as he held her in his arms.

White as wax, she threw back her head and tenderly closed her eyes. And, clasping her as though she were dead, he took a step; his knee encountered a low sofa, that slid away escaping him. Carlos followed the wide sofa as it rolled off, and he stumbled as he did so, for her silk train had got wrapped around his feet. Then he bumped against the pedestal upon which the Count elevated his inspired forehead. A long sigh died amid the sound of crushed skirts.

A moment later both of them were standing up: Carlos alongside the bust, scratching his beard, looking embarrassed and already vaguely regretful; she before the Louis XV mirror, tidying her curls with trembling fingers. Suddenly, in the hall, the voice of the Count sounded. She turned abruptly and ran to Carlos. With her long, bejewelled fingers she took his face in her hands and placed two sparkling kisses on his hair and eyes. Then, easily, she sat down on the sofa and was talking of Cintra and laughing loudly when the Count entered followed by a bald-headed old man who was busy blowing his nose in an enormous Indian silk handkerchief. On seeing Carlos in the boudoir the Count looked pleasantly surprised and gave him a long, warm handshake, insisting that he had been thinking of him only that morning in Parliament.

'Then why did you come back so late?' exclaimed the Countess, who had immediately taken possession of the old man and was smiling and gesticulating with animation and cordiality.

'Our Count spoke,' said the old man, his eye still shining with enthusiasm.

'You spoke?' she exclaimed, turning to him with delighted interest.

It was true, he had spoken! And without notice! However, when he had heard Torres Valente (a man of letters, but a madman, no practical sense!) when he had heard him defending compulsory gymnastics in the schools, he had risen. But friend Mala must not imagine that he had delivered a speech.

'Come now,' cried the old man waving his handkerchief. 'It was one of the best I have ever heard in the Chamber! A splendid speech!'

The Count protested modestly. No! He had simply put in a word of good sense and good principle. He had merely inquired of his illustrious friend Torres Valente if in his opinion our sons, the heirs to our estates, were destined to become clowns.

'Oh! What wit, Countess!' exclaimed the old man. 'How I wish you had heard this sally! It was the way he delivered it! Such *chic*!'

The Count smiled and turned aside to thank the old man. Yes, that was all he had said. And then, replying to other reflections of Torres Valente's, who did not want to see the instruction in high schools and colleges 'impregnated with the Catechism', he had assailed him cruelly.

'Terribly!' cried the old man in dark tones as he got his handkerchief ready to blow his nose again.

'Yes, terribly! I turned to him and told him this: "The noble lord ought to realize that our country will never recapture its place at the head of civilization if we, the legislators, are to lay an impious hand on high schools, colleges and institutions of learning in order to replace the Cross with the trapeze . . ."'

'Wonderful!' hooted the old man delivering a dreadful snort into his handkerchief.

As Carlos rose he declared that the Count's irony was quite enchanting.

And when he took leave of him the Count was not contented with a simple handshake: he put his arm round his waist and called him his dear Maia. The Countess smiled, her look still humid, and with a remnant of pallor as she fanned herself languidly and leaned back on two cushions of the sofa – below the bust of her husband with his noble brow.

10

ON A HOT afternoon three weeks later, when the sky was gloomy with thunder and just as a few big drops of rain had begun to fall, a cab stopped slowly at the corner of the Patriarcal, its green blinds mysteriously drawn, and Carlos stepped out. Two people passing by looked at each other and grinned as though they had caught him emerging awkwardly from some suspicious doorway. And, as a matter of fact, that old cab with its yellow wheels had indeed just ceased to be a verbena-scented love-nest in which Carlos had ridden along the Queluz Road for two whole hours in the company of the Countess de Gouvarinho.

She had got down in Amoreiras Square. And Carlos was taking advantage of the solitude of the Patriarcal to get away from that old carriage with its hard seat. He had suffocated inside it for the past hour rather than risk opening the windows; his legs had gone to sleep; and he had been satiated with so many crumpled silks and the interminable kisses she placed on his beard.

Until that afternoon they had, for the past three weeks, met in a house in Rua de Santa Isabel that belonged to one of the Countess's aunts, who had gone to Oporto with her maid, and left the key to the house and the care of her cat with her niece. The good aunt was a little old woman called Miss Jones – a saint, a militant disciple of the Anglican Church, a missionary for the propagation of her faith; and every month she took a proselytizing journey through the provinces distributing bibles, wrenching souls from the darkness of Catholicism and purifying, as she put it, the swamp of Papacy. The moment one stepped on to the staircase one sensed that sweet, sad, faint aroma characteristic of devotion and elderly virginity. A big card hung on the landing bearing a motto in letters of gold interlaced with purple lilies, appealing to those who entered to persevere in the path of the Lord! Carlos entered and tripped immediately over a mountain of bibles. The whole room was packed with them: they lay in piles on top of the furniture; they overflowed from old hat-boxes; they were mixed up with pairs of galoshes; they had wandered into the hip-bath. All of them were in the same format, wrapped in black binding like battle-armour, sullen and aggressive. The walls were resplendent, decked with cards printed in coloured lettering that irradiated harsh verses from Scripture, stern moral counsels, cries from the psalms, insolent threats of hell-fire.

And in the midst of all that Anglican piety, on the night-table beside a small, hard, virginal iron bed, stood two bottles of cognac and gin that were almost empty. Carlos had drunk the saintly old maid's gin; and her hard bed had become as disorderly as a battlefield.

Then the Countess had begun to be afraid of a neighbour, a woman called Borges, who visited her aunt and was the widow of a former steward of the Gouvarinhos. On one occasion when they lay languorously smoking cheroots on Miss Jones's chaste bed, three enormous thumps on the door thundered through the house. The poor Countess nearly fainted; Carlos ran to the window and saw a man moving away with a plaster statuette in his hand and others inside a basket. But the Countess vowed it was the Borges woman who had sent the Italian with his images to give those three knocks, hurling them into the house like three warnings, three moral alarm signals. And she would return no more to the aunt's blessed cot. So that afternoon, as there was so far no other refuge, they had sheltered their love in that hansom cab.

But Carlos returned enervated, limp and already feeling the first yawns of satiety in his spirit. It was hardly three weeks since those verbena-scented arms had thrown themselves about his neck. Now, as he walked along the promenade of S. Pedro de Alcantara, under the light drizzle falling on the foliage of the avenue, he wondered how he might extricate himself from her tenacity, her ardour, her weight. For the Countess was becoming absurd with her eager, audacious determination to invade his entire life, to assume the largest and deepest place in it, as though that first kiss they had exchanged had united not only their lips for one instant, but also their destinies – and for ever. Again that afternoon she had repeated those words, stammeringly, leaning against his chest, her eyes drowned in beseeching tenderness: 'If you wanted, how happy we could be! What a wonderful life we could have together! Just the two of us alone!' And

this much was clear: the Countess had conceived the extravagant notion of eloping with him and going off to live in an
eternal dream of idyllic love in some corner of the world, as remote as possible from Rua de S. Marçal. If he wanted! No, by
God, he did not in the least want to elope with Madame the
Countess de Gouvarinho!

But this was not all! In addition she was demanding, ego-
tistical and given to the tumultuous explosions of a jealous temperament; already more than once in those two short weeks
she had thrown a scene over a trifle, talked of dying and dissolved in tears . . . Ah, but in even those tears there was nevertheless a certain voluptuousness that made the satin of her neck
seem even more tender! What really disturbed him, however,
were certain looks that crossed her face, a nervous gaze from her
dry eyes that revealed the passion that mounted in those thirty-
three-year-old woman's nerves, a passion that scorched her to
the depths of her being. Certainly this love affair had brought
yet one more luxury and one more perfume into his life. But its
charm lay in remaining facile and serene and no more than skin-
deep. If, for the slightest thing, her eyes were to brim with tears
and she were to talk of dying; if she were to wring her hands
and beg to elope with him – then, good-bye! Everything was
ruined; the Countess with her verbena, her flame-coloured hair
and her sobs became nothing but an encumbrance.

The shower had stopped and a patch of watery blue appeared
among the clouds. Carlos was making his way down the Rua de
S. Roque when he came upon the Marquis emerging from a
confectioner's looking dismal and holding a parcel in his hand,
his neck wrapped in an enormous white silk scarf.

'What's the trouble? A cold?' asked Carlos.

'Everything,' said the Marquis walking beside him as slow as
death. 'I went to bed late. Fatigue! An oppression in the chest!
Hoarse throat! Pains in my side! Frightful! . . . I've just brought
some sweets!'

'Don't be foolish, man! What you need is roast beef and a
bottle of burgundy – isn't it today that you're supposed to dine
with us at Ramalhete? And you'll even meet Craft and Damaso
– let's go down the Rua do Alecrim. It's stopped raining now
– we'll have a brisk walk along the Aterro, and you'll be cured
by the time we arrive!'

267

The poor Marquis shrugged his shoulders. No sooner did he feel the slightest indisposition – a pain, a shiver – than he immediately believed himself 'finished', as he put it. For him the world began to come to an end. He would be overwhelmed with Catholic terrors and an anguished preoccupation with Eternity. On such days he would shut himself up in his room with his chaplain, with whom he sometimes, despite everything, ended up playing draughts.

'In any case,' he said, cautiously removing his hat as they passed the door of the Church of Martyrs, 'just let me go to the Grémio first – I want to write a note to Manuelita, so that the girl won't be waiting for me.'

Then, distracted and sorrowful, he asked for news of that libertine, Ega. The libertine was still up there in Celorico, under the maternal roof, listening to Father Seraphim belch and taking refuge, so he said, in great art. He was composing a comedy in five acts to be entitled *The Swamp* – written to revenge himself on Lisbon.

'The worst of it will be,' muttered the Marquis after a pause, as he wrapped himself more closely in his scarf, 'if I'm like this on Sunday for the races!'

'What?' exclaimed Carlos, 'are the races on Sunday?'

As they went down the Chiado the Marquis proceeded to explain that the races had been brought forward at the request of Clifford, the great Cordova sportsman, who was entering two English horses. It was a bit humiliating to have to depend on Clifford. But after all Clifford was a gentleman and he and his thoroughbred horses and his English jockeys were the only serious feature of the Belem Hippodrome. In the absence of Clifford it would be an affair of nags and hacks.

'Don't you know Clifford? A fine chap! A bit affected, but worth his weight in gold!'

As they entered the patio of the Grémio the Marquis extended his arm to Carlos.

'Feel the pulse.'

'The pulse is excellent – go and deliver that blow to Manuela, while I wait for you here.'

So the races were on Sunday – only five days away! And *she* would be there, he would meet her at last! During these last three weeks he had caught sight of her twice: once while he stood talking to Taveira at the door of the Hotel Central she had come out on to a balcony wearing a hat and pulling on a long black glove; the second time had been on a rainy afternoon a few days ago when she had stopped at the door of the Mourão on the Chiado in a hired coupé, and had stayed and waited while the coachman took a casket-shaped package tied with a red ribbon into the shop. She had seen him on each occasion; and her eyes had rested on his for a moment – and it had seemed to Carlos that the last time her look had lingered a little as though abandoning itself, soaking itself in a delicate sweetness as it rested on his. Perhaps it was an illusion, but his impatience decided him to carry out his old idea – unpleasant though it might be – of being introduced by Damaso to Castro Gomes. Poor Damaso had at first been troubled by this request; with the expression of a dog defending his bone he reminded Carlos at once about the deplorable conduct of Castro Gomes, who had failed to come as he had promised three weeks earlier to leave his card at Ramalhete. But Carlos scorned such severe formalities between men – Castro Gomes seemed a man of taste and a sportsman; it was not every day that someone appeared in Lisbon who knew how to knot his tie correctly; and it would be pleasant even for Damaso himself if they were all to gather once in a while with Craft, with the Marquis, to smoke a cigar and talk of horses. This decided Damaso and he ended by proposing to take Carlos to the Hotel Central one afternoon. Carlos, however, did not wish to enter the hotel following at Damaso's heels, hat in hand. And so they decided to wait until the races, where the Castro Gomeses intended to be present. 'There, in the weighing-in enclosure,' said Damaso, 'an introduction will be more *chic* – really fantastically *chic*!'

'Let's hope it doesn't rain on Sunday!' murmured Carlos as the Marquis came out, more wretched than ever, and more closely wrapped in his scarf.

They went on down the road in the direction of the Ferregial. Beside the pavement just above the Grémio stood a hired coupé whose white-gloved coachman waited by the door. Carlos glanced casually towards it; and he saw the adorably fair face of a child leaning out the window and smiling at him with a lovely smile that dimpled its cheeks. He recognized her at once. It was Rosa – Rosicler; and she did not content herself merely with smiling and turning her sweet blue eyes to him; she put her little **head** out and waved to him excitedly. He could just glimpse a **light** profile like that of a statue and a wavy lock of fair hair inside the black-lined coupé. Carlos took off his hat and made a deep bow feeling so disturbed that his footsteps wavered. *She* nodded her head slightly and something luminous – a confused flood of emotion – seemed to spread itself across her face. And fleetingly, as though from mother and daughter at the same time, a warm emanation of regard seemed directed towards him.

'My God! Does that belong to you?' asked the Marquis who had noticed the effect on Madame Gomes.

Carlos flushed.

'No, it's a Brazilian lady whose little daughter I attended.'

'Huh! That's what I call gratitude!' grunted the other from inside the folds of his scarf.

As they walked in silence along the Ferregial, Carlos turned over an idea that had come upon him suddenly when he had received that sweet look. Why not have Damaso take Castro Gomes to Olivais one morning to view Craft's collection? He would be there, they would open a bottle of champagne and they would discuss antiquities. Then, quite naturally, he would invite Castro Gomes to lunch at Ramalhete in order to show him the great Rubens and his old Indian bedspreads. In this way, even before the races, a comradeship would arise between them, perhaps even a certain familiarity.

The Marquis wanted to take a cab in the Aterro for fear of the air from the river; and their silence continued as far as Ramalhete. The Marquis, again uneasy, fingered his throat. Carlos ruminated over that slow nod of the head, that look, that lively flush of colour – as he debated inwardly with himself. Perhaps she had not known who he was till that moment. But after waving at him so excitedly, Rosa, still all smiles, had turned to her mother and had surely told her that there was the doctor who had cured her and her doll – and then the lovely colour had mantled her cheek and deepened, as though in happy surprise and chaste perplexity at the knowledge that this man she had observed had already somehow been admitted to her intimacy, had kissed her daughter, had even sat on the edge of her bed.

Then he began to reconsider his plan, now vaster in scale and more brilliant, for the visit to Olivais. Why should she not go to see Craft's curiosities as well? What a delightful afternoon they would spend, what a party it would be, what an idyllic meeting! Craft would arrange a dainty lunch on his old Wedgwood service. Carlos would be placed beside her at table. And afterwards they would go and see the garden already in flower; or they would take tea in the Japanese pavilion that was lined with straw mats. But what most appealed to him was to view Craft's two drawing-rooms with her, stopping together here and there over a lovely *faience* or some rare piece of furniture while each sensed the sympathy of their hearts rise like a perfume through the harmony of their tastes. He had never seen her so beautiful as this afternoon inside the coupé with its dark lining, against which the whiteness of her profile shone more purely than ever. On the lap of her black dress had lain the lighter colour of her gloves; and on her hat a white feather had curled.

The cab halted at the door of Ramalhete, and now they were among the silent tapestries of the hallway.

'How does she know the Crugeses?' asked the Marquis abruptly with a suspicious tone as he divested himself of his scarf.

Carlos looked at him like someone suddenly awoken.

'She? Who? That lady? How does she know Cruges? Why, you're right! That was Cruges's house! The carriage was outside Cruges's house! Perhaps somebody who lives on another floor?'

'Nobody does,' said the Marquis as he went in the direction of the corridor, 'but in any event she's quite a woman!'

Carlos found the expression odious.

In the corridor the petulant voice of Damaso could be heard through the open door of Afonso's study, talking loudly about 'handicaps' and 'dead heats' – and they found him discoursing with conviction and authority about the races, as a member of the Jockey Club. From his seat in his old armchair Afonso listened to him, courteous and beaming, with the Reverend Bonifácio on his lap. Craft sat in one corner of the sofa leafing through a book.

Damaso at once sought the Marquis's support. Was it not a fact, as he had just been telling Senhor Afonso da Maia, that these were to be the best races ever to have been run in Lisbon? Eight horses had been put down for the Great National Prize alone – six hundred *milréis*! And, besides, Clifford was bringing Mist.

'Ah! By the way, Marquis, you must come to the Jockey Club on Friday night to help us finish the handicap.'

The Marquis had drawn a chair up to Afonso in order to retail the history of his ailments to him; but Damaso placed himself between them, still talking about Mist, declaring that Mist was *chic*, wanting to bet five pounds on Mist against the field – and at last the Marquis turned round wearily and said that Senhor Damaso was giving himself foolish airs. Betting on Mist indeed! It was the duty of every patriot to bet on the horses of Viscount de Darque – the only Portuguese breeder worthy of the name.

'Don't you agree, Senhor Afonso da Maia?'

The old man sat and smiled and stroked his cat.

'This patriotism,' he said, 'could be put to better use in organizing a good bullfight instead of races.'

Damaso raised his hands to his head. A bullfight! So, Senhor Afonso da Maia preferred bulls to horse-racing, Senhor Afonso da Maia, who was practically an Englishman –

'A simple Beira man, Senhor Salcêde, a simple Beira man, and proud of it! If it so happened that I took up domicile in England, it was because my king, as he then was, put me out of my homeland . . . But it's true! I own to that Portuguese weakness! I prefer bulls. Each nation has its particular sport, and ours is the bull – the bull with plenty of sunshine, a feast-day atmosphere, fresh water and fireworks. But d'you know, Senhor Salcéde, the advantage of the bullfight? It's a great school of strength, courage and dexterity. In Portugal there's no institution that equals the importance of the amateur bullfight. And believe me, if among this melancholy generation there are still to be found in Lisbon a few lads with a bit of muscle, a straight spine and the ability to administer a good punch, it is due to the bull and the amateur bullfight!'

The Marquis clapped his hands enthusiastically. That was talking! There you had the philosophy of the bull! Of course, the bullfight was a great physical education! And only idiots talked of finishing with the bullfight. Oh, fools, thus would they eliminate the last of Portuguese valour!

'We haven't the games of dexterity that other nations have!' he exclaimed, striding round the room and forgetting his ills. 'We have neither cricket, nor football, nor running, like the English; nor have we gymnastics as they have in France; we haven't got the compulsory military service that makes the German solid. We have nothing capable of giving a lad a bit of fibre – only the bullfight! Take away the bullfight, and all we'll have left will be spineless mediocrities, crawling round the Chiado! Don't you agree, Craft?'

A convinced reply came from the other corner of the sofa where Carlos had gone to sit and was talking to Craft in a low voice:

'What, the bull? Of course! In this country the bull should be what schooling is abroad – free and compulsory!'

Meanwhile Damaso was earnestly assuring Afonso that he too was very fond of bulls. Ah, as far as patriotism and that sort of thing went, nobody could outdo him – but racing had a style all its own. The Bois de Boulogne on the day of the Grand Prix, eh? It was enough to dazzle one!

'D'you know,' he exclaimed, turning suddenly to Carlos, 'it's a shame you haven't a four-in-hand and a mailcoach. We could all go in it. Everybody would rave about it.'

Carlos also thought to himself that it was a pity he didn't have a four-in-hand. But he joked and said he thought it more appropriate to the Jockey Club that everyone should go in an omnibus.

Damaso let his arms fall in discouragement and turned to the old man.

'You see, Senhor Afonso da Maia! That's why nothing's ever done properly in Portugal! Nobody wants to compete so that things should turn out well. It's not possible to do anything this way. As for myself, now, this is my idea – each person in a country should contribute as far as possible towards civilization!'

'Excellent sentiments, Senhor Salcêde!' said Afonso da Maia. 'That is a great and noble dictum.'

'Well, isn't it true?' exulted Damaso, swelling with pleasure. 'And therefore, I, for instance – '

'Yes, you – you!' the cries showered on him from all sides. 'What have you done for civilization?'

'I've ordered a white dress-coat for the day of the races – and I shall be wearing a blue veil on my hat!'

A footman came in bearing a letter for Afonso on a salver. Still grinning at Damaso's notions about civilization, the old man

273

put on his glasses and scanned the first lines – all the merriment died from his face and he rose at once, after carefully depositing the heavy Bonifácio on the cushion.

'Now, that's what I call elegance! That's what I call knowing how to behave!' exclaimed Damaso, waving his arms at Carlos. 'That grandfather of yours, my boy, is fantastically *chic*!'

'Leave Grandfather's *chic* alone for a moment – come here, I want to talk to you about something!'

He opened one of the french windows onto the terrace and took Damaso outside and told him rapidly of his plan for the visit to Olivais and the lovely afternoon they would spend at the manor with Castro Gomes. He had already spoken to Craft who had agreed, found the idea delightful, and was going to fill the place with flowers. And now all that remained was for friend Damaso to invite the Castro Gomeses, as though it were all his own idea.

'Hang it all,' muttered Damaso suspiciously, 'you're desperately keen to meet her!'

But at last he agreed that it would be fantastically *chic*! And he saw a great opportunity for himself – while Carlos and Craft went around showing the curiosities to Castro Gomes and talking to him about horses, he – marvellous! – he would take her for a walk around the estate – and who knows what luck might not hold in store for him!

'Well, I'll go and see them tomorrow. I'm sure they'll accept right away. She's mad about antiques.'

'And you'll come to let me know whether they accept – '

'I'll come and tell you . . . You'll love her! She's read a lot and she understands literature – sometimes her conversation confuses even me!'

The Marquis came up to call them inside impatiently, for he wanted to shut the french window and was worried again about his throat. Before dinner he insisted on going to Carlos's room to gargle with salt and water.

'So this is Portuguese strength?' cried Carlos, catching merrily hold of his arm.

'My weakness is my throat,' replied the Marquis freeing himself and glaring fiercely. 'And yours is sentiment. And Craft's is respectability. And Damasozinho's is foolishness. In Portugal everthing is Weakness and Co.'

Carlos chuckled and drew him into the corridor. As they entered the hall they suddenly came upon Afonso talking to a woman all dressed in mourning who kissed his hand, half kneeling, and choked with tears; beside her another woman, her eyes brimming too, was rocking a little child in a shawl, a child that looked sick and moaned. Carlos hesitated in embarrassment and the Marquis's hand went instinctively to his pocket. But the old man, thus surprised in his charity, immediately led the woman towards the stairs; they went down, huddled together, blessing him in a murmur of sobs. Afonso turned to Carlos and spoke in a voice that was almost apologetic and still quivered:

'These calls upon one never cease . . . Still, it's a bad case – and the worst of it all is that as much as one might do, it's never enough. The world is a very badly organized place, Marquis.'

'Yes, indeed! It's very badly organized, Senhor Afonso da Maia,' responded the Marquis with feeling.

At about two o'clock the following Sunday, just as fireworks were being set off from the direction of the Hippodrome, Carlos drew up at the end of Belem Square in his eight-spring phaeton, accompanied by Craft, who had come to stay at Ramalhete for the two days of the races. One of the servants got down to buy the weighing-in ticket for Craft at a badly-made wooden booth that had been erected the previous day and contained a little man with a big grey beard.

The day was already hot, with a dark-blue sky and one of those shining festival suns that inflame the stones in the street, gild the dull dust in the air, throw mirror-like sparkles on to windows and give to all the city that white, chalk-like glitter, monotonously alive and implacable, that tires and somewhat saddens the soul in the slow summer hours. In Jeronimos Square, silent and scalding with light, an unharnessed omnibus waited next to the church door. A labourer with a child in his arms, his wife at his side in her flowered shawl, strolled along there, gazing at the road and at the river, leisurely enjoying his Sunday. Disconsolately, an urchin urged the purchase of race programmes that nobody wanted to buy. The drinking-water woman sat in the shade, without customers, delousing a child. Four heavy municipal guards on horseback patrolled the emptiness at walking pace. And in the distance the gay outbursts of fireworks died incessantly in the hot air.

Meanwhile the coachman continued to lean over the counter of the booth, unable to obtain change for a pound. Craft had to jump from the box and go and put in a word. But Carlos felt impatient and tickled the mares' rumps, as shiny as satin, with his whip and took a quick, nervous turn round the square. All the way from Ramalhete he had driven this way – irritated and silent. The whole week had been a discouraging one since that evening when he had arranged with Damaso to visit Olivais. Damaso had vanished into thin air without even sending Castro Gomes's reply. And his pride had kept him from seeking out Damaso. The days had passed drearily; the gay idyll at Olivais had remained unrealized; and now he did not even expect to see her at the races. And that festive Sunday, the bright sun, the streets filled with people dressed in cashmere and holiday silks, all filled him with melancholy and unease.

A cab passed in which sat two individuals wearing flowers in their lapels and pulling on their gloves; then a dog-cart driven by a fat man in dark glasses nearly ran into the arch. Craft at last returned with his ticket, after having been rebuked by the man with the prophetic beard.

Beyond the arch the dust choked them. Ladies leaned from the windows and looked out from under parasols. More municipal guards filled the road.

At the entrance to the Hippodrome – a ruined opening in the wall surrounding a small park – the phaeton had to draw up behind the fat man's dog-cart, which could not itself proceed because the space in front of it was occupied by the cab, from which one passenger, with a flower at his breast, was shouting furiously at a policeman. Did they want him to go and call Senhor Savedra? Senhor Savedra, who was a member of the Jockey Club, had told him he could go in without paying for the carriage. Only the previous night in Azevedo's pharmacy he had received this assurance. Did he want to call Senhor Savedra? The policeman waved his arms in embarrassment. And the passenger took off his gloves and was about to open the cab door to go and hit the man, when a municipal guard trotted up on his great charger, his fist raised, and insulted the fat man and sent the cab wheeling off. Another municipal guard interfered brusquely. Two ladies fled into a doorway, terror-stricken and clutching their skirts. And through the tumult and the dust, a barrel-organ could be heard farther ahead, dolefully playing an air from *La Traviata*.

The phaeton went in behind the dog-cart from which the fat man, his red face swelling with fury, still swore to get his own back on the municipal guard.

'All this is most decently arranged,' murmured Craft.

The Hippodrome rose smoothly in front of them on a hill, and after the hot dust of the pavement and the raw, chalky glitter it seemed fresh and spacious with its arena already a little scorched by the June sun, and here and there a poppy shining red. A light, restful breeze reached it slowly from the river.

In the centre, nearly lost in that vast green space, a tight knot of people stood silhouetted black in the sunshine, surrounding a group of carriages from which shone the pale colours of parasols, the gleam of a lantern glass and the white coat of a coachman. Beyond, on either side of the royal tribune that was lined with the red baize of government-office desks, stood the two public grandstands, constructed of badly nailed planks, like stalls in a fairground. The one on the left was empty and needed painting, and the light betrayed the chinks between the boards. The one on the right was daubed on the outside in light blue, and a row of ladies, nearly all of them in dark dresses, leaned against the rails while others were scattered on the lower steps; the remainder of the benches were deserted and sad, and the pallor of the wood deadened the gay colours of the few summer dresses. Occasionally a slight breeze agitated the blue flags on top of the two masts, and a great silence rained down from the sparkling sky.

The enclosure containing the royal tribune was surrounded by a wooden fence against which stood infantry soldiers with their bayonets gleaming in the sun. And when Carlos looked at the sad ticket-collector at the entrance, inside an enormous white waistcoat stiff with starch that practically reached to his knees, he recognized the servant he employed at his laboratory.

They had no sooner taken a few steps than they met Taveira at the door of the buffet where he had been consoling himself with a glass of beer. He wore a posy of yellow carnations in his buttonhole, and white spats – and he was eager to liven up the

277

races. He had already seen Mist, Clifford's mare, and had decided to back it. What a head it had, my boys, what slender legs . . .

'Upon my word, it quite took my fancy! And I've decided – this is a big day – this has got to be livened up. I bet three *milréis*. Will you take it, Craft?'

'Well, later perhaps – let's go and have a look around first.'

The sloping enclosure between the tribune and the course was occupied only by men, people from the Grémio, from the ministries, from the Casa Havanesa. For the most part they were dressed casually in light-coloured coats and bowler hats; others, more stylish in frock-coats, with binoculars hanging round their necks, seemed embarrassed and almost repentant of their elegance. They talked in low voices as they slowly paced the grass and puffed idly at their cigarettes. Here and there someone stood still with his hands behind his back and gazed languidly at the ladies. Two Brazilians beside Carlos were complaining at the price of tickets and found 'all this killingly boring!'

The track facing them was deserted, guarded by two soldiers. Close to the rope on the farther side was the knot of people with the carriages in their midst, and no sound came from them as they stared dismally under the weight of that June sun. A youth with a lazy voice was shouting fresh water for sale. And there in the distance the broad Tagus glistened all blue, as blue as the sky in that finely powdered light.

The Viscount de Darque, wearing the phlegmatic air of a fair man who is beginning to grow plump, came up to shake Carlos and Craft by the hand. And as soon as they mentioned his horses (Rabino, the favourite, and the other one), he shrugged his shoulders and closed his eyes like a man sacrificing himself. Well, what the devil, the fellows had insisted – but the fact was he wouldn't be in a position to enter a decent horse in his colours for another four years! And for that matter, he was not breeding thoroughbreds for the miserable Belem course – his friends must not suppose he was as patriotic as all that. No indeed! His aim was to go to Spain and beat the horses of Caldillo . . .

'Well, we'll see – give me a light. This is all quite ghastly. And then, hang it, what are races without *cocottes* and champagne? It simply won't work with all these stodgy people and fresh water . . .'

At that moment one of the race commissioners, a large beard-less youth, red as a poppy and dripping with sweat under a white hat that was pushed back on his neck, came to inform Darque that he was 'urgently required at the weighing-in to settle a doubtful point'.

'I'm the encyclopaedia,' said Darque once more shrugging his shoulders in resignation. 'Every now and again one of these Jockey Club gentlemen appears to leaf through my pages. You can imagine, Maia, the state I'm in after a race: I need a new binding . . . !'

And off he went, laughing at his joke, urged forward by the commissioner who patted him familiarly on the shoulder and called him a dandy.

'Let's go and take a look at the women,' said Carlos.

They slowly walked the length of the grandstand. All those ladies mentioned in the society columns of the newspapers, the ladies of the opera boxes and the Gouvarinho's Tuesdays – all were there, leaning over the rail in a mute row and looking about themselves vaguely as if gazing from a window on the day of a procession. For the most part they wore dresses sober enough for church. Here and there the shadow of one of those plumed hats in the Gainsborough style, just then coming into fashion, accentuated the sallow colour of some little face. And in the candid light of afternoon, in the fresh air of that open hill, the complexions seemed withered, worn, flabby and dull with powder.

Carlos greeted Taveira's two sisters, thin, fair little things, both correctly turned out in checks. Then the Viscountess de Alvim, plump and white, her black bodice gleaming with tiny beads, and at her side her dear inseparable friend, Joaninha Vilar, who grew constantly plumper, a sweet lassitude showing in her heavy-lashed eyes. Ahead were the Pedrosos, the banker's ladies, wearing light colours and taking an inordinate interest in the races – one with a programme in her hand, the other standing with binoculars and studying the course. To one side, convers-ing with Steinbroken, stood the Countess de Soutal, looking dishevelled and as though she might have mud on her skirts. Silent on a lonely bench sat Vilaça with two ladies in black.

The Countess de Gouvarinho had not yet arrived. Nor was there any sign of that other for whom Carlos's eyes sought rest-lessly and hopelessly.

279

'It's a garden of withered camellias,' said Taveira, quoting Ega.

Meanwhile Carlos had gone to speak to his old friend Dona Maria da Cunha, who had beckoned to him a few moments earlier with her look, with her fan and with her maternal smiles. She was the only lady who had dared to descend from that window-like shelter of the stand and come and sit down below among the men; but she could not stand the boredom of it up there, waiting conspicuously for 'the passage of the procession', as she put it. And now, still lovely under her grey hair, she was the only person there who seemed to be enjoying herself, very much at ease, with her feet resting on the bar of a chair, her binoculars on her lap, greeting all and sundry, calling the men her 'dear boys'. She was accompanied by a relative whom she presented to Carlos, a Spanish lady who would have been pretty but for the black shadows under her eyes, that reached to the middle of her cheeks. Hardly had Carlos sat down beside her than Dona Maria at once questioned him about that libertine Ega. The libertine, said Carlos, was up there in Celorico composing a comedy to revenge himself on Lisbon, to be called *The Swamp*.

'Does Cohen come into it?' she asked with a laugh.

'We all come in, Dona Maria. All of us are inhabitants of the swamp – '

At that instant, behind the enclosure, a desultory ran-tan-tan of cymbals and drums broke into the 'Liberal Anthem' and mingled with it were the commanding voice of an officer and the thud of rifle-butts. Then, between ranks of golden epaulettes, the King appeared on the royal tribune, smiling and wearing a velvet coat and a white hat. Here and there a few persons greeted him very offhandedly. The Spanish lady took Dona Maria's binoculars, stood up and in very leisurely fashion started to scrutinize the King. Dona Maria considered the music ridiculous – it gave the races the atmosphere of a fairground, and besides how silly it was to play the anthem as though it were a military parade!

'And isn't this anthem dreadful?' said Carlos. 'D'you know Ega's definition, Dona Maria? His theory about anthems? It's wonderful!'

'That Ega!' she said, now all smiles and delight.

'Ega says that the national anthem is the musical definition of the character of a people. The compass of the national anthem, he says, depicts the spiritual direction of the nation. Now, Dona Maria, just consider the different anthems on the basis of Ega's notion: the *"Marseillaise"* marches forward carrying a naked sword; "God Save the Queen" advances drawing a royal train – '

'And the 'Liberal Anthem'?'

'The "Liberal Anthem" saunters along in a dress coat.'

Dona Maria was still chuckling when the Spanish lady sat down again and serenely restored her binoculars to her lap.

'He has the face of a good person,' she murmured.

'Who? The King?' exclaimed Dona Maria and Carlos simultaneously. 'An excellent person!'

Meanwhile a bell sounded, its peal lost in the air above, and there appeared on the indicator-board the numbers of the two horses who were to run for the first prize in kind. They were No. 1 and No. 4. Dona Maria wanted to know their names, for she wished to bet and win five *tostões* from Carlos. But as Carlos rose to fetch a programme she touched his arm.

'Never mind, my boy,' she said, 'here comes our Alencar with a programme. Just look at him! Now, see if you can tell me of anyone else around nowadays with that same sentimental, poetic air . . .'

The poet, in a new suit of light cheviot that made him look younger, pearl-grey gloves and his ticket in his buttonhole, advanced fanning himself with his programme and already smiling from afar at his good friend Dona Maria. He carried his hat, and his bare-headed mane was well-combed that day and gleamed with oil. When he reached her he lifted her hand to his lips gallantly.

Dona Maria had been one of his lovely contemporaries. Very ardently they had danced the mazurka together in the salons of Arroios. She spoke to him in tones of easy intimacy. He addressed her as 'dear friend' or 'dear Maria'.

'Let me just see the names of those horses, Alencar – come along, sit down here and keep me company.'

He pulled over a chair, laughing at her interest in the races, she who had always been known as an enthusiast for the bulls – Well, the names of the horses were Jupiter and Escoces.

'I don't like either of those names; I shan't bet! Well, what d'you think of it all, Alencar? Our Lisbon is beginning to come out of its shell.'

Alencar desposited his hat on a chair, passed a hand over his vast bard's forehead and confessed that really all this did have a certain air of elegance, it did breathe a perfume of the Court. And then, over there, was the wonderful Tagus, not to mention the importance of horse-breeding . . .

'Isn't that true, my Carlos? You, who so thoroughly comprehend these matters, you who are a master sportsman, you know that breeding – '

'Yes, quite! Breeding – very important,' said Carlos absently, raising his eyes once more to the stand.

It was nearly three o'clock and now, most certainly, *she* would not be coming; and the Countess de Gouvarinho had not appeared either. An immense lassitude began to invade him. He answered the sweet smile given to him from the grandstand by Joaninha Vilar with a slight nod of the head; he began to contemplate going back to Ramalhete to end up the afternoon in tranquillity in his dressing-gown, with a book, remote from this tedium.

Meanwhile the ladies were still arriving. The little Sá Videira girl, daughter of the rich shoe-merchant, passed on the arm of her brother; a doll-like creature, she wore a somewhat sulky expression, disdainful of everything, and spoke loudly in English. Then there was the wife of the Minister of Bavaria, the Baroness de Craben – immense, decked out like a peacock, with her massive Roman matron's face, her skin covered in tomato-coloured patches and bursting out of a dress of blue grosgrain with white stripes; and the Baron skipped along behind her, diminutive, jovial, wearing a big straw hat.

Dona Maria da Cunha rose to speak to them; and for a second the Baroness's voice could be heard, like a turkey's thick gobbling, finding that *c'était charmant, c'était très beau!* The Baron, amid little skips and little smiles, *trouvait ça ravissant!* And, confronted by these foreigners who had failed to greet him, Alencar concentrated on preserving the pose of a great national figure, twirling the points of his moustaches and rearing even higher his bare forehead.

When they had gone up to the stand and good Dona Maria had sat down again, the poet indignantly pronounced that he abominated Germans! What an air of superciliousness she had worn as she looked at him, that Minister's lady with her barrel-

282

like figure, exuding sweat from every seam in her dress! Huh! The insolent whale!

Dona Maria smiled and looked at the poet fondly. Then she suddenly turned to the Spanish lady.

'Concha,' she said in Spanish, 'permit me to present Dom Tomás de Alencar, our great lyric poet . . .'

At that instant some of the most sportive of the young men – those who wore their binoculars round their necks – hurried towards the rope round the course. Two horses passed at an easy gallop, almost neck and neck, under the furious lashes of two jockeys with big moustaches. A voice could be heard saying that Escoces had won. Others declared it had been Jupiter. And in the weary, disappointed silence that fell there arose more clearly through the air the flutes of the band playing the waltz from *Madame Angot*. Some people had kept their backs turned and had gone on smoking and staring at the grandstand, where the ladies were still leaning over the rail waiting for that procession. At Carlos's side a gentleman summed up his feelings by saying the whole thing was a fraud.

And when Carlos got up to go and find Damaso, Alencar was already engaged in animated conversation with the Spanish lady, talking of Seville, of *malagueñas* and of the great heart of the poet Esponceda.

Carlos's only thought now was to rout out Damaso and discover why the visit to Olivais had fallen through; then he would go home to Ramalhete, and hide this strange and childish melancholy that befogged him, mixed with irritability, making him detest the voices that addressed him, the ran-tan-tans of the music, and even the calm beauty of the afternoon. But as he rounded the corner of the grandstand he bumped up against Craft, who detained him to present a strong, blond young man with whom he had been conversing merrily. It was the celebrated Clifford, the great sportsman of Cordova. People crowded round them, hypnotized by that Englishman whose name had become a legend in Lisbon, a race-horse owner, a friend of the King of Spain, the most stylish of men. Clifford was very much at his ease, somewhat affected, wearing a simple blue flannel jacket as though he were in the country; and he laughed very heartily with Craft at recollections of their days together at Rugby. Then, very cordial, he thought he remembered Carlos. Hadn't they met nearly a year ago in Madrid, at a dinner-party in Pancho Calderon's house? Of course! Their handshake this time was more intimate – and Craft wanted them to go and water that flower of friendship with a bottle of bad champagne. The awe around them grew.

The buffet was installed under the naked planks of the grand-stand, with no floor, no decoration, no flowers. At the back there was a bar-counter with bottles and plates of cakes on it. And two harassed and dirty menials hurriedly flattened slices of bread for sandwiches on the cheap counter with their hands damp from beer froth.

When Carlos and his two companions entered, a lively group stood against one of the beams supporting the steps of the stand, with glasses of champagne in their hands. They included the Marquis, the Viscount de Darque, Taveira, a pale youth with a black beard who carried the red starter's flag rolled up under his arm, and the beardless commissioner with his white hat tilted even farther back on his neck, his cheeks more inflamed, his collar limp now with sweat. It was he who had provided the champagne – and no sooner had he caught sight of Clifford coming in than up he rushed with his glass in the air, making the beams tremble as he raised his powerful voice:

'To the health of our friend Clifford! The first sportsman of the Peninsula, and one of our own! Hip, hip, hurrah!'

Glasses were lifted in a clamour of hurrahs, among which, vibrant and enthusiastic, could be picked out that of the starter. Clifford thanked him smiling and slowly drew off his gloves, while the Marquis took Carlos to one side by the arm and hastily presented the commissioner, his cousin Dom Pedro Vargas.

'How d'you do?'

'All the sporting chaps should be acquainted – ' exclaimed the commissioner, 'this is the true brotherhood – the rest is the mob!'

And immediately he raised his glass on high and bellowed with such energy that more blood flowed to his cheeks:

'To the health of Carlos da Maia, the most elegant man in the land! The best hand at the rein – hip, hip, hurrah!'

'Hip, hip, hurrah!'

And once more it was the voice of the starter that delivered the most vibrant and enthusiastic hurrah.

An employee knocked at the door of the buffet and summoned

the commissioner. Vargas tossed a pound on to the counter and went off shouting from outside, his eyes ablaze:

'It's getting warm, fellows! By God! What's needed is liquid! And you down there, head waiter! Senhor Manuel, send for some ice. Go on, send someone! Go yourself, away with you – Haaah!'

Meanwhile, as Craft's champagne was being uncorked, Carlos had been inviting Clifford to dine at Ramalhete that night. The other accepted, moistening his lips on the glass, finding it an excellent thing to continue the tradition of dining together whenever they met.

'Well, well – here's the General!' exclaimed Craft.

Everyone looked round. It was indeed Sequeira, with a face like a red pimento, clad in a short frock-coat that made him look bulkier than ever, a white hat over one eye and a big whip under his arm.

He accepted a glass of champagne and was very pleased to make the acquaintance of Senhor Clifford.

'And what do you have to say to this boring affair?' he cried immediately as he turned to Carlos. As far as he was concerned, he was completely satisfied – in fact he was jumping with joy! These insipid races, with no horses or jockeys worth the name, and half a dozen folk around, all yawning, this made him certain there would be no more races, that probably the Jockey Club would collapse too – and a good thing too! People would be released from the burden of an entertainment that was not in accord with national custom. Racing was simply for the purpose of betting. Had they bet? No! Then it was all a waste of time. In England, in France, that was another story! There it was a game, like roulette, like cards – there were even bankers known to be bookmakers on the side! That was something like it.

The Marquis put down his glass and attempted to soothe the General with talk of breeding good horses, developing new strains – but the other shrugged his shoulders indignantly.

'What nonsense are you trying to tell me? Are you really trying to make out that you're breeding horses for the benefit of the cavalry? Well, just you try and mount the army on racehorses! It's not the horse that can run best that you want on active service, it's the horse that has most stamina – anything else is fairy-tales! Racehorses are freaks, like a bull with two heads. It's all fairy-tales! In France they even give them champagne – what d'you think of that!'

At each utterance his shoulders shook furiously. Then with one long gulp he emptied his glass of champagne, repeated that he had been very pleased to meet Senhor Clifford, turned on his heels and went out puffing, holding his whip more tightly under his arm – its tip quivering as though avid to thrash somebody.

Craft grinned and patted Clifford on the shoulder.

'D'you see? We old Portuguese don't care for innovations in sport – we're all for the bull!'

'And with reason,' said the other gravely as he preened himself above his collar. 'Only the other day at Granja the King of Spain was saying to me – '

There was suddenly an uproar outside and loud voices crying 'Order!' A lady, passing with a small boy, fled inside the buffet, overwhelmed. A policeman passed at a run.

A riot had started.

Carlos and the others hurried out and there, at the foot of the royal tribune, they saw a group of men – and Vargas, waving his arms. Men came rushing curiously from the weighing-in enclosure, excited, tripping, standing on tiptoe; others came from the carriage enclosure, leaping over the ropes of the course despite the thrusts of the police. Soon there was a tumultuous mob in tall hats and light suits, pushing against the steps of the royal stand, where, resplendent in gold braid, one of the King's aides-de-camp stood bareheaded and looked calmly on.

Carlos elbowed his way forward and at last, in the centre of the mob, he saw one of the individuals who had run for the prize in kind – the one who had ridden Jupiter – still in riding boots and now wearing a fawn coat on top of his jockey's jacket. He was furious and raging, and his insults were directed at Mendonça, judge of the races, who stood speechless and with glazed eyes. The jockey's friends tugged at him and urged him to lodge a protest. But he stamped his foot, tremulous, livid, and shouting that he didn't give a damn for protests! He had lost the race only because of a trick! The only protest in such a case was the whip! For what was taking place in that hippodrome was nothing but favouritism and daylight robbery.

Part of the crowd grew indignant at such brutal accusations.

'Away with him! Away with him!'

Others took the side of the jockey; and all around other quarrels arose – violently. A man dressed in grey cried that Mendonça had decided in favour of Pinheiro, who had ridden Escoces, because of his close friendship with him; another gentleman, wearing binoculars round his neck, declared that this was an infamous accusation. And the two faced one another, fists clenched, accusing each other furiously of being scum!

All the while a stocky man wearing a big spotted collar tried to push his way in, waving his arms, and exclaiming in a voice that was hoarse and imploring:

'For heaven's sake, gentlemen . . . Just a minute . . . I've got experience! I've got experience – '

Suddenly the booming voice of Vargas dominated everything, like the bellow of a bull. Hatless, his face livid, he shouted at the jockey that he was unworthy to be there among decent people. When a gentleman doubted the judge of a race, he put in a protest! But to come and declare that people here were robbers was worthy only of scum and ruffians like him. He should never have been admitted to membership of the Jockey Club! The other man, held by his friends, stretched out his thin neck as though he were about to bite, and spat out a foul word. Then Vargas, elbowing people aside, opened up a space, rolled his sleeves up and bellowed:

'Repeat that! Just repeat that!'

All at once the mass of people stirred, bumping against the boarding of the royal stand and groaning in tumult. There were cries of 'Order' and 'Death'; hats waved on high; and one could hear the dull thud of blows.

Amid the uproar police whistles shrilled furiously; ladies caught up their skirts and fled across the track, desperately seeking their carriages; and through the hippodrome there swept the gross breath of low brawling, as all the artificial veneer of civilization and the forced assumption of decorum collapsed.

Carlos found himself beside the Marquis who stood there pallid, exclaiming: 'This is incredible! Simply incredible!'

On the contrary Carlos found it picturesque.

'Picturesque indeed, man! It's a crying shame, in front of all these foreigners . . .'

Meanwhile the knot of people was dispersing, slowly obeying an officer of the guard, a tiny but determined youth, who stood on tiptoe and was counselling everyone in the voice of an orator to 'gentlemanliness' and 'prudence'. The jockey in the fawn coat went off, limping, his nose dripping blood, supported on the arm of a friend; and the commissioner went on down the course, with a retinue behind him, triumphant, collarless and putting his crumpled hat away in a case. The band struck up the march from the *Prophet* and the wretched race judge, Mendonça, leaned in a daze against the royal stand, with his arms hanging limply by his sides, as he stammered out the remains of his amazement:

'This could only happen to me! This could only happen to me!'

The Marquis continued to vociferate in a group that had now been joined by Clifford, Craft and Taveira:

'Well, does this convince you? What have I always said? This country is good only for brawls and fairgrounds – races, like other civilized amenities you find abroad, in the first place require an educated populace. At heart we are nothing but a lot of *fado*-singers. What we really love is wine, guitars, brawling and back-slapping! And that's the truth of the matter!'

Clifford, who stood beside him, had maintained his gentlemanly demeanour more severely than ever throughout all the tumult, and now he bit a smile and assured his hearers in consoling tones that similar conflicts occurred everywhere – but, deep down, he seemed to regard the whole thing as ignoble. He even said he was going to withdraw Mist. And some thought he was right! What the deuce! It was degrading for a fine thoroughbred creature to race in a hippodrome where there was neither order nor decency, where at any moment the flash of knives might be seen.

'Just a moment,' said Carlos, summoning Taveira to one side. 'Have you by any chance seen that animal, Damaso? I've been searching for him for over an hour.'

'He was there, on the other side, just a little while ago, in the carriage enclosure, with Salazar's Josefina. He looks most extraordinary – he's wearing a white frock-coat and a veil on his hat!'

But a short while later when Carlos wanted to cross, the course was closed. The Grand National Prize was about to be run. Numbers had already gone up on the indicator, and the sound of a bell died in the air. Rabino, one of Darque's horses, ridden by a jockey in his red and white colours, was coming down led by a groom and accompanied by Darque. People stopped to examine its legs with a serious look, affecting to understand these matters. Carlos stopped for a moment too and admired it; it was a lovely dark chestnut, nervous and light, but it had a narrow chest.

Then, turning back, he suddenly caught sight of Countess de Gouvarinho, who must have just arrived. She stood talking to Dona Maria da Cunha dressed in an English outfit, close-fitting and simple, all in white cashmere, a creamy white against which her great, dark musketeer's gloves contrasted dashingly. Her black hat was swathed in the narrow pleats of a white veil that was rolled round her head and còvered half her face, giving it an oriental look that did not sit well with her short nose and flame-coloured hair. But all the men near by stared at her as though at a picture.

The moment she saw Carlos, the Countess was unable to hold back the smile and the light in her eyes that illumined her. Involuntarily she took a step towards him; and for a moment they stood isolated, talking in low voices while Dona Maria observed them, beaming, already full of benevolence, already prepared to bestow her maternal blessing on them.

'I nearly didn't come,' said the Countess a little nervously. 'Gastão has been so unpleasant today! And probably I have to go to Oporto tomorrow.'

'Oporto?'

'Papa wants me there; it will be his birthday – poor dear, he's getting old and I've had such a sad letter from him. It's two years since he's seen me – '

'Is the Count going?'

'No.'

She smiled at the Minister of Bavaria who had bowed to her as he passed in little bounds; then, looking penetratingly into Carlos's eyes, she added:

'And there's something I want.'

'What?'

'I want you to come too.'

At that very moment Teles da Gama stopped beside them with his programme and a pencil in his hand.

'Would you like to enter the monster pool, Maia? Fifteen tickets at ten *tostões* each – they're betting furiously up there on the corner of the grandstand. That brawl did them good! It shook their nerves and woke everyone up – wouldn't you like to join in too, Countess?'

Yes, the Countess would enter the pool as well. Teles da Gama wrote down her name and went off burdened with duties. Then Steinbroken came up, all florid, wearing a white hat and a ruby horseshoe in his tie – more erect, blonder, more English on this solemn day of official sport.

'*Ah, comme vous êtes belle, Comtesse! Voilà une toilette merveilleuse, n'est-ce pas, Maia? Est-ce que nous n'allons pas parier quelque chose?*'

Thwarted, eager to speak to Carlos, but smiling nevertheless, the Countess lamented that she already had a fortune at stake – but still, she was always willing to bet five *tostões* with Finland. What horse was he backing?

'*Ah, je ne said pas, je ne connais pas les chevaux. D'abord, quand on parie –* '

Impatient, she offered him Vladimiro. Then she had to shake hands with another Finn. He was Steinbroken's secretary: a slow, languid, blond youth who bowed silently before her, letting his gold-rimmed monocle slip out of his light, vacuous eye. At almost the same time up hurried Taveira to tell them excitedly that Clifford had withdrawn Mist.

Seeing her thus surrounded, Carlos drew away. But Dona Maria's gaze had not left him, and it beckoned him, more affectionate and lively than ever. She pulled at his sleeve when he reached her side, and made him stoop down so that she could whisper delightedly in his ear:

'She's very stylish today!'

'Who?'

Dona Maria raised her shoulders impatiently.

'Well now, who? Whom should I mean, indeed! You know perfectly well, dear boy – the Countess – most appetizing!'

'Very elegant indeed!' replied Carlos coldly.

He stood beside Dona Maria and slowly took out a cigarette. Then, almost indignantly, he considered the Countess's words. Go with her to Oporto indeed! This was just one more bold demand, the same impertinent tendency to make free with his time, his actions, his life! He felt like going back to her and drily saying no, brusquely, giving no reasons or explanations, being brutal.

Now she was coming slowly towards him in the silent company of Steinbroken's lanky secretary, and she enveloped him in a happy look that annoyed him still further, for that serene brightness and calm smile gave away her certainty of his submission.

And she was indeed certain. Hardly had the Finn moved lazily away than right there, beside Dona Maria, she calmly began speaking in English and pointing to the course as though commenting on Darque's horses. She described the delightful plan she had contrived. Instead of leaving for Oporto on Tuesday she would go on Monday night in a reserved compartment and accompanied only by her confidante, her Scots maid. Carlos would take the same train. When they reached Santarém they would both get out and go very simply to spend the night in a hotel. The following day she would go on to Oporto and he would return to Lisbon.

Carlos stared at her in stunned, dumbfounded amazement. He had not anticipated such impetuosity. He had supposed she wanted him in Oporto hidden at the Hotel Francfort for romantic outings to Foz, or furtive visits to some hovel – But the idea of a night in a hotel at Santarém!

Finally he shrugged his shoulders indignantly. How could she imagine that, on a railway line where one constantly encountered one's acquaintances, she could get out with him at Santarém station, take his arm conjugally and go off with him to an inn? But she had thought out all the details. Nobody would know her. She would be disguised in a big waterproof and a false wig.

'A wig?'

'Hush – here comes Castão,' she murmured abruptly.

Sure enough, the Count was standing behind him and embracing him tenderly around the waist. Immediately he wanted friend Maia's opinion of the races. Pretty lively, wasn't it? And nice dresses too . . . A certain air of luxury . . . There was certainly nothing for anyone to be ashamed of! Here was proof positive of what he had always maintained: that all the refinements of civilization adapted themselves well in Portugal.

'Our moral soil, Maia, like our physical soil, is blessed soil!'

The Countess went back to Dona Maria. And Teles da Gama walked past again in the noisy duty imposed on him by the formation of his pool. He called Carlos to come to the grandstand in order for him to draw his ticket and bet with the ladies.

'Oh, Gouvarinho! Come along too, man!' he exclaimed. 'Hang it! One needs to liven this thing up! It's patriotic!'

And for the sake of patriotism the Count condescended.

'It is a good thing,' he said as he took Carlos by the arm, 'to encourage elegant diversions. I have already pointed this out in the Chamber: luxury is conservative.'

Above, in a corner, among a group of ladies, they did in fact encounter some animation – and it seemed almost scandalous in that silent expectant grandstand. The Viscountess de Alvim was industriously folding pool tickets; a Russian secretary's little wife, with pretty light-blue eyes, desperately bet five *tostões*, half-crazy, already deeply involved and searching frantically for her programme. The Pinheiro sister, the thinner one, with a light dress of Pompadour wreaths that made hollows in her collar-bone, was delivering pretentious opinions in English about the horses; and Taveira, with damp eyes amid all those skirts, talked about ruining the ladies and living at their expense. All the men elbowed their way forward and wanted to make bets with Joaninha Vilar, who stood with her back against the railing of the grandstand, plump and lazy, and smiled with her head thrown back, her eyelashes drooping and seeming to offer her appetizing little dove-like breast to all those greedy outstretched hands.

Teles da Gama in the meantime was organizing merry confusion. The tickets were folded and a hat was needed – and the gallants then pretended an inordinate love for their headgear, not wishing to confide them to the nervous hands of the ladies. One youth in deep mourning even exceeded himself by clutching the brim of his hat with both hands and shouting.

The Russian secretary's little wife ended by impatiently offering her small son's sailor-hat – he was an obese child, deposited to one side like a bundle. It was Joaninha Vilar who took the tickets round, smiling and shaking them lazily, while Steinbroken's secretary, as though performing an office, gravely collected the coins in his big hat as they dropped with a silvery tinkle one by one. And the draw itself was the entertaining highpoint of the pool! Only four horses were registered and there were fifteen entries, so eleven blank tickets existed to terrorize everyone. All wanted No. 3, *Rabino*, Darque's horse and the favourite for the National Prize. Each greedy little hand that delayed in the bottom of the cap, stirring and groping for the papers, caused merry indignation and much laughter.

'The Viscountess is searching too much! She folded them – she knows them! Probity is required, Viscountess!'

'*Ah, mon Dieu, j'ai Minhoto, cette rosse!*'

'*Je vous l'achète, Madame!*'

'Oh, Dona Maria Pinheiro, you've taken two numbers!'

'*Ah! Je suis perdue – blanc!*'

'Me too, we must make another pool! Let's make another pool!'

'Yes, yes! Another pool!'

And then the vast Baroness de Craben, on a step above, that she occupied like a throne in solitary state, rose with her ticket in her hand. She had drawn Rabino, and in her supercilious fashion she affected not to understand her good luck and asked what Rabino was. When the Count de Gouvarinho explained very earnesly to her the significance of Rabino, that Rabino was practically the national pride, she showed her teeth and condescended to growl from the depths of her bosom that *c'était charmant*. Everyone envied her; and the immense whale again took her throne, fanning herself majestically.

Suddenly there was surprise; while they had been drawing the tickets the horses had started off and were passing the grandstand neck-and-neck. Everyone rose with binoculars in hand. The starter was still on the course with his red flag dipped towards the ground, and the rumps of the horses disappeared round the curve, lustrous in the light, under the fluttering jackets of the jockeys.

Then the sound of voices fell; and in the hush the lovely afternoon seemed to extend itself more gently, more calmly than ever. Through the dustless air in which there was no longer the tremor of strong rays, everything took on delicate relief; the grass was a warm green on the hill facing the grandstand; from time to time in the group of carriages there scintillated the glass of a lantern, the glint of harness, and standing up on a carriage-box there was silhouetted a figure in a tall hat. The horses raced away on the green track, smaller now, finely drawn in the light. Far off, the white of the houses became covered over in a pale pink; and the distant horizon sparkled with the gold of the sun and gleams from the glassy river that was drowned now in a luminous mist; the bluish tones of the hills seemed almost transparent, as though made of precious gems.

'It's Rabino!' cried someone standing on a step behind Carlos. Darque's red and white colours were in fact running ahead. The two next horses were even; and finally, at a sleepy gallop, came Vladimiro, another of Darque's horses, a light bay that looked nearly white in the light.

The Russian secretary's wife clapped her hands and called to Carlos, who in fact had drawn Vladimiro's number in the pool. She had Minhoto, a melancholy nag belonging to Manuel Godinho, and they had made a complicated bet on the two horses that involved gloves and almonds. Already her lovely light-blue eyes had sought those of Carlos several times; and now she was touching his arm with her fan, joking and triumphant.

'*Ah, vous avez perdu, vous avez perdu! Mais c'est un vieux cheval de fiacre, votre Vladimiro!*'

A cab-horse indeed! Vladimiro was Darque's best horse! Perhaps it would still be Portugal's only glory, as Gladiator in former days had been the only glory of France. Perhaps it might even yet replace Camoes.

'*Ah, vous plaisantez!*'

No, Carlos was not joking. He was, in fact, ready to bet everything on *Vladimiro*.

'You'll back Vladimiro?' cried Teles da Gama, turning round quickly.

To amuse himself, and scarcely knowing why, Carlos said he would take on Vladimiro. There was amazement all around and everyone wanted to bet and exploit that rich man's whim of backing a green pony, not even a thoroughbred, that Darque himself called a nag. He smiled, accepted and ended by raising his voice and proclaiming Vladimiro against the field. From all sides they called to him, greedy for plunder.

'Monsieur de Maia, ten *tostões.*'

'Certainly, Madame.'

'Oh, Maia, half a sovereign.'

'At your service.'

'Maia, me too! Listen, me too! Two thousand *reis.*'

'Senhor Maia, ten *tostões.*'

The horses in the distance were rounding the bed as the ground rose. Rabino was already out of sight – and Vladimiro was tailed off and seemed to be tiring. A voice could be heard saying that he was lame. Then Carlos, who was continuing to take on Vladimiro against the field, felt a slow tug at his sleeve. He turned; it was Steinbroken's secretary, who had approached slyly to take part in the raid on Maia's purse, and he proposed two sovereigns in his own name and in that of his superior, as a collective bet by the Legation, a bet by the Kingdom of Finland.

'C'est fait, Monsieur!' exclaimed Carlos with a laugh.

Now he had begun to enjoy himself. He had merely glanced at Vladimiro, but he had liked the horse's light head and its broad, deep chest. But, above all, he was betting in order to put some more life into that corner of the grandstand and to observe the greedy gleam that came into the eyes of those covetous women. Teles da Gama, at his side, approved and found all this patriotic and chic.

'It's Minhoto,' Taveira shouted suddenly.

A change had indeed taken place as the horses rounded the bend. Rabino had suddenly lost ground; he had been tired by the climb and was now short of breath. It was Minhoto, the obscure little horse of Manuel Godinho, that now forged ahead, admirably ridden by a Spanish jockey and eating up the course in an unflagging effort. Directly behind came Darque's red and white colours; at first it looked as though it were still Rabino; but, caught suddenly by an oblique ray of sunshine, the horse assumed the lustrous tones of light bay and to everyone's astonishment it was Vladimiro! The race now lay between him and Minhoto.

Godinho's friends rushed up to the course and threw their hats in the air.

'Minhoto! Minhoto!'

Those around Carlos who had bet against Vladimiro also urged Minhoto on, standing on tiptoe next to the parapet of the grandstand, stretching out their arms to him, urging him on.

'Go on Minhoto! That's it! Keep it up, boy! Bravo! Minhoto! Minhoto!'

The Russian clapped her hands, all nerves and hoping to win the pool. Even the enormous Craben reared herself up, dominating the grandstand and filling it with her blue and white grosgrain; the Count de Gouvarinho, at her side, stood up too, smiling, contentment filling his patriot's breast at the sight of those competing jockeys, those waving hats, that spark of civilization.

Suddenly below, at the foot of the grandstand among the young men who encircled Darque a cry went up:

'Vladimiro, Vladimiro!'

In a desperate burst the horse had drawn even with Minhoto, and now they were approaching at a furious pace, their light colours gleaming brightly, neck and neck, eyes bulging under a shower of whiplashes.

Teles da Gama, his bet forgotten, and all for Darque, his best friend, shouted for Vladimiro. The Russian stood up on a step leaning on Carlos's shoulder, pale and excited, and was urging Minhoto on with little cries and taps of her fan. The agitation in that corner of the grandstand spread down to the enclosure where a row of men could be seen leaning against the rope of the course with their arms waving. On the other side was a row of pale faces fixed in brief anxiety. Ladies had stood up in the carriages. And coming across the hill to see the finish, two horsemen raced at full speed gripping their low hats with their hands.

'Vladimiro, Vladimiro!' here and there isolated cries again rose.

The two horses were approaching with a muffled thud of hooves and raising a gust of wind.

'Minhoto! Minhoto!'

'Vladimiro! Vladimiro!'

They were finishing – and suddenly Vladimiro's English jockey, all aflame and lifting the horse, which seemed to be flying, outstretched and gleaming, from between his legs, made his whip whistle triumphantly, and with a true aim he shot him past the winning-post, two heads in front of Minhoto and covered with foam.

There was lamentation around Carlos – a long, slow groan. Everyone had lost; he took the pool; he took the bets; he gathered in everything. What luck! What a chance! An Italian attaché, the pool's treasurer, turned pale as he surrendered a handkerchief filled with silver; and from every side little hands gloved in pearl-grey or brown sulkily threw him their lost bets, a shower of coins that he gathered up smiling in his hat.

'Ah! Monsieur,' exclaimed the vast wife of the Bavarian Minister in fury, 'beware! You know the saying – luck at gambling – '

'*Hélas, Madame,*' said Carlos resignedly offering her his hat.

And again a subtle finger touched his arm. It was Steinbroken's secretary, slow and silent, bringing him his money and the money of his superior, the bet of the Kingdom of Finland.

'How much d'you win?' exclaimed Teles de Gama, over-whelmed.

Carlos did not know. Gold was now shining at the bottom of the hat. Teles counted, his eyes gleaming.

'Twelve pounds!' he said, marvelling and looking respectfully at Carlos.

Twelve pounds! The figure was passed round with a murmur of surprise! Twelve pounds! Below, Darque's friends were waving their hats and still cheering. But indifference and a slow tedium were returning. The young men fell back yawning in their chairs with an exhausted air. The music, spiritless too, mournfully played selections from *Norma.*

Carlos stood on a step of the grandstand glancing through his binoculars over the carriage enclosure and trying to discover Damaso. People were beginning to disperse over the hill. The ladies had resumed their melancholic immobility at the back of their carriages with their hands on their laps. Here and there a shabby dog-cart made a short trot across the grass. Eusèbio-zinho's two *espanholas,* Concha and Carmen, sat with scarlet sun-shades in a victoria. And individuals with hands behind their backs stared at a charabanc with four horses harnessed in the Daumont style, where a nurse with a laundress's kerchief sat among a sad-looking family and suckled a child covered in lace. Two shrill-voiced urchins were peddling casks of fresh water.

Having failed to discover Damaso, Carlos descended from the grandstand – and at precisely that moment he came upon him face to face as he approached the stairways, red and blazing, in his famous white frock-coat.

'You creature, where the devil have you been?'

Damaso gripped him by the arm and stretched up on tiptoe to whisper in his ear that he had been on the other side with a divine wench, Salazar's Josefina – fantastically *chic*! Beautifully dressed! It looked as though he had a woman!'

'Ah! you scoundrel, you Sardanapalian!'

'It's the struggle for life – come on up to the grandstand! Come along! I haven't had a chat yet today with the high life . . . But, you know, I'm furious. They've made fun of my blue veil! This is a land of swine! Immediately they set about one with mockery, jokes and ribaldry! They're scum! I had to take the veil off – but I've made up my mind! At the next races I'll appear naked! Yes, naked! This country is the disgrace of civilization! Aren't you coming? Well, good-bye.'

But Carlos detained him.

'Listen a moment, man, I've something to say to you – what about that visit to Olivais? You never came back. We'd arranged that you were to go and invite Castro Gomes and that you'd be back bringing the answer . . . You neither came nor did you let us know – and Craft waiting. Well? Altogether the behaviour of a savage!'

Damaso flung up his arms. Didn't Carlos know? Great news! He had not returned to Ramalhete as arranged, because Castro Gomes couldn't go to Olivais. He had been about to leave for Brazil. In fact he had left that Wednesday. The most extraordinary thing – he'd arrived to deliver the invitation and His Excellency had informed him that he much regretted it but he was leaving the next day for Rio! His luggage was already packed; a house had already been taken for his wife where she would live and wait for three months – and he had his passage in his pocket. All of a sudden, between Saturday and Monday. A determined fellow, that Castro Gomes!

'And off he went – ' he exclaimed, turning to compliment the Viscountess de Alvim and Joaninha Vilar who were coming down from the grandstand. 'Off he went, and she's already moved to the house. Only the day before yesterday I went there to call on her, but she was not at home. D'you know what I'm afraid of? That in the first few days, on account of neighbours and as she is on her own, she won't want me to go there often. What d'you think?'

'Perhaps – where does she live?'

Damaso described Madame's establishment in a few words. And, very remarkable, she lived in the Cruges's building! Mama Cruges had let that first floor furnished for many years now; last winter Bertonni the tenor had been there with his family. A well-arranged house. Castro Gomes had been lucky.

'And it's very convenient for me, there beside the Grémio . . .

Well, but won't you come back up to chat with the female tribe? Good-bye. Madame Gouvarinho's as *chic* as can be today! And simply begging for a man! Good-bye!'

Facing Carlos stood the Countess de Gouvarinho in Dona Maria's group, who had now been joined by Madame Alvim and Joaninha Vilar. She beckoned him incessantly with a restless eye as she tortured her great black fan. But he did not obey her at once and halted at the foot of the steps of the grandstand, vaguely lighting a cigarette, troubled by Damaso's words that had made his heart leap. Now that he knew she was alone in Lisbon, living in the same house as Cruges, it seemed that he already knew her and he felt very close to her. Now that he could enter her doorway at any moment, and tread the same steps she trod. Possibilities of a meeting already shone in his mind: an exchanged word, small things, as subtle as threads, but which would begin to link their destinies. And the childish temptation at once arose to go there then, that very afternoon, that instant, and as a friend of Cruges enjoy the right to mount her stairs and pause in front of her door — catch a voice, a sound at the piano, some sign of her life.

But the Countess's look would not let him go. At last, unwillingly, he approached her. She rose at once, left her group and took a few steps with him across the grass. Again she started speaking of the trip to Santarém. Carlos answered very drily that the whole project was an insane one.

'Why?'

Why, for heaven's sake! For every possible reason. The danger, the discomforts, the ridiculousness — For her, as a woman, it might be all right to have picturesque fantasies of romance, but it was up to him to have common sense.

She bit her lip and all her blood rushed to her face. There was no common sense there for her. She could see only coldness. When she would be risking so much he could for one night very well face the discomforts of an inn —

'But it's not that — '

Then what was it? Was he afraid? There was no more danger than in those visits to her aunt's house. Nobody would be able to recognize her, with different-coloured hair, lots of veils, disguised in a big waterproof. They would arrive at night, go into the room, and not leave it, served only by the Scots girl. The

299

following day she would go on to Oporto on the night train, everything would be over.

In that insistence she was the man, the seducer with the vehemence of an active passion, tempting him, arousing his desire, while he seemed like the hesitating and fearful woman. And Carlos felt this. His prolonged resistance to one night of love now threatened to become grotesque. At the same time the warmth of voluptuousness that emanated from that breast as it rose and fell beside him, and for him, gradually made him feel limp. Finally he looked at her meaningfully; and as though desire had at last been suddenly lit in him by the brief flame that flickered in her eyes, black, humid, devouring, promising a thousand things – he spoke to her, his face pale:

'Very well, then. Tomorrow night at the station.'

At that moment catcalls went up around them: a solitary horse was coming up at a lazy gallop and passed the post unhurriedly as though down an avenue of the Campo Grande on a Sunday afternoon. All around people were asking what race was that in which only one horse ran when, far off, as though emerging from the lovely light of the sun that descended on the river, there appeared a poor, white nag, forcing itself and panting in a painful effort under the desperate whiplashes of a jockey in purple and black. When it finally arrived the other gentleman rider had already come indolently from the finishing-line at walking pace, and was now conversing with friends who leaned against the rope of the course.

Everybody laughed. And the race for the King's Prize thus grotesquely ended.

There was still the Consolation Prize – but now all that fictitious interest in horses had vanished.

In the calm and radiant beauty of the afternoon some of the ladies had imitated Viscountess de Alvim and descended to the weighing-in point, tired of the calm in the grandstand. More chairs were procured, and here and there upon the trodden grass groups formed that were enlivened by some light dress or by a gay hat feather; and there was conversation and casual smoking as though in some winter salon. Round Dona Maria and the Alvim woman a great picnic expedition to Queluz was being planned. Alencar and Gouvarinho were discussing educational reform. Among the diplomats and youths with binoculars round their necks the horrible Craben was delivering from the great depths of her chest opinions on Daudet, whom she found *très agréable*. When Carlos at last left, the enclosure, in the clear, fresh air of the hill and with the races forgotten, was taking on the atmosphere of a soirée, with the murmur of voices, a motion of fans and in the distance the music playing a Strauss waltz.

Carlos looked everywhere for Craft and found him at last in the buffet with Darque and others, drinking champagne again.

'I still have to go back to Lisbon,' he told him, 'and I'm going in the phaeton. I am going to abandon you wretchedly – you'll have to find your own way back to Ramalhete – '

'I'll take him!' cried Vargas at once, his tie all dishevelled. 'I'll take him in the dog-cart. I'll look after him. Craft will be in my care! D'you want a receipt for him? To the health of Craft, an Englishman after my own heart – hurrah!'

A little later Carlos was going down the Chiado in the phaeton at a brisk trot and making a turn into the Rua de S. Francisco. He drove with a delicious and singular feeling of perturbation, certain that she was alone in Cruges's house. That last look she had given him seemed to shine ahead of him, beckoning him, and a tumultuous awakening of nameless hopes hurled his soul skywards.

When he drew up in front of the gate someone inside her windows was slowly drawing the blinds. A shadow of dusk was already falling in the silent street. He threw the reins to the coachman and crossed the patio. Never had he visited Cruges, never had he climbed this staircase; and he found it horrible, with its uncarpeted cold stone steps, the bare and dilapidated walls glimmering sadly in the beginnings of dusk. He stopped on the first-floor landing. Here it was that she lived. And he stood and stared naïvely and devotedly at the three doors painted blue – the one in the middle was blocked by a long wicker bench, and a bell-chain hung with a huge ball from the one on the right. There was not a sound from inside – and, combined with the movement of the blinds that he had seen being shut, this heavy silence seemed to encircle with solitude and impenetrability the persons who lived within. A tremor of disappointment passed over him. What if now, alone without her husband, she were to embark upon the life of a recluse and a solitary? What if he were never to meet her eyes again?

Slowly he climbed up to Cruges's floor. He hardly knew what he was going to say to the maestro to explain this odd, un-expected visit – it was a relief when the little maid came to tell him that Master Victorino had gone out.

When he was back in the street Carlos took up the reins and drove the phaeton slowly towards Library Square. Then he re-turned, at walking pace. Now there was a vague light from a lamp behind the white blind. He looked at it like a man looking at a star.

He returned to Ramalhete. Craft, who was covered in dust, was just getting out of a public cab. For a moment they stood there at the door while Craft searched for change for the coach-man and told Carlos about the end of the races. One of the riders for the Consolation Prize had fallen almost beside the finishing line, but had not hurt himself; and at the last, just as they were leaving, Vargas, in his third bottle of champagne, had punched a buffet waiter.

'Thus,' said Craft as he made up his change, 'today's races ran true to the old Shakespearian principle of "all's well that ends well".'

'A punch,' said Carlos with a laugh, 'certainly makes a good full stop.'

In the courtyard the old watchman waited, his hat off, with a letter in his hand for Carlos. A servant had delivered it just a few moments before Carlos had arrived.

There was a woman's English handwriting on the broad en-velope sealed wth a crest. Carlos opened it there and then, and at the first line he at once made such a lively movement, he showed such delighted surprise, his face so lit up, that Craft questioned him with a smile:

'An adventure? An inheritance?'

Red-faced, Carlos put the letter in his pocket and murmured:

'Only a note from a patient . . .'

It was indeed only a patient and only a note, but it began: 'Madame Castro Gomes presents her compliments to Senhor Carlos da Maia and begs him to . . .' Then in a few brief words she asked him to come as early as possible the following morning to see a member of the family who was indisposed.

'Good, I'll go and dress,' said Craft. 'Dinner's at seven-thirty, eh?'

'Yes, dinner . . .' answered Carlos, scarcely knowing what he was saying and wreathed in ecstatic smiles.

He rushed to his rooms. There beside the window, without even taking off his hat, he read her note once more, blissfully contemplating the handwriting, voluptuously seeking the scent of the paper.

It was dated that same day in the afternoon. So when he had passed before the door, she had already written to him; her thoughts had already rested on him – even if it had only been as she penned the simple letters of his name. It was not she who was sick. Had it been Rosa she would not have so coldly said 'a member of the family'. It was perhaps that splendid black man with the grey hair. Perhaps Miss Sarah, bless her for ever, who wanted a doctor who understood English . . . In any case, there was somebody lying in bed there to whom she herself would lead him through the inside corridors of that house – that only a few moments ago he had felt to be closed to him, as if impenetrable for ever! And now, this adorable note, this delicious request to go to her house – now that she knew him, that she had seen Rosa throwing him her bold greeting – took on a deep, disturbing significance.

Had she not wished to understand or accept the distant love that his eyes had clearly offered, as luminously as they had been able, in those fleeting instants when they had met hers – then she could have called another doctor, some practitioner or other, a stranger. But no! Her look had answered his, and she was opening her door to him – and what he felt at this notion was an ineffable gratitude, a tumultuous impulse of all his being to fall at her feet, and lie there kissing the hem of her dress devotedly for eternity, without wanting anything more, without asking for anything else.

When Craft came down a few moments later in evening dress – fresh, white, starched, correct – he found Carlos still covered in the dust of the road, his hat on his head, pacing about the room, in this radiant commotion.

'You're sparkling, man!' said Craft, stopping before him with his hands in his pockets and contemplating him for a moment from above his resplendent collar. 'You're afire! You look as though you've a halo round your head! Something or other very good has happened to you!'

Carlos stretched himself and smiled. Then he gazed at Craft for a moment in silence, shrugged his shoulders and murmured:

'One never knows, Craft, whether what happens to one is, in the final analysis, good or bad.'

'Usually it's bad,' replied the other coldly as he went up to the looking-glass and adjusted the knot of his white tie.

BOOK
2

1

THE FOLLOWING MORNING Carlos rose early and went on foot from Ramalhete to the house of Madame Gomes in Rua de S. Francisco. On the landing, where the distant light from the skylight was fading into a penumbra, waited an old woman wrapped in a mean black shawl with a scarf over her head – a melancholy figure seated in a corner on a rush-seated bench. Through the open door an ugly yellow-papered corridor could be seen. Inside, a hoarse clock was striking ten.

'Have you knocked?' asked Carlos, raising his hat.

The old woman muttered in a tired sick voice from the shadow of the scarf which fell over her eyes: 'Yes, sir. And they have already had the goodness to answer. Senhor Domingos, the servant, won't be a minute.'

Carlos waited, pacing slowly back and forth across the landing. From the second floor came the cheerful noise of children playing; above, Cruges's boy was scrubbing the stairs with a great din and shrilly whistling a *fado*. One long minute dragged by, and then another – interminable. The old woman gave a little weary sigh from within the blackness of the scarf. Away inside the house a canary broke into song; and then Carlos tugged impatiently on the bell-pull.

A servant with ginger whiskers and correctly buttoned flannel jacket appeared at a run, carrying in his hand a serving-dish covered with a napkin. When he saw Carlos he stopped in such amazement that some of the gravy from the roast meat splashed from the dish on to the floor.

'Oh, Senhor Dom Carlos da Maia, sir, do come in! What a surprise! Be good enough to wait just a moment please and I'll show you into the drawing-room. Here, take this, Senhora Augusta, take it quick and don't spill any more! Madam says she'll send the port later . . . I beg Your Excellency's pardon . . . This way, sir . . .'

He pulled aside a heavy curtain of red rep and showed Carlos into a tall, spacious room with blue sprigs of flowers on the wallpaper and two balconies looking on to Rua de S.

Francisco. As he hurriedly pulled up the two thin white blinds he asked Carlos if he did not remember him. And when he turned round smiling, hastily pulling down his sleeves, Carlos recognized the ginger whiskers. It was in fact Domingos, an excellent footman who had been employed at Ramalhete at the beginning of the winter, and had left because of patriotic and jealous rows with the French chef.

'I didn't see you clearly, Domingos,' said Carlos. 'The landing is a little dark. Now I remember perfectly of course . . . So you are here now, are you? Are you happy here?'

'I think I'm very happy indeed, sir. Senhor Cruges lives up above, too, you know.'

'Yes, yes, I know.'

'If Your Excellency will be patient enough to wait just a moment, I'll go and tell Senhora Dona Maria Eduarda . . .'

Maria Eduarda! It was the first time Carlos had heard her name, and it seemed ideal to him, perfectly matching her serene beauty. Maria Eduarda. Carlos Eduardo . . . Their names were similar. Who could tell it would not presage a merging of their destinies too!

Domingos, in the meantime, had stopped once again, with his hand on the heavy curtain over the door, to tell him with a smile and a tone of confidence: 'It's the English governess who's ill.'

'Ah, the governess?'

'Yes, sir, she has had a slight temperature since yesterday, and a heavy feeling on her chest.'

'Ah . . .'

Domingos made another slight movement with the curtain, in no hurry, studying Carlos in admiration.

'And is the old gentleman, your grandfather, well, sir?'

'Very well, thank you, Domingos.'

'He's a fine gentleman, that one! There's no other gentleman like him in Lisbon!'

'Thank you, Domingos, thank you.'

When the servant finally left the room, Carlos took off his gloves and wandered slowly around the room, deeply interested in everything. The floor had a fresh mat down. Near the door was an ancient grand piano shrouded with a whitish cover; on a bookstand beside it, full of music scores, sheets of music and illustrated magazines, stood a Japanese vase where three beautiful lilies were fading. All the chairs were covered in red rep, and at the foot of the sofa lay an old tiger skin. As in the Hotel Central, the scant furnishings of a rented house had received touches of comfort and taste: new cretonne curtains, which harmonized with the blue of the wallpaper, had replaced the original curtains of muslin; a small Moorish chiffonier which Carlos remembered having seen a few days ago in old Abraham's had been introduced to fill one wall which had been rather bare; the plush cloth on an oval table in the centre of the room could scarcely be seen beneath beautifully bound books and albums, two Japanese bronze owls, and a Dresden china flower-basket – delicate artistic objects which surely did not belong to Mother Cruges. And there seemed to linger in the air, caressing the carefully arranged things and distinguishing them with a particular charm, that vague perfume in which jasmine was dominant and which Carlos had sensed in the rooms of the Hotel Central.

But what attracted Carlos most was a pretty screen in unbleached linen embroidered with flowers, which was placed beside the window to make a secluded cosy corner. There was a low chair there in scarlet satin, a large foot-cushion, a sewing table strewn with interrupted work, fashion magazines, a piece of embroidery rolled up, and skeins of coloured wools spilling out from a basket. And there, comfortably curled in the soft chair, was the famous little Scots terrier bitch which had so often appeared in Carlos's dreams, trotting lightly along the Aterro behind a radiant figure, or nestled up asleep in a soft lap . . .

'Bonjour, Mademoiselle,' he said quietly, hoping to capture her affection.

The little bitch sat up sharply in the chair, ears cocked, and flashing, from behind tousled strands of hair, two beautiful jet eyes full of an almost human penetration and distrust of the stranger. For a moment Carlos feared she would start barking, but the little bitch was suddenly overcome with love, and sprawled over in the chair, paws in the air, quite indecent, abandoning her stomach to be fondled. Carlos was about to stroke her and make a fuss of her when a light step sounded on the mat. He turned and there was Maria Eduarda before him.

It was like an unexpected apparition – and he bowed his head low, less to greet her than to conceal the tumultuous wave of blood which he felt rush to his face. She, tall and white and simply dressed in a black serge dress with a straight white collar like a man's, and a rosebud with two leaves at her breast, sat down near the oval table, while she finished unfolding a little lace handkerchief. At her bidding, Carlos sat himself embarrassed on the edge of the rep sofa. And after a moment's silence, which seemed to him profound, almost solemn, Maria Eduarda spoke, in a rich, slow voice, with a caressing tone of gold.

Through his confusion, Carlos realized vaguely that she was thanking him for the kindness and attention he had shown towards Rosa; and the more he looked at her the more charms he found, and further features of her perfection.

Her hair was not blonde, as it had seemed from afar in the sunlight, but two tones of chestnut, light and dark, and it was thick and lightly waved over the forehead. In the great dark light of her eyes was something at once both very grave and very sweet. She had a habit of familiarly crossing her hands over her knees at times as she spoke. And through the tight serge sleeve which ended in a white cuff, he sensed the beauty, the whiteness, the softness, and almost the warmth of her arms.

She stopped speaking. Carlos, as he was about to speak, felt the blood rush to his cheeks as before. And although he knew from Domingos that it was the governess who was sick, he found in his confusion only one timid question to ask:

'It is not your daughter who is sick, is it, senhora?'

'Oh no! Thank God!'

And Maria Eduarda told him, just as Domingos had done, that the English governess had been indisposed for two days, with difficulty in breathing, a cough and a slight temperature.

'We thought at first it was a cold which would pass, but yesterday evening she grew worse and now I'm anxious that you should see her.'

She got up and went to pull an enormous bell-rope which hung beside the piano. Her hair, taken up behind, left a curling golden down exposed on the milk-white neck. As she walked among that rep-covered furniture, beneath the grubby plaster ceiling, her whole person seemed more radiant to Carlos, a nobler, almost inaccessible beauty; and he thought that he would never dare, in that room, stare at her so frankly, with such obvious devotion, as when he met her in the street.

'What a pretty little terrier you have, senhora!' he said when Maria Eduarda had sat down again; and he put into these simple words, spoken with a smile, a note of tenderness.

She responded with a charming smile that made a dimple appear in her chin and gave a sweeter tenderness to her serious features. Then gaily, clapping her hands together, she called into the screen:

'Niniche! You're being complimented. Come and say thank you!'

Niniche appeared, yawning. Carlos found the name Niniche pretty. And it was a coincidence, for he had had a little Italian greyhound also called Niniche.

At this point the maid entered – the tall freckle-faced girl with a petulant expression whom Carlos had already seen in the Hotel Central.

'Melanie will show you Miss Sarah's room,' said Maria Eduarda. 'I won't accompany you, because she is so shy, and is so full of scruples about making a nuisance of herself, that with me in the room she is likely to deny everything, and say there is nothing whatever the matter with her . . .'

'Of course, I understand,' murmured Carlos, smiling, enchanted with the whole affair.

And it seemed to him then that something special shone in her eyes as she looked at him, something sweet and vivacious for him alone.

Hat in hand he walked along the intimate corridor with familiar step, and as he noticed little details of domestic life, he felt a joy as if of possession. Through a half-open door he caught sight of a bath and, hanging beside it, large Turkish bath-towels. A little farther ahead, there were bottles of mineral waters from St-Galmier and Vals lined up on a table, as if they had been recently unpacked. He discerned behind these simple everyday things evidence of tasteful living.

Melanie pulled aside an unbleached linen curtain and showed him into a bright fresh room; there he found poor Miss Sarah sitting up in a little iron bed, with a blue silk bow at her neck and her hair as smooth and carefully brushed as if she were about to attend Sunday service at the Presbyterian chapel. Her English newspapers were scrupulously folded on the bedside table beside a glass holding two beautiful roses, and everything in the room shone with a severe orderliness – from the portraits of the English royal family displayed on a lace cloth on the chest of drawers, to her well-polished boots carefully sorted and lined up on a pine-wood shelf.

Carlos had no sooner sat down than she declared between bouts of coughing, and with two rosy patches of shame in her cheeks, that there was nothing wrong with her. It was her mistress, such a good woman and so solicitous about her, who had obliged her to take to her bed. For her part she was most displeased at having to remain there idle, useless, now that Madame was alone like that, in a house without a garden. Where was the child to play? Who could take her out? Ah, this was a prison for Madame . . . !

Carlos consoled her as he took her pulse. Then, when he stood up to examine her with the stethoscope, the poor girl flushed all over in distress, clasping her clothes over her breast, and asking if this was absolutely necessary . . . Yes, most definitely it was necessary. He found her right lung slightly affected and while he tucked her up, he made a few inquiries about her family. She said she was from York, the daughter of a clergyman, and had fourteen brothers and sisters: the boys were in New Zealand and they were all as strong as athletes. She had turned out the weakest of the lot, and when her father saw that she weighed only eight stone at seventeen, he began teaching her Latin, preparing her for a post as governess.

Anyway, asked Carlos, there had never been any chest complaints in the family? She smiled. Oh no, never! Mama was still alive. Papa had died at an advanced age from a kick by a mare.

Carlos in the meantime had stood up and was watching her reflectively, hat in hand. Then suddenly, without apparent reason, she was overcome with emotion and her small eyes became misty. And when she heard that so much attention was necessary, that she would have to remain in her room for another fortnight, she became even more distraught and two timid tears slipped from under her lashes. Carlos finished by patting her hand paternally.

'Oh, thank you, sir!' she whispered in English, quite overcome by it all.

In the drawing-room, Carlos found Maria Eduarda seated beside the table arranging sprays of flowers, with a large basket of flowers on a chair at her side and her lap full of carnations. A brilliant ray of sunlight, falling across the mat, came to rest at her feet, and Niniche, stretched out there, shone as if she were made of strands of silver. In the street below, that lovely sunny morning, a barrel-organ was gaily playing a waltz from *Madame Angot*. From the floor above, the noise of children playing and running about had begun again.

'Well?' she asked at once, turning round with a bunch of carnations in her hand.

Carlos set her at ease. Poor Miss Sarah had a touch of bronchitis with just a slight temperature. She needed care and attention, however.

'Of course! And she must take something, too, mustn't she?'

She immediately deposited the carnations from her lap into the basket and went and opened a little ebony writing-desk that stood between the windows. And she herself set out the paper for him to write the prescription on, and put a new nib in the pen. These attentions stirred Carlos as profoundly as if they were caresses.

'Oh, senhora,' he murmured, 'a pencil would do.'

When he sat down, his eyes lingered with affectionate interest upon these familiar objects on which the sweetness of her hands had rested – an agate seal on an old accounts book, an ivory knife with silver monogram beside a little Saxe bowl full of stamps; and over all there was an orderliness in keeping with her perfect profile. The barrel-organ in the road had stopped playing and upstairs the children no longer chased about. And while he slowly wrote, Carlos heard the soft fall of her steps on the mat, heard her quietly move the position of the vases.

'What pretty flowers you have,' he said, turning his head as he very leisurely and distractedly blotted the prescription.

She stood beside the Moorish chiffonier where she had placed a yellow Indian vase, and was arranging foliage around two roses.

'They give an air of freshness to the room,' she said. 'But I imagined there would be prettier flowers in Lisbon. There is nothing to compare with the flowers in France, don't you agree?'

He did not answer at first, lost in gazing at her, thinking how delightful it would be to stay for ever there in that room of red rep, full of brightness and full of silence, watching her arrange green leaves around roses!

'There are beautiful flowers in Cintra,' he murmured at last.

'Ah, Cintra is charming,' she said, without raising her eyes from her arrangement. 'It would be worth coming to Portugal merely to see Cintra.'

At this moment the rep curtain was pushed aside and Rosa came running in, all in white with little black silk stockings, a wave of black hair falling down her back, and her great doll in her arms. When she saw Carlos, she stopped abruptly, delighted, her beautiful eyes full upon him and Cricri, who wore only a vest, hugged tighter in her arms.

'Don't you know this gentleman?' asked her mother, seating herself once more before her basket of flowers.

Rosa smiled, and her little face grew pink. She had an unusual charm as she appeared at this moment, all black and white like a swallow, a lithe little figure of peculiar grace, with great blue eyes and a maidenly blush on her face. When Carlos approached with hand outstretched to renew the acquaintance, she rose on tiptoe and gaily offered him her lips fresh as a rosebud. Carlos dared do no more than touch her lightly on the forehead.

Then he shook hands with his old friend Cricri. This suddenly reminded Rosa of what had brought her there at a run.

'It's her *robe-de-chambre*, Mama! I can't find Cricri's *robe-de-chambre*. I can't dress her. Do you know where her *robe-de-chambre* is?'

'Just listen to the untidy girl!' said her mother, looking at her with a slow tender smile. 'If Cricri has her own special wardrobe and chest of drawers, I don't see why things should be lost. Do you, Senhor Carlos da Maia?'

He, with prescription in hand, also smiled, not saying a word, touched by that intimacy in which he felt himself included.

The child went over to her mother, rubbing against her arm and continuing in a languid, lazy little voice:

'Go on, tell me . . . Don't be nasty . . . Go on, where's her *robe-de-chambre*? Tell me . . .'

Lightly, with the tips of her fingers, Maria Eduarda straightened the white silk bow which caught up her hair. Then she spoke in a more serious tone.

'All right, that's enough now. Be quiet. You know I have nothing to do with Cricri's clothes. You should be tidier. Go and ask Melanie.'

Rosa obeyed immediately, she too, serious now, acknowledging Carlos as she passed, with a ladylike: '*Bonjour, Monsieur.*'

'She's delightful!' he murmured.

The mother smiled. She had finished arranging her bowl of carnations, and now she attended to Carlos, who had put the prescription on the table, and had leisurely seated himself in an easy chair to speak of the diet Miss Sarah should have, and the syrup of codeine which should be taken every three hours.

'Poor Sarah!' said she. 'It's funny, isn't it, but she came with the premonition, almost the certainty, that she was going to fall ill in Portugal!'

'Then she's going to hate Portugal!'

'Oh, she is already horrified by it! She finds it too hot, and there are unpleasant smells everywhere, and the people are dreadful. She's frightened of being insulted in the street . . . Altogether she is extremely unhappy here, and dying to leave.'

Carlos laughed at these Anglo-Saxon antipathies. Although, to tell the truth, Miss Sarah was quite right in much of this criticism.

'And are you satisfied with Portugal, senhora?'

'Yes, I have to be. It is my country.'

Her country! And there was he thinking she was Brazilian.

'No, I'm Portuguese.'

And for a long moment there was silence. She had taken a large black fan with painted red flowers on it from the table, and was opening it slowly. And Carlos felt, without knowing why, a new sweet joy enter his heart. Then she began to speak of the journey, which had been very pleasant. She loved travelling by sea, and it had been wonderful to arrive that morning in Lisbon, with the sky deep blue and the sea all blue too, and to feel already the warmth of the balmy climate . . . But as soon as they had disembarked, everything began to go badly. Their lodgings were bad at the Hotel Central. Niniche had frightened them badly one night with an attack of indigestion. Then straightway there had been that accident.

'Yes,' said Carlos,' 'that accident of your husband's in the Praça Nova . . .'

She looked surprised. How did he hear about it? Ah, of course, through Damaso.

'You are great friends, I believe.'

After a moment's hesitation, which she perceived, Carlos murmured:

'Yes, Damaso is often at Ramalhete. As a matter of fact, though, he is a young man I have known only a few months.'

She opened her eyes wide in astonishment.

'Damaso? But he told me that you had known each other from infancy, that you were even related.'

'Pure imagination. But if it makes him happy . . .'

She too smiled, and lightly shrugged her shoulders.

'And you, senhora,' Carlos went on, not wanting to speak of Damaso any more, 'how do you find Lisbon?'

She liked it well enough, found the meridional tone of white and blue very pretty. But there were so few comforts! There was an atmosphere in the life here which she had not yet been able fully to understand – was it simplicity or poverty which caused it?

'Simplicity, senhora. We have the simplicity of savages.'

She laughed.

'I wouldn't say that. But they seem to be like the Greeks: they are satisfied to nourish themselves on an olive – and the exquisite blue sky . . .'

This seemed an adorable remark to Carlos and his whole heart fled out to her.

Maria Eduarda complained above all of the houses, so lacking in comfort, so devoid of taste, so slovenly. The one she was living in was a disgrace. The kitchen was atrocious, the doors did not close. There were some pictures in the dining-room of little boats and hills, which put one off one's food.

'Besides that,' she added, 'it's dreadful to have no garden or yard where the child could run and play.'

'It's not easy to find a house like this and with a garden,' said Carlos.

He glanced round at the walls, at the grubby plaster of the ceiling, and suddenly remembered Craft's villa, with its view of the river, its spaciousness, the cool paths of acacia.

Fortunately Maria Eduarda was renting the house only by the month, and was thinking of going to spend the rest of the time she had to stay in Portugal on the coast.

316

'As a matter of fact,' she said, 'that is what my doctor in Paris, Dr Chaplain, advised.'

Dr Chaplain? Carlos knew Dr Chaplain very well. He had listened to his lectures, had visited him personally at his home in Maisonettes, near St-Germain. He was a great teacher, an outstanding man.

'And so kind-hearted!' she said with a bright smile, and eyes that shone.

And this shared feeling seemed to draw them closer together: each at that moment adored Dr Chaplain; and they continued to talk of him at length, enjoying through this trifling affection for an old physician a nascent harmony of spirits.

Dear Dr Chaplain! What fine kind features. Always wearing that little silk cap, and always with a big flower in his buttonhole. And moreover the greatest physician that had appeared in Trousseau's generation.

'And Madame Chaplain,' went on Carlos, 'is a charming person. Don't you think so?'

But Maria Eduarda did not know Madame Chaplain.

Within the house, the hoarse clock was chiming eleven. And Carlos stood up, his fleeting, unforgettable, delicious visit at an end.

They exchanged their civilities of departure, and a light flush spread over his face once more as he touched her smooth, cool hand. He would leave his regards to Mademoiselle Rosa. Then, at the door, with his hand already on the curtain, he turned once more to receive, as a final souvenir, the gentle glance with which she followed him.

'Until tomorrow, of course!' she exclaimed, with her beautiful smile.

'Until tomorrow, to be sure!'

Domingos was already on the landing in dress-coat, smiling and neat.

'Is it anything to worry about, senhor?'

'No, it's nothing very much, Domingos. Pleased to see you here.'

'And I to see Your Excellency. Until tomorrow, senhor.'

'Until tomorrow.'

Niniche appeared on the landing too. Carlos bent down to stroke her affectionately, and she too received a radiant:

'Until tomorrow, Niniche!'

Until tomorrow! And as he returned to Ramalhete this was the only clear idea he could distinguish through the luminous haze he moved in. Now his day was ending, but when the long hours had passed and the weary night was over, he could penetrate again that red rep room where she would be waiting for him in the same serge dress, encircling still the roses with green leaves . . .

All along the Aterro, amid the dust of summer and the clatter of carts, he saw only this room, with its new floor-covering, cool, clear and still; sometimes a phrase she had pronounced sung in his memory, in all the golden glory of her voice; or he could see the stones of her rings glittering as she fondled Niniche's silky coat. She seemed even lovelier now that he knew her graceful, delicate smile; she was full of intelligence and good taste, and the poor, ill, old woman at the door, to whom she had sent port, proved her goodness. And what pleased him most of all was that he would no longer have to go sniffing round the city like a lost dog, hunting for those beautiful black eyes; now he had only to mount a few steps and the door of her house would be opened to him. Everything in life had suddenly become easy, harmonious, all doubts and impatience gone.

Back in his room at Ramalhete, Baptista handed him a letter. 'The Scots girl brought it just after you had left, sir.'

It was from the Countess. Half a sheet of paper with no more than a pencil-written 'All right'. Carlos screwed it up, furious. The Countess! He had scarcely remembered her since the day before, in this radiant tumult in which his heart was plunged. And it was on tonight's train, just a few hours away, that they were to set off together to Santarém, to hide in an inn and make love! He had faithfully promised her this; she was no doubt already making ready with the atrocious wig, with the enveloping waterproof; everything was 'all right' . . . At this moment he considered her ridiculous, stupid, despicable. Oh, it was as clear as day that he would not go, that he would never go, never! But he had to put in an appearance at Santa Apolónia Station and stammer some clumsy excuse, witness her grief, watch her eyes fill with tears. What a nuisance it all was! He loathed her.

When he went in to lunch Craft and Afonso, already seated at table, happened to be talking of Gouvarinho and the articles he solemnly continued to publish in the *Jornal de Comércio*.

313

'What an ass the man is!' hissed Carlos, releasing upon the political literature of the husband the anger he felt against the wife's amorous importunities.

Afonso and Craft looked at him, amazed at such violence. And Craft censured his ingratitude. For there was no doubt about it, there was no other man on the face of the earth with such an enthusiasm for Carlos as that unfortunate statesman had.

'You have no idea, Senhor Afonso da Maia. He worships him. It's sheer idolatry.'

Carlos shrugged his shoulders impatiently. And Afonso, well-disposed now towards this man who so wholeheartedly admired his grandson, murmured kindly: 'Poor soul, I suppose he is inoffensive enough . . .'

Craft clapped with delight: '*Inoffensive!* That is admirable, Senhor da Maia! *Inoffensive*, applied to a statesman, to a member of the Upper House, a minister, a policy-maker – that's the best I've heard for a long time! And that is just what he is – *inoffensive*. That's what they all are . . .'

'Chablis?' inquired the footman.

'No, I'll have tea.' And he added, 'That champagne we drank yesterday at the races, for the sake of patriotism, upset my system completely. I must keep to a milk diet for a week.'

Then they continued to talk of the races, of Carlos's winnings, of Clifford, of Damaso's blue veil.

'The person who was really well-dressed yesterday was the Countess de Gouvarinho,' said Craft, stirring his tea. 'That creamy white with touches of black suited her to perfection. A turn-out eminently suited to a race-meeting . . . *C'était un œillet blanc panaché de noir* . . . Didn't you think, Carlos?'

'Mmm,' grunted Carlos, 'she looked all right . . .'

Again the Countess! It seemed as if there would never now be a conversation in his presence when the name of the Countess did not arise, and there would be nowhere to turn where the Countess did not bar the way. And there and then, seated at table, he decided he would never see her again, but would write a brief, polite note, refusing to go to Santarém, and not even bother to find an excuse.

But once in his room, seated before a sheet of paper, he smoked a long cigarette and could find no phrase that was neither puerile nor brutal. He did not even feel sufficiently affable to

319

be able to address her with a banal 'Dearest'. He was suddenly overcome by an indefinable physical revulsion from her: a whole night of her exaggerated verbena perfume would be intolerable, and he recalled how the skin of her neck, which had formerly seemed satin-like, had a certain viscousness, a certain yellowish tone, beyond the line of face-powder. He decided not to write to her after all. He would go to Santa Apolónia that night, and just as the train was due to depart, he would rush up to the carriage-window and hastily stammer out an excuse; there would be no time for weeping and recriminations; a swift hand-clasp and off, good-bye, for ever . . .

But what a sacrifice that night, when the hour approached to go to the station, to drag himself from the comfort of his easy-chair and leave his cigar! He flung himself into his coupé in desperation, cursing that evening in the blue boudoir when, all because of a rose and a certain becoming dress the colour of autumn leaves, he had found himself in her arms on a sofa . . .

He arrived at Santa Apolónia just two minutes before the express was due to leave. He hurried to the far end of the entrance hall which was almost empty now, to buy a platform ticket. And there he had to wait an age, watching the two slow slack hands on the other side of the glass fumble with change.

He entered the waiting-room at last – only to collide with Damaso, who wore a hat with the brim turned down and a travelling-bag strung crosswise over his shoulder. Damaso clasped his hands, overcome with emotion.

'Oh, my dear boy! Have you really taken all this trouble? How did you know I was leaving?'

Carlos did not disillusion him, and stammered that Taveira had told him, that he had met Taveira . . .

'Well, this is the last thing I was expecting,' exclaimed Damaso. 'There was I this morning, snug in bed, when the telegram arrived. I was furious! I mean, you can imagine how I felt, to get such bad news!'

It was only then that Carlos realized that he was dressed in heavy mourning – crape round his hat, black gloves, black spats, a black band on his kerchief . . . He murmured with embarrassment:

'Taveira told me you were going, but he didn't explain any further. Has someone of your family died?'

'My uncle Guimarães.'

'The communist? The one in Paris?'

'No, his brother, his elder brother, from Penafiel. Just wait here a minute, I'll be right back. I'm going to the bar to fill my brandy flask. I completely forgot my brandy with all the worry . . .'

Passengers were still arriving, out of breath, dressed in dust-coats, clutching hat-boxes in their hands. Porters sluggishly trundled along luggage. At one window stood a gentleman with a large corporation and an embroidered cap, surrounded by a whole company of political friends who waited respectfully and in silence. In a corner a lady sobbed beneath a veil.

Carlos, seeing a carriage labelled 'reserved', imagined the Countess must be there. But a guard hurled himself forward, furious, as if he were profaning a sanctuary. What did he want? What did he want there? Did he not know that carriage was reserved for Senhor Carneiro?

'I didn't know.'

'You should've known! You should've asked!' the other grumbled, still trembling with indignation.

Carlos inspected several other compartments where people crowded in, jostling each other as they put up their parcels; in one compartment two individuals were quarrelling over seats, calling each other insolent and ill-bred. Farther on, a child kicked and bawled on its nurse's lap.

'My dear boy, who the devil are you searching for?' exclaimed Damaso gaily, appearing suddenly from behind Carlos and slipping his arm round his waist.

'No one . . . I just thought I saw the Marquis.'

Immediately Damaso began complaining about what a dreary nuisance it was to have to go to Penafiel.

'And right now when I particularly needed to be in Lisbon! I've been having devilish good luck with the ladies lately, my boy! Fiendish good luck!'

A bell clanged. Damaso immediately gave Carlos a tender clasp, leapt into his compartment and stuck on his head a little silk cap. Then, hanging out of the window, he continued his confidences. What upset him most was to leave that nice little adventure in Rua de S. Francisco. The pest upon it! Just now that everything was going so well, the chap in Brazil, and she there, right at hand, two steps from the Grémio!

Carlos scarcely heard him as he stared distractedly at the great glass clock-face. Suddenly Damaso, at the carriage-window, gave a start of surprise.

'Look, there are the Gouvarinhos!'

Carlos started too. The Count, in a bowler proper for the journey, and an off-white jacket, approached leisurely, as befitted a director of the Company, talking with a station employee of elevated rank and adorned with gold braid, who was charged with the transport of His Lordship's cardboard hat-box. And the Countess, in a splendid travelling-coat of chestnut-coloured foulard, with a grey veil covering her face and hat, followed behind with her Scottish maid, carrying in her hand a bouquet of roses.

Carlos hurried towards them, the picture of amazement.

'You here, Maia?'

'Off on a journey, Count?'

It was true. He had decided to accompany the Countess to Oporto on the occasion of her father's birthday. A last minute decision which nearly made them miss the train.

'Shall we have the pleasure of your company, Maia? Are you coming too?'

Carlos explained rapidly that he had come to the station solely to shake the hand of poor Damaso who was off to Penafiel on account of the death of an uncle.

Leaning from the window, with his black-clad hands hanging outside, poor Damaso was greeting the Countess, gravely, funereally. And the good Gouvarinho had to go at once to shake his hand and offer his condolences.

Alone for this brief instant with the Countess, Carlos could only murmur: 'How exasperating!'

'The confounded man!' she hissed, with her eyes flashing through the veil. 'Everything all arranged and then at the last moment he insists on coming!'

Carlos accompanied them to the reserved compartment, in another carriage that they were coupling on especially for His Lordship. The Countess took her seat in the corner near the window. And when the Count, in a tone of icy politeness, advised her to sit facing the engine, she showed her irritation by sharply flinging aside her bouquet and settling herself more deliberately in the cushions; a stony look of anger passed between them.

322

Embarrassed, Carlos asked: 'Will you be staying long?'

The Count replied with a smile to disguise his bad mood: 'A couple of weeks perhaps. A little holiday.'

'Three days at the most,' she retorted coldly in a voice as keen as a knife.

The Count was livid and made no response.

The doors were all closed now and a silence had fallen over the platform. The engine whistle pierced the air and the long train, with a dry screech of taut brakes, began to move, with people still at the windows, stretching out for a final hand-clasp. Here and there a white handkerchief fluttered. The glance the Countess darted at Carlos held the tenderness of a kiss. Damaso was shouting his regards to Ramalhete. The mail coach slipped by, illuminated, and with another piercing whistle, the train merged into the night.

Carlos, alone in the coupé returning to Ramalhete, felt a triumphant joy at the Countess's departure and the unexpected journey of Damaso. It was like a providential banishment of all impediments; and Rua de S. Francisco became a place of seclusion – with all the charms and complicities that that entailed.

He left the carriage at the Cais de Sodré and went on foot up Ferregial to pass in front of the windows in Rua de S. Francisco. All he could see was a vague strip of light between the half-closed shutters. But this was enough. He could imagine in detail now the tranquil evening she was spending in the wide room furnished in red rep. He knew the names of the books she read, and the music she had on the piano; and the flowers which exhaled their fragrance there he had seen her arrange that morning. Would her thoughts dwell a moment upon him? Naturally: the illness in the house would oblige her to remember the hours the medicine was to be taken, the instructions he had given her, the sound of his voice; and when she spoke with Miss Sarah she would doubtless pronounce his name. Twice he walked the length of Rua de S. Francisco, and he made his way home under the star-strewn sky slowly, meditating upon the sweetness of that great love.

Every day then, for weeks, he spent this delicious, splendid, perfect hour – his visit to the English Miss.

He leapt out of bed, singing like a canary, and embarked on

323

his day with a feeling of triumph. The mail arrived, invariably bringing a letter from the Countess, three sheets of paper from out of which fell some little withered flower. He left it lying there on the carpet, and would have been at a loss to describe the contents of the letter. All he was aware of, and that only vaguely, was that three days after she had arrived in Oporto, her father, old Tompson, had had a fit and she was retained there to nurse him. Then, carrying two or three of the finest flowers from the garden wrapped in tissue paper, he would set off for Rua de S. Francisco, always in the coupé now for the weather had changed and one gloomy day followed another, all rain and south-westerly winds.

At the door Domingos welcomed him with a brighter smile every day. Niniche rushed from within the house, leaping up at him enthusiastically; he picked her up and kissed her. He stood a moment waiting in the drawing-room and glanced an affectionate greeting at the furniture, the bowls of flowers, the neat orderliness of things; then he went over to the piano to examine the music she had been playing that morning, or the book she had left interrupted with an ivory knife between the pages.

She came in. And every day her smile and the golden voice with which she wished him 'Good morning' seemed to Carlos more charming, more penetrating. She generally wore a dark dress of simple style: only occasionally the severity was enlivened by a collar of superb antique lace, or a belt with a stone-encrusted buckle, and this sedate attire seemed most beautiful to Carlos, and like an expression of her spirit.

They began by speaking of Miss Sarah, and the miserable wet weather which was so unfavourable to her condition. As they talked, still standing, she would adjust the position of a book or slightly move a chair which was not straight; she had a restless habit of constantly rearranging the symmetry of objects – and automatically, as she passed, of flicking away with the magnificent lace of her handkerchief imaginary dust from the furniture which had already been scrupulously dusted and polished.

She always accompanied him now to Miss Sarah's room. As he walked beside her along the yellow corridor, Carlos felt disquieted by the caress of this intimate jasmine perfume which seemed to emanate from the movement of her skirts. At times she would familiarly open the door of a room, barely furnished with only an old sofa: it was here that Rosa played, where Cricri's things were kept, her prams and her kitchen utensils. They would find the little girl dressing the doll or in deep conversation with it; or else she would be sitting in the corner of the sofa, lost in admiration of some picture-book she held open on her knees. She would run up to Carlos and offer him her little mouth to be kissed; and her whole person exhaled the freshness of a flower.

In the governess's room, Maria Eduarda would seat herself at the foot of the white bed, and poor Miss Sarah, still coughing badly, still embarrassed and continually making certain that the silk sheet was properly covering her neck, would straightway declare that she was well. Carlos joked with her, insisting how lucky she was to be tucked up in bed there during this miserable winter weather, with care and attention all round, some nice sentimental novels to read and a tasty Portuguese diet. She would turn grateful eyes to Madame and sigh: 'Oh yes, I am very comfortable.'

And then she would be touched with emotion again.

Right from the start, Maria Eduarda had settled down in her scarlet chair when they returned to the drawing-room, and, talking with Carlos, had very naturally picked up her embroidery, as if in the presence of an old friend. How profoundly happy he was to see her unfold her canvas! It was to be a pheasant with brilliant plumage, but so far the only part embroidered was the branch of the apple tree on which he perched, a fresh vernal bough covered with little white flowers, like in an orchard in Normandy.

Carlos sat beside the pretty little ebony bureau, occupying the oldest, most comfortable of the red rep easy-chairs, the springs of which gave a creak from time to time. Between them was the sewing-table with the *Ilustrada* or some fashion magazine lying upon it; sometimes, during a moment's silence, he would glance at the illustrations, but the graceful hands of Maria, shining with jewels, would be drawing strands of wool through the canvas. Niniche lay at her feet, peering up at them at times through the fine hair over her muzzle, from beautiful grave black eyes. In these days of rain and cold and the noise of dripping gutters outside, that corner by the window, with the peacefulness of the leisurely work on the canvas, the slow friendly voices and an occasional easy silence, had an air of intimacy and tenderness.

But there was nothing intimate in their conversation. They talked of the charm of Paris, of London where she had spent four dismal winter months, of Italy where she longed to go, about books and artistic topics. Of novels, she preferred Dickens, and Feuillet pleased her less because he smoothed over everything, even the pangs of love. Although educated in a strict convent in Orléans, she had read Michelet and Renan. Moreover she was not a practising Catholic; churches only attracted her from the aesthetic, artistic point of view and because of the music and lights and the charming month in praise of the Virgin in France, when the churches were embellished with the lovely flowers of May. Her ideas were very forthright and clear-sighted, with an underlying tenderness which drew her towards everything weak or suffering. That was why she admired the Republic, as it seemed to her the régime which showed most concern for the lowly. Carlos laughingly declared her a Socialist.

'Socialist, legitimist, Orléanist,' said she, 'anything as long as people don't go hungry.'

But was this possible? Even Jesus himself, who had so many sweet illusions, had stated that there would always be poor . . .

Jesus lived a long time ago; Jesus did not know everything. A lot more was known today; men were far wiser. It was necessary to construct some other society, and quickly, in which misery no longer existed. In London, sometimes, when the snow was thick, there were little children huddled in doorways, shivering and moaning with hunger. It was horrible! And what about Paris? People only saw the boulevards, but what poverty and distress there was behind!

Her beautiful eyes almost filled with tears. And every one of her words brought with it the complex generosities of her soul – as a single breeze wafts the many scattered fragrances of a garden.

Carlos was delighted when Maria asked his co-operation for her works of charity, begging him to go and see the sister of her ironing-woman who had rheumatism, and the consumptive son of Senhora Augusta, the old lady he had met on the landing. Carlos carried out these requests as fervently as if he were performing a religious duty. And in her acts of mercy he saw a resemblance with his grandfather. As with Afonso, any suffering of animals caused her consternation. One day he met her coming from the Praça de Figueira, indignant almost to the extent of desiring revenge, through having seen in the poultry stalls fowls and rabbits cooped up in baskets, suffering the torture of immobility and hunger for days on end. Carlos conveyed such charming wrath to Ramalhete, and passionately chided the Marquis, who was a member of the Society for the Protection of Animals. The Marquis, just as indignant, swore justice, spoke of imprisonment, of exile on the coast of Africa . . . And Carlos, deeply moved, sat thinking what a far-reaching influence a true heart can have, even when it is unattached to anything.

One afternoon they spoke of Damaso. She found him unbearable, with his petulant tone, his bulging eyes, his senseless questions: Do you find Nice elegant, senhora? Do you prefer the Chapel of St John the Baptist to Notre Dame, senhora?

'And he will insist on speaking about people I don't know! The Countess de Gouvarinho and the Countess de Gouvarinho's tea-parties, and the particular affection that the Countess de Gouvarinho has for him. And this goes on for hours! At times I fear I'll fall asleep.'

Carlos went scarlet. Why had she to bring up between them the name of the Countess, of all people? He grew more composed when he heard her simple candid laughter. She could certainly have no idea who the Countess was. But in order to thrust away immediately this name which had sprung up between them, he began to talk of M. Guimarães, Damaso's famous uncle, the friend of Gambetta, the man with such influence in the Republic . . .

'Damaso told me you know him well . . .'

She raised her eyes and coloured slightly.

'M. Guimarães? Yes, I know him quite well. We have not seen very much of each other recently, but he was a great friend of Mama.'

And after a momentary silence and a brief smile, she began to pull the long strands of wool through again.

'Poor Guimarães! Unlucky man! His influence in the Republic goes no farther than translating news articles from Spanish and Italian newspapers for the *Rappel*, and this is his means of livelihood. Whether he is Gambetta's friend or not I couldn't

327

say; Gambetta has such extraordinary friends. But Guimarães, although I admit he is a good honest man, is a grotesque fellow, a sort of Republican Calino. And so very poor! If Damaso, who is so rich, had the least decency or any feeling for him at all, he wouldn't let him live in such a wretched state.'

'So all this talk of Damaso's about his uncle's carriages and his uncle's luxurious living . . . ?'

She shrugged her shoulders silently; and Carlos felt an unbearable loathing for Damaso.

Gradually an intimacy was creeping into their conversations. She wanted to know how old Carlos was; he spoke to her of his grandfather. And during these delightful hours, while she sat silently piercing the canvas, he told her of his past life, his plans concerning his career, his friends, his travels . . . She was acquainted now with the beauties of Santa Olávia, the Reverend Bonifácio, the eccentricities of Ega. One day she asked Carlos to explain to her in full the idea of his book, *Medicine, Ancient and Modern*. She approved whole-heartedly of his idea to paint the portraits of the great doctors, benefactors to humanity. Why should only warriors and the strong be glorified? Saving the life of a child seemed to her a far more worthy and beautiful thing than the battle of Austerlitz. And these words, which she uttered with such simplicity, without even raising her eyes from her embroidery, pierced Carlos's heart and remained there a long time, throbbing and shining.

And so he found he had made a full confession of his own life, and yet knew nothing of her past, not even where she had been born, nor the street she had lived in in Paris. He never heard her mention her husband's name, nor speak of a friend or a joyous event in her household. In France, where she lived, she seemed not to have either interests or home – she was, indeed, like the goddess of his imagination, without previous contacts with Earth, descended from a golden cloud, to encounter there, in that furnished apartment on Rua de S. Francisco, her first experience of human emotions.

In the very first week of his visits, they had spoken of affection. She frankly believed that there could exist between man and woman a pure immaterial friendship, born of the friendly harmony of two discriminating spirits. Carlos declared that he too had faith in the possibility of such beautiful unions, which were wholly to be admired, were wholly right – as long as there was added a touch, be it ever so light, of tenderness. This would enrich them with a fragrance to increase their charm yet not diminish their sincerity . . . And through these somewhat diffuse words, murmured between stitches of embroidery and with slow smiles, it had been subtly established that between them there should exist such a feeling as this – chaste and legitimate, smooth and painless.

What did Carlos care? As long as he could spend that hour in the cretonne-covered easy-chair, watching her embroidering and chatting of things which were interesting, or which were made interesting by the grace of her person; as long as he could see her face, slightly coloured, bowed with the grave beauty of a caress over the flowers he brought her; as long as he could feel his soul comforted by the certainty that her thoughts followed him sympathetically throughout the day, from the very moment he left that adored room of red rep – his heart was completely and splendidly satisfied.

He never really considered that that ideal friendship, of such chaste intentions, was the surest way to lead her, sweetly deceived, to ardent arms. In the dazzling wonder which overcame him, as he saw himself suddenly admitted to an intimacy which he had considered impenetrable, his desires fled: at times, far from her, they went so far as to dare to hope for a kiss, or a fleeting caress with the tips of his fingers; but no sooner had he crossed her threshold and received the calm regard of her dark eyes, than he fell once more into innocent devotion, and would have considered it a bestial affront to touch even the folds of her dress.

This was undoubtedly the most pleasantly exciting period of his whole life. He felt the creation within himself of a thousand fine things all keenly fresh and novel. He had never imagined it could be so pleasant to contemplate the heavens on a clear starry night, or walk through the garden in the morning to select an opening rose. He bore a constant smile in his soul, a smile repeated on his lips. The Marquis noticed the adoring, benedictory air . . .

At times he wondered, as he paced his room, where this great love would lead him. He did not know. Before him stretched the three months she would be in Lisbon, when no one but he would be in Lisbon, when no one but he would occupy the old chair beside her embroidery. Her husband was far away, separated by leagues of uncertain sea. And then he was rich, and the world was large . . .

He retained his fine ideas of work, and desired that his day should be made up of only noble hours – that those that did not belong to the pure bliss of love should belong to the healthy pleasures of study. He would go to his laboratory and add a few lines to his manuscript. But before his visit to Rua de S. Francisco he was unable to quiet his restless, hopeful spirit, and after returning from there, he spent the day going over what she had said, and what he had answered, her gestures, the charm of her smiles . . . So he would smoke and read poetry.

Every night in Afonso's study there would be whist. The Marquis would be battling with Taveira at dominoes – both utterly lost in this vice, descending in their rancour to insults. After the races Steinbroken's secretary began to frequent Ramalhete, but he was a useless creature, he could not even sing Finnish ballads as his superior could. Sunk in the depths of an armchair, wearing evening dress and monocle in eye, he would swing his leg and silently stroke his long sad moustache.

The friend Carlos liked to see come in was Cruges, who came from Rua de S. Francisco and brought something of the air Maria Eduarda breathed. The Maestro knew Carlos went there every morning to see the 'English Miss', and often, quite innocently, unaware of the heartfelt interest with which Carlos listened to him, brought him the latest news of his neighbour.

'I left our neighbour playing Mendelssohn. She has a certain skill and expression, has our neighbour. She's got what it needs . . . And she certainly understands Chopin.'

If he did not put in an appearance at Ramalhete, Carlos would call for him at his house: they would go to the Grémio, smoke a cigar in the big isolated room, and talk of the neighbour. Cruges found her the very epitome of the *grande dame*.

They generally met the Count de Gouvarinho who had come to see (as he put it with a flash of irony) what was happening 'in Senhor Gambetta's territory'. He seemed younger lately, more spritely in his movement, with the light of hope shining in his glasses, and on the lofty forehead. Carlos asked after the Countess. She was up in Oporto, performing her filial duties.

'And your father-in-law?'

The Count lowered his radiant face a moment, to murmur gravely and resignedly: 'Bad.'

One afternoon while Carlos was talking to Maria Eduarda, and fondling Niniche who had come to sit on his knees, Romão drew the curtain discreetly aside, and in a low embarrassed voice, with an air almost of complicity: 'It's Senhor Damaso!'

She looked up at Romão surprised, almost scandalized at such behaviour.

'Well, show him in then!'

And Damaso, chubby and beaming, bounded into the room, covered in mourning and with a flower in his buttonhole. He entered with a familiar air, hat in hand and dangling on a string a large parcel done up in grey paper. But when he saw Carlos there, looking quite at home with the little dog on his lap, he stopped short, eyes bulging foolishly. Eventually he managed to free his hands of the cumber, went over to Maria Eduarda and greeted her almost off-handedly – to turn immediately to Carlos with arms open wide, and all his astonishment overflowed as he shouted:

'Fancy seeing you here, man! This *is* a surprise! I'd never have believed such a thing! You're the *last* person . . .'

Maria Eduarda, somewhat disturbed at such an outcry, hastily indicated a seat, and interrupting her embroidery for a moment asked if he had had a good journey.

'Excellent, senhora. I'm a little tired of course, I have come straight from Penafiel. As you can see,' pointing to his mourning, 'I have been through most distressing times.'

Maria Eduarda murmured a cool, vague word of sympathy. Damaso lowered his eyes to the carpet. He had come back from the country full of health and colour, and as he had shaved off the beard he had been growing for months in imitation of Carlos, he seemed chubbier and more well-fed than ever. His fat thighs filled his black cashmere trousers to bursting point.

'And will you be with us for long now?' asked Maria Eduarda.

He drew his chair a little closer to hers, and smiled once more.

'No one could drag me out of Lisbon now, senhora! Why, anyone could die . . . I mean, I'd be really rattled if someone close died, believe me. But what I meant is that it won't be easy to drag me away from here!'

Carlos continued calmly stroking Niniche's soft coat. There

was a short silence. Maria Eduarda picked up her embroidery again. And Damaso, after smiling and coughing and smoothing his moustache, stretched out his hand to pat the little dog seated on Carlos's knees. But Niniche, who for some moments had been watching him with a suspicious eye, leapt up and began to bark furiously.

'*C'est moi, ami . . . Alors*, Niniche . . .'

Maria Eduarda had to rebuke Niniche severely, for she continued to growl and keep an eye on the hated Damaso even curled up once more in Carlos's lap.

'You've forgotten me,' he said embarrassedly, 'how strange . . .'

'She knows you perfectly well,' remarked Maria Eduarda very seriously. 'But I don't know what you did to her, that she hates you so. There's always this disgraceful scene.'

Damaso stammered, his face scarlet: 'Oh, really, senhora! What did I do to her? Just loved her, caressed her . . .'

Then, unable to contain himself any longer, he spoke ironically, bitterly, of Niniche's new friendships. There she lay, in the arms of another, while he, the old and trusted friend, was cast aside.

Carlos laughed.

'Oh, Damaso, don't accuse her of ingratitude now, if Senhora Dona Maria Eduarda says she has always detested you.'

'Always!' exclaimed Maria.

Damaso also smiled, but he was livid. Then, taking out his black-bordered handkerchief and wiping his lips and his sweating forehead, he reminded Maria Eduarda that she had disappointed him on the day of the races. He had waited for her all afternoon.

'It was the day before departure,' she said.

'Oh yes, of course, your husband . . . And how is Senhor Castro Gomes? Have you had news from him?'

'No,' she answered, with her eyes on her work.

Damaso fulfilled other obligations. He asked after Mlle Rosa. And then after Cricri. One mustn't forget Cricri.

'Well, it was your loss,' he continued, suddenly loquacious, 'for the races were stupendous. We haven't met since the races, have we, Carlos? Oh yes, at the station. Well, isn't it right what I say? Weren't they *chic*? You know, senhora, there is one thing you can be certain of, and that is that there is no prettier racecourse anywhere. A view right out to the mouth of the river, a delicious view. You can even see the boats coming in. Isn't that so, Carlos?'

Yes,' answered Carlos with a smile. 'It's not properly a race-course. And it's true that the horses aren't properly speaking racehorses either. And then again there aren't jockeys. And no betting . . . But it's true that there's no public either . . .'

Maria Eduarda laughed gaily.

'What is there then?'

'You can see the ships coming in, senhora . . .'

Damaso protested, his ears bright pink. No, that was too bad. No, senhor, no, senhor! They were very good races. Just like the ones abroad, the same rules and everything.

'Why,' he added, very serious, 'they even speak English at the weighing-in!'

He repeated once more that the races were *chic,* and then, finding nothing further to say about them, spoke about Penafiel, where it had rained so much that he had been obliged to stay stupidly indoors and read.

'A real nuisance! If there'd been any women there to have a bit of a chat with . . . But not likely! Hideous creatures! And I'm not one to put up with washerwomen and barefoot wenches. There are men who like that type. But not me, that's one thing you can be sure of.'

Carlos blushed, but Maria Eduarda appeared not to have heard, as she sat attentively counting the stitches of her embroidery.

Suddenly Damaso remembered that he had brought a little present for Senhora Dona Maria Eduarda. But she mustn't think it was anything very special . . . It was really more for Mlle Rosa.

'Still, let's dispense with the mystery. D'you know what it is? It's wrapped up here in this grey paper. Six little barrels of egg sweet from Aveiro. It's a confectionery famous even abroad. And only the type made in Aveiro is really *chic.* You should ask Carlos, senhora. Isn't that so, Carlos? Isn't it a delicacy known even abroad?'

'Most certainly,' murmured Carlos, 'most certainly.'

He put Niniche down and got up to retrieve his hat.

'Already?' asked Maria Eduarda, with a smile for him alone. 'Until tomorrow then.'

333

And she turned to Damaso, expecting to see him get up too. But he remained settled in his chair, apparently intending to stay longer, swinging a leg familiarly. Carlos offered him the tips of his fingers.

'*Au revoir,*' said the other. 'Regards to Ramalhete. I'll be turning up there soon!'

Carlos went down the steps, furious.

The imbecile was staying, imposing his presence in such unmannerly fashion, so obtuse that he could not see the utter tedium he induced, her icy tolerance! And what was he staying for? What other crude banalities was he going to bring forth, in slang, with his legs crossed? And suddenly he remembered what Damaso had said to him the evening of Ega's dinner, at the door of the Hotel Central, with respect to Maria Eduarda, and his method with women, which was 'grab them when you can'! Suppose that idiot, a beast of a fellow hot with desire, suddenly attempted to insult her? The idea was foolish perhaps, but it held him there a moment on the landing, listening for sounds from above, with ferocious ideas of waiting there for Damaso, and forbidding him ever to tread those stairs again. And at the least encouragement, to smash his brains out, there on the stone stairs.

But he heard the door open upstairs and hurried out, ashamed to be caught there listening. Damaso's coupé was waiting in the street. Carlos felt an irresistible curiosity about how long Damaso would stay with Maria Eduarda. He walked quickly to the Grémio, and had barely opened its glass door when he saw Damaso come out of the doorway, leap into his coupé and slam the door. He had an air of having been ejected and Carlos suddenly felt sorry for the grotesque creature.

After supper that night, when Carlos sat ensconced in an easy-chair alone in his room, smoking and reading a letter received from Ega that morning, Damaso suddenly appeared. And without waiting even to put down his hat, he exclaimed in the same amazed tone of the morning: 'Tell me what happened! How the devil did I come to find you there with the Brazilian today? How did you get to meet her? What happened?'

His head still resting on the back of the chair and hands crossed over Ega's letter on his knees, Carlos, good-humoured now, said in a gently reproving and paternal tone: 'So you go and lay before a lady your lubricious opinions on the washer-women of Penafiel!'

'That's got nothing to do with it. I know perfectly well what I'm about!' cried Damaso, scarlet-faced. 'Come on, I want to know. What the deuce! I reckon I have a right to know. How did you get to know her?'

Carlos, quite unperturbed, closed his eyes and made as if to remember, and then began in a slow, solemn, recitative tone:

'It was a mild spring evening, as the sun was sinking behind clouds of gold, when a messenger arrived to grasp, exhausted, the bell-rope of Ramalhete. He bore in his hand a letter, secured with heraldic seal, and the expression on his face – '

Damaso, annoyed by this time, flung his hat down on the table.

'I should have thought it would have been more decent to drop all the mystery.'

'Mystery? You're obtuse today Damasco. You go into a house where there's a person who's been gravely ill for a month, and you're surprised, wonder-struck, to find the doctor there! Who did you expect to see there? A photographer?'

'Who's ill then?'

Carlos explained in a few words about the English girl's bronchitis while Damaso, sitting on the edge of the sofa, nibbling on an unlighted cigar, looked on suspiciously.

'And how did she know where you lived?'

'The same way as you know where the king lives, where the Customs House is, on what side shines the evening star, where lie the fields that once were Troy . . . This sort of thing is learnt in elementary school.'

Poor Damaso strode uncomfortably across the room.

'She's got Romão with her now, who used to be my servant,' he murmured after a short silence. 'It was I who recommended him. She pays a lot of attention to what I say.'

'Yes, she has him there for a few days, while Domingos is visiting his family. But she is going to dismiss him, for he's a fool, and you've taught him bad ways.'

Damaso flung himself down on to the sofa then and confessed that when he had entered the room and seen Carlos there, with the little dog curled up on his lap, he had been curious. But now he could see that it was through illness, well, that explained everything. But at first it seemed as if something funny was going on. When he was left alone with her, he had considered putting a question or two, but then he thought perhaps it was not delicate, and anyway she was in a bad mood.

He went on, lighting his cigar: 'But she improved as soon as you left; she seemed more at ease. We laughed a lot together. I stayed until quite late, some two hours more; it was almost five when I left. Another thing: has she ever spoken about me?'

'No. She is a person of excellent taste, and knowing that we are acquainted she would not have dared speak ill of you.'

Damaso looked at him, horrified.

'I like that! She could have spoken well of me!'

'No, she is a person of good sense, too, and would not have done that either.'

And jumping up, Carlos clasped Damaso round the waist, patting him and asking after his dear uncle's will, and on what love affairs, and travels, and luxurious horses he was going to spend his millions.

Damaso remained cold and sulky in the face of such endearments, and looked at him with suspicion.

'You know, I think you're something of a scoundrel . . . No one is to be trusted!'

'Everything on this earth, my dear Damaso, is but appearance and deceit!'

They made their way into the billiards-room to have a 'reconciliatory game'. And gradually, under the influence which Ramalhete always had upon him, Damaso grew calmer, already his old smiling self again, and enjoying once more his close friendship with Carlos amidst that solemn luxury, addressing him again as 'dear boy'. He asked after Senhor Afonso de Maia. He wanted to know if the handsome Marquis had appeared there of late. And Ega, how was the famous Ega?

'I have just received a letter from him,' said Carlos. 'He is coming back; we might have him with us by Saturday.'

Damaso listened in astonishment.

'Good heavens, man, that's curious! And I met the Cohens today! They arrived two days ago from Southampton . . . Is it my turn?'

He played, and missed a cannon.

'Well, that's how it is. I met them today, and spoke with them for a moment. Raquel looks better, a bit plumper. And she wore an English outfit with white bits on it, and pink bits. Really *chic*, she looked just like a little strawberry! And so Ega's coming back is he? Well, well, dear boy, that'll be a bit more scandal!'

2

ON SATURDAY WHEN Carlos returned to Ramalhete from Rua de
S. Francisco, he found Ega installed in his room. He was dressed
in a suit of light-coloured cheviot and wore his hair long.

'Now don't go round telling everybody,' he cried; 'I'm in Lisbon incognito.'

And after clasping his friend in greeting, he confessed he was
in Lisbon for only a couple of days for some good food and
good conversation. And he was counting on Carlos to furnish
him with these pleasures, right there in Ramalhete.

'Have you a room for me? I'm at the Hotel Espanhol at the
moment, but I haven't even opened a case yet. A tiny room will
be enough, with a deal table – big enough to write a masterpiece
on.'

Of course! There was the room above, where he had stayed
after leaving Villa Balzac. And it was more luxurious now, for it
had acquired a beautiful Renaissance bed and a copy of Velasquez's 'Los Borrachos'.

'An excellent den to create art in! Velasquez is one of the
patron saints of naturalism. By the way, do you know who I came
back with? The Countess de Gouvarinho. Old man Thompson
was at death's door, got better, and the Count went to fetch
her. I thought she looked thin, but no less vivacious. And she
talked about you constantly.'

'Ah,' murmured Carlos.

Ega, monocle in eye and hands in pockets, looked contemplatively at Carlos.

'It's true, you know. She spoke of you constantly, irresistibly,
immoderately! You haven't told me about this. You followed my
advice, eh? Very nice body, I'll bet. And what's she like in bed?'

Carlos flushed, called him coarse, and swore his relations with
the Countess had never been more than superficial. He'd been there
occasionally to drink a cup of tea with her; and at the hour when
everyone promenaded in the Chiado he had, with the rest of
Lisbon, chatted a while with the Count on the corner of
Loreto Square about public affairs. Nothing more.

'You're lying to me, you rake!' said Ega. 'But it doesn't matter. Nothing will escape my Balzacian eye on Monday. We're having dinner there, you know.'

'We . . . ? Who's "we"?'

'We. I and you, you and I. The Countess invited me in the train. And the Count, characteristically for a member of that species, added straightway that we must have "our Maia" there too! *His* Maia, *her* Maia . . . A most holy alliance! A most convenient state of affairs!'

Carlos looked at him severely.

'You have come back from Celorico obscene, Ega.'

'It's what one learns in the bosom of our holy mother Church.'

But Carlos had a piece of news which would shatter him too. Ega, however, already knew. It was the Cohens' arrival, wasn't it? He had read about it that morning, in the 'high life' section of the *Gazeta Ilustrada*. There it was stated respectfully that their Excellencies had returned from their trip abroad.

'And what impression did it make on you?' asked Carlos laughing.

His friend shrugged his shoulders brusquely.

'One more – cuckold in the city.'

And as Carlos accused him once more of bringing back filthy language from Celorico, Ega, slightly flushed, perhaps sorry for his words, launched into critical considerations, calling for the social necessity of giving things their proper name. What was the use of the great naturalist movement of the century? If vice continued, it was because an indulgent and romantic society gave it names which beautified it, idealized it, What scruples could a woman have about cuddling and kissing an outsider between conjugal sheets, if all the world sentimentally called this a romance, and the poets sang its praise in gilded strophes?

'By the way, how's your comedy, *The Swamp*, going?' asked Carlos, who had disappeared for a moment into the bathroom.

'I abandoned it,' said Ega. 'It was too ferocious. Besides, it plunged me again into the rottenness of Lisbon, immersed me in human excrement once more. It distressed me . . .'

He stopped before the long mirror, gave a glance of discontent at the light jacket and the cheap patent-leather boots.

'I need a completely new outfit, Carlinhos. Poole's, naturally, sent you a new summer suit; I must examine the latest lines in high fashion. There's no doubt about it – I've the deuce of a shabby style at the moment!'

He passed a brush over his moustache and continued in the direction of the bathroom: 'Well, dear boy, I'm going to fling myself into the *Memoirs* again. You'll see realms of sublime art created here in this room you are putting at my disposal, in front of Velasquez. Incidentally, I must go and greet old Afonso, seeing that he will be giving me bed and board.'

They found Afonso de Maia in his study, in his old arm-chair, with an old collection of *Ilustração francesa* open on his knees, showing the pictures to a pretty little boy, very dark, with lively eyes and curly hair. The old man was happy to learn that Ega was coming to enliven Ramalhete for a while with his flights of fantasy.

'I've no fantasy left, Senhor Afonso de Maia.'

'Then enlighten the house with your clear reasoning,' answered the old man, smiling. 'We're in need of both things here, John.'

Then he introduced the little gentleman at his side, Sr Manuelinho, a charming young neighbour of his, son of Vicente the builder. Manuelinho came along sometimes to relieve Afonso's solitude, and the two of them looked at picture-books and had philosophical talks. He was, at that moment, unable to explain how it was that General Canrobert (whose elegant posture on a rearing horse they had been admiring), if he had ordered so many people to be killed in battle, had not been sent to prison . . .

'It's obvious,' exclaimed the quick little boy promptly, with his hands folded behind him: 'If he ordered people to be killed, he ought to have been locked up in prison!'

'Hmmm, Ega, my friend,' said Afonso, laughing, 'what am I to answer to such beautiful logic? Look, my child, now that we have these two gentlemen here who are graduates of Coimbra, I'm going to study the case carefully. You go and look at the pictures over there on the table . . . Then it will nearly be time for you to be off inside to Joana, to have your tea.'

Carlos helped the little boy to sit up at the table with the great illustrated volume, and thought how much his grandfather, with that affection of his for children, would love to know Rosa!

Afonso, in the meantime, was also asking Ega about his comedy.

What! Abandoned already? When was our good John going to stop writing incomplete scraps of masterpieces? Ega complained about the country, about its indifference to art. What original spirit would not lose heart, seeing all around it the dense bourgeois mass, lethargic and crassly ignorant, disdaining intelligence, incapable of interest in any noble idea, in any well-turned phrase?

'It's not worth it, Senhor Afonso da Maia. In this country, in the midst of this prodigious national imbecility, the man of good sense and taste should restrict himself to growing his vegetables with all care and attention. Look at Herculano . . .'*

'Well, then,' returned the old man, 'at least grow your vegetables. That's a service you'd be doing to public nourishment. But you don't even do that!'

Carlos, very serious, agreed with Ega.

'The only thing to do in Portugal,' he said, 'is grow vegetables until there is a revolution which will bring to the surface some of the strong, living, original elements which are imprisoned in its depths. And then if we find that there is in fact nothing locked up in there, let us resign voluntarily from our position as an independent country, for which we have no suitable elements, and become a fertile, stupid Spanish province – and grow more vegetables!'

The old man listened with a melancholy air to his grandson's words, in which he sensed a disintegration of will, a glorifying of his inertia. He ended by saying: 'Well, you two make the revolution then. But for God's sake, do something!'

'Carlos's work is no mean accomplishment,' laughed Ega. 'He parades his person, his fashionable dress and his phaeton, and so educates public taste!'

The chiming of the Louis XV clock interrupted them, reminding Ega that he still had his case to fetch from the Hotel Espanhol before dining. In the corridor he confessed to Carlos that before going to the Espanhol, he was going to rush over to Fillon, the photographer, to see if he could get a becoming photo.

'A photo?'

'A surprise which must be off within three days to reach Celorico for the birthday of a little creature who sweetened my exile.'

* Alexandre Herculano: famous historian of the nineteenth century who retired to the country, tired of city life.

341

'Oh, Ega!'

'It's horrid, I know, but what's to be done? She's the daughter of Father Correia, and a publicly recognized daughter, in addition to which she is married to a rich landowner of the district, a most odious reactionary. So you see, this double blow struck at Religion and Property . . .'

'Ah, well, in that case . . .'

'No man, my friend, should shirk the duties democracy imposes upon him!'

It was drizzling the following Monday when Carlos and Ega got into the closed coupé to go to dinner at the Gouvarinhos'. Carlos had seen the Countess only once since her return, at her house, and it had been an unpleasant half-hour, with both ill at ease; there had been a cold kiss or two and endless recriminations. She had complained of his letters, which had been infrequent and dry. They were unable to come to any agreement regarding plans for the summer – the Countess had to go to Cintra where a house had already been rented, while Carlos spoke of his duty to accompany his grandfather to Santa Olávia. The Countess found Carlos absent-minded; he found her demanding. Then she sat on his knees for a moment – and that delicate light body weighed on Carlos like a cumbersome lump of bronze.

Finally the Countess had wrenched from him a promise to meet her, that very Monday morning, in the house of her aunt who was in Santarém, for she always had the perverse desire to clasp him in her naked arms on days when she was later to receive him formally in her drawing-room. But Carlos had failed to appear – and now, rolling along the road towards her house, he felt an anticipatory impatience at the complaints he would have to listen to in the window-recesses, and the empty lies with which he would be obliged to respond.

Suddenly Ega, who had been silently smoking, buttoned up in his summer jacket, slapped Carlos's knee, and half-joking, half-serious, inquired: 'Tell me something, if it is not an inviolable secret. Who is this Brazilian lady you are spending every morning with?'

Carlos looked at Ega for a moment in amazement.

'Where did you hear this?'

'Damaso told me. Or, rather, it was Damaso who snarled the news at me, for it was between clenched teeth, pounding a poor sofa in the Grémio, with his face an apoplectic hue, that he told me everything.'

'And what's everything?'

'Everything. That he had introduced you to a Brazilian woman he was angling for, and you, taking advantage of his absence, had wheedled your way in there, and wouldn't budge now.'

'It's a lot of lies!' cried Carlos, out of patience.

Ega replied, still smiling, 'Then "what is truth", as old Pilate asked the so-called Jesus Christ?'

'The truth is that there is a lady whom Damaso supposes to be passionately fond of him, as he always supposes, and who, when her English governess caught bronchitis, sent for me to look after her. She is still not better and I go to see her every day. Madame Gomes, which is the lady's name, and who, incidentally, is not at all Brazilian, cannot tolerate Damaso, as no one can, and has shut her doors to him. This is the truth, but perhaps I'll pull Damaso's ears for him.'

Ega murmured simply, 'So that's how history's written . . . A lot of good believing historians then!'

They continued in silence to the Gouvarinhos' house, Carlos fuming with anger towards Damaso. So the fine delicate veil with which he had been sheltering his love had been torn aside by that imbecile! Now Maria Eduarda's name would be spoken in the Grémio; what Damaso had said to Ega he would repeat to others, in the Casa Havanesa, in the Silva Restaurant, probably even in brothels. The supreme interest of his life would thus be constantly disturbed henceforth, ruined by the vile prating of Damaso!

'It looks as if we have other company,' said Ega, as they entered the hall and saw a grey overcoat and ladies' cloaks lying over a couch.

The Countess was waiting for them in the little room at the end, called the 'room of the bust'. She was dressed in black with a black velvet ribbon around her neck, on to which were pinned three diamond stars. A magnificent basket of flowers almost filled the table, where a few English novels were scattered and a *Revista dos dois Mundos* was on show with an ivory knife between its pages. As well as the good Dona Maria da Cunha and the Baroness de Alvim, there was another lady whom neither Carlos nor Ega knew, fat and dressed in scarlet; and standing talking in a low voice to the Count, hands behind his back, was a tall, grave, wan-looking man with a very thin beard and wearing the Order of Conceição.

The Countess, colouring slightly, held out to Carlos a limp, indifferent hand: all her smiles were for Ega. And the Count immediately took possession of dear Maia, to introduce his friend Senhor Sousa Neto. Sr Sousa Neto had already had the pleasure of hearing of Carlos da Maia as a distinguished doctor, an honour to the University . . . That was the great advantage of Lisbon, put in the Count, everyone had heard of everyone else, so one could appreciate characters more easily. In Paris now, this was impossible: there was so much immorality in that city, such slackness . . .

'One never knows who one is inviting home!'

Ega, sunk in the sofa, between the Countess and Dona Maria, stretched his legs to display his star-embroidered socks, and was making the ladies laugh by recounting the story of his exile in Celorico, where he had whiled away the time writing sermons for the curate: the curate preached them, but the sermons, wrapped in mystical language, were really revolutionary declarations which the holy curate launched with fervour, smiling down from the pulpit . . . The lady in red, sitting opposite with her hands folded in her lap, listened to Ega aghast.

'I thought you had already left for Cintra,' said Carlos, coming to sit beside the Baroness. 'You are always the first.'

'How can you imagine me going to Cintra in this weather?'

'No, you're right. It's dreadful.'

'What is there in the way of news?' she asked, slowly opening her great black fan.

'I don't think there has been any news in Lisbon, senhora, since the death of Senhor Don João VI in 1826.'

'Well, there is your friend Ega now, for instance.'

'That's true. There is Ega. How do you find him, Baroness?'

She did not bother to lower her voice to reply: 'As I have always found him an extremely presumptuous fellow, and have never liked him, I cannot really give an opinion.'

'Oh, Baroness, how lacking in charity you are!'

The footman announced dinner. The Countess took Carlos's

arm, and as they crossed the main drawing-room she was able to say bitterly, under cover of the mutter of voices and the soft rustle of silk trains: 'I waited half an hour, but I realized straightway that you must be amusing yourself with the Brazilian.'

In the dining-room, a somewhat sombre room, with wine-coloured paper and darkened still further by two antique panels portraying a gloomy landscape, the oval table, surrounded by carved oak chairs, shone bright and white between two gilt candlesticks. Carlos sat at the Countess's right, with Dona Maria da Cunha on his other side, looking rather old this evening, smiling somewhat wearily.

'What have you been doing all the time that no one has set eyes upon you?' she asked, unfolding her napkin.

'Wandering around, senhora . . .'

Opposite Carlos, Sr Sousa Neto, who wore three enormous coral studs in his shirt-front, was observing, while he stirred his soup, that the Countess must have noticed great changes in the streets and buildings during her stay in Oporto. The Countess, unfortunately, had scarcely left the house during the whole time she was in the city, but the Count, he indeed had admired the signs of progress there. And he began enumerating them: he praised the view from the Crystal Palace; he spoke of the ancient antagonism that existed between Lisbon and Oporto – more than once he had compared it with the rivalry between Austria and Hungary. And throughout these grave pronouncements, cast down as it were from above, with weight and the voice of superiority, the Baroness and the lady in scarlet, who sat on either side of him, spoke of the Salesian Convent.

Carlos, eating his soup in silence, was considering the words of the Countess. She too, then, knew of his friendship with 'the Brazilian'. It was evident that Damaso's base defamatory chatter had reached her. And by the time the servant offered him Sauterne, he had decided to give Damaso a thrashing.

Suddenly he heard his name mentioned. At the end of the table, a lazy, sing-song voice was saying: 'Senhor Maia is the one who should know. Senhor Maia has been there.'

Carlos put his glass down briskly. It was the lady in scarlet who was addressing him, smiling and showing some very pretty teeth under the moustache on the pale middle-aged face. No

345

one had introduced her, and he did not know who she was. He smiled too, and asked:

'Where, senhora?'

'In Russia.'

'In Russia? I'm afraid not. I have never been in Russia.'

She looked a little disappointed.

'Oh, they told me you had. I can't remember who it was, but it was someone who knew . . .'

The Count, at the end of the table, explained to her kindly that friend Maia had only been as far as Holland.

'A very prosperous country, Holland! Inferior in no way to our own. I personally knew a Dutchman who was an excessively learned man.'

The Countess had lowered her eyes, idly crumbling a piece of bread, suddenly more serious, drier, as if the calm voice of Carlos, there at her side, had rekindled her grudges. He, after slowly tasting his Sauterne, turned to her very naturally and smiled.

'You see how things are, Countess! I hadn't the slightest idea of going to Russia. There are innumerable things they say that are not true. And if some ironic allusion is made to them, one understands neither the allusion nor the irony.'

The Countess did not answer immediately, but gave a silent order with her eyes to the footman. Then with a pale smile she answered:

'But there is always some fact at the bottom of what they say, or some half-fact which is true. And that is sufficient. At least it is sufficient as far as I am concerned.'

'Then you are childishly credulous, Countess. I can see that you believe that once upon a time there was a king whose daughter had a star on her head – '

But the Count interrupted. He wanted his friend Maia's opinion. It was about a book by an Englishman, a Major Bratt, who had travelled Africa and then treacherously published unpleasant things about Portugal. The Count saw envy at the root of this – the envy all nations harbour against Portugal, because of the importance of our colonies, and our vast influence in Africa . . .

'It's evident,' said the Count, 'that we have neither the millions nor the fleet that the English have. But we have our glories: Prince Henry was a man of the first order, and the taking of Ormuz a masterpiece. And I, who know something about colonial systems, can assure you that there are no colonies today so potentially rich, so intent on progress or so liberal as ours! Don't you agree, Maia?'

'Yes, perhaps, it's possible . . . There's a great deal of truth in that.'

But Ega, who had been somewhat silent, fixing his monocle in his eye from time to time, and smiling towards the Baroness, now gaily declared himself against all the explorations of Africa, against all these long geographic missions. Why not leave the Negro peacefully alone with his idols? What harm did the existence of savages do to the order of things? On the contrary, they gave the Universe a delicious abundance of the picturesque! This mania of the French and bourgeoisie for reducing all nations and races to a uniform type of civilization was making the world abominably monotonous. It wouldn't be long before a tourist, at enormous expense and sacrifice, would make his way to Timbuktu. And for what? Only to find there Negroes in top hats reading the *Journal des Debats*.

The Count gave a superior smile. And good Dona Maria, aroused out of her apathy, fluttered her fan, and turned in delight to Carlos: 'Oh this Ega! This Ega! So witty! So *chic*!'

Then Sousa Neto, gravely putting down his cutlery, solemnly inquired of Ega: 'Are you then in favour of slavery, sir?'

Ega assured Sr Sousa Neto that he was certainly all in favour of slavery. The lack of comforts in life had begun, in his opinion, with the liberation of the negroes. Only he who was wholly feared was wholly obeyed. That was why it was impossible to get one's shoes properly polished nowadays, one's rice properly cooked, one's staircase thoroughly cleaned – because there were no longer black servants whom one could legitimately whip . . . There were only two civilizations where man had managed to live with reasonable comfort, and those were the Roman and the civilization among the New Orleans planters. Why? Because in both the first and the second there had existed absolute punishment!

For a moment Sr Sousa Neto was at an utter loss. Then he dabbed his napkin over his lips, prepared himself and faced Ega: 'Then you, sir, at your age, and with your intelligence, do not believe in progress?'

'Not I, sir!'

The Count gently interrupted with a smile: 'Our Ega here simply wants to make a paradox. And he's right to do so, quite right, for he makes brilliant paradoxes.'

Jambon aux épinards was being served. For a moment they spoke of paradoxes. According to the Count, another person who made really brilliant paradoxes, and ones difficult to maintain, extremely difficult, was Barros, the minister.

'Immensely talented fellow,' murmured Sousa Neto respectfully.

'Yes, and forceful,' said the Count.

But he was not speaking so much now of Barros's talent as a parliamentarian, but rather as a statesman. He spoke of his social accomplishments, his *esprit* . . .

'Why, only this winter we heard a brilliant paradox of his! It was in Senhora Dona Maria da Cunha's house. Don't you remember, Senhora Dona Maria? Oh, this wretched memory of mine! Teresa, can't you remember that paradox of Barros's? Good Lord, now what was it? Well, anyway, it was a paradox most difficult to maintain. This memory of mine! Don't you remember, Teresa?'

The Countess did not remember. And while the Count anxiously sorted through his memories, hand to head, the lady in scarlet returned to the subject of Negroes, and black footmen, and a black cook that an aunt of hers had, Aunt Vilar . . . Then she began to complain bitterly of modern servants: ever since her Joana had died, who had been with her for fifteen years, she had not known what to do, had been quite out of her mind, with one disappointment after another. In six months she had had no less than four new girls. And what slovenly, self-important, immoral hussies they were! A sigh almost escaped from her breast, and disconsolately munching a scrap of bread, she murmured:

'Have you still got Vicenta, Baroness?'

'Why shouldn't I still have Vicenta? Vicenta's part of the household. And it's Senhora Dona Vicenta, if you don't mind.'

The other woman looked at her for a moment, envious of such happiness.

'And is it Vicenta who does your hair?'

Yes, it was Vicenta who did her hair. She was getting old, poor soul, but as stubborn as ever. Now there was the craze for learning French. She already knew the verbs. It was enough to make one die of laughing to hear Vicenta reciting *j'aime, tu aimes* . . .

'The Baroness, I see,' put in Ega, 'has begun with the most necessary verbs.'

Naturally, said the Baroness, that was the most important of all. But it was not going to be a lot of use to Vicenta at her age!

'Ah,' exclaimed the Count, almost dropping his cutlery, 'now I remember.'

He had at last remembered the wonderful paradox Barros had invented. Barros said that dogs, the more you taught them . . . But no, that wasn't it!

'This wretched memory of mine!' he wailed. It was about dogs though. Something really brilliant, philosophical even!

Talking of dogs reminded the Baroness of Tommy, the Countess's greyhound, and she inquired after Tommy. She hadn't seen dear Tommy for ages. The Countess did not wish to talk of Tommy, poor thing! He had some nasty little things growing in his ears – really horrible . . . She had sent him to the Institute, and there he had died.

'This galantine is delicious,' remarked Dona Maria da Cunha, leaning towards Carlos.

'Really delicious.'

The Baroness, on the other side, also declared the galantine was perfection itself. The Countess's eyes gave an order to the footman to serve the galantine a second time, then hastily replied to Sr Sousa Neto who, talking about dogs, was referring now to the Society for the Protection of Animals. Sr Sousa Neto approved of it wholeheartedly, considered it a sign of progress. He even thought the government ought to give it a subsidy.

'For it's my belief that it is prospering. And it deserves to, Countess, believe me, it deserves to. I have studied this question, and of all the societies that have recently been founded here, in imitation of those in existence abroad, like the Geographic Society for example, I consider the Society for the Protection of Animals certainly one of the most useful.'

He turned to Ega.

'Do you belong, sir?'

'To the Society for the Protection of Animals? No, sir, but I belong to the other, the Geographic Society. I'm one of those protected.'

The Baroness gave a gay laugh. But the Count became extremely serious: he belonged to the Geographic Society, and considered it a pillar of the State, believed in its civilizing mission, and loathed such irreverence. But the Countess and Carlos had also laughed, and suddenly the ice which held them there reserved, side by side, feigning solemnity, broke under the warmth of that shared laughter, and the brightness of the exchanged glance. The champagne was served; her face was slightly flushed. Her foot, without her realizing how, brushed against Carlos's; they smiled again; and as the rest of the table was engaged in conversation on the classical concerts that there were going to be at the Price, Carlos took the opportunity of asking her in a low voice, with a note of friendly rebuke:

'What's all this foolishness about the Brazilian? Who told you that?'

She admitted straightway that it had been Damaso. Damaso had come to her with tales of Carlos's enthusiasm for this lady, of the whole mornings he spent there, every day, at the same hour . . . In short, Damaso had made it clear that there was an affair going on.

Carlos shrugged his shoulders. How could she believe what Damaso said? She ought to know his idle chatter, his stupidity.

'It's perfectly true that I go to the house of this lady – who, incidentally, is no Brazilian, but as much of a Portuguese as I am – but it is because her governess is very ill with bronchitis, and I am the family doctor. It was Damaso himself who took me there in my capacity as doctor.'

A smile spread over the Countess's face, a radiance which seemed to emanate from the sweet relief she felt in her heart.

'But Damaso said she was so pretty!'

Yes, she was very pretty. But so what? A doctor could scarcely demand, through loyalty to his personal attachments and fear of causing them anxiety, a certificate of ugliness before entering a patient's house!

'But what is she doing here?'

'She is waiting for her husband, who is in Brazil on business and will shortly be back. They are very distinguished people and very rich too, I believe. They will be going away soon, and apart from that I know very little about them. My visits have been those of a doctor; I have only spoken to her of Paris and London and her impressions of Portugal.'

The Countess drank in these words with delight, captured by the tenderness in his eyes as he murmured them; and her foot pressed hard against Carlos's in a passionate reconciliation, with all the warmth she would have liked to put into an embrace, if only she could have embraced him at that moment.

The lady in scarlet had in the meantime returned to the subject of Russia. What shocked her was that it was such an expensive country, and there was such a lot of danger because of dynamite, and a delicate constitution must suffer terribly with all that snow in the streets. It was only then that Carlos realized that she was the wife of Sousa Neto, and she was talking about their son, an only child, who had been nominated second secretary for the legation at St Petersburg.

'Do you know him, dear boy?' whispered Dona Maria to Carlos, behind her fan. 'He is the most awfully stupid creature. He can't even speak French. Still, he's no worse than the rest. The number of fools, nincompoops and bores sent to represent us abroad is enough to make you weep. Don't you think so dear boy? Ours is an unfortunate country.'

'Worse than unfortunate, senhora, far worse. It's a country of fops.'

The dessert was over. Dona Maria looked at the Countess, with her weary smile; the lady in scarlet stopped speaking, prepared to move, her chair already drawn back a little from the table; and the ladies arose, just as Ega, still on the subject of Russia, was finishing a story he'd heard from a Pole, which proved the Tsar was a stupid fellow.

'Liberal though, for all that, and quite progressive,' murmured the Count, standing.

The men, alone now, lit their cigars and the footmen served coffee. Then Sousa Neto, cup in hand, came over to Carlos to express once more the pleasure he had had in making his acquaintance.

'I also had the pleasure of knowing your father, sir, long ago Pedro, Senhor Pedro da Maia his name was, I believe. I was just beginning my public career then. And how is your grandfather, sir? Is he well?'

'Very well, thank you.'

'Such a fine gentleman. And your father was, well, what we might call a really elegant man about town. I also had the pleasure of knowing your mother.'

He stopped abruptly in embarrassment, lifting his cup to his lips. Then, slowly, he turned to hear better what Ega was discussing with Gouvarinho about women. It was about the wife of the Secretary at the Russian Legation, with whom he had found the Count conversing that morning in Calhariz Square. Ega found her delicious with her vivacious lithe little body, those great green-blue eyes . . . And the Count, who also admired her, praised above all her intelligence and culture. This, in Ega's eyes, detracted from her, for woman's duty was first to be beautiful and second to be stupid. The Count agreed effusively that he disliked women with literary minds; yes, there was no doubt that woman's place was beside the cradle, not in the library.

'I won't say it is disagreeable for a woman to be able to converse on a few light subjects, on a magazine article, or on a . . . For example, when a new book is published . . . I don't say when we are dealing with a Guizot, or a Jules Simon . . . But, for instance, when we are dealing with a Feuillet, or a . . . In short, a lady must be talented. Don't you think so, Neto?'

Neto gravely replied: 'A lady, especially when she is young, should have a few accomplishments.'

Ega protested passionately. A woman with accomplishments – above all, literary accomplishments, able to converse on Sr Thiers, or Sr Zola – is a monster, a freak that ought to be in a circus. Women should have two accomplishments: know how to cook well and love well.

'You are acquainted with the remarks of Proudhon, of course, Sr Sousa Neto?'

'I cannot remember the exact text, but . . .'

'But anyway, you know the substance of Proudhon perfectly?'

The other gentleman, clearly disliking such interrogation, murmured very drily that Proudhon was an author of great renown.

But Ega insisted with treacherous impertinence: 'You must have read, as we have all done, Proudhon's great pages on love?'

Sr Neto, scarlet now, put his cup down on the table. And he

tried to be sarcastic, to crush that stripling who was so literary and audacious.

'I did not realize,' he said with an infinitely superior smile, 'that this great philosopher had written upon such scabrous subjects!'

Ega flung his arms into the air in dismay.

'Oh, Sr Sousa Neto! Do you mean to say that you, the head of a family, find love a scabrous subject?!'

Sr Sousa Neto was thoroughly embarrassed. Very upright, very dignified, speaking from the great height of his very considerable bureaucratic position, he said:

'It is my custom, Sr Ega, never to enter arguments, and to respect the opinions of others, however absurd they seem . . .'

And he practically turned his back on Ega, and addressed Carlos, wanting to know, in a voice still a little strained, whether he intended to stay long in Portugal this time. The two spoke for a while about travelling, as they finished their cigars, and Sr Neto deplored the fact that his numerous duties prevented him from visiting Europe. This had been his ideal as a child, but now, with his many public duties, he found himself tied to his desk. And there he stayed, without even having seen Badajoz . . .

'And which do you prefer, sir, Paris or London?'

Carlos really did not know, could hardly compare them. They were two such different cities, two civilizations so distinct . . .

'In London,' remarked the Counsellor, 'there's coal everywhere . . .'

Yes, agreed Carlos with a smile, there was quite a lot of coal, especially on the fires when it was cold.

Sr Sousa Neto murmured: 'And the cold there must be considerable all the time! Such a northern climate!'

He sat for a moment, sucking his cigar, his eyes closed. Then he came out with the sagacious and profound observation: 'A practical people, an essentially practical people.'

'Yes, they are rather practical,' Carlos answered vaguely, making a move towards the drawing-room where he could hear the lilting laughter of the Baroness.

'And tell me another thing,' continued Sr Sousa Neto, full of interest and intelligent curiosity. 'Do you find there, in England nice literature like ours, serial-writers and first-rate poets?'

353

Carlos dropped his cigar end into the ashtray and replied coolly: 'No, there's none of that.'

'That's what I've always thought,' said Sousa Neto. 'A purely business-minded race.'

They went into the drawing-room. It was Ega who was making the Baroness laugh. He was sitting opposite her, talking about Celorico again, recounting a soirée in Celorico with picturesque details of the authorities, and of a priest who had killed a man and who sang sentimental *fados* at the piano. The lady in red sat on the sofa alongside with her arms dropped in her lap, listening open-mouthed to Ega's eloquence as she might have watched the capers of a clown. Dona Maria was seated at the table turning the pages of an *Ilustracão* with an air of weariness. When she saw Carlos enter and look round for the Countess, she called him over and told him quietly that she had gone inside to look at Charlie, her little boy.

'Ah, yes,' said Carlos, sitting down beside her, 'how is our pretty little Charlie?'

'She says he has a slight cold, is somewhat off-colour today.'

'And you too, Senhora Dona Maria, seem a little off-colour today.'

'It's the weather. I'm at the age when good or bad moods come as a result of the weather. At your age other things are important. Incidentally, to change the subject, has Madame Cohen returned too?'

'She has returned,' said Carlos, 'but not *too*. *Too* implies complicity. And Madame Cohen and Ega have returned at the same time purely by chance. Anyway this is old history, like the loves of Helen and Paris.'

At that moment the Countess re-entered the room looking slightly flushed and with a large black fan open. Without even sitting down, and directing her words to Senhora Sousa Neto, she began complaining immediately that she had not found Charlie looking very well. He was so hot, so restless. She was frightened he was sickening for measles.

Then turning swiftly towards Carlos, she said with a smile: 'I'm ashamed to ask, but if I could trouble Sr Carlos da Maia to come and look at him for a moment. I know it is dreadful, really, to ask you to look at a patient straightway after dinner . . .'

'Oh, Countess!' he exclaimed, already on his feet.

He followed her. In a small room at one side, the Count and Sr Sousa Neto were ensconced in a sofa, smoking and talking. 'I'm taking Sr Carlos da Maia to see our little boy.'

The Count made to get up, not fully comprehending. But she had already gone. Carlos followed her long black silk train in silence through the billiard-room, which stood with the gas lamps alight and empty, under the eyes of four stern and elaborately arranged ladies of the Gouvarinho family. Off this room, behind a heavy green curtain, was a small study, containing an old armchair, some books in a glass-fronted case, and a little bureau illuminated by a table-lamp with a pink lace shade. And there, she abruptly stopped and flung her arms around Carlos's neck, her lips clinging fiercely to his in an ardent lingering kiss which ended in a sob. He felt a shudder run through that beautiful body before it went limp in his arms.

'Tomorrow,' she murmured, scarcely able to get out the words, 'in Aunty's house at eleven.'

'If you wish.'

Released from his arms, the Countess remained for a moment with her hands covering her eyes, waiting for the languor and vertigo which had reduced her face to a waxen pallor to pass. Then, with a weary smile, she apologized: 'How foolish I am . . . Let's go and see Charlie.'

The little boy's room was at the end of the corridor. And there, in a small iron bed, beside the maid's larger one, Charlie lay serenely sleeping, with one small arm hanging over the side, and his pretty fair curls strewn over the pillow like an angel's halo. Carlos briefly felt his pulse, and the Scots maid, who had brought a light from the chest of drawers, smiled happily: 'The child has been so well these last few days . . .'

They returned. In the study before entering the billiard-room, the Countess, with her hand on the curtain, again offered her insatiable lips to Carlos. She reaped a hasty kiss. And as she passed through the antechamber where Sousa Neto and the Count were still immersed in some grave discussion, she said to her husband: 'The child is sleeping. Senhor Carlos da Maia thinks he looks well.'

The Count de Gouvarinho slapped Carlos affectionately on the shoulder. And the Countess stood there for a moment chatting, allowing herself to calm down in that friendly penumbra before having to face the bright lights of the drawing-room. Then, as they were talking of exercise, Carlos invited S. Sousa Neto to join him in a game of billiards, but Sr Nousa Neto had not held a cue since Coimbra, since University. Carlos was about to call Ega when Teles da Gama arrived from the Price. And immediately after him came Count Steinbroken, so the rest of the evening was spent in the *salon*, around the piano. The minister sang Finnish airs and Teles da Gama played *fados*.

Carlos and Ega were the last to make their departure, and that after a brandy and soda which the Countess, like the strong Englishwoman she was, also drank. Outside, buttoning his coat, Carlos was finally able to put the question he had had on his lips all evening:

'Ega, who's that fellow, that Sousa Neto, who wanted to know whether there is literature in England too?'

Ega looked at him in amazement.

'But didn't you guess? Didn't you see right away? Couldn't you realize immediately who in this country would have been capable of asking such a question?'

'I don't know. There are so many people who might.'

And Ega, radiant, replied: 'A high official in an important State department.'

'Which?'

'Which? Which do you expect? Education!'

The following day at five o'clock Carlos ordered the coupé to drive full-speed to Rua de S. Francisco. He had stayed later than he had intended in Aunty's house with the Countess, retained by her interminable kisses, and now he looked at his watch every minute, fearing that Maria Eduarda had gone out on such a fine summer's day, so luminous and warm. As it happened, her hired carriage stood at the door, and Carlos leapt up the stairs, furious with the Countess and particularly with himself who was so weak, so passive, allowing himself to be drawn back like that into those demanding arms, which daily felt heavier to him and which now failed to move him at all.

'Madam has just arrived,' said Domingos, who had arrived back three days ago and had not yet ceased beaming.

Maria Eduarda sat on the sofa, still wearing her hat and pulling off her gloves, and greeted him with a becoming blush, and affectionately rebuked him.

356

'I waited for you for half an hour before going out. Ungrateful creature! I thought you had deserted us!'

'Why? Is Miss Sarah worse?'

She looked at him in scandalized amusement. Miss Sarah indeed! Miss Sarah was recovering perfectly well. But it was not the visits of the doctor they looked forward to now, but the friend, and they had missed him.

Carlos could find no answer in his confusion, and turned to Rosa who was looking at a new picture-book, and all the tenderness and infinite gratitude he felt, but did not dare to show to the mother, he revealed in the caress he gave the child.

'Mama has just bought me these stories,' explained Rosa, quite serious and still attached to her book. 'I'll tell you them later . . . They're animal stories.'

Maria Eduarda got up, slowly untying the ribbons of her hat.

'Will you have a cup of tea with us, Senhor Carlos da Maia? I'm dying for a cup of tea. What a lovely day, isn't it? Rosa, you stay here and tell Senhor Carlos da Maia about our drive while I go and take my hat off.'

Carlos, alone with Rosa, sat down beside her, drawing her attention away from the book, and taking her two hands.

'We went to the Estrela,' said the child. 'But Mama wouldn't stay long because she thought you might come!'

Carlos kissed her hands, one after the other.

'And what did you do when you got there?' he asked, with a little sigh of pure happiness.

'I ran about, and there were some little baby ducks.'

'Were they pretty?'

The little girl shrugged her shoulders: 'Mucky things.'

Mucky things! Whoever had taught her such an ugly expression?

Rosa laughed. Domingos had. And Domingos said other funny things like that. He said Melanie was a tart . . . Domingos was very funny.

Carlos explained to her that a pretty child like her, with such pretty clothes, too, should not use words like that. Only ragged, tattered people spoke like that.

'But Domingos isn't ragged and tattered,' answered Rosa solemnly.

Then suddenly she remembered something else, and clapped

357

her hands and jumped between Carlos's knees, her eyes sparkling.

'And he brought me some crickets from the market! Domingos brought me some crickets! If only you knew how frightened Niniche is of crickets! It seems incredible, doesn't it? I never saw such a cowardly creature!'

She looked at Carlos for a moment, and then added gravely: 'It's Mama's fault. She spoils her so. It's a shame!'

Maria Eduarda entered at this moment, patting her hair in place, and hearing the end of the conversation, wanted to know who it was that she spoilt. Niniche? Poor Niniche, only that morning she had punished her.

Rosa burst out laughing at this, clapping her hands.

'Do you know how Mama punishes him?' she exclaimed, pulling Carlos's sleeve. 'Do you know? She makes her voice gruff, and says to her in English: "Bad dog! Dread-ful dog!"'

She looked enchanting as she shook her finger threateningly at Niniche and imitated the stern voice of her mother. Poor Niniche, believing she was in fact being scolded, slunk off under the sofa in disgrace. And Rosa had to get down on her knees on the tiger-skin to console her, hugging her and insisting that she was not really a bad dog, a dreadful dog; she was only showing what Mama did.

'Go and give her some water, she must be thirsty,' said Maria Eduarda, moving over to her scarlet armchair. 'And tell Domingos to bring us some tea.'

Rosa and Niniche ran out of the room and Carlos went to occupy the usual rep chair by the window. But for the first time since the beginning of their friendship there was an uneasy silence. Then she began to complain of the heat as she absent-mindedly unrolled her embroidery. Carlos remained silent, as if for him that day there was only one possible pleasure, only one word which could have any meaning; and that word hung on his lips but he dared not utter it, yet almost feared it could be guessed, for his heart was so full.

'It seems this embroidery will never come to an end,' he said at last, impatient to see her serenely busy with her wools.

With the canvas unfolded on her knees, she answered without raising her eyes: 'But why should it come to an end? The pleasure lies in creating the work, doesn't it? A stitch today, another tomorrow – it's like company. Why do you want to arrive at the end straight away?'

A shadow fell over Carlos's face. He sensed a discouraging allusion to his love in these words, uttered in such a light tone over the embroidery – an allusion to the love which was filling his heart just as the wool was covering that canvas, the simultaneous production of the same fair hands. Did she want to keep him there, lingering on like the embroidery, always a little more and always incomplete, kept tucked away in the sewing-basket to comfort her moments of loneliness?

He said to her with feeling: 'It is not like that. There are certain things which only exist when they reach completion, and only then do they give the full happiness which is sought in them.'

'This is all very complicated,' she murmured, blushing. 'It is very subtle.'

'Would you like me to explain it more clearly?'

At this moment Domingos, drawing aside the curtain announced that Sr Damaso was there.

Maria Eduarda gave a short little gesture of impatience.

'Tell him I am not receiving visitors!'

They heard the slam of a door break the silence. And Carlos thought uneasily that Damaso must have seen his coupé driving up and down in the street below. Heavens above! What wouldn't he go babbling now, humiliated like this, with his spitefulness! At this moment Damaso's experience seemed almost incompatible with the tranquillity of his love.

'That's another inconvenience of this house,' Maria Eduarda was saying. 'Just here, right next to the Grémio, a stone's throw from the Chiado, it is too accessible to importunate persons. Nearly every day now I have to repel this assault on my door! It is intolerable.'

Then at a sudden idea, flinging her embroidery into the work-basket and crossing her hands over her knees, she said:

'Tell me something I've been wanting to ask. Couldn't I find a little house somewhere, a cottage, where I could spend the summer? It would be so good for the child! But I don't know anyone here, I don't know whom I could ask . . .'

Carlos remembered Craft's lovely house in Olivais, just as on the other occasion when she had shown a desire to live in the

359

country. Craft had recently, in fact, spoken again and more pur-
posefully, of his old idea of selling the house and getting rid
of his collection. What a superb residence for her, both rural
and artistic; it would be so in keeping with her tastes. An irresistible temptation came to him.

'Actually I know of a house . . . and so delightfully situated
that it should be just right for you.'

'And it's to be let?'

Carlos no longer hesitated.

'Yes, I think it could be arranged.'

'That would be wonderful!'

She had said, 'That would be wonderful!' and that decided
him, for it seemed mean and unkind to offer her a hope and
not to try to fulfil it with all his might.

Domingos came in with the tea-tray. And while he placed it
on a little table in front of Maria Eduarda near the window
Carlos got up, and walked about, thinking of beginning negotiations immediately with Craft; he would buy his collection of
antiques, rent the house for a year and offer it to Maria Eduarda
for the summer months. And at this moment he considered
neither difficulties nor money. All he saw was her joy as she
walked with the little girl among the beautiful trees in the garden. And how much more beautiful Maria Eduarda would be
when surrounded by the noble severe lines of the Renaissance
furniture.

'More sugar?' she asked.

'No, that's just right. Thank you.'

He came and sat in his old armchair, and as he took his cup –
common white china with a blue band – he remembered the
magnificent gold and crimson service of old Wedgwood that
Craft had. Poor lady! So delicate and buried there among all
that rep, sullying her lovely hands with old Mother Cruges's
shabby things.

'And where is this house?' asked Maria Eduarda.

'In Olivais, very near here, just an hour's drive away.'

He explained the place in detail, adding, with his eyes on her
and an uneasy smile: 'Here I am providing the rope to hang
myself with! Because if you settle in that house and the hot
weather arrives, when shall we see you again?'

She looked surprised.

'But where's the problem, with your horses and carriages, and practically nothing to do all day?'

So it seemed natural to her that he should continue in Olivais the visits he had been making in Lisbon! And it seemed to him then impossible to renounce this charming intimacy that was being so generously offered, and would doubtless be all the sweeter in the solitude of a village. By the time he finished his cup of tea it was as if the house, the furniture and trees already belonged to him, and so to her. And he had a delightful few moments describing to her the tranquility of the country house, the acacia avenue leading up to it and the beauty of the dining-room with its two windows looking on to the river.

She listened to him enthralled.

'Oh, this is just like my dreams! I'll be a different person from now on, full of hope. When can I know definitely?'

Carlos looked at his watch. It was too late now to go to Olivais. But he would go early the very next morning to speak to the owner, a friend of his.

'Such a lot of trouble for my sake!' she said. 'Really, how can I thank you!'

She said no more but her beautiful eyes rested on his, as if forgetful for a moment, and letting irresistibly escape something of the secret which she held in her heart.

He murmured: 'Whatever I did I should be more than repaid if you looked at me again like that.'

She flushed deeply.

'Don't say that.'

'It's not necessary anyway. For you know perfectly well that I adore you, adore you, adore you!'

She got up abruptly and he too, and there they remained, silent, anxious, their eyes fastened on each other as if some great change had come over the universe and they waited there, in suspense, for the key to their destinies. And then it was she who spoke, with a great effort, almost on the point of dropping; she stretched out trembling hands to him as if wanting to drive him away.

'Listen! You know what I feel about you, but listen to me! Before it is too late there is something I want to tell you.'

Carlos saw her trembling, saw her pale . . . and neither understood her words nor even heard them. He simply felt, and in a flash, that the love he had confined within his heart had at last broken out, triumphant, and, striking her heart through the seemingly impenetrable marble of her breast, had called forth a similar flame. He saw only that she trembled, saw only that she loved him. And grave and strong as if in the act of possession, he slowly took her hands which she had given him, suddenly submissive, subdued, without strength. And he kissed them one after the other, slowly, the palms and the fingers, unable to say more than: 'My love! My love! My love!'

Maria Eduarda sank down slowly on to her chair, and without withdrawing her hands, imploring him with eyes full of passion and misted with tears, in a final weak supplication: 'There is something I want to tell you!'

Carlos was already kneeling at her feet.

'I know what it is!' he exclaimed with ardour, his face close to hers, and he prevented her from saying any more for he was sure he guessed her thoughts. 'You don't have to say – I know perfectly what you feel. I have thought the same thing so often! A love like ours cannot live in the conditions in which other common loves survive. It's as if when I tell you I love you, I am asking you to be my wife before God.'

She drew back her hand, looking at him anxiously, as if she did not understand. And Carlos went on in a low voice, with her hands in his, infusing her with the emotion which was making him tremble.

'I have always thought of us as living in a world of our own, far from here, far from everyone, all present bonds broken, our love above all human friction, seeking our happiness in some corner of the world alone and for ever. We'd take Rosa, naturally – I know you could not bear to be separated from her. And we'd live like that, just the three of us, in paradise!'

'Good Lord! Run away?' she murmured in astonishment.

Carlos stood up.

'What else can we do? What else would be worthy of our love?'

Maria did not answer, as she sat motionless, her face lifted towards his, wax-like in its pallor. Then gradually an idea seemed to sweep through her, a wild, bewildering hope which stirred her entire being. Her eyes shone brighter and larger and yet were apprehensive.

Carlos was about to speak again when a quiet footfall on the mat detained him. It was Domingos coming for the tea-tray: and for a moment, a seemingly interminable moment, there passed between those two beings, shaken by a veritable storm of passion, the homely movements of a servant clearing away empty tea-cups. Maria Eduarda abruptly fled behind the cretonne curtains and laid her face against the window-pane. Carlos went and sat on the sofa, to leaf nonchalantly through an *Ilustração* which he held in trembling hands. And he could think of nothing, did not even know where he was. Only the day before, only seconds ago, he had said ceremoniously, as they talked together, 'my dear senhora'; then there had been a glance exchanged; and now they must flee together and she had become the object of greatest importance in his life, his soul's secret spouse.

'Is there anything else you need, madam?' asked Domingos.

Maria Eduarda answered without turning her head.

'Nothing.'

Domingos left the room and the door closed behind him. Then she crossed the room to where Carlos sat on the sofa, waiting for her with arms outstretched. And it was as if she were obeying only the impulse of her tenderness, and all her doubts were stilled. But yet once more she hesitated before that passion which was ready to take possession of her whole being, and she murmured almost sadly:

'But you know so little about me! You know so little for us to run away like this, making an irreparable break with everything to create a new destiny together.'

Carlos took her hands and pulled her gently down to sit beside him.

'Enough to adore you above all else, and want nothing more in life.'

Maria Eduarda sat pensive for a moment as if listening to the last faint struggling in her heart. Then she uttered a heavy sigh.

'Well, let it be so, then. Let it be so. There was something I wanted to tell you, but it doesn't matter. It's better like this.'

What else could they do, Carlos wanted to know, radiant in his certainty. It was the only worthy, serious solution there was. And they had nothing to hinder them; they loved each other, they trusted in each other completely; he was rich and the world was wide . . .

363

And she repeated, more firmly now, quite decided, and as if their resolution was driven every moment farther into her soul, piercing it through and through and for ever:

'Let it be so, then! It's better like this!'

They stayed a moment silent, looking at each other entranced.

'Tell me you are happy, at least,' said Carlos.

She flung her arms round his neck, and their lips met in an ardent, infinite kiss which was almost spiritual in its ecstasy. Then Maria Eduarda slowly opened her eyes and said very softly:

'Good-bye. Leave me now. Go.'

He took his hat and left.

The following day Craft, who for a week now had not been to Ramalhete, was walking in the grounds before lunch when Carlos appeared. They shook hands, spoke for a moment of Ega and the arrival of the Cohens.

Then Carlos, making a wide gesture to take in the house, garden and all the horizon, asked with a smile: 'Would you like to sell me all this Craft?'

Craft replied without blinking, hands still in pockets: '*A la disposición de usted . . .*'

And they concluded the business there and then, strolling along a little path between box hedges and flowering geraniums.

Craft would sell Carlos all the furniture, both modern and antique, for 2,500 sovereigns to be paid in instalments; he would keep only a few rare pieces of Louis XV which would form part of the new collection he was planning – a homogeneous collection of eighteenth-century furniture. And as Carlos had no room in Ramalhete for this vast accumulation of bric-à-brac, Craft was to rent him the house and grounds in Olivais for a year.

After that they went in to lunch. Carlos never considered for a moment the enormous expenses he was incurring, simply to offer a summer residence, for two short months, to someone who would have been content with a simple cottage and a couple of trees. On the contrary, when he passed through the rooms, now with an owner's eyes, he found everything unhandsome, unworthy, and began to think of modifications, touches here and there in better taste.

How gaily he rushed to Rua de S. Francisco when he left

Olivais, to tell Maria Eduarda that he had managed to arrange a delightful country house for her! Rosa, who had seen him dismount from the balcony, ran to meet him on the landing: he picked her up and they entered the drawing-room like that – she perched triumphantly in his arms. He could not contain himself, and revealed his 'wonderful news' to the child there and then, telling her she was to have two cows and a goat, and flowers, and trees for a swing . . .

'Where is it? Tell me, where is it?' exclaimed Rosa, her beautiful eyes sparkling, and her little face aglow with laughter.

'A long, long way away . . . You need a carriage to get there and you can see the boats on the river . . . And you go in through a big gate and there's a mastiff on guard . . .'

Maria Eduarda appeared carrying Niniche.

'Mama! Mama!' shouted Rosa, running up to her and clutching her skirt. 'He says I'm going to have two little goats and a swing. Is is true? Tell me, tell me, where is it? Tell me . . . Are we going right away?'

Maria and Carlos shook hands, looking at each other without a word. And there, beside the table, with Rosa leaning on his knees, Carlos told her of his visit to Olivais. The owner of the house was willing to rent it from the following week. And there she was suddenly with a picturesque, salubrious and elegantly furnished house.

Maria Eduarda seemed surprised and almost suspicious.

'I suppose I must take bed- and table-linen.'

'But everything's there!' exclaimed Carlos gaily. 'Or almost everything! It's just like a fairy-tale. The lamps are burning, the vases are full of flowers . . . It only means taking a carriage and you're there.'

'There's just one thing. I should like to know how much this paradise is going to cost me.'

Carlos blushed scarlet. He had not foreseen that she would talk of money – and that she would expect, most naturally, to pay for the house she was to live in. So then he preferred to confess everything. He told her how Craft had been wanting to get rid of his collection of antiques and rent the house for nearly a year; he and his grandfather had repeatedly thought of acquiring a large part of the furniture and china, to finish furnishing Ramalhete and add to Santa Olávia. He had finally decided on the purchase when he had visualized the happiness he could thus offer her for a few months that summer, with such an elegant house, such a comfortable home . . .

'Rosa, run along inside now,' said Maria Eduarda after a moment's silence. 'Miss Sarah is waiting for you.'

Then, looking seriously at Carlos, she remarked:

'So if I had not shown desire to live in the country, you would not have gone to all this expense?'

'I should have gone to the same expense. I should also have rented the house for six months or a year. Where have I now to put all Craft's things? What perhaps I should not have done is buy, along with the rest, bed- and table-linen, furniture for servants' quarters, and so on.'

And he added laughing: 'If you'd like to compensate me for this, however, we could discuss the matter now . . .'

She slowly lowered her eyes and reflected:

'At any rate your grandfather and your friends will learn in a few days' time that I am going to move into this house. And they will realize that you bought it for me to move into . . .'

Carlos tried to catch her eye but she remained pensive, looking away from him. It made him feel uneasy to see her withdraw like that from the absolute communion of interests he had hoped to establish with her, the woman his heart had espoused.

'Don't you agree with what I did? Be frank . . .'

'Of course I do. How could I not approve anything you do, anything coming from you? But . . .'

He came to her aid, clasping her hands and aware of his triumph.

'There are no buts! My grandfather and friends still know only that I have a country house, unable to be used for the time being, and that I have rented it to some lady. And if you really wish, we could have my steward deal with the business. My dear friend, it would be wonderful if our affection could pass beyond this world, far from people's eyes and protected from all suspicions. But this cannot be! Someone always gets to know something even if it's only the coach-driver taking me to your house every day, or the servant who opens your door to me. There is always someone to intercept a glance; there is always someone to guess where you have come from at certain hours of the day. The gods in the old days arranged these things far better

– they had a cloud which made them invisible. But we are not gods, fortunately . . .'

She smiled.

'So many words to convert one already converted!'

And a long kiss settled everything.

Afonso da Maia thoroughly approved the purchase of Craft's collection. 'It's an asset,' he said to Vilaça, 'and it means we can finish furnishing Santa Olávia and Ramalhete tastefully.'

But Ega, annoyed that he had not been consulted about the transaction, resented the step and spoke of it as an extravagance. What made him particularly indignant was that behind this unexpected purchase of a country gouse he sensed a further symptom of the grave, deeply-guarded secret he had already discerned in Carlos's life. Two weeks he had been at Ramalhete and Carlos still had not taken him into his confidence! Ever since their days at Coimbra he had acted as Carlos's secular confessor: even when travelling abroad Carlos would send Ega a report of the most trivial adventures in love. The affair with the Countess de Gouvarinho, which Carlos had at first tried rather feebly to screen in mystery, had eventually been related to him in full; he had even read her letters and been in Aunty's house.

But of this other secret he as yet knew nothing – and he considered himself offended. He saw Carlos set off every morning for Rua de S. Francisco, carrying flowers; he saw him arrive home afterwards, as he commented, 'oozing with ecstasy'; he noticed the periods of silence denoting a profound happiness, and that vague air, both light and serious, smiling and superior, of the man who feels himself loved intensely. And he, Ega, knew nothing about it.

A few days later, when they were alone together, talking of their plans for the summer, Carlos alluded to Olivais, remarking enthusiastically on certain of Craft's most valuable pieces, on the peacefulness of the house, on the excellent view of the Tagus . . . He had really got a little bit of paradise for a mere handful of money.

It was late at night and they were in Ega's room. Ega, pacing up and down with hands thrust in the pockets of his dressing-gown, shrugged his shoulders, sick and tired of these eternal praises of Craft's wretched house.

'This all sounds like a shopkeeper's idea of paradise,' he exclaimed. 'For a touch of nature: Scotch kale; for decoration: the old cretonne curtains in the study, discoloured now after three good soakings to get them clean . . . A bedroom as lugubrious as a chapel . . . A drawing-room as cluttered as a storehouse. Apart from the Dutch cabinet and a plate or two, the whole lot is just an archaic rubbish heap. God, how I loathe bric-à-brac!'

Carlos answered calmly and reflectively from the depths of his armchair: 'The curtains are hideous, it's true. But I am going to redecorate a little, make it more comfortable to live in.'

Ega stopped in his tracks, his glistening monocle on Carlos.

'To live in? Are you going to have guests then?'

'I'm going to let it.'

'Let it! To whom?'

And the silence Carlos maintained, as he exhaled the smoke of his cigarette with his eyes on the ceiling, infuriated Ega. He bowed low, almost to the ground, and said sarcastically:

'My most humble apologies. The question was a brutal one. I acted like one trying to break open a locked drawer. The tenant of a building is always a delicate secret, a matter of heart and honour which no one ought dare to try to extort, nor even allow the wings of imagination to brush against! I behaved uncivilly! Heavens! I was almost shamefully rude!'

Carlos remained silent. He understood Ega's feelings and almost regretted his rigid reserve. But it was as if modesty bound him, prevented him from even pronouncing Maria Eduarda's name. All his other affairs he had related to Ega – it was these confidences indeed which constituted perhaps the greatest pleasure the affairs had given. This time, however, it was not a simple adventure. There was something almost religious in this love of his and, like all true devotees, he was averse to discussing his faith. But on the other hand he was tempted at the same time to talk of her to Ega, to bring alive, visible as it were to his own eyes, outlining with words and bringing into relief, the divine confusion which filled his heart. And wouldn't Ega learn everything sooner or later anyway, from the gossip of others? Better for him to tell the story, in a brotherly fashion. But he still hesitated, and lit another cigarette. Ega had picked up his candlestick and had sulkily begun to light it.

'Don't be stupid, don't go to bed yet. Come and sit down,' said Carlos.

And he told him everything, in a mass of detail, from the first time he had seen her at the entrance of the Hotel Central, on the evening of the supper in honour of Cohen.

Ega heard him without a word, buried in the depths of the sofa. He had expected a trivial little romance – one of those which are born with a kiss and die with a yawn; and now, from the tones in which Carlos spoke of his great love, he realized it to be something profound, all-absorbing and eternal – something which for good or evil would become his irremediable destiny. He had imagined a Brazilian woman sophisticated by Parisian life, a pretty, frivolous creature who, with husband far away in Brazil and a handsome young man on the sofa beside her, had simply and joyfully accepted the circumstances. But she had turned out to be a woman full of character, passionate and capable of sacrifices and even heroism. As always on these dramatic occasions, his patter dried up, he was lost for words, and when Carlos finished, the good Ega could only inquire clumsily,

'So you're going to skedaddle with the lady?'

'Skedaddle, no! To live with her far from here, most definitely.'

'It's staggering!'

But what else could they do? In some three months' time, Castro Gomes would be back from Brazil. And neither Carlos nor she would ever accept one of those atrocious, shabby situations where the woman belongs to both husband and lover, at different hours. There was only one decent dignified solution left to them – to flee together.

Ega, after a short silence, murmured thoughtfully:

'For the husband, perhaps, it is not so amusing to lose wife and daughter and little dog all at the same time.'

Carlos got up and took a step or two around the room. Yes, he also had thought of that side of the question, but he felt no remorse, supposing one could feel remorse in the absolute selfishness which envelops one at the height of passion. He did not know Castro Gomes personally, but he could well guess the type, he could easily reconstruct him from the things Damaso and Miss Sarah had said. Castro Gomes was not a serious-minded husband: he was a dandy, a vain fellow, a *gommeux*, a man interested

369

mainly in sport and *cocottes*. He had married a beautiful woman, his passion had worn itself out, and he had returned to club life and his little affairs on the side . . . You had only to look at him and the way he dressed and acted, and you could straightway see what a shallow character he was.

'What's he like as a man?' asked Ega.

'A swarthy supercilious little Brazilian . . . A *rastaquouère*, the real Café de la Paix type . . . It's possible he'll feel his vanity wounded a little when this happens, but he's a fellow who'll soon console himself at the Folies Bergères.'

Ega made no reply. He thought that a man who spent his life in clubs, and especially one whom the Folies Bergères would console, might indeed worry little over the loss of a wife, but he could still love his daughter very much.

Then another idea occurred to him and he added: 'What about your grandfather?'

Carlos shrugged his shoulders.

'Grandfather will have to be a little upset for me to be profoundly happy; as I should have to sacrifice the most important thing in my life if I were to save him this displeasure. That's how the world is, Ega. And I, on this particular matter, am not willing to make sacrifices.'

Ega absent-mindedly rubbed his hands together, eyes on the ground, repeating the same words, the only ones his active mind could produce at such a dramatic moment:

'It's staggering!'

3

CARLOS HAD LUNCHED early and was on the point of leaving in the coupé when Baptista came in to announce that Sr Ega wished to speak to him on an important matter and could he therefore wait a moment. Sr Ega was shaving.

Carlos immediately supposed that it was something to do with Madame Cohen. She had been in Lisbon for two weeks now and Ega had not seen her and spoke of her only rarely. But Carlos had sensed that he was nervous and restless. Every morning Ega showed his disappointment when he received his mail and there was only a newspaper or letters from Celorico. In the evenings he went the rounds of two or three theatres which now, at the beginning of the summer, were almost completely deserted, and when he returned it was a further disappointment to hear the servants affirm that no, there had definitely been no letters for him. Ega had obviously not resigned himself to losing Rachel, and was longing to meet her; and the disagreeable fact that she had not somehow let him see that her heart still felt some nostalgia for their past happiness gnawed away at him bitterly. Only the day before Ega had turned up for dinner in a disturbed state: he had met Cohen in Rua do Ouro and it seemed as if 'that swine' had looked at him insolently and shaken his cane. Ega swore that if 'that swine' dared to look at him again like that, he would smash him to pieces, mercilessly and publicly, there in the centre of town.

In the antechamber the clock struck ten and Carlos, impatient to leave, was about to go up to Ega's room. But at that moment the mail arrived with a *Revista dos Dois Mundos* and a letter for Carlos. It was from the Countess de Gouvarinho. Carlos had just finished reading it when Ega appeared in slippers and jacket.

'I want to speak to you on a very important matter, dear boy.'

'Read this first,' said his friend, passing over the Countess's letter.

The Countess complained bitterly that Carlos had twice failed to turn up at Aunty's house, and without a word of explanation or apology. She was deeply offended at this, it was brutal behaviour and she was now summoning him, 'in the name of all the sacrifices she had made for him' to appear in Rua de S. Marcel on Sunday at midday, that she might have a definitive explanation before she left for Cintra.

'An excellent opportunity to bring the affair to an end!' exclaimed Ega, handing back the letter to Carlos, after inhaling the perfume of the paper. 'You neither go nor answer. She goes off to Cintra, you to Santa Olávia, you don't see each other any more and that's the end of that. An end like all great things, like the Roman Empire or the River Rhine – a gradual, imperceptible dispersion.'

'That's just what I am going to do,' said Carlos, drawing on his gloves. 'God! What a nuisance the woman is!'

'And shameless too! To call such things "sacrifices"! She drags you to Aunty's house twice a week, indulges in all manner of extravagances there, drinks champagne, smokes cigarettes, ascends into a seventh heaven, goes into ecstasies of pleasure, and then dolefully lowers her eyes to the ground and calls all this "sacrifices". She needs a good beating!'

Carlos shrugged his shoulders with resignation, as if one could only expect fraud and incoherence from the Countess de Gouvarinho – indeed from the world as a whole.

'But what's this you have to tell me?'

Ega adopted a grave air, leisurely selected a cigarette from the box and buttoned up his jacket.

'Have you seen Damaso lately?'

'He's never come back,' answered Carlos. 'I believe he's sulking. Whenever I see him at a distance I wave a finger at him in a vague friendly way.'

'You'd do better to wave a cane at him. Damaso's going round everywhere talking of you and this lady, your friend. You he calls a scoundrel, and her far worse. It's the same old story: he says he introduced you there, and then you pushed your way in, and as it's all a question of money with this lady and you happen to be the richer, she has passed him over for you. You see how he's dirtying your name. And this is spread around the Grémio and the Casa Havanesa, with the foulest sort of details, and the question of money always brought in. It's atrocious. You must put a stop to it.'

Carlos went extremely pale and said simply: 'Justice will be done.'

He went downstairs furious. It seemed to him that a disgusting insinuation like that about money could only be punished adequately by death. And for a moment, with his hand on the bolt of the carriage-door, he thought of going straight to Damaso's house and exacting a bloody vengeance.

But it was almost eleven o'clock and he had to go to Olivais. On the following day, Saturday, a day far brighter and more solemn than other days, Maria Eduarda was at last to visit Craft's house. The day before it had been arranged that they would spend the hot afternoon hours there in the cool unstaffed house amid the trees. He had begged this of her in trembling hesitation and she had consented immediately, smiling and natural. That morning he had sent two servants to Olivais to air the rooms, dust and fill the house with flowers. Now he was going there, the devotee, to see if the goddess's sanctuary was embellished to perfection! And now there was Damaso trampling across his carefully tended plans once again, just as he was completely happy, profaning and obscuring the brilliance of his love!

All the way to Olivais his mind was occupied unceasingly in devising vague and violent ways to get rid of Damaso. His love would have no peace while that wretched fellow wandered round repeating his slander at every street corner. He would have to insult him in such a way, so publicly, that he would not dare show his vile chubby face in Lisbon again. When the coupé stopped at the garden-gate, Carlos had reached the decision that he would give him a good thrashing with his cane one afternoon in the Chiado in full view of everybody.

But by the time he had reached Lisbon again he had regained his calm. He had trod the beautiful avenue of acacias which her feet would tread tomorrow; he had glanced long and lovingly at the bed which was to be hers – a richly draped bed raised on a small platform and surrounded by curtains of gold brocade, with the serious splendour of a pagan altar . . . In a few hours' time they would be alone together there in that silent isolated house; during the summer their love would be concealed from inquisitive eyes in that cool country retreat and in three months' time they would be far away in Italy, beside some clear lake, amid the flowers of Isola Bella . . . In the face of such soul-stirring delights, what could Damaso matter, fat and despicable, filling the billiards-room of the Grémio with his coarseness and slang! By the time he reached Rua de S. Francisco, he had decided that if he saw Damaso he would continue to acknowledge him as before, with a wave of the tips of his fingers . . .

Maria Eduarda had gone for a drive to Belém with Rosa but had left a note asking him to come along that evening *pour un bout de causerie*. Carlos slowly descended the stairs, putting away this little piece of paper, like a precious relic, into his wallet. He emerged from the door at the same time as Alencar, all in black and gloomy and pensive, appeared opposite coming from the Travessa de Parreirinha. When he caught sight of Carlos, he stopped with arms outstretched; then, as if remembering something, he swiftly lifted his eyes to the windows above.

They had not met since the day of the races and the poet clasped his Carlos to him effusively – and began to speak of himself in great detail. He had been to Cintra again, and in Colares with his old friend Carvalhosa. How he cherished the memory of that magnificent day he and Carlos and the Maestro had spent together in Seteais! Ah, Cintra was a jewel! He had a slight chill unfortunately. And in spite of Carvalhosa's company (such a deep, learned man) and in spite of his wife's excellent musical talents (dear Julinha, like a sister to him!) he had grown somewhat bored. He was clearly getting old . . .

'To tell the truth,' said Carlos, 'you are looking a little worn. The usual luminous air is missing . . .'

The poet shrugged his shoulders.

'As it is written in the Gospel . . . Or is it the Bible? No, it's St Paul . . . St Paul or St Augustine? Anyway, the authority is of no importance here. In one of these sacred books it is affirmed that this earth is a vale of tears . . .'

'In which people do their share of laughing,' finished Carlos gaily.

The poet shrugged his shoulders again. Tears or laughter, what did it matter? It was all feeling, all living! Only the day before he had said just this same thing in the Cohens' house.

And suddenly he stopped in the middle of the road and touched Carlos's arm.

'Speaking of the Cohens, tell me something, dear boy, with all frankness. I know you are a close friend of Ega's and the devil

374

knows there's no one admires his talent more than I do! But really, do you think it right for him to rush back to Lisbon as soon as he hears of the Cohens' arrival? After all that happened . . . ?'

Carlos assured the poet that Ega had only learnt of the Cohens' return from the *Gazeta Ilustrada* some hours after his own arrival. And besides, if two people were unable to live in the same city just because there had been some friction between them, human society was going to come to an end.

Alencar did not answer but walked slowly beside Carlos, with head bowed. Then he stopped again and frowned.

'There's another thing I wanted to ask you. Has there been any tiff between you and Damaso? I ask because the other day he came out with a few remarks and insinuations in the Cohens' house. I said to him immediately, "Damaso, Carlos da Maia, the son of Pedro da Maia, is like a brother to me." And Damaso shut up. He shut up because he knows me, and knows I'm a person not to be played with where matters of the heart and loyalty are concerned!'

Carlos answered simply: 'No, there's nothing that I know about. I haven't even seen Damaso lately.'

'Well, let me tell you,' continued Alencar, taking Carlos's arm. 'I thought about you a great deal in Cintra. I even composed a little thing which is not too bad and which I dedicated to you. It's a simple piece, a landscape, a sketch of Cintra at sunset. I wanted to prove to these adherents of the New Idea that this is one poet who knows how to carve out modern verse and give the realistic touch when it's necessary. Wait – I'll recite it to you if I remember. The piece is called, "On the way to Capuchos".'

They had stopped and the poet had cleared his throat to recite when who should appear but Ega, coming up the hill dressed in country apparel with a beautiful white rose ornamenting his blue flannel jacket.

He and Alencar had not met since the fatal evening at the Cohens'. And if Ega held a strong resentment against the poet, believing him to be the inventor of the vile 'obscene letter' legend, Alencar loathed Ega for the secret certainty that he had been the divine Rachel's beloved lover. Both turned pale; their handshake was limp and icy, and they stood in silence, all three, while Ega nervously spent an eternity lighting a cigar from Carlos's match. But it was he who spoke first, affecting a friendly superiority:

'You're looking well, Alencar!'

The poet was also affable, slightly haughty as he fingered his moustache and replied:

'Not so bad. And what are you doing these days? When are we going to have these *Memoirs*, old man?'

'I'm waiting for the country to learn to read first.'

'You'll wait a long time! You should ask your friend Gouvarinho to hurry things up – he is the man dealing with education. Ah look, there is the gentleman himself, looking as grave and empty as a column in the official papers.'

The poet pointed with his cane to the other side of the street where Gouvarinho was slowly approaching, talking to Cohen; and at their side, with white hat and waistcoat, swaggered Damaso, smiling and pot-bellied, surveying the Chiado like a conqueror contemplating his dominions. That unctuous, tranquilly triumphant air immediately irritated Carlos, but when Damaso stopped opposite and turned his back, feigning to laugh aloud with Gouvarinho, Carlos could not contain himself and crossed the road.

It was brief and cruel: he shook Gouvarinho's hand and acknowledged Cohen; then without lowering his voice he coldly warned Damaso: 'Listen, if you continue to talk about me and people of my acquaintance the way you have been doing, which I find displeasing, I'll give you a good box on the ears.'

The Count hastily put himself between the two men.

'Maia, for heaven's sake, man! Here, in the Chiado!'

'There's nothing to worry about Gouvarinho,' said Carlos, putting a hand on his arm, quite calm and serious. 'I'm just warning this imbecile here.'

'I don't want any trouble, I don't want any trouble,' stammered Damaso, livid, backing into a newsagent's.

And Carlos serenely returned to his friends after having taken his leave of Cohen and shaken Gouvarinho's hand.

He was simply a little pale; Ega was more agitated, for he suspected he had seen, in a glance of Cohen's, an intolerable provocation. Only Alencar had noticed nothing, and continued to talk on literary matters, explaining to Ega the concessions that could be made to naturalism.

376

'I was just saying to Ega here: it's quite evident that when we are dealing with scenery we must imitate reality. You can't describe a chestnut tree *a priori* as you could a soul . . . And that's just what I do. Here's the poem about Cintra now, that I dedicated to you, Carlos. It is realistic, naturally, it's realistic. What else, if I'm describing a scene! Let me recite it. I was just about to, Ega, when you appeared. Unless of course it would bore you . . .'

Bore them indeed! They even turned into Rua de S. Francisco, which was quieter, to hear better. And there, moving slowly forward, one step at a time, the poet breathed his eclogue. It was in Cintra, at sunset: an English lady, her hair floating loose, all in white, is seated on a donkey which ambles along a pathway overlooking a valley; the birds are singing quietly; butterflies flutter around the honeysuckle; then the English lady gets down off her donkey and gazes enraptured at the heavens and at the peaceful houses. It is at this point, in the third tercet, that the 'realistic note' of which Alencar had been boasting, appears:

At the sleeping flower and the chaste white cloud she gazes,
While the smoke from the houses coils in the air
And the donkey at her side, pensive, grazes.

'There you have the touch, the naturalistic note: "And the donkey at her side, pensive, grazes". That is stark reality, you can just see a pensive donkey. There's nothing so pensive as a donkey. It's these little details of nature that you have to notice. You can see now, can't you, how you can have realism, and good realism, without coming out with obscenities. How do you like my little work?'

Both praised it highly – Carlos sorry that he had not completed Damaso's humiliation by giving him a few strokes of his cane, and Ega thinking that one of these afternoons, there in the Chiado, he'd have to set about Cohen for sure. As they were returning to Ramalhete, Alencar, his good humour restored now, accompanied them as far as the Aterro. And all the way he talked, expounding the plan he had for a historic novel where he would paint the great figure of Afonso de Albuquerque, but from the human side, more intimate than usual: Afonso de

377

Albuquerque in love; Afonso de Albuquerque alone at night on the stern of his galleon before a blazing Ormuz, kissing between sobs a withered flower . . . Alencar thought this would be sublime.

After supper Carlos was dressing to go to Rua de S. Francisco when Baptista entered to say that Sr Teles da Gama was there and wanted to speak to him urgently. Not wishing to receive him there, in shirt-sleeves, Carlos asked to have him shown into the scarlet and black study. And when he entered a moment later he found Teles da Gama admiring the beautiful Dutch *faiences*.

'You have this arranged exquisitely, Maia,' he exclaimed. 'I'm mad about porcelain. I must come back one day when I have more time, and see all this in daylight. But today I'm in a hurry; I come on a mission. Can't you guess?'

Carlos could not.

So Teles da Gama withdrew a step and announced with a gravity in which flickered a smile:

'I have come to ask you, on behalf of Damaso, if you intended to insult him in what you said today. That's all. My mission is simply that: to ask you if you intended to insult him.'

Carlos looked at him, quite serious.

'What? If I intended to insult him when I threatened to box his ears? Not at all: all I intended was to box his ears.'

Teles da Gama bowed low.

'That was precisely what I told Damaso: your intention was no more than that. Anyway, that brings my mission to an end. How well you have this arranged! What's that great plate over there – majolica?'

'No, an old Nevers. Go and have a close look. It's Thetis carrying the arms of Achilles. It's magnificent – and very rare. And see this Delft here with the two yellow tulips. It's a beautiful piece.'

Teles da Gama gave a long look at these exquisite objects, and picked up his hat from the sofa.

'Charming, this is really charming! So your only intention then was to box his ears? No intention of offending?'

'None at all of offending, but every intention to box his ears. Won't you have a cigar?'

'No, thank you.'

'A drop of brandy then?'

'No. Complete abstention from alcohol and alcoholic drinks. Well, good-bye, my dear Maia!'

'Good-bye, my dear Teles!'

The following day, on a resplendent July morning, Carlos leapt from his coupé with a bunch of keys in his hands and stood before the garden-gate of Craft's house. Maria Eduarda was to arrive at ten o'clock, alone, in a hired carriage. The gardener had been given a couple of days off and had gone to Vila Franca; the house was not yet staffed and the windows were closed. And over all the road and house hung one of those heavy solemn village silences when one can feel the humming of ox-flies in the air.

The gate opened into a cool, sweet-smelling avenue of acacias. At one side could be discerned through the foliage the summer-house which had been a whim of Craft's; it had a wooden roof and was painted red and furnished inside in Japanese style. At the end of the avenue lay the house, freshly whitewashed, with balcony windows and green blinds and three steps leading up to the front door flanked by blue china pots full of carnations.

He inserted the key in the lock of that discreet villa with unnecessary caution, but the simple act was for him a delicious pleasure. He opened the windows, and the bright light which entered seemed permeated with a rare sweetness and a jubilation greater than on other days, as if prepared especially by the good Lord to illumine this glad day. He hurried to the dining-room to see if the flowers he had brought the day before to decorate the table were still fresh. Then he returned to the coupé for the box of ice he had brought from Lisbon, all wrapped in flannel and sawdust. Along the road, silent at that hour, a solitary country lass passed, mounted on her mare.

He had scarcely put away the ice when he heard the slow approach of the carriage. He went to the cretonne-curtained study, which opened on to the corridor, and stood there in hiding because of the coach-driver, and peeped through the door. Then a moment later he saw her coming up the acacia avenue, tall and beautiful, dressed in black with a half-veil as thick as a mask. Her little feet climbed the three stone steps, and then her voice came quiet and tense:

'Êtes-vous là?'

He appeared and they stood a moment at the door of the study, fervidly clasping hands without a word, deeply moved, dazzled.

'What a lovely morning!' she said at last, pink and smiling.

'A lovely morning indeed!' repeated Carlos, looking at her in rapture.

Maria Eduarda sank wearily on to a chair beside the door to still the agitation in her heart.

'This is all very comfortable, quite enchanting,' she said, looking slowly around her at the cretonnes and the Turkish divan covered with a Brousse cloth, at the grass-fronted bookcase full of books. 'I shall be in heaven here.'

'But I haven't even thanked you for coming yet,' murmured Carlos, gazing at her distractedly. 'I haven't even kissed your hand . . .'

Maria Eduarda began to take off her veil, and then her gloves, talking about the road from Lisbon. She found it long and exhausting. But what did it matter? Once installed in that cosy little haven she would never go back to Lisbon!

She put her hat on the divan and stood up, radiant and gay.

'Let's go over the house, I'm dying to see these marvellous things of your friend Craft! It is Craft he's called, isn't it? *Craft* means industry!'

'But I haven't even kissed your hand yet,' Carlos reminded her, smiling in supplication.

She offered him her lips and was held fast in his arms.

And Carlos, slowly kissing her eyes and her hair, told her how happy he was and how he felt far more that she belonged to him there between the old walls of that country-house which separated them from the rest of the world.

She let him kiss her and asked gravely:

'Is all this true? Really true?'

Was it true! Carlos gave a sigh which was almost sad.

'What can I say? Must I repeat those words of Hamlet: "Doubt everything, doubt that the sun doth move, but never doubt I love".'

Maria Eduarda freed herself from his arms, slowly and nervously.

'Let's go and see the house,' she said.

They began with the second floor. The staircase was old and

ugly but the rooms above were bright and gay, with fresh matting on the floors, light paper on the walls and with a view over the fields and river.

'Your rooms will be the richly-furnished ones below, of course,' said Carlos. 'But Rosa and Miss Sarah will be very comfortable here, don't you think?'

She went through the rooms slowly, examining the cupboard space, feeling the softness of the mattresses, scrupulously attentive to the well-being of the people in her care. Occasionally she asked for something to be changed, and it seemed as if the fond, smiling man at her heels were no more than an old landlord.

'That room with two windows at the end of the corridor would be best for Rosa. But the child cannot sleep in that enormous ebony bed!'

'Then we'll change it!'

'Yes, it could be changed. And we need a big room for her to play in when it's very hot. If there weren't that partition between the two small rooms . . .'

'We'll have it knocked down!'

He rubbed his hands together contentedly, ready to have the whole house rebuilt for her sake; and she, intent on having her household well accommodated, agreed to the modifications.

They went down to the dining-room. And there, standing before the famous carved-oak chimney, flanked by two black Nubian figures like caryatids, with their gleaming crystal eyes, Maria Eduarda began to find Craft's taste eccentric, almost exotic. Carlos admitted that Craft's taste was hardly perfect, hardly that of an Athenian: he was simply a Saxon touched by a ray of southern sun. But there was nevertheless talent in his eccentricity.

'Ah, but the view is wonderful!' she exclaimed, moving over to the widow.

Outside the balcony grew a clump of ox-eye daisies and alongside these another of vanilla, heavily scenting the air. Before them stretched a carpet of lawn in need of cutting and slightly yellowed by the July heat; and there, between two large shady trees, a wide cork bench had been placed for whiling away the hours of siesta. A close row of bushes shut off the grounds on that side like a hedge. Then the hill swept down with other little farms tucked out of sight and a factory chimney; and there at the bottom lay the river shimmering blue and silent in the sun and stretching as far as the hills of the upper reaches of the Tagus, also rising blue in that brilliant clear summer sky.

'This is really enchanting,' she repeated.

'It's heaven. Didn't I tell you so? We must give the house a name. What are we going to call it? "Ville-Marie"? No. "Château-Rose"? No, not that either. It sounds like a wine. We had better baptize it definitely with the name we have already suggested. We'll call it "Hideaway".'

Maria Eduarda thought the name original. They should have it painted in red on the gate.

'Exactly, and with arms showing a creature in its hideaway,' laughed Carlos. 'Showing a creature looking blissfully selfish and bearing the words: "Please don't disturb!"'

But she had stopped with a smile of delighted surprise before the table laden with fruit with two chairs pulled up and crystal glittering among the flowers.

'It's like the wedding in Cana!'

Carlos's eyes shone.

'It's our wedding!'

Maria Eduarda blushed very pink and bent her head to choose a strawberry and then a rose.

'Would you like a little champagne?' exclaimed Carlos. 'With ice? We have ice, we have everything here! There is nothing missing, not even the blessing of the Lord . . . Just a little drop of champagne, come!'

She accepted. They drank from the same glass; and again their lips met in a passionate kiss.

Carlos lit a cigarette and they continued their inspection of the house. The kitchen pleased her immensely, all tiled in the English manner. In the corridor Maria Eduarda stopped before a bullfighting display: a black bull's head, swords and goads, crimson silk capes, with something of the grace of their wearers retained in their folds . . . Beside these things hung a yellow bullfight poster bearing the name of Lagartijo. This delighted her, like a flash of fiery Spanish sun and fiesta.

But the strident air of sensual luxury of the room which was to be hers did not please her at all. It received its light from a room lined with tapestries, where the loves of Venus and Mars were worked into the weave of the wool; over the communicating door hung a heavy wrought-iron lamp of the Renaissance, and at that hour, illuminated by a shaft of sunlight, the place shone like the interior of a heathen temple which had been converted into a lascivious harem. Walls and ceiling were completely covered with a heavy golden brocade and a velvet carpet in the same rich tone made a pavement of living gold – plainly to be trodden by the naked feet of some amorous goddess. The four-poster bed, raised on a platform and covered with a yellow satin bedspread embroidered with golden flowers and surrounded by solemn yellow curtains in old brocade, filled the little room completely, a splendid severe piece of furniture clearly destined for the voluptuous grandeur of a tragic passion of the times of Lucretia or Romeo. And there it was that Craft, with an Indian silk kerchief tied round his head, had snored away his seven hours, tranquil and alone.

But Maria Eduarda did not like this excessive yellow. And she received a sudden shock on noticing looming out of all that gold from a very old, dark, indistinct painting, a livid decapitated head set in its own blood on a copper plate. And yet another note of eccentricity appeared in a corner – on an oaken column an enormous stuffed owl gazed at the couch of love with evil meditation in its two round ominous eyes. Maria Eduarda could not imagine sleeping peacefully in such an atmosphere.

Carlos seized the owl and column and thrust them into a corner of the corridor, and offered to change the brocades and line the bedroom instead in a sunny pink satin.

'No, I'm getting used to all this gold already. Just that picture with the head and blood – ugh! How horrible!'

'Now I look at it carefully,' said Carlos, 'I believe it's our old friend St John the Baptist.'

In order to undo the disheartening impression made by the bedroom, he led her to the great drawing-room where Craft had arranged his most valuable things. Maria Eduarda, however, still discontent, considered it over-furnished and too much like a museum.

'It's to see, admire and then leave. One could not sit and talk here.'

'But this is just the raw material!' cried Carlos. 'You can

make an adorable sitting-room out of this. What's our artistic skill for otherwise? Look at that cabinet and its exquisite central part! It's beautiful!'

Almost filling the far wall stood Craft's 'divine piece', a carved cabinet from the time of the Hanseatic League – a luxurious sombre affair constructed majestically: at the base four warriors, armed like Mars, flanked the doors, each one depicting in low relief either the assault on a city or an encampment; the upper part was guarded at its four corners by the four evangelists, Matthew, Mark, Luke and John, inflexible figures wrapped in those violently-agitated garments which prophetic winds always seem to blow; then, on the cornice stood an agricultural composition with ears of corn and bunches of grapes and ploughshares; and amid these objects of toil and plenty reclined two fauns in careful symmetry, indifferent to the heroes and saints as they played their reed-pipes in bucolic rivalry.

'What do you say?' asked Carlos. 'What a superb piece of furniture! A complete poem from the Renaissance: fauns and apostles, wars and georgics! What could one put in a cabinet like this? If I had any letters from you, it's here, as though on a high altar, that I'd keep them.'

She did not answer, only smiled as she wandered slowly among these things belonging to the past, with their cold beauty, exhaling the indefinable sadness of a luxury now dead: like exiles from their marble palaces stood exquisite pieces of Italian Renaissance furniture inlaid with cornelian and agate which shone with a soft jewelled glow against the black of ebony or the satin-like pink woods; there were long nuptial chests painted in purple and gold with miniature forms of the Graces, where popes' and princes' gifts had rested; stately Spanish chiffoniers adorned with polished metal and crimson velvet, with mysterious interiors like little chapels, full of niches and tortoiseshell cloisters ... Here and there a brilliant satin drapery covered in golden flowers and birds illuminated the dark green of the walls; or on a corner of an Oriental carpet woven in severe tones and depicting a line or two from the Koran, a pastoral minuet was being danced in Cythera on the silk of an open fan ...

Maria Eduarda finished by seating herself wearily in a Louis XV armchair, a wide noble seat designed for regal panniers, covered in Beauvais tapestry and seeming still to retain a faint aroma of powder.

Carlos felt triumphant when he saw Maria's admiration. Well, did she still consider that purchase made in a burst of enthusiasm an extravagance?

'No, there are some adorable things here. I don't know if I shall dare to live a tranquil rustic life amid all these rare objects though!'

'Don't say that,' exclaimed Carlos with a laugh, 'or I'll set fire to the lot!'

But what really captivated her were the beautiful *faiences*, perfect pieces of fragile, immortal art scattered over the marble of the console-tables. One in particular claimed her attention, a splendid Persian goblet of a rare design, with a border of black cypresses, each one sheltering a brilliantly coloured flower. This reminded her of brief smiles which appear between long periods of sorrow. Then there were the sumptuous pieces of majolica, strident and dissimilar in design, full of famous characters – Charles V crossing the Elbe, Alexander crowning Roxanna; there were the pretty Nevers pieces, some ingenuous, some serious, and the Marseilles voluptuously exhibiting a fat red rose as if flaunting a state of nudity; the Derby with their gold borders on the deep blue like a tropical sky; the Wedgwood, milky-white and pink, with the subtle glimpses of colour seen on a shell under water . . .

'Just one more thing,' said Carlos, seeing her sit down again. 'You must meet the guardian spirit of the house!'

There in the centre, on a wide pedestal, was a bronze Japanese idol, a bestial god, naked, bald and obese, a broad grin on his swollen face. His belly was distended triumphantly in the indigestion of a whole universe and his two soft flabby little legs were like the flaccid flesh of a foetus. And this monster squatted in triumph on a fabulous animal with human feet that bowed a submissive neck to the ground, and in its snout and slanting eye showed the dumb resentment of its humiliation.

'And to think that entire generations have come and knelt before this grotesque creature, prayed to him, kissed his navel, offered him their riches, died for him . . .'

'Love felt for a monster is considered more meritorious, I believe, isn't it?' asked Maria.

385

'Then you can't consider love for you very meritorious.'

They sat on a low wide divan beside the window, full of cushions and surrounded by a white silk screen which made a cosy modern corner amid all that luxury of the past; and because she complained of feeling rather hot, Carlos opened the window. Beneath the window-sill grew a large clump of ox-eye daisies; just in front in an old stone stand on the lawn blossomed a red-flowering cactus, and from the branches of a walnut tree a welcome coolness descended.

Maria Eduarda went to lean against the window and Carlos followed her; they stood there together, silent, deeply happy, filled with the sweetness of their solitude. A bird sang quietly and then stopped. She wanted to know the name of a little village that lay glistening white in the sun on the blueish hill in the distance. Carlos did not remember. Then he playfully picked a daisy and inquired of it, '*Elle m'aime, un peu, beaucoup . . .*' She snatched it from his hands.

'Why do you need to ask the flowers?'

'Because you have not yet told me yourself, plainly, as I want to hear you tell me.'

He caught her round the waist and they smiled at each other. Then Carlos, his eyes lost in the depths of hers, murmured quietly and entreatingly: 'We have not yet seen the bath-room . . .'

Maria Eduarda let herself be led through the great drawing-room with his arm around her, then through the tapestry-hung room where Mars and Venus made love in the woods. The baths were at one side, the tiled floor enlivened by an old red Caramanian carpet. Carlos, still holding her close, laid a long kiss upon her neck. She abandoned herself to his ardour and her eyes closed heavily in surrender. They entered the warm gold-coloured bedroom. Carlos unfastened the curtains over the chapel-like arch – curtains of a light silk through which filtered a sunny pale gold light – and for a second they stood quite still, alone at last, without even touching, as if suspended, even suffocated by the fullness of their happiness.

Then, 'That horrible head!' she cried.

Carlos pulled the cover off the bed and concealed the sinister painting. Then every sound was stilled, and the isolated house slept among its trees, a long sleep in the calm of the July afternoon . . .

It was Afonso da Maia's birthday the next day, Sunday. Almost all the friends of the house had dined at Ramalhete and were having coffee in Afonso's study, the windows of which were open to the night. It was a warm night, starlit and serene. Craft, Sequeira and Taveira walked on the terrace smoking. In a corner of a sofa Cruges sat listening religiously to Steinbroken gravely describing the progress made in music in Finland. And the group around Afonso, who sat stretched out in his old armchair with pipe in hand, talked about the countryside.

At supper Afonso had announced his intention of going to visit the old trees of Santa Olávia towards the middle of the month, and a great pilgrimage of friendship to the banks of the Douro had immediately been arranged among the company. Craft and Sequeira would accompany Afonso, and the Marquis promised to visit him in August, 'in the melodious company', as he put it, of his friend Steinbroken. Dom Diogo hesitated, apprehensive about the long journey and the dampness of the village. Now they were trying to persuade Ega to go too, with Carlos, when Carlos had finished collecting the material for his book, a task which was retaining him in Lisbon, tied to his desk. But Ega resisted the idea. The country, in his opinion, was good only for savages. As man becomes more civilized, he grows away from nature; and the realization of Progress, of this Paradise on Earth which the Idealists predicted, he had imagined as an enormous city covering the entire globe, all houses and stone, with only here and there a little sacred rose-garden to supply the blossoms to perfume the altar of Justice.

'And what about corn? And fresh fruit and vegetables?' asked Vilaça laughing, with a touch of mischief in his voice.

Did Vilaça really imagine, retorted Ega, that in a couple of centuries' time they would still be eating vegetables? This plant-eating habit was a vestige of the animal still in man. With time the complete and civilized being would be nourished purely by artificial products in little bottles or in tablet form, made in state laboratories . . .

'The country,' suggested Dom Diogo, gravely twirling his moustache, 'has a certain advantage for society: it is good for a picnic, or a donkey-ride, or a game of croquet. Where would society be without it?'

'Oh, yes,' scoffed Ega, 'as a drawing-room with trees in it, I agree the countryside is acceptable.'

Ensconced in an armchair, smoking languidly, Carlos smiled in silence. All through dinner he had been like that, with a vague smile for everything in general, and a delicious air of languor. At this point the Marquis, who had already spoken to him twice, only to encounter the same radiant abstractedness, burst out impatiently:

'For goodness' sake, man, say something! You've got a most extraordinary look tonight, like some pious soul who's just been fed the host!'

Everyone studied Carlos: Vilaça thought he looked healthier and happier; Dom Diogo, with the air of one who knows about such things, sensed a woman in the picture, and envied him his youth and vigour. Afonso looked at his grandson with tenderness as he slowly filled his pipe.

Carlos got up at once to escape that affectionate scrutiny.

'It's true,' he said, stretching himself a little, 'I have felt languid and dull today. It must be the beginning of summer . . . But I must shake myself out of it! What about a game of billiards, Marquis?'

'Certainly, Maia. If that will bring you to life again . . .'

They went out and Ega followed them. No sooner were they in the corridor than the Marquis stopped as if he had just remembered something and asked Ega point-blank what was the latest news of the Cohens. Had he seen them recently? Was everything over? For the Marquis, the soul of loyalty, secrets did not exist. Ega told him that the affair had finished and now Cohen prudently lowered his eyes when they met.

'I asked,' said the Marquis, 'because I have seen Madame Cohen twice recently.'

'Where?' inquired Ega eagerly.

'In the Price, and both times accompanied by Damaso. The last time was just this week. And there was Damaso, all close and intimate, chatting away. He came and sat next to me for a few minutes but he didn't take his eyes off her. And she, on her side, with that haughty look of hers, constantly watching him through her lorgnette. There's something going on there, there's no doubt about that. That Cohen's predestined.'

Ega went livid, twisted his moustache nervously and finally said: 'Damaso is on very friendly terms with them. But perhaps he's having a try . . . I wouldn't be at all surprised. They're suited to one another.'

In the billiards-room, while the players lazily took their turns, Ega walked unceasingly up and down, obviously greatly disturbed, chewing on his cigar which had gone out. Suddenly he stopped in front of the Marquis, and his eyes were blazing.

'When did you say you last saw this sluttish daughter of Israel?'

'Tuesday I believe it was.'

Ega gloomily began his pacing again.

At this moment Baptista appeared at the door and with a wordless glance called Carlos over. Carlos came, somewhat surprised.

'There's a cabman outside,' said Baptista quietly. 'He says there's a lady in a carriage who wants to speak to you.'

'What lady?'

Baptista shrugged his shoulders. Carlos, cue in hand, looked at him in alarm. A lady! It must be Maria. What in heaven's name could have happened to bring her to Ramalhete at nine o'clock at night!

He sent Baptista to run and fetch a hat, and just as he was, in evening jacket and without a coat, he hurried anxiously downstairs. In the hall he met Eusèbiozinho who had just arrived and was carefully dusting his half-boots. Carlos did not even stop to speak but ran out to the coupé, standing at the private entrance to his rooms, all closed and silent, mysterious and alarming . . .

He opened the carriage-door. From the corner of the old carriage a black form wrapped in a lace mantilla, leant out to stammer nervously: 'It's only for a second! I want to talk to you!'

What a relief! It was the Countess de Gouvarinho! Then Carlos spoke brutally in his indignation.

'What damned fool's trick is this? What do you want?'

He was about to slam the door but she was pushing it open from inside, desperate to retain him; and then, unable to control herself, she burst out, there in front of the cabman who was calmly occupying himself with the buckle of the trace:

'Whose fault is it? Why are you treating me like this? Come inside, just for a second! I must talk to you!'

Carlos got in, furious.

'Drive round the Aterro,' he called to the driver. 'Slowly!'

The old coach started off down the hill; and for a moment in the darkness inside, backing away from each other on the narrow seat, they could only repeat the same bitter, brusque words above the noise of the rattling windows.

'How indiscreet! How ridiculous!'

'And whose fault is it? Whose fault?'

The coupé rolled more silently now on the macadam surface of the Santos ramp. And Carlos, already repenting of his harshness, turned towards her, and gently, in a tone almost as affectionate as formerly, reproved her for her recklessness. Wouldn't it have been wiser to have written?

'What for?' she cried. 'You wouldn't have replied. You just ignore my letters as if they were from someone begging charity.'

She was hot and breathless and pulled the mantilla from her head. As the coupé swayed leisurely and silently from side to side along the river edge, Carlos could hear her breathing, tumultuous gasps full of anguish. He sat there motionless and silent, horribly uncomfortable, catching a confused glimpse through the misty windows of the masts of boats on the sleepy sad stretch of river. The pair of horses seemed to be dropping to sleep, and her complaints went on and on, full of bitterness.

'I ask you to come to Santa Isabel and you don't come . . . I write to you and you don't even answer . . . I want a straightforward explanation, but you don't appear. Nothing, not even a card, not a word, not a hint of what's happened. Such a brutal show of contempt, so ill-mannered! I shouldn't have come, I know, but I couldn't help it. I just couldn't! I wanted to know what I had done. What is it? What have I done?'

Carlos felt her eyes, shining through a film of tears, seeking his in supplication. And without even the courage to look at her he murmured miserably:

'Really, my friend . . . Things speak for themselves, surely. Explanations aren't necessary.'

'Yes they are. I must know if this is just a passing mood, ill-humour you will get over, or if it is something definite, the end!'

He fidgeted in his corner, unable to find a kind way of telling her that he no longer had any desire for her. Finally he declared it was not ill-humour. His feelings for her had always been the highest; he was hardly likely to stoop to fits of sulkiness now.

'Then you mean this is the end?'

'No, not the end either. A definite parting, for ever, no . . .'

'Then it's just a passing mood? Why?'

Carlos did not answer. She shook his arm in desperation.

'But say something! Say something, in heaven's name! Don't be a coward, have the courage to tell me what's the matter!'

Yes, she was right. He was being a coward, it was unworthy of him to sit there like that, gauche and dissimulating in the shadows, stammering mean little excuses. He wanted to be strong, speak clearly.

'Well, here's the truth of the matter. I felt our relations should change somewhat . . .'

And again he hesitated. The truth melted away on his lips as he felt that woman at his side trembling with agony.

'By change, I mean . . . we could transform what has up to now been just a passionate whim and the sort of thing that cannot last, into a friendship which is both nobler and more agreeable.'

And gradually the words became easier, capable, persuasive, above the slow rumble of the wheels. Where could such a relationship lead? To the usual conclusion. One day everything would be discovered and their beautiful romance would end in shame and scandal, or else, through guarding their secret for too long, they would fall into a dull, almost conjugal union lacking both interest and elegance. And it was clear that if they continued to meet, here, there, in Cintra and so on, their social circle, ever inquisitive and tittle-tattling, would come to discover their affection. And was there anything more revolting for a person who had pride and delicacy, than a love affair that all the world knew about, even the cab-drivers in the square? No . . . common sense, and good taste even, pointed to a separation. She would be grateful to him later. Naturally this first breaking of a pleasant habit was disagreeable, and he himself felt far from happy about it. That's why he had not had the courage to write to her . . . But there, they must be strong, and not see each other for a few months at least. Then, gradually, what had been no more than a fragile fancy, full of uneasiness, would become a firm, secure and enduring friendship.

He stopped; then in the silence he heard her, slumped in the corner of the coupé like some wretched half-dead thing, huddled in her shawl, softly crying.

It was an intolerable moment. She wept humbly, without any violence, a slow, apparently endless sobbing. And Carlos could only repeat the same dull banal words:

'Don't be silly, don't be silly!'

They were moving along in front of a row of houses, now they were passing the gas-works. A brightly-lit tram hurried by with ladies dressed in light dresses. It was a warm starlit summer's night and people were wandering peacefully among the trees. She continued to weep.

That slow sobbing at his side began to move him and at the same time he almost loathed her for not being able to control these interminable tears which were tearing his heart. And he had been so happy there in Ramalhete, in his armchair, smiling at everything round him in that delicious state of lassitude!

He took her hand, hoping to calm her, full of pity – and impatience!

'Really there is no need for this. It's quite absurd. All this is for your own good . . .'

She stirred then, and wiped her eyes, and blew her nose loudly between heavy sobs. And then suddenly, in an impulsive burst of passion, she flung her arms round his neck, clasping him to her frenziedly, crushing him against her breast.

'Oh, my love! Don't leave me, don't leave me! If only you knew! You're the only happiness I've ever had in my life. I'll die, I'll kill myself! What have I done? No one knows about our love . . . And what if they did? I'd sacrifice everything for you, life, honour, everything! Everything!'

His face was wet with her tears, and he yielded, feeling that warm uncorseted body move on to his lap, and cleave to his body in a fury of desire, with ardent, wild kisses which took his breath away . . . Suddenly the cab stopped. And for a moment they stayed as they were: Carlos motionless, she sunk over him, her breast heaving.

But the cab remained still. Carlos extricated an arm and, letting down the window, found they were in front of Ramalhete

392

again. The driver, obeying their order, had driven round the Aterro, slowly, come back up the ramp and returned to the door of the house. For a moment Carlos felt tempted to get out and finish that long torment abruptly there and then. But it seemed too cruel. And hopelessly, detesting the woman, he shouted to the driver:

'Round the Aterro again, and keep moving!'

The carriage heaved resignedly round in the narrow street and rolled off again: again the cobbled roadway set the windows rattling; again, more smoothly, they descended the Santos ramp.

She began to kiss him once more. But her kisses had lost the flame that for a moment had made them almost irresistible. Now Carlos felt only weariness, an immeasurable longing to get back to his room, to the repose which she had invaded and dragged him from to torture him with these recriminations, with this tear-stained ardour . . . And suddenly, as the Countess hung on his neck, stumbling over her words as if she were out of her mind, he saw Maria Eduarda, a vivid, resplendent figure illuminating his soul, sitting at that moment in her red rep room, thinking of him, trusting in him, remembering the happiness of the previous day when Hideaway, full of their love, had slumbered, white among the trees . . . Then he felt a revulsion for the Countess and brutally pushed her to the corner of the carriage.

'That's enough! This is absurd. Our affair's over, and there's nothing more to say!'

She stopped for a moment as if stunned. Then she trembled, gave a nervous little laugh and pushed him back, pinching his arm.

'Right! Leave me! Leave me for the other one, for the Brazilian! I know all about *her* – an adventuress with a ruined husband and who needs someone to pay her dressmaker's bills!'

He turned on her with clenched fists as if he would beat her, and in the dark carriage, where a faint scent of verbena already hung, the eyes of each, unseen by the other, flashed hatred. Carlos banged furiously on the window, but the carriage did not stop. The Countess tried frantically to open the window on her side, hurting her fingers in the process.

'You'd better get out!' she said breathlessly. 'I can't bear being in here with you! I can't bear it! Driver! Driver!'

The old cab drew to a halt. Carlos leapt out and slammed the door, and without a word or even raising his hat, he turned his back and made his way to Ramalhete with long strides, still quivering and bitter in the still peace of the summer night.

4

IT WAS ON a Saturday that Afonso da Maia left for Santa Olávia. Early the same morning, which she considered auspicious, Maria Eduarda had installed herself in Olivais. And Carlos, returning from Santa Apolónia, where he had gone to see off his grandfather, said gaily to Ega:

'So here we are to stay and roast in the city of marble – and filth!'

'Better that,' replied Ega, 'than mincing around meditating in white shoes in the dust of Cintra!'

But on Sunday, when Carlos returned to Ramalhete at night-fall, Baptista announced that Senhor Ega had left just a few moments before for Cintra, taking with him only one or two books and clothes-brushes wrapped in a newspaper. Senhor Ega had left a letter, and told Baptista: 'Baptista, I'm going to pasture.'

The letter, written in pencil on a sheet of foolscap, said:

'I was suddenly overcome by a horror of the dross of Lisbon and an infinite longing for nature and greenery. The remains of animality, in this civilized and over-civilized being, calls out to roll in the grass, to drink from little brooks and be lulled to sleep in the swaying boughs of a chestnut tree. May the kind Baptista send on by bus tomorrow the case with which I had no desire to overload Mulato's carriage. I shall be gone for only three or four days. Time enough to chat a while with the Absolute, high up by the Capuchos, and see how the forget-me-nots are getting on beside the gentle lover's fountain . . .'

'Pedant!' growled Carlos, indignant at Ega's ungrateful desertion. And flinging aside the letter: 'Baptista! Senhor Ega says here that he wants a box of cigars sent – Imperiales. Send him Flor de Cuba. Imperiales are deadly. The beast doesn't even know how to smoke!'

After supper Carlos leafed through the *Figaro*, read a page or two of Byron, tried his hand at billiards in the empty room, whistled a *malagueña* on the terrace – and finally went out, with no destination in mind, towards the Aterro. Ramalhete was miserable like that, silent and dark, open to the heat of the night. He found himself making his way involuntarily to Rua de S. Francisco. Maria Eduarda's windows were also open and dark. He went up to the floor where Cruges lived. Master Vitorino was not in.

Cursing Ega, he went to the Grémio, where he found Taveira, jacket over his shoulders, reading the news. Nothing was happening in old Europe – just a few Nihilists hanged. Taveira was off to the Price.

'Come along with me, Carlinhos! They've got a pretty girl there who goes into a tank of water with crocodiles and snakes. I'm mad about these animal women! This one's not too easy though – she's brought her fancy man with her. But I've already written to her, and she gives me the eye a bit from the tank.'

He dragged Carlos off with him and as soon as they were in the Chiado he brought up the subject of Damaso. Hadn't he seen this flower of manhood lately? Well, this flower was going round proclaiming that Maia, after the Chiado incident, had offered him humble, cowardly excuses through a friend . . . A terrible fellow, that Damaso! He looked and sounded and acted like a child's rubber ball! The harder you flung him to the ground, the more triumphantly he'd bounce up again!

'Anyway, he's a treacherous rat, and you'd better be careful of him.'

Carlos shrugged his shoulders and laughed.

'No,' said Taveira seriously, 'I know my Damaso. When we had that scrap in Lola Gorda's house, he acted like the coward he is, but afterwards he did all he could to make my life a misery. He's capable of anything. The day before yesterday I was having supper in the Silva and he came and sat with me for a few minutes and straightway started on you, with gossip and threats.'

'Threats? What did he say?'

'He said you pretend you've got spunk but in a very short while you're going to find someone who'll teach you a lesson. That there's a monumental scandal brewing and he wouldn't be surprised to see you with a bullet through your head before very long.'

'A bullet?'

'That's what he said. You can laugh, but I know. If I were you, I'd go along to Damaso and say to him: "Look little

Damaso, flower of my heart, let me just warn you that from this moment onwards, every time I have any unpleasantness to put up with I'm going to come here and break one of your ribs; I should therefore take great care." '

They had reached the Price. A gay, gaping Sunday crowd filled the room right up to the back rows where young men sat in shirt-sleeves with bottles of wine; and there was loud coarse laughter at the antics of the clown with his painted red and white face who was touching the feet of a girl on horseback and then licking his fingers and turning up his eyes as if he had tasted ambrosia. She, a thin, serious creature with flowers in her hair, rested in the wide saddle upon a cloth of gold as her white horse, biting its rein, was led slowly round by an assistant; and all round the arena the foolish lecherous clown accompanied her, clasping his hands over his heart in a besotted supplication, his fat thighs wobbling in his sequin-studded bloomers. One of the company, in gold striped trousers, gave him a push in affected jealousy, and the clown fell full length with a loud bang as he hit the ground amid bursts of laughter from the children and a fanfare from the band. The heat was overpowering and the cigar smoke wafted up continuously to form a haze below the ceiling where the flames from the gas-lights flickered. Carlos found the atmosphere objectionable and made for the door.

'At least wait and see the crocodile woman,' called Taveira.

'I can't. The smell in here will kill me!'

But at the door he was stopped by the open arms of Alencar who was just arriving with another man, a tall old fellow with white whiskers and dressed in mourning. The poet was amazed to see his Carlos there. He had imagined him in Santa Olávia! He had even seen it in the papers.

'No,' said Carlos. 'It was Grandfather who went yesterday. I don't feel in the mood just yet for communing with nature.'

Alencar laughed, his cheeks slightly flushed and a glow in the hollow eye which suggested gin. At his side the bewhiskered ancient put on his black gloves.

'Well, with me it's just the opposite,' exclaimed the poet. 'I'm in need of a dose of pantheism. Beautiful, beautiful nature! The woods! The fields! So perhaps I'll spoil myself and be off to Cintra next week. The Cohens are there, they've rented a very pretty little house just past the Vitor.'

The Cohens! Carlos understood immediately Ega's disappearance and his 'longing for greenery'.

'Listen,' said the poet quietly, pulling him to one side. 'Don't you know this friend of mine? Your father thought a lot of him and the three of us had some good times together. He wasn't anyone important, he used to hire out horses. But here in Portugal especially in those days people were very good-natured and the aristocrat mixed with the muleteer. But what the deuce! You must know him! He's Damaso's uncle!'

Carlos could not remember him.

'It's Guimarães, the one from Paris!'

'Oh, the communist!'

'Yes, he's very much a republican, a man of humanitarian ideas, friend of Gambetta, writes in the *Rappel*. An interesting fellow! He's come here to see about some lands he's inherited from his brother, that other uncle of Damaso's who died a few months ago. And he's going to stay a while, I believe. Anyway, we had dinner together tonight, imbibed a little and were even talking about your father. Would you like me to introduce him?'

Carlos hesitated. Perhaps another time would be better, when they could smoke a leisurely cigar together and talk over the past.

'Excellent idea! You'll like him. He knows his Victor Hugo well and hates the sight of the clerical crew. Very broad-minded man, very broad-minded!'

The poet shook Carlos's two hands heartily, and Sr Guimarães raised his crape-bound hat slightly.

All the way back to Ramalhete Carlos thought about his father and the past, suddenly brought alive again by that old gentleman, one time horse-hirer and fellow-reveller of his father! And with these ideas came another which in the last few days had stubbornly dogged him and tormented him, a thought which amid all his radiant happiness had yet caused a pang of grief . . . Carlos thought of his grandfather.

It had been decided now that he and Maria Eduarda would leave for Italy at the end of October. Castro Gomes had stated in his last bleak, pretentious letter from Brazil that he would be 'making an appearance in Lisbon along with the refinements of the cold season, towards the middle of November'; and before that happened they had to be far away among the verdure of Isola Bella, hidden in their love and separated by it from the world as effectively as by the walls of a cloister. All this was simple, and indeed his heart deemed it almost legitimate and the idea filled his life with splendour. There was only one snag – his grandfather.

Carlos was going off with Maria, was going to achieve perfect felicity; but he was going to destroy once and for all old Afonso's happiness, and the noble peace and calm which had brought him such a contented old age. He was a man of bygone eras, austere and pure, one of those strong souls which would never know a moment of weakness, and in this frank, manly, clean-cut solution to a problem of indomitable love he would see only – libertinism! The natural espousal of souls, as something over and above fictitious civil laws, would mean nothing to him; and he would never understand this subtle sentimental ideology, with which they, like all transgressors, tried to cloak their errant ways. As far as Afonso was concerned he would be simply a man who was taking away another man's wife and another man's child, who was disrupting a family, destroying a home, and descending to concubinage. All the subtleties of passion, however beautiful and strong they were, would burst like soap-bubbles against the fundamental concepts of Duty, Justice, Society and Family, which stood solid as marble and upon which he had based his life for nearly a century. And it would break upon him like a horrible fatality: already his son's wife had run away with another man, leaving behind her a corpse, and now his grandson was doing the same, snatching away another man's family. The history of his family had thus become a repetition of adulteries and flights and dispersals under the vicious goad of the flesh! All the hopes Afonso had built around him would seem to have come to nothing, been dragged in the mud. In Afonso's embittered imagination he would from henceforth be a fugitive, a useless wastrel who had severed the roots which bound him to his native land, renounced the life which raised him in the esteem of his countrymen, a man who lived in foreign hotels and spoke a foreign tongue, surrounded by an equivocal family which sprang up like weeds over a ruin.

Sobering, tormenting thoughts, ever-present and implacable, which would poison his grandfather's last years of life. But what else could he do? It was as he had said to Ega: life was like that! He possessed neither the heroism nor saintliness which made sacrifice easy. And what did grandfather's displeasure spring from, after all? From prejudice. And he had rights to his happiness, by God! Rights bestowed by nature!

He had reached the end of the Aterro. The silent river merged into the darkness. Before very long *the other one* would be sailing in along this river from Brazil, *the other one* who even forgot to send a kiss to his daughter in his letters! Ah, if only he never returned! A providential wave might carry him away. Then everything would be so easy, so perfect and crystal-clear. What did the world want with this dried-out creature? It would be like an empty sack dropping into the sea. Ah, if only he were to die! And Carlos forgot his problems, transported with the vision of Maria calling to him, waiting for him, free, serene, smiling, covered in mourning . . .

Back in his room Baptista, watching him fling himself into an armchair with a weary, disconsolate sigh, coughed cheerfully and turned up the light and said: 'It seems rather lonely here now, without Senhor Ega . . .'

'It's lonely all right, and miserable,' murmured Carlos. 'We must shake ourselves out of it. I've already mentioned we'll probably be travelling this winter, haven't I?'

No, the master hadn't mentioned it.

'Well, perhaps we'll be going to Italy. Would you like to go back to Italy?'

Baptista reflected.

'The last time I didn't have a chance to see the Pope. And before I die I'd quite like to see the Pope.'

'Of course. We'll have to see to that. You must see the Pope.'

Baptista thought for a moment, then asked, casting a glance at himself in the mirror: 'One has to wear full dress to see the Pope, I believe?'

'Yes, I advise you to wear full dress. What you really want for occasions like this is the Order of Christ . . . I must see if I can't arrange the Order of Christ for you.'

Baptista stood for a moment in amazement. Then he blushed scarlet and said full of emotion: 'I'm most obliged to you, sir. There are people round here who have it who probably don't deserve it as much as I do . . . They say there are even barbers . . .'

'You're right,' replied Carlos seriously. 'It would be a disgrace. What I must try to get for you is the Order of the Conception!'

Every morning now Carlos travelled the dusty road to Olivais. To save exhausting his own horses in the excessive heat, he used the carriage belonging to Mulato, Ega's favourite driver, who would leave his pair of horses in the Hideaway's old stables and spend the hours till Carlos's return to Ramalhete loafing round the taverns.

Generally at midday, after lunching, Maria Eduarda would hear the coach rolling along the silent road and come to meet Carlos at the door at the top of the flower-lined steps, under the new pink awning. She always wore light-coloured dresses now in the country; sometimes there would be a flower, Spanish-fashion, in her hair, and the fresh healthy country air was giving a warmer tone to the ivory complexion. Every day Carlos was dazzled afresh by her simple radiant beauty as she stood there amid sunlight and foliage. As he closed the creaking gate Carlos felt himself immediately enveloped by an 'extraordinary moral euphoria' as he put it, in which his whole being seemed to move more easily, more smoothly, in a permanent atmosphere of harmony and sweetness. But his first kiss was always for Rosa, who ran up the acacia path to meet him, her heavy wave of black hair bobbing on her shoulders and Niniche at her side leaping and yelping with joy. He picked Rosa up. Maria, under the pink awning in the distance, smiled at them. Everything seemed peaceful and familiar in the luminous air of the garden.

Inside, the house had already taken on a more delicate air. Now they could use the large salon which had lost its museum-like formality, its atmosphere of bygone luxury: the flowers Maria had arranged in the vases, a newspaper which lay forgotten on a table, the embroidery wools, the simple rustling of her fresh dresses, had already conferred a subtle warmth and femininity to even the most stiff-necked Charles V chiffoniers, ornamented with burnished iron. And it was here that they sat talking until the time for Rosa's lessons.

Then Miss Sarah would appear, grave and reserved, always dressed in black with a silver horseshoe on her straight masculine collar. She had recovered her doll-like rosiness, and her lowered lashes wore an even more pronounced air of virginal shyness under the smooth puritan hair style. Plump and with a bosom like a well-fed pigeon's filling out the severe bodice, she looked wholly content with the slow, calm village life. But those dry brownish olive groves hardly seemed like country to her: 'It is very arid, very hard,' she said, with a vague yearning for the damp green hills of England and for the dim grey skies covered in mist.

At two o'clock punctually Rosa's long lessons began in the rooms upstairs. Then Carlos and Maria would take refuge, more at their ease, in the Japanese summer-house which Craft's love for Japan had bid him build at the end of the acacia path, taking advantage of a bucolic spot shaded by two chestnut trees. Maria had taken a fancy to this nook and called it her *pensadouro*. It was built entirely of wood, with a single circular window and a pointed Japanese roof where the branches rustled – so softly that above the sound one could hear the cheeping of birds. Craft had covered the floor with fine Indian mats, and it was furnished soberly with one lacquered table and some Japanese china; the roof was concealed under a yellow silk drapery which was caught up at the four corners like the rich festoons of a princely tent; and the whole light summer-house seemed to have been constructed for the sole purpose of sheltering a soft low divan, which had the languor of the harem about it, was deep enough for any sort of dream, wide enough for any kind of sloth.

They would enter – Carlos carrying a book he had chosen in the presence of Miss Sarah, and Maria Eduarda with a piece of embroidery or sewing. But book and embroidery immediately fell to the floor, and their lips and arms clung together impetuously. She dropped to the divan; Carlos knelt before her on a cushion, trembling and impatient after the control imposed by the presence of Rosa and Sarah – and there he stayed, clinging to her waist, stammering a thousand and one puerile and ardent things between the long kisses which left them both limp with their eyes closed in a sweet swoon. She wanted to know what he had done during the long, long night of separation. And Carlos had nothing to tell her save that he had thought of her and dreamt of her . . . Then silence reigned; the sparrows outside twittered, the doves cooed on the light roof, and Niniche, who always accompanied them, lay curled up in a corner following their murmurings and their silences with a black suspicious eye shining from behind the silver hair.

Outside, on these calm, airless days, the dry garden, all dusty green, would sleep under the motionless leaves, under the weight of the sun. The only sound from behind the closed shutters of the white house, were the lethargic strains of the piano as Rosa practised her scales. And in the summer-house too there was a full, contented silence – broken only by a languorous sigh from the silken cushions of the divan, or by a more than usually ardent and lingering kiss. It was Niniche who would drag them out of this sweet torpor, tired of sitting there quiet, confined within those hot wooden walls, breathing air already impregnated with that indefinable aroma which had a touch of jasmine in it.

Slowly, wiping her hands over her face, Maria would get up – but then fall again at Carlos's feet in infinite gratitude. Dear God, what this moment of separation cost her! Why did it have to be like this? It seemed so unnatural, they being espoused as they were, that she should stay there all night alone with her desire for him, while he went off to sleep without her caresses, in solitude, at Ramalhete! And still they remained there, in an ecstatic silence, while their eyes lingered on each other's, continuing the kiss that expired on their weary lips. Niniche it was who made them move eventually, Niniche trotting impatiently back and forth from door to divan, growling, threatening to bark.

Maria often felt uneasy as they returned. What must Miss Sarah think of their siestas, shut in like that, without a sound, behind a closed window? Melanie had been in Maria's service since childhood and was in her confidence; good Domingos was an imbecile and didn't count; but Miss Sarah? Maria confessed with a smile that she felt rather ashamed when she met the English girl's eyes at table – such innocent eyes under the smooth virginal hair. Of course if the good girl so much as muttered a disapproving sound or gave the slightest frown, she would straightway receive her ticket on the next Royal Mail bound for Southampton! Rosa would not be sorry, she had no affection for her governess. But she was such a good, serious girl, and she admired her mistress so! She would not like to lose the respect of such a serious-minded girl. So they decided to get rid of Miss Sarah, pay her regally and replace her at a later date in Italy with a German governess, for whom they would be a married couple, 'Monsieur et Madame'.

But gradually they felt the need for a more intimate, more

complete relationship. These brief hours on the divan, with the birds singing above and the garden full of sun and life, no longer satisfied them. They longed for the bliss of a full night together when their arms could entwine without encountering garments, when everything around, people and light, slept. And it was so simple! The tapestry room which adjoined Maria's bedroom had french windows which opened on to the garden; the governess and servants went up to their rooms on the floor above at ten o'clock, and the house settled down to sleep. Carlos had a key to the gate and the only dog in the house, Niniche, was already a loyal confidante of their kisses.

Maria desired this night together as ardently as he did. One night, as dusk was falling and they were returning from a cool walk in the fields, they tried the duplicate key – which Carlos had already promised to have gilded – and he was surprised to find the old gate, which always creaked abominably on its hinges, now swung back in oiled silence.

He came that very night, leaving Mulato, a discreet driver whose pockets he was fattening with tips, in the village to collect him in the morning. It was a close, sultry sky, without a single star; and on the water burst the pale brilliance of a lightning-flash from time to time. Carlos, creeping along with unnecessary caution close to the wall, felt a vague intimidating melancholy now that he was actually approaching this so ardently desired moment of possession. He was almost trembling as he opened the gate, and stopped abruptly after the first steps when he heard Niniche barking furiously from within the house. But everything grew still and from the window in the corner which led on to the garden he saw a reassuring light. There he found Maria in a lace nightgown standing by the glass door, almost smothering the still growling Niniche in her arms. She was extremely nervous and anxious to feel him at her side, so that she did not want to go in immediately, and they stayed there for a moment, sitting on the steps with Niniche who had calmed down now and was licking Carlos. A pitch-black night enshrouded everything; only far down on the water, a lonely wan light flickered in the darkness from a ship's mast. Maria, nestling close to Carlos, sheltering in him, gave a long sigh, and her eyes explored uneasily those silent shadows where the familiar bushes of the garden seemed to lose all reality and dissolve into the gloom.

404

'Why don't we go to Italy now?' she asked suddenly, reaching for Carlos's hand. 'If we are going, why not go immediately? It would avoid all this secrecy and fear.'

'Fear of what, my love? We are as safe here as we should be in Italy, or China even. Still, we can go earlier if you like. You decide when; you set the day!'

She didn't answer, but let her head fall on Carlos's shoulder. He added slowly:

'At any rate, you realize I must go to Santa Olávia first, to see my grandfather.'

Maria gazed distractedly into the gloom again, as if seeing there the presentiment of a future where everything would be dark and confused.

'You have Santa Olávia and your grandfather and your friends . . . I haven't got anybody!'

Carlos held her closer, moved by her words.

'You haven't got anybody indeed! To say such a thing to me! But I won't say you are being unfair, or even ungrateful; it's just nervousness, and what the English call the rash adulteration of a fact.'

She stayed nestled against Carlos's breast, as if she were in a swoon.

'I don't know why, but I'd like to die . . .'

A brilliant flash of lightning lit up the river. Maria was frightened and they went into the bedroom. There the candles in the two candelabra shone upon the damask and the yellow silk draperies and filled the tepid, faintly perfumed air with all the ardent splendour of a sanctuary: and the lace-bordered sheets on the opened bed gave a chaste snow-white freshness to the amorous and flame-coloured opulence. Outside, far out over the sea, a roll of thunder sounded slow and heavy. But Maria no longer heard the night, for she was in Carlos's arms. Never had she desired him, adored him so much! It seemed her avid kisses wanted to reach farther than the flesh, penetrate and devour his very soul. And all night, amid these splendid brocades, with her hair loose, and looking divine in her nakedness, she seemed to have turned into the goddess he had always imagined her, and she had at last claimed him, clasping him to her immortal breast, soaring with him now in a celebration of love, high above on clouds of gold.

When he left in the morning it was raining. He found Mulato in a drunken sleep in a tavern, so he had to put him inside the carriage and take the reins himself back to Ramalhete. But wrapped in a cloak the tavern-keeper had lent him, drenched to the skin and humming for joy, he felt sublimely happy.

A few days later, as he was walking with Maria in the lanes around Hideaway, Carlos noticed a little house to let at the side of the road. It occurred to him that it might be a good idea to take it, and so avoid those disagreeable morning departures when Mulato, drowsy and half-drunk, shook the life out of the carriage on the stony road back to Ramalhete. They went to see the house: there was one large room which would make a comfortable enough retreat once it was furnished with carpet and curtains. He took it there and then, and Baptista came the following day with furniture to put this new little nest in order.

Maria sounded almost sad as she remarked: 'Yet another house!'

'This is the last,' promised Carlos, laughing. 'No, it's the last but one – we still have one more, the real one, our own, far away, I don't know where . . .'

They began to see each other every night now. Punctually at half past nine, Carlos would leave Hideaway smoking his cigar, with Domingos ahead to light his way and close the gate behind him and take out the key. He would make his way to his cottage where a single servant looked after him – the young son of the gardener of Ramalhete. A loose carpet covered the wooden floor and apart from the bed there was only a table, a striped sofa and two cane-seated chairs. Carlos whiled away the hours that separated him from Maria by writing to Santa Olávia and often to Ega, who had taken permanent root in Cintra.

He had received two letters from him, and those entirely occupied with Damaso. Damaso was seen everywhere with Madame Cohen; Damaso had made himself look a fool in a donkey-race; Damaso had sported a veiled hat in Seteais; Damaso was a filthy beast; Damaso, in the patio of the Vitor, would cross his leg and familiarly speak of 'Rachel'. It was a matter of public duty to give the man a thrashing!

Carlos shrugged his shoulders and found such jealousy unworthy of Ega. And for whom? For that stuck-up Israelite, that indolent sweet-as-syrup female who'd had a caning from her husband! 'If she has, indeed, stooped from you to Damaso, you must behave as you would with a cigar that drops in the mud; you cannot retrieve it of course; you must let the lad who picks it up smoke it in peace – to get angry with the lad, or with the cigar, is idiotic.' But generally when he wrote to Ega he spoke only of Olivais, and the walks he had taken with Maria, and the things she had said, and her charm, her distinction . . . But to his grandfather he found nothing to say: in the ten lines or so he addressed to him he described the heat and advised him not to overtire himself, sent his regards to his guests and gave him messages from Manuelzinho – whom he never saw.

When he had no letters to write he would lie on the sofa with an open book and his eyes on the hands of the clock. At midnight he would leave the house, wrapped in a hooded coat and with stick in hand. And his steps echoed across the lonely fields with a vague melancholy of secrecy and guilt . . .

One night when the heat was excessive Carlos, tired out, fell asleep on the sofa, and only woke with a start when the clock on the wall was drearily striking two o'clock. How infuriating! There was his night of love gone! And Maria was waiting anxiously for him for certain, imagining all kinds of accidents! He snatched up his stick and went running off up the lane. Then, as he stealthily opened the garden-gate, he thought perhaps Maria had fallen asleep by now, and Niniche might start barking; he crept very carefully, with muffled steps, up the acacia path. And suddenly, at his side, from the grass under the branches, he heard a man's ardent, heavy breathing and the sound of kisses. He stopped, utterly amazed. His first impulse was to smash his stick down on those two animals writhing on the lawn there, defiling the poetic retreat of his love. In the darkness a glimpse of white skirt moved and he heard a dazed voice gasp in English: 'Oh yes, oh yes . . .' It was the English girl!

Oh, good heavens above, it was Miss Sarah! Stunned, Carlos stole back through the gate, shut it softly, and went a little way off to wait in a recess of the wall, screened by the overhanging branches of an ash tree. And he trembled with indignation. He must tell Maria about this abominable affair immediately! He didn't want her to keep this immoral creature a moment longer beside little Rosa, sullying the innocence of his angel. Such hypocrisy was incredible, so astute and methodical she was, never losing her composure for an instant. Only a day or two before he had seen the creature turn her eyes away from a drawing in the *Ilustração*, where a chaste shepherd and his shepherdess were depicted kissing each other in a bucolic grove. Now here she was grunting and rolling on the grass!

On the dark road, just outside the gate, a cigarette glowed. A man passed, big and heavy, with a blanket flung round his shoulders. He looked like a labourer. The good Miss Sarah was evidently not fussy then! There she was, spruce and clean and very correct in her appearance with her carefully smoothed puritan locks, accepting just anybody, it didn't matter how coarse and dirty as long as it was male! And for months now she had been deceiving them like that with her two completely separate lives! By day, virginal, severe, always blushing, with her Bible in her sewing-basket; by night, while the child slept and with her daily tasks over, the saint became a beast and with shawl flung round her shoulders, off she'd be, up the garden and down on the grass with anyone! What a fine story for Ega!

He returned to the gate, opened it slowly and once more, deadening the sound of his steps, walked up the dark acacia path. He was beginning to feel doubtful now about telling Maria about the abominable affair. In spite of himself, he realized that Maria too was waiting for him, her bed invitingly open in the silent, sleeping house; and he too was penetrating the darkness, furtively, like the man in the blanket . . . Of course their case was different! There was all the difference in the world between the divine and the bestial! Yet he feared awakening Maria's delicate scruples by showing her, parallel to their own refined love affair conducted among golden-hued brocades, this other rude love, as secret and illegitimate as her own, enacted animal-like in the grass . . . It would be like showing her an image of her own guilt, somewhat turbid and coarser, but similar in outline, deplorably similar . . . No, he would say nothing. And the child? Oh, in her conduct with Rosa, Miss Sarah would continue the same assiduous puritan as always, grave and orderly as ever.

A light still showed through the glass doors; he tossed a little earth at the windows and then knocked softly. Maria appeared, untidily wrapped in a gown, fastening her hair which had come undone, and half asleep.

'Why are you so late?'

Carlos slowly and tenderly kissed the beautiful heavy eyes, almost closed now under the weight of sleep.

'I fell asleep like a fool while I was reading. Then when I did arrive I thought I heard footsteps in the garden and I had a look round. Just my imagination, of course.'

'We ought to have a watchdog,' she murmured, stretching herself.

Sitting on the edge of the bed, her arms hanging and inert, she smiled at her own laziness.

'You're so tired, darling! Shall I go?'

She pulled him to her warm, perfumed bosom:

'*Je veux que tu m'aimes beaucoup, beaucoup, et longtemps . . .*'

He did not return to Lisbon the following day and turned up early at Hideaway. Melanie, who was dusting the summer-house, said that Madame, a little tired that morning, was having her chocolate in bed. He entered the salon: in front of the open window, seated on the cork bench, Miss Sarah was sewing under the shade of the trees.

'Good morning,' said Carlos, going over to the balcony, full of curiosity as to how she would appear this morning.

'Good morning, sir,' she answered with her usual shy, modest air.

Carlos spoke of the weather. Miss Sarah found the heat already unbearable at that hour. Fortunately the view of the river down there was refreshing to the senses.

And last night was terribly close, wasn't it, insisted Carlos, lighting a cigarette. He had not been able to sleep. What about her?

Oh, she had slept like a top. Carlos inquired whether she had had pleasant dreams.

'Oh yes, sir!'

Oh yes! But now it was a chaste *yes* with no moans but downcast eyes. And she was so correct, so prim and so apparently virginal! It was really extraordinary! And Carlos, twirling his moustaches, thought what well-formed white breasts she must have!

So the summer was passing in Olivais. At the beginning of September Carlos had a letter from his grandfather telling him that Craft would be arriving at the Hotel Central the following Saturday, and he hurried there early that morning to hear the latest news from Santa Olávia. He found Craft already up and standing before the mirror, shaving. In a corner of the sofa sat Eusèbiozinho, who had arrived the night before from Cintra and was also staying at the Central; he sat now in silence, covered in mourning, cleaning his finger-nails with a pen-knife.

Craft had returned from his visit absolutely enchanted with Santa Olávia. He could not understand how Afonso, a robust north-countryman, could tolerate the Rua de Janelas Verdes and the stuffy little garden of Ramalhete! And he had been treated regally. His grandfather, bursting with good health, had offered them hospitality which brought to mind Abraham and the Bible. Sequeira was in top form, eating so much that he was rendered useless after dinner, groaning fit to burst from the depths of an armchair. He had met old Travassos while he was there, who spoke continually with tears in his eyes, of 'the talent of our dear colleague Carlos'. And the Marquis was looking splendid, clasping to him with parental affection all the petty aristocracy of Lamego, and in love at the moment with a boat-girl. Then there were the superb dinners, a few rabbit-hunts, a pilgrimage, girls dancing in the church-square, nights spent listening to the guitar, days spent watching the husks stripped off the maize – all the sweet pleasures of a Portuguese idyll . . .

'But we must have a serious talk about Santa Olávia,' finished Craft, going into the washing recess to give himself a shampoo.

'And what about you?' asked Carlos, turning to Eusèbiozinho. 'You've been in Cintra, haven't you? What's been going on there? How's Ega?'

Eusèbiozinho got up, putting away his pen-knife and straightening his glasses.

'He's there in the Vitor, very witty as always. He's bought himself a donkey. Damaso's staying there too. But you don't see much of him, he never leaves the Cohens' side. It hasn't been so bad on the whole, quite warm . . .'

'Were you with the same prostitute this time – Lola?'

Eusèbiozinho flushed scarlet. God forbid such a thing! He had been staying most respectably in the Vitor! He'd seen Palma with a Portuguese girl, it's true. He had a newspaper now, *The Devil's Trumpet..*

'*The Trumpet?*'

'Yes, the Devil's,' said Eusèbiozinho. 'It's a paper full of quips and scandal. It already existed under the name of *The Whistle* but now it's in Palma's hands and he's going to enlarge the format, put more jokes into it . . .'

'All in all, something filthy and greasy – like himself . . .'

Craft reappeared at this moment, drying his head. And while he dressed, he spoke of a journey he had been planning in Santa Olávia. Now that he no longer had Hideaway and his house in Oporto needed a lot of redecorating, he was thinking of spending the winter in Egypt, sailing up the Nile, in spiritual communication with the Pharaonic past. Then perhaps he'd go on to Baghdad and see the Euphrates and Babylonia.

So that's why I noticed that book over there on the table,' exclaimed Carlos, '*Nineveh and Babylonia.* What the deuce, old man! Do you enjoy these things? I personally have a horror of dead races and civilizations. Only life interests me.'

'That's because you're a sensualist,' said Craft. 'And talking of sensualism and Babylonia, will you have lunch with me at the Bragança? I have to meet an Englishman there, the one who looks after the mines. But we'll have to go by way of Rua d'Ouro as I want to drop in at my agent's den for a moment. And let's get going, it's midday!'

They left Eusèbiozinho downstairs in the lounge adjusting his lugubrious dark glasses to peer at the news. As soon as they were outside, Craft put his arm through Carlos's and told him that the serious matter he had mentioned regarding Santa Olávia was his grandfather's visible disappointment that he had not yet visited him.

'Your grandfather did not say anything to me, but I know he is very unhappy about it. And there is no excuse, as it only means a couple of hours' journey. You know how he adores you. What the deuce! *Est modus in rebus.*'

'Definitely,' murmured Carlos. 'I ought to have gone. But what do you expect, my friend? Still, that's that: I must make an effort! Perhaps I'll go up next week with Ega.'

'That's it. It will please him so much. Stay there for a few weeks . . .'

411

'*Est modus in rebus*: I'll see if I can manage a few days.'

Craft's agent's den was just opposite the Montepio, the state-operated pawnshop. Carlos waited for a few moments, strolling by the shops and glancing in the windows, when suddenly he saw Melanie coming out of the Montepio, with a plump matron in a red hat at her side. Surprised to see Carlos, she crossed the road and stood as if she had been caught red-handed at something. She blushed, and without waiting for his question, stammered that Madam had given her leave to come to Lisbon and she had been accompanying her friend. An old carriage drawn by a pair of white horses was standing there at the sidewalk. Melanie hastily jumped in and the old vehicle crumbled off towards Terreiro do Paço.

Carlos watched it go in amazement. And Craft, joining him at that moment, recognized the ramshackle old calèche belonging to Torto from Olivais – a vehicle he had used occasionally when he'd come to parade himself in Lisbon.

'Was it someone from Hideaway?' he asked.

'A maid,' answered Carlos, still astonished at Melanie's strange embarrassment.

They began to walk, then he stopped and lowered his voice under the noise of the traffic.

'Tell me, did Eusèbiozinho say anything about me, Craft?'

Craft confessed that Eusèbiozinho had no sooner entered the room than he had begun informing him, mincing matters somewhat, of the mysterious life Carlos was leading in Olivais.

'But I silenced him,' went on Craft, 'by telling him I was so little inquisitive that I had never even got round to reading *The History of Rome* . . . Anyway, you still ought to go to Santa Olávia.'

Carlos spoke to Maria that evening about the visit he owed to his grandfather. She gravely agreed that he should go and regretted having selfishly kept him there for so long, far from the other people who loved him.

'But, my dear, it won't be for long, will it?'

'For two or three days at the most. And naturally I'll bring Grandfather back with me. He's not doing anything up there, and I don't want to have to go up there again.'

Then Maria threw her arms round his neck and, very quietly and shyly, confessed a secret desire she had: she longed to see

412

Ramalhete! She wanted to visit his rooms and the garden and all those places where he had thought of her so often in despair, believing her cold and inaccessible.

'Tell me, would you like me to come? But it must be before your grandfather returns. Shall we?'

'I think it's a wonderful idea! There's only one danger. I'll probably never let you out again and keep you there and devour you in my den.'

'Would to God that you would!'

They arranged that she should have dinner at Ramalhete the evening Carlos was going to Santa Olávia. At dusk she would take him to Santa Apolónia in the coupé and then continue back to Olivais.

This was on Saturday. Carlos came to Ramalhete early, and his heart beat fast with the same delicious sensation as before a first rendezvous, when he heard Maria's carriage stop at the door and her dark clothes rustle along the cerise-coloured carpet which lined the discreet stairway to his rooms. The kiss they exchanged in the antechamber had all the profound tenderness of a first kiss.

She went to the dressing-table to take off her hat and tidy her hair. He could not stop kissing her; he caught her round the waist and, faces close together, they smiled into the mirror, delighted with the youthful reflections there. Then, impatient and curious, she went through his rooms very thoroughly, even visiting the washing recess; she read the titles on books, smelt the perfume in bottles, and opened the silk curtains of the bed. On a Louis XV chest of drawers there was a silver salver piled with photographs which Carlos had forgotten to hide – the Hussar colonel's wife in riding habit; Madame Rughel *décolletée* and several others. She plunged her hands into this profusion of memories with a sad smile. Carlos laughed and begged her not to look at these 'misguided wanderings of my heart'.

'Why not?' asked Maria gravely. She knew quite well that he had not descended from the clouds, pure as a seraph. There were always photos in a man's past. On the other hand she was sure he had never loved any of the others as he loved her.

'It's almost sacrilege to talk of these chance affairs in terms of love,' murmured Carlos. 'They're merely like rooms of inns where one has spent a night.'

413

Maria was studying the photo of the Hussar colonel's wife. She found her extremely pretty! Who was she? Was she French?

'No, she came from Vienna. She was the wife of an agent of mine, a business-man . . . They were quiet folk, lived in the country . . .'

'Ah! A Viennese . . . They say the women of Vienna have a special charm.'

Carlos drew the photograph out of her hand. Why must they talk of other women? There was only one woman for him in the whole world, and he was holding her there now, close to his heart.

They went all over Ramalhete, even on to the terrace. She liked Afonso's study particularly, with its damask furnishings like a prelate's chamber and the severe atmosphere of studious calm. 'I don't know why,' she murmured, giving a long slow glance over the heavy book-shelves and the crucified Christ, 'I don't know why, but your grandfather frightens me!'

Carlos laughed. What nonsense! If Grandfather knew her he would pay court to her with all the gallantry in the world! He was a perfect saint! And a handsome old man too!

'Was he a man of passionate love affairs?'

'I don't know; perhaps. But I believe Grandfather has always been a puritan.'

They went down to the garden, which also pleased her, quiet and bourgeois as it was, with its little waterfall cascading with a gentle babbling rhythm. They sat a moment under the old cedar, beside a rustic stone table with barely discernible letters carved in it and an ancient date; Maria found the trilling of the birds in the branches above prettier than any other birds' song she had heard; then she picked a branch to take back with her as a souvenir.

Just as they were, bareheaded, they went to see the coachhouses: the gate-keeper stood, cap in hand, gaping in amazement at the lady, so lovely and so fair, and the first he had ever seen in Ramalhete! Maria fondled the horses, and especially Tunante, who had brought Carlos so many times to Rua de S. Francisco. For Carlos these simple gestures had all the incomparable grace and tenderness of the perfect wife.

They returned to Carlos's private staircase, which Maria found

414

mysterious with heavy cerise velvet carpeting it like a coffer, deadening the sound of skirts. Carlos swore that no other skirts had ever passed there – unless you counted the ones worn by Ega once when he dressed up as a fisherwoman.

He left her for a moment in his room while he went to speak to Baptista; but when he returned he found her sitting in a corner of the sofa, looking so dejected and crestfallen that he took her hands in alarm.

'What's the matter, my love? Don't you feel well?'

She slowly raised her eyes which glistened behind a mist of tears.

'To think that you are leaving this beautiful house, and your comfortable life and peace and friends – all for me! It makes me sad, it's such a weight upon my conscience!'

Carlos knelt at her side, smiling at her scruples, calling her silly, and kissing dry the tears which rolled down her cheeks. Did she consider then that the little waterfall in the garden and a few worn carpets were worth more than she?

'All I regret is sacrificing so little, my dear Maria, when you are sacrificing so much!'

She gave a bitter little shrug of her shoulders.

'I!'

She ran her fingers through his hair and pulled him to her bosom, then began to speak quietly, as if to herself, to calm the hesitations and doubts in her heart.

'No, it's true. There's nothing else in the world as important as our love! Nothing in the world! If it is true and strong, all the rest is vain and futile, nothing else matters . . .'

Carlos silenced her with kisses and led her to the bed – where he had often thought of her in despair as of an unapproachable goddess.

At five o'clock they began to think of dinner. The table had been laid in a small room which Carlos had for some time been meaning to redecorate with draperies of pearl and tea-rose coloured satins. But it had not yet been arranged and the walls were still papered in dark green. Carlos had recently hung his father's painting there – a nondescript portrait showing a pale youth with large eyes and yellow suède gloves and a whip in his hand.

Baptista served them, already wearing his light travelling suit. The small round table looked like a basket of flowers; the champagne stood in ice in a silver bucket and on the sideboard the dish of sweet rice bore Maria's initials.

Such careful attentions made her smile with tenderness. Then she noticed Pedro da Maia's portrait and studied the discoloured face which time had turned livid, and from which the languid black Arabian eyes looked out scornfully.

'Who's that?' she asked.

'My father.'

She went closer to examine it more carefully, lifting a candle to see better. She didn't think Carlos took after his father. And turning to him gravely as he uncorked a bottle of old Chambertin with great reverence:

'Do you know whom you remind me of sometimes? It's extraordinary but it's true. You remind me of my mother!'

Carlos laughed, delighted with such a similarity that bound them closer together, and flattered him at the same time.

'You're right,' she said, 'for Mama was very beautiful. But it's true, there's something about the forehead, and the nose . . . But most of all in certain gestures, your way of smiling . . . And another way you have of looking vague, absent-minded . . . I've thought about it a lot.'

Baptista came in with a Japanese tureen. And Carlos gaily announced a Portuguese-style dinner. M. Antoine, the French chef, had accompanied his grandfather, and he had been left with Micaela, the other cook, whom he considered marvellous and who retained the cooking traditions of the nuns of the time of Dom João V.

'So to start with, my dear Maria, you have a chicken broth such as you would only eat in Odivelas in Mother Paula's cell, on nights of mystical union . . .'

The dinner was delicious. When Baptista left them they clasped hands for an instant over the flowers. Never had Carlos found Maria so pretty, so perfect: her eyes seemed to emit even more tenderness than usual; in the single rose which she wore on her breast he perceived her unfailing taste. And the same desire assailed them both – to stay there for ever, in those comfortable bachelor rooms with Portuguese suppers from the era of Dom João V served informally by Baptista.

'I feel like missing the train,' said Carlos, as if imploring her approval.

416

'No, you must go. We must not be selfish. Just be sure you don't forget to send me a long telegram every day. Telegrams were invented for separated lovers, Mama used to say.'

Then Carlos began to joke again about his supposed likeness to her mother. And bending down to cool the champagne in the ice, he said:

'It's strange that you have never told me before. But then you have never spoken about your mother at all.'

A slight flush tinged Maria Eduarda's face. Oh, she had never spoken of her mother because the subject had never arisen.

'Anyway, there's nothing very exciting to tell,' she went on. 'Mama came from Madeira, she was not rich, she married . . .'

'In Paris?'

'No, she married in Madeira, to an Austrian who had gone there with a brother who was consumptive. He was a very distinguished man, he saw Mama, who was extremely beautiful, they fell in love, *et voilà* . . .'

She said this slowly, without lifting her eyes from her place, cutting a chicken wing.

'Then if your father was Austrian, my love, you are Austrian too,' exclaimed Carlos. 'Perhaps you are one of these Viennese women that you say have such charm!'

Yes, she supposed, as far as the legal aspect was concerned, she was Austrian. But she had never known her father, she had always lived with her mother, always spoken Portuguese and always considered herself Portuguese. She had never been in Austria and couldn't even speak German.

'No brothers or sisters?'

'I had a little sister but she died when she was small. I don't remember her, but I have a picture of her in Paris. She was so pretty!'

At this moment a carriage stopped in the road below. Carlos, surprised, ran to the window, napkin in hand.

'It's Ega!' he cried. 'The rascal's back at last from Cintra!'

Maria also got to her feet, looking uneasy. For a moment they stood there, looking at each other, hesitating as to what to do. But Ega was like a brother to Carlos. He had only been waiting for Ega to return from Cintra to take him to Hideaway. It was even better that they should meet here, easily and naturally.

'Baptista!' called Carlos, hesitating no longer. 'Tell Senhor Ega that I am having dinner and to come in here.'

Maria sat down again, very pink, hastily arranging the pins in her hair, which had been put up in a hurry and was a little disarranged.

The door opened – and Ega stopped short in amazement, quite intimidated, with his white hat and white sunshade and a grey-wrapped bundle under his arm.

'Maria,' said Carlos, 'here, at last, you have my dear friend Ega.'

And to Ega he said simply: 'Maria Eduarda.'

Ega in confusion was trying to put aside the parcel to shake Maria Eduarda's hand which she was offering him, pink-faced and smiling. But the grey paper, clumsily tied, fell open – and a shower of fresh Cintra cheese-cakes rolled and squashed on to the flowered carpet. At this, all embarrassment was dispelled amid a burst of merry laughter – while Ega disconsolately opened wide his arms over the ruins of his dessert.

'Have you eaten?' asked Carlos.

No, he hadn't had dinner yet. But he'd already caught sight of a national delicacy – egg dessert – which he found particularly inviting after the horrible cuisine of the Vitor. What cooking! Lugubrious dishes, translated from the French into slang, like the comedies shown at the Ginásio.

'Then to the attack, man!' cried Carlos. 'Quick, Baptista! Bring back the chicken broth! Oh, there's still time! Did you know I'm off to Santa Olávia today?'

'Of course I knew. I received your letter; that's why I came. But I cannot eat like this, all covered in dust, and with such a bucolic jacket too . . . Have the broth kept hot, Baptista! Look, have everything kept hot, because I'm as hungry as an Arcadian shepherd!'

Baptista had served coffee, and the lady's carriage, which was to take them to Santa Apolónia, was already waiting ready with his case outside. But Ega wanted to talk, assured them that they had time and took out his watch. It had stopped. He said that in the country he went by the sun, as the flowers and birds did.

'Are you staying in Lisbon now?' asked Maria Eduarda.

'No, senhora, at least only long enough to do my duty as a

citizen and walk up and down the Chiado two or three times. Then I must return to the grass. Cintra is beginning to be interesting for me now that there is hardly anyone there. Cintra in the summer, full of bourgeois, reminds me of an idyll blotched with grease marks.'

But Baptista was pouring Carlos a glass of Chartreuse now and insisting that he should not linger unless he was deliberately intending to miss the train. Maria got up immediately and went inside to put on her hat. The two friends, left alone, were silent for a moment as Carlos slowly lit his cigar.

'How long will you be away?' asked Ega finally.

'Three or four days. And don't you go back to Cintra before I return. We need to talk . . . What the devil have you been doing there?'

Ega shrugged his shoulders.

'I've been absorbing fresh air and picking flowers, and murmuring: "How delightful all this is!" from time to time, and so forth.'

Then, leaning over the table and sticking an olive, he went on: 'Apart from that, nothing. Damaso's there. And always with the Cohen woman, as I told you in my letters. There's obviously nothing between them – it's just done to annoy me. That Damaso's a swine! And I'm only waiting for an opportunity. I'll throttle him!'

He gave a sharp tug on his cuffs and a flush of anger spread over his tanned face.

'I still speak to him, of course, shake his hand and call him "dear Damaso", and so on, but I'm only waiting for an opportunity. The animal must be annihilated. It's a moral duty, a matter of public cleanliness, to wipe out that nasty blob of human sludge.'

'Who else was there?' asked Carlos.

'Who are you interested in? The Countess de Gouvarinho. But I only saw her once. She has been making few appearances, poor soul, now that she's in mourning.'

'In mourning?'

'For you.'

He stopped. Maria had returned, her veil down, just finishing buttoning her gloves. Then Carlos sighed resignedly and put out his arms for Baptista to help him on with a light travelling coat.

419

Ega gave a hand and begged him to convey his filial respects to Afonso and regards to fat Sequeira.

He went down with them, hatless, and, as he shut the carriage door, promised Maria Eduarda a visit to Hideaway as soon as Carlos was back from the craggy Douro region.

'Now don't go back to Cintra before I return!' shouted Carlos. 'And see Micaela looks after you!'

'All right, all right!' returned Ega. 'Have a good journey! At your service, senhora . . . Until we meet again at Hideaway!'

The coupé set off. Ega went up to his room where a servant was preparing his bath. In the deserted room below, amid the flowers and remains of the meal, the candles continued to flicker, emphasizing against the dark canvas the pallor of Pedro da Maia and the melancholy eyes.

The following Saturday, about two o'clock, Carlos and Ega, still at table, were finishing their cigars and talking of Santa Olávia. Carlos had arrived back that morning, alone. His grandfather had decided to stay among his time-honoured trees until the end of the autumn, which was proving so gentle and luminous a season that year.

Carlos had found him very gay and strong, in spite of a touch of rheumatism which had finally obliged him to give up his cold showers. And the old man's hearty, resplendent health was a great relief to Carlos: he felt his departure with Maria to Italy in October would not seem so ungrateful, would be altogether simpler. Moreover he had a little plan, as he told Ega, whereby he could achieve the greatest desire of his life without paining his grandfather too much, without disturbing the peace of his old age. It was a simple enough little plan: he would set off alone for Madrid to begin a certain 'professional trip' abroad, which he had already prepared his grandfather for while he was in Santa Olávia. Maria would stay on at Hideaway for a month. Then she would take the boat to Bordeaux, and there Carlos would meet her and they could at last begin their life of happiness and romance perfumed by the flowers of Italy . . . In the spring he would return to Lisbon, leaving Maria installed in her snug little retreat; then gradually he would reveal to his grandfather this relationship which bound him by his honour and obliged him to spend long months every year in another country which had become his heart's native soil. And what could his grandfather say? He would simply accept the situation, the more unpleasant aspects of which he would not see anyway, attenuated as they would be by distance and his love for his grandson. It would just be a vague and little understood love affair away in Italy. And regrettable simply because it took his grandson away from him for months at a time; and each year he would console himself by thinking of the fragility and short duration of human idylls. And Carlos also counted upon the benevolence which softens the sternest souls when they are but a few steps from the tomb. He considered his little plan very clever. And Ega too approved of it.

Then they went on to the gayer subject of where the love-nest should be. Carlos clung to his original romantic idea of a cottage on the edge of a lake. But Ega was against a lake. To have the ever-calm, ever-blue water of a lake before one's eyes every day would surely endanger the permanence of passion. In the continued quiet of an unchanging landscape, two solitary lovers, he said, who were neither botanists nor keen on fishing, would be driven to live exclusively on each other's desires, and from there only draw all their ideas, sensations, occupations, jokes and silences. And what the deuce, man! Not even the hardiest love could stand that! Two lovers, whose only occupation was loving each other, should settle in a city, in a big busy creative city where the man has his clubs and gossip, museums, ideas and the smiles of other women during the day, and the woman has her shops and avenues, theatres and the attentions of other men; so that at night, when they are together again, not having spent the whole long day observing each other, and each one bringing with him or her a breath of the vibrant life they have experienced, they find delight once more in the comfort of their solitude, and an ever-new sweetness in their embraces.

'Personally,' went on Ega, getting to his feet, 'if I were carrying off a woman, it wouldn't be to any lake, nor to Switzerland nor even to the Sicilian mountains that I'd go; but to Paris, to the boulevard des Italiens, over on that corner by the Vaudeville with windows looking out on real life, just a step away from the *Figaro* offices, and the Louvre, philosophy and wit. There's my doctrine for you! . . . And here comes our friend Baptista with the mail.'

It was not the mail. It was just a card that Baptista was bringing in on the salver; and he was so disturbed that he announced that 'there was a person outside, in the antechamber, in a carriage, waiting . . .'

Carlos glanced at the card and went terribly pale. Then he took it up and looked at it again, slowly as if stunned, his fingers trembling. Then he tossed it over to Ega without a word.

'Good God!' gasped Ega, horrified.

It was Castro Gomes!

Carlos got up abruptly and decisively.

'Show him in. Into the main salon!'

Baptista pointed to the flannel jacket Carlos had worn for lunch and asked in a low voice whether his master would like his frock-coat.

'Fetch it!'

Alone, Ega and Carlos looked at each other anxiously for a moment.

'It's not a challenge, that's obvious,' stammered Ega.

Carlos made no reply. He studied the card again: the man was called Joaquim Álvares de Castro Gomes; beneath his name, Hotel Bragança had been written in pencil. Baptista returned with the frock-coat, and Carlos went out slowly buttoning it, without another word to Ega who was standing at the table, stupidly wiping his hands on his napkin.

In the main salon, lined with brocades the colour of autumn moss, Castro Gomes was examining, with one knee on the edge of the sofa, the magnificent Constable portraying the Duchess of Runa, splendid and strong in her scarlet velvet hunting costume. At the sound of Carlos's steps on the carpet, he turned, white hat in hand, smiling and apologizing for so familiarly scrutinizing the superb Constable . . . Very stiffly, Carlos made a gesture inviting him to sit down. Smiling and affable, Castro Gomes leisurely accepted. In the buttonhole of the tight frock-coat he wore a rosebud; his patent-leather shoes shone above the linen spats; the lean suntanned face terminated in a pointed beard, and his hair was growing thin at the parting; his very smile seemed somehow dry and weary.

'I have a *chic* little Constable in Paris,' he said without the least trace of embarrassment, in a drawl of r's which the Brazilian accent softened. 'But it is only a small landscape with two little figures. To tell the truth, I don't find him a very entertaining painter. Still, he gives a distinguished tone to a collection. One must keep him.'

Carlos sat in front of him on a chair, with fists clenched tight on his knees, as immobile as a block of marble. A suspicion was gradually forming in his mind as he heard the other's affable tone, a suspicion which wounded him and struck him with an irrepressible burst of anger. Castro Gomes knew absolutely nothing of the affair! He had arrived, disembarked, gone straight to Olivais, and slept there! He was the husband, he was young, and he had held her in his arms! Her, Maria! And now here he was, as calm as you like, flower in buttonhole and talking about Constable! Carlos's one desire at that moment was that the other man should insult him!

Castro Gomes in the meantime was politely apologizing for arriving like that, without so much as an introduction or even requesting an interview.

'The motive which brings me here, however, is so urgent, that although I arrived only at ten this morning from Rio de Janeiro, or rather from the Lazareto,* here I am already! And tonight if it's possible, I depart for Madrid.'

Relief flooded Carlos's heart. So he had not seen Maria Eduarda then; those dry lips had not touched her! And the marble rigidity relaxed; he began to listen with attention and moved his chair a little closer.

Castro Gomes had in the meantime put aside his hat and was drawing out of an inside pocket a wallet with a large gold monogram on it. Slowly he went through the papers until he found a letter. Then, letter in hand, he went on calmly:

'I received this anonymous letter in Rio de Janeiro just before I left. But you mustn't believe it was this which led me to cross the Atlantic so quickly. That would have been most ridiculous. I should also like to assure you that the contents of the letter leave me completely indifferent. Here it is. Would you like to read it yourself, or shall I read it to you?'

Carlos muttered with an effort: 'Please read it.'

Castro Gomes unfolded the paper and turned it a moment between his fingers.

'As you can see, it is an anonymous letter with all the usual

* Former house of quarantine in Lisbon.

423

sordid characteristics: cheap, blue-lined paper, vile writing, vile ink, vile smell – altogether an odious document. And this is the information it has to impart:

' "Sir: A man who has had the honour of shaking Your Excellency's hand," I would have done without such an honour, "who has had the honour of shaking Your Excellency's hand and recognizing what a gentleman you are, feels it his duty to warn you that your wife, before the eyes of all Lisbon, is the mistress of a young man very well known here, Carlos Eduardo da Maia, who lives in a house called Ramalhete in Janelas Verdes. This famous character is extremely rich and has bought a country-house in Olivais expressly to instal your wife there. He goes there every day, often stopping until dawn, a fact that scandalizes the whole neighbourhood. So your honourable name, sir, is being dragged through the mud of the streets of the capital." '

'That is all the letter says; and I must add, for I know it as a fact, that everything written here is unquestionably exact. Senhor Carlos da Maia is known publicly, in the eyes of all Lisbon, as the lover of this lady.'

Carlos got up, completely composed. And opening his arms slightly, accepting entirely all his responsibilities, he answered: 'Then I have nothing more to say, except that I am at your service!'

A wave of colour passed swiftly over the pale olive features of Castro Gomes. He folded the letter, and very slowly put it back into his wallet. Then he smiled coldly, and replied:

'I beg your pardon. Senhor Carlos da Maia knows as well as I do that if the matter had to have a violent solution, I should not have come here in person, to your house, and read you this letter. The case is quite different.'

Carlos dropped back into his chair, astonished. That honeyed drawl was becoming intolerable to him. A confused fear of what might come from those lips, smiling there with an impenetrable pallor, struck terror into his heart. He had a sharp desire to cry out to him to stop or to kill him, or if not to get out of that room where his presence seemed futile – or obscene!

Castro Gomes smoothed his moustache and went on in the same slow voice, choosing his words with care and precision.

'Things are like this, Senhor Carlos da Maia. There are people in Lisbon who do not know me of course but they know that at this moment somewhere, in Paris or Brazil or hell perhaps, exists a certain Castro Gomes who has a pretty wife, and this pretty wife has a lover here in Lisbon. This is most disagreeable, particularly as it is untrue. And you will appreciate that I cannot have this reputation of unhappy husband hanging over me any longer, especially as I don't deserve it and am not legally entitled to it. That is why I have come here to tell you quite frankly, as one gentleman to another, and as I intend to tell others, that the lady is not my wife.'

Castro Gomes waited for a moment for Carlos da Maia's reponse. But Carlos's face remained still, impenetrable, with only the eyes shining out brightly from the blanched face. Finally, with an effort, he lowered his head slightly as if taking in quite placidly this revelation which made any other comment between them vain and superfluous.

But Castro Gomes had shrugged his shoulders lightly and resignedly as one who attributes all ill to the hand of Destiny.

'It's the way life goes . . . Senhor Carlos da Maia will understand – it's the old story. I have been living with this lady for three years; when I had to go to Brazil last winter I brought her to Lisbon with me rather than come alone. We went to the Hotel Central. You can understand that naturally I wasn't going to confide my personal affairs to the manager of that establishment. The lady had arrived with me, she slept with me, she was therefore to all intents and purposes my wife, as far as the hotel staff were concerned. As the wife of Castro Gomes she stayed at the Central; as the wife of Castro Gomes she later rented a house in the Rua de S. Francisco; as the wife of Castro Gomes she also then took a lover. She assumed the role of Castro Gomes's wife throughout, even in circumstances which were particularly unpleasant to Castro Gomes . . . And, heavens above, we can't really blame her for that, can we? To find herself suddenly given an excellent social position and spotless name, and then declare for the simple sake of honesty that that position and name were merely borrowed and she was little Miss Nobody, not wife, only mistress – was too much to ask of any normal human being. And anyway, to be quite fair, she was not morally obliged to give explanations to the shopkeeper who sold her her butter or the landlady who rented her the house: to no one at all, in fact, in my opinion, except possibly to a father who

425

wished to present his little convent-bred daughter . . . Also, I admit the fault has been mine to an extent: very often, even in quite delicate matters, I have let her use my name. It was under the name of Castro Gomes that she hired the English governess. English women are so fussy! And that one particularly is such a serious girl. Anyway, all this is past now. And the important thing now is to withdraw solemnly the name I lent her; and she will be left with her own, Madame MacGren.'

Carlos got up, ashen-faced. And with his hands clutching the side of the chair so tightly that they almost tore the cloth, he asked: 'There's nothing more, I presume?'

Castro Gomes bit his lip at such an obvious dismissal.

'Nothing,' he said, taking his hat and getting up extremely slowly. 'I should emphasize, however, so that you will not harbour unjust suspicions against me, that the lady was no maiden I seduced and then refused to redress. The little one she's got with her isn't mine. I have only known the mother for three years. She left another man's arms for mine. I can say without insulting anyone that she was just a woman I paid.'

So he completed Carlos's humiliation. He had had a splendid revenge. Carlos brusquely pulled back the curtain without a word. And confronted with this further piece of rudeness – further evidence of the other's mortification – Castro Gomes comported himself admirably: he bowed, and smiled, and murmured: 'I am leaving tonight for Madrid, and I shall carry with me the extreme regret of having made your acquaintance under such unfortunate conditions . . . So unfortunate for me.'

The precise light footsteps were absorbed by the tapestries of the antechamber. Then, below, a carriage-door slammed, and a carriage rolled away down the hill.

Carlos sat slumped in a chair by the door, his head in his hands. The slow cloying words of Castro Gomes which still echoed in his ears left him only with the stunned sensation that something that had been very beautiful, resplendent and sublime, had suddenly fallen and shattered to pieces in the mud, splashing him with vile, intolerable stains. He felt no pain, simply an utter astonishment which descended over his entire being at this gross ending to a divine dream. He had rashly joined his soul to another that was noble and perfect, and they had flown together high among clouds of gold; then suddenly a voice spoke

426

full of r's; the two souls faltered, then pitched into the mire; and he was left holding in his arms a woman he did not know, a woman whose name was MacGren.

MacGren! She was MacGren!

He got up with his fists clenched; and his pride rose in sudden fury against her ingenuity which had kept him so timid for months, so tremulous and anxious, following that woman like some divine star – a woman who would have offered herself naked to any man in Paris who had a thousand francs in his pocket! It was horrible! And he remembered now, hot with shame, the pious emotion he had felt as he entered the red rep room in Rua de S. Francisco; the tenderness and charm with which he had watched those hands, which he had supposed the chastest in the world, drawing the embroidery wool back and forth – the ideal, diligent, withdrawn mother; he remembered the veneration which had held him from brushing even the edge of her dress which to him had seemed like a virgin's tunic whose rigid folds not even the coarsest beast would dare to disarrange! Oh fool! Fool! And all the time she had been laughing at the simplicity of that poor provincial from the Douro! Oh, how ashamed of his bashful courteous addresses of 'Senhora'!

And it would have been so easy, from the very first day in the Aterro, to see that that goddess, who had suddenly stepped out of the clouds, was in fact no more than mistress of the Brazilian! But no, this absurd romantic passion had put between his eyes and the dearest, most revealing details a golden haze of the sort that gives the sternest, blackest mountains the appearance of being made of precious stone! Why had she chosen as her doctor, to enter her house and her intimacy, the very man who had looked at her with an obvious flush of desire on his face? Why had she never spoken, during those long conversations every morning in Rua de S. Francisco, of her friends in Paris and of her home? Why, at the end of two months, had she so precipitously abandoned herself to him at his first 'I love you', without any of the usual preludes to love which grow gradually and then bloom like a flower? Why had she accepted a furnished house with the same facility as she accepted his flowers? And there were other things too, little details it is true, but ones which would not have escaped the notice of the simplest of fellows: flamboyant jewellery of the sort of showy

427

luxury that a *cocotte* would appreciate; the book entitled *Explanation of Dreams* at her bedside; the familiarity with Melanie . . . Now even the ardour of her kisses seemed to derive not from sincerity and passion but from the science of sex! But it was all over, fortunately! The woman he had loved and her seductive appeal had suddenly vanished in the air like a dream, a radiant but impure dream from which that Brazilian had generously awoken him. The woman was only a MacGren after all. Ever since he had first seen her his love had been like the very blood coursing in his veins; now it drained away through the incurable wound in his pride which could never be healed.

Ega appeared at the door, still white in the face:

'What happened?'

Carlos's fury exploded.

'It's extraordinary, Ega, absolutely extraordinary! The vilest, most despicable thing imaginable!'

'Did he ask you for money?'

'Worse than that!'

And pacing the room impulsively, Carlos unburdened himself and told Ega everything without reticence, using the same blunt words Castro Gomes had used, which, repeated and revived by his own lips, seemed to furnish him with fresh sources of humiliation and disgust.

'Has anything more repulsive ever happened to anyone?' he asked at last, flinging out his arms in a helpless appeal to Ega, who had sunk on to the sofa in astonishment. 'Can you imagine anything more sordid? And yet at the same time more ridiculous? It's enough to break one's heart. Or make one burst with laughter. Wonderful! There was the little fellow on the sofa, just where you are, flower in buttonhole, and saying in such a friendly manner: "Look, that creature's not my wife, you know, just a little thing I pay . . ." Do you understand? That character pays her! How much is a kiss, I wonder? A hundred francs. Here's a hundred francs . . . Ghastly!'

And he began distractedly pacing up and down again, still relieving his feelings, repeating everything in Castro Gomes's words which he contorted into an even greater ugliness.

'What do you say, Ega? Come on, out with it, man. What would you do? It's horrible, isn't it?'

Ega, who was reflectively cleaning his monocle, hesitated, and then remarked that considering things coolly, as befitted men of their times and 'their world', there was really nothing there to evoke anger or pain . . .

'Then you haven't understood the first thing,' shouted Carlos. 'You don't see my position at all!'

Oh yes, Ega understood perfectly that it was horrible for a man, at the precise moment when he was about to unite heart and soul with a woman, to learn that others had had her for so much a night. But this really simplified matters, made them altogether more favourable. What had been a complicated drama was now just a pleasant little pastime. Carlos need no longer have remorse about disorganizing a family; he no longer need become an exile, nor hide his sins in some sunny corner of Italy; now he was not bound for ever by his honour to a woman to whom perhaps love would not always bind him . . . All these, my God! were advantages.

'And her dignity?' cried Carlos.

Yes, but dignity and purity had not decreased to so great an extent after all, for before the visit of Castro Gomes she had been a woman about to run away from her husband – which, without being too harsh, was neither very pure nor very dignified . . . The humiliation was, of course, annoying – but not more so than that of a man who has a *Madonna* which he cherishes with devotion, supposing it to be by Raphael, then one day discovers that the divine canvas was fashioned in Baia, by an individual called Castro Gomes! But it seemed to him that as far as he and society were concerned the effect of all this was that up till now Carlos had had a beautiful mistress with definite disadvantages and now, without any disadvantages at all, he still had a beautiful mistress.

'What you should do, my dear Carlos – '

'What I'm going to do is write her a letter, enclosing the price of two months' sleeping with her.'

'What romantic brutality! This has already happened before, though, in *La Dame aux Camélias*. And I fear you are not viewing the matter in the proper philosophical light – '

Carlos broke in impatiently: 'All right, Ega, let's not say any more about it. I'm in a vile state of nerves! I'll see you later. You're having supper here, aren't you? Good, see you later.'

He was marching out of the room and about to slam the door

when Ega, calm now, and slowly getting up from the sofa, re-marked:

'The fellow went off in that direction.'

Carlos turned, his eyes flashing.

'To Olivais? He went to see her?'

It seemed so. At least he had ordered the cab to drive to Craft's house. In order to see Castro Gomes, Ega had hidden himself in the watchman's hut. He had seen him leave and light a cigar. He was indeed one of those *rastaquouères* who, in that unfortunate city where anyone is tolerated, go to the Café de la Paix for their *groseille* – coarse, hard fellows. It was the watchman who had told him the individual seemed very pleased with him-self and had ordered the cabman to drive to Olivais.

Carlos seemed utterly shattered.

'This is disgusting! Perhaps they'll make a deal, after all. I feel as you described your state some time ago: "My soul's fallen into a latrine. I need a bath inside!" '

Ega murmured gloomily: 'There's getting to be such a demand for moral baths that I can see we'll have to have a special establishment in the city to provide them.'

In his room, Carlos walked up and down in front of the table where a sheet of white paper lay with the date and the words *Dear Senhora* written, at the cost of great effort, in a firm, strong hand. But he couldn't think of another suitable word. He had decided to send her a cheque for two hundred pounds, insultingly generous payment for the weeks he had spent in her bed. But he wished to add a couple of biting lines which would wound her more than the money – and the only words which occurred to him were words of wrath which betrayed his love.

He looked at the blank sheet, and the banal *Dear Senhora* gave him a heart-rending nostalgia for her whom only the day before he had called 'beloved', for the woman who was not yet called MacGren, who was perfect and whom an insuperable passion, stronger by far than reason, had stirred and overcome. And this love for his noble and loving Maria Eduarda who had suddenly been transformed into MacGren, false concubine of another, was infinitely greater now that it was unattainable – like the love one feels for a dead person which throbs more

430

violently beside the cold tomb. Ah, if only she could appear once more clean and pure, from the mud in which she had sunk, once more Maria Eduarda with her chaste embroidery! He would surround her with the tenderest love to compensate for the married status she would no longer deserve. He would treat her with such veneration – to make up for the respect the superficial and convention-bound world would deny her! And she had everything to command love and respect – she had beauty and charm, intelligence, gaiety, maternal appeal, goodness and taste . . . And for all these sweet, strong qualities, she was just an imposter!

But why? Why? Why had she entered this long deception, embroidered upon day after day, lying about everything, from the modesty she feigned to the name she used?

He clasped his head between his hands, and life seemed intolerable. If she lied, where could there be truth? If she had betrayed him like that, with those innocent eyes, the whole world might be just one big fraud. Put a bunch of roses in a vase, and they emit the plague! Walk towards a patch of fresh green grass, and you'll find it conceals a swamp! Any why, why these lies? If, from the first day when he, tremulous and impassioned, had seen her, contemplating her embroidery as one contemplates a saintly action – if she had told him that she was not Castro Gomes's wife but only his mistress, would his passion have been any the less? It was not some priest's stole which gave beauty to her body and value to her caresses. Why then these shameless shady lies, so that now he even feared her kisses and her very sighs were feigned? And this artifice had almost led him to exile himself, giving his whole life for a body which others had paid a mere few pounds for! And for this woman, hired by the hour like cabs, he was going to make his grandfather's last years a misery, ruin his own life and limit his freedom!

But why? Why this banal farce, the theme of so many comic operas, of the *cocotte* who pretends to be a lady? Why had she done it, with her honest-sounding words, her pure profile and her motherly tenderness? For money? No. Castro Gomes was richer than he, and could more easily satisfy her worldly cravings for fine clothes and carriages. Had she thought Castro Gomes was going to leave her, and wanted to have another well-lined pocket ready at her side? Then it would have been much simpler to have said: 'I'm free. I love you. Take me freely, as I give myself.' No, there was something else there, something secret, tortuous, impenetrable. What he would give to discover what it was!

Gradually he was feeling the need to go to Olivais. Yes, it was not enough to revenge himself like this, arrogantly throwing in her lap a cheque wrapped in an insult! What he must do, for his complete satisfaction, was drag out the secret of that infamous farce from the depths of her turbid soul. Only this would calm his bitter torment. He wanted to enter Hideaway once again, see what this other woman called MacGren was like, hear her words. Oh, he wouldn't be in the least violent, or recriminatory, but serene and smiling! Just so that she would tell him the reason for that long, laborious, futile lie. Just so that he could ask dispassionately, 'Well, my fine lady, why all this double-dealing?' And then watch her cry . . . Yes, his love made him long to see her cry. He wanted to see the agony that he had experienced in the great salon the colour of autumn moss, while Castro Gomes rolled his r's, repeated in her breast, on which he had slept so peacefully, oblivious of all else, that beautiful breast, so divinely beautiful . . .

On a sudden decision he pulled the bell-cord. Baptista appeared, buttoned-up in his frock-coat and with a resolute air as if ready and prepared to be of service in that crisis he guessed was passing.

'Baptista, run along to the Hotel Central and ask if Senhor Castro Gomes has returned. No – listen, wait at the door of the Central until that individual that was here goes in . . . No, it's better to ask. Oh, just find out if he's back, or is in the hotel. And as soon as you're sure, get back here at top speed with a cab. Get a reliable driver, as I want to go on to Olivais!'

He calmed down after this. It was an immense relief not to have to write the letter and find biting words to wound her. He tore the paper slowly to pieces. Then he made out a cheque for two hundred sovereigns 'To the bearer'. He would take it himself. Oh, he wasn't going to fling it romantically in her lap! He would leave it on a table in an envelope addressed to Madame MacGren. And suddenly he felt sorry for her. He could see her opening the envelope with two great tears slowly, silently rolling down her face. And tears came into his own eyes.

432

At that moment Ega inquired from outside if he would be disturbing him.'

'No, come in!'

And he continued pacing back and forth in silence, with his hands in his pockets, while his friend, also silent, went to lean against the window which looked out over the garden.

'I must write to Grandfather and let him know I have arrived,' murmured Carlos at last, stopping in front of his writing-desk.

'Give him my regards.'

Carlos sat down and listlessly picked up his pen – but soon flung it down again. He crossed his hands behind his head, leant against the back of the chair, and closed his eyes as if exhausted.

'Do you know something I'm sure about?' Ega remarked suddenly from the window. 'It was Damaso who wrote that anonymous letter to Castro Gomes!'

Carlos looked at him.

'Do you think so? Yes, perhaps . . . Mmm, who else would it be?'

'There's no one else, dear boy. It was Damaso for sure!'

Carlos recalled what Taveira had told him – the mysterious allusions Damaso had made regarding a scandal he was preparing, a bullet he was going to get through the head . . . Damaso had therefore been sure the Brazilian would come, and that there would be a duel.

'The infamous wretch must be destroyed!' cried Ega, suddenly furious. 'There's no safety, no peace in our lives while that blackguard lives!'

Carlos made no reply. Ega went on raging, his face pale, releasing the hatred which had been accumulating day after day.

'I've not murdered him because I haven't had any pretext. If I were given a pretext – an insult or even an audacious glance – I'd get him, I'd destroy him! But you'll have to do something, you can't leave things like this! It's not right. Some blood must be shed. Just think what an infamous cur he is – an anonymous letter! Our peace and happiness is constantly exposed to the attacks of Senhor Damaso. Things can't stay like this. All I'm sorry about is that I haven't a pretext! But you have; take advantage of it and destroy him!'

Carlos shrugged his shoulders vaguely.

'He needs a good hiding, it's true. But he's only been vile

433

with me because of my relations with this lady; and as the affair is now over, everything concerned with it is over too. *Parce sepultis.* And he was right, after all, when he called her a fraud.'

He banged his fist down on the table, got up and said with a bitter smile, as if infinitely weary of everything:

'It was Senhor Damaso Salcêde who was right, after all.'

All his anger flashed up again at the thought. He looked at his watch. He needed to see her at once, to insult her immediately.

'Have you written to her?' asked Ega.

'No, I'm going personally.'

Ega looked at him aghast. Then he began pacing again, silent, eyes on the carpet.

It was getting dark when Baptista returned. He had seen Senhor Castro Gomes get out of a cab and order his luggage to be sent down; and the cab to take his master to Olivais was waiting down below.

'Right. Good-bye!' said Carlos, looking dazedly for his gloves.

'Aren't you having supper?'

'No.'

In a few moments he was on his way to Olivais. The gas-lamps were already alight. He sat on the narrow seat, nervously lighting cigarettes which he could not smoke, and already suffering in anticipation the difficult, painful meeting ahead. He did not even know how he was to address her: if 'Senhora' would be better, or 'my dear friend', with an air of superior indifference. And at the same time he felt a vague pity for her which made him relent a little. He could see her, faced with such icy manners, pale and trembling, her eyes full of tears. And these tears that he had been looking forward to, now that he was so near to seeing them fall, troubled and grieved him. For a moment he thought of turning back. It would be far more dignified, after all, to write a few disdainful words and be rid of her once and for all. Perhaps he would not send the cheque – a brutal insult from a man of wealth. Hypocrite she might be, but she was still a woman, nervous and imaginative, and perhaps she had loved him disinterestedly. A letter was definitely more dignified. And now the words he should have written came to him, sharp and precise. Yes, he should have said that although he was ready to give his

434

life to a woman who had surrendered herself to him for love, he was not willing to sacrifice even his moments of leisure to a woman who offered herself merely as part of her profession. It was simpler, and it was conclusive. Then he would not have to see her, would not have to put up with explanations and tears.

His strength of purpose was weakening. He banged on the window to have the carriage stop and allow him to reflect for a few moments quietly, without the incessant rumble of the wheels. But the driver did not hear and the swift trotting of the horses continued along the dim road. Carlos let him go on, hesitant once more. Then as he recognized, looming out of the gloom, spots he had passed when his heart was gay and his passion at its height, his anger returned – less against Maria Eduarda than against this lie she had invented which had irreparably destroyed the greatest happiness of his life. It was this lie which he loathed now, seeing it like something material and tangible, enormous in size and ugly in colour, crushing his heart. Ah, if it wasn't for this little unforgettable thing between them, like an indestructible block of granite, he could take her in his arms again, if not with the same confidence, at least with the same ardour. Whether wife or mistress of another man, what did it matter? Because a priest's blessing had not been muttered over them in Latin, had his kisses defiled her skin more, or made it less fresh? No, it was that lie, that initial lie, spoken the very first day he had gone to Rua de S. Francisco and which like a ferment had then corrupted everything that came afterward, the charming conversations, the silences, walks, siestas in the garden, the kisses behind the gold-coloured curtains. Everything fouled, contaminated by that first lie she had uttered with a smile and calm, innocent eyes.

He was stifling. He was about to let down the window, whose strap was missing, when the cab stopped abruptly in the deserted road. He opened the door. A woman with a shawl over her head was speaking to the driver.

'Melanie!'

'Ah, monsieur!'

Carlos jumped out. They were near the house, just at the bend in the road where the wall receded a little under an ash tree in front of the aloe hedge surrounding the olive-groves. Carlos shouted to the driver to go on and wait outside the garden-gate.

435

And he remained there, in the dark, with Melanie wrapped in her shawl.

What was she doing there? Melanie was greatly agitated; she explained she had been sent to the village to get a carriage as her mistress wanted to go to Lisbon, to Ramalhete. She had thought the cab was empty.

And she wrung her hands thankfully – it was such a relief! How fortunate he had come! Her mistress was terribly upset, she had eaten nothing and couldn't stop weeping. Senhor Castro Gomes had turned up unexpectedly, and her mistress, poor soul, said she wanted to die!

Carlos, walking along close to the wall, began to question Melanie. How had the other man behaved? What had he said? How had he left? Melanie had heard nothing. Senhor Castro Gomes and her mistress had spoken alone in the Japanese summer-house. When he had left Senhor Castro Gomes had said good-bye to Madam, very calmly and friendly, smiling and with some comment on Niniche. Her mistress was as pale as death though! When the man left she had almost fainted.

They were close to Hideaway now. Carlos drew back, hat in hand, breathing heavily. His pride was lost under the terrible desire to know. He had to know! And he asked for details, he let Melanie into the painful secrets of his heart. *Dites toujours, Melanie, dîtes!* Did her mistress know that Castro Gomes had been to see him in Ramalhete, had told him everything?

Of course she knew, that's why she had wept, said Melanie. Oh, how often she had warned her mistress that it was better to tell the truth! She was a great friend of hers, had waited on her ever since she was a little girl, had even been there when her daughter was born. And she had told her so, even in Olivais!

Carlos lowered his head in the benevolent shadow of the wall. *Melanie had told her so!* So she and her maid had discussed this trick she had played on him, like conspirators! These words of Melanie, whispered from beneath the shawl, destroyed the last fragments of the beautiful dream he had valued so dearly, raised upon clouds of gold. Nothing remained now. Everything lay shattered in filth and mud.

His heart was so heavy that for a moment he thought of

436

returning to Lisbon. But *she* was there behind that black wall, sobbing with grief and wishing for death . . . He moved slowly towards the gate.

And now, all his pride dispelled, he put more intimate questions to Melanie. Why hadn't Maria Eduarda told him the truth?

Melanie shrugged her shoulders. She didn't know; her mistress did not know herself! She had lived in the Central as Senhora Gomes; she had rented the house in Rua de S. Francisco as Senhora Gomes; she had received him as Senhora Gomes . . . And somehow she had let things go on like that, talking with him, falling in love with him, coming to Olivais . . . And then it seemed too late, she dared not confess then, caught up in the lie, fearful of the consequences.

But didn't she ever think, asked Carlos, that one day everything would be discovered?

"*Je ne sais pas, monsieur, je ne sais pas,*' murmured Melanie, almost in tears herself.

Then there were other points. Did she not expect Castro Gomes? Didn't she suppose he would return? Did she never speak about him?

'*Oh non, monsieur, oh non!*'

Since the gentleman began to visit Rua de S. Francisco every day her mistress had considered herself dissociated from Senhor Castro Gomes. She never spoke of him again nor allowed anyone else to speak of him. The little girl used to call Senhor Castro Gomes *petit ami*, but now she never mentioned him; they had told her that there wasn't a *petit ami* any more.

'But she still wrote to him,' said Carlos. 'I know she still wrote to him.'

Yes, Melanie believed she did. But letters without feeling. Her mistress was so scrupulous about things that she had not spent a cent of Castro Gomes's money since she moved to Olivais. She had kept the letters of credit he sent her unopened, and returned them this evening. Didn't he remember that day he had met her at the door of the Montepio? Well, she had gone there with a French friend of hers to pawn a diamond bracelet of her mistress's. Her mistress lived off her jewels now; there were others in the pawnshop.

Carlos stopped, moved by this new piece of information. But why ever had she lied then?

437

'*Je ne sais pas,*' said Melanie. '*Je ne sais pas . . . Mais elle vous aime bien, allez!*'

They had arrived at the gate. The cab was waiting. And at the far end of the acacia-bordered avenue the door of the house was open, letting out a feeble, cheerless light from the corridor. Carlos thought he saw Maria Eduarda pass through this patch of light, wrapped in a dark cloak and wearing a hat. She must have heard the carriage. What a terribly nervous state she must be in!

'Go and tell her I'm here, Melanie, go on!'

The girl fled. And he, walking slowly under the acacias, could hear in the sombre silence the violent beating of his heart. He went up the three stone steps, which seemed now to belong to an unknown house. Inside, the corridor was deserted, while the Moorish lamp shone upon the display from the bull-ring. He went no farther. Melanie, her shawl in her hand now, came to tell him that her mistress was in the tapestry room.

Carlos went in.

There she stood, still with her cloak on, very pale and with all her soul concentrated in the tear-filled eyes. She ran to him, snatched up his hands, not able to utter a word, sobbing, trembling violently.

Carlos could only murmur, futile and stupid in his agitation:

'I don't know why you're crying. I don't know why. There's no reason to cry.'

Eventually she managed to gasp:

'Listen to me, for God's sake! Don't say anything, let me tell you everything. I was going to see you, I'd sent Melanie to get a carriage. I was going to see you. I never had the courage to tell you before! I was wrong, I know, it was horrible! But listen, don't say anything yet, forgive me, it wasn't my fault!'

Again the words were interrupted by a fit of sobbing. And she dropped on to the sofa, weeping bitterly, shaken by the violence of it, her hastily arranged hair falling into disorder.

Carlos stood there unable to move. His heart seemed to stand still with doubt and surprise. He could not unburden his feelings. He only felt how low and brutal it would be to leave the cheque which he had in his wallet and which filled him with shame. She lifted her head, her face wet with tears, and murmured with a great effort:

438

'Listen to me! I don't know how to tell you – there's so much, so much . . . ! You mustn't go, sit down, listen to me.'

Carlos slowly pulled forward a chair.

'No, here, next to me. So I'll have more courage. Have pity on me, please, please, that's all I ask!'

He yielded to the appeal in the tear-filled eyes, and sat down in the opposite corner of the sofa, apart from her, bitterly distressed. Then, very quietly, her voice hoarse from weeping and without looking at him, she began to talk as if she were in the confessional – a hesitant and confused account of her past interrupted by broken sobs and shame which made her bury her face in her hands.

She wasn't to blame! It wasn't her fault! He should have asked that man that knew all about her. It was her mother's fault! It was horrible to have to say it, but it was because of her that she had met and run away with the first man, the Irishman. She had lived with him for four years as if she were his wife, completely faithful and withdrawn from the world, devoting herself to the house. He was going to marry her but he had been killed in the war with the Germans, in the Battle of St-Privat. And she had been left with Rosa, and her mother who was ill then, and no means at all after having sold everything. At first she had worked. In London she had tried to give piano lessons. But everything had failed; for two days they had been without a fire, and lived on dried fish. And Rosa was without food! To see the child with nothing to eat! Ah, he'd never understand what that was like! They had been helped back to France, and there she had met Castro Gomes! It was horrible, but what else was there to do? She was utterly lost . . .

She slid off the sofa and dropped at his feet. And he remained motionless, silent, his heart torn by different emotions: he felt a deep pity for all the wretchedness she had undergone – the suffering as a mother, the seeking for a job, hunger – all these things made her dearer to him than before, whereas knowledge of this other man, the Irishman who had suddenly appeared, debased her still further in his eyes.

She went on talking of Gastro Gomes. She had lived with him for three years, honestly, with never a disloyal thought or action. It was he who had obliged her to go out and about, joining him in nightly revels.

Carlos could bear no more. He pushed away her hands which sought his. He wanted to get out, get far away!

'Oh no, don't send me away!' she cried, clinging to him desperately. 'I know I don't deserve anything! I'm the most wretched of women! But I hadn't the courage to tell you, my love! You're a man, you don't understand these things. Look at me! Why don't you look at me? Just a second, don't turn your face away, have pity on me . . .'

No, he dared not look at her. He feared those tears, the agony in her face. The warmth of her breast, rising and falling against his knees, was dispelling his pride and spite, his jealousy and notions of dignity . . . And then, unconsciously, unwillingly, his hands took hers. She immediately and frenziedly covered his fingers and sleeves with kisses, and implored from the depths of her misery a moment's mercy.

'Tell me you forgive me! You are so good! Just one word! Only, tell me you don't hate me, and then I'll let you go! But tell me first. And look at me, just once, as you used to . . .'

And now it was her lips which sought his. And the weakness Carlos felt enveloping him suddenly burst into fury against himself and against her. He shook her roughly and cried:

'But why didn't you tell me? Why didn't you tell me? Why this long, persistent lie? I'd have loved you just the same! Why, why did you lie?'

He pushed her away and she fell prostrate on the floor. And standing above her, he flung out the same desperate complaint.

'It's the lie that has forced us apart, your horrible lie! Your lie and only that!'

She pulled herself up very slowly, barely able to stand, a pallor like death on her face.

'But I wanted to tell you,' she whispered, crushed with grief, her arms hanging limply at her sides. 'I wanted to tell you. Don't you remember, that day when you came late, when I spoke of a house in the country, and you told me for the first time that you loved me? I said to you then, "There is something I must tell you", but you wouldn't let me finish. You thought you knew what it was. You thought I wanted to tell you I wanted to belong only to you, far away from everything else. And then you said that we would go, and live happily there . . . Don't

440

you remember? It was then I was tempted! I wouldn't say anything and let myself be taken away, and then much later, years later, when I had proved what a good wife I was, worthy of your respect, I'd confess everything and say "Now send me away if you wish!" Oh it was wrong of me I know. But it was such a temptation, I couldn't resist. If you hadn't spoken of our going away together, I would have told you everything. But as soon as you spoke of our going away, I saw another sort of life, a great hope – I don't know what! And apart from everything else, I could put off the horrible confession! Then, I don't know how to explain it, it was as if the heavens had suddenly opened – I saw myself with you in a house of our own. It was such a temptation! It would have been horrible, at a moment when you loved me so much, to go and say, "You can't do this for me; I'm just a poor wretch that hasn't even got a husband . . ." What more can I explain? I couldn't face losing your respect. It was so wonderful to be looked up to. Still, it was wrong of me, terribly wrong. Now here I am, utterly lost, and everything's finished!'

She collapsed on to the floor, like a broken defeated thing, and hid her face in the sofa. Carlos walked slowly to the far end of the room and then returned with the same reproach as always, the *lie*, the *lie*, persistent, repeated day after day . . . Only sobs came in answer.

'Why didn't you tell me, at least afterwards, here in Olivais, when you knew you meant everything to me?'

She lifted a weary head.

'What do you expect? I was afraid your love would change, that it would become different. I could imagine you losing your respect for me. I could just see you coming in here without bothering to remove your hat, no longer feeling the same love for the child, wanting to pay for the housekeeping. I regretted it but kept postponing the day. I used to say, "Not today, just one day more, I'll tell him tomorrow." And so it went on. I can hardly understand it myself – it's so horrible!'

Neither of them spoke. Then Carlos heard Niniche at the door, crying to enter. He let her in, and the animal ran straight to the sofa where Maria sat huddled in a corner sobbing, and leapt up and tried to lick her hands, sensing something wrong. Then she stood close, as if on guard, watching distrustfully out of her sharp little black eyes, as Carlos began to pace restlessly to and fro again.

A long painful sigh from Maria made him stop. He stood a moment looking at that picture of humility and grief. Thoroughly upset, with his lips trembling, he murmured:

'Even if I could forgive you, how could I ever believe you again? There would always be this horrible lie between us! There would be no more confidence or peace.'

'I've never lied to you except in this one thing, and that was only because I loved you so!' she answered gravely from the depths of her prostration.

'No, you lied to me about everything! Everything was a lie, your marriage was a lie, your name was a lie, your whole life was a lie. I'd never be able to believe you again! How could I, if even now I have doubts as to the cause of these tears?'

Indignation drew her to her feet, tall and proud. Her eyes were suddenly dry of tears, and flashed out from the marble whiteness of her face.

'What do you mean by that? That these tears have some other cause? That my pleas are dishonest? That I am pretending everything, just to keep you, hold on to you, in order to have another man to keep me now that I've been cast off?'

He stammered: 'No, no! No, I didn't mean that!'

'And what about me?' she cried, moving towards him, suddenly supremely dominant, the splendour of truth shining from her face. 'What about me? Why should I believe in this great passion you have sworn that you have? What was it you loved in me after all? Go on, tell me! Was it the wife of another man, or my name, or the titillating thrill of adultery perhaps, or my fashionable clothes? Or was it myself, my body, my soul and my love for you? I am the same woman, look at me! These arms are the same, this breast is the same! Only one thing is different: my passion! That's greater, unfortunately, infinitely greater.'

'Oh, if only this were true!' cried Carlos, wringing his hands.

Maria fell at his feet, her arms outspread to him.

'I swear by the soul of my daughter, by the soul of Rosa! I'll love you, I'll adore you madly, frantically, till I die!'

Carlos shuddered. His whole being reached out to her;

and he felt an impulse to let himself drop on to that breast that panted at his feet, even if it were an abyss into which he was dropping his whole life. But suddenly the idea of the *lie* flashed across his eyes again and froze him. He moved away from her, beating his fists against his head in despair, repelled by that little indestructible thing which wouldn't disappear and which interposed itself like an iron barrier between himself and his happiness!

She was still kneeling, motionless, staring at the floor. Then, in the carpeted stillness of the room, her voice arose, painful and tremulous:

'You're right, everything is finished! You don't believe me, so everything's finished! You'd better go. No one will ever believe me again. Everything's over for me. I've no one else in the world now. I'll leave tomorrow, I'll leave everything. You must give me time to settle things. Then, what else is there to do? I'll go . . .'

Unable to go on, she fell to the floor with arms outstretched, weeping bitterly.

Carlos turned, his heart pierced. Fallen and helpless there in her dark dress, she seemed like some poor creature that has been flung out of house and home into some corner to face alone all the rigours of the world. Then modesty and pride, family dignity – everything was swept away by a great wave of pity. Obscuring all her weaknesses he saw only her beauty, her grief, her supremely loving soul. A burst of generosity, of unsparing kindness, mingled with his passion. He bent down and said softly with his arms open wide:

'Maria, will you marry me?'

She looked up bewildered. But Carlos was offering her his arms, and he was waiting to enclose her within them again, this time for ever. Then she got up, stumbling over her skirts, and dropped into his arms, covering him with kisses, half crying and half laughing, giddy and dazed with excitement.

'Marry you? *You?* Oh, Carlos! And live with you always, always? Oh, my love, my love! And look after and serve you and adore you, and be just yours? And poor Rosa too! No, no, you can't marry me, it's impossible, I'm not worth it! But if you really want, why not? We'll go far, far away together, Rosa and I and you. And you must be our friend, for

443

we haven't anyone else in the world ... Oh God! Oh God! ...'
    She went pale and slipped heavily into his arms in a swoon:
and her long hair, which had come unfastened, shone in the
light with flashes of gold as it trailed on the ground.

5

MARIA EDUARDA AND CARLOS – who spent the night in his
cottage in Olivais – had just finished lunch. Domingos had served
coffee and placed Carlos's cigarettes and the *Figaro* beside him.
The two windows were wide open and not a leaf stirred in the
sultry air. The morning was overcast and the slow tolling of bells
which echoed far across the fields emphasized the melancholy in the
air. Miss Sarah sat listlessly sewing on the cork bench under the
trees while Rosa played beside her on the grass. And Carlos, who
had come in informal dress appropriate to his new conjugal role –
silk shirt and flannel jacket – drew his chair a little closer to Maria's,
took her hand and began to fondle it and play with her rings.

'Now, my love, what do you think? Have you decided yet
when you want to leave?'

The night before, in tender murmurs between kisses, she had
shown her desire not to alter their original plan of a romantic
little nest in Italy amid the flowers of Isola Bella – only now they
would not have to hide a guilty love but enjoy instead the tranquility of a legitimate happiness. And after all the uncertainties
and torments that had beset Carlos since the day he had first encountered Maria Eduarda in the Aterro, he too eagerly looked
forward to the moment when he could settle down finally in the
comfort of a love with no more doubts and disappointment.

'For my part I'd slip away tomorrow. I'm longing for peace.
I'm even eager for some idleness! But you, you tell me, when
would you like to go?'

Maria did not answer. But her eyes smiled in gratitude and
love. Then, without withdrawing her hand from Carlos, who was
still caressing it, she called through the window to Rosa.

'I'm coming, Mama, just a minute! Give me some crumbs . . .
There are some sparrows here who haven't had any lunch.'

'No, come here right away.'

She came to the door, dressed all in white, pink-cheeked and
with one of the last roses of summer tucked into her sash, and
Maria drew her over to stand between them, to rest against
their knees. Then, tying afresh her hair-ribbon which had worked

loose, Maria asked her very seriously whether she would like Carlos to come and live with them altogether and stay there at Hideaway. The little one's eyes filled with surprise and delight.

'What! Be here always, always, even in the night-time, all night? And have his bags and cases and things here?'

They murmured, 'Yes.'

Then Rosa jumped up and down and clapped her hands for joy, wanting Carlos to go immediately and fetch his bags and cases and things.

'Listen,' said Maria, still grave, holding the child against her knees, 'would you like him to be your daddy, and be with us always, for us both to love and obey?'

Rosa lifted a keen little face towards her mother, whose own face had lost its smile.

'But I can't love him more than I do already!'

They both kissed her, their emotion bringing tears to their eyes. And Maria Eduarda, for the first time in Rosa's presence, leant over to kiss Carlos lightly on the forehead. The child stared in amazement first at her friend then at her mother. Then she seemed to comprehend everything, and slipping from between Maria's knees, went to snuggle up against Carlos and inquired sweetly and shyly:

'Do you want me to call you Papa, just you and no one else?'

'Just me,' he answered, enfolding her in his arms.

Thus they obtained the consent of Rosa, who then rushed back to the garden, slamming the door behind her, and with hands full of cakes for the birds.

Carlos got up and, holding Maria's head gently between his hands, studied her deeply, right to her very soul, and murmured in raptures: 'You're perfect!'

Sorrowfully she detached herself from that adoration which disturbed her.

'Listen: I still have a great deal to tell you, unfortunately. Let's go to our summer-house. You haven't anything to do, have you? Anyway, even if you have, today is mine. You go, and take your cigarettes. And I'll be with you right away.'

Going down the steps into the garden, Carlos stopped for a moment to look around him and feel the veiled softness of the grey sky. And life, enwrapped like that in the soft mist where nothing either shone or sung, seemed adorable to him, woven of a delicate sad poetry, and so appropriate to the union of two hearts which were no longer preoccupied with the world and were indeed out of favour with it; there they could abandon themselves together in an everlasting dream of love among the silence and the shade . . .

'It looks as if we're going to have rain, André,' he remarked, as he came upon the old gardener clipping the box hedge.

Old André pulled off his hat in embarrassment. Ah! A drop of water was just what they needed after the drought! The poor old earth was really thirsty! Was everyone in the house well? The lady? And the little girl?

'They're all fine, thank you, André.'

And wishing to see everyone around him as happy as he himself was and the dry soil that was soon to be assuaged, Carlos slipped a sovereign into the hand of old André, who stood dazed, and not daring to close his fingers over the extraordinary piece of gold that glittered there in his palm.

When Maria came into the summer-house, she brought with her a sandalwood chest. She put it on the sofa, made Carlos comfortable beside it, and lit him a cigarette. Then she sat herself at his feet in the humble attitude of one about to confess.

'Are you all right like that? Would you like Domingos to bring you a brandy and water? Then listen to me now, I want to tell you everything.'

It was her whole life she wanted to recount. She had thought of writing it all down in an enormous letter, as they do in novels. But she had decided after all to devote a whole morning to telling him personally, while she nestled at his feet.

'You're all right then, aren't you?'

Carlos waited, deeply moved. He knew that those beloved lips were about to divulge revelations which would be grievous to his heart – and a bitter blow to her pride. But these confidences of her life would enable him to possess her more completely: when he knew her as she was in the past he would feel she was his entirely. And deep down he was sharply curious about these things which would distress him and humiliate her.

'Yes, go on. Afterwards we'll forget it all for ever. But now tell me. Where were you born after all?'

She had been born in Vienna, but she remembered very little of her childhood, and almost nothing about her father, except the fact that he was very noble and very handsome. She had had a younger sister called Heloísa who had died at the age of two. Mama, later, when she was a girl, wouldn't let her inquire into the past; she always said that churning up memories was as bad as shaking up a bottle of old wine. All she remembered of Vienna was vague avenues of trees and soldiers dressed in white uniforms, and a house full of gilt and mirrors where people danced. Sometimes she was left alone there for a while with her grandfather, a sad, timid little old man who sat tucked away in corners and told her stories about the sea. Then they went to England, but she only remembered crossing a noisy hum of streets one rainy day, wrapped in furs and sitting on the knees of a footman. Her first clear memories dated from Paris: Mama, a widow now, was in mourning for the grand-father; and she had an Italian nanny who took her to play every morning with a hoop and a ball in the Champs-Elysées. At night she would see her Mama, *décolletée*, in a room full of lights and satins; and a fair-haired, somewhat abrupt man, who was always stretched out on the sofas smoking, would sometimes bring her a doll and call her Mademoiselle Triste-coeur because she was always so grave. Later her mother put her in a con-vent near Tours, for although at that age she could sing to a piano accompaniment the waltzes from *La Belle Hélène*, she could not yet spell. And there in the gardens of the convent, full of beautiful lilacs, her mother had parted from her in a fit of weeping, and at her side, to console her no doubt, waited a grave-looking gentleman with waxed moustaches to whom the Mother Superior spoke with veneration.

At first her mama had visited her every month, spending two or three days at a time in Tours; she would bring her a host of presents – dolls and chocolates and embroidered handker-chiefs and fancy dresses which the strict rules of the convent forbade her to wear. Then they would go for rides in a carriage around the outskirts of Tours, and there were always officers on horseback to escort them, who addressed Mama by the intimate '*tu*'. The Mother Superior and the teachers in the convent dis-liked these outings, and disliked the way Mama awoke their sleeping corridors with her laughter and rustling silks, but at the same time they seemed to fear her, and called her Madame la Comtesse. Mama was very friendly with the general in charge at Tours, and she visited the Bishop. Monseigneur always gave her face an affectionate pat whenever he visited the convent and referred with a smile to *son excellente mère*. Then Mama began to appear less at Tours. She was away a whole year travelling in Germany and scarcely wrote; one day she returned, thin and dressed in mourning, and stayed all morning with her, hugging her and weeping.

But on her next visit she looked younger again, more brilliant, gayer, and brought with her two fine white greyhounds, and spoke of making a poetic pilgrimage to the Holy Land and all the Far East. Maria was nearly sixteen then, and her diligence and sweet serious manner had won the affection of the Mother Superior who at times looked at her sorrowfully and stroked her hair which was tied back into two plaits according to the rules, and professed the desire to keep her there for ever at her side. '*Le monde,*' she said, '*ne vous sera bon à rien, mon enfant!*' One day, however, a lady appeared to take her back to Paris and Mama – a lady called Madame de Chavigny, a poor aristocrat with white curls who looked like an illustration representing severity and virtue.

How she had cried when she left the convent! And how much more would she have cried if she had known what she was about to encounter in Paris!

Mama's house, in the Parc Monceaux, was really a gaminghouse, but disguised under an elegant sober luxury. The footmen wore silk stockings; the guests, whose names featured in the French nobility, chatted of the races, of the Tuileries, of speeches in the senate; and the gaming-tables were resorted to afterwards as to a more piquant entertainment. She always retired to her room at ten o'clock; Madame de Chavigny, who had stayed on as her companion, went with her early every morning to the Bois in a dark dowager's coupé. Gradually, however, the fine varnish began to crack. Poor Mama had fallen under the yoke of a M. de Trevernnes, a dangerous fellow by reason of his personal charm and grievous lack of honour and common sense. The house declined rapidly into a noisy tarnished bohemianism. When Maria awoke early with the healthy habit of her convent days, she found men's coats strewn over the sofas; on the marble consoles, cigar-ends and champagne stains; and from some distant room sounded the clink of money as a

449

baccarat game went on in the morning light. As she lay in her room one night she suddenly heard shouts and the hasty dispersal of people on the stairs; she came down to find her mother stretched out on the carpet in a swoon. Later, amid a flood of tears, she said simply that 'something unfortunate had occurred.'

They moved then to a third floor flat in the Chaussée-d'Antin. And a suspicious-looking set of people she had not seen before began to visit them: there were Wallachians with great moustaches, Peruvians with false diamonds, Roman counts who kept their grubby cuffs hidden in their sleeves . . . Sometimes there would appear amid this crowd a 'gentleman' – who did not take off his jacket, as if he were at a *café-concert*. One of these was a young Irishman called MacGren . . . Madame de Chavigny had left them since they no longer had the satin-cushioned coupé; and Maria, alone with her mother, gradually and fatally began to take part in the night life of drinks and baccarat.

Mama used to call MacGren 'the baby'. He was indeed a happy, impetuous child. He fell in love with her immediately with all the ardour and effusion and impulsiveness of an Irishman, and promised to marry her as soon as he was free – for MacGren, still a minor, lived mainly on the liberal gifts of a wealthy, eccentric grandmother who lived in a vast country house in Provence and kept a private zoo. And in the meantime, dismayed to see her living there among those Wallachians perpetually smelling of gin, he tried to persuade her to go away with him. He wanted to take her away to Fontainbleau, to a little cottage he often spoke about, covered with climbing plants, and live there peacefully awaiting his majority, which would bring him an income of two thousand sovereigns. It was a false position, certainly, but preferable to remaining in that depraved brutal atmosphere which caused her to blush at every moment. At this time Mama seemed to be losing her head completely: she quarrelled with the maids and drank champagne '*pour s'étourdir*'. To satisfy M. de Trevernnes's wants, she pawned her jewels, and almost every day jealousy of him drove her to tears. Finally there was real trouble: one night they had to bundle up their clothes in a bag in a hurry and spend the night in a hotel. And worse, far worse than everything else, M. de

450

Trevernnes began to look at her in a manner which frightened her.

'My poor Maria!' murmured Carlos, pale-faced, taking hold of her hands.

She stayed quite still for a moment, unable to speak, with her face resting on his knees. Then wiping away the tears that had clouded her eyes, she continued:

'I have MacGren's letters here, in this chest. I have kept them to justify myself, if that is possible. In all of them he begs me to go to Fontainebleau with him; he calls me his wife and swears that as soon as we are together we'll go and kneel before his grandmother and beg her indulgence . . . A thousand promises! And he was sincere! What else is there to say? One morning Mama went off with a group of doubtful friends to Baden. I was left alone in Paris in a hotel. I feared Trevernnes would come, I was desperately frightened, and all alone! I was so terrified I thought of buying a revolver. But it was MacGren who came instead.'

And she had gone away with him, calmly, as his wife, taking all her baggage. Mama rushed back from Baden to Fontainebleau, a distracted tragic figure, cursing MacGren, threatening him with prison, vowing she'd thrash him. Then she burst into tears. MacGren, like a big baby, clasped and kissed her, and also wept. Finally Mama had hugged them both close to her heart, forgiven them everything and called them 'children of her soul'. She spent the day in Fontainebleau, radiant again, and told them of the spree they'd had in Baden; she was already planning to move into their cottage and live with them in blissful grandmotherly tranquillity. That was in May; that night MacGren had let off fireworks in the garden.

Their first year was simple and peaceful. Her only desire was that Mama would come and live with them quietly. When she pleaded with her, Mama would grow pensive and say, 'You're right. We'll see!' But then she'd be sucked back into the whirlpool of Paris – from where she emerged one morning in a fiacre, dazed and distressed, dressed in a fine fur over an old skirt, to beg a hundred francs! Eventually Rosa arrived, and her sole preoccupation from that moment was to legalize the union. But MacGren, childishly afraid of his grandmother, kept frivolously postponing marriage. He was a real baby, and spent his mornings

451

catching birds with birdlime! But at the same time he was terribly stubborn. She gradually lost all respect for him. One morning in the beginning of spring Mama arrived at Fontainbleau exhausted, weary of life. She had finally parted from Trevernnes. But she recovered almost immediately, and began to adore MacGren, showering him so effusively with caresses and finding him such a darling, that it was sometimes embarrassing. The two spent the day with glasses of brandy, playing bezique.

Suddenly war broke out with Prussia. MacGren waxed enthusiastic and, in spite of their supplications, rushed off to enlist in the battalion of Zouaves at Charette. His grandmother, moreover, had approved of this indication of his love of France and, with a letter in verse in which she extolled Joan of Arc, had enclosed a large sum of money. Rosa had croup at this time and Maria, who scarcely left the sick-bed, bothered little with news of the war. She only knew vaguely about the first battles that had been lost on the border. One morning her mother had burst into the room in her night-gown, looking stunned: the army had capitulated in Sedan, and the Emperor had been taken prisoner! 'It's the end of everything, the end of everything!' her mother had cried in terror. She went to Paris for news of MacGren; in Rue Royale she had had to take refuge in a doorway before a wild screaming crowd who shouted and sang the *Marseillaise* around a carriage where a man sat waxen pale with a scarlet scarf around his neck. And a terrified individual at her side had told her that the mob had gone to fetch Rochefort from prison, and proclaim the country a republic.

She discovered nothing of MacGren. Then followed days of alarm. Luckily Rosa was getting better. But poor Mama was an object of pity: she had suddenly grown old and gloomy and lay stretched in a chair murmuring only, 'It's the end of everything, the end of everything!' And it did indeed seem as if it were the end of France. Every day meant another battle lost; whole regiments were taken prisoner and packed into cattle-trucks to be sent full speed to German garrisons; the Prussians were marching on Paris . . . They could not remain in Fontainbleau; the long winter was beginning and so, with the money from things they sold in a hurry and the money McGren had left, they departed for London.

This had been a whim of Mama's. And in London, lost in the

enormous strange city, and ill too, she had let herself be led by the foolish ideas of her mother. They took an expensive furnished house in the wealthy quarter, in Mayfair. Mama talked of organizing a centre of resistance there for Bonapartist refugees; but in reality what the poor woman hoped to do was set up a gaming-house in London. But these were different times! The Imperialists, without an Empire now, no longer played baccarat. And the two women, with no income and continually paying out money to maintain the costly house and three servants, soon found themselves with enormous debts and no more than one five-pound note to pay them. And there was MacGren somewhere in Paris surrounded by half a million Prussians. They had to sell their jewels and clothes and even their furs, and take three poorly furnished rooms in the poor quarter of Soho. These were typical mean London lodgings in all their dirty solitary gloom; there was a single maid, grimy as an old rag, a few damp logs smoking badly in the fireplace, and for supper an unappetizing piece of cold lamb and beer from the shop on the corner. Eventually they no longer had even the bare shilling for the lodgings. Mama, wasted and weeping, never stirred from her narrow bed. Maria sometimes went at dusk, wrapped in a waterproof, to the pawnshop with bundles of clothing (even underwear, and vests!) so that Rosa should at least not go without her glass of milk. The letters Mama wrote to former supper-companions at the Maison d'Or either went unanswered or brought them a half-sovereign wrapped in a scrap of paper, which brought the humiliation of charity.

One Saturday night she went out in a thick fog to pawn a lace night-gown of Mama's and got lost in the vast city, lost in the yellow gloom, shivering with cold and hunger and persecuted by two brutes who stank of alcohol. In order to lose them she jumped into a cab which took her home. But she hadn't a penny to pay the cabman and her landlady lay snoring in a drunken stupor in her cubicle. The man grumbled and she burst into tears there on the door-step. Then the cabman, moved by her distress, got down from his box and offered to take her to the pawnshop for nothing, and there they would settle their account. They went, and the poor man would only accept a shilling; and believing her French, went so far as to curse the Prussians and insisted on offering her a drink.

In the meantime she looked for work of any kind – sewing, embroidery, translating, copying manuscripts . . . But it was hopeless. Work was scarce during that severe winter; a host of Frenchmen had suddenly appeared, as poor as she, all fighting for a crust of bread. And Mama never stopped weeping; and worse than her tears were her constant hints of how one could easily live in comfort and luxury in London if one was young and pretty . . .

'What do you think of that for a life, my love?' she asked, clasping her hands in distress.

Carlos kissed her in silence, his eyes moist.

'Anyway it was all over at last,' Maria Eduarda continued. 'Peace was proclaimed, the siege ended. Paris was accessible again. The only difficulty was how to return.'

'And how did you?'

One day in Regent Street she chanced to meet a friend of MacGren's, another Irishman who had often dined with them at Fontainebleau. He went to see them in Soho and in the face of such misery, of the pot of watery tea and the reheated lamb bones placed over cold coals, he began, as any good Irishman would, by cursing the English and swearing to spill blood. Then he promised them, with lips trembling, his devoted service. The poor boy also had to struggle for his existence, but he was an Irishman and he set off there and then, armed with all his cunning, to earn somehow in hostile London the small amount of money necessary to see them back to France. And he returned that very night, exhausted and triumphant, brandishing three bank notes and a bottle of champagne. Mama nearly fainted with joy when she saw the gold-capped bottle of Clicquot after so many months of black tea. They bundled up their bits and pieces. In Charing Cross Station, when they were about to leave, the Irishman took Maria aside and, twisting his moustache and stumbling over the words, informed her that MacGren had died in the battle of St-Privat . . .

'Why tell you any more? In Paris I started to look for work again. But everything was in chaos. The Commune was set up almost immediately. We went hungry many a time, I can tell you. But still, it wasn't London and it wasn't winter, nor exile. We were in Paris again, and sharing our suffering now with friends of former times. It was not so terrible as before. But

Rosa began to grow thin and wasted. It was torture to see her growing pale and wan, dressed in rags and living in an attic. And Mama had already started complaining of the heart trouble which eventually killed her. The work I had found was poorly paid and was only enough for the rent of the house and to keep us barely alive. I myself began to grow ill with worry and the hopelessness of it all. But I kept fighting. Mama was a pitiful sight. And Rosa would not live much longer if she didn't have a different life with fresh air and the minimum comfort . . . I met Castro Gomes at the house of an old friend of Mama's, a woman who had not suffered at all in the war, not even at the hands of the Prussians. She gave me sewing to do. The rest you know. I can't even remember it myself. I was carried away . . . I used to watch Rosa sometimes, poor little thing, horribly quiet in her corner and still hungry after she'd scraped clean her meagre dish of bread and milk . . .'

She could not go on. She burst into tears and fell on to Carlos's knees. And he, stirred by this tale of misery, could only stroke her hair with trembling hands and promise her that he would make up for all this suffering.

'But listen,' she said, wiping her eyes. 'There's just one thing more I want to say. And it's the gospel truth, I swear it – I swear by Rosa's soul! My heart was not involved in either of these two affairs. It remained untouched always, it never felt or desired a thing, never, until I saw you. And there's something else I want to tell you . . .'

She hesitated, blushing deeply. Her arms were round Carlos's neck and she hung from him, her eyes on his. And it was even more softly that she whispered the last, absolute confession wrung from her innermost being.

'Not only was my heart untouched but my body was always cold, as cold as marble . . .'

He clutched her to him fiercely, and their lips clung together for long silent moments, completing with a new and almost virginal emotion the perfect communion of their souls.

A few days later Carlos and Ega were on their way in a victoria to Olivais.

Carlos had spent the entire morning in Ramalhete recounting to Ega the impulse which had driven him again, and definitively

this time, in the role of husband, into Maria's arms; and with
the absolute confidence he shared with Ega, he had even revealed
her story in all its painful yet justifying details. Then, as the heat
of the day had passed he suggested they went to Hideaway for
supper. Ega got up and walked round the room and hesitated
before replying. Finally he passed a brush slowly over his
jacket and murmured, as he had done at intervals during
Carlos's long recital: 'Extraordinary! What a strange thing life
is!'

And now as they rolled along the road, cooled by a soft
breeze from the river, Carlos continued to speak of Maria and
their life at Hideaway – a veritable hymn of happiness bursting
from his heart.

'It's a fact, Ega my lad, I feel I know almost perfect happiness
at the moment!'

'And doesn't anyone at Hideaway know anything yet?'

No one – except Melanie, Maria's confidante – so much as suspected the profound alteration which had taken place in their
relationship. And they had agreed that Miss Sarah and Domingos,
the first witnesses of their friendship, should be regally recompensed and dismissed from their service at the end of October when they departed for Italy.

'And you'll marry in Rome?'

'Yes. Or anywhere where there's an altar and a priest. And
there's no lack of those in Italy . . . But there's one nasty snag
hampering all this happiness. That's why I said "almost" just
now. The terrible snag is Grandfather.'

'Too true – old Afonso. Haven't you any idea yet how you're
going to break the news to him?'

Carlos had no idea at all. All he felt was that he lacked the
courage to tell his grandfather: 'This woman whom I am about
to marry has erred severely in her past.' And then, as he had
realized, it would be useless anyway. Grandfather would never
understand the complicated and fatal although justifiable motives
which had led Maria on. Even if he recounted them all in detail
he would only see a vague fragile romance, contrary to
his own strong and candid nature. The ugliness of her sins
would simply wound him and he would be unable to appreciate serenely how irresistible were the motives. It would take
a more flexible, more worldly character than Grandfather had to

understand this case of a noble spirit caught in an implacable net of fatal circumstances. Old Afonso was a block of granite; one could hardly expect from him the subtle discriminations of a modern casuist. All he would see from Maria's life was the tangible fact that she had fallen into the arms of two men. And it would be on this which he would base his opposition as head of the household. What was the good then of his making a confession to the old man, when it would undoubtedly lead to a conflict of feelings and an irreparable domestic separation?

'Don't you agree, Ega?'

'Don't talk so loud. Remember the driver.'

'He doesn't understand decent Portuguese, especially our style. I said, don't you agree?'

Ega struck a match against the sole of his shoe to light his cigar, and muttered: 'Yes, old Afonso's granite true enough.'

So Carlos had designed another plan, a subtler one: he would simply hide Maria's past from the old man, and let him get to know her personally. They would marry secretly in Italy, and later return – she to Rua de S. Francisco and he to Ramalhete. Then Carlos would take his grandfather to the house of a good friend of his, a lady he had met in Italy, Madame de MacGren. There he would surely be captivated at once by Maria's charms, all the attractions of her delicate, serious nature, perfect simple little dinners, straightforward ideas, Chopin, Beethoven, etc. And to complete the conquest of one who adored children, there would be Rosa . . . Then when Grandfather was wholly enamoured of Maria, the little girl and everything in general, he would say to him frankly one morning: 'This superior and most adorable being has a stain upon her past, but I have married her, and considering how worthy a creature she is, did I not do right in choosing her as my wife, after all?' And Grandfather, seeing how irremediable the case was, and with all an old man's tenderness and indulgence to defend Maria, would be the first to admit that this marriage, if it were not the best according to the rules of the world, was at least the best according to the interests of the heart.

'Don't you agree, Ega?'

Ega sat deep in thought, shaking the ash from his cigar. It occurred to him that Carlos had adopted the same complicated

plan for his grandfather as Maria Eduarda had tried with him
– and he was even unconsciously imitating her subtle reasoning.

'And that's the end of it,' went on Carlos. 'If he decides to
be indulgent and accept things, all well and good, we'll have a
big party at Ramalhete. If he doesn't, that's just too bad. Each
one of us will have to live his own life, with grandfather revering
the virtues of family and conventions, and I the rights of the
heart.'

Then seeing Ega still did not speak, he insisted:

'What do you think? Go on, tell me. You're painfully short of
ideas today, old man!'

His friend shook his head as if he were wakening from sleep.

'Would you like me to give you my opinion? Quite frankly?
What the deuce, we're two men discussing the matter like men!
This is what I think: your grandfather is nearly eighty and
you're twenty-seven or somewhere about that. It's painful to say
this, and no one says it with more sorrow than I do, but your
grandfather will die one day . . . Well then, wait until then.
Don't marry. Imagine she had a father who was very old and
stubborn and inflexible, who loathed the sight of Senhor Carlos
da Maia and his neat little beard. Wait a while, continue visiting
Hideaway in Mulato's cab; and let your grandfather finish his old
age in peace, free of disillusion and pain.'

Carlos twirled his moustache in silence, seated well back in
the victoria. Never in all these days of anxiety had such a simple
sensible solution occurred to him. That's what he would do –
wait! He owed it to his grandfather to spare him the pain. Maria,
like any woman, was naturally eager to have her lover converted
into her husband by the sacred bond which purifies everything
and which no force can undo. But he too would prefer a legal
consecration that wasn't hasty and underhand. And then again,
being so honest and generous, she would surely understand their
supreme obligation not to mortify that saintly old man. And
finally she must appreciate his loyalty, as firm and pure as a
diamond. She had his word and from that moment they were
as married, not before an altar and recorded in a church register,
but by his honour and in the unshakeable communion of their
hearts.

'You're right!' he cried at last, slapping Ega's knee. 'You're absolutely right! You're a genius to think of such a thing! I shall wait – but in the meantime . . . ?'

'What do you mean, in the meantime?' laughed Ega. 'That's up to you, not me!'

Then he went on more seriously:

'While you wait you have plenty of the vile metal which makes existence noble. You set up your wife – because she is your wife from today onwards – either here in Olivais or anywhere else, with all appropriate comfort and dignity. And just let things go! There's nothing to stop you from going off on your nuptial trip to Italy now. Then you come back, and just let things go! It's only common sense – it's what Sancho Panza would advise you! What the devil have you got in that parcel that smells so appetizing?'

'A pineapple. Well, that's what I'll do then, my dear fellow – wait and let things go. It's a wonderful idea!'

An idea it definitely was! And most in keeping with Carlos's nature. Why should he indeed involve himself in a tangle of domestic problems just through an excess of romantic chivalry? Maria was fully confident in him; he was young and rich, and the world would open out before them, eager to fulfil their desires. All he had to do was just let things go on as they were.

'You're right, Ega. And Maria will be the first to see the sense and convenience of this. I'm rather sorry to have to postpone setting up my new life and home. But still, it'll have to be so. Grandfather's happiness comes before anything else. And now let's hope Maria's got a worthy dinner to celebrate the new idea!'

Ega grew apprehensive of this meeting with Maria Eduarda as they neared Hideaway. It made him uneasy to think of the embarrassment she would feel and surely be incapable of hiding, aware that as an intimate friend of Carlos, Ega must know of her past and sufferings and relationship with Castro Gomes. This was the reason he had hesitated in coming to Hideaway. But to have stayed away from her would have been to betray an almost offensively charitable desire to spare her humiliation. So he had decided to take the plunge. Who if not he should be the first to hasten to shake the hand of Carlos's fiancée? And apart from everything else he had an infinite curiosity to see her at home, at table, this beautiful creature with the nobility of carriage of a modern goddess! Nevertheless he was feeling nervous as he jumped down from the victoria.

But they were soon at ease. Maria sat embroidering on the steps leading to the garden. She started and blushed deeply when she caught sight of Ega, who was fumbling uneasily for his monocle. They shook hands silently and diffidently. But Carlos had unwrapped the pineapple and in the burst of enthusiasm all their constraint disappeared.

'It's magnificent!'

'What a gorgeous thing! Look at the delicious colours!'

'And what a fragrance! It perfumed the entire road!'

Ega had not been back to Hideaway since the fatal night of the soirée at the Cohens' when he had drunk and raved so. And he reminded Carlos now of the journey in the storm in the ancient cab, the grog Craft had prepared for him, the cold turkey supper . . .

'I suffered profoundly here, senhora, dressed as Mephistopheles!'

'Was Marguérite the cause?'

'Who else would one suffer for in this impassioned world, senhora, if not for Marguérite or for Faust?'

But Carlos wanted him to come and admire the new splendours of Hideaway. And it was in quite familiar fashion that Maria led him through the rooms, regretting the fact that he had come so late, with the summer and the flowers nearly over. Ega was noisily enthusiastic over the changes. So Hideaway had lost its sad cold museum-like air! One could speak there freely at last!

'The man's an absolute barbarian, Maria!' exclaimed Carlos, looking radiantly happy. 'He has a horror of art. He's a Philistine, a Semite!'

A Semite? Ega considered himself an enlightened Aryan! That was why he would never be able to live in a house where every chair had the gloomy solemnity of bewigged ancestors.

'But surely these pretty objects of the eighteenth century remind you rather of lightness and spirit and charming manners?' argued Maria, laughing.

'Do you think so?' asked Ega. 'All these gilt and flowery pieces, all this rococo seems to stem from a wild frivolous vivacity. No! We live in a democracy! And there's nothing like

460

large fat leather easy chairs and polished mahogany for expressing the simple, solid, good-hearted gaiety of the democracy.'

And laughing and chattering light-heartedly about furniture they went down to the garden.

Miss Sarah was walking between the box hedges, eyes lowered and a closed book in her hand. Ega, who knew all about her nocturnal ardours, studied her eagerly through his monocle; and when Maria bent down to cut a geranium, he conveyed to Carlos in a single silent gesture his admiration for the bright pink lips and the full rounded breasts like a well-fed pigeon's. Then, at the end of the garden, near the bower, they found Rosa playing on a swing. Ega seemed dazzled by her beauty, the velvety freshness of a white camellia. He begged a kiss from her. But she insisted, and most seriously, that he take the glass out of his eye first.

'But it's to see you better! So I can see you better!'

'Then why don't you have one in both eyes? You can only see half of me like that.'

'Charming child! Charming!' murmured Ega, although privately he thought the child forward and impudent. Maria glowed.

And this gay intimacy was further developed during dinner. Carlos, speaking right at the beginning of the meal of the country and a chalet he intended building in Cintra, near the Capuchos, had said: 'When we are married . . .' And Ega had referred to this future in a way most pleasing to Maria. Now that Carlos was settled in a stable happiness, he said, he would have to start working! And he reminded them of their former idea of the circle, represented by a magazine which would guide literature and educate taste, raise the standard of politics and rejuvenate worm-eaten old Portugal! Carlos, by reason of his temperament and his fortune (and even his figure, laughed Ega) should direct this movement. And what a supreme pleasure this would give old Afonso da Maia!

Maria listened, attentive and serious. She saw that Carlos, with a full interesting life, would elevate their union most splendidly and demonstrate her fecund and purifying influence.

'You're right, you're quite right!' she agreed enthusiastically.

'And this is apart from the fact that the country needs us,' went on Ega. 'As our beloved and utterly stupid Gouvarinho says, the country has no proper staff. How can it have if people like

461

us, who have all the gifts, are content to drive our **dog-carts**
and write the intimate life of atoms? It's I, senhora, who am
doing this, writing this biography of an atom! No, this dilettantism is absurd. There we are in bars and books always
calling the country a lot of trash. But what the deuce! Why don't
we work to rebuild it, to remake it to our own taste, reshape it
to our own ideas? You don't know this country, senhora! It's
wonderful! It's like a shapeless lump of wax of the best quality.
It's merely a question of who works it. Up till now the wax
has been in rough, rotten, vile and unfeeling hands. We must
work it with the hands of artists, with *our* hands in fact. We'll
make a jewel of this little country!'

Carlos laughed and went on preparing the pineapple on a tray
with orange juice and Madeira wine. But Maria did not like
his laughing. Ega's idea seemed to her a dignified one – a duty of
a noble order. She was almost ashamed, she said, of having
encouraged Carlos's laziness. And now that he was to live amid
calm and tenderness, she wanted to see him working, outstanding,
influential.

'The romantic period has indeed come to an end,' said Ega
with a smile, leaning back in his chair. 'And now . . .'

But Domingos was serving the pineapple. And when Ega tried
it, he burst out with enthusiasm. Ah, it was delicious! Wonderful!

'How did you do it? With Madeira?'

'A spot of genius,' laughed Carlos. 'Tasty, isn't it? Now tell
me honestly whether all I could do for civilization would be
worth this plate of pineapple! It's for these things that I live!
I wasn't born to create civilizations . . .'

'You were born,' agreed Ega, 'to pluck the flowers of this plant
of civilization which the multitude waters with its sweat! And
to tell the truth, so was I, dear boy!'

'No, no! Maria won't have you speaking like that!'

'This sort of talk spoils everything. And Senhor Ega, instead
of perverting Carlos, ought to inspire him.'

Ega protested, his eyes languid and smiling. If Carlos needed
a muse to inspire him, *he* wasn't the person – a bearded graduate
in law . . . His muse was *toute trouvée*!

'Ah, and what magnificent pages and noble ideas a paradise
like this could produce!'

462

And with an indolent caressing gesture he took in Hideaway and the tranquillity of the groves and the beauty of Maria . . . Then in the drawing-room, while Maria played a Chopin nocturne and he and Carlos finished off their cigars at the door to the garden and watched the moon rise, Ega declared that ever since the beginning of dinner, he too, had been toying with the idea of marrying! There was really nothing like marriage and a home, a little nest . . .

'When I think, my dear fellow,' he said, chewing gloomily on his cigar, 'that nearly a whole year of my life was given to that Israelite who likes to take a beating . . .'

'What is she doing in Sintra?' asked Carlos.

'Wallowing in debauches. There's not the slightest doubt that she's given her heart to Damaso . . . You know what *heart* means in this case . . . Can you imagine such lowness? She's downright obscene!'

'And you adore her,' said Carlos.

His friend made no reply. Then, in the house again, in a sudden loathing of the bohemian and romantic life, he extolled in solemn sonorous tones the family and work and man's duties – while he drank numerous glasses of cognac. When he left at midnight he stumbled twice in the avenue of acacias, slightly dizzy by now and quoting Proudhon. And when Carlos helped him into the victoria (which he wanted open in order to communicate with the moon), Ega still clutched his arm to talk again of their magazine which was to be like a strong wind of spiritual energy and virile virtue which they were to set blowing through the country. Finally, stretched back on the seat and taking off his hat to catch the cool night breeze, he added:

'Just one more thing, Carlinhos. See if you can't get hold of the English miss for me. There are delicious vices lurking beneath those downcast eyes . . . See if you can't manage it for me . . . Go on, then, off you go, cabbie! *Caramba*, what a night!'

Carlos was delighted with this first supper with a friend at Hideaway. He had not intended to present Maria to his close friends until after their marriage and return from Italy. But now their 'legal union' was postponed, was something remote and almost lost in the vagueness of the future. As Ega had said, he ought to wait, let things go . . . And in the meantime Maria and he could hardly live there in isolation all winter without the sociable warmth of friends around them. One morning, therefore, when he met Cruges, who had formerly been Maria's neighbour and given him news of 'the English lady', he asked him to supper at Hideaway the following Sunday.

The maestro turned up in a cab late in the afternoon, dressed in dress-coat and white tie: and the light informal suits which Carlos and Ega were wearing straightway put him ill at ease. Any female, apart from the Lolas and the Conchas, embarrassed him and reduced him to silence. Maria, with her bearing of a *grande dame,* as he put it, intimidated him to such an extent that he stood before her without a word, scarlet-faced and fiddling with the linings of his pockets. Before dinner Carlos offered to show him the garden. The poor maestro, catching his ill-made dress-coat on the bushes, did his utmost to find some compliment about the beautiful position, but all that came out were inexplicably slipshod clichés: 'charming place', 'nice little nest' . . . And this in turn made him furious, and he sweated profusely, unable to understand how such shabby comments, so contrary to his delicate artist's nature, could pass his lips. When he sat down to dinner he was suffering a most ungracious fit of spleen and taciturnity! Even a controversy on Wagner and Verdi, which Maria generously contrived for him, failed to open those stony lips. Carlos did his best to draw him out by recounting the trip to Cintra when he had been looking for Maria in the Lawrence, and he had found instead the fat matron with a moustache and a little dog in her arms, arguing fiercely with her companion in Spanish. But to every cheerful question of Carlos's: 'Do you remember, Cruges?' 'Isn't that right, Cruges?' – the scarlet-faced maestro only muttered a sour 'yes'. He was like a funereal clog there at Maria's side. The dinner was a failure.

They decided to go out for a short ride in the break after coffee. And Carlos was just picking up the reins, and Maria sitting back buttoning her gloves, when Ega, fearful of the evening air, jumped out of the brake and back to the house for his coat. At that moment they heard a horse trotting towards them along the road, and the Marquis appeared.

This was a pleasant surprise for Carlos, who had not seen him all that summer. The Marquis stopped, taking off his wide-brimmed hat with great ceremony when he saw Maria.

'I thought you were in Golegã!' exclaimed Carlos. 'Cruges here told me you were there. When did you get back?'

He had returned the day before. He had gone to Ramalhete – quite deserted. Now he had come to Olivais to see one of the Vargas brothers who had just got married and had taken a house there to spend the first few weeks of married life.

'Which one, the fat one, the racing one?'

'No, the lean one, the yachting one.'

Carlos leant over to study the Marquis's little mare, a well-marked, pretty brown bay.

'Is this new?'

'Yes, she's a little palfrey of Darque's. Would you like to buy her? I'm a little heavy for her, and she'd pull a dog-cart.'

'Ride round and let me see.'

The Marquis rode round, sitting well in the saddle and showing off the mare to advantage. Carlos thought she moved well. Maria murmured, 'Very pretty, a fine head . . .' Then Carlos introduced the Marquis de Sousela to Madame MacGren. He pulled up beside the carriage, hat in hand, to shake Maria's hand, and while they waited for Ega, who was taking an interminable time getting his jacket, they talked of the summer and Santa Olávia, of Olivais and Hideaway. It was such a long time since the Marquis had been there! The last time he had come he had been a victim of Craft's eccentricity.

'Just imagine,' he said to Maria Eduarda, 'this Craft invited me to lunch. When I arrive the gardener tells me that Senhor Craft, plus valet and cook, have gone to Oporto; but Senhor Craft has left a note for me in the drawing-room. I go to the drawing-room and I see a sheet of paper hanging from the neck of a Japanese idol, bearing these words, more or less: "The god Chi has the honour of inviting the Marquis, in the name of its absent master, to pass to the dining-room where he will find on a sideboard cheese and wine, which should be sufficient lunch for a strong man." And that's what I had for lunch. And rather than eat alone, I shared it with the gardener.'

'I hope you had your revenge!' laughed Maria.

'You can be sure I did, senhora. I invited him to dinner, and when he arrived from Hideaway here, my door-keeper told him that I had gone away and that there was neither bread nor cheese in the house . . . As a result of that Craft sent me a dozen magnificent bottles of Chambertin. But I've never set eyes on the god Chi again.'

The god Chi was still there, hideous and obese. And Carlos naturally invited the Marquis to revisit his old friend Chi that evening on his return from the Vargas's house.

The Marquis arrived at ten o'clock and they spent a charming few hours together. He shook Cruges out of his gloom immediately, dragging him off masterfully to the piano; Maria sang; and the conversation was witty. Their hideaway of love sparkled until late with the first party that had taken place there.

These happy gatherings were at first, as Ega described them, dominical; but autumn was growing chilly and soon the trees of Hideaway would shed their leaves, so Carlos increased them to two a week – their old University holidays – Sundays and Thursdays. He had discovered an excellent Alsatian cook, who had been brought up according to past traditions, who had served under the Bishop of Strasbourg, and whom the extravagances of a son and various other misfortunes had drawn to Lisbon. And Maria composed her dinners with the most delicate of art: the Marquis considered the day when he dined at Hideaway his 'day of civilization'.

The table shone; and the tapestries, representing groves of trees, enclosed them in a cool shade like that of a woodland retreat where, by some strange chance, silver candelabra glittered. The wines came from the excellent cellars of Ramalhete. And everything in heaven and earth was ardently discussed there – except Portuguese politics, which was considered an indecorous subject among people of good taste.

Rosa put in an appearance at coffee, exhaling the charm of a fresh flower from her smile and uncovered arms and fluffy dresses over black silk stockings. The Marquis adored her and was a rival of Ega, who had begged her hand in marriage from Maria, and who was now composing a sonnet in her honour. Rosa, however, preferred the Marquis, and found Ega 'very . . .' – and she completed her opinion by gesturing with a little curved finger in the air, as much as to say he was very odd.

'There you are!' he exclaimed. 'Just because I am more civilized than the other fellow! It's a case of simplicity unable to comprehend the sophisticated.'

'No, you poor fellow,' they corrected him. 'It's because you're so unoriginal! It's nature repelling convention!'

They drank to Maria's health. She smiled, happy among her new friends, and divinely beautiful. She generally wore dark colours and the incomparable splendour of her skin shone white from the modestly cut neckline.

Then they decided to have some celebrations. One Sunday when the bells were chiming in the distance and fireworks were whistling into the air, Ega lamented the fact that his austere philosophical principles prevented him, too, celebrating that village saint who had no doubt been in life a charming obstinate old fellow, full of illusions and gentleness. But then, he added, must it not have been on just such a clear day, bright under such a fine sun-filled sky, that swords were crossed in the battle of Thermopylae? Why not let off a bunch of fireworks in honour of Leonidas and his three hundred? And they let off their fireworks to the eternal glory of Sparta.

After that they celebrated other historical dates. The anniversary of the discovery of the Venus de Milo was commemorated by a flaming balloon. On another occasion the Marquis brought a group of famous *fado*-singers from Lisbon, all packed close in one cab – Pintado and Vira-vira and Gago; and after supper, until quite late, five guitarists sobbed out the saddest of Portuguese airs, with the moon shining bright on the river.

When they were alone, Carlos and Maria spent their mornings in the Japanese summer-house for which they had a special affection seeing that it was their first rendezvous, and in that little cosy nook their hearts beat stronger and nearer to one another. Carlos had replaced the straw wall-mats by beautiful straw- and pearl-coloured Indian bedspreads. One of his major occupations these days was to embellish Hideaway: he never came from Lisbon without bringing some little Saxe figure, or a piece of ivory or china – like a happy bridegroom finishing the adorning of his nest.

In the meantime Maria never stopped reminding him of Ega's intellectual plans: she wanted him to work and acquire a name for himself. This would be a great source of inner pride to her, and the supreme joy of his grandfather. So, in order to content her (rather than to satisfy the demands of his own spirit), Carlos turned again to some literary articles on medicine he was writing for the *Gazeta Médica*.

He worked in the summer-house in the mornings. He took along drafts and books and the famous manuscript of his *Medicine, Ancient and Modern*. And he found it delightful to sit there in a light silk jacket with his cigarettes beside him and around him the cool rustle of trees – polishing his phrases while she sat embroidering in silence at his side. His ideas sprung forth with more originality and the style acquired more colour in that cool satin-lined summer-house which was perfumed with Maria's presence. Maria respected this work as if it were something noble and sacred. In the mornings it was she herself who cleaned away the faint film of dust which blew in through the window on to his books; she tidied the white sheets of paper and carefully put out new pens; she was even embroidering a satin-covered feather cushion so the writer would be more comfortable in his enormous tooled-leather chair.

One day she offered to make a fair copy of an article. Carlos, delighted with her neat handwriting, which was almost comparable with the legendary hand of Damaso, began to use her as his copyist, feeling on account of this more attachment to a work in which she took a part. What pains the poor creature took! She bought a special paper for the job, a smooth ivory-coloured paper, and with her little finger crooked in the air, set about transcribing Carlos's weighty considerations on Vitalism and Transformism, with as much delicacy as if she were creating a piece of lace. And a kiss paid her handsomely. At times Carlos gave Rosa her lessons – one day on history, making the facts picturesque as if they were a fairy-tale; another day it would be geography, when he fascinated the child with tales of countries where black people lived, and ancient rivers which flowed beside the ruins of sanctuaries. This was Maria's greatest pleasure. She listened with a religious silence and seriousness to that beloved creature teaching her daughter. The work slipped from her fingers – and her eyes misted with tears as she watched how engrossed Carlos was, and how fascinated the child was as she sat at his feet absorbing stories of Jeanne d'Arc or of the caravels which had gone to India.

About the middle of October Afonso da Maia spoke of returning from Santa Olávia, as soon as some alterations he was
having made to the old part of the house and the coach-house
were finished. Recently he had been seized by the urge to rebuild – it was rejuvenating, he said, to feel the new wood and
smell the fresh paint. Carlos and Maria were also thinking of
leaving Olivais. Filial duty forbade Carlos to remain there when
his grandfather returned to Ramalhete. Apart from that, late
autumn was turning dark and stormy, and Hideaway was hardly
idyllic in those conditions with the garden stripped bare and
inundated with water, and a mist hanging over the river; also
there was only one fire in the house – in the cretonne-curtained
study – apart from the sumptuous fireplace in the dining-room
which, between its Nubians, sent out vile clouds of smoke whenever Domingos tried to light it.

One morning at this time Carlos, who had stayed late with
Maria and then been unable to sleep in his flimsy cottage because of a storm outside and the lashing of the gusts of wind
and rain, arose at nine and went to Hideaway. Maria's windows
were still closed; the morning was growing clear; the garden was
gleaming from its bathe, and the fine blue air shone with the
beautiful silent grace of a winter's day. Carlos was strolling
about, looking at the pots of chrysanthemums when he heard the
bell of the gate ring. It was the postman. Carlos had written
to Cruges a few days before to ask if the flat in Rua de S. Francisco would be vacant when the cold set in in December, and
now, expecting a reply, he went to open the gate, accompanied
by Niniche. But the mail today consisted only of a letter from
Ega and two newspapers – one addressed to him, and one to
'Madame Castro Gomes, c/o Sr Craft, Olivais'.

As he wandered along between the acacias, he opened the
letter from Ega. It bore the previous day's date and had been
written 'at night, in a hurry.' He wrote: 'Read in this vile paper
I am sending you the superb Tacitus-like piece of prose it con-
tains. But don't get alarmed: I managed with pecuniary aid to
suppress the lot, all except two copies which went, one to Hideaway and the other (ah! the supreme logic of constitutional
habits!) to the Palace, to the Head of State! But not even this
will reach its destination. Anyway I have a strong suspicion as
to the gutter this filth issued from, and we need to take pre-

cautions. Come right away! I'll wait for you till two o'clock. And as Iago said to Cassius, "Put money in thy purse".'

Carlos uneasily unwrapped the paper. It was called *The Devil's Trumpet*, and paper, lay-out, the numerous italics, the worn-out type – all revealed baseness and vulgarity. On the front page two pencil crosses marked an article which Carlos could see at a glance was dotted here and there with his name. And he read this: ' "Hello there, Senhor Maia, sir! Don't you go to the consulting room these days? Don't you visit the sick in the district now, you rogue?" This taunt was flung in the Chiado, at the door of the Havanesa, at our famous Maia of the English horses, Maia of Ramalhete, chock-full of *chic* . . . And a little bird who happened to be passing heard the following wisecrack: "Our Maia finds it cosier to cuddle in the skirts of a married lady of Brazilian extraction, who is neither Brazilian nor married and who the simpleton Maia has set up in a house away over near Olivais, to enjoy the *fresh air*! It takes all sorts to make a world! The poor fellow thought he'd made a conquest; but he's the laughing-stock of men of good taste here, for what the tart likes is not his handsome eyes but his handsome pocket . . . This nitwit (who capers around on nags of Albion, as if he were a marquis, *the* Marquis!) believed he'd caught a lady of elegance, a lady from the boulevards of Paris, and married withal, and titled! And he's found all he's got (and this is enough to make people laugh fit to burst their bellies!) – he's found all he's got is a well-worn *cocotte* that a Brazilian brought to our shores, as he was fed up with her, to pass on to us . . . And it was Maia who got landed with her! Poor fool! All he got was what others had finished with, because the hussy had already, before charming Maia, had a bit of a good time in Rua de S. Francisco with one of our brighter lads, but he had cleared off too, for, like us, he prefers the lovely Spaniards . . . But Maia's only rubbish anyway. And as that is the state of things, we say "beware", for the Devil here has his trumpet ready to proclaim to all the world the fine deeds of All-conquering Maia! So good luck there, Senhor Maia, sir!'

Carlos stood motionless between the rows of acacias, the paper clenched in his hand, furious and speechless, as if he had just received a handful of mud in his face! It was not so much anger at seeing his love abased by the vulgar publicity of this sordid paper, it was the horror of feeling those cheap slang expressions that only Lisbon was capable of producing, splattering their putridness like dirty grease over Maria and him and the splendour of their passion . . . He felt himself soiled. And one idea only penetrated his confusion – he must kill the brute who had written it.

Kill him! Ega had suppressed the edition, so he must know the journalist responsible. It was of no importance whatsoever that the two copies he held in his hand were the only ones extant. He had had mud flung in his face. It was the same whether the insult was proclaimed aloud through every square, or hurled at him privately on a single sheet. And whoever had dared such a thing must be brought low, annihilated!

He decided to go immediately to Ramalhete. Domingos was polishing silver at the kitchen window and whistling as he worked. When Carlos told him to go to Olivais for a coach, the good fellow looked at his watch and reminded him:

'You'll have Torta's cab here at eleven, that Madam ordered to take her to Lisbon.'

Carlos remembered then that Maria had arranged the day before to go to Aline and the bookshops. Another nuisance, just the day when he needed to be free – he and his cane! But Melanie, passing by at that moment with a jug of hot water, said that her mistress had not yet dressed, and perhaps would not be going to Lisbon after all. And Carlos began his pacing again – backwards and forwards on the grass carpet between the walnut trees.

Finally he sat down on the cork bench, unwrapped the *Trumpet* addressed to Maria and slowly reread the vile prose: in this copy destined for her, the slang seemed even more insulting and intolerable, demanding a bloody vengeance. It was really incredible that anyone should dare to fling such filth at so quiet and inoffensive a woman. And his indignation spread from the journalist who had spat out this despicable article to the putrid society which had produced such a creature. Every city had its vermin of course. But only Lisbon, only vile Lisbon, with its moral corruption, its social debasement, its complete lack of good sense and good taste and its low tricks and slang, could produce a *Devil's Trumpet*

And in the midst of this moral indignation, a sharp biting pain

471

pierced him. Yes, all Lisbon society might make a cesspool of
that perfect corner of his world – but was there actually any
calumny in what had been written? No. It was simply Maria's
past, which she had cast off like a dirty torn garment, which he
himself had interred, covering it over with his love and even his
name – and which someone had exhumed to expose it to the
daylight in all its tatters and stains. And this would threaten
his life henceforth, a menace hanging over him. In vain might
he forgive, in vain might he forget. All the world around him
knew. And at any time interest or evil could write another such
article.

He got up, shaken. And there, under the leafless trees which
during the summer had whispered over them and refreshed
them with their shade, where he had strolled with Maria – the
elected companion of his life – Carlos asked himself for the
first time whether domestic honour and social honour and the
purity of the men from whom he was descended, and the dignity
of the men who would be his descendants, permitted him to
marry her.

Devote all his affection and his future to her, certainly! But
marry . . . And suppose he had a son? His son one day might
read in some *Devil's Trumpet* that his mother had once been
the mistress of a Brazilian after being the mistress of an Irishman. And if his son, indignant, should cry out 'Calumny!' he
would have to lower his head and murmur 'Truth!' And his
son would see himself attached for ever to a mother whose sacrifices and charm were not known, but whose errors were cruelly
known to all the world.

And she too! If he called upon her reason, so upright and
honest, showing her how some vile *Devil's Trumpet* could one
day wound a son of theirs with insults and derision, she herself
would willingly release him from his promise and be content to
slip into Ramalhete by his private stairway lined in cerise-
coloured velvet, as long as she knew a strong unchanging love
awaited her above. She had never again, all that long summer,
referred to a union different from that which bound their hearts
so loyally and peacefully now. No, Maria was no devotee, worried
about mortal sin! What did the priest's blessing matter to her?

Perhaps, but after offering her this blessing at the most
dramatic moment of their long love, was he now to say to her,

'Sorry, this was just a piece of childishness that we had better forget'? No, nor would his heart want such a thing. Rather did it bend before her, bend in warmth and generosity before her, while his cautious sober reason argued. She was everything his soul yearned for, her arms were everything his body could desire; where she was not there could be no happiness, and the only wise thing to do was bind himself to her definitively by the strongest possible link – his name – however much the *Devil's Trumpet* thundered through the air. And thus he would fling a glorious challenge in the face of the world, affirming the omnipotence of the one and only kingdom of Passion! But first he'd kill that journalist! He paced up and down, flattening the turf. And all his problems resolved themselves at last in a great fury against the infamous rogue who had slavered upon his love and who had for an instant caused such torment and doubt.

Maria opened a window near him. She was dressed in dark clothes ready to go out; and it only wanted her tender smile and the full warm beauty of those splendid shoulders, which rose out of the close-fitting cloth, for Carlos to feel an immediate loathing for those disloyal and cowardly thoughts to which he had abandoned himself for a brief moment under the leafless trees . . . He ran to her. The kiss he gave her, long and tender, bore all the humility of a supplication for forgiveness.

'What's the matter? Why so serious?'

He smiled. He denied being serious, in the sense of solemn. Perhaps a little annoyed. He had received a letter from Ega – another of Ega's perpetual complications. And he had to go to Lisbon now, and stay the night there in all probability.

'All night?' she cried, with disappointment in her voice and placing her hands on his shoulders.

'Yes, very likely. It's infuriating! One must always expect the unexpected with Ega's affairs. You're going to Lisbon today, aren't you?'

'I am now, most definitely. If you want me to, that is.'

'It's a nice day. But it will be cold on the road.'

These were just the days Maria liked, these wintry days with a bright sun and a fresh wind which made her feel lighter and more alive.

'Right,' said Carlos, throwing away his cigarette. 'Let's have lunch, my dear . . . Poor Ega must be howling with impatience.'

While Maria went to hurry Domingos up, Carlos wandered slowly across the wet grass to the low row of bushes which enclosed Hideaway at one side like a hedge. From there the ground swept downhill dotted with little farms and white walls, olive groves and a tall factory chimney with smoke curling out. Farther off shone the cold blue stretch of river and behind that the darker blue of the hills with a white cluster of houses nestling at the edge of the water, sharp and clear in the soft transparent air. He stood still for a moment, gazing over the scene. And that village of whose name he had no idea, so quiet and restful under the winter sun, gave Carlos a sudden desire for calm and obscurity in some hidden corner of the world beside a strip of water, where nobody knew him and there were no *Devil's Trumpets*, and where he could enjoy the peace that a simple, poor fellow enjoyed, under his humble roof, with a woman who loved him.

Maria called to him from the dining-room window where she was leaning out picking one of the last climbing roses.

'Beautiful weather for a long journey, Maria,' said Carlos as he approached across the grass.

'Lisbon's very beautiful now, though, too, with this sun . . .'

'Yes, I suppose so, apart from the Chiado, with all its scandal-mongering and petty politics and the rest of the horrors . . . For my part I fancy a hut in Africa at the moment!'

They sat long over lunch after all. It was just on one when Torto's cab set off along the road which was still shining wet from the night's rains. Going downhill, just out of the town, they met a cab which was panting up the hill. Maria thought she caught a glimpse of a white hat and Ega's monocle. They stopped. And it was in fact Ega, who had also recognized Hideaway's cab and was now leaping over the puddles with long stork-like legs, calling to Carlos.

But when he saw Maria he stopped in embarrassment.

'What a nice surprise! I was just coming to see you. It was such a fine day, I said to myself – '

'Right. You'd better pay off your cab and come along with us,' Carlos interrupted, fixing Ega with anxious eyes as if to discover what motive had brought him there so impatiently.

Inside their cab, Ega, unable to give vent to his feelings about the *Trumpet* in front of Maria, began to talk, under

Carlos's searching eyes, about the winter and the floods in the Ribatejo ... Maria picked up a book. Terrible, two little babies had been drowned in their cots, vast numbers of cattle had been lost, a real disaster!

At last Carlos could contain himself no longer: 'I received your letter.'

Ega hastened to assure him: 'Everything's arranged! The matter's settled! And really my purpose in coming out here was purely a bucolic one.'

Maria discreetly looked out of the window to the river. Ega then made a rapid gesture with his fingers, indicating 'money, it's just a question of money'. Carlos reassured him and Ega returned to the subject of the floods in the Ribatejo and the literary and artistic evening that they were going 'to commit' in the Trindade in aid of the distressed. It was to be a vast solemn official affair. Parliamentarian tenors, literary nightingales, pianists decorated with the order of Santiago, all the sentimental sweet-voiced elements of constitutionalism were 'going to attack'. The king and queen would attend, garlands of camellias were already being woven to decorate the room. He, demagogue though he was, had been invited to read a chapter of his *Memoirs of an Atom*. He had modestly refused, there being nothing sufficiently idiotic in it to please the capital. But he had recommended Cruges, and the maestro was going to wake the crowd to a frenzy – or lull them to sleep – with one of his 'Meditations'. Then there was to be a social poem by Alencar. Everything, in fact, pointed to an immense orgy.

'And Senhora Dona Maria should go too!' he went on. 'It's going to be supremely picturesque. You'll have a chance to see all romantic, liberal Portugal there *à la besogne*, all bow-tied in white and giving all they've got in them to give!'

'Yes, you really ought to go,' laughed Carlos. 'If Cruges is playing and Alencar is reciting, it's practically our party!'

'But of course!' shouted Ega, searching excitedly for his monocle. 'If there are two things that are worth seeing in Lisbon, it's a Lenten procession and a poetic evening!'

They were passing the Largo do Pelourinho. Carlos called out to the coachman to stop at the end of Rua do Alecrim: they were going to get out and pick up the tram there to Ramalhete.

But the cab stopped before it reached the hill, outside a

tailor's shop. And there stood a tall old gentleman dressed in mourning with white apostle-like whiskers, putting on his gloves. When he saw Maria, who was looking out of the window, a look of surprise crossed the old man's face; then with a slight colour in the pale broad cheeks, he gravely took off his hat, an enormous curly-brimmed hat of the 1830s, with a crape ribbon round the crown.

'Who's that?' asked Carlos.

'It's Damaso's uncle, Guimarães,' said Maria, who was also slightly flushed. 'How strange that he's here!'

Ah yes! The famous M. Guimarães of the *Rappel*, the intimate friend of Gambetta! Carlos remembered now having met the patriarchal gentleman in the Price with Alencar. He too greeted him; the old man once more lifted, this time with an even graver air, the sombre carbonari hat. Ega snatched up his monocle to study this legendary uncle of Damaso's, who helped to govern France; and when they had taken their leave of Maria and the cab was on its way up Rua do Alecrim, and they were crossing the road to the Hotel Central, he turned again, fascinated by those manners, those austere, revolutionary's whiskers.

'Fine type! And magnificent hat, don't you think? Where the devil did Dona Maria meet him?'

'In Paris. This M. Guimarães was a great friend of her mother's. Maria has already spoken to me about him. He's a poor wretch, and neither friend of Gambetta's nor anything. He translates articles from Spanish newspapers for the *Rappel*, and goes hungry.'

'But what's all this Damaso says then?'

'Damaso's a liar. But let's get down to business. This foul *Trumpet* that you sent me, tell me about it.'

They strolled slowly along the Aterro and Ega told the story of the vile piece. He had received the *Trumpet* the afternoon before in Ramalhete. He already knew the scurrilous paper, already knew personally the proprietor and editor, a so-called Palma *Cavalhão* to distinguish him from another worthy gentleman called Palma *Cavalhino*. He realized immediately that if the prose was Palma's, the inspiration came from elsewhere. Palma knew nothing of Carlos nor Maria nor the house in Rua de S. Francisco, nor Hideaway. It was hardly likely that he'd

476

write, for intellectual fulfilment, an article that could only bring him unpleasantness and possibly blows. He had simply been paid to publish the article. And where money is concerned, he who pays almost always wins. So, working on this solid principle, he had rushed off to capture Palma in his den.

'You know his den too, then?' asked Carlos horrified.

'Not so well as all that. I found out from the Secretary of Justice, an individual who had had some dealings with him over the publication of religious almanacs.'

He had made his way to his den then, and there found things nicely arranged by an accommodating Providence. First, after producing five or six copies, the machine, worn out by printing other such scurrilous pieces, had had a breakdown. Then again Palma was furious with the gentleman who had ordered the article, who had not played straight in the most serious matter of lucre. So no sooner had Ega proposed buying the complete edition than the worthy journalist extended a large nail-bitten hand, trembling with hope and gratitude. He had given him five sovereigns and promised him a further ten.

'It's dear, I know, but what else was there to do?' went on Ega. 'I wasn't calm enough, I should have haggled more. And when I asked for the name of the gentleman who had commissioned the article, Palma, poor wretch, explained that he had a Spanish girl he was keeping and that his landlord had put up the rent, and that Lisbon was frightfully expensive and that literature in this miserable country . . .'

'How much does he want?'

'A hundred *milreis*. But probably if we threaten him with the police he'll accept forty.'

'Give him the hundred, give him anything as long as I have the name. Who do you think it is?'

Ega shrugged his shoulders and drew a slow line on the path with his cane. And more slowly still, he suggested that the author must have been someone familiar with Castro Gomes; someone who used to frequent Rua de S. Francisco; someone who knew about Hideaway; someone who had a bitter desire, for vengeance or jealousy's sake, to wound Carlos; someone who knew Maria's history; and finally someone who was a coward.

Carlos stopped, pale-faced.

'You've described Damaso!' he exclaimed.

Ega shrugged his shoulders again, and went on scratching at the ground.

'Perhaps not. Who knows! Anyway let's go and find out. I finished the deal by arranging to meet Palma at three o'clock in the *Lisbonense*. And you'd better come along too. Have you money on you?'

'If it's Damaso, I'll murder him!' muttered Carlos.

He found he had not brought enough money. So they took a cab to Vilaça's office. His steward had gone to a baptism in Mafra. Carlos had to go and borrow a hundred *milreis* from old Cortés, his grandfather's tailor. When they finally arrived at the *Lisbonense* at nearly four o'clock, Palma was standing at the door lighting a cigarette. He wore a mended velvet jacket and light cashmere trousers clinging to his thighs, and leisurely offered his hand to Carlos – who ignored it. And Palma, with his hand hanging limply in the air, yet unoffended, declared he was just about to leave, as he was tired of sitting waiting upstairs in front of a cold grog. And he was sorry too that Senhor Maia had had the inconvenience of coming all this way.

'I thought I'd finished the little deal with our friend Ega here. Anyway if you like, gentlemen, we'll go upstairs to a private room so we'll be more at ease, and we'll have a drink.'

As he followed him up the gloomy staircase, Carlos realized he had seen those thick-lensed glasses and flabby drab-coloured face before. Of course, he had been in Cintra with Eusèbiozinho and the two Spanish girls on that day when Carlos had been trailing the countryside, like a lost dog, in search of Maria! This made Sr Palma seem even more loathsome. Above, they entered a cubicle with a barred window through which slipped in the dirty light of a courtyard below. On a grubby table-cloth spattered with fat and wine, several plates stood around a cruet with flies in the olive oil. Sr Palma clapped his hands and called for gin to be brought.

Then, jerking up his trousers, he began: 'Well, I trust we are all gentlemen here. As I have said to our friend Ega here, in all this entire business – '

Carlos stopped him, significantly tapping the edge of the table with his cane: 'Let's get to the point. How much money do you want to tell me who commissioned that article in the *Trumpet*?'

478

'To tell us who and prove it!' joined in Ega, who was studying an engraving on the wall portraying naked women at a river's edge. 'The name's not enough. Naturally you're a friend and we trust you, Palma, but what the deuce, you'd hardly expect us to believe you if you told us the fellow was Dom Luis de Bragança!'*

Palma shrugged his shoulders. Obviously he'd have to give proof. He might have other defects, but he wasn't a swindler! In matters of business he believed in frankness and sincerity. If they came to an agreement he would hand them over the proofs there and then, for they were scorching his pocket! There was the letter from his friend commissioning the little joke, the list of people to whom the *Trumpet* was to be sent, and a pencil draft of the article.

'Do you want a hundred *milreis* for this lot?' asked Carlos.

Palma hesitated a moment, adjusting his glasses with flabby fingers. But at this point the waiter entered, bringing the bottle of gin; then the editor of the *Trumpet* liberally offered his guests a drink and even pulled up chairs for them to sit on. Both refused – Carlos standing at the table where he had finally deposited his cane, and Ega wandering over to another engraving depicting two friars getting drunk. When the waiter left the room, Ega went up to the journalist and tapped him on the shoulder in a friendly way.

'A hundred *milreis* is a tidy sum, Palma, old fellow! And understand we're offering you this out of kindness. Because articles of this sort, if they were taken to court, would have you behind bars! Of course this is a different case: you had no intention to offend, we know – but it would put you behind bars all the same! It was a case like this that sent Severino off to Africa. Down in the hold of a big ship with a sailor's meagre ration and an occasional lash of the whip. Distasteful, most distasteful . . . That's why I wanted to resolve the matter here in a friendly, gentlemanly fashion.'

Palma, with eyes lowered, was stirring lumps of sugar into his gin. He sighed, and finally, looking somewhat crestfallen, decided that as he was dealing with gentlemen, and they were all friends together, he'd accept the hundred *milreis*.

Carlos immediately took out of his pocket a handful of sov-

* King of Portugal, 1861-89.

479

ereigns which he let fall in silence, one by one, onto a plate. And
Palma, excited by the clink of gold, straightway unbuttoned his
jacket and took out his wallet which was decorated with a heavy
silver monogram and the enormous crest of a viscount. His
fingers shook but finally he managed to unfold and hold out
three papers. Ega, who was standing by in suspense, with an
eager monocle in his eye, gave a shout of triumph. The writing
was Damaso's!

Carlos examined the papers slowly. There was a short letter
written in slang from Damaso to Palma, enclosing the article
and advising him 'to liven it up a bit'. There was the draft of
the article written out in Damaso's laborious hand, with phrases
added afterwards. There was the list, again written by Damaso,
of the people who were to have a copy of the *Trumpet*, which
included the Countess de Gouvarinho, the Brazilian Minister,
Dona Maria da Cunha, the King, all the friends who frequented
Ramalhete, Cohen, various officials, and the prima donna Fancelli . . .

Palma, in the meantime, nervously drummed with his fingers
on the cloth beside the gleaming gold. And it was Ega who
stirred him into life, after glancing at the documents over Carlos's
shoulder.

'Rake in your cash, Palma, old fellow! Business is business,
and it's getting cold lying there!'

The touch of gold moved Palma. If he had known he was
dealing with a gentleman like Senhor Maia, he wouldn't have
accepted – *caramba!* on his word of honour he wouldn't! But
still! It had been a friend of his, Eusèbio Silveira, who had spoken
to him about it. And then there was Salcêde. And both of them
had laughed and said it was only a joke, that Senhor Maia would
not mind, and promised this and that . . . Anyway, he had
allowed himself to be persuaded. And then both Salcêde and
Silveira had behaved shabbily.

'It was a bit of luck the press went wrong! Or I'd have been
in a nice mess now! And I would've been sorry, on my word
I would, I would have been really sorry. Still, it's over and done
with now! Nothing very terrible's come of it and I've made a
bit to help my rotten life out.'

Again his eye ran over the money he was clutching in his
hand; then he emptied his glass in one noisy, consoling gulp.

Carlos had put away the letters and had his hand on the door. But he turned to put one final question.

'So my friend Eusèbio Silveira had a hand in the business, too?'

Sr Palma loyally insisted that Eusèbio had only spoken on Damaso's behalf.

'Eusèbio, poor wretch, only came as envoy. Damaso and I don't exactly hit it off together. We've not been on very good terms since we had a few words in Biscaínha's house. Just between ourselves, I promised him a box round the ears and he shut up. After a while though we got on speaking terms again when I was doing "Highlife" in the *Verdade*. He came and asked me very civilly, on behalf of the Count de Landim, if I'd write a few kind words about a birthday ball. Then when it was Damaso's birthday I did the same for him. He bought me a dinner and now we're on better terms. But he's no good, that one. As for Eusèbiozinho, he was no more than his envoy, poor wretch!'

Without a further word or gesture to Palma, Carlos turned his back and left the cubicle. The editor nodded a farewell in the direction of the door; then, not in the least offended, he turned blithely back to his gin, giving another heave to his trousers. Ega in the meanwhile slowly lit a cigar.

'You do all the editing yourself now, don't you, Palma?'

'Silvestre helps.'

'Which Silvestre?'

'The one that goes with Pingada. I don't think you know him. He's a lean boy, not bad-looking . . . But what a bore, and he writes drivel. But he knows a few things about society folk. He was with the Viscountess de Cabelas for a time, whom he called "my Cabeluda", "my hairy one" . . . Silvestre's a real wit at times! And he knows a tidy few things about society folk, the capers some of our aristocracy get up to, their affairs, swindles . . . Haven't you ever read anything of his? Trash really. I always have to polish up the style . . . What there was in this issue was a nice little article of mine, a modern thing, just what I like, with a bit of the realistic touch . . . Still, it'll be all right for next time. And another thing, Ega, I'm grateful to you, you know. Whenever you want, I and the *Trumpet* are at your service!'

Ega offered him his hand.

481

'My thanks, noble Palma! Adiós!'

'*Pues vaya usted con Dios, Don Juanito!*' rejoined the worthy gentleman with great wit.

Downstairs Carlos was waiting inside a coupé.

'Now what?' asked Ega at the window.

'Now jump in and we'll go and settle Damaso.'

Carlos had already sketched out a plan for settling him. He intended challenging Damaso as being the proven author of an insulting article in a newspaper. The duel would be with either sword or rapier – one of those weapons whose flashing movement used to drain the colour from Damaso's cheeks in the fencing-room at Ramalhete. If, as was extremely unlikely, he decided to fight, Carlos would puncture him just enough somewhere between his fat cheeks and his stomach to keep him in bed for a few months. Otherwise the only satisfaction Carlos would accept from Sr Salcede would be a document from him stating simply: 'I, the undersigned, am an unprincipled scoundrel.' And for help in these matters Carlos was counting on Ega.

'Thank you! Thank you! Let's go right away!' cried Ega, rubbing his hands, his eyes alight with joy.

But he reminded Carlos that these funereal formalities required another second, and suggested Cruges, a passive, adaptable soul. But the maestro was not to be contacted, for the maid always insisted that Master Vitorino was not at home . . . They decided to go to the Grémio, and send a note from there summoning Cruges 'for a very urgent matter of art and friendship'.

'And thus,' said Ega, continuing to rub his hands, while the cab trotted off in the direction of Rua de S. Francisco, 'thus we finish off our Damaso.'

'Yes, this persecution has got to stop. It's getting to be ridiculous. And with one neat lunge or a letter, we'll have the scoundrel out of the way for a time at least. I'd prefer a sword-thrust. Otherwise I'll leave it to you to compose the terms of a really strong letter.'

'You'll have a good letter, don't you worry!' assured Ega, with a grim smile.

After writing and sending off the note to Cruges they sat and waited for him in the reading-room at the Grémio. The Count de Gouvarinho and Steinbroken stood talking together by the window. And they received a surprise. The Finnish Minister welcomed *cher* Maia with outstretched arms, for he had not seen him since Afonso had gone to Santa Olávia. Gouvarinho greeted Ega full of smiles, renewing the friendship they had struck up in Cintra during the summer. But the handshake he gave Carlos was brief and cold. Carlos had sensed a cooling in their relations a few days before when they had met in Loreto Square and Gouvarinho had murmured an indifferent 'How are you, Maia?' Ah, this was different from the effusion and familiar pats on the back that he had received when he and the Countess used to smoke cigarettes in Aunty's bed in Santa Isabel. Now that Carlos had deserted the Countess, the Rua de S. Marçal and the comfy sofa where he had once collapsed amid a rustle of crumpled skirts, the husband sulked as if he too had been deserted.

'I've missed those fascinating discussions we had in Cintra!' he said, giving Ega the friendly clap on the back with which he had formerly favoured Maia. 'They were first class!'

They were really ferocious arguments they'd had in the courtyard at the Vitor, about literature, religion, morals . . . Why, one night they had even lost their tempers over the divinity of Christ!

'That's right!' agreed Ega. 'You talked as if you were wearing the robes of a religious brotherhood that night . . .'

The Count smiled. Heaven forbid! Nobody realized more than he did the amount of legend there was in the sublime stories of the Gospel. But they were legends which served to console the human soul. That's what he had objected to in his friend Ega's arguments . . . Would philosophy and rationalism ever be capable of consoling a weeping mother? No. Well then . . .

'Anyway it was marvellously stimulating!' he finished, looking at his watch. 'I must confess that I find a high-minded discussion on religion or metaphysics really delightful. That's my real vocation – delving deep into such problems.'

In the meantime Steinbroken, erect in his blue frock-coat with a spray of rosemary in his lapel, clasped Carlos's hands:

'*Mais vous êtes encore devenu plus fort!* . . . *Et Afonso da Maia, toujours dans ses terres?* . . . *Est-ce qu'on ne va pas le voir un peu cet hiver?*'

He was sorry he had been unable to get to Santa Olávia. But how could he? The Royal Family had been staying in Cintra

483

and he had been obliged to pay court and accompany them. Then he had had to pay a flying visit to England and he had only just returned.

Yes, Carlos had seen it in the *Gazeta Ilustrada*.

'*Vous avez lu ça? Oh, oui, on a été très aimable, très aimable pour moi à la Gazette . . .*'

They had mentioned his departure and then his arrival with particularly well-chosen, friendly words. Of course one would hardly expect anything else, considering the sincere affection which bound Portugal and Finland . . . '*Mais enfin on avait été charmant, charmant . . .*'

'*Seulement,*' he went on, smiling politely and turning to include Gouvarinho in the conversation, '*on a fait une petite erreur . . . On a dit que j'étais venu de Southampton par le Royal Mail . . . Ce n'est pas vrai, non! Je me suis embarqué à Bordeaux, dans les* Messageries. *J'ai même pensé à écrire a M. Pinto, redacteur de la* Gazette, *qui est un charmant garçon . . . Puis, j'ai réflechi, je me suis dit: "Mon Dieu, on va croire que je veux donner une leçon d'exactitude à la* Gazette, *c'est très grave . . ." Alors, voilà, très prudemment, j'ai gardé le silence . . . Mais enfin c'est une erreur: je me suis embarqué à Bordeaux.*'

Ega murmured that History would see that the error was corrected one day. The Minister gave a modest smile, and made a gesture as if to beg History not to trouble itself. Then Gouvarinho, lighting a cigar, and glancing furtively at his watch again, asked if his friends had heard anything about the ministerial crisis.

This came as a surprise to both men, as they had not read the papers. But what was the crisis about, asked Ega, at such a calm period with the Houses closed and everyone content and the autumn weather so fine . . . ?

Gouvarinho shrugged his shoulders modestly. There had been a ministerial meeting late the night before, and this morning the Prime Minister had gone to the palace in ceremonial dress, determined to hand over power. That was all he knew. He had not discussed the matter with his friends, nor had he even gone to the Party's headquarters. As at other critical moments he had withdrawn from the scene, held his peace and was waiting . . . He had been there all morning with a cigar and the *Revista dos Dois Mundos*.

Carlos considered such abstention was hardly patriotic.

'Because, after all, Count, if your friends come to power . . .'

'That's precisely the reason I don't wish to put in an appearance,' answered the Count, the colour rising to his cheeks. 'I have my pride, and reasons for having it, perhaps. If my experience and my voice and name are needed, then my colleagues know where I am, and they must come for me.'

He broke off, nervously chewing on his cigar. And Steinbroken, in the presence of these political topics, softly withdrew into the window recess and began to wipe his glasses, impenetrable, observing most carefully the neutrality of which Finland was so proud. Ega had not got over his amazement: why had a government like that fallen – a government with a majority in the Houses, with peace throughout the country, the support of the army, the blessing of the Church, the protection of the *Comptoir d'Escompte?*

Gouvarinho fondled his goatee reflectively and murmured in answer: 'The Government was worn-out.'

'Like a tallow candle?' laughingly inquired Ega.

The Count hesitated. He wouldn't quite say like a tallow candle. Tallow inferred obtuseness. And there was plenty of talent in this government. There was no doubt there was some really powerful talent there.

'That's a good one!' roared Ega, throwing his arms in the air. 'It's extraordinary how every politician in this blessed country has tremendous talent. The opposition insists that the ministers, whom they are always insulting profusely, are, in spite of the idiotic things they do, men of first-class brains and talent! And for their part, the majority declares that the Opposition, whom they are constantly accusing of stupidness, is excessively rich in talent! This regardless of the fact that the rest of the world considers the country rotten through and through. And so we have the outrageously comic result that the country, which by unanimous agreement is the most incompetently governed in all Europe, is bursting with talent! I suggest the following: seeing that the talented men are never any good, let's try the imbeciles for a change!'

The Count smiled condescendingly at these fantastic exaggerations. And Carlos, eager to be agreeable, asked him, lighting his cigar at his: 'What portfolio would you prefer, Gouvarinho, if your friends came to power? Foreign Affairs, I presume?'

The Count made a large gesture of denial. It was hardly likely that his friends would need his political experience. He was a man devoted to study and theory now. And besides, he was not sure his work and property and health and habits would allow him to take up the burden of a governmental office. And apart from anything else Foreign Affairs did not tempt him in the least.

'Never,' he declared decisively. 'To be able to raise one's voice in Europe, as Minister of Foreign Affairs, one needs an army of a couple of thousand men behind one, and a fleet of torpedo ships. We are weak, unfortunately. And I'm not one for second-rate jobs or for a Bismarck or Gladstone to tell me: "This is the way things are to be!" . . . Don't you agree, Steinbroken?'

The Minister coughed and stammered: '*Certainement . . . C'est très grave . . . C'est excessivement grave . . .*'

So Ega then suggested that his friend Gouvarinho, with his geographical interest in Africa, would make an original, enterprising, broad-minded Minister of the Navy . . .

The Count's face shone with pleasure:

'Yes, I might consider that . . . But I tell you this, my dear Ega, all the really fine things, all the great things have already been done. The slaves have been freed, and taught all they need to know of Christianity; they've got custom-houses there now . . . It's all been done, you see. However, there are still a few interesting details to see to . . . Luanda, for example – I mention this as a very small point, mind – the final touch that progress gives. Luanda, for example, needs a theatre, as a civilizing element.'

At this moment a servant approached to tell Carlos that Senhor Cruges was waiting below in the hall. The two friends immediately went to meet him.

'Extraordinary fellow, Gouvarinho!' said Ega, going down the stairs.

'And this,' remarked Carlos with worldly disdain, 'is one of the best politicians we have. All things considered and taking into account all the things one sees and hears, perhaps he's even *the* best!'

They found Cruges at the door in a light jacket, rolling a

cigarette. Carlos asked him to go home at once and put on a black frock-coat. The maestro stared at him in surprise.

'Are we going to a dinner?'

'No, to a funeral.'

And then, without mentioning Maria, he briefly told the maestro that Damaso had published an article in the *Devil's Trumpet* (the whole edition of which had been suppressed so that it was not possible to show him the foul piece) – an article in which the mildest thing he called Carlos was 'scoundrel'. So Ega and he, Cruges, were going to Damaso's house for satisfaction or his life.

'Hmmm,' muttered the maestro. 'What am I supposed to do? I don't know the first thing about these matters.'

'You must wear your black frock-coat and scowl,' said Ega. 'Then come with me. Don't say a thing, address Damaso as "sir", second me in everything I propose, and never relax the scowl nor take off your frock-coat.'

Without a further word Cruges left to clothe himself in black frock-coat and solemnity. But in the middle of the road he turned back.

'Oh, Carlos, I've had a word at home. The first floor is vacant and has been freshly papered . . .'

'Thanks. But now go and make yourself gloomy, quick!'

The maestro hurried off and a cab, coming along at a fast trot, pulled up short in front of the Grémio. Teles da Gama jumped out and with his hands still on the door-handle, shouted to the two friends.

'Where's Gouvarinho? Is he upstairs?'

'Yes. Any news?'

'They've fallen. Sá Nunes has been nominated!'

And he hurried into the courtyard. Carlos and Ega made their slow way to Carlos's house. Carlos lifted his eyes and thought of the afternoon of the races when he had come in the phaeton from Belém to see those windows: it had been growing dark, and behind the closed shutters a light had sprung on, and he had gazed at it as if it were some inaccessible star. How things change!

They returned to the Grémio just as Gouvarinho and Teles were jumping into the waiting calèche. Ega stopped and let his hands fall to his sides.

'There goes Gouvarinho hastening to power, arranging to have *La Dame aux Camélias* played in the backwoods. God help us!'

At last Cruges appeared buttoned in a solemn frock-coat, top hat on and wearing patent-leather boots. They crowded into a hard narrow cab in which Carlos was going to take them to Damaso's house. As he wanted to dine in Olivais that evening he would wait for them by the bandstand in the Estrella Garden to learn the result of 'the dust up'.

'And be swift and terrible!'

Damaso's house, old and single-storied, had an enormous green door with a wire bell-pull that sounded a mournful convent-like bell inside. The two friends waited a long time before they heard the shuffling steps of Damaso's slovenly Galician, who, freed now from pomp and Carlos, was no longer tortured by patent-leather boots. In a corner of the yard a small door opened into the light of a little garden which seemed to be used as a dump for old boxes and empty bottles and other refuse.

The Galician, recognizing Sr Ega, immediately led them up a straw-matted stairway and along a wide musty-smelling corridor. Then, his slippers flapping, he went ahead of them to the far end of the corridor where an open door let in a shaft of light. Almost immediately there came a shout from Damaso: 'Is that you, Ega? Come along in, man! What the deuce . . . ! I'm just dressing . . .'

Embarrassed by such bursts of familiarity and effusion, Ega gravely lifted up his voice from the corridor: 'That's all right, we'll wait.'

But Damaso insisted from the door, as he stood in shirt-sleeves, crossing his braces: 'Come in, man! What the deuce, I've nothing to be ashamed of — I've got my trousers on!'

'There's someone important here,' called Ega, to put an end to the business.

The door closed and the Galician came to open the door of the drawing-room. The carpet was identical to those in Carlos's rooms at Ramalhete. And all around were reminders of the former friendship with Maia: a picture of Carlos on horseback in an ornate frame of china flowers; one of the Indian bedspreads bought from the Medeiros sisters, a green and white affair draped over the piano and pinned in place by Carlos; and on a Spanish escritoire under a glass bell stood a woman's new satin slipper, which Damaso had bought in the Serra after hearing Carlos say one day that in every young man's room there should be some discreetly placed relic of love . . .

Untouched by these *chic* finishing touches, hastily added under Maia's influence, the solid furniture of Salcêde senior stood stiff and straight, all mahogany and blue velvet; and there was a marble console with a gilt bronze clock on which Diana fondled a greyhound, and a costly mirror with visiting cards and photographs of singers and invitations stuck in the frame. Cruges was about to examine these documents when the jaunty steps of Damaso sounded in the corridor. The maestro hastened to Ega's side, who was planted comfortably in front of the velvet sofa with his top hat in his hand.

Seeing him, the worthy Damaso, who was all buttoned up in a blue frock-coat with a camellia bud in his buttonhole, laughingly flung his arms in the air:

'So this is the "someone important", is it? You will have your jokes! And here I am putting my frock-coat on . . . I almost wore my decorations!'

Ega stopped his chatter with a serious voice:

'Cruges is no more important than us, but the matter which brings us here is very important; it's a very serious, delicate matter.'

Damaso stared at his two friends, noticing now their strange behaviour, their dry, solemn manner, their black attire. And he took a step back, the smile completely gone from his face.

'What the deuce is all this about? Take a seat, take a seat!'

His voice petered out, and he sat on the edge of a low armchair beside a table full of richly bound books, waiting anxiously with his hands on his knees.

'We have come here,' began Ega, 'on behalf of our friend Carlos da Maia.'

A wave of blood rushed to Damaso's plump cheeks and up to the parting of his hair crimped tightly by the curling-iron. And he couldn't find a word to say as he sat there horrified, suffocated, stupidly rubbing his knees.

Ega went on slowly, sitting upright on the sofa:

'Our friend Carlos da Maia complains that you have published, or you ordered publication of, an article which was extremely injurious to him, and to a lady of his acquaintance, in the *Devil's Trumpet*.'

'Me? In the *Trumpet*?' burst out Damaso, stuttering wildly. 'What *Trumpet*? I've never written in newspapers, thank the Lord! That's good, that is, in the *Trumpet* indeed . . .'

Ega coldly produced a wad of papers from his pocket, and began to place them one by one in front of Damaso, on the table beside a magnificent edition of the Bible, illustrated by Doré.

'Here's the letter sending the draft of the article to Palma *Cavalhão*. Here also, in your own hand, is a list of the people to whom the *Trumpet* was to have been sent, from the King to Fancelli . . . Apart from this we have Palma's statement: "Damaso did not only commission the article but is practically the author of it . . ." Our friend Carlos da Maia, having been insulted, demands satisfaction by arms . . .'

Damaso gave a leap in his chair, and so suddenly that Ega moved back, half expecting a blow. But Damaso was in the middle of the room now, looking dazed and waving trembling arms in the air.

'So Carlos is challenging me, is he? *Me!* What have I done to him? He's the one that played a rotten trick on me! He's the one – you two know, don't you?'

And he burst into a loquacious rush of complaint, beating his breast, his eyes swimming with tears. It was Carlos, Carlos, who had mortally offended him! All winter long he had begged him to introduce him to a really *chic* Brazilian lady who had lived in Paris and had been leading him on . . . And he, Damaso, good-hearted as he was, had promised: 'Don't worry, I'll introduce you!' And then what had Carlos done? He had taken advantage of a sacred moment, a time of mourning, when Damaso had had to go north to an uncle's funeral, to wheedle himself inside the Brazilian's house . . . And there had been so much scheming that the poor lady had been persuaded to shut her door to him, Damaso – intimate friend of her husband. *Caramba!* He was the one who should have challenged Carlos! But no! He'd been thoughtful, he had wanted to avoid a scandal for the sake of Sr Afonso da Maia. He had complained about Carlos's behaviour, it's true. But only in the Grémio and the

Casa Havanesa, among friends . . . And then for Carlos to do a thing like this!

'Challenging me! Me, whom all the world knows!'

He stopped, suffocated. And Ega, holding out his hand, placidly observed that they were getting away from the point. Damaso had conceived, drafted out and paid for the article published in the *Trumpet*. This he did not deny, nor could he deny, for the proof was there before him on the table; apart from this they had Palma's statement –

'That shameless rat!' shouted Damaso, carried off by another burst of indignation which stunned him and made him whirl round, stumbling against the furniture. 'The unprincipled cur! I'll have it out with him all right! This question with Carlos is nothing – we'll soon settle things, we're both gentlemen . . . But you wait till I see Palma! This is the traitor I'd like to tear apart! I've given that man half-sovereigns, even seven *milreis* once! And treated him to suppers and cab-rides! He's such a scoundrel that he borrowed Zeferino's watch once to go to a christening and then pawned it! And he does a thing like this to me! I'll slaughter him! Where did you see him, Ega? Come on, man, tell me! I want to catch him right away and thrash the life out of him . . . I won't have people squealing on me!'

Ega, with the calm patience of one who realizes he has got his man, reminded him once more of the futility of rambling on in this way: 'We'll never settle the matter like this, Damaso . . . The point is this: you insulted Carlos da Maia, and either you publicly retract this insult or else settle the matter by a duel.'

Damaso, however, was not listening, but appealing in desperation to Cruges who had not moved from the velvet sofa where he sat painfully rubbing his two new patent-leather shoes one against the other.

'Fancy Carlos! A man who called himself a friend of mine! I was everything to him. I even used to copy things out for him . . . You saw, didn't you, Cruges? Didn't you? Go on, say something, man! Don't all be against me! I'd even go and get boxes of his from the customs at times . . .'

The maestro lowered his eyes, his face scarlet with embarrassment. And Ega, fed up with this stalling, gave a final summons:

'In short, Damaso, are you going to retract or fight?'

'Retract?' stammered the other, drawing himself up in a painful effort to affect dignity – and trembling in the process. 'Retract what? That's good, that is! Am I a man to retract?'

'Of course not. Then you'll fight . . . ?'

Damaso staggered back a step, quite distraught.

'I fight? I'm no man to fight duels! It's fists for me! Let him come here. I'll show him I'm not afraid of him – I'll pulverize him.'

He gave short little jabs with his fists as he danced back and forth on his short fat legs. He wished Carlos was there now: he'd slaughter him! But a duel . . . ! This duel business in Portugal was ridiculous – they always ended in a mockery!

Ega meantime, as if his mission were over, was buttoning his frock-coat and collecting up the papers which were scattered over and around the Bible. Then he calmly made the final statement with which he had been charged: if Sr Damaso Salcêde refused to retract and also rejected satisfaction by arms, Carlos da Maia warned him that henceforth wherever they encountered each other, whether in the street or in the theatre, he would spit in his face . . .

'Spit in my face!' shouted Damaso, stepping back as if the saliva were already upon him.

Then suddenly, horrified, covered with beads of perspiration, he rushed up to Ega and clasped his hands frantically:

'Oh João, João, you're a friend of mine. For the sake of our friendship, get me out of this scrape!'

Ega showed generosity. He released himself from Damaso's grip and pushed him gently into a chair, calming him with friendly pats on the shoulder. And he declared that since Damaso had called upon their friendship, Carlos's envoy, exigent of necessity, would therewith disappear and in his place become the comrade of the times of the Cohens and the Villa Balzac. Would Damaso like his advice then? He ought to sign a letter declaring that everything he had had published in the *Trumpet* about Sr Carlos da Maia and a certain lady was of his own invention and utterly false. This was the only way he could save himself. Otherwise, one of these days in the Chiado or in the S. Carlos Theatre, Carlos was going to spit in his face. And when that happened, Damasozinho would have to fight by sword or pistol, if he did not want to be pointed out in all Lisbon as an incomparable coward . . .

492

'And as you know, you're as good as dead, fighting with either of these weapons.'

Damaso lay limp in the depths of the chair, looking at Ega and listening with a stupefied expression on his face. He loosely lifted his arms and murmured from out of his terror:

'Right then, João, I'll sign, I'll sign . . .'

'It'd be the best thing for you. Get some paper then. You're upset at the moment, I'll compose it for you.'

Damaso got up weak-kneed, casting a vague, vacant glance around the room.

'Writing paper? Is it for a letter?'

'Yes, of course – a letter to Carlos!'

The poor wretch's footsteps died away down the corridor, heavy and defeated.

'Poor devil!' murmured Cruges, painfully rubbing a hand over his shoes again.

Ega silenced him with a severe *ssshh!* Damaso returned with his sumptuous monogrammed and crowned paper. To enclose the distressful little scene in silence and secrecy, he pulled close the curtain behind him; and as the vast expanse of velvet unfolded it showed the Salcêde arms: a lion, a tower, a steel-protected arm and underneath, in letters of gold, the formidable motto: 'I am strong'! Ega straightway cleared a space on the table, sat down, and in large letters dated and addressed the paper . . .

'I'll do the draft, then you can copy it.'

'All right,' agreed Damaso, thoroughly shaken, wiping his face with his handkerchief.

Ega began to write slowly and lovingly. And in the embarrassing silence, Cruges finally stood up and limped over to the mirror where cards and photos were displayed stuck between the mirror and the frame. These were Damaso's social glories, the documentary proof of the *chic* which was the passion of his life: cards from titled personages, photos of singers, invitations to balls, entry cards for the races, diplomas proving him a member of the Naval Club and the Jockey Club and the Pigeon-Shooting Club – there were even cuttings from newspapers announcing his birthday and the arrivals and departures of Sr Salcêde, 'one of our most distinguished sportsmen'.

Unhappy sportsman! That sheet of paper Ega was scribbling

493

upon was filling him with growing terror. Good God! Why so much fuss about a letter to Carlos, who was, after all, a close friend? One line would do: 'My dear Carlos, don't be angry, I'm sorry, it was only a joke.' But no! A whole page of small writing with added afterthoughts. And now Ega was turning over the sheet, dipping the pen in the ink as if humiliations were to pour from it without a stop.

Damaso could hold himself no longer, but thrust his face over the table, almost on to the very paper: 'Ega, this isn't for publication, is it?'

Ega reflected a moment, pen poised: 'Probably not. No, I'm certain of it. When he sees you're sorry Carlos will naturally let it lie forgotten at the bottom of a drawer.'

Damaso heaved a sigh of relief. This certainly seemed the most decent action among friends! He really wanted to show how sorry he was, anyway! The article was a piece of foolishness, he admitted now . . . But there it was – where women were concerned, he had always been impetuous, irrascible as a lion.

Less anxious, he fanned himself with his handkerchief, ready to enjoy life once more. He even lighted a cigar and got up without a noise and went over to Cruges, who, limping around the various curiosities the room had to offer, had come to rest, with one painful foot in the air, by the books of music on the piano.

'Done anything new lately?' asked Damaso.

Cruges, very red in the face, mumbled that he hadn't done anything.

Damaso stood still a moment, chewing his cigar. Then casting an anxious glance at the table where Ega was writing interminably, he murmured over the maestro's shoulder:

'A mess like this, imagine! I wouldn't mind except for people I know . . . But see if you can't arrange things so that Carlos keeps that tucked away in his drawer.'

Ega got up at that moment and made his way slowly to the piano, rereading to himself what he had written.

'Excellent – this will settle everything!' he cried at last. 'It will go as a letter to Carlos – it's more correct like that. Then you copy it out and sign it. Listen: "Dear Sir," – you'd better address him like that seeing that it's a case of honour – "Dear Sir, Your friends João da Ega and Vitorino Cruges have ex-

494

pressed the indignation you felt at an article in the *Devil's Trumpet* which I drafted and ordered to be published, and I am therefore writing to declare that this article contained only untruths and incoherences. My only excuse is that I composed and sent it to the offices of the *Trumpet* when I was in the most complete and utter state of intoxication . . ." '

He stopped. He did not turn towards Damaso, who, dumbfounded, had let his arms fall to his sides and his cigar fall to the ground. It was to Cruges that he spoke, adjusting his monocle.

'Do you think it's too strong? I said this as it seemed the only way to preserve our friend Damaso's dignity.'

And he developed the idea, showing how clever and generous he was, while Damaso, confounded, bent to pick up his cigar. Neither Carlos nor he would want Damaso to declare in a letter (that could be made public) that he had published such libel because he was a slanderer. He would have to justify the slander, therefore, by offering a reason which could be regarded as accidental and uncontrollable and would therefore remove all responsibility from the action. And what better reason could a worldly fellow like Damaso, a reputed spark, give than being drunk at the time? Drunkenness was nothing to be ashamed of. Carlos himself, and all of them there, men of honour and good taste, had been drunk at one time or another. Without going back to the Romans, who had considered it a matter of hygiene and luxury, many great historical figures had drunk too much. It was considered so *chic* in England, that Pitt, Fox and a few others never spoke in the House of Commons without being drunk. And what a drunkard Musset was! You could see all history, literature and politics alike were soaked in booze! So if Damaso stated he was drunk, his honour was safe. He was an honourable gentleman who had gone on a spree and committed an indiscretion. Nothing more!

'Don't you think, Cruges?'

'Er, yes, he was drunk, perhaps,' muttered the maestro uncomfortably.

'And don't you think so too, Damaso, quite sincerely?'

'Er, yes, I was drunk, perhaps,' stammered the unhappy creature.

Ega recommenced the reading: ' "Now that I am sober, I

495

recognize, as I have always recognized and declared, that you, sir, have a most honourable character; and the other people whose characters I saw fit to sully in this moment of drunkenness, are worthy only of my respect and highest praise. Furthermore I declare that should I ever again utter an insulting word against you, sir, neither you nor anyone else should pay more attention to it than you would to an involuntary flush of alcohol – for, due to a hereditary failing which frequently appears in my family, I find myself repeatedly in a state of drunkenness. I am, sir, with all respect, etc." ' He spun round on his heels, deposited the draft on the table and, lighting his cigar at Damaso's, explained in a friendly fashion what had led him to include the confession of incorrigible and garrulous drunkenness. It was a further desire to guarantee "our Damaso's" future peace from disturbance. By attributing all the imprudences he could possibly commit to a habit of hereditary intemperance for which he could not be blamed any more than he could for being short and fat, Damaso was protecting himself *for ever* from any more provocations from Carlos.

'You've got a temper, Damaso, and a quick tongue! One of these days you'll be forgetting yourself again, you'll let drop a word against Carlos in the Grémio or somewhere. Without this precaution we'd have this whole business again, the spit in the face, the duel. From this moment on Carlos can never complain again. Here we have the explanation to cover everything – a drop too much, a drop taken under the influence of hereditary drunkenness. Like this you obtain the most desirable thing of the nineteenth century – irresponsibility! And there's no shame as far as your family's concerned, for you haven't any family. What do you say – is this all right?'

Poor Damaso listened to him overwhelmed, incapable of understanding these high-sounding phrases about 'hereditary' and the 'nineteenth century'. One single desire dominated him – to finish with this business and continue again his lazy peaceful life, free from rapiers and ignominy. He shrugged his shoulders helplessly.

'What else can I do? To avoid gossip . . .'

And he sat himself down, put a new nib in his pen, selected a sheet of paper in which the monogram stood out particularly clearly, and began to copy the letter in his magnificent copperplate.

Ega meanwhile, with frock-coat unbuttoned and cigar smoking, circled the table, eagerly following the words being copied out by Damaso's diligent hand, adorned with a large signet ring. For a moment panic seized him: Damaso had stopped, with pen vacillating. Confound it! Had some hidden shred of dignity and revolt been awoken after all in that great flabby heap?

Damaso looked at him with lustreless eyes: 'Is drunkenness spelt with one "n" or two?'

'Two, Damaso, two,' answered Ega affectionately. 'You're getting on fine . . . What beautiful writing you have!'

And the unfortunate fellow smiled admiringly at his handwriting, head on one side as he proudly surveyed this talent of his.

When he had finished Ega checked it and put in the punctuation. The document had to be *chic* and perfect.

'Who's your notary, Damaso?'

'Nunes, in Rua do Ouro. Why?'

'Oh, nothing. It's just a detail that is always asked in these cases. A mere formality . . . Well, my friends, as far as paper and writing and style are concerned the little letter's superb!'

He put the letter in an envelope with large letters on it claiming 'I am strong' and tenderly buried it in the depths of his frock-coat. Then picking up his hat and slapping Damaso on the shoulder with gay, playful familiarity, he went on:

'Well, I think we can congratulate ouselves, Damaso! This could have ended up outside the city somewhere in a pool of blood! As it is it's wonderful. *Adeus.* Don't bother to come to the door. The big evening's on Monday, isn't it? Everybody'll be there, I suppose! No, don't bother, man. *Adeus.*'

But Damaso insisted on accompanying them along the corridor, silent, withdrawn, downcast. And on the landing he retained Ega a moment to ask anxiously: 'This is not to be shown to anyone, is it, Ega?'

Ega shrugged his shoulders. The document belonged to Carlos. But Carlos was such a fine fellow, such a generous fellow!

The uncertainty which was undermining the poor fellow drew a sigh from Damaso.

'And to think I called that man my *friend*!'

'Life is full of disillusions, Damaso old fellow!' remarked Ega, leaping gaily down the steps.

497

When the cab stopped in Estrella Gardens, Carlos was waiting for them impatiently by the iron gate, worrying about getting to Olivais for dinner. He jumped in, tripping over the maestro, and shouted to the driver to get to Loreto Square as quickly as possible.

'Now, my friends, are we to have blood or not?'

'We've something much better,' cried Ega above the rattle of the wheels, flourishing the envelope.

Carlos read Damaso's letter, and was shocked.

'But this is incredible! It's a disgrace to human nature!'

'Damaso doesn't belong to the human species,' laughed Ega. 'What the devil did you expect? That he'd fight?'

'I don't know. But it's disgusting. What are we going to do with this?'

Ega considered it should not be published as it would only awaken curiosity and encourage gossip about the article in the *Trumpet* which had cost them thirty pounds to suppress. But Carlos ought to keep the letter and use it as a threat to hold over Damaso and so keep him harmless for a good many years.

'I'm more than revenged,' concluded Carlos. 'You keep it: it's your work, do what you like with it.'

Ega took it with pleasure, while Carlos, slapping the maestro on the knee, wanted to know how he had comported himself during this call of honour.

'Hopelessly!' cried Ega. 'With expressions of pity for the accused; without a shred of propriety; slumped over the piano; clutching his shoe with his hands – '

'What do you expect?' cried Cruges, unable to contain himself any longer. 'You tell me to put on formal dress and I wear new patent-leather shoes, and they've been killing me all afternoon!'

And unable to stand the offending shoe any longer, he tore it off, heaving an enormous sigh of relief.

The following day after lunch, while a strong south-westerly wind beat lashes of rain against the windows, Ega sat ensconced in a deep armchair in the smoking-room, with his feet to the fire, rereading Damaso's letter; and gradually there arose a deep sorrow that such a colossal document of human cowardice,

498

so interesting both for psychology and for art, should stay un-used for ever in the darkness of a drawer! What an effect, what a superb effect it would make if this confession of 'our distinguished sportsman' should appear one day in the *Gazeta Ilustrada* or in the new newspaper *A Tarde* in the 'Highlife' column, under this title: 'A Case of Honour'! And what a lesson it would be, what a worthy act of social justice!

All that summer Ega had loathed Damaso, convinced since their stay in Cintra that he was Madame Cohen's lover, and that for this fat-bottomed imbecile she had forgotten for ever the Villa Balzac and their mornings together on the black satin bedspread, his tender kisses, the poems of Musset that he had read her, the tasty little lunches of partridge – such a number of poetic delights. But what made Damaso really unbearable was his radiant fanfaronade of 'I am the favourite'; and that air of possession he wore as he walked at Rachel's side along the roads in Cintra, dressed in white flannel; the secrets he always had to whisper to her over her shoulder; the disdainful little wave of the hand he casually gave him, Ega, as he passed . . . It was loathsome! He hated him: and across this loathing flickered desire for vengeance – a beating, dishonour or ridicule which would make Sr Salcéde appear despicable, grotesque, as deflated as a punctured balloon, in the eyes of Rachel.

And now he had this godsend of a letter in which the man solemnly declared himself a drunkard: 'I am a drunkard, I am always drunk!' That was what Sr Salcêde had written on his gold monogrammed paper, cringing in fear like a miserable little street dog hiding its tail between its legs before a threatening stick. No woman could fail to be affected by this.

And was such a decisive document to be locked away in a drawer?

He could not publish it in the *Gazeta Ilustrada* or *A Tarde*, unfortunately, for Carlos's sake. But why shouldn't he show it 'privately', like a psychological curiosity, to Craft and the Marquis, to Teles and Gouvarinho and Cohen's cousin? He could even let Taveria have a copy, who had had a grudge against Damaso ever since a dispute with him in Fat Lola's house, and would read it 'privately' in the Casa Havanesa, in the billiards-room of the Grémio, in the Silva, in the dressing-rooms of actresses . . . And at the end of a week Senhora

Dona Rachel would know, without a doubt, that the chosen one of her heart was, by his own confession, a slanderer and drunkard! Wonderful!

It was so wonderful that he hesitated no more but went up to his room to copy out Damaso's letter. But scarcely had he begun when a servant brought him a telegram from Afonso da Maia, announcing that he would be arriving next day at Ramalhete. Ega had to go out and send a telegram to Olivais to notify Carlos.

Carlos turned up that night very late and chilled to the bone, with a vast amount of baggage because he was leaving Olivais for good. Maria Eduarda was also returning to Lisbon, to the first floor of Rua de S. Francisco which had been freshly carpeted by Mother Cruges, and which they had taken for six months. Carlos was feeling very saddened at the departure from Hideaway. After supper, sitting at the fireside finishing off his cigar, he went over a never-ending stream of memories of those happy days – his cottage and the morning bath in the tub, the celebrations in honour of the god Chi, the Marquis's guitar parties, the long chats over coffee with the windows open and the moths fluttering round the lamps . . . Outside the cold winter-driven showers beat against the windows in the silence of the black night. They both ended up in silence, thoughtfully gazing at the fire.

'There wasn't a single leaf on the trees when I took a last turn round the garden this afternoon,' said Carlos at last. 'Don't you always feel the melancholy of these late October days?'

'Terribly! murmured Ega mournfully.

The morning was clear and white next day when Ega and Carlos, still drowsy and shivering with cold, arrived at Santa Apolónia. The train had just come in. Amongst the people trickling out of the open doorways they picked out Afonso at once with his old velvet-collared cape, clinging to his cane and refusing the offers of men with gold-trimmed hats who were recommending the Hotel Terreirense and the Pomba d'Ouro. Behind came M. Antoine, the grave French chef, wearing a tall hat and carrying in one hand the basket in which travelled Bonifácio.

Carlos and Ega found the old man looking wearier and more

aged, but they praised his appearance and robust strength as they greeted him. He shrugged his shoulders and complained that he had experienced fits of dizziness and a vague tiredness since the end of the summer.

'You're the ones who are really looking well,' he went on, hugging Carlos again and smiling at Ega. 'But what sort of ingratitude was this, John, that kept you here all summer long, without even the briefest visit to Santa Olávia? What have you been doing? What have you both been doing?'

'Thousands of things,' Ega responded gaily. 'Plans, ideas, headlines . . . Above all the plan for a *Revista*, a form of higher education which we intend to launch with a thousand horsepower! Still, we'll tell you all about it at lunch.'

And at lunch, to justify their staying in Lisbon, they talked of the *Revista* as if it were already organized and the articles ready for press – so precisely did they describe the tendencies, the critical slant, the lines of thought on which it would be based. Ega had already prepared a piece for the first number – 'The Capital of the Portuguese.' Carlos was contemplating a series of English-style essays under the title: 'Why the Constitutional System failed here.' Afonso listened in delight to those fine ambitions to controversy and wanted to help finance this great work. But Ega thought Sr Afonso de Maia ought to step into the ring and offer too the fruits of his wisdom and experience. The old man laughed. What! Compose prose – he who hesitated before even drafting a letter to his steward? Anyway all he had to say to his country as the result of his years of experience could be condensed into three brief pieces of advice: to the politicians: 'Less liberalism and more character'; to the men of letters: 'Less rhetoric and more ideas'; to his countrymen in general: 'Less progress and more morals'.

Ega was thrilled! There, right there, was the outline for the spiritual reform which the *Revista* should propagate! They would have to adopt his phrases as their symbolic motto and have them inscribed in gold letters on the cover – for Ega wanted the *Revista* to be original right from the cover. The conversation then turned to the exterior of the *Revista*: Carlos wanted it pale blue with Renaissance lettering; Ega insisted they should model it on the *Revista dos Dois Mundos*, with the colour more canary-yellow. And now, stimulated by their Latin imagination, it was not only to please Afonso da Maia that they were giving a more distinct shape to the original vague plan.

Carlos cried to Ega, with his eyes alight: 'This is really serious! We must see about arranging an editorial office right away!'

Ega flung his arms about: 'Immediately! And furniture! And machines!'

All morning they busied themselves in Afonso's study, drawing up a list of collaborators. But there were difficulties at once. Almost all the writers suggested displeased Ega as they lacked the plastic Parnassian touch and style, of which he wanted the *Revista* to be the impeccable model. And as for Carlos, certain men of letters seemed absolutely impossible to him – though he hesitated to admit that what he found repugnant about them were their social shortcomings and ill-fitting clothes.

One thing at least was decided: the editorial offices. They would be furnished luxuriously with sofas from Carlos's consulting-room and some of the bric-à-brac from Hideaway: and over the door (adorned with a liveried keeper) a black varnished board with the words *Revista de Portugal* in large letters picked out in gold. Carlos smiled and rubbed his hands, thinking how happy Maria would be to know about this decision which would thrust him, as she desired, into activity again, into the absorbing struggle of ideas. Ega could already imagine the canary-coloured magazines piled high in the bookshops, discussed avidly at the evening sessions in Gouvarinho's house, handled with fear by politicians in the House . . .

'We're going to stir Lisbon up a bit this winter, Sr Afonso da Maia!' he shouted, flinging his arms towards the ceiling.

And the old man was the happiest of them all.

After supper, Carlos asked Ega to accompany him to Rua de S. Francisco (where Maria had settled in that morning) to carry the news of their great plan. But at the door they encountered a cart unloading cases; and Domingos, who was helping the carters, announced that his mistress was still dining – and on a corner of the table without a cloth. Ega felt he should not enter with the house in such disorder.

'See you later,' he said. 'I'll go and find Simão Craveiro perhaps and tell him about the *Revista.*'

He went slowly up the Chiado and read the news in the Casa

Havanesa. When he came to the corner of Rua Nova da Trindade
a hoarse-voiced man, enveloped in an oversize jacket, offered him
a ticket. Other vendors around shouted from outside the Hotel
Aliança:

'Tickets for the Ginásio! Get 'em cheap here! Tickets for
the Ginásio! Tickets for sale!'

There was a bustle of carriages with liveried attendants. The
gas lamps of the Ginásio glowed with an air of festivity. And
as he crossed from Loreto Square Ega came face to face with
Craft, who wore a white tie and flower in his buttonhole.

'What's all this?'

'A charity do, I don't know exactly what,' answered Craft.
'Something arranged by the ladies; the Baroness of Alvim sent
me a ticket. Come along and help me bear my charitable cross
to Calvary.'

Ega bought a ticket in the hopes of being able to flirt with
the Baroness. In the foyer of the Ginásio they met Taveira
pacing up and down and smoking in solitude as he waited for
the first play, *Forbidden Fruit*, to finish. Craft suggested 'the
bar and a glass of gin'.

'What's the latest news on the Ministry?' he asked as soon as
they had sat down in a corner.

Taveira did not know. These two long days had been full of
scheming: Gouvarinho wanted Public Works and so did Videira.
There was talk of a terrible scene over Syndicates in the house
of the Prime Minister who had ended by banging his fist on the
table and shouting: 'This isn't Azambuja Wood!'*

'Swine!' muttered Ega with loathing.

Then they talked of Ramalhete, of the return of Afonso, of
the reappearance of Carlos. Craft thanked the Lord that there
would be a house again that winter with fires where one could
spend an intelligent civilized hour.

Taveira joined in with a sparkle in his eye: 'They say we're
going to have an even more interesting centre, in Rua de S.
Francisco! It was the Marquis who told me. Madame MacGren
will be entertaining.'

Craft did not even know she had returned from Hideaway.

'She came back today,' said Ega. 'Don't you know her? She's
a delightful woman.'

* Pinhal de Azambuja: forest outside Lisbon formerly infested by bandits.

'So I believe.'

Taveira had caught a glimpse of her in the Chiado. She looked a beauty. And a pleasant nature too, it seemed.

'Delightful,' repeated Ega.

But *Forbidden Fruit* had finished and men were crowding into the foyer amid a low hum of voices, lighting their cigars. Ega left Craft and Taveira with their gin and hurried to the stalls to look for the Baroness Alvim's box.

Scarcely had he lifted the curtain and raised his monocle to his eye, however, when he caught sight of Madame Cohen in the front row, all in black with a great white lace fan; behind her he saw the black side-whiskers of her husband; and opposite her, leaning against the velvet-covered rail, frock-coated and with a huge grin on his chubby face and a fat pearl in his shirt-front, was friend Damaso, the drunkard!

Ega fell limply into the nearest chair and, forgetting entirely about the Baroness, his mind in confusion, he sat staring at the curtain covered with advertisements and ran his fingers nervously over his moustache.

A bell had begun to ring and people were leisurely returning to their seats. One fat, surly-looking gentleman stumbled over Ega's knee; another, with light gloves and an affected politeness, begged permission to pass. Ega heard nothing, understood nothing; his eyes, which had wandered a little at first, were fastened upon the Cohens' box and they would not move now, held there by an emotion which took away his colour.

He had not seen her since Cintra, where he had caught sight of her from afar, in light-coloured dresses under the green of the trees; and now here, dressed in black, hatless, with that perfect neck gleaming white out of the modestly-cut dress, she had become *his* Rachel again, of the divine times of the Villa Balzac. In the same way he had sat watching her every night in the São Carlos Theatre from Carlos's box, his head leaning against the wooden partition, his whole body bathed in happiness. There she was with her gold lorgnette on its little gold chain. She seemed paler, more delicate, but the remembered languor was in the heavy eyes, and the romantic, faded-lily look; and, as before, her magnificent heavy locks fell in an attractive semi-fastened heap upon her shoulders, giving a suggestion of nakedness . . . Amidst the tuning-up of the fiddles and the scrape of chairs, Ega was swept by the wave of memories which took away his breath and he saw again the wide bed at the Villa Balzac, remembered their kisses and their laughter, the partridges they had eaten as they sat in their underwear on the edge of the sofa, the delicious melancholy of those evenings when she furtively went away, covered in veils, and he remained, tired out, in the poetic twilight of the room, humming *La Traviata*.

'Would you kindly excuse me, Senhor Ega?'

It was a wan-looking gentleman with a thin beard who was claiming his seat. Ega got up in confusion without recognizing Sr Sousa Neto. The curtain lifted. At the edge of the stage a lackey winked his eye at the audience and proceeded, duster under arm, to pass on some confidential remarks about his mistress. And Cohen, standing up now and filling half the box, slowly stroked his whiskers with a well-tended hand displaying a sparkling diamond.

Ega, with a superb show of indifference, directed his monocle on the stage. The lackey had scuttled off in alarm at the furious ringing of a bell; and a shabby sour little shrew dressed in a green dressing-gown and with her hat askew, burst on to the stage, frantically shaking her fan and scolding a quaint little girl who stamped her foot and shrieked: 'I'll always love him! I'll always love him!'

It was irresistible. Ega peeped out of the corner of his eye at the box: Rachel and Damaso had their heads together as in Cintra and were whispering and smiling. And everything within Ega suddenly exploded into a terrible loathing of Damaso! Leaning against the doorpost he gritted his teeth in a bitter desire to go up there and spit on those fat cheeks.

He could not take his burning eyes off them. On stage an old general, gouty and grumbling, shook a newspaper and shouted for his tapioca. The stalls laughed. Cohen laughed. And it was at that moment that Damaso, who was leaning over the edge of the box with his hands, in gloves of *gris-perle*, hanging over, caught sight of Ega, smiled at him and gave a little condescending petulant wave of the fingers, as he had in Cintra. This struck Ega like an insult. And only the day before the coward had clutched his hands, trembling all over and crying: 'Save me . . .!'

Suddenly an idea occurred to him and he patted his pocket where he had put the wallet containing Damaso's letter the evening before. 'I'll fix you!' he muttered. And he left at once and set off down Rua da Trindade, crossed into Loreto Square like a hurled stone, and darted through a lamp-lit gateway in Camões Square. It was the offices of *A Tarde*.

The smell was vile in the courtyard of this elegant newspaper. On the unlit stone stairway he passed an individual with catarrh who told him Neves was upstairs talking. Neves, member of the House and director of *A Tarde*, had, during a holiday a few years ago, shared an apartment with him in the Largo do Carmo, and ever since that gay summer when Neves had borrowed but never repaid a loan of three sovereigns, the two had addressed each other by the intimate '*tu*'.

He found him in an enormous room lit with unshaded gas lamps, sitting on the edge of a table overflowing with papers, his hat pushed back, and holding forth to a group of provincials who stood listening to him as if they were his disciples. In the window recess two men listened to a lean young man in a light cheviot jacket, with bristling hair which seemed as if it had been whipped up by the wind, who waved his arms around like a windmill on a hilltop. Seated near by, a bald fellow laboriously scrawled on a strip of paper.

When he saw Ega (an intimate friend of Gouvarinho) in his office there, on a night of scheming and crisis, Neves stared at him with such inquisitive eyes that Ega hastened to assure him:

'It's nothing to do with politics; it's a personal matter. Don't let me interrupt. We'll talk afterwards.'

Neves finished the insult he was casting at José Bento – 'that great oaf who had let out everything to the mistress of Sousa e Sá, a member of the Upper House' – and then impatiently leapt from the table, linked his arm in Ega's and dragged him to a corner.

'What is it then?'

'Just this, in two words: Carlos da Maia was insulted by a well-known individual here. Nothing very interesting. A smutty paragraph in the *Devil's Trumpet* over a question of horses. Maia demanded apologies. The other fellow gave him them in a fantastic contemptible letter which I want you to publish.'

Neves's curiosity was kindled.

'Who is it?'

'Damaso.'

Neves stepped back in amazement.

'Damaso? Never! This is absolutely extraordinary! I was only dining with him this evening! What does the letter say?'

'Everything. He begs pardon, declares he was drunk, in fact that he's a drunkard by profession . . .'

Neves waved his hands about in indignation.

'And you want me to publish this, man? Damaso – our political ally! And even if he weren't, it's not a party matter, it's a simple question of decency. How could I do a thing like that! If it were a record of a duel, an honourable thing, dignified explanations . . . But a letter where the man declares he's a drunk! You're pulling my leg!'

Ega frowned, furious. But Neves, his face purple, was still revolted at the idea of Damaso declaring himself drunk.

'It can't be! It's absurd! There's a story behind this somewhere. Let's see the letter.'

And after a glimpse at the paper, at the large flourish of the signature, he gave a triumphant shout.

'This isn't Damaso, and it's not Damaso's writing! "Salcêde"! Who the devil's "Salcêde"? That's not *my* Damaso!'

'Well, it's mine!' retorted Ega. 'Damaso Salcêde, a fat fellow . . .'

His friend flung his arms in the air:

'Mine's Guedes, man, Damaso Guedes! There's no other! What the deuce, when you say Damaso, you mean Guedes . . .'

He gave a deep sigh of relief.

'You scared the life out of me! Imagine, at a moment like this, with all this business of the ministry, a letter like that written by Guedes . . . If it's Salcêde, good, that's the end of the matter! Wait a minute . . . Isn't he a podgy fellow, a fop with a place in Cintra? Ah, him! A rascal who caught us in the last election – made Silvério spend more than thirty *milreis* . . . Oh certainly, at your service! Pereirinha, see to Senhor Ega here. He has a letter which he wants published tomorrow, in large type on the front page.'

Senhor Pereirinha reminded him of the article of Sr Vieira da Costa on 'Reform of Custom Duties'.

'Put it in later,' shouted Neves. 'Questions of honour before anything else!'

And he returned to the group he had left, where they were

now discussing the Count de Gouvarinho. He perched himself on the table again and burst in with the authoritative voice of the leader, declaring Gouvarinho had great gifts as a parliamentarian!

Ega lit a cigar and considered for a moment those individuals who gaped with awe at the word of Neves. They were no doubt members of the House who had been drawn to Lisbon by the crisis, dragged out of the peace and quiet of their farms and little towns. The youngest, dressed in fine cashmere, had an enormous fat face bursting with blood, jocund, coarse, and reminding one of healthy fresh air and roast pork. Another, slimmer, with jacket flung over curved shoulders, had a stubborn horse-like chin; two well-shaved tanned priests smoked cigarettes. All of them had the air, at the same time dull and suspicious, which characterizes the provincial man lost among the cabs and plotting of the big city. They went there at night, to their party paper, to learn the latest news, get inside information – some hoping for a job, others seeking to safeguard local interests, others out of sheer idleness. Neves was for these 'a man of great talent'; they admired his verbosity and tactics; they were no doubt proud to be able to quote in the shops of their towns their friend Neves, the journalist, the director of *A Tarde*. But cutting across this admiration for him and pleasure at being one of his intimates, one noted a vague fear on their part in case he should draw them to a window and touch them for a loan. Neves was now praising Gouvarinho's oratory. He hadn't the vision, the pureness, the historical syntheses of José Clemente! Nor the poetry of Rufino! But there was no one like him for delivering taunts which wound and stick in the skin and burn! And that was the great thing in the House – to have barbs and know how to thrust them!

'Do you remember that sally of Gouvarinho's about the trapeze, Gonçalo?' he shouted, turning towards the window to the boy in the light jacket.

Gonçalo, his black eyes darting with wit and malice, thrust his lean neck out of a slack collar and cried: 'The one about the trapeze! That was a good one! Tell the boys!'

The 'boys' stared wide-eyed at Neves, waiting for the trapeze sally. It had been in the Upper House during the Education Reform Bill. Torres Valente had been talking, that madman who wanted gymnastics taught at school and schoolgirls doing physical exercises. Gouvarinho had got up and barked:

'Senhor Presidente, I should like to say just one word. Portugal will for ever leave the path of progress where she has shone so brightly, the day we substitute with impious hand the trapeze for the cross in our schools!'

'Hear! Hear!' grunted one of the priests with deep satisfaction.

And amid the murmur of admiration which arose a yelp broke forth from the fat boy who was shaking his shoulders and jeering from the round tomato-face.

'Well, gentlemen, I reckon this Count de Gouvarinho's a sanctimonious devil!'

And all around smiles twinkled on the faces of those foxy, liberal gentlemen from the provinces who considered the aristocrat rather too attached to the cross. But Neves was on his feet, gesticulating wildly:

'Sanctimonious! So our fat boy here considers him sanctimonious! Gouvarinho sanctimonious! Naturally he has all the ideas of the century; he's a rationalist, a positivist . . . but what matters here is the repartee, parliamentary tactics! As soon as that fellow from the majority comes out with the trapeze, our friend Gouvarinho, even if he were as atheist as Renan, beats him down with the cross! That's what I call parliamentary strategy, don't you, Ega?'

Ega murmured through a haze of cigar smoke: 'Yes, indeed, the cross is still useful for things like that.'

At this point the bald individual, who had pushed away his strip of paper, stretched himself and now fell back exhausted against the back of the chair and remarked that Senhor João de Ega was stuck up today, not talking to his friends . . .

Ega went over to the amiable fellow, such a humorous man, so warm and well-loved by everybody.

'Well, working on the masterpiece, Melchior?'

'I'm trying to write something on Craveiro's book, *Mountain Songs,* and I can't find the right words. I just don't know what to say!'

Ega, hands in pockets, laughed and chaffed friend Melchior.

'Nothing! You're just small-town reporters, pen-pushing columnists. All you have to say about a book like Craveiro's is where it is sold and how much it costs.'

Melchior looked at Ega ironically, his hands crossed behind his neck.

'Where do you suggest we should write of books then? In the catalogues?'

No, in the critical magazines; or otherwise in newspapers – on condition they were real newspapers and not cheap rags containing a load of political rubbish as dull as ditchwater, or filled with wisecracks and badly translated French novels, and the rest of the space devoted to birthdays, announcements, petty court-cases and the winning numbers of the Misericordia lotteries. And as there were neither serious newspapers nor critical magazines in Portugal, books should not be reviewed anywhere.

'It's true,' agreed Melchior. 'No one talks of anything, no one ever seems to think of anything.'

And they had their reasons, thought Ega. Some of this silence must certainly originate from the natural desire that mediocre people have to refer as little as possible to the great ones: shabby, grovelling envy! But generally speaking, the silence of the newspapers towards books derived mainly from the fact that they had abandoned all serious critical work and become simply vulgar sheets of common information, and they were aware of their incompetence.

'Of course, I don't mean you, Melchior. You're one of us and one of the best! But your fellows, my friend, keep silent because they realize they are incompetent.'

Melchior shrugged his shoulders with a weary, disbelieving air.

'And they keep silent too because the public doesn't care, nobody cares.'

Ega, excited now, protested. The public didn't care! That was odd. So the public didn't care to hear about the books they were buying at the rate of three thousand, six thousand copies? And considering the population of Portugal, this was equivalent to one of the big successes of Paris or London, caramba! No, friend Melchiorzinho, no, no. This silence spoke more clearly and loudly than the words: 'We are incompetent. We are stupefied by the news that Senhor Counsellor has left or Senhor Counsellor has arrived, and by the "Highlife" page, by the charming ladies, by the scrappy, slangy leading article, by all this filthy prose we grub about in. We can't, we don't know how to speak any longer about a work of art or a historical piece, or of this beautiful book of verse or that beautiful travel book. We have neither phrases nor ideas. Perhaps we aren't by nature cretins – but have just been cretinized. The work of art passes high above us while we wallow here below in the mire.'

'So there you have it, Melchior, there you have the words of the silent choir of journalists!'

Melchior listened in rapture and smiled, with his head back as one listens to a beautiful aria. Then, clapping his hand down on the table, he cried: 'By Jove, Ega, you speak well! Have you never thought of standing for Parliament? I was only saying to Neves the other day, "Ega's the man! Ega's the one to let fly the witticisms à la Rochefort. He'd be wonderful!"'

And while Ega laughed contentedly and relit his cigar, Melchior picked up his pen again.

'You're on form today! Come on now, tell me what I'm to say about this book of Craveiro's!'

Ega wanted to know what friend Melchior had already written. No more than three lines: 'We have received the latest book of our glorious poet Simão Craveiro. This delightful volume which sparkles with all the genius of our distinguished writer, is published by the active publishers . . .' Melchior had got stuck here. He did not like the word 'active'. Ega suggested 'enterprising'. Melchior changed it and read:

'. . . published by the enterprising publishers . . .' No, he didn't like it. He flung his pen down dejectedly. That was enough! He was not in the right mood. And anyway it was late and he had his girl waiting.

'I'll leave it till tomorrow . . . The worst of it is I've already been on the thing five days! Drat it! You're right – people get stupefied. And it makes me mad! Not for the book's sake – I couldn't care less for the book – but for Craveiro's sake; he's a nice chap, and belongs to our party too!'

He opened a drawer and took out a brush with which he began to scrub away at his jacket. Ega was about to help him clean off some of the whitewash from his shoulders when the drawn nervous face of Gonçalo thrust itself between them with its shock of hair perpetually stuck up as if caught by a gust of wind.

511

'What's Egazinho doing in our newspaper den?'

'Brushing down Sampaio here. I've also been listening to Neves, hearing the witty remark of Gouvarinho . . .'

Gonçalo leapt back with a sparkle of malice twinkling in his dark bright eyes.

'About the cross? Wonderful! But there's a better one, much better!'

He slipped his arm through Ega's and pulled him towards the window.

'Have to keep our voices low because of the lads from the provinces. There's another excellent remark of his. I can't remember it exactly – Neves'll tell it to you word for word. It's about Liberty, leading in the great steed Progress. Anyway, an equestrian image! Liberty with his jockey's boots on and Progress in all its trappings! Superb! What a blockhead the man is! And the others, dear boy, the others! You weren't in the House when they discussed the question of Tondela? Extraordinary! The things they said! Enough to make you die of laughing! And I nearly did! All this politics, and São Bento, and rhetoric and lawyers' talk – they kill you! They are saying it's no worse here than in Bulgaria. A lot of nonsense! There couldn't ever have been such riff-raff in the whole universe!'

'Riff-raff in which you wallow!' observed Ega, laughing.

His companion drew back in horror.

'Now let's distinguish! I wallow in it through necessity, as a politician; and I poke fun at it as an artist!'

But Ega considered this discord between intelligence and character a disgrace to the country. Here was friend Gonçalo considering, as any intelligent man would, that Gouvarinho was an imbecile –

'A downright ass,' corrected Gonçalo.

'A downright ass then! And yet here you are, as a politician, wanting this ass as minister, and you support him with your votes and speeches every time he brays or kicks.'

Gonçalo ran his hand over the erect tuft of hair, his face creased in a frown.

'But it has to be like this. It's a question of party discipline and solidarity. We have certain commitments. The Palace wants him, it likes him . . .'

He peered round and whispered into Ega's ear: 'There are syndicates and bankers and concessions in Mozambique in question . . . Money, dear boy, omnipotent money!'

And as Ega bent his head in defeat, full of respect, his companion clapped him on the shoulder and went on, his eyes alight with cunning and cynicism:

'My dear fellow, politics today are a very different matter from what they used to be. We've done the same as you literary people. In the old days literature was all imagination and fantasy and ideals. Now it's reality, experience, positive facts, documents. Well, here in Portugal politics have taken up the realist trend. In the time of the Regeneradores and the Históricos,* politics meant progress, transport, liberty, verbiage. We've changed all that. Today it's plain fact – money, money! Filthy lucre! Dough, Cash – the stuff of our souls, dear boy! Marvellous money!'

He stopped, for there was a sudden silence in the room, and his shout of 'Money! Money!' seemed to reverberate through the hot gas-lit air, echoing and lingering like an alarm bell awakening covetousness, calling on the cunning far and wide to plunder the helpless Fatherland.

Neves had disappeared. The gentlemen from the provinces were dispersing, some putting on their jackets, others lazily giving a perfunctory glance at the papers on the table. Gonçalo abruptly bid Ega farewell and, spinning round on his heels, also left, amicably clasping one of the priests as he went and addressing him as 'rogue'.

It was midnight. Ega left. And as he sat in the cab taking him to Ramalhete, he began, calmer now, to reflect that the result of the publication of the letter would be to awaken a voracious curiosity throughout all Lisbon. No one would believe it was merely a 'question of horses' as Neves had done, distracted as he had been by the political crisis that night. Damaso would doubtless try to excuse himself, when questioned, with horrible stories of Maria and Carlos; and an intolerable light of scandal was going to shine on things better left in darkness. He was probably preparing all manner of trouble and vexation for Carlos – and all because of this petty hatred he had for Damaso. There couldn't be anything meaner and more selfish! Going up to his

* Two opposing political parties of the mid-nineteenth century.

rooms he decided to return to the offices of *A Tarde* next morning and prevent publication of the letter.

But that night he dreamed of Rachel and Damaso. He saw them rolling along a never-ending road between orchards and vineyards, lying together in an ox-cart on a straw mattress displaying the rich lascivious black satin bedspread from the Villa Balzac; the two lay clasped together kissing under the cool shade of the overhanging branches to the sound of the squeaking wheels. And the cruellest feature of the unpleasant dream was that Ega, without losing his consciousness and manly pride, was one of the oxen drawing the cart! The ox-flies stung him, the yoke weighed heavily on his neck, and the louder the kisses behind him, the more he stretched up his head and dribbled, shook his horns and lowed pitifully to the heavens!

Uttering these cries of agony he awoke, and his fury against Damaso increased, nourished by the incoherences of the dream. Apart from this, it was raining. And he decided not to return to the offices of *A Tarde* after all, but let the letter be published. Besides, what did it matter what Damaso said? The article in the *Trumpet* was out of existence now and Palma well paid. And who would ever again believe in a man who had declared himself in the newspapers a slanderer and drunkard?

Carlos thought the same when Ega told him, after lunch, of his resolution of the night before when he had seen Damaso in the box looking jeeringly at him, whispering with the Cohens.

'I could see, without the slightest doubt, that he was talking about you, and Senhora Dona Maria, and all of us, recounting all manner of horrors. That finished it, I didn't hesitate a moment longer. The justice of God can wait! We'll have no peace till we've got rid of the man!'

Yes, Carlos agreed, perhaps. He was only worried lest his grandfather, hearing of the scandal, should be displeased to find his name mixed up in all that sordid business of the *Trumpet* and drunkenness.

'He doesn't read *A Tarde*,' said Ega. 'It will be a very vague distorted tale by the time he hears anything about it, if he hears anything at all.'

All Afonso did in fact hear was something confused about Damaso directing some unpleasant words at Carlos in the Grémio, and then afterwards publishing in a newspaper that he had been drunk at the time. The opinion of the old man was that if Damaso was intoxicated (and how else could he have insulted Carlos, who had been his friend), his statement revealed extreme loyalty and an almost heroic love of truth!

'Here's something we never expected,' remarked Ega, in Carlos's rooms. 'Damaso turns righteous!'

The friends of Ramalhete, knowing nothing about the article in the *Trumpet,* approved the annihilation of Damaso. Only Craft felt that Carlos would have done better to give him a thrashing privately; and Taveira considered it cruel that they'd told the poor fellow, with a rapier at his throat, 'Your dignity or your life!'

But the scandal was forgotten a few days later. There were other things to interest the Chiado and the Casa Havanesa. The government had finally been formed. Gouvarinho was in the Admiralty; Neves in the Court of Audit. The newspapers of the fallen government had already begun, as was the custom, to find the country irrevocably lost, to make sarcastic references to the King . . . And the final faint echo of Damaso's letter came on the day before the concert at the Trindade – a paragraph in the selfsame *A Tarde* which noted in the following kind words:

'Our friend and distinguished sportsman, Damaso Salcêde, is leaving shortly for a pleasure trip to Italy. We wish our elegant tourist happiness in his delightful excursion to the land of song and art.'

6

AFTER SUPPER IN Rua de S. Francisco, Ega, who had lingered in the corridor hunting for his cigar-case in his coat pockets, returned to the drawing-room and inquired of Maria, who was sitting at the piano: 'Then you're definitely not coming to the show at the Trindade?'

She turned to answer lazily between chords of the slow waltz she was playing.

'I'm not really interested. And I'm tired . . .'

'It's a bore,' remarked Carlos from a vast armchair where he lay, eyes shut, contentedly smoking.

Ega protested. So was it annoying to have to climb the Pyramids of Egypt. But one would suffer if one did not, for it's not every day of the week that a Christian can clamber up a monument five thousand years old. Now at this show Dona Maria would for only ten *tostões* be able to see something equally rare – the sentimental soul of a people naked, although in evening dress, revealing itself on the stage.

'Come, courage! All we need is a hat, a pair of gloves, and off we go!'

She smiled and pleaded laziness and fatigue.

'Right,' cried Ega. 'But I mustn't miss Rufino. Come, Carlos, move yourself!'

But Carlos begged mercy.

'Just a few more minutes! Let Maria play a few notes of *Hamlet*. We have time . . . Rufino and Alencar and the ones that matter will only do their stuff later.'

So Ega too yielded to the cosy peaceful warmth and settled himself on the sofa with a cigar to listen to Ophelia's song, the sad dreamy words of which Maria was now singing:

'*Pâle et blonde,*
Dort sous l'eau profonde . . .'

Ega adored this old Scandinavian ballad. But he was also fascinated by Maria who had never seemed to him so beautiful: the light dress which she wore fitted her as if it were moulded to her body; in the light of the candles on the piano, which illuminated the pure profile and added a note of gold to the hair, the incomparable marble splendour of her skin was revealed in its perfection. Everything about her tonight was harmonious and healthy and sublime. And how ardent her passion must seem in contrast to the calmness of her outward appearance! Carlos was definitely the happiest man in the land. Ease and pleasure surrounded him. He was rich, intelligent, had the health of a young ox, and spent his life adoring and being adored; he had only the necessary number of enemies to show his superiority; never had he suffered from dyspepsia; he fenced well enough to be feared, and conscious of his strength was not even irritated by public folly. A fortunate fellow indeed!

'Who is this Rufino anyway?' asked Carlos, stretching his legs farther along the carpet, when Maria finished her song.

Ega did not know. He had heard he was a member of the House, a graduate, an inspired creature.

Maria, who was looking for some Chopin nocturnes, turned to them and inquired: 'Is this the great orator you spoke about at Hideaway?'

'No, no! That was another one, a real orator, a friend of ours from Coimbra – José Clemente, a man of eloquence and ideas . . . This Rufino is an odd, long-bearded fellow, member for Monção and sublime in the art, which was formerly a national one and is today more particularly provincial, of composing and uttering in theatrical, pompous tones, sonorous combinations of words.'

'I loathe that,' snorted Carlos.

Maria too found it intolerable that a man should twitter away, devoid of ideas, like a bird on the branch of a tree.

'It all depends on the occasion,' remarked Ega, glancing at his watch. 'A Strauss waltz also has no ideas, but at night in the drawing-room with ladies, it's delightful.'

Oh no! Maria considered this empty rhetoric always debased the human word, which should, of its nature, be used to express ideas. Music was different – it spoke to the senses. If you sang a march to a child it would laugh and jump around on your lap –

'And if you read it a page of Michelet,' finished Carlos, 'the little angel gets bored and starts to yell.'

'Yes, perhaps,' considered Ega. 'All this depends on the latitude and the customs it produces, of course. Every Englishman, no matter how cultured and intellectual he might be, has a weakness for brute strength, for athletes and sports and muscles of iron. And we Latins, however critical we are, like melodious phrases. For my part, I love a bit of rhetoric at night when the room's full of light and the ladies are there and the men are in evening clothes.'

And with his appetite thus awoken, he got up to put on his jacket and fly to the Trindade for fear he'd miss Rufino.

Carlos retained him with another idea: 'Wait. I've thought of something better. Let's have our soirée here. Maria will play, Beethoven, we'll recite Musset, Hugo, the Parnassians – and we have Father Lacordaire if you fancy eloquence. We'll spend the evening in a superb idealistic orgy!'

'And we have better chairs!' added Maria.

'And better poets,' went on Carlos.

'Good cigars!'

'Excellent brandy!'

Ega flung his arms in the air in despair. That's how a citizen was perverted, preventing him from encouraging native letters with treacherous promises of tobacco and drinks! Moreover it wasn't only for literary reasons that he must attend the show – Cruges was playing one of his *Autumn Meditations* and Cruges must have a clap.

'Not another word!' cried Carlos, jumping up out of the armchair. 'I'd forgotten Cruges! It's a case of duty! Let's go.'

And a few moments later, having kissed the hand of Maria, who remained at the piano, the two walked slowly down the street, surprised at the beauty of this winter's night, so clear and still. Carlos glanced back twice at the lighted windows.

'I'm very glad,' he cried, linking his arm in Ega's, 'that I've left Olivais. Here one can at least have one's friends along for a bit of talk and literature.'

He intended arranging the drawing-room with rather more taste and comfort, and converting the room leading off it into a smoking-room hung with his Indian textiles, and having a set day for his friends to dine there. In this way, he could make the old dream come true – form a centre of art and dilettantism . . . And then they must launch their *Revista*, which was to be the supreme intellectual frolic. They could look forward to a really *chic* winter, as the deceased Damaso would say.

'And all this,' summed up Ega, 'is a way of civilizing the country. Really, dear boy, we are going to become valuable citizens!'

'If they want to put up a statue to me,' said Carlos gaily, 'I hope they'll put it up here in Rua de S. Francisco. What a magnificent night!'

They reached the door of the Trindade Theatre at the same moment as a white-bearded figure descended from a hired cab – a figure dressed in mourning and a large wide-brimmed hat such as they used to wear in the 1830s. He put his change in his pocket and passed the two friends without noticing them.

'That's Damaso's uncle – the demagogue! Splendid type!'

'And, according to Damaso, one of the family drunkards,' laughed Carlos.

Upstairs there was a sudden burst of applause. Carlos handing his coat to the doorman, feared it might be Cruges.

'Impossible,' cried Ega. 'That sort of applause is reserved for rhetoric!'

And true enough, when they arrived at the top of the flower-lined stairs and entered the foyer, where two dress-coated individuals were creeping back and forth on the tips of their toes, whispering – they heard a bombastic, quavering provincial voice evoking from the stage in a sing-song manner 'the religious soul of Lamartine'!

'It's Rufino – he's been wonderful!' commented Teles da Gama who stood in the doorway, with his cigar hidden behind his back.

Carlos, indifferent to the proceedings, remained standing beside Teles, but Ega, tall and lean, went striding down the red-carpeted aisle. On both sides rows of heads strained forward, transported, spellbound. Spectators filled the cane-seated chairs right up to the stage bordered by ladies' hats displaying a variety of feathers and flowers. Round about, leaning against the slender pillars supporting the gallery, were figures from the Grémio, the Casa Havanesa, Ministry Departments – some with white tie, some in evening jackets – and all reflected in the mirrored walls. Ega noticed Sr Sousa Neto pensively listening and supporting on finger and thumb his wan-looking face with its scant whiskers; farther on was Gonçalo with his hair standing on end; over there was the Marquis, his neck wrapped in a white silk scarf; and farther off still, in a little group, were gathered friends from the Jockey Club – the two Vargas, Mendonça, Pinheiro – all attending to this 'sport' of eloquence with a mixture of wonder and tedium. Above, behind the velvet parapet of the gallery, a row of ladies could be discerned languidly fanning themselves; behind them rose their accompanying gentlemen, among whom he recognized Neves, the new Counsellor, grave, arms crossed, a camellia bud in the buttonhole of his ill-fitting jacket.

The gas was stifling and the stark light vibrated in the bright room of a pale tone of canary-yellow broken by the reflections from the mirrors. Here and there a timid catarrhal cough severed the silence and was hastily stifled in a handkerchief. And at the far end of the gallery in a box made out of partitions, with cherry-coloured velvet curtains, two gold-backed chairs stood vacant in all the regal solemnity of their scarlet damask.

Meanwhile, on the platform, Rufino, transmontane lawyer, swarthy and bearded, flung open his arms as he extolled an angel, 'The Angel of Alms', whom he had glimpsed far up in the blue, beating its satin wings. Ega did not understand, confined between a very fat priest who dripped with perspiration and a lieutenant in dark glasses.

Finally he could control his curiosity no more: 'What's he talking about?' The priest answered him, his face shining and alight with enthusiasm: 'It's all about charity and progress! He's been superb but he's nearly done now, unfortunately!'

It seemed as if it were, indeed, the peroration. Rufino snatched out his handkerchief and slowly wiped his forehead; then he darted to the front of the stage and turned towards the royal chairs with such an ardent gesture of inspiration that the top of his drawers peeped out from under his waistcoat. It was then that Ega suddenly comprehended. Rufino was praising a princess who had given six hundred *milreis* to the victims of the flood in Ribatejo, and was going to organize a bazaar in their favour in the Tapada Gardens. But it was not only this superb example of charity which dazzled Rufino – because he, 'like all men educated by philosophy who have the true mental orientation of their times, he saw not only the poetic beauty of the great facts of history, but also their social significance. The mob would smile in simplicity and rapture at the incomparable poetry of the fine-gloved hand extended towards the poverty-stricken. He, however, a philosopher, discerned a deep and beautiful consequence blossoming from these delicate fingers of a princess . . . What, gentlemen? The resurrection of Faith!'

Suddenly a fan fell from the gallery, followed by a yell from a fat lady below, which led to a murmuring and a brief flutter of excitement. Dom José Sequeira, director of the proceedings, immediately stood upon the stage steps, his red silk band on his arm, darting his little squint eyes fiercely towards the undisciplined corner where scattered laughter had broken out. Other gentlemen, indignant at the interruption, called 'Silence!' 'Outside!' 'Ssshhh!' And from the front row rose the ministerial face of Gouvarinho, anxious for the restoration of order, his glasses shining fiercely. Ega looked for the Countess and found her eventually, seated farther off in a blue hat between the Baroness Alvim, all in black, and the vast mauve-satin covered shoulders of the Baroness de Craben. The murmurs ceased and Rufino, who had slowly wet his lips with a glass of water, advanced a step, smiling, with a white handkerchief in his hand.

'I was saying, ladies and gentlemen, that considering the mental direction of this century . . .'

But Ega felt stifled, crushed, sick of Rufino and with the impression that the priest at his side smelt. He could tolerate no more, and made his way back to relieve his feelings upon Carlos.

'Can you imagine an ass like that?'

'Terrible,' agreed Carlos. 'When's Cruges playing?'

Ega did not know: the programme had all been changed.

'And you've got the Countess here: she's over there in blue. I'm looking forward to seeing the meeting afterwards.'

But both turned to answer a discreet: '*Bonsoir, messieurs . . .*' behind them. It was Steinbroken and his secretary, solemnly dressed in evening clothes, walking on their tiptoes with their crush hats clasped in their hands. Steinbroken began straightway to complain of the absence of the royal family.

'*M. de Cantanhede, qui est de service, m'avait cependant assuré que la reine viendrait . . . C'est bien sous sa protection, n'est-ce pas, toute cette musique, ces vers? . . . Voilà pourquoi je suis venu. C'est très ennuyeux . . . Et Alphonse de Maïa, toujours en santé?*'

'*Merci.*'

The silence in the hall was impressive. Rufino, with gestures like one drawing slow noble lines on a canvas, was describing the sweetness of a village, the village where he had been born, at sunset. And his voice dropped, became tender, died away amid the little sounds of twilight. Steinbroken touched Ega on the shoulder very gently. He wanted to know if this was the great orator of whom they had spoken. Ega confirmed patriotically that this was one of the finest orators in Europe!

'In what genre?'

'In the sublime, in the genre of Demosthenes!'

Steinbroken raised his eyebrows in admiration and spoke in Finnish to his secretary who languidly lifted his monocle; and with their crush hats under their arms, eyes closed, and as respectful as if they were in a temple, the two Finnish attachés stood listening, waiting for the sublime.

In the meantime, Rufino, with his hands dropped to his sides, was confessing a weakness of his soul! In spite of the poetic atmosphere of his native village where the violets in the field and nightingales in the bushes proved unquestionably the existence of God, he had been pierced by the thorn of disbelief! Ah, how many times at nightfall when the bells of the old church tower were calling the faithful to evening prayer and the harvesters were singing in the valley, had he passed the cross in the church square and the cross of the cemetery, casting at them a cruel cold Voltairean smile!

A shiver of emotion passed over the audience. Voices gasping with delight could barely utter their little cries of admiration.

It was in this state, tormented by doubt, that Rufino had heard a cry of horror resound throughout Portugal! What had happened? It was Nature attacking her children! And throwing out his arms like one struggling amidst a catastrophe, Rufino described the flood. Here a cottage was destroyed, a flower-covered love-nest; down there in a hollow came the mournful lowing of cattle; farther off the black waters were sweeping away a rosebud and a cradle . . .

Hoarse fervent 'Bravos' broke from heaving breasts. And around Carlos and Ega individuals turned passionately one to another, a common enthusiasm lighting up their faces: 'What eloquence! By Jove! Sublime!'

Rufino smiled, drinking in this emotion which was the work

of his words. Then he respectfully turned towards the solemn, empty royal seats.

Seeing the anger of Nature implacable, he had turned his eyes towards the natural shelter, to the exalted place whence salvation descends – towards the Throne of Portugal! And suddenly, dazzled, he had seen the white wings of an angel hovering over him. It was the Angel of Alms, ladies and gentlemen! And whence had it come? Whence had it received the inspiration of charity? Whence had it come with its golden locks? From the books of science? From the chemical laboratories? From the anatomical amphitheatres, where the soul is brutally denied? From the arid schools of philosophy which turn Jesus into a precurser of Robespierre? No! He had dared to inquire of the angel as he humbly knelt upon the ground. And the Angel of Alms had answered, pointing to the divine spaces: 'I come from there.'

A murmur of rapture ran through the crowded rows. It was as if the plaster roof suddenly opened and the angels sang on high. A shiver of poetry and devotion ran through the ladies.

And so Rufino ended with a lofty certitude in his soul. Yes, ladies and gentlemen! From that moment onward, doubt had been like mist which the sun – their radiant Portuguese sun – disperses in the air. And now, in spite of the ironies of science, in spite of the haughty contempt of a Renan, a Littré, a Spencer, he, who had received the divine confidence, could, with hand on his heart, assert to all in a loud voice – that Heaven existed!

'Hear! Hear!' roared the sweaty priest in the aisle.

And all over the hall, in the stifling heat of the gas-lamps, the gentlemen from Ministry departments, from the Arcade, from the Casa Havanesa, clapped their hands and shouted, proudly affirming the existence of Heaven.

Ega was laughing, amused at the spectacle, when he heard near by a cry of anger. It was Alencar, gloomily stroking his moustache.

'What do you think of him, Tomás?'

'Nauseating!' growled the poet.

He trembled with fury! On a night of poetry like that when men of letters should show themselves for what they were, sons of democracy and liberty, it was simply disgusting to see that scoundrel licking the feet of the royal family!

Down at the front by the stage steps there was a flurry of embraces and compliments for Rufino who shone with pride and sweat. And men slipped out of the doors, still aglow, taking out their cigar-cases from their pockets. Then Alencar slipped his arm through Ega's.

'Listen, I've been looking for you. Guimarães, Damaso's uncle, has asked me to be introduced to you. He says it's something serious, very serious. He's downstairs in the bar with a grog.'

Ega looked surprised. Something serious?

'Right, let's go down and have a grog too. What are you reciting, Alencar?'

'"Democracy",' the poet answered with a certain reserve as they went down the stairs. 'A new little thing, you'll see . . . A few hard truths about this bourgeoisie.'

They arrived at the door of the bar just as Sr Guimarães was coming out, buttoning his frock-coat, with his hat over his eye and a cigar in his mouth. Alencar introduced them gravely.

'My friend, João de Ega . . . My old friend Guimarães, a fine fellow and veteran of the Democracy.'

Ega moved to a table and politely drew out a stool for the veteran of the Democracy, and asked whether he'd prefer brandy or beer.

'I've just had my quota,' answered Guimarães drily, 'and that will last me all night.'

A waiter wiped over the marble table-top and Ega ordered a beer. And immediately, putting aside his cigar and smoothing his whiskers to assure that his face was rightly grave for the occasion, Sr Guimarães began slowly and solemnly: 'I am Damaso Salcêde's uncle, and I asked my old friend Alencar here to introduce us in order to summon you to look at me clearly and tell me if you think I have the face of a drunkard – '

Ega understood the situation immediately, and in a frank, friendly tone, cut him short: 'You are referring to a letter your nephew wrote, I presume.'

'A letter which you dictated! A letter which you forced him to sign!'

'I?'

'He assures me of it, sir!'

Alencar broke in: 'Lower your voices, confound it! This is an inquisitive country!'

Sr Guimarães coughed and drew his chair closer to the table. For some weeks, he went on, he had been out of Lisbon dealing with the inheritance of his brother. He had not seen his nephew as he only met that imbecile when forced to. The day before he was in the house of a friend of his, Vaz Forte, when he had chanced to glance at the *Futuro*, a Republican newspaper which was not badly written but short of ideas. And there on the first page, in enormous type, under the heading 'Highlife Happenings', was his nephew's letter. Senhor Ega could imagine his fury! He had written a letter to Damaso right there in Forte's house, more or less on these lines: 'I've read your infamous statement. If you don't write another tomorrow, for every newspaper, declaring that you had no intention of including me among the drunkards of your family, I shall come and break every bone in your body, one by one. So beware!' 'That was what I wrote. And do you know what his reply was, sir? I have it here. It's a human document, as friend Lola says. Here it is . . . enormous paper, gold monogram, coronet and all. What an ass the fellow is! Would you like me to read it?'

Ega laughingly nodded and he read, slowly and emphatically: ' "My dear uncle, The letter you speak of was written by Sr João da Ega. I would naturally be incapable of such disrespect towards my beloved family. It was he who grabbed me and forced me to sign and in all the confusion I didn't know what I was doing and signed to avoid further unpleasantness. It was a trap my enemies had set for me. My dear uncle, who knows only too well how fond I am of him – I was even going to send you half a barrel of Colares wine last year if I'd known your address in Paris – won't be angry with me, I know. Unhappy man that I am! If you like you can talk to this João da Ega who caused my downfall. But I can assure you I'll wreak such a vengeance on him that it will never be forgotten! I've been in such a quandary I haven't decided what yet; but at any rate our family will be avenged, for I'll allow no one to trifle with my dignity . . . And the reason I didn't do so before I left for Italy, the reason I didn't stand up for my honour, is that with all these troubles I've had an awful bout of dysentery for the past few days, and have hardly been able to stand on my two feet. This on top of my moral distress!" '

'Are you laughing, Senhor Ega?'

525

'What do you want me to do?' spluttered Ega at last, his eyes full of tears. 'Of course I'm laughing, and Alencar's laughing and you must be laughing too! It's extraordinary! This dignity, this dysentery . . .'

Sr Guimarães, perplexed, looked at Ega, looked at the poet snorting under his long moustache, and finally said: 'Well, we know it's a numbskull who wrote the letter, but the fact remains . . .'

So then Ega appealed to Sr Guimarães' common sense, to his experience in matters of honour. Could he imagine two gentlemen going to a man's house with a challenge, grabbing him by the wrist and forcing him to sign a letter where he declares himself a drunkard?

Sr Guimarães, mollified by that appeal to his tact and experience, confessed that such a thing would be most unusual – at least in Paris.

'And in Lisbon too, sir! What the deuce, this is not Kaffir Land! And perhaps you'd tell me another thing, Senhor Guimarães, as one gentleman to another: what do you think of your nephew? Do you consider him irreproachably truthful?'

Sr Guimarães stroked his beard and stated frankly: 'He's an out-and-out liar.'

'There you are then!' shouted Ega triumphantly, flinging his arms in the air.

Again Alencar intervened. The question appeared to be satisfactorily concluded. All that was wanted now was for the two to shake hands like brothers, like good democrats.

Standing up, he poured his gin down his throat. Ega smiled and offered his hand to Sr Guimarães. But the elderly demagogue, with a shadow still on the wrinkled face, wanted Sr João da Ega to declare – if he was certain of the fact – there in front of their friend Alencar, that he didn't consider Sr Guimarães had a drunkard's face.

'Oh, my dear sir!' cried Ega, banging on the table with a coin to call a waiter. 'On the contrary! With the greatest pleasure I'll proclaim here in front of Alencar and to the four winds that your face is that of a perfect gentleman and a patriot!'

Then they exchanged a hearty handshake and Sr Guimarães assured Sr João da Ega of his great satisfaction in having met him, such a talented and liberal young man. And whenever the gentleman required anything, either political or literary, he had only to write to him at the address known throughout the world: Editor's Office, *Rappel*, Paris!

Alencar had gone. And the two left the bar exchanging impressions of the show. Sr Guimarães was nauseated with the sanctimoniousness and sycophancy of Rufino. When he had heard him prating about the wings of the princess and the cross in the church square, he had almost called out: 'How much are they paying you for this, you miserable wretch?'

But Ega had suddenly stopped on the stairs, and was taking off his hat.

'Oh, Baroness, are you deserting us?'

It was the Baroness Alvim who was coming down the stairs with Joaninha Vilar, tying the wide ribbons of her green plush cape. She complained of an excruciating headache, although she'd enjoyed Rufino immensely. But a whole night of literature – what a bore! And now, to make matters worse, there was an awful man playing classical music –

'It's Cruges, a friend of mine!'

'Oh, a friend of yours, is he? Well, you should have advised him to play something like "Pirolito".'*

'You grieve me, Baroness, with this contempt of yours for the masters of music . . . Won't you let me accompany you to your carriage? Bad luck . . . A very good night to you, Senhora Dona Joana! At your service, Baroness! And may the Lord relieve you of your headache!'

She stopped on the stair, wagging her fan at him reprovingly.

'Don't be hypocritical, Senhor Ega. You know quite well you don't believe in the Lord.'

'I beg your pardon. May the devil relieve you of your headache, Baroness!'

The elderly democrat had discreetly disappeared. And from the foyer Ega saw Cruges on the stage at the far end of the room, seated on a low stool which caused the long tails of his dress coat to trail upon the ground; his pointed nose was almost sticking into the music as his skilful fingers moved over the keys. Ega tiptoed up the aisle, unobstructed now, practically empty; the air was cooler, and weary ladies yawned behind their fans.

He stopped beside Dona Maria da Cunha, surrounded by a

* A very simple popular song of the time.

troop of friends – the Marchioness de Soutal, the two Pedrosos, Teresa Darque. And the good lady touched his elbow to inquire who the long-haired musician was.

'A friend of mine,' answered Ega. 'A great pianist, Cruges.'

Cruges . . . The name rippled along the row of ladies, who did not know him. And was that a piece of his, that thing he was playing?

'It's Beethoven, Senhora Dona Maria da Cunha, the Pathétique Sonata.'

One of the Pedroso's didn't catch the name of the Sonata, and the Marchioness de Soutal, very beautiful and very serious, leisurely inhaling from a little bottle of smelling salts, told her it was the *Sonata Pateta, Fool's Sonata*. There was a ripple of stifled laughter from all along the line. *Sonata Pateta!* That was wonderful!

From the end of the row the fat Vargas, the racing one, pushed forward his enormous poppy-red hairless face: 'Very good, Marchioness. Very witty!'

And he passed on the joke to other ladies who turned and smiled at the Marchioness, amid the flutter of their fans. She sat in triumph, beautiful and serious, wearing an old black velvet dress, inhaling her salts – while a few seats away a grey-bearded music-lover turned enormous angry gold rimmed glasses upon the disorderly row.

Meanwhile, throughout the room, the whispering was growing louder. The coughers barked more freely. Two gentlemen had opened their *A Tarde*. And slumped over the keys, with his coat collar sticking up, poor Cruges sweated in shame and embarrassment at that noisy inattention, and hit the notes in haste and confusion.

'A complete fiasco!' declared Carlos, who had come up to Ega and the row of friends.

What a charming surprise for Dona Maria da Cunha! So at last Sr Carlos da Maia, the Gloomy Prince, was to be seen again! What had he been doing all summer? Everyone had been waiting for him in Cintra – one waiting most anxiously . . . A furious 'Ssshh!' from the grey-bearded man silenced her. And at that moment Cruges, after two brusque chords, pushed away his stool and stole away from the stage, wiping his hands on his handkerchief. Here and there rose a little clapping, feeble claps

528

for courtesy's sake amid many a sigh of relief. Ega and Carlos ran to the door, where the Marquis, Craft and Taveira were already waiting, to embrace and console poor Cruges who was shaking all over with a haggard look on his face.

In the expectant silence reigning over the hall, a very tall, very lean gentleman appeared on the stage, manuscript in hand. Someone at Ega's side said that it was Prata, who was going to talk on 'The Agricultural State of the Province of Minho.' Behind him a servant placed a two-branched candlestick on the table: Prata, profile silhouetted in the light, pored over his notebook; and from between the sorrowful nose and the large sheets of paper slipped a slow mumbling, a prayer-like muttering which had the somnolent air of a novena, from which stood out an occasional phrase like a groan – 'wealth of cattle' . . . 'division of property' . . . 'a fertile, unprotected region' . . .

A stealthy exodus now began, which not even the 'ssshh' of the director of the proceedings, standing vigilant upon a step of the stage, could control. Only the ladies remained, and an elderly bureaucrat or two straining forward towards the murmur of prayer, with a hand cupped over the ear.

Ega, who had also escaped the 'luxuriant paradise of the Minho', found himself beside Sir Guimarães.

'Rather a bore, eh?'

The democrat agreed that the last apeaker had not been very entertaining. Then, in a more serious tone, grasping a button of Ega's coat: 'I hope you didn't get the impression, a few minutes ago, that I support my nephew, or that I care twopence about him . . . ?'

Oh, definitely not! Ega had seen immediately that Sr Guimarães had no family love for Damaso.

'Disgust's what I feel for him, sir, disgust! When he went to Paris for the first time and learnt I was living in an attic, he never so much as visited me. The imbecile gives himself airs and acts the aristocrat. And as you know, he's the son of a usurer!'

He pulled out his cigar-case and went on gravely:

'His mother's a different matter! My sister came from a good family. She made that unfortunate marriage but she came from a good family. But as you can see, as far as I'm concerned all this business of aristocracy and titles and coats of arms is pure *blague*, just *blague*! Still facts are facts, and we can't change the history of Portugal: the Guimarães da Bairrada have blue blood in their veins.'

Ega smiled in cordial assent.

'You're leaving shortly for Paris, I believe?'

'Tomorrow, for Bordeaux. Now this scurvy crowd of the Marshal de MacMahon and the Dukes of Broglie and Descazes are finished, one can breathe again there.'

Teles and Taveira passed at that moment, arm in arm, and they turned to observe with interest that austere old gentleman dressed all in black, who was speaking in a low voice to Ega about Marshals and Dukes. Ega noticed their attention: the democrat's frock-coat, incidentally, was of new cashmere; his top hat shone; and Ega was pleased to be seen there talking with that correct and venerable gentleman, who clearly impressed his friends.

'The republic was definitely in danger for a while,' he remarked, walking beside Sr Guimarães.

'Absolutely lost! And there was I, *I*, my dear sir, about to be expelled from the country because of a few little home truths I expressed at an anarchist meeting. I've even been told that at a cabinet meeting Marshal de MacMahon, who's a coarse fellow, beat his fist on the table and cried, *"Ce sacré Guimaran, il nous embête, il faut lui donner du pied dans la derrière"*! I wasn't there, so I don't know, but that's what they told me. As the French can't pronounce Guimarães and I can't stand their bungling my name, I always sign myself Guimaran in Paris. When I went to Italy two years ago, I became Mr Guimarini. And if I had to go to Russia for any reason now, I'd be Mr Guimaroff . . . I can't bear to have people bungling my name!'

They had reached the door of the hall again. An air of abandonment and boredom hung over the empty seats in the hard gas-light; and on stage Prata continued with a hand in his pocket and his nose in his manuscript, though not a word could be distinguished now from the lips of the poor lean scarecrow. But the Marquis, wrapping himself up in his silk scarf as he made his exit, told Ega as he passed that the little man was very practical, he knew his stuff and had even brought Proudhon into it.

Ega and the democrat continued their slow walk around the

foyer where the whisper of the ill-concealed conversations was growing louder amid furtive puffs of cigars. And Sr Guimarães laughed at the idea that Proudhon should be quoted there in that second-rate theatre, to illustrate a talk on manures in the Minho.

'Oh, Proudhon's accepted among us now as the classic monster,' laughed Ega. 'Even Counsellors of State know that he considered property was robbery and God an evil . . .'

The democrat shrugged his shoulders.

'A great man! A giant among men! They're the three notables of this century: Proudhon, Garibaldi, and my *compadre*.'*

'Your "*compadre*"?' cried Ega in astonishment.

It was the nickname by which Sr Guimarães called Gambetta in Paris. Gambetta never saw him without shouting in Spanish, '*Hombre! Compadre!*' and he'd reply '*Compadre! Caramba!*' That's why he called him by this nick-name, and Gambetta laughed. Ah, he's a good fellow, and frank and patriotic as they come!

'A giant among men, my dear sir! The greatest of them all!'

Ega supposed that Sr Guimarães, being connected as he was with the *Rappel*, would bow to the cult of Victor Hugo.

'Ah, he's not a man, my friend, he's a whole world . . .'

And Sr Guimarães lifted his head a little higher and added very gravely: 'A whole world! And not three months ago he said something to me – *me*, my friend – that went straight to my heart!'

Seeing with delight the curiosity and interest on Ega's face, the democrat described in detail this glorious moment which still moved him deeply.

'It was one night at the *Rappel*. I was there writing when he came in limping a bit, but his eyes shining with that infinite goodness of his, that majesty! I got up as if a king had entered the room – no, not a king! If it had been a king I'd have kicked his backside. I got up as if he were a god! God, no! There's no god who'd make me get up! Anyway, I got up. He looked at me, and gave a little wave of the hand like this, and said, smiling, with that something of genius that is his: '*Bonsoir, mon ami!*" '

* Literally the godfather of one's children (from the parents' point of view).

531

And Sr Guimarães took a few dignified steps in silence, as if that '*Bonsoir*' and '*mon ami*', recollected like that, made him feel more acutely his sense of importance in the world.

Suddenly Alencar, who had been gesticulating wildly to a group of friends, came over to them, his face pale, his eyes aflame.

'What do you think of this disgrace? That shameless scoundrel's been up there half an hour with his pieces of paper, mumbling and grumbling . . . And everyone's leaving; there won't be anyone left! I'll have to recite to a lot of cane seats!'

And he disappeared, grinding his teeth, to relieve his fury on others.

But a faint hand-clapping within the hall made Ega turn. The stage was unoccupied again, and the two candles flickered in the candlestick. A notice stated in big letters that there would be 'an interval of ten minutes' – like in a circus. And at that moment the Countess de Gouvarinho came out on the arm of her husband amid a wave of greetings, of bowed heads and well-raised hats of bureaucrats. The master of ceremonies bustled around to find chairs for the worthy personages. The Countess, however, had seen Dona Maria da Cunha who was standing in a window recess with the Marchioness de Soutal and the Pedroso ladies. Ega immediately crossed to the little group of friends, and waited until the ladies had kissed each other.

'Well, Countess, are you still feeling very moved by Rufino's eloquence?'

'Very tired . . . And how hot it is!'

'Terrible. The Baroness de Alvim left a short while ago with a headache.'

The Countess's eyes looked weary and faint wrinkles could be discerned at the corners of her mouth.

'I'm not surprised. This is hardly amusing. Still, nowadays one has to carry one's cross!'

'If only it *were* a cross, senhora!' cried Ega. 'Unfortunately it's a lyre.'

She laughed. And the face of Dona Maria da Cunha, looking younger and livelier that night, lit up with a big smile, full of affectionate admiration for Ega, who was one of her favourites.

'Oh, Ega! You're always so full of life! Tell me something! Where's your friend Maia these days?'

Ega had seen her a few minutes before inside, with her hand on Carlos's sleeve, whispering to Carlos . . . But he played innocent.

'He's here, around somewhere, listening to all this literature.'

Suddenly the pretty, languid eyes of Dona Maria da Cunha lit up with a spark of mischief: 'Talk of the devil . . . In this case it's talk of the angel: here comes our Gloomy Prince!'

And there was Carlos, who had stopped before the open arms of Gouvarinho who was welcoming him with an enthusiasm which seemed to foretell an awakening of the old friendship . . . This was the first time Carlos had seen the Countess since the night when he had left her in the Aterro, abandoned her for ever, slamming the cab door with hatred as she sat inside weeping. Both lowered their eyes as they held out their hands. And it was she who tried to put an end to their embarrassment by opening her large ostrich feather fan.

'How dreadfully hot it is!'

'Terribly,' said Carlos. 'But be careful of the draughts from this window.'

She forced her white lips into a smile.

'Is that a doctor's advice?'

'No, my dear lady, these aren't my consulting hours! This is merely Christian charity.'

But suddenly the Countess called to Taveira who was laughing, titillated, with the Marchioness de Soutal, to scold him for not having turned up on Tuesday at Rua de S. Marçal. Surprised at such a show of interest and such familiarity, Taveira went very red in the face and stammered that he had not known, that it was his ill-luck, that something had turned up . . .

'Anyway, I didn't imagine you would begin receiving so soon, Countess. I remember last year . . .'

But he stopped. The Count de Gouvarinho had turned and placed an affectionate hand on Carlos's shoulder, asking him for his opinion of 'our Rufino'. He, the Count, had been delighted! And delighted above all with the range of tone and emotion – that extremely difficult art of passing from the solemn to the light, descending from passion to puns. Extraordinary!

'I've heard great politicians – Rouher, Gladstone, Canovas, and the rest – but they have none of these flights of language, this opulence of style. Everything's dry – both ideas and facts. They don't reach the soul! What about that image full of ardour and respect of the Angel of Alms, descending slowly on her satin wings? First class!'

Ega could not restrain himself: 'I think your genius is an imbecile.'

The Count laughed, as one laughs at the foolish words of a child.

'It's a matter of opinion.'

And he held out his hands to Sousa Neto and Darque and Teles da Gama, and the others of the innermost circle – while his political friends from the Party and the House – Gonçalo, Neves, Vieira da Costa – stood a little farther off, unable to touch the Minister they had created, now that he was talking and laughing with society ladies and gentlemen. Darque, who was related to Gouvarinho, wanted to know how friend Gastão was coping with his new responsibilities. The Count remarked to his admirers that at the moment he had done no more than study the elements on which he could rely to attack the problems . . . The government, however, was most unfortunate concerning matters of work. The Prime Minister was out of action for a week in bed with catarrh. Now his colleague on Finance had a fever –

'How is he? Is he better? When will he be up?' came the solicitous questions on all sides.

'He's about the same. He's going to Dafundo tomorrow. But he doesn't consider himself out of action. I said to him yesterday, "You go to Dafundo, take your papers and documents . . . In the mornings go for a stroll, get plenty of fresh air, then at night, after supper, in the candlelight, amuse yourself by trying to sort out these problems of Finance!" '

A bell rang. Don Jose Sequeira, red in the face from his labours, came forcing his way to the heart of the group to announce the end of the interval to the Count and offer his arm to the Countess. She, in passing, reminded Carlos, with the delicate simplicity of one performing a duty, of her Tuesday at-homes. He bowed in silence. It was as if the shared past – the sofa which had slipped beneath him, Aunty's house in Santa Isabel, the cabs which she had filled with her verbena perfume – were something read in a book by both of them and then for-

534

gotten. Behind her, her husband followed, head and glasses held high, like the Representative of Power at a party of the Intelligentsia.

'Well, sir, the lady's got some nerve!' commented Ega as he moved away with Carlos.

'What the devil do you expect? She's had her hour of passion and foolishness and now she calmly continues her routine.'

'And in the routine,' finished Ega, 'she bumps into you at every step, who's seen her in her nightshirt! What a world!'

Alencar appeared at the top of the stairs on his way back from the bar, his hollow eyes shining more brightly with gin, and with coat over arm he was ready to declaim. The Marquis came over to join them, enveloped in his white silk scarf, complaining even more hoarsely of his bad throat. It was getting worse, he'd have real trouble with that throat of his one day, he was sure of it.

Then, gravely studying Alencar, he asked:

'Here, this thing you're going to recite – "Democracy"; is it politics or sentiment? If it's politics, I'm off. If it's sentiment, humanity, the saintly labourer, fraternity and all the rest of it, I'll stay, as I like it and it might even do me good.'

The others assured him it was sentiment. The poet removed his hat and combed his fingers through the fluffy inspired grey locks.

'Let me explain, my friends. The one can't exist without the other; look at Danton! But still, I'm not talking about these lions of the Revolution now. Look at Passos Manuel! Of course, we need logic, but by Jove! I can't stand politics without any heart and a bit of the infinite!'

Suddenly, penetrating the silence of the room, a voice louder than Rufino's bellowed, and the great names of Don João de Castro and Afonso de Albuquerque echoed across the room. Everyone moved to the door in curiosity. It was a fat rogue with a pointed beard and a camellia in his buttonhole. With his fist clenched in the air as if he were waving the national flag, he deplored vociferously that they, the Portuguese, having in their possession that noble estuary of the Tagus and such glorious traditions, should squander, indifferent, the sublime inheritance of their ancestors!

'God, Patriotism!' cried Ega. 'Let's get out quick!'

535

But the Marquis held them back, for he liked a bit of patriotism.

And it was the poor Marquis the patriot seemed to address as he raised his little fat body on tiptoe and bellowed. Who was there now who, with sword clasped in one hand and cross in the other, would leap aboard a caravel and carry the Portuguese name over unknown waters? Who was there now heroic enough to emulate the great João Castro, who had torn up all his fruit trees from his garden in Cintra, such was the disinterestedness of the poet's soul?

'The wretch wants to deprive us of our dessert,' cried Ega.

Laughter broke out around. And the Marquis turned his back, sickened by such paltry patriotism. Others yawned behind their hands, thoroughly and completely bored with 'all our glories'. As Carlos, retained there purely to applaud Alencar, suggested to Ega they go downstairs and while away their impatience in the bar, he caught sight of Eusèbiozinho who was descending the stairs, hastily donning an off-white coat. He had not met him since the infamous article in the *Trumpet* for which he had been the 'envoy'. And the anger he had felt against him that day was reawakened now in an irresistible desire to thrash him.

He said to Ega: 'While we're waiting for Alencar, I'll just go and teach that blackguard a lesson.'

'Leave him,' advised Ega. 'He's not responsible for what he does.'

But Carlos was already running down the stairs. Ega followed him nervously, fearing he might do something violent. At the door Eusèbio turned in the direction of the Carmo. And they caught him up in the Largo da Abegoaria, deserted at that hour under the forlorn light of a couple of gas-lamps. When he saw Carlos descend upon him without even a coat and with his white shirt front showing up in the darkness, Eusèbio shrank back and stammered: 'Well, well, you here . . . ?'

'So, you filthy little rat!' began Carlos in a low voice. 'You were mixed up in that *Trumpet* business, were you? I ought to tear you apart, bone by bone!'

He caught him by the arm, though without rancour. But no sooner could he feel that sluggish trembling flesh beneath his own firm hand, than all the old loathing surged to the surface – the desire he'd felt as a small boy whenever the Silveiras had brought him to their house, to jump on him, to tear him to pieces. So now he shook him furiously, as he used to then, and felt a pleasure in his fury. The poor widower, thin and frantic, leapt about, his black glasses flying, his crêpe-banded hat falling on the flag-stones. Finally Carlos flung him against the door of a coach-house.

'Help! Police!' shrieked the poor fellow.

Carlos was grasping him by the throat when Ega intervened. 'That's enough now! Stop it! Our friend's had enough.'

He picked up Eusèbiozinho's hat. Shaking and puffing, Eusèbio grovelled for his umbrella. And to finish the matter, Carlos's boot sent him sprawling on the stones and into the gutter on top of some horse manure.

The square was deserted and the gas-flames low in the tarnished lamps. The two friends calmly returned to the theatre. In the foyer, full of lights and plants, they met the patriot with the pointed beard who was surrounded by friends and on his way to the bar; he was wiping his face and neck and exclaiming with the air of a weary conqueror: 'Phew! It was hard work, but I stirred their hearts!'

Alencar must be reciting now! The two friends leapt up the stairs, and there was Alencar walking on to the stage with the candles aflame behind him.

Slim and sombre-looking in that canary-coloured light, the poet cast a pensive glance around the hall, a slow, hollow-eyed glance: and a silence hung pregnant in the face of such melancholy and solemnity.

' "Democracy",' announced the author of 'Elvira', with as much pomp as if he were uttering a revelation.

Twice he passed his white handkerchief over his whiskers and then dropped it upon the table. And raising his hand in a wide, protracted gesture, he began.

'A park it was. Moonlight
On the tall trees,
Full of love and secrets . . .'

'There, what did I tell you?' cried Ega, touching the Marquis's elbow. 'It's sentiment all right . . . I bet it'll be the banquet.'

537

It was in fact the banquet already described in the 'Flower of Martyrdom', a romantic banquet in some vague garden where wines from Cyprus circulated and brocade trains swept the ground between magnolia trees and from the waters of the lake rose strains of music to the accompaniment of violins. But very soon the serious social idea of the poem appeared: while everything is 'laughter and toasts and lascivious murmurs', under the moonlit trees, outside the gilt railings of the park, alarmed by the barking of the mastiffs, a frail woman clothed in rags weeps as she clasps to her lean breast her child who cries for bread. And the poet, shaking back his locks, asked why there should still be people hungry in this proud nineteenth century. Had the desperate efforts of men to attain justice and equality ever since Spartacus availed nothing? For what had served then the cross of the great Martyr, standing tall on the hillside among the firs:

> 'The sun's rays die,
> The sorrowful wind grows still . . .
> And the eagles wheeling
> Among the clouds are watching
> The Son of Man die!'

Silence and suspicion hung over the room. Alencar, his hands fluttering in the air, lamented that all the accumulated genius of generations had been impotent for this simple thing: to give bread to a hungry child!

> 'It pierces the heart!
> It astounds the conscience!
> That all the wealth of human science
> Cannot answer the dread question!
> Time passes by
> But no light appears,
> And on one side I see hunger
> And on the other indigestion!'

Ega choked, covered his mouth with his handkerchief, and swore he would burst with laughter! *Indigestion!* Never had such an extraordinary word appeared on the lyrical heights! And grave gentlemen around also smiled at such coarse realism. One joker suggested there was bicarbonate of soda for indigestion.

'Not for mine there isn't,' grumbed a greenish-complexioned gentleman who was unbuckling his waistcoat.

But everyone fell silent at the terrible 'Ssshh!' the Marquis uttered, as he loosened his scarf in the excitement and tenderness that humanitarian poetry always awoke in him. Meanwhile on the stage Alencar had found the solution to human suffering! It was a Voice which had emerged from the depths of the centuries, and though stifled always, had gradually been increasing in strength from the times of Calvary to the Bastille. And then, solemn behind the table with a preacher's persuasion and a soldier's firmness, as if that honest piece of mahogany were at one and the same time pulpit and barricade, Alencar lifted his head in a magnificent challenge to Danton and uttered the awe-inspiring words: Alencar wanted the Republic!

Yes, the Republic! Not the Republic of the Terror and of hatred but one of gentleness and love. The one where the smiling millionaire opens his arms to the labourer! The one which is Dawn, Consolation, Refuge, Mystical Star and Dove.

> 'Dove of Brotherhood,
> Which extends its snowy wings
> Over the human mire
> And enwraps its children
> In blessed Equality!'

An impassioned 'Bravo!' echoed from the gallery, and then to quiet it, 'Silence!' from stern-faced individuals. So now Ega flung his skinny hands high in the air and shouted audaciously: 'Bravo! Excellent! Bravo!'

Then pale-faced from his daring, he fitted his monocle in his eye and declared to his companions: 'Such democracy is absurd. But I'm not letting those bourgeois give themselves airs! I'll give him my applause first!'

And his two lean hands went up again, up high, next to the hands of the Marquis which thundered his appreciation. Other spectators round about, not wishing to seem less democratic than

539

Ega and that aristocrat of such renowned lineage, immediately added their own lusty 'Bravos'. Uneasy eyes were beginning to be cast from all sides of the room towards this revolutionary group. But silence fell once more, grave and expectant, when Alencar (for inspiration had forewarned him of bourgeois intolerance) asked in raging strophes what it was that they detested, what it was they feared, in the sublime advent of the Republic? Was it the gift of bread to the child? Was it the liberal hand extended to the people? Was it hope? Was it the dawn?

'Do you fear the bright light?
Are you afraid of the A.B.C.?
Then punish him who reads,
And become again the vile plebs.
Retrogress in History,
Turn out the gas from the streets,
Let the children run naked,
And bring back the scaffold into use!'

More hand-clapping broke out, stronger now and sincere, for the audience was at last responding to the charm of such humanitarian and sonorous lyricism. The Republic and its dangers did not matter any more. The lines rolled out, clear and ringing; and the waves of sentiment swept through the more positive spirits. And at such a sympathetic response Alencar smiled, opened wide his arms and announced one by one – and it was as if pearls were dropping from his lips – the gifts the Republic would bring. Under its banner – not red, but white – he saw the countryside covered with crops, the hunger of everyone satisfied, the nations singing in the valleys under the smiling eyes of God. Ah yes, because Alencar did not want a Republic without God! Democracy and Christianity, like a lily clasping a stem of wheat, completed one another. The hill of Calvary became the platform of the Convention. And there would be no need of cardinals nor missals nor novenas nor churches: the Republic, made entirely of purity and faith, would pray in the fields while the full moon was the Host, and the nightingales intoned the 'Tantum ergo' in the branches of the laurels. And everything would prosper, everything shine: the world of Love would replace the world of Conflict.

540

'The plough replaces the sword
And Justice laughs at Death,
Learning is vital and secular
And the Bastille razed to the ground.
The tiara rolls in the mud,
The Lily of Equality blooms forth
And a new Humanity plants a Cross
On ground where men formerly fought.'

There was such a response of 'Bravos' that the gas-lamps
flickered. It was the Latin passion for verse, for sonority, for
romantic Liberalism, for the image which whistles into the air
and bursts in brilliance, like a firework, conquering everything,
making every heart leap, sending departmental chiefs shouting
their admiration as they leant forward over their ladies in their
enthusiasm for a republic in which nightingales existed! And
when Alencar raised his arms to the roof and, with a semblance
of the *preghiera* in his husky voice, called down to earth this
dove of Democracy, which had arisen out of the darkness of
Calvary and was sweeping down now amid waves of light –
the souls of his audience were bathed in tenderness, a quiver of
ecstasy passed through them. The ladies relaxed in their chairs
and they half-turned their faces towards heaven. Cool breaths
of air, as in a chapel, wafted momentarily through the oppressive
heat of the room. The rhymes dissolved as if into murmurs of
litany addressed to a star-crowned, satin-gowned statue. And
one scarcely knew if this Being whom they were praying to and
waiting for was the Goddess of Liberty or Our Lady of
Sorrows.

Alencar in the meantime was watching her descend, spreading
abroad a sweet perfume. Her divine feet were touching earthly
vales. From her fertile breast brimmed universal plenty. Everything blossomed again, everything was rejuvenated:

'The roses have a rare scent!
The fruits are sweeter far,
Shades and veils both are rent
From the soul which glows like a star . . .
Pain now flees in alarm,
Hunger and war disappear,

Man sings his joy on earth
And Christ smiles down to us here . . .'

A deafening ovation shook the canary-coloured walls. Wild young men leapt on their chairs; two white handkerchiefs fluttered. And the poet, weary now and quivering with emotion, moved down the steps into the ardent arms of admirers. Breathless, he murmured, 'My boys, dear friends . . . !' When Ega ran up with Carlos, crying: 'You were marvellous, Tomás!' Alencar was overcome with emotion and tears lept to his eyes.

And all down the aisle the ovation continued – pats on the back, handshakes from grave gentleman, congratulations from all. Gradually he lifted his head with a proud smile which displayed his bad teeth, feeling himself the Poet of Democracy, consecrated now, anointed by triumph, charged with the unexpected task of freeing souls! Dona Maria da Cunha plucked his sleeve when he passed and murmured in delight that she had found his poem, 'beautiful, beautiful!' And the poet, dazzled by success, replied: 'We need light, Maria!' Teles da Gama came up to slap him on the back and assure him he had "trilled magnificently." Alencar, wholly lost, stammered 'Sursum corda, Teles, my friend, sursum corda.'

Ega inquired after Carlos, who had disappeared after congratulating Alencar. Taveira said Carlos had gone to the bar. Then, below, a boy explained that he had seen Sr Don Carlos take a cab and go up the Chiado.

Ega stood at the door, wondering whether or not to take on the rest of the show. At that moment he saw Gouvarinho, the Countess on his arm, descending the stairs: his face bore an expression of annoyance. His Excellency's lackey hurried to call his coupé. And when Ega approached to ask with a smile how they had liked Alencar's triumphant democratic piece, Gouvarinho's anger, restrained with difficulty up to now, exploded from between clenched teeth: 'Admirable poetry, but indecent!'

The coupé was approaching. He had only time to growl, as he shook Ega's hand: 'To talk of barricades and promise the earth to the plebs at a society show, under the patronage of the Queen, and in front of one of His Majesty's ministers, is downright indecent!'

The Countess was already stepping into a carriage, catching up her long silk train behind her. The minister stepped angrily into the shadowed coupé after her. And alongside trotted his braid-trimmed courier on a white nag.

Ega was about to return up the stairs. But the Marquis appeared, enveloped in an enormous overcoat, fleeing from a long-whiskered poet who was on stage reciting sweet little verses to some sweet big eyes – and the Marquis loathed poems on the parts of the human body. Then it was Cruges who emerged from the bar, buttoning his coat. So, faced with such a dispersal of all his friends, Ega decided to leave too, and go and have his grog at the Grémio with the maestro.

They saw the Marquis into a cab and set off slowly down Rua Nova da Trindade, enjoying the strange charm of that starless winter's night which was as mild as if it had been warmed by the breath of May.

They were passing the entrance of the Hotel Aliança when Ega heard someone hurrying after them and a voice call: 'Oh, Senhor Ega! Just a moment, Senhor Ega!' He stopped, and recognized the curved hat and the white beard of Sr Guimarães.

'I'm so sorry!' panted the demagogue. 'But I saw you walking along and wanted to have a few words with you as I'm leaving tomorrow.'

'That's all right. Cruges, you go on, I'll catch you up.'

The maestro stopped at the corner of the Chiado. Sr Guimarães apologized again: it was just a word he wanted with him.

'You're a great friend of Sr Carlos da Maia's, I believe, sir. Like two brothers, they say.'

'Yes, we're great friends.'

The road was deserted except for a few boys standing at the lighted entrance of the Trindade. In the darkness the tall façade of the Hotel Aliança cast an even darker shadow over them. Sr Guimarães, however, lowered his voice cautiously.

'The case is this: you know, sir – or perhaps you don't know – that I was a close friend of Sr Carlos da Maia's mother in Paris. You are in a hurry, so I don't want to go into that now. All I wanted to say is that some years ago she gave me a coffer to look after which she said contained important papers. Afterwards, naturally, both of us had plenty of other things to think about, the years went by, and eventually she died. To put the matter briefly, as I know you're in a hurry: I still have this box in my possession and I brought it here accidentally when I came to

543

Portugal recently to see about my brother's inheritance. And it suddenly occurred to me today – there in the theatre in fact – that the best thing to do would be to hand it over to the family.'

Cruges was getting impatient.

'Are you going to be much longer?'

'Just a moment!' called Ega, curious now about these papers and the coffer. 'Please go on.'

Then Sr Guimarães explained what he wanted. As he knew how close the two men were, he'd thought it a good idea to hand the coffer over to Sr João da Ega for him to restore to the family.

'Of course!' replied Ega. 'I'm staying at the Maia's house actually, at Ramalhete.'

'Ah, good! Then perhaps you'll send a reliable servant along tomorrow to pick it up. I'm at the Hotel de Paris in Pelourinho Square. Or better still: I'll take it there myself, it's no trouble, even though it's my last day.'

'No, certainly not! I'll send a man along!' insisted Ega, offering the democrat his hand.

He shook it warmly.

'Thank you very much indeed! I'll enclose a card and you can give it to Senhor Carlos da Maia, or his sister.'

Ega looked at him in amazement.

'His sister? What sister?'

Sr Guimarães looked at Ega, also with considerable surprise. And slowly dropping his hand, repeated: 'What sister? Why, *his* sister – Maria!'

Cruges, who was tapping his foot with impatience, shouted from the corner: 'I'm going on to the *Grémio*.'

'I'll join you later, then.'

Sr Guimarães was stroking his long whiskers with black kid-gloved fingers and staring at Ega in an effort to understand. And when Ega slipped his arm in his and suggested they had a little talk together as they walked to Loreto Square, the democrat hesitated a moment with apparent suspicion.

'It seems to me,' said Ega with a nervous smile, 'that we're talking at cross purposes. I've known Maia since he was little, I'm even living in his house at the moment, and I can assure you he has no sister whatsoever . . .'

544

Then Sr Guimarães mumbled some confused apologies – which disturbed Ega even more. Sr Guimarães had supposed it was no secret, that all the sister's goings-on had been forgotten since there had been a reconciliation.

'As I saw Senhor Carlos da Maia with his sister and you, sir, a few days ago, all together in the same carriage at the Cais do Sodré – '

'What! That lady? The one with us in the carriage?'

'Of course!' snapped Sr Guimarães, sick of this muddle they were in. 'That same lady – Maria Eduarda Monforte, or Maria Eduarda Maia, just as you wish, whom I've known since she was a child and whom I've had on my lap many a time; who ran away with MacGren and then lived with that beast of a Gastro Gomes . . . That same lady!'

They were in the middle of the Loreto under the gas-lamp. And Sr Guimarães suddenly stopped sharp when he saw the eyes of Ega staring at him in horror and a terrible pallor covering his face.

'Didn't you know anything about this?'

Ega took a deep breath and removed his hat without answering. The other man finally shrugged his shoulders in embarrassment. Well, he could see he'd been foolish! People should never meddle in the affairs of others! Still, that was that! Sr Ega must imagine it was all a nightmare after the frightful poetry they'd been listening to! He apologized most sincerely – and wished Sr João da Ega a very good night.

Ega in a sudden flash could see the whole catastrophe: and he clung anxiously to Sr Guimarães' arm, fearful that he would run away, disappear, taking with him for ever his evidence, these papers he spoke of, Monforte's coffer – and with these things the certainty which he craved for. And as they strolled slowly across the Loreto he stammered something to justify his emotion, to tranquillize the man, to enable him to draw from him all he knew, the proofs, the whole truth.

'You see, Senhor Guimarães . . . These are such delicate matters that I supposed they weren't known to anyone else. So I was dumbfounded, absolutely stupefied when I heard you suddenly talk of them like that with such frankness. Because, you know, just between ourselves, that lady is not known here in Lisbon to be Carlos's sister.'

Sr Guimarães flung out a hand in relief. Ah, so that was it! Sr Ega had just been playing with him? Well, he'd certainly acted excellently. And of course these matters *were* serious and needed all sorts of veils and concealment. Yes, he could understand, he could understand perfectly! And really, considering the Maias' position in Lisbon society, the lady was not exactly a person he could introduce as his sister.

'But it wasn't her fault, my dear sir! It was her mother's — that extraordinary mother that the devil gave her!'

They were going down the Chiado now. Ega stopped a moment, devouring the old man with frenzied eyes: 'Did you know this lady, Madame Monforte, very well, Senhor Guimarães?'

Oh, extremely well! He had known her in Lisbon — but only from afar, as the wife of Pedro da Maia. Then this disaster had happened, when she ran away with the Italian. He'd left the country for Paris that year too, with Clemence, a seamstress from the Levaillant, and what with one thing and another, business matters and bad luck, he'd stayed there indefinitely. Still, it wasn't his life they were talking about . . . Only later had he met Madame Monforte, one night at the Bal Laborde: and their friendship had begun there. The Italian had already died in a duel at that time, and something to do with the bladder had finished off old Monforte. She was with a young fellow called Trevernnes at that time, living very elegantly in a pretty house in the Parc Monceaux. An extraordinary woman! And he wouldn't forget what he owed her! When his little friend Clemence had fallen ill with consumption, Madame Monforte brought her flowers and fruit and wine, sat and kept her company, watched over her like an angel. She certainly had a generous heart, that woman! The little one, Dona Maria, was seven or eight then, and as pretty as a picture. There was another child too — the daughter of the Italian, a lovely little thing. A really lovely little thing — but she died in London, that one.

'And I carried Maria in my arms many a time, my dear sir. I don't know if she still remembers a doll I once gave her, that spoke, said "Napoléon" . . . That was the time of the Empire — even the dolls were imperialists! Then when she was in the convent in Tours I went to see her with her mother. In those days my principles prevented me entering these religious dens, but nevertheless I went with her mother. And when she ran away

546

with the Irishman, MacGren, it was to me her mother rushed, furious, wanting me to call the Police Commissioner to arrest the man. Finally she took a fiacre to Fontainebleau and was reconciled, and they even lived together. Oh, it was a mess, the whole business.'

A weary sigh escaped from Ega, who dragged his feet along, overcome with shock.

'And this lady had no idea who her father was, of course . . .'

Sr Guimarães shrugged his shoulders.

'She didn't even know that people called Maias existed! Madame Monforte had always told her her father was an Austrian nobleman whom she had married in Madeira. A terrible mix-up, my dear sir, a dreadful mix-up!'

'It's horrible,' murmured Ega.

But still, said Sr Guimarães, what else could Madame Monforte do? What the deuce, man, it would be somewhat hard to confess to your daughter, 'I ran away from your father, and because of that he killed himself!' It wasn't so much a question of shame – the girl could see her mother had lovers and she herself had one by the time she was eighteen, poor child – but because of the death, the corpse, the blood . . .

'Not even to me,' cried Sr Guimarães, stopping in the deserted street and throwing out his arms. 'Not even to me did she ever say a word of her husband, or Lisbon, or Portugal. I remember one occasion in Clemence's house when I referred to a horse of Pedro da Maia's, a sorrel which she used to ride. A superb animal! But I never mentioned her husband – only the horse. Well, my dear sir, she beat her fan on the table, and shrieked like a wild thing: *"Dîtes donc, mon cher, vous m'embêtez avec ses histoires de l'autre monde!"* And I suppose they were stories from another world. I'm sure towards the end of her life she had convinced herself that Pedro da Maia had never existed. A foolish creature! She even took to drink at the end. Still, that's all finished now. She had a generous heart and behaved splendidly towards Clemence. *Parce sepultis!*'

'It's horrible,' muttered Ega again, taking off his hat and running a shaky hand through his hair.

His only desire now was to have all the proof, all the details. So he spoke of the papers and this coffer belonging to Mme Monforte. Sr Guimarães had no idea what it contained: he wouldn't have been surprised if it was simply dressmakers' bills or cuttings from the *Figaro* which mentioned her name.

'It's a small box she gave me the day before she set off for London with her daughter. It was during the war. Maria was already living with the Irishman, and had the little girl then too – Rosa. Then the Commune took over and there was the series of misfortunes. When Mme Monforte returned to Paris, I was in Marseilles. That was when poor Maria started living with Castro Gomes – rather than die of hunger, I believe. I went back to Paris later, but I didn't see her mother – she was already very ill by then. And there was Maria stuck to that vile Castro Gomes, a pedant of a man, a *rastaquouère* – just the sort that should have gone to the guillotine. If I saw her it was only to acknowledge her from a distance, like the other day when I saw her in the carriage with you, sir, and her brother . . . So here I am with the papers still. And to tell the truth, I haven't thought anything more about them with all this political business. Still, now they're at the family's disposal.'

'If it's no trouble to you,' suggested Ega, 'I'll walk with you to your hotel and pick them up now.'

'No trouble whatsoever! We're on our way and the matter will be over and done with.'

They walked for a time in silence. The show must have finished. Carriages were rumbling down the Chiado. Two ladies and a gentleman, waving his arms and talking loudly of Alencar, passed them. Sr Guimarães took his cigar-case slowly out of his pocket, then stopped to light a match.

'So Dona Maria is regarded simply as a relative? How did she find out? What happened?'

Ega, walking along with his eyes on the ground, trembled as if he had been brusquely awoken. And he began to stammer some confused story which caused him to blush in the darkness. Yes, Maria Eduarda was considered a distant relative of the family. They had found out through the steward. She had broken with Castro Gomes and the past. The Maias gave her an allowance and she lived in retirement in Olivais, as the daughter of a Maia who had died in Italy. Everyone was very fond of her; Afonso da Maia adored the little girl . . .

And suddenly infuriated with all this dishonesty, into which he had even dragged the name of that fine old gentleman, he burst out:

'God! My God! It's frightful!'

'A tragedy!' Sr Guimarães summed up gravely.

When they reached the Largo do Pelourinho, he asked Ega to wait a moment while he went up to get Mme Monforte's papers.

Alone in the square, Ega lifted up his arms to heaven in dumb surrender to his feelings, a release from the nervousness and anxiety in which he had drifted like a somnambulist from the Loreto. And all he could feel was the absolute authenticity of Guimarães' story, so compact, so flawless, without a weakness which would undermine it and cause it to fall to pieces. The man had known Maria Monforte in Lisbon, while she was still the wife of Pedro da Maia, shining on her sorrel horse; he had met her in Paris after she had run away, after the death of her first lover and then living with others; he had carried her little daughter in his arms – the little girl who'd been given dolls . . . And since then he had never lost sight of Maria Eduarda: he had followed her career in Paris, in the convent at Tours, in Fontainebleau with the Irishman, in the arms of Castro Gomes – and finally in a hired cab with him and Carlos da Maia a few days ago in the Cais do Sodré. All this corresponded with the story Maria Eduarda herself had told. And over and above all this towered the monstrous certainty that Carlos was the lover of his sister!

Guimarães had not returned. A light went on on the second floor at an open window. Ega began to pace slowly about the square. Gradually he began to grow incredulous about such an outrageous thing. Was it likely that such a thing should happen to a friend of his, in a street in Lisbon, in a house let by Mother Cruges? Impossible! Such horrific things only happened in a muddled society, in the tumult of the Middle Ages! In a bourgeois society, with abundant police and records and laws and documents, with the registration of births and marriages – impossible! No, it couldn't happen in contemporary life that two children, separated by a mother's madness, after a brief moment together in the cradle, should grow up in distant lands, be educated, follow their individual destinies – all for what? To meet and sleep together, but in concubinage! It wasn't possible! Such incidents belonged to books – subtle inventions of art – to instil fear in human hearts . . . He lifted his eyes to the lighted window where Sr Guimarães was obviously searching in his cases for the papers. There was the man with his story, and not the least inconsistency anywhere which could destroy it! And little by little that bright light above seemed to illuminate the whole calamity, reveal its development. Yes, it was basically probable. This child, daughter of a woman who had taken her away with her, grows up, becomes the lover of a Brazilian, comes to Lisbon, lives in the city. In a neighbouring part of the city lives another child of this same woman, a child that was left by her and who grew to manhood. His fine features and sophistication stand out in our shabby, provincial city. She, for her part, tall, fair and beautiful, dressed by Laferrière, the flower of a superior civilization, outshines the crowds of short, dark-skinned women here. In the few square yards of the Baixa, the Alterro, where one can't help meeting everybody else, their two paths fatally cross; and because of abundant charm, too fatally they become attracted to each other! Could there be anything more natural? If she had been ugly and cheaply dressed, and he had been an insignificant little fellow in a bowler hat, they would never have noticed each other and would have followed their separate destinies. But as it was, it was natural that they should get to know each other and probable that they should fall in love . . . Then one day Sr Guimarães comes by and the terrible truth is made known.

The door of the hotel creaked in the dark and Sr Guimarães stepped forward with a silk cap on his head and a package in his hand.

'I couldn't find the key to the case, I'm so sorry. It's always like that when you're in a hurry. Still, here's the famous coffer at last.'

'Right, right . . .'

It was a box like a cigar-box and the democrat had wrapped it in an old number of the *Rappel*. Ega slipped it in his coat pocket, and put out his hand to Sr Guimarães as if any further words between them were superfluous. But Sr Guimarães insisted on accompanying him to the corner of Rua do Arsenal, in spite of his informal cap. The night was almost oriental in its soft calm for anyone fresh from Paris, and he, with the habits of a newspaperman, never went to bed early, never before two or three in the morning . . .

Then strolling along leisurely with his hands in his pockets and a cigar between his teeth, Sr Guimarães returned to the

subject of politics and the show. Alencar's poem, whose title
had given him high hopes, had seemed to him very weak after
all.

'All swank and flash, all talk of liberty, and yet no proper
attack, not one good blow at this trash of a monarchy and the
court . . . Don't you agree?'

'Yes, yes, you're quite right,' murmured Ega, looking round in
the hopes of seeing a cab.

'It's like the Republican newspapermen we have around here
. . . All empty talk! Nothing but hot air! As I've said to them:
"Infernal wretches, why don't you attack social problems?"'

Fortunately a coach was coming clattering along slowly from
the Terreiro do Paço. Ega gave the old democrat a hasty handshake, wished him a good journey and gave the driver the address
of Ramalhete. But Sr Guimarães still clung to the carriage door,
to advise Ega to make a trip to Paris. Now that they had struck
up a friendship he wanted to introduce him to all the people
there . . . And Sr Ega would see! There was none of that
grandiose Portuguese pose there, no shabby imbecile characters
giving themselves airs and twirling their moustaches. There, in
the first nation of the world, everything was gaiety and fraternity
and wit in abundance.

'And you'll find me at the offices of the *Rappel*! Known
throughout the world! As for the parcel, I can put my mind at
rest now.'

'You can, you can . . .'

'Your humble servant, dear sir . . . Give my regards to Dona
Maria!'

As he rode along the Aterro, the fearfully distressing question which repeated itself was 'What shall I do?' What was he to
do, God above, with that terrible secret he held, which he alone
possessed now that Sr Guimarães was leaving, disappearing for
ever? And as he viewed in horror the terrible predicament in
which this revelation was going to throw the man he most esteemed in all the world, his first instinct was to keep the secret
to himself, let it die with him. He wouldn't say anything about it;
Sr Guimarães would be swallowed up in Paris; and those who
loved each other would continue to love each other. In that
way he could avoid an atrocious crisis in Carlos's life, and his
own sufferings as a friend. What a ruthless thing to do, to ruin

551

the life of two innocent and adorable creatures by flinging in their faces proof of their incest!

But at this idea of incest, all the consequences of his silence burst like fearful living flames before his eyes out of the darkness of his thoughts. Could he calmly witness the life of these two people, knowing that it was incestuous? Could he go to Rua de S. Francisco, sit there happily at table, glimpse through the curtains the bed in which they slept – and know that sin and sordidness was the result of his silence? Impossible . . . But had he then the courage to go to Carlos the next day and say to his face, 'Look, do you know you're your sister's lover?'

The carriage stopped at Ramalhete. Ega entered, as was his custom, up Carlos's private stairway. Everything was dark and silent. He lit a candle and pulled aside the curtain to Carlos's apartments. He walked a few timid steps, which seemed to echo gloomily, into the room. The light caught a mirror which shone in the shadows of the bed recess. And the light fell upon the bed, with its long smooth cover between silken curtains. Then the idea that Carlos was at that moment in Rua de S. Francisco, sleeping with a woman who was his sister, pierced him with such sharpness, produced such a vivid, palpable image, that he could see them clearly with their arms entwined, lying naked . . . All Maria's beauty and Carlos's elegance disappeared. All that remained were two animals, sprung from the same womb, coupling in a corner like two dogs on heat!

He hurried to his room, away from that vision which grew still brighter and clearer in the ill-lit corridor. He bolted his door and hastily, with trembling hand, lit the six candles on his dressing-table, one by one. And now the need to tell Carlos everything seemed more urgent and inevitable. But at the same time he felt less able to go and face Carlos and destroy his life and happiness with this revelation of incest. He just could not! Let someone else tell him! He would be there afterwards, faithful and devoted, to console him, share in his pain. But the supreme calamity of Carlos's life was not coming to him by words from *his* lips! Let someone else tell him! But who? A thousand incoherent, mad ideas passed through his head. Ask Maria to go away, disappear . . . Write an anonymous letter to Carlos, with all the details of Guimarães' story . . . And gradually this anxiety and confusion was turning into a hatred of Sr Guimarães. Why

552

had the fool spoken at all? Why had he insisted on committing other people's private papers to him? Why had Alencar ever introduced the man? Ah, if it weren't for Damaso's letter . . . Everything stemmed from Damaso's cursed letter!

Moving restlessly around the room, his eyes fell on an envelope lying on his bedside table. He recognized Vilaça's writing – and didn't even open the letter . . . An idea had suddenly occurred to him. Tell Vilaça everything! Why not? He was the Maias' steward. There had never been any secrets in the house from him. And this extraordinary complication concerning a lady of the family, supposed dead and suddenly appearing – who better to solve it than the faithful steward, the old confidant, the man chosen by inheritance and destiny to receive all the secrets and share in all the interests of the house? And without deliberating any longer, he pounced upon this means to salvation, which at least calmed him, lifted from his heart the overwhelming, crushing burden . . .

He would get up early and go to Vilaça's home. He wrote on a sheet of paper: 'Wake me at 7', and went downstairs along the long stone corridor where the servants slept, and stuck the note in his servant's keyhole.

He returned to his room calmer, and opened Vilaça's letter. It was one brief sentence reminding his friend Ega that payment of a two-thousand-*milreis* loan from the Banco Popular was due in two days' time.

'Hell, everything together!' cried Ega furiously, crumpling up the letter and flinging it to the ground.

7

PUNCTUALLY AT seven o'clock the servant woke Ega. He sat up
with a start when he heard the door open, and suddenly all the
gloom and worry of the night before – Carlos, his sister, the
happiness of that household brought to a sudden end – also stirred
up in his soul with a start, as if they too were awakening from
sleep. The french doors were open and a livid silent dawn air
seeped in through the curtains. Ega sat looking around him for
a moment, shivering and disconsolate; then cravenly snuggled
down between the sheets again, enjoying the warmth and comfort before going out to face the miserable day ahead.

And gradually, in the snug warmth of the bedclothes, it began
to seem less urgent to him and less useful to rush along, half
asleep as he was, to Vilaça's house. What was the use of
going to Vilaça? There was no problem of money here, or peti-
tions, or legal questions – nothing requiring the experience of a
steward. It meant simply introducing one more bourgeois into
a secret which was so terribly delicate that even he had been
alarmed to hear of it. And nestling down farther under the bedclothes, with only his nose out in the cold, he muttered to
himself: 'It would be stupid to go to Vilaça!'

Couldn't he rather summon up enough courage to tell Carlos
everything himself, right away that morning, in a straightforward
manly fashion? Was the matter really so alarming as it had
seemed the night before – the complete destruction of a man's
life? In a little village called Vouzeias near his mother's country
house in Celorica, there had been a similar case, with a brother
and sister who were, unknowing, about to marry. Everything
came out when the papers were being got together for the banns.
For a day or two the pair were utterly dumbfounded, as Father
Serafim said, but eventually they laughed about it in a friendly
fashion, highly amused to call each other 'brother' and 'sister'.
The boy, a handsome youth, said later that 'there was nearly a
real mix-up in the family'. Here the matter had gone a step farther, and the couple's sensibility was subtler, but their hearts
were still free from blame, they too were absolutely innocent.

Why then should Carlos's life be ruined for ever? The unawareness of their sin would leave them free from remorse, and with the first shock over, what reason had they for continued grief? It was only their pleasure that would be finished. It was no more than an ordinary disappointment in love then. Nothing like as bad as if Maria had been unfaithful to him with Damaso.

The door opened, and Carlos appeared.

'What's this dawn awakening then? Baptista's just told me downstairs. Some adventure? A duel?'

His coat was fully buttoned and the collar turned up – concealing the white tie of the night before; he had surely come straight from Rua de S. Francisco in the cab Ega had heard stop outside a few moments before.

Ega sat up sharply in bed, reaching out a hand for his cigarettes on the table beside him, and murmured with a yawn that he had arranged a trip to Cintra with Taveira the night before. That's why he'd asked to be called. But now, he didn't know, he'd woken rather tired.

'What's the day like?'

Carlos went to pull the blinds. There, on the desk, in full view in the light of day, lay Mme Monforte's box wrapped in the *Rappel*. Ega had a sudden idea: 'If he notices it, and asks about it, I'll tell him everything!' His poor heart began to beat violently, terrified at this decision. But the blind, somewhat stiff, rose at last and a sun-ray bathed the table in light – and Carlos turned back without noticing the coffer. It was an immense relief to Ega.

'So you're off to Cintra?' said Carlos, sitting on the foot of his bed. 'Not a bad idea . . . Maria was only talking yesterday of going to Cintra . . . Hold on! . . . Let's all go together! We could all go in the brake.'

And he looked at his watch, calculating the time it would take to get the horses ready and advise Maria.

'The only thing is,' Ega went on in confusion, taking his monocle from the table, 'Taveira said something about going with a couple of girls . . .'

Carlos shrugged his shoulders and grimaced with distaste. How sordid, going to Cintra with a couple of wenches in the daytime! At night perhaps, after a few drinks, that was a different matter . . . But in the pure light of day! Who was it – fat Lola?

Ega plunged into a complicated story, wiping his monocle on the corner of his handkerchief. They weren't Spanish girls – they were a couple of decent girls, seamstresses . . . He'd promised a long time ago to go to Cintra with one of them – the daughter of Simões, a deceased upholsterer . . . Very serious people . . .

Faced with such seriousness and solemn promises, Carlos dropped the idea of going to Cintra.

'Right, let's not talk any more about it! I'm going to have a bath, and then to business! And if you do decide to go, bring me back some cheese-cakes for Rosa – she loves them.'

When Carlos had left, Ega crossed his arms in despair, utterly disconsolate, recognizing only too well that he would never have the courage to 'tell him everything'. What was he to do? And once more he drifted back into the more comfortable idea of going to Vilaça and handing over to him Mme Monforte's box. There was surely no more honest nor practical man; and with that mediocre bourgeois spirit of his, who better to face such a catastrophe calmly and dispassionately? This phlegmatic temperament of Vilaça's finally decided him.

He leapt impatiently out of bed and rang the bell. And as he waited for the servant he slipped his dressing-gown over his shoulders and went to examine the Monforte coffer. It was indeed like a cigar-box and was wrapped in a paper with tattered dirty edges and the remains of a seal on which could be discerned what was undoubtedly the Monforte crest: *'Pro amore'*. On the lid, in a woman's poor handwriting, was written: 'Monsieur Guimaran, à Paris'. Hearing the servant's steps he snatched up a towel hanging on a near-by chair and covered the box. And in half an hour he was rolling along the Aterro in an open carriage, feeling more cheerful as he took in a deep breath of that fine fresh morning air which he so rarely enjoyed.

Things began badly. Vilaça had already left the house and his servant did not know whether he had gone to his office or over to Alfeite. Ega set off for the office in Rua da Prata. But Sr Vilaça had not arrived yet.

'When's he likely to be here?'

The clerk, a lank youth, nervously twisting a string of coral that hung across his waistcoat, stammered that Sr Vilaça should not be long, if he hadn't taken the nine o'clock boat to Alfeite . . . Ega left in despair.

'Right,' he called to the cabman, 'drive to the Café Tavares.'

In the Tavares, still deserted at that hour, a boy was sanding the floor. And while he waited for his meal, Ega glanced at the papers. They all spoke briefly of the charity show and promised full details on this brilliant artistic performance later. Only the *Gazeta Ilustrada* went on in solemn phrases, to call Rufino grandiose and Cruges promising; with Alencar the *Gazeta* separated the philosopher from the poet: they reminded the philosopher most respectfully that not all the idealist aspirations of philosophy, beautiful as mirages in the desert, are socially practicable; but to the poet, creator of such exquisite images, such inspired stanzas, the *Gazeta* wholeheartedly shouted 'Bravo! Bravo!' There were further absurdities. Then followed a list of people whom the *Gazeta* had seen there, among which 'stood out the handsome, monocled profile of João da Ega, always outstanding in verve'. Ega smiled and stroked his moustache. His steak arrived at that moment, smelling delicious and sizzling in its earthenware dish. Ega put his *Gazeta* aside thinking, 'Not bad at all, this paper!'

The steak was excellent, and after a cold partridge, a little pineapple dessert and a cup of strong coffee, Ega felt the black cloud which had been hovering over him since the day before lift a little. Really, he thought, lighting a cigar and glancing at his watch, all the tragedy meant, if it was looked at in a practical manner, was the loss to Carlos of a beautiful mistress. And wouldn't such a loss, though heart-rending now, afterwards have its compensations? There had been that shadow over Carlos's future up till now – the promise of marriage which bound him by his honour to a woman who was very attractive but who had a past full of Brazilians and Irishmen. Her beauty romanticized everything: but for how much longer would this charm last, this radiance of a goddess on earth? Might this discovery of Sr Guimarães not be a providential way out? In a few years' time Carlos would be consoled, as serene as if he had never suffered a thing – and free and rich, with the world at his feet!

The café clock struck ten. 'Right, let's get on with it,' thought Ega.

Again the cab drove to Rua da Prata. Sr Vilaça still had not come, and the clerk was beginning to think he had indeed gone to Alfeite. Faced with this uncertainty, Ega suddenly felt depressed again, and without courage. He dismissed the cab and with the package containing the coffer under his arm, he made his way along the Rua do Ouro to the Rossio, stopping inattentively in front of a goldsmith's, or glancing at the book-covers in the bookshops. The gloom of the night before, temporarily dispersed, descended again upon him, more densely than before. He saw no providential liberations now, no compensations . . . All he could see, as if actually hovering in the air around him, was the horror of Carlos sleeping with his sister.

He returned to Rua da Prata, and once more went up the dirty stone stairway; and there on the landing, outside the green-shuttered door, he found Vilaça who was leaving in a hurry, and buttoning his gloves.

'At last, man!'

'Ah, you are the friend who was looking for me? Can you hold on a bit, because I've got Viscount Torral waiting for me.'

Ega almost gave him a push. Confound the Viscount! This was something urgent, extremely serious! But Vilaça did not move from the door and went on buttoning his gloves with the same business-like, hurried air.

'Look, my friend, you can see how things are! The man's waiting for me! I have an appointment at eleven.'

Ega, furious, clutched hold of his sleeve, thrust his face next to his and murmured tragically that it was to do with Carlos and was a matter of life and death! At that Vilaça crossed the office in great alarm and showed Ega into a cubicle narrow as a corridor, at the side, with a cane couch in it and a table with dust-covered books and a cupboard at the far end. He shut the door and pushed his hat to the back of his head.

'Right, what is it?'

Ega gestured towards the door, indicating that the clerk might be listening. The steward opened the door, called to the lad to go to the Hotel Pelicano and ask the Viscount Torral if he would be so good as to wait for half an hour. Then shutting and bolting the door, he put again the same fearful question: 'What is it?'

'It's something dreadful, Vilaça, really dreadful . . . I hardly know where to begin.'

Vilaça, extremely pale now, slowly put his umbrella down on the table.

'Is it a duel?'

'No. It's this. You know Carlos has been seeing a lot of a Senhora MacGren, who came to Portugal last winter, and has been staying here?'

A Brazilian lady, the wife of a Brazilian, who had spent the summer in Olivais? Yes, Vilaça knew. He'd even spoken to Eusèbiozinho about it.

'Ah, Eusèbio! Well, she wasn't Brazilian after all! She was Portuguese, and his sister!'

Vilaça dropped on to the couch, clutching his hands together in amazement.

'Eusèbio's sister!'

'No, not Eusèbio's, man! Carlos's!'

Vilaça, unable to understand, did not utter a word, but stared at Ega who was wandering up and down the cubicle murmuring: 'Sister, legitimate sister!' He finally sat down on the couch and quietly, very quietly in spite of their privacy, described his meeting with Guimarães at the concert, and how the terrible truth had come out casually, in a single word, at the corner of the Aliança. But when he spoke of the papers given to Sr Guimarães by Mme Monforte, put away for years and never reclaimed, and which Sr Guimarães now suddenly and urgently wanted to restore to the family, Vilaça, crushed and stupefied up to this point, woke up and burst out:

'There's a trick here! It's just to get money!'

'Get money? Who?'

'Who?' cried Vilaça passionately, on his feet now. 'This woman, this Guimarães, the whole crowd of them! You don't understand . . . If a sister, a legitimate authentic sister of Maia's turns up, it means some four hundred contos or more for her!'

They two stood gazing at the idea which, in spite of himself, shocked Ega. But as the steward returned to the subject of the four hundred contos with a tremor in his voice, and suggested they had come across a wily pair, Ega gave a gesture of disagreement.

'I don't think there's the least possibility of that! She is incapable, absolutely incapable of such scheming. Anyway, if it were a question of money, why should she pretend to be his sister, since Carlos has already promised to marry her?'

Marry her! Vilaça threw up his hands in disbelief. What! Sr Carlos da Maia offer his hand and name to this creature who

559

had been living with a Brazilian? In the name of all things holy! But a further suspicion penetrated his amazement, he saw here another case of their wiliness.

'No, Vilaça! No, sir!' insisted Ega, out of patience now. 'If it were a question of documents and she had them, either real or false, she would have brought them forward before, not slept with her brother first!'

Vilaça slowly lowered his eyes. An awful apprehension was stealing over him at the thought of that great house, which was his pride, being torn apart and half seized by an adventuress. But as Ega, in a fearfully nervous state, reminded him that it was not a question of documents, nor legality nor the fortune – the steward had another idea, and his face lit up anew.

'Just a minute, there's something else! Perhaps she's the daughter of the Italian!'

'So what? It comes to the same thing.'

'No, it doesn't!' shouted the steward, bringing his fist down upon the table. 'She is not the legitimate daughter of a Maia and cannot claim a farthing from this house! Ah, there we have it!'

Ega shook his head disconcolately. No, that wasn't the case either, unfortunately. She was the daughter of Pedro da Maia. Guimarães had known her from the time he had carried her in his arms as a child, he had given her dolls when she was seven, and before that when she was only four or five and the Italian had been staying in the house as a result of the shot he'd received. The Italian's own daughter had died as a baby in London.

Vilaça dropped glumly back on to the couch.

'Four hundred contos! What a windfall!'

Ega returned to the main point. If there was no legal certainty yet, there was at least a strong suspicion. And they could not let poor Carlos innocently wallow in that sordidness any longer. It was therefore necessary to inform him of everything that very night.

'And you, Vilaça, are the man to tell him.'

Vilaça jumped so much that the sofa slid against the wall.

'Me?'

'Yes, you. You're the steward of the house!'

What was this if not a question of filiation and inheritance? Who was the man to deal with these legal matters if not the steward?

The blood rushed to Vilaça's face and he murmured: 'God, man, you put me in a spot!'

No, Ega merely put him in the place where Vilaça, as steward, should logically and professionally be.

Vilaça protested, stuttering in his confusion. What the deuce! He wasn't shirking his duties! But he just didn't know anything! What could he say to Sr Carlos da Maia? 'Your friend Ega told me this, and a certain Guimarães told him last night in the Loreto . . .' There wasn't anything else he could say . . .

'Then say that.'

The other man's eyes flamed: 'Say that! Say that! My God, sir, you want some nerve to do that!'

He jerked down his waistcoat and marched puffing and blowing to the other end of the room where he was brought up sharp by the cupboard. He turned and looked at Ega again.

'You can't go to a man with a story like this without proof. Where's the proof?'

'Oh, Vilaça, excuse me but you're being obtuse! What did I come here for but to bring you the proofs, what there are, good or bad I don't know, and the story of Guimarães and this little box with Madame Monforte's papers in it?'

Vilaça, mumbling under his breath, went over to examine the box, turning it over in his hands, deciphering the legend of the seal: *'Pro amore'*.

'Well, are we going to open it?'

Ega had already drawn up a chair to the table. Vilaça cut the paper, worn at the corners, in which the box was wrapped. And what appeared was in fact an old cigar-box, held by two tacks, full of papers, some in bundles secured by ribbons, others loose in open envelopes which bore the monogram of Monforte under a Marquis's crown. Ega undid the first bundle. They were letters in German which he did not understand, written in Budapest and Karlsruhe.

'Right, this doesn't help us much . . . Let's try something else.' Another package, whose pink knot Vilça carefully untied, was an oval box containing a miniature of a man with reddish moustache and side-whiskers, buttoned up in a white uniform with a tall gold collar. Vilaça thought the picture pretty.

'Some Austrian officer,' snored Ega. 'Another lover . . . *Ça marche. . . .*'

561

They were taking out the papers one by one, with the tips of their fingers, as if they were handling relics. A large envelope crammed with dressmakers' bills – some paid, some not – interested Vilaça deeply, who went through them, horrified at the prices, at the infinite variety of items of luxury. Bills for six thousand francs! Two thousand francs for one dress! Another bundle was a surprise: they were letters from Maria Eduarda to her mother, written from the convent in a careful, round, ornate writing, full of devoutly grave little phrases, obviously dictated by the good sisters: and in these compositions, virtuous and cold like formal essays, the only sign of the girl's sincerity was a little dried flower pinned to the top of the paper.

'We'll put these aside,' murmured Vilaça.

Then Ega impatiently emptied the whole contents of the box on to the table and spread out the papers. And among the letters and bills and visiting cards, they found a large envelope addressed in blue ink to: 'My daughter Maria Eduarda'. Vilaça ran his eyes over the enormous sheet of paper inside, a grand official-looking affair with the same gold monogram over the Marquis's coronet. When he handed it to Ega, he seemed as if he were suffocating, and his ears were bright red.

Ega read it out aloud very slowly:

'As Maria is still weak from giving birth to her daughter, and as I too am not feeling very well with these sharp pains in my side, I feel it prudent for what might happen in the future to make a declaration here which belongs to you, my beloved daughter, and which only Father Talloux (M. l'abbé Talloux, coadjuteur à Saint-Roch) knows as I told him two years ago when I had pneumonia. It is the following: I declare that my daughter Maria Eduarda, accustomed to sign herself Maria Calzaski, supposing this to be the name of her father, is Portuguese and the daughter of my husband Pedro da Maia, from whom I separated of my own free will, bringing the child with me to Vienna, and after to Paris, and who is now living in Fontainebleau with Patrick MacGren whom she is going to marry. And the father of my husband was my father-in-law Afonso da Maia, widower, who lived in Benfica and also in Santa Olávia, beside the River Douro. All this can be confirmed in Lisbon, for the papers must be there; and my mistakes, the consequences of which I see now, should not prevent you, my dear daughter, from having the posi-

tion and fortune which belong to you. I am, therefore, making
this declaration which I sign, in case I am unable to do so
before a notary, which I intend to do when I am better. And
should I die, though God forbid it! I beg my daughter's pardon
for everything. And I herewith sign with my married name –
Maria Monforte da Maia.'

Ega looked across at Vilaça. The steward could only mutter
with his hands crossed on the table:

'What a mess! What a mess!'

Ega stood up. Right! Now everything was simple. All Vilaça
had to do was hand this document to Carlos without comment.
But Vilaça scratched his head troubled by a further doubt:

'I don't know if this paper would be considered legal proof in
a court . . .'

'What d'you mean, legal, court . . . !' cried Ega violently.
'It's enough to stop him sleeping with her again!'

A timid knock at the door stopped him short, nervous. He
turned the key. It was the clerk who whispered through the
crack: 'Senhor Carlos da Maia was downstairs in his carriage
when I came in, and he asked for Senhor Vilaça.'

Panic! Ega frantically clutched Vilaça's hat. The steward
snatched up the Monforte papers with both hands and flung
them into a drawer.

'Perhaps I'd better tell him you're not in,' suggested the
clerk.

They stood listening, still pale from the shock. They heard
Carlos's dog-cart rattle off along the street, and they breathed
again. But now Ega was sorry he had not asked Carlos up and,
there and then, without more ado, without any more cowardice,
told him everything, with the paper before them. The worst
would have been over then.

'Things have to be done slowly, my friend,' said Vilaça, wiping
his forehead with his handkerchief, 'slowly and methodically.
People have to be prepared and take a deep breath before they
take the plunge.'

Anyway, said Ega, further conversation was futile. The other
papers in the box had lost their interest after that confession
by Mme Monforte. All that was needed now was for Vilaça to
appear that night at Ramalhete at half past eight or nine
o'clock, before Carlos left for Rua de S. Francisco.

'But you must be there, my friend!' cried the steward, appalled at the task in front of him.

Ega promised. Vilaça gave a little sigh. Then, on the landing where he had come to accompany Ega, he muttered:

'Imagine a thing like this! Just imagine! And I was feeling so pleased at the thought of dining there tonight.'

'And I to be dining with them in Rua de S. Francisco!'

'See you tonight.'

'Until tonight.'

Ega did not dare to return to Ramalhete that day, to sit at table with Carlos, watching his happiness and peace, and feel as night approached the calamity that was about to descend upon him. He went to beg a bite from the Marquis, who since the evening of the concert had stayed at home with his throat well wrapped. At half past eight he supposed Vilaça would be at Ramalhete and he left the Marquis, who had settled down with the Chaplain for a game of draughts.

That beautiful day, which had become overcast in the afternoon, had now turned into a night of drizzle which chilled the streets. Ega took a cab but as he stopped at Ramalhete, feeling extremely nervous, he met Vilaça in the doorway, umbrella under his arm and tucking up his trousers before going out into the rain.

'Well?' cried Ega.

Vilaça put up his umbrella and whispered:

'I wasn't able . . . He said he was in a great hurry and hadn't time to listen.'

Ega stamped his foot in desperation.

'What did you expect me to do? Grab hold of him and force him to listen? We left it till tomorrow. I'll be here at eleven.'

Ega strode up the stairs, muttering to himself: 'Confound it, we'll never get out of this mess!' He went to Afonso's study – but did not enter. Through a gap in the half-drawn curtains he saw a corner of the room, warm and comfy in the soft rose-hued light falling on the damask: the cards lay waiting on the whist-table; on the sofa embroidered in self-coloured silk sat Dom Diogo, limp and faded, twirling his moustache. And, engaged in some dispute, the voice of Craft muttering through his pipe and the slower voice of Afonso who sat calmly in his easy-chair intermingled and were drowned by Sequeira who roared furiously: 'But if any disorder broke out tomorrow, it would be this army, which you gentlemen consider no more than a bunch of vagrants fit only to be disbanded, it would be this army that would protect you. It's all very well to talk, and be very philosophical! But you'd feel the difference when the trouble started and there weren't half a dozen bayonets at the ready!'

Ega went to Carlos's rooms. The candles were still burning; there was an aroma in the air of cologne water and cigar-smoke. Baptista told him that Sr Dom Carlos had left just ten minutes before. He had gone to Rua de S. Francisco! He had gone there to sleep. Ega, tense and disquieted at the thought of the long, miserable night ahead of him, felt a need to dull the senses, dispel the ideas which were torturing him, with some vigorous excitement. He had not dismissed the cab, so he left now for the S. Carlos Theatre. And he finished up by going to Augusto's for supper with Taveira and two girls, Paca and Carmen Filósofa, and drinking abundant quantities of champagne. At four o'clock he was drunk and laid out on the sofa, muttering sentimentally to himself snatches of Musset's poem to Malibran. Taveira and Paca, sitting together in the same chair, he looking the typical tender lady's man, and she *muy caliente*, were pecking at little bowls of jelly. And Carmen Filósofa, glutted and unbuttoned, her tight corset already laid aside in a *Diário de Notícias*, was beating her knife on the edge of her plate, carolling away, staring at the gas-lamps:

> '*Señor Alcade mayor,*
> *No prenda usted los ladrones . . .*'

He awoke later on at nine beside Carmen Filósofa in a room with big wide windows which let in all the melancholy of that grey rainy morning. And while he waited for the closed cab that the servant had gone to fetch, poor Ega, disgusted and vexed at his state, with his tongue coated and his feet bare upon the carpet, gathered together his scattered garments and had only one firm idea – to flee from all that into a deep bath, cool and perfumed, where he could cleanse himself of the nauseating viscous sensation of Carmen and the orgy of the previous night.

He went to take this purificatory bath at the Hotel Bragança

565

to be washed and ready to meet Carlos and Vilaça at eleven. But he had to wait for the clean linen that the coachman, with a note to Baptista, had gone to fetch from Ramalhete. Then he lunched, and it was just striking midday when he stopped outside the private entrance to Carlos's rooms with his dirty linen in a bundle.

He met Baptista crossing the landing with a basket of camellias. 'Is Vilaça here?' asked Ega in a low voice, and walking on tiptoe.

Yes, Sr Vilaça had been in there for some time. Had Sr Ega received the clean linen? He'd sent a suit too, for at these times it always makes one feel fresher . . .

'Yes, thank you, Baptista. Thank you very much!'

Ega was thinking, 'Right, Carlos knows by now. The barrier's passed.' But he hesitated a little longer, taking off his gloves and coat with cowardly indecision. Finally, his heart beating fast, he pulled aside the velvet curtains. A silence weighed upon the antechamber; the heavy rain beat against the glass doors, through which the dark shapes of the garden trees could be seen. Ega lifted up the other curtain, embroidered with the Maia arms.

'Ah, it's you!' cried Carlos, getting up from his work-desk, with a number of papers in his hand.

He seemed to have maintained a firm and manly attitude; only his eyes shone strangely with a dry gleam and looked anxious and bigger in the pallid face. Vilaça, sitting facing him, passed an Indian silk handkerchief over his forehead with a slow, weary movement. The table was scattered with the Monforte papers.

'What the devil sort of mix-up's this that Vilaça's been telling me?' cried Carlos, crossing his arms in front of Ega, his voice trembling very slightly.

Ega stammered: 'I didn't have the courage to tell you . . .'

'Well, I have to hear! What the devil did this man tell you?'

Vilaça got up at once. He got up with the haste and timidity of a recruit being relieved from a dangerous post, and asked permission, if they did not require him any more, to return to his office. The two friends would obviously prefer to talk in private. And the Monforte papers were there. If he were needed they'd find him in Rua da Prata or his home . . .

'And you'll understand,' he added, rolling the silk handkerchief up in his hands, 'that I took the liberty of coming here to

talk to you as it was my duty, as a confidant of the family . . .
That was Ega's opinion here too . . .'

'Of course, Vilaça, thank you!' replied Carlos. 'If it's necessary, I'll send for you.'

The steward, handkerchief in hand, glanced slowly round the
room. Then he peered underneath the table. He looked very surprised. And Carlos followed his timid, searching steps around
the room impatiently.

'What is it, man?'

'My hat. I thought I'd put it here. I must have left it outside.
Right, if you need anything . . .'

No sooner had he left the room, still darting worried glances
into the corners, than Carlos closed the curtain violently. And
turning to Ega and dropping wearily into a chair, he demanded:
'Right, out with it!'

Ega, seated on the sofa, began with his meeting with Sr
Guimarães down in the bar of the Trindade, after listening to
Rufino. The man wanted an explanation of Damaso's letter about
the hereditary drunkenness . . . Everything had been explained
away and the beginnings of a sort of friendship had sprung
up . . .

But the curtain moved again and once more Vilaça's face
emerged.

'I'm terribly sorry, but my hat . . . I can't find it – I could
have sworn I left it here . . .'

Carlos checked a curse. Then Ega began the search too, looking
behind the sofa and in the window recess. Carlos, in desperation,
even lifted the curtains of the bed to see if it was there. And
Vilaça, scarlet-faced and distressed, even examined the washing-
recess.

'Imagine it disappearing like that! Perhaps I left it in the
antechamber after all. I'll go and see again. I'm so sorry.'

The two were by themselves once more. And Ega started
again, telling how Guimarães had spoken to him during the intervals about various things – the concert, politics, Papa Hugo, etc.
Then Ega had looked for Carlos to go on to the Grémio for a
few minutes; and had eventually left with Cruges. They'd passed
in front of the Aliança –

Once more the curtain lifted. Baptisa begged pardon, but:
'Senhor Vilaça can't find his hat. He says he left it in here.'

567

Carlos got up, furious, clutching the back of his chair as if he were going to break it over Baptista's head.

'Go to the devil the pair of you! Let him go home without his hat! Give him one of mine! But get out!'

Baptista made a solemn retreat.

'Go on, finish!' said Carlos, dropping back into his chair, paler than ever.

And Ega recounted the long terrible conversation with Guimarães in detail, from the moment when the man had chanced to speak just as he was leaving, just as he was shaking his hand, about 'Maia's sister'. Then he had handed over the Monforte papers at the door of the Hotel de Paris in the Pelourinho . . .

'And there it is, I don't know anything more than that. Imagine the sort of night I had! But I just hadn't the courage to tell you. I went to Vilaça . . . I went to Vilaça with the hope above anything else of his knowing something, or having some document which would make nonsense of Guimarães's tale . . . He hadn't anything, didn't know anything. He was as thunderstruck as I was!'

In the brief silence which followed, a heavier shower of rain, flooding the greenery in the garden, dashed against the windows. Carlos got up abruptly, his whole being in revolt.

'And do you actually think this is possible? D'you believe this could happen to a man like me or you, in a street in Lisbon? I meet a woman, I look at her, I get to know her, I sleep with her and out of all the women in the world, she had to be my sister! It's not possible. And no Guimarães, no papers nor documents will convince me it is!'

And as Ega remained silent in his corner of the sofa, with his eyes lowered, he cried out: 'For God's sake say something! Say you doubt it too! It's extraordinary. You all believe this as if it were the most natural thing in the world, and all over the city brothers and sisters were sleeping together!'

Ega murmured: 'Something like this nearly happened near our house in Celorico.'

At that moment, without a sound to signal his approach, Afonso da Maia appeared between the curtains, leaning on his cane and smiling about something which evidently amused him. It was Vilaça's hat still.

'What the devil have you two done with Vilaça's hat? The poor man was wandering around in distress. I had to lend him one of mine. It came down over his eyes, and we had to stuff it with handkerchiefs – '

But then he noticed the anguish in his grandson's face. And the embarrassment of Ega whose eyes did not dare to meet his, but flickered anxiously towards Carlos. All the laughter left his face as he stepped slowly into the room.

'What's the matter? Has anything happened?'

Then Carlos, totally selfish in his passion and without a thought of the cruel shock he was going to give the old man, and driven by the hope that his grandfather, witness of the past, would know something to give the lie to this story of Guimarães, and these papers of Mme Monforte – went towards him and burst out:

'Yes, something extraordinary, Grandfather! Perhaps you'll know . . . You must know something to get us out of this mess! It's this, in brief: I know a woman who arrived in Lisbon some time ago, and lives in Rua de S. Francisco. Now suddenly I find she's my legitimate sister! A fellow's come along who knows her, who has some papers . . . The papers are here. They're letters and a declaration of my mother's. It's a real mess, and there's a pile of proof . . . What's all this mean? Didn't this sister of mine whom my mother took with her die? You must know, Grandfather!'

A tremor ran through Afonso da Maia and he clutched his cane tight and at last dropped heavily into a chair beside the curtain. And there he sat dumbly staring at his grandson and at Ega, with a glazed look in his eye.

'This man's a fellow called Guimarães,' went on Carlos. 'He's an uncle of Damaso's. He spoke to Ega, and it was Ega he gave the papers to . . . Tell Grandfather, Ega; tell him from the beginning . . .'

Ega recounted the lengthy story in brief. And the most important point, he finished, the most decisive point was that this Guimarães – who had no reason to lie and only mentioned these things by chance, by pure chance – had known this lady since she was a little girl, as the daughter of Pedro da Maia and Maria Monforte. And he had never lost sight of her. He had watched her grow in Paris, he had carried her in his arms, he had given her toys. He had visited her at the convent with her mother. He had even been to the house she'd lived in in Fontainebleau, as the wife of MacGren.

'And finally,' interrupted Carlos, 'he saw her again the other day in a carriage with Ega and me . . . What do you think, Grandfather?'

The old man spoke with a great effort, as if the words as he uttered them were tearing his heart.

'The lady, of course, doesn't know anything about this?'

Ega and Carlos both shouted together: 'No, nothing at all!' According to Guimarães, her mother had always concealed the truth from her. She supposed she was the daughter of an Austrian, and originally signed herself Calzaski.

Carlos, who was sorting among the papers on the table, held one out to his grandfather.

'Here's my mother's statement.'

The old man fumbled for his glasses from his waistcoat pocket, his poor fingers trembling helplessly; he read the paper slowly, growing paler at every line and breathing with more and more difficulty. When he finished he let his hands, still clutching the paper, drop on his knees, and looked crushed, lifeless. Eventually the words came, slow and heavy: he didn't know . . . What Mme Monforte said here might well be true, he couldn't tell. This lady in Rua de S. Francisco could in fact be his granddaughter . . . He didn't know . . .

And Carlos's shoulders drooped, also overwhelmed at the certainty now of the calamity which had fallen upon him. His grandfather, witness of the past, knew nothing! That statement, the whole story of Guimarães, remained intact and irrefutable. There was nothing, no memory of man, no written document, to dispute it. Maria Eduarda, then, was his sister! And the old man and his grandson, facing each other there, seemed struck and broken by the same pain, born of the same idea.

At last Afonso got up, leaning heavily upon his cane, and went and replaced the paper on the table. He glanced, though without touching them, at the papers strewn around the cigarbox. Then slowly passing his hand over his forehead, he repeated:

'I don't know any more than you . . . I always thought this child had died. We made extensive inquiries. She herself said her daughter had died, and even showed someone or other a portrait . . .'

'That was the other younger one, the Italian's daughter,' said
Ega. 'Guimarães told me about that. This one lived. This one
was seven or eight then, four or five years after the Italian
turned up in Lisbon. It was this one.'

'This one,' repeated the old man.

He gave a little gesture of resignation, sighed deeply and went
on: 'Right! All this must be carefully thought about. I think it
would be a good idea to call Vilaça back. Perhaps he ought to go
to Paris . . . And we must calm ourselves before anything else.
No one's died after all, have they? No one's died . . .'

His voice trembled and died away. He put out his hand to
Carlos who kissed it in choked silence, and the old man pulled
his grandson towards him and laid his lips on his forehead. Then
he moved towards the door, but his steps were so uncertain that
Ega hastened to help him.

'Take my arm, sir.'

Afonso leaned heavily upon him. They crossed the silent antechamber where the rain continued to beat upon the window-
panes. The great curtain embroidered with the Maia arms fell
to behind them. Then Afonso, disengaging his arm from Ega's,
whispered with his face close to the young man's, giving vent at
last to his horror:

'I've heard of this woman! She lives in Rua de S. Francisco,
and spent the summer in Olivais. She's his mistress!'

Ega stammered, 'No, no, Senhor Afonso da Maia!' But the old
man put his finger on his lips, indicating that Carlos was inside
and could hear. And he moved away, doubled over his cane,
overcome by that implacable destiny which, after wounding him
when he was young and strong with his son's tragedy, was
finally crushing him in his old age with the disgrace of his grandson.

Ega, nervous and exhausted, returned to Carlos who had resumed his agitated pacing which shook the floor and made the
bottles on the marble console tinkle. Ega stood silently beside the
table, running through the rest of Mme Monforte's papers: there
were letters, a little morocco-bound address book, visiting-cards
from members of the Jockey Club and senators of the Empire.
All at once Carlos stopped in front of him, desperately wringing
his hands.

'Two people are in absolute heaven and some nonentity, some

idiot, some Guimarães, says a couple of words, hands over a few papers and shatters these two lives for ever! Oh, Ega, isn't it horrible!'

Ega risked a trite consolation.

'It would be far worse if she had died.'

'Why?' cried Carlos. 'If she'd died, or I had, the object of our love would have finished, it would turn to grief and nostalgia which is another matter. Like this though, we are alive, but dead as far as each other is concerned, though the passion uniting us still lives! You don't suppose that just because it's suggested she's my sister, I love her less than I loved her yesterday, or in a different way, do you? Of course I don't! My love's not going to accommodate itself to new circumstances like that, and suddenly turn into friendship. Never! And I never want it to!'

His love was rebelling, defending itself, not willing to die just because the revelations of some Guimarães and a cigar-box full of old papers suddenly declared it was impossible, and ordered the fire quenched!

There was a further silence. Ega lit a cigarette and sank down into a corner of the sofa. Weariness was encroaching on him, a weariness springing from all this emotion and the night out at Augusto's and the drowsy awakening in Carmen's bedroom. The room was growing gloomier in the light of the winter afternoon. Ega closed his eyes. But only to be awoken again almost immediately by a further exclamation from Carlos, who stood before him again, wringing his hands as before.

'And this isn't the worst of it, Ega! The worst of it is that we still have to tell her, her, Ega!'

Ega had already thought of this. And she had to be told right away, without any vacillations.

'I'll go there and tell her myself,' said Carlos.

'You?'

'Who else? D'you want Vilaça to go?'

Ega frowned.

'What you ought to do is catch the night train to Santa Olávia and write telling her everything from there. You'll be safer like that.'

Carlos flung himself into an easy chair with a great sigh of weariness.

Yes, perhaps that was the best thing to do – the night train tomorrow. He'd already thought of that too, it was certainly best. But right now he felt dreadfully tired.

'So do I,' said Ega, stretching himself. 'And we can't do anything more now, we'll only sink farther into the muddle. The best thing to do is to calm ourselves. I'm going to lie down for a while.'

'See you later.'

Ega went up to his room, stretched out on top of the bed and, weary as he was, rapidly fell asleep. He awoke late at the sound of the door opening. It was Carlos who came in, lighting a match. It had grown dark and the dinner-bell was ringing downstairs.

'And there's this wretched dinner to make matters worse!' said Carlos, lighting the candles on the dressing-table. 'No chance of slipping out to a bar to talk things over quietly. And I even invited Steinbroken yesterday.'

Then, turning to his friend, he asked: 'Ega, d'you think my grandfather knows everything?'

Ega jumped off the bed and went over to the wash-basin, rolling up his sleeves.

'I'll tell you what I think. I think your grandfather suspects something. The news struck him like the news of a disaster. And if he hadn't suspected anything it wouldn't have caused him any more surprise than the simple discovery of a lost granddaughter.'

Carlos uttered a long sigh. They went down to dinner.

Downstairs they found, apart from Steinbroken and Dom Diogo, Craft, who had come 'to beg a bite'. And over that table, usually so gay, and covered with flowers and light, hovered a cloud of melancholy that night, while the conversation was all about illnesses – Sequeira was suffering from rheumatism, the poor Marquis was getting worse . . .

Afonso, in his study, complained of a bad headache which accounted for his worn-out look and pallor. Carlos, whom Steinbroken thought looked 'off-colour', explained that he too had had an awful night. Then Ega, in order to liven up the meal, asked friend Steinbroken what he had thought about Rufino – the great orator of the charity show. The diplomat hesitated. He had been considerably surprised to learn that Rufino was a politician, a member of the House. Those gestures, the strip of shirt showing at the stomach, the imperial and the boots – hardly seemed typical of the statesman.

'*Mais cependant, cependant . . . Dans ce genre là, dans le genre sublime, dans le genre de Démosthène il m'a paru très fort . . . Oh, il m'a paru excessivement fort!*'

'What about you, Craft?'

The only part of the show Craft had enjoyed was Alencar's poem. Ega impatiently shrugged his shoulders. What rubbish! Surely there wasn't anything more comical than that romantic comedy of Alencar's, that soft fair republic all dressed in white like Ophelia, praying in the fields under the benevolent eye of God . . . But Craft found all this excellent, on the grounds that it was sincere. What was always revolting in exhibitions of Portuguese literature? Why, the scandalous lack of sincerity. No one, either in verse or prose, ever seemed to behave in what they were ardently declaiming, beating their breasts with their fists. It was like that the night before. Rufino did not seem to believe in the influence of religion; nor did the man with the pointed beard seem to have any faith in the heroism of the Castros and Albuquerques; and not even the poet of the pretty little eyes seemed to believe in the prettiness of those same little eyes. All false! All counterfeit! But what a difference with Alencar! He had a real faith in what he sang about, in the Brotherhood of Peoples, in the Republican Christ, in His devout Democracy crowned with stars.

'This Alencar must be getting on in years,' observed Dom Diogo, rolling little pellets of bread between his long pale fingers.

At his side Carlos finally woke up out of his silence.

'Alencar must be some fifty years old.'

Ega swore he must be at least sixty. As far back as 1836 he was publishing raging verse and calling upon death in remorse for the number of virgins he had seduced.

'Yes, I heard about this man many years ago,' murmured Afonso slowly.

Dom Diogo, raising his glass to his lips, turned to Carlos. They were very close friends within the circle of distinguished young men of that time. Alencar often used to go to Arroios with poor Dom João da Cunha – God keep his soul – and various others.

They were a bright young set, and all around the same age. Nothing of that lot left now . . . nothing at all!

Carlos lowered his eyes. Everyone grew silent. An air of sadness passed over the flowers and lights as if sent from the depths of this past they spoke about, full of tombs and grief.

'And what about poor Cruges? What a fiasco!' cried Ega, trying to shake off the gloom.

Craft considered the fiasco well deserved. Why had he tried to give Beethoven to that crowd brought up on rubbishy Offenbach? But Ega would not permit such contempt for Offenbach, who was one of the finest manifestations in modern times of scepticism and irony. Steinbroken accused Offenbach of not knowing counterpoint. Ega finished by saying that there was nothing in art so beautiful as the *fado*. And he called to Afonso in order to rouse him:

'Isn't that so, Senhor Afonso da Maia? You're like me, one of the *fado* faithfuls, loyal to our great national creation.'

'Yes, indeed,' answered the old man, lifting a hand to his head, as if to justify his listless, disinterested air. 'There is a great deal of poetry in the *fado*.'

Craft, however, attacked the *fado*, the *malagueñas*, the *peteneras* – all this meridional music which seemed to him one vast sobbing warble, prolonged to infinity with sterile sluggish *aieeees*. He remembered one night, for example, hearing a *malagueña*, one of those famous *malagueñas* sung in perfect style by a lady from Málaga. It was in Madrid, in the house of Villa-Rubia. The lady sat herself at the piano, muttered something about *tomb* and *gloom*, and then broke into a never-ending *ã-ã-ã-ã-ah* . . . Well, gentlemen, he got rather bored with this, went into another room, watched a whole rubber of whist, leafed through a thick album, discussed the Carlist war with General Jovellos – and when he returned, there was the same lady, with carnations in her locks and eyes on the ceiling, sobbing out the same *ã-ã-ã-ã-ah* . . . !

Everyone laughed. Ega protested energetically, completely aroused now. Craft was just a dry Englishman, brought up on the flat breast of Political Economics, incapable of understanding the world of poetry that an *aieee* could contain! But he wasn't speaking of *malagueñas*. It wasn't up to him to defend Spain. Spain had more than enough liveliness and knife-play to con-

575

vince Craft and his fellow Britons . . . The question there was the *fado*.

'Where have you ever heard the *fado*? In drawing-rooms, with piano accompaniment . . . Of course I quite agree, it's insipid like that. But listen to it played by three or four guitars at night in the country with a beautiful moon above. Like at Olivais this summer when the Marquis took along Vira-Vira! D'you remember, Carlos?'

And he stopped suddenly, immediately sorry for having carelessly mentioned Hideaway. Carlos did not answer and a shadow fell across his face. Craft snorted that on a beautiful moonlit night all country sounds were beautiful, even frogs croaking. And once more a strange depression flooded the room; the footmen were serving dessert.

Then in the silence, Dom Diogo remarked pensively, with the majesty of a nostalgic lion remembering a great past:

'Another music very *distingué* in the old days were the monastery bells. It was just as if they were bells you were listening to. You don't hear them now.'

The dinner finished bleakly. Steinbroken had returned to the absence of the royal family at the show – a fact which had disquieted him since the preceding evening. No one there was at all interested in the Court. Then Dom Diogo came out with a fussy story about the Infanta Dona Isabel. It was a relief when the footmen brought round the large silver bowl and jug of scented water.

After coffee, served in the billiards-room, Steinbroken and Craft began a game of billiards – with the stake at fifteen *tostões* to make it more interesting. Afonso and Dom Diogo had withdrawn to his study. Ega had buried himself in a soft easy chair with the *Figaro*. But before very long the magazine slipped to the floor and he closed his eyes. Then Carlos, pacing thoughtfully up and down smoking, glanced at the sleeping Ega and slipped out behind the curtain.

He was going to Rua de S. Francisco.

But he was in no hurry and wandered along the Aterro wrapped in a fur coat, finishing off his cigar. The sky had cleared and a sliver of moon shone between scraps of white cloud which were being swept along by a sharp north wind.

Alone in his room that afternoon Carlos had decided to speak personally to Maria Eduarda, justifying his decision as the only one his dignity and reason would allow. Neither he nor she was a weak-spirited child, needing the most terrible crisis of their lives to be resolved by Ega or Vilaça; both were strong and sufficiently firm-willed to be able to find their own way, with dignity and reason, out of this distress which would tear their lives asunder. That's why he, and he alone, was going to Rua de S. Francisco.

Of course it was going to be terrible to see her there in that room, still warm from their love, now that he realized she was his sister. But why not? Were they then two religious, eternally preoccupied with thoughts of the devil, to be horrified by the sin into which they had unconsciously fallen, and anxious to rush away and hide their carnal horror of each other in distant convents? No! And was it necessary to put the many leagues from Lisbon to Santa Olávia between them, in order not to fall into the former weakness, if their eyes should meet, glowing with the same fire? No! Both had enough strength to subdue their hearts to reason, bury them as if under a cold hard stone, and so completely that they would never more feel revolt or sorrow. And so he could easily return to that room, still warm from their love.

In any case, why was he appealing to reason and their courage? He wasn't going to reveal all the truth to her at once, say a pathetic farewell, a dramatic farewell, and open between them an abyss of passion and pain. On the contrary! All that afternoon he had been seeking a means of softening the blow and revealing gradually the horror he must tell the poor creature. And finally he had found a way, though a cowardly and complicated one. But so what? It was the only one, the sole one which, by its careful preparation, would spare her the brutality of a sudden revelation. And this way was only possible if he himself went, quite dispassionately and resolutely, to Rua de S. Francisco.

That's why he was going; and all along the Aterro, slowing down his steps, he went over his plan, rehearsing to himself the words he would use. He would go into the room with a great show of haste, and tell her how a piece of business concerning the house, a complicated affair with some land-stewards, obliged him to leave for Santa Olávia in a few days' time. And he would leave the house at once on a pretext of having to hurry to Vilaça's house. He could even add: 'I won't be long, only a moment, see you later.' One thing bothered him. Suppose she kissed him? He decided to exaggerate his haste and keep his cigar in his mouth and his hat on his head . . . And out he'd go, never to return. Poor thing: she would wait up until late, listening to every carriage that passed by. The following night he would go away to Santa Olávia with Ega, and leave her a note explaining that he had received a telegram obliging him to take the next train. He might even add: 'I'll be back in two or three days.' And there he was, parted from her for ever. He would write straightway from Santa Olávia, in a somewhat confused and troubled tone, speaking of family documents unexpectedly discovered, proving them to be closely related. All this would be brief, vague, unclear. Finally, in another letter he would reveal the whole truth and send her her mother's statement; then, explaining that a separation was necessary while the doubts were being cleared up, he would suggest she return to Paris. Vilaça would deal with the money question and give her three or four hundred pounds for the journey. Ah, this was all so complicated and cowardly! But this was the only way. And who, if not he, could try to do things in a tactful, tender way?

Amid this tumult of thoughts he suddenly found himself in the Travessa da Parreirinha, in front of Maria's house. He could see a faint light through the curtains of the drawing-room. The rest of the house was in darkness – the window of the narrow little dressing-room and the chrysanthemum-filled balcony of her bedroom.

And that silent façade which only showed one single sleepy light was gradually filling him with uneasiness and discomfort. It was fear of the soft penumbra within, full of warmth and that perfume which had a touch of jasmine in it. He did not enter, but continued slowly along the pavement in front of the house, thinking of certain details inside – the wide deep sofa with its silk cushions, the lace frills around the dressing-table, the white curtains of her bed. He stopped in the wide beam of light issuing from the Grémio, and went in automatically, attracted by the simplicity and security offered by that stone-floored entrance with its large gas-lamps and no penumbras and perfumes.

In the lounge downstairs he sat glancing, uncomprehending, through the news telegrams on the table. A waiter passed and he ordered a cognac. Teles da Gama who came from an inner room whistling, with his hands in his coat pockets, stopped to ask if Carlos was going to the Gouvarinhos on Tuesday.

'Perhaps,' answered Carlos.

'Do come! I'm trying to get some people along. It's Charlie's birthday that day. Everyone'll be going and there's supper too.'

The waiter entered with the tray and Carlos, standing beside the table, stirring the sugar in the glass, remembered that afternoon when the Countess, slipping a rose in his buttonhole, gave him the first kiss; he saw again the sofa where he had fallen with a rustle of crumpled silk . . . How vague and remote it all seemed.

He finished the drink and left. Walking along on the same side as the house, he no longer saw the perturbing façade with its dim disturbing light flickering at the window. The front door was shut and the gas-lamp burnt on the landing. He went up the stairs, and stair by stair the beating of his heart sounded louder to him than his footsteps. Melanie, who opened the door to him, said that her mistress had felt a little tired and gone to lie down for a while – and the drawing-room seemed deserted with its candles out and the embroidery lying idle in its basket, the books arranged in cold order upon the table where the lamp cast a tenuous light from beneath the yellow lace shade.

Carlos took off his gloves slowly, again uneasy before that sleepy withdrawal. But suddenly Rosa ran in, laughing and skipping, with her hair bobbing round her shoulders and her arms wide open. Carlos caught her up with the usual greeting: 'Here comes my little mountain goat!'

But then, as she hung there in the air, with her feet kicking, the idea suddenly flashed through his mind that this was his niece, this child bore his name! He let her down, indeed almost dropped her, and stared at her as if he were seeing that delicate ivory-complexioned face, where his own blood ran, for the first time.

'What are you looking at me like that for?' she cried, backing away and smiling with her little hands clasped behind the fluffy skirts.

He could not understand: she seemed another Rosa, and min-

gled with his uneasiness was a nostalgia for the old Rosa, the
daughter of Madame MacGren, to whom he used to tell stories
of Joan of Arc, whom he used to push on the swing under the
acacias at Hideaway. In the meantime her smile grew brighter,
the little teeth gleamed white and the blue eyes shone with
tenderness as she watched him there so grave and silent, and
expected him to start some game or to boom out with the voice
of Carlos the Great . . . She had the same smile as her mother
and the same dimple in the chin. Carlos suddenly saw in her all
Maria's charm and grace. And he caught her up in his arms
again, but so violently and with such rough kisses on her hair
and cheeks that she struggled to get away, and cried out with
fright. He let her go immediately, fearing that he had been un-
chaste.

Then very seriously, he asked: 'Where's Mama?'

Rosa rubbed her arm, with a frown on her forehead.

'Horrid! You hurt me!'

Carlos stroked her hair with a hand that still trembled.

'Go away with you, don't be such a baby. Mama doesn't like it.
Where is she?'

The little girl, placated immediately, leapt around and caught
his wrists so that he should skip with her.

'Mama went to lie down. She says she's very tired – and then
calls *me* a lazybones! Come on, jump with me! Don't be miserable!'

Out in the corridor came Miss Sarah's voice:

'Mademoiselle!'

Rosa placed a finger on her laughing lips.

'Tell her I'm not here! Go on – just to make her angry! Tell
her!'

Miss Sarah lifted up the curtain and discovered her immediately, hiding behind Carlos, crouching to make herself small.
The governess smiled benevolently, and murmured: 'Good evening, sir.' Then she said it was nearly half past nine and that
Mademoiselle should remember she'd had a cold and ought to
go to bed. Carlos pulled Rosa's arm gently and stroked her affectionately so that she should obey Miss Sarah.

But Rosa shook him off, indignant at such betrayal.

'You never do anything! Mean old thing! Well, I shan't say
good-bye, so there!'

She marched sulkily out of the room, swerving out of reach of her governess who smiled and held out her hand to her, and in the corridor burst into bitter, angry tears. Miss Sarah smilingly excused the little girl. It was the cold which made her impertinent. But she wouldn't have dreamed of behaving like that in front of her mother.

'Good night, sir.'

'Good night, Miss Sarah.'

By himself again, Carlos wandered around the room for a few moments. Finally he lifted the tapestry which shut off the small dressing-room. There, in the darkness a mirror flickered pale in the shaft of light from a street-lamp. Very quietly he opened the bedroom door.

'Maria, are you asleep?'

There was no light in the room, but the same street-lamp shining dimly through the blinds picked out from the gloom the white curtains surrounding the bed. And from there a sleepy voice answered:

'Come in! I was very tired so I came to lie down. What's the time?'

Carlos did not move, his hand still on the door-handle.

'It's late and I must go and find Vilaça. I just came to tell you I might have to go to Santa Olávia tomorrow, for two or three days.'

A movement beyond the curtaining made the bed creak.

'To Santa Olávia? How miserable – why? So suddenly! Come in! Come over here!'

Carlos made one silent step on to the carpet. He could still hear the faint creaking of the bed. And now the warm shadows seemed charged with that perfume of hers which he knew so well, and he felt lost in it, felt it enter into his soul with the hopeless seduction of a new caress and perturb him most strangely. But he went on stammering out his insistence that he must see Vilaça that night.

'It's such a bother, just on account of some land-stewards and water problems.'

He touched the bed, and sat down on the very edge, suddenly overcome with weariness which robbed him of the strength to continue with these inventions of land-stewards and water; it was as if they were mountains of iron to be moved.

'I felt so sleepy after supper, so lazy. But now you're going off suddenly like this . . . What a shame! Give me your hand!'

He groped among the white bedclothes – and encountered a knee, the shape and gentle warmth of which he felt through the silk sheet; and there he left his hand, forgotten, open and slack, as if dead, in a sudden dulling of all his will and consciousness which left him with only the sensation of that warm soft skin where his palm rested. A sigh, a little sigh like that of a child, escaped from Maria's lips and faded away in the shadows. Carlos felt the warmth of her desire, weakening him like the fierce heat issuing from an abyss which had suddenly opened at his feet. He still whispered, 'No, no!' but she lifted her arms, entwined his neck and pulled him towards her with a murmur like the continuation of a sigh, and a trembling, whispered 'dearest'. Unresisting, like a dead thing driven by the wind, he dropped on to her breast. He felt her open mouth upon his own dry lips, and he caught her to him furiously, crushing her, devouring her, in a despair which shook the bed.

Ega at this time was just waking up in the billiards-room where he lay still stretched out in the armchair into which he had fallen in his weariness. Yawning and still drowsy, he dragged his steps to Afonso's study.

A cheerful fire was burning there and Bonifácio lay toasting himself in front of it on the bearskin rug. Afonso was playing whist with Steinbroken and Vilaça, but so absent-minded and confused was he that twice an annoyed Dom Diogo had snorted that if his headache dulled his wit so much, it would be better if they stopped their game! When Ega appeared, the old man lifted troubled eyes.

'Where's Carlos? Gone out?'

'Yes, I believe he left with Craft,' said Ega. 'They spoke about going to see the Marquis.'

Vilaça, shuffling with his usual slow meticulousness, also glanced with curiosity at Ega. But Dom Diogo was tapping impatiently on the table and grumbling, 'Come along, come along! Worrying about others won't get us very far!' Ega stayed there a moment, yawning idly and following the slow fall of the cards. Finally, listless and bored, he decided to go to bed and read; he stopped a moment before the bookshelves and went out with an old number of *Panorama*.

The next day at lunch-time he went to Carlos's room and was astonished to learn from Baptista who, sensing trouble, had been gloomy since the day before, that Carlos had gone on horseback, very early, to the Tapada.

'That's good! And didn't he leave any message about going to Santa Olávia?'

Baptista looked at Ega in amazement.

'To Santa Olávia? No, sir, he didn't say a word about such a thing. But he left a letter for you to see. I believe it's from the Marquis. And he said he'll be there at six. I think it's for dinner.'

It was, in effect, a visiting-card from the Marquis, reminding Carlos and Ega that it was the anniversary of his 'unhappy birthday', and said that he expected them at six, to help him eat a chicken prepared in accordance with his diet.

'Right, we'll see each other there,' said Ega, going down into the garden.

What an extraordinary thing! There was Carlos out riding, and dining with the Marquis as if nothing had happened to disturb his carefree bachelor's life! He was sure now that Carlos had gone to Rua de S. Francisco the night before. Good God! Whatever had happened? He went up into the house at the sound of the lunch-bell. The footman announced that Sr Afonso da Maia had had a cup of tea in his bedroom and had not come down. Everyone was staying out of sight. For the first time at Ramalhete Ega sat by himself at the large table reading the *Gazeta Ilustrada*.

At six o'clock that evening in the room of the Marquis (who had his neck wrapped in a lady's boa of marten fur) Ega found Carlos and Darque and Craft around a fat boy who was playing the guitar, while at their side the Marquis's steward, a handsome black-bearded man, played draughts with Teles.

'Have you seen Grandfather?' asked Carlos, shaking Ega's hand.

'No. I lunched alone.'

The dinner, accompanied by an abundant supply of the superb wines from the Marquis's estates, soon grew very gay. And no one laughed more nor drank more than Carlos, suddenly revived as it were out of a gloomy despondency to a nervous gaiety – which disturbed Ega, who heard a false note in the laughter, a sound like cracked glass. But Ega himself grew considerably excited at dessert with a splendid 1815 port. Then they played baccarat in which Carlos, again gloomy and with his eyes constantly on his watch, had a triumphant success – 'the devil's luck' as Darque called it, as he indignantly changed his last twenty-*milreis* note. At midnight, however, the Marquis's steward relentlessly reminded the company of the doctor's orders, which had set this limit to the birthday party. There was a hasty donning of coats then, with Craft and Darque complaining that they had been drained dry and hadn't even money for the tram. The others made a subscription which they collected in their hats, muttering blessings on their benefactors.

In the cab taking them home Carlos and Ega sat each in his corner, smoking in silence. Only halfway along the Aterro did Ega seem to wake up.

'So what's happening after all? Are you going to Santa Olávia, or what are you doing?'

Carlos fidgeted in the darkness. Then slowly, as if profoundly weary, he answered: 'Perhaps I'll go tomorrow. I haven't said anything to her yet, I haven't done anything. I decided to give myself forty-eight hours to calm myself, and consider things carefully . . . We can't talk with the noise of these wheels.'

Again they both fell silent in their separate corners.

At home, as they made their way up the velvet-lined stairway, Carlos declared he was exhausted and suffering from a bad headache.

'We'll talk tomorrow, Ega. Good night.'

'See you tomorrow.'

Ega awoke in the early hours feeling extremely thirsty. He got out of bed and had emptied the flask on the dressing-table when he thought he heard a door slam below in Carlos's apartment. He listened. Then, shivering, he crept back between the sheets. But he was wide awake now with a strange, foolish idea which persecuted him for no reason whatsoever, which disturbed him and made his heart beat loud in the silence of the night. He heard three o'clock strike. The door banged again, and then a window; it was obviously the wind which had risen. But he could not sleep again, tossing and turning in a terrible restlessness, with that idea stuck in his mind and torturing him. He leapt out of bed in despair, slipped on a coat and crept quietly down to Carlos's rooms on tiptoe and with a hand shading the light. In the antechamber he stopped, and listened with his ear against the curtain for the calm respiration of a sleeper. There was a complete and heavy silence. He dared to enter: the bed was made and empty; Carlos had gone out.

He stood looking stupidly at the smooth bedspread and lace-edged sheet carefully unfolded by Baptista. He had no more doubts. Carlos had gone to finish off the evening at Rua de S. Francisco! He was there, he was sleeping there! And a single idea penetrated his horror – to flee, escape to Celorico, refuse to witness any longer such unparalleled infamy!

The following day, a Tuesday, was wretched for poor Ega. Fearful lest he meet Carlos or Afonso, he got up early, stole down the stairs like a thief and went to lunch at the Tavares. In the afternoon, in the Rua do Ouro, he saw Carlos pass in his brake with Cruges and Taveira, hastily invited most surely so that he should not have to eat alone with his grandfather. Ega dined gloomily at the Universal. He returned to Ramalhete only at nine o'clock to dress for the soirée at the house of Gouvarinho, who had stopped his carriage that morning in the Loreto to remind him that it was Charlie's birthday. And with his coat on, and crush hat in his hand, he went into the little Louis XV drawing-room where Cruges was playing Chopin and Carlos had settled down to a game of bezique with Craft. He wanted to know if his friends had any message for the noble Count and Countess de Gouvarinho.

'Have a good time!'

'Outshine them all, Ega!'

'I'll be along for supper,' promised Taveira, stretched out in an armchair with a *Figaro*.

It was two o'clock when Ega returned from the soirée where he had amused himself by flirting outrageously with the Baroness de Alvim, who after the champagne at supper, overcome by such charm and wit, had presented him with two roses. Outside Carlos's room, Ega lit his candle and was seized with curiosity: was Carlos there? But he was ashamed at such spying and went up the stairs, determined, as he had been the night before, to get away to Celorico. In his room he carefully put the Baroness's roses in a glass in front of the mirror. And he was beginning to undress when he heard steps in the dark corridor, heavy, slow steps which came nearer and finally stopped outside his door. He called out in fright, 'Who's there?' The door creaked open. And Afonso da Maia appeared, pale-faced, with a jacket over his night-shirt, and a candlestick with a dying candle in it in his hand. He did not enter. He merely inquired in a hoarse trembling voice:

'Where's Carlos? Was he there?'

Ega stammered, embarrassed in his shirt-sleeves, that he did not know. He had only dropped into the Gouvarinhos' for a moment. Carlos had probably gone later with Taveira to supper.

The old man closed his eyes as if he would faint, and put out a hand to support himself. Ega hurried over to him.

'Don't distress yourself, Senhor Afonso da Maia!'

'What do you want me to do? Where is he? He's stuck there with that woman. You needn't worry, I know, I've had spies on him . . . I've sunk to that, but I couldn't stand not knowing. And he was there last night until morning, and he's sleeping there now . . . Was it for such a horror that God has let me live so long?'

He shook his head in revolt and pain. And his steps fell slow and heavy once more along the corridor.

Ega stood at the door, horror-struck. Then he undressed slowly, decided to tell Carlos very simply the next day before he left for Celorico that his infamy was killing his grandfather and had forced him, his best friend, to go away rather than witness it any longer.

As soon as he woke, he pulled his case into the middle of the room and piled armfuls of clothes on the bed to be packed. And for half an hour he tackled this task in his shirt-sleeves, angry thoughts of Carlos mingling with memories of certain glances that the Baroness had given him the evening before, and which made his departure regrettable. A cheerful sun bathed the balcony in golden light. Eventually he opened the french doors to breathe in the fresh air and admire the beautiful blue of the winter's day. The season enhanced the city's beauty so! Already Celorico, and his home there and Padre Serafim, threw their shadow over his soul from afar. Looking down he saw Carlos's dog-cart harnessed to Tunante, who was pawing the ground, enlivened by the fresh air. It was Carlos no doubt who was going out early – so as not to meet him or his grandfather.

Fearing that he might not catch him all day, Ega ran down to his rooms. Carlos was locked in the bathroom. Ega called but his friend made no reply. Finally Ega beat on the door and shouted, unable to hide his irritation.

'Have the goodness to listen to me! Are you going to Santa Olávia or not?'

After a moment, Carlos called above the noise of falling water:

'I don't know . . . Perhaps . . . I'll tell you later.'

Ega could contain himself no longer.

'Things can't stay like this indefinitely . . . I've had a letter from my mother, and if you're not going to Santa Olávia, I'm going to Celorico. This is absurd! We've been like this for three days now!'

But he repented of his violence when he heard Carlos's humble weary voice, beseeching him from within:

'Ega, for the sake of our friendship, have a little patience with me. I'll tell you later . . .'

Ega was overcome by one of his emotional attacks, and his eyes grew moist. He stammered:

'All right! All right! I only shouted because there's a door between us. There's no hurry!'

And he hurried back to his room, full of pity and tenderness, with a large tear clinging to his eyelashes. He could feel now the torture in which poor Carlos was struggling, under the sway of a passion which had till then been legitimate and which at a bitter moment had suddenly turned monstrous, though without losing anything of its charm and intensity. He was human and weak, and unable to stop being swept along by that violent impulse of love and desire which drove him before it like a tempest! He'd yielded, succumbed to those arms which innocently continued to call him. And there he was now, appalled at his sin, driven out of the house, spending the day away from his friends and family, wandering tragically around like an excommunicated man who fears to encounter pure eyes which reflect the horror of his sinfulness . . .

And in the same house poor Afonso, who knew everything and was dying of grief! But could he, a guest of happier times, leave now that a wave of disgrace was breaking over the house where he had been welcomed more generously than in his own house? It would be a base action! He began to unpack his case again, and furious in his selfishness at these bitter happenings which were sweeping him off his feet, he arranged his clothes in the drawers once more with the same anger with which he had emptied them.

'The Devil take women, and life, and everything!'

By the time he had dressed and gone down, Carlos had disappeared. Baptista, with sorrowful frowning face, sure now that something terrible had happened, stopped him to remark:

'You were right, sir. We're going to Santa Olávia tomorrow, and taking enough clothes for a long stay . . . This winter's begun badly!'

The next morning in the darkness at four o'clock, Carlos quietly closed behind him the door of Rua de S. Francisco. And in the cold street he felt more keenly the fear which had visited him in the shadows of the bedroom as he had dressed beside the sleeping Maria – the fear of returning to Ramalhete! It was this fear which had driven him out of the house the day before, trotting round all day in the dog-cart and eventually dining gloomily with Cruges in a private room at Augusto's. It was fear of his grandfather, fear of Ega, fear of Vilaça; fear of the dinner-bell which would call them together; fear of his bedroom where at any moment one of them could raise the curtain, enter, and observe his soul and secret . . . He was sure now that they knew everything. And even if he went away that night to Santa Olávia, putting between himself and Maria a barrier of distance as insurmountable as the highest wall, never again would the infamy he was indulging in be erased from the memory of these men, his closest friends. His moral life was ruined. Why, then, leave, if he was fleeing from passion without any hope of finding peace? Wouldn't it be more logical to kick aside all human and divine laws, carry off Maria in her innocence and plunge once and for all into this crime which had become part of his life?

That was what he had thought the night before. That was what he had thought . . . But then he had envisaged another horror, the supreme punishment awaiting him in the solitude in which he had chosen to bury himself. He had already sensed its approach even; he had glimpsed a presage of the future the night before; and again that night as he lay beside Maria who was asleep, tired out, he felt, like the first cold breath of death, a presentiment of what might come.

He could feel emerging from the depths of his being a satiety, only tenuous now, yet nevertheless already perceptible, since he knew they were of the same blood! A material uncontrollable carnal repugnance, which ran through him like a shudder. First it had been the perfume she wore, which surrounded her and hung between the curtains and clung to his suit and skin, and formerly had excited him and now annoyed him – last night he'd soaked himself with eau-de-cologne to get rid of it. Then it had been her body, which he had always adored like some ideal statue, that had suddenly appeared to him as it was in reality – too big, too muscular, large-limbed like a savage Amazon, with all the abundant beauty of an animal of pleasure. In the sleek, shining hair he suddenly saw the wildness of a lion's mane. Her movements in bed that night had reminded him alarmingly of a wild beast, slow and jealous, stretching itself before devouring him . . . When her arms had clasped him, crushing him against her firm full breasts, he had still felt the bestial fire she kindled in his veins. But scarcely had the last sigh died on her lips, than he had begun to draw away from her to the edge of the bed with a strange fear running through him: motionless, huddled in the clothes and lost in the depths of an infinite sadness, his mind had wandered to another life he could lead, far from here, in a simple house all open to the sun, with a legitimate wife, a domestic angel, petite and shy and modest, a woman who did not cry out lasciviously nor use such a warm, heavy perfume! And unfortunately he no longer doubted it – if he went away with her, he would very soon be beset by the indescribable horror of physical nausea. And then, with the passion which was the cause of his crime dead, and bound for good to a woman who sickened him (who was, incidentally . . .) – what would there be left to do? Only kill himself!

But having slept with her for just one night fully conscious of their blood-relationship, could he begin his life again in tranquillity? Even if he had sufficient cold-bloodedness and strength to wipe out this memory – it would not die as far as his grandfather and his friends were concerned. That loathsome secret would remain between them sullying, spoiling everything. Henceforth existence could only offer him intolerable bitterness . . .

But God Almighty! What was there to do, what was there to do? Oh, if only someone could advise him, could console him! When he arrived at the door of his house, his only desire was to fling himself at the feet of a priest, pour forth the troubles of his heart and implore his sweet mercy! But Lord! Where was there a saint?

The lights were still burning in front of Ramalhete. He opened the door quietly. Very stealthily, step by step, he crept up the stairs, muffled with the cerise velvet. Groping for a candle on the landing he suddenly glimpsed through the open curtain a light moving at the far end of the room. He jumped back with a start and stood there in a recess. The light was coming nearer, growing larger: slow, heavy steps moved almost soundlessly across the carpet. The light emerged in front of him, and behind it his grandfather in shirt-sleeves, a great mute, livid, spectral form. Carlos stood stock-still holding his breath; and the old man's eyes fell upon him – wan red eyes full of horror which lingered on him, went right through him to the very depths of his soul, reading there his secret. Then, without a word, with his white head trembling, Afonso crossed the landing where the light on the velvet gleamed blood-red, and his steps died away, slow, muffled steps fading away as if they were the last he would tread on this earth!

Carlos entered his room in darkness and stumbled over a sofa. And there he let himself sink, his head buried in his arms, unthinking and unfeeling, seeing only the old man pass and pass again before him, like a phantom dragging itself along, with the reddish light in his hand. Gradually a great weariness was overcoming him, an inertia, an infinite lack of will where only one desire emerged – the desire of death came to him. Death would be the perfect cure, the only safe refuge. Why shouldn't he go forward and seek it? A few grains of laudanum that night and he would enter into perfect peace . . .

For a long time he sat meditating on this idea which offered him relief and consolation, as if he had been driven by a fierce storm and now saw before him a door open and silence and warmth within. A noise, the chirping of a bird at the window, made him aware of sun and day. He got up and undressed very slowly, feeling immensely weak. And he dropped into bed and sunk his head into the pillow to regain the sweetness of that inertia which was like a foretaste of death; he would have liked never again to see the light nor feel any earthly thing in all the hours that remained to him of life.

The sun was high, there was a noise, and Baptista burst into the room: 'Oh, Senhor Dom Carlos, oh, Master Carlos! Your grandfather's ill in the garden! He won't wake up!'

Carlos leapt out of bed and flung a coat round him. The housekeeper, clutching hold of the banister in the antechamber, called out in distress: 'Hurry, boy, for God's sake, Dr Azevedo, next door to the baker's.' And a boy he bumped into in the corridor as he ran past, shouted: 'He's at the end of the garden, near the fountain, Senhor Dom Carlos, at the stone table!'

Afonso da Maia was there in that corner of the garden under the branches of the cedar; he was sitting on the cork bench, fallen forward over the rough table with his face between his arms. His hat had rolled on to the grass; around his shoulders was his old blue cloak with the collar turned up. All around, on the leaves of the camellias and the sandy paths, shone the golden winter sunlight, and from out of a bed of shells sighed the little fountain of water.

Carlos caught up the old man's face, waxen now and stiff; the eyes were closed and a trickle of blood showed at the corners of the long snow-white beard. Carlos dropped on his knees on the damp earth, shaking the old man's hands and crying: 'Grandfather! Grandfather!' He ran to the tank and sprinkled him with water.

'Call someone! Call someone!'

Again he felt his heart – but he was dead. He was dead, already cold, that body which, older than the century, had resisted the years and storms so splendidly, like a great strong oak. There he had died alone, with the sun already high, on that rough stone table where he had lain his weary head.

When Carlos got up Ega appeared, dishevelled, and wrapped in a dressing-gown. Carlos caught hold of him and broke into a fit of weeping. The servants stood around gazing in alarm. And the housekeeper, distraught, wandered along the rose-paths sobbing with her hands to her head: 'Oh my poor dear master! Oh my poor dear master!'

The gatekeeper came running up out of breath with Dr Azevedo, whom he had fortunately met in the street. He was no more than a boy, fresh from medical school, thin and nervous

591

with very curled tips to his moustache. He gave an embarrassed 'Good morning!' all around to the servants, to Ega and Carlos, who did his best to calm himself though his face was bathed in tears. Then, having pulled off his gloves, he examined the whole of Afonso's body with great care and attention, which in fact he exaggerated as he felt the anxious, expectant eyes of all those present on him. Finally, coming up to Carlos and passing his fingers nervously over his moustache, he murmured a few technical terms. Anyway, he said, his colleague must already have realized that everything was unfortunately over. He was truly sorry . . . if they needed him for anything he'd be most pleased –

'Thank you,' stammered Carlos.

Ega, in his house-slippers, walked a few steps with Dr Azevedo to show him to the gate.

Carlos in the meantime remained before the old man, no longer crying but simply lost in awe at that sudden ending! Images of his grandfather while he was alive and strong, sitting smoking his pipe beside the fire, or watering his roses in the early morning, flashed by in confusion, leaving him more and more dejected. He felt then a desire to end his own life, and lean like that on the stone table, without having to make any more effort or to feel any more grief in his life, but drop instead, like his grandfather, into everlasting peace. A ray of sunlight, falling from between the thick branches of the cedar, came to rest on Afonso's dead face. The birds, for a few brief moments frightened silent, had begun to sing again. Ega went up to Carlos and touched his arm.

'We must take him up to the house.'

Carlos kissed the limp cold hand. And slowly, with trembling lips, he tenderly lifted his grandfather's shoulders. Baptista ran to help; Ega, clumsy in his large dressing-gown, got hold of the old man's feet. They carried him across the garden, over the terrace, through his study where his armchair waited in front of the lit fire, in a silence broken only by the servants' steps as they hurried to open doors and help when Carlos or Ega flagged under the weight of the enormous body. The housekeeper was already in Afonso's bedroom spreading a silk bedspread over the simple iron bed without curtains. And there they laid him, on the pale embroidered foliage of the blue silk spread.

Ega lit two silver candlesticks: the housekeeper knelt at the bedside, counting her beads; M. Antoine, with his white chef's hat in his hand, stood at the door beside a basket of camellias and hot-house palms. Carlos in the meantime wandered round the room, shaken by deep sobs, and turned every few minutes with a last, absurd hope to feel the old man's pulse and heart. In his velveteen jacket and great white shoes, Afonso looked even stronger and larger as he lay stiff upon the narrow bed; between the white cropped hair and the long unruly beard, the skin took on the tone of old ivory with the wrinkles carved out as by a chisel; the shrivelled white-lashed eyelids were closed with the serenity of one who had finally found peace; and as they placed him there, one hand dropped upon his heart, with the simple natural attitude of a man who had always been ruled by his heart.

Carlos was lost in this painful contemplation. And what grieved him most was that his grandfather had gone for ever, just like that, without a word of farewell between them, without the exchange of one kind word. Nothing! Only that look of anguish when he had passed him with his candle in his hand. He was walking even then to death! His grandfather knew everything, this was what had killed him! The certainty of this beat upon his soul with a long incessant and gloomy hammering. His grandfather had known everything, it was this that had killed him!

Ega came up to him to point out the way they were dressed – he in a dressing-gown, Carlos with a jacket thrown over his night-shirt.

'We must go down and dress ourselves.'

Carlos stammered: 'Yes, we must dress ourselves . . .'

But he did not move. Ega took his arm and led him gently out. Carlos walked like a sleepwalker – wiping his forehead and beard absent-mindedly with his handkerchief. And when they were in the corridor he suddenly wrung his hands in despair, his face covered with tears again, and burst out an agonized confession of his guilt:

'Ega, my dear Ega! Grandfather saw me this morning when I came in! And he passed without a word . . . He must have known everything – that's what killed him!'

Ega pulled him away and consoled him, rejecting such an idea. What rubbish! His grandfather was nearly eighty years old and had a weak heart. How many times had they spoken in dread of such a thing since his return from Santa Olávia? It was absurd to make himself even unhappier with such an idea!

Carlos murmured slowly, as if to himself, with his eyes on the ground:

'No! It's strange, but it doesn't make me unhappier. I accept it as a punishment. I want it to be a punishment. And I feel very small and humble before Him who punishes me like this. This morning I was considering killing myself. But not now. My punishment is to live, crushed and broken. What really grieves me is that he didn't say good-bye.'

Again the tears fell, slower now, less bitter, less desperate. Ega led him to his room as if he were a child. And he left him there on a corner of the sofa with his handkerchief over his face, steadily and quietly weeping, the tears seeming to wash him and relieve him of all the confused nameless troubles which had weighed upon him these last days.

At midday Ega had just finished dressing when Vilaça burst into the room, his arms open wide.

'What happened? What happened?'

Baptista had sent the messenger boy to fetch him but the lad had not been able to tell him much. Now downstairs poor Carlos had embraced him, wet with tears and unable to tell him anything, begging him to go to Ega who would explain. And there he was.

'But how did it happen so suddenly?'

Ega explained how they had found Afonso that morning in the garden, head down on the stone table. Dr Azevedo had come but everything was already over.

Vilaça lifted his hands to his head.

'A thing like that! I can tell you what it was! It was that woman, that woman who appeared, who killed him! He was never the same after that shock. It wasn't anything else! It was that!'

Ega replied, automatically shaking eau-de-cologne on his handkerchief: 'Yes, perhaps that shock, and his eighty years and too little attention and a disease of the heart . . .'

They discussed the funeral, which was to be simple as befitted the simple man he had been. Ega thought the body could stay in the Marquis's tomb until it could be moved to Santa Olávia.

Vilaça scratched his chin, hesitated, then said:

'I've got a tomb. It was Senhor Afonso da Maia himself who had it erected to the memory of my father – God keep his soul. Now he could stay there for a few days perfectly well. Like that we would not have to ask favours of anyone, and I personally should be greatly honoured.'

Ega agreed. Then they fixed other details about invitations, the time, the key to the coffin . . . Finally Vilaça, glancing at his watch, got up with a sigh.

'Right, I'll see to these unhappy details. And then I'll be back as I'd like to see him again for the last time when he's dressed. Whoever'd have thought such a thing! Only yesterday I was playing cards with him. I even won three *milreis* off him, poor soul!'

A wave of nostalgia swept over him and he hurried from the room with his handkerchief to his eyes.

When Ega went downstairs he found Carlos, dressed in full mourning, seated at his writing-desk in front of a sheet of paper. He flung down his pen and got up.

'I can't do it! You write to her – just a couple of words.'

Without a word Ega took the pen and wrote a short note:

'Dear Senhora, Afonso da Maia died suddenly in the early hours of this morning. You will appreciate that at a time like this Carlos can do no more than ask me to pass on this unfortunate news to you. I am, etc. . . .' He did not read it to Carlos. And as Baptista came in at that moment with their lunch on a tray, Ega asked him to send the boy with the note to Rua de S. Francisco. Baptista whispered over Ega's shoulder:

'You won't forget the mourning for the servants, will you?'

'Senhor Vilaça is already seeing to it.'

They drank their tea hurriedly from the tray. Then Ega wrote notes to Dom Diogo and Sequeira, Afonso's oldest friends; and it was two o'clock when the men arrived with the coffin to lay out the corpse. But Carlos would have no mercenary hands touch his grandfather. It was he and Ega, helped by Baptista, their sense of duty overcoming their emotion, who courageously washed and dressed him and laid him in the great satin-lined oak coffin where Carlos put a miniature of his grandmother Runa. Later, with the aid of Vilaça, who had returned 'to have a last look at his master', they carried him down to his study which Ega had not wanted to alter or decorate and which therefore retained its austere air of studious peace, with its scarlet damask, its carved bookshelves and the books strewn over the ebony writing-desk. The only modification was to place together two large tables and cover them with a black velvet cloth embroidered in gold with the family arms. Above, the Rubens *Christ* opened His arms above the red sunset. Twelve silver candlesticks burned around the coffin. Broad palm leaves from the greenhouses were crossed at the head of the coffin between sprays of camellias. And Ega lit a little incense in two bronze perfuming braziers.

The first of Afonso's old friends to appear that night was Dom Diogo, solemnly attired in dress-coat. Leaning on Ega, awed at the sight of the coffin, he could only murmur, 'And he was seven months younger than me.' The Marquis came a little later, well-wrapped in rugs and bearing a large basket of flowers. Craft and Cruges had not known; they had met coming up Santos Ramp and their first surprise had been to see the gate of Ramalhete shut. Sequeira was the last to arrive, as he had spent the day at his country house, and he clasped first Carlos and then Craft; he was momentarily stunned and, with a tear shining in each bloodshot eye, he stammered, 'He's been my friend for so many years! I can't live much longer now!'

And the night of the wake began, slow and silent. The twelve flames of the candles burnt high in funereal solemnity. The friends exchanged a whispered word or two with their chairs drawn close together. Gradually the heat and the aroma of incense and the exhalation of the flowers obliged Baptista to open one of the terrace windows. The sky was full of stars. A slight wind rustled the leaves in the garden.

Quite late Sequeira, who sat with his arms crossed and had not moved from his easy chair, had a fit of giddiness. Ega took him into the dining-room and comforted him with a glass of brandy. There was a cold supper laid there with wines and sweetmeats. Craft arrived with Taveira who had learnt of the unhappy event in the office of *A Tarde*, and had rushed along with hardly time for dinner. Sequeira revived with a little Bordeaux and a sandwich and recalled the past, the glorious days when he and Afonso were young. But he stopped abrutly when he saw Carlos enter, pale and aimless like a sleepwalker and mutter, 'Yes, help yourselves to something, do . . .'

He toyed with something on a plate, walked round the table,

and left. He wandered distractedly into the antechamber where all the candelabra were alight. A lean black figure emerged from the stairs. Two arms embraced him: it was Alencar.

'I've never been here on a happy occasion, yet here I am in the moment of sorrow!'

And the poet made his way along the corridor on tiptoe as if down the aisle of a temple.

Carlos in the meantime wandered round the antechamber. In the corner on a divan was a great wreath of flowers with a card attached. He recognized Maria's writing. He did not touch it but returned to the study. Alencar, standing before the coffin, with his hand on Ega's shoulder, was murmuring, 'The soul of a hero has left us!'

The candles were burning down. A feeling of weariness hung in the air. Baptista ordered coffee to be served in the billiards-room. And there, with his coffee before him, Alencar, surrounded by Cruges, Taveira and Vilaça, also began to talk of the past, of the glorious days of Arroios, of the ardent young men of those days.

'Can you imagine, my lads, another family like these Maias, with their souls of lions, generous and valiant! Everything seems to be dying out in this miserable country! Splendour has gone, passion has gone . . . Afonso da Maia! Ah, I can see him now at the window of his palace in Benfica, with his white satin cravat, that noble face of a Portuguese of former times . . . Now he has gone! And my poor Pedro too! *Caramba!* My wretched heart is heavy!'

His eyes grew misty and he took a large draught of brandy.

Ega, after a sip of coffee, returned to the study where the scent of incense spread a church-like melancholy over the room. Dom Diogo snored, stretched out on the sofa; opposite him Sequeira was also dozing with his head fallen forward over his crossed arms, and his face was flushed with blood. Ega woke him gently. The two friends, after embracing Carlos, left in the same carriage smoking cigars. The others also, one by one, were taking their farewells of Carlos and putting on their coats. The last to leave was Alencar who, in a moment of emotion in the courtyard, kissed Ega, still lamenting the past and former companions.

'It's you, dear boys, the younger generation, whom I rely upon now. Don't cast me aside! Or, by Jove, whenever I feel like visiting my friends, I'll be obliged to go to the cemetery. Good-bye now. Don't catch cold here!'

The funeral took place the following day at one o'clock. Ega, the Marquis, Craft and Sequeira carried the coffin to the door, followed by a group of friends, among whom stood out the Count of Gouvarinho looking extra solemn with his Grand Cross. The Count de Steinbroken, accompanied by his secretary, carried a bouquet of violets in his hand. A long row of carriages filled the narrow road and was lost to view as it wound its way through other neighbouring streets; people crowded at the windows all around; police shouted at the coach-drivers. Finally the hearse carrying the coffin began to move, followed by two carriages belonging to the family, unoccupied and with their lanterns draped with hanging crape veils. Behind followed the hired carriages with the guests who buttoned up their dress-coats and pulled up the windows against the cold and damp of the misty day. Darque and Vargas rode in the same coupé. Gouvarinho's courier trotted by on his white nag. And in the deserted road, the great gate of Ramalhete finally closed for a long period of mourning.

When Ega returned from the cemetery he found Carlos tearing up papers in his room, while Baptista busied himself on his knees closing a leather travelling-case. When Ega entered, rubbing his hands and pale and shivering with cold, Carlos closed the drawer full of letters and suggested they go into the smoking-room where there was a fire.

As soon as they were in, Carlos pulled the curtain shut and turned to Ega: 'Would you object to going to speak to her?'

'No. Why? What do you want me to tell her?'

'Everything.'

Ega pulled an armchair over to the fireplace and stirred up the coals. At his side Carlos gazed into the fire and went on:

'I want her to go away, to go back to Paris right away. It would be stupid for her to remain in Lisbon. And until it's been settled what belongs to her, she must be given an allowance, a good allowance. Vilaça's coming here shortly to discuss these details. Anyway, you'll take her five hundred pounds for the journey tomorrow.'

Ega murmured: 'Perhaps it might be better for these money matters if Vilaça were to go instead of me – '

'For God's sake, Ega! Why make the poor creature blush before Vilaça?'

There was a silence. Both looked into the dancing flames.

'It's going to be very hard for you, isn't it, Ega?'

'Not so bad . . . I'm beginning to grow immune. It's just a matter of shutting the eyes, swallowing these extra distasteful moments, and then being able to rest. When are you coming back from Santa Olávia?'

Carlos did not know. He hoped that Ega, with his mission in Rua de S. Francisco completed, would go and while away a few boring days with him in Santa Olávia. Later on his grandfather's body would have to be moved up there.

'And then when all this is over, I'm going to America, and Japan; I'm going to do that stupid and always efficacious thing which is called distracting oneself.'

He shrugged his shoulders, went slowly to the window where a shaft of wan sunlight hung, for the mist of the morning had cleared. Then turning back to Ega who was stirring the coals again: 'Of course I wouldn't dare to ask you to come, Ega. I'd like to, but I wouldn't dare!'

Ega slowly replaced the tongs, stood up and held his arms open to Carlos, overcome by emotion.

'What the deuce, man, dare! Why ever not?'

'Then come!'

Carlos's whole soul went into these words, and as he embraced Ega, two large tears ran down his face.

Ega reflected a moment. Before going to Santa Olávia, he would have to make a pilgrimage to the country estate at Celorico. The East was expensive. He would have to wring a few credit notes out of his mother first. And when Carlos insisted he would have enough to keep the two in luxury, Ega, very serious, stopped him.

'No, certainly not! My mother's rich too. A trip to America and Japan is a form of education. And it's Mama's duty to complete my education. What I will accept is one of your leather cases.'

When Carlos and Ega, acompanied by Vilaça, arrived at Santa Apolónia Station that night, the train was on the point of departure. Carlos barely had time to jump into his reserved compartment, while Baptista, clasping the travelling rugs and helped with a push from the guard, clambered desperately into another carriage, though not without protest from the passengers already crowding it. The train immediately started off. Carlos leant out of the window to shout to Ega: 'Send a telegram tomorrow and let me know what happened!'

On his way back to Ramalhete with Vilaça, who was going to collect and seal up Afonso da Maia's papers, Ega spoke straight-way of the five hundred pounds which he was to give Maria Eduarda the following day. Vilaça had been informed of this by Carlos too. But frankly, between friends, didn't Ega think such a sum excessive, for one short journey? Apart from this Carlos had mentioned paying this lady a monthly allowance of four thousand francs – a hundred and sixty pounds! Now wasn't that some-what exaggerated? For one woman, one simple woman . . .

Ega reminded him that this simple woman was legally entitled to far more.

'Ah yes,' agreed the steward. 'But all this about legality has got to be thoroughly studied yet. Let's not talk about it. I'm not very keen on talking about this!'

Then, when Ega referred to the fortune Afonso da Maia had left, Vilaça provided details. Theirs was certainly one of the greatest houses in Portugal. The inheritance of Sebastião da Maia alone gave an income of fifteen contos. Their property in Alentejo, with the alterations there that Vilaça's father had supervised, had trebled its value, although Santa Olávia was an expense to keep up. But their estates near Lamego were wealthy.

'There's plenty of money there,' he cried with satisfaction, slapping Ega's knee. 'And that, my friend, say what they like, makes up for anything.'

'It makes up for a lot, I agree.'

As they entered Ramalhete, Ega thought with sorrow of the happy friendly home that used to exist there and that was now gone for ever. In the antechamber his steps rang out sombrely as if in a deserted house. A vague smell of incense and phenol still hung in the air. On the chandelier in the corridor only a single drowsy light glowed.

'There's an air of ruin over the place already, Vilaça.'

'A nice comfortable little ruin, I must say,' replied the stew-ard, glancing round at the tapestries and divans, and rubbing his hands and shivering from the cold night air.

They went into Afonso's study where they stood for a moment

warming themselves in front of the fire. The Louis XV clock struck nine – then its silver minuet tinkled out for a moment and died away. Vilaça got ready to begin his work. Ega said he was going to his room to straighten his papers and tidy up two years of his youth.

He went up. Scarcely had he placed the light on the chest of drawers when he heard far off, down at the end of the silent corridor, a long drawn-out groan, a desolate, infinitely sad noise. His hair stood on end with terror. That mournful moaning was coming from near Afonso da Maia's room. Finally, remembering that the whole house was awake, full of servants and lights, Ega dared to step out into the corridor, with his candlestick in his tembling hand.

It was the cat! It was Bonifácio who stood outside Afonso's room, scratching the closed door and mewing pitifully. Ega drove him away, furious. Poor Bonifácio ran off, fat and slow, with his fluffy tail trailing on the ground; but he returned again at once, and clawing at the door and brushing against Ega's legs, began again to mew his poignant lament, as pathetic as any cry of human grief as he wept for the master who had once held him on his lap and stroked him – but who had suddenly disappeared.

Ega hurried to the study and asked Vilaça to stay the night at Ramalhete. The steward consented, moved by the tale of the mourning cat. He left the pile of papers on the table, went to warm his feet at the dying fire. Then, turning to Ega, still pale from his fright, who had sat on the self-embroidered sofa – the former seat of Dom Diogo – he murmured slowly and gravely:

'Three years ago, when Senhor Afonso asked me to begin re-decorating this house, I reminded him, according to an ancient legend, that the walls of Ramalhete were always fatal to the Maias. Senhor Afonso da Maia laughed at the idea of omens and legends . . . But fatal they were!'

The following day, carrying the Monforte papers and the money in notes and sovereigns which Vilaça had handed him at the door of the Bank of Portugal, Ega mounted the steps of Rua de S. Francisco, his heart beating fast but nevertheless determined to be strong and confront the crisis calmly. Domingos, in a black tie, moving on tiptoe, pulled aside the curtain to the drawing-room. And no sooner had Ega deposited Mme Monforte's cigar-box on the sofa, than Maria Eduarda entered, pale-faced and dressed in black, and holding out her two hands to him.

'How is Carlos?'

Ega stammered: 'You can imagine, at a moment like this . . . It was terrible, so sudden like that . . .'

A tear trembled on Maria's dark-shadowed eyes. She had not known Sr Afonso da Maia, she had never even seen him. But she suffered to feel Carlos's suffering . . . How he had adored his grandfather!

'It was sudden then?'

Ega procrastinated by giving full details. He thanked her for the wreath. He told her of the groans and affliction of poor Bonifácio.

'And how's Carlos?' she repeated.

'Carlos has gone to Santa Olávia, senhora.'

She wrung her hands in surprise and distress. To Santa Olávia? Without a note, without a word? Fear increased her pallor in the face of this hasty departure which seemed almost like desertion. Finally she murmured, with an air of resignation and confidence which she did not feel: 'Yes, of course, at a moment like this, one doesn't think of others . . .'

Two tears ran slowly down her cheeks. And faced with this humble dumb grief, Ega grew disconcerted. For an instant, with his fingers nervously fiddling with his moustache, he watched Maria weep in silence.

Finally he rose, went to the window, turned and opened his arms in anguish before her: 'No, it's not that, senhora! There's something more, there's something else! These have been terrible days for us! Days of agony . . .'

Something else? She waited, her large eyes on Ega, her whole soul in suspense.

Ega took a deep breath.

'Do you remember a Guimarães who lives in Paris, an uncle of Damaso's?'

Maria slowly nodded in surprise.

'This Guimarães was very friendly with your mother, wasn't he?'

The same short silent nod. But poor Ega still hesitated, his face white and frowning, smarting with embarrassment.

'I'm speaking to you about these matters, senhora, because Carlos asked me to . . . Lord knows it grieves me . . . It's horrible, I don't know where to begin – '

She clasped her hands together in anguished supplication. 'For the love of God!'

At that moment Rosa very gently lifted up a corner of the curtain, with Niniche at her side and her doll in her arms. Her mother cried out impatiently: 'Go inside and leave me alone!'

The little girl stood still in terror while her pretty eyes filled with tears. The curtain fell, then from the far end of the corridor came a burst of sobbing.

Ega had one desire only, a desperate desire to finish the business.

'You'd recognize your mother's handwriting, wouldn't you? Well look, I've got a statement of hers here which refers to you. This Guimarães had this document with other papers which she entrusted to him in 1871, on the eve of the war . . . He kept them till now and wanted to return them to you but didn't know where you lived. Then he saw you a couple of days ago in a carriage with me and Carlos. It was just at the end of the Aterro, remember? In front of the tailor's, when we were coming in from Hideaway. Well, Guimarães went to the Maias' steward, and gave him these papers to hand to you. And you can imagine everyone's amazement when we learnt you were a relation of Carlos's, and a very close relation at that.'

He blurted out this story standing, almost out of breath and jerking about with brusque nervous gestures. She, livid and overcome with a vague fear, scarcely understood. She could only murmur weakly, 'But . . .' Then she stopped, alarmed, her eyes voraciously devouring Ega's clumsy movements as he leant over the sofa and tremblingly undid the Monforte cigar-box. Finally he turned to her with a paper in his hand, his words tumbling over each other in his confusion.

'Your mother never told you . . . She had a very good reason of course . . . She'd run away from Lisbon, from her husband . . . I'm telling you in this brutal manner, senhora, do forgive me, but this isn't the moment for mincing matters. Look, here it is – you'll recognize your mother's handwriting. It is her handwriting, isn't it?'

'It is,' said Maria, making to take the paper.

'Excuse me!' cried Ega, snatching it back. 'I'm a stranger here! I can't let you read this until I've left the room.'

It was an inspired idea which saved him from having to witness the terrible shock, the horror of the things she was about to learn. And he insisted. He would leave her all her mother's papers. She would read them when he had left and understand the atrocious truth. Then, taking out of his pocket the two heavy piles of sovereigns and the envelope containing the promissory note for Paris, he put everything on top of the table with Mme Monforte's declaration.

'Just two words more. Carlos thinks it would be better if you left at once for Paris. You have a right, as your daughter has, to part of the fortune of the Maia family, which is your family now. In this packet is a promissory note for immediate expenses in Paris. Carlos's steward has already reserved you a carriage. When you decide to leave, please send a message to me at Ramalhete and I'll be at the station to see you off. I think that's everything. And now I must leave you.'

He quickly picked up his hat and went over to take her cold, limp hand.

'Everything's fate! You're young, life still has a lot to offer you, and you have your little girl to comfort you . . . I just don't know what else there is to say . . .'

Choking, he bent to kiss the hand she silently and absent-mindedly let him take as she stood upright there in her mourning, with the still pallor of a piece of marble. He fled.

'To the telegraph office,' he called to the coachman in the street.

It was only when he reached Rua do Ouro that he began to grow calm and take off his hat and breathe more normally. Then he began to think of all the consoling words he should have offered Maria Eduarda: she was young and beautiful; her sin was an unconscious one; time heals all grief; and one of these days, reconciled to her fate, she would realize she belonged to a distinguished family, with a handsome fortune, in the very pleasant city of Paris, where a pair of pretty eyes and a few thousand-franc notes can always be relied upon to provide a pleasing life.

'She's in the position of a beautiful rich widow,' he concluded aloud to himself in the coupé. 'There are far worse situations.'

He dismissed the coupé when he left the telegraph office. In that soothing light of a winter's day, he returned to Ramalhete on foot, to write the long letter he had promised Carlos. Vilaça was already there with a velveteen cap on his head, sorting out Afonso's papers, and paying the servants' wages. They dined late, and were sitting smoking in front of the fire in the Louis XV furnished room when a footman announced that there was a lady below, in a carriage, asking to see Sr Ega. For a moment there was panic. They supposed it was Maria, come to some desperate decision. Vilaça still hoped she might bring some news which would change everything, would rescue them from 'their appalling loss'. Ega was trembling as he went downstairs. It was Melanie in a hired cab, wrapped up in a great ulster, with a letter from Madame.

By the light of the lantern Ega opened the envelope which bore one small white card with the information written in pencil: 'I have decided to leave for Paris tomorrow.'

Ega overcame his curiosity to ask Melanie how her mistress was. He leapt up the stairs and, followed by Vilaça, who had been waiting and watching in the antechamber, ran to Afonso's study to write to Maria. On a black-bordered sheet of paper he wrote (apart from details regarding baggage) that the carriage was reserved as far as Paris, and that he would have the honour of seeing her in Santa Apolónia. Then, about to write the envelope, he stopped with his pen raised. Should he put 'Madame Mac-Gren', or 'Dona Maria Eduarda da Maia'? Vilaça thought the former name preferable, as she was not yet legally a Maia. But neither was she properly MacGren, returned Ega.

'Leave it! Let it go without anything. She'll think you forgot.'

So he took down the letter as it was. Melanie put it in her muff. And leaning out of the carriage window, she inquired in an appropriately sorrowful voice, on behalf of her mistress, where the gentleman was buried.

Ega fixed his monocle upon her, undecided as to whether he found Maria's curiosity indiscreet or touching. Finally he gave the required information. Afonso lay in Prazeres, on the right at the far end where there was an angel with a torch. The best thing to do was to ask the cemetery-keeper where the Vilaças' tomb was.

'*Merci, monsieur, bien le bonsoir.*'

'*Bonsoir,* Melanie.'

The following day in Santa Apolónia Station, Ega, who had come early with Vilaça, had just got rid of his luggage to the Douro, when he caught sight of Maria who was coming in, leading Rosa by the hand. She was wrapped in a vast dark fur, with a double veil as thick as a mask, and the same sort of mourning veil covered the little girl's face and was tied in a bow on top. Miss Sarah, in a light check ulster, carried a stack of books under her arm. Behind came Domingos, looking very red-eyed and bearing a bundle of rugs, and at his side Melanie, all in black with Niniche in her arms. Ega hurried towards Maria Eduarda and took her arm and led her in silence to a reserved compartment with all its blinds drawn. At the door she slowly pulled off a glove, and without a word held out her hand.

'I'll see you again at Entroncamento,' said Ega. 'I'm going up north too.'

A few people stared with curiosity at such a seemingly beautiful lady wearing all black and looking so miserable, getting into that luxurious, closed mysterious carriage. And no sooner had Ega closed the door than Neves, the one from *A Tarde* and the Court of Audit, broke away from a group of friends and shook his arm impatiently.

'Who is she?'

Ega pulled him away up the platform before whispering tragically in his ear: 'Cleopatra!'

The politician snorted angrily: 'Fool!' Ega moved away. Outside his compartment Vilaça was waiting, still stunned by the figure of Maria Eduarda, so melancholy and noble. He had never seen her before. She was like some queen in a novel.

'She staggered me, I can tell you! By Jove, she's a beautiful woman! We're at a loss through her, but she's really a fine piece!'

The train started. Domingos stood weeping into a coloured handkerchief. And Neves, counsellor of the Court of Audit, still furious with Ega, surreptitiously made an obscene gesture at him as the train slipped past.

At Entroncamento Ega knocked on the windows of the reserved carriage which remained shut and lifeless. It was Maria herself who opened the door. Rosa was sleeping. Miss Sarah was reading in one corner with her head resting on a cushion. And Niniche, startled by the intruder, barked furiously.

'Would you like anything, senhora?'

'No, thank you.'

They lapsed into silence. Ega slowly took out his cigar-case and rested his foot on the steps. Provincial folk wandered around the dimly-lit station muffled in capes. A porter trundled a luggage-cart. Ahead, the engine paused for a while in the shadows. And two individuals strolled in front of the compartment casting indolent inquiring glances at that magnificent woman so grave and sombre, in her black fur.

'Are you going to Oporto?'

'To Santa Olávia . . .'

'Ah!'

Then Ega mumbled with his lips trembling: *'Adeus!'*

She clasped his hand tight, silent, choking back tears.

Ega crossed between the soldiers with their capes rolled over their shoulders, hastening to the bar for a drink. At the door of the buffet he turned again and raised his hat. She, still standing, lightly moved her hand in a slow farewell. And that was the last time he saw Maria Eduarda, a tall, silent woman, all black against the light, at the door of the compartment which was to carry her away for ever.

8

SOME WEEKS LATER, during the first days of the New Year, the *Gazeta Ilustrada* carried this information in its 'Highlife' column: 'The distinguished sportsman Sr Carlos da Maia, and our friend and collaborator, João da Ega, left yesterday for London, where they will shortly set sail for North America and from there continue their interesting journey to Japan. Numerous friends went aboard the *Tamar* to say farewell to our tourist friends. We saw among others the Minister of Finland and his secretary, the Marquis de Sousela, the Count de Gouvarinho, Viscount Darque, Guilherme Craft, Teles da Gama, Cruges, Taveira, Vilaça, General Sequeira, our glorious poet Tomás de Alencar, etc. etc. Our friend and collaborator João da Ega promised us at the final handshake to send us letters with his impressions on Japan, that delightful country whence come the sun and fashion. This is indeed great news for all who appreciate discerning observation and spirit. *Au revoir!'*

After these affectionate lines (in which Alencar collaborated) the first news of the 'travellers' was received in a letter from Ega to Vilaça from New York. It was short and dealt with business. But he added a postscript entitled 'General Information for our Friends'. Here he described the fearful crossing from Liverpool, the persistent sorrow of Carlos, and New York covered in snow under a brilliant sun. And he continued: 'The inebriation of travelling is taking hold of us, determined to tread this small Universe of ours until our sorrows cease. We plan to go to Peking, cross the Great Wall, and then Central Asia, the Merv Oasis and Khiva as far as Russia; from there we'll go through Armenia and Syria and so down to Egypt and revive our spirits in the sacred Nile; up then to Athens to greet Minerva from the heights of the Acropolis; over to Naples; have a look at Algeria and Morocco, and finally drop full length into Santa Olávia round the middle of '79, to rest our weary limbs. I'll not scribble more because it's late and we're going to the Opera to see Patti in *The Barber.* Lots of warm embraces to all our dear friends.'

Vilaça copied out this paragraph and carried it in his wallet to show the intimates of Ramalhete. All wholly approved and admired such fine adventures. Only Cruges, appalled at the vastness of the Universe, murmured gloomily: 'They won't return.'

But one fine March day a year later, Ega reappeared in the Chiado. And what a sensation he caused! He looked splendid, tanned and healthy and a little heavier, full of verve, with the most assiduous care and attention paid to his toilet; he'd brought back endless stories and anecdotes about the East, would no longer tolerate anything in art or poetry that did not come from Japan or China, and promised a great work, 'my book', entitled, in the manner of a solemn heroic chronicle, *Journey across Asia.*

'And Carlos?'

'Wonderful! He's installed in Paris in a magnificent apartment in the Champs-Élysées, living the life of an artistic Renaissance prince.'

But to Vilaça, who knew their secrets, Ega confessed that Carlos was still badly shaken. He lived and laughed and drove his phaeton in the Bois – but there at the bottom of his heart, bleak and disturbing, lay the memory of 'that terrible week'.

'Still, the years fade away Vilaça,' he went on. 'And with the years, everything on this earth gradually fades away too – excepting China . . .'

And that year faded. People were born, people died. Harvests ripened, leaves dropped. And more years went by.

At the end of 1886 Carlos went to Seville to spend Christmas at the house of a friend of his from Paris, the Marquis de Vila-Medina. And from this estate of Vila-Medina, called La Soledad, he wrote to Ega announcing that after an exile of nearly ten years, he had decided to return to old Portugal to see the trees in Santa Olávia and the wonders of the Avenue. Apart from which he had a wonderful piece of news which would astound Ega: and if that made him aflame with curiosity, he must come and meet him with Vilaça, and eat the delicious pork of Santa Olávia.

'He's going to get married,' thought Ega.

It was three years (when he had last visited Paris) since he had seen Carlos. Unfortunately he was unable to rush straight up to Santa Olávia, for he was confined to his room in the

Bragança with a sore throat after a fantastically entertaining supper he had had with Silva on Twelfth Night. Vilaça, however, took a letter from him to Carlos in Santa Olávia, where he told him of his illness and begged him not to linger with the pork among the rocky hills of the Douro, but hasten to the capital to tell him the great news.

And Carlos did stay only a short time in Resende, and one mild shining morning in January 1887 the two friends, together at last, had lunch in the Hotel Bragança with the two windows open to the river.

Ega was recovered now and radiant once more, and with uncontrollable excitement and drinking coffee after coffee, picked up his monocle again and again to admire Carlos and his 'unchangeableness'.

'Not a white hair, not a wrinkle, not a shadow of weariness! That's Paris, dear boy! Lisbon drags one down. Look at me, just look at this!'

With a bony finger he pointed to the two deep furrows at the side of his nose in the hollow face. And what appalled him most was the bald patch which had begun a couple of years before and was growing larger and shone now on the top of his head.

'Look at this degrading situation! Science has an answer to everything now except baldness! Civilizations come and go, and baldness remains! It's already beginning to take on the look of a billiard ball, don't you think? What's the cause of it?'

'Idleness,' laughed Carlos.

'Idleness, indeed! What about you, then?'

Anyway, what could one do in such a country? On his return from France this last time he had considered going into the Foreign Office. He had always had the gift of the gab, and now that poor Mama was lying in her great tomb in Celorico, he also had the cash. But then he had reflected. What did being a Portuguese diplomat really mean? Just another form of idleness, passed abroad, with a permanent conviction of one's insignificance. Rather the Chiado than that!

And when Carlos suggested politics, occupation of the useless, Ega burst out in indignation. Politics! That had become morally and physically disgusting since business fever had attacked constitutionalism like some form of phylloxera. Politicians were just marionettes which made certain gestures and took certain atti-

tudes because two or three financiers were behind them pulling
the strings. Of course they could still be neat little well-
polished marionettes. But, well! That was just the horrible part
of it. They had no personality, no manners, they did not wash,
they did not clean their fingernails . . . An extraordinary thing,
which occurred nowhere else, not even in Romania or Bulgaria!
The three or four drawing-rooms in Lisbon which received anybody, it didn't matter who they were, excluded the majority of
politicians. And why? Because the ladies found them revolting!

'Look at Gouvarinho! Does he receive his fellow politicians on
his Tuesday visiting-days?'

Carlos, who had been smiling, enchanted by Ega's bitterness,
sat up sharply.

'Ah, Gouvarinho! And how is our fine friend?'

Ega wandered round the room and gave the latest news. The
Countess had inherited some sixty contos from an eccentric aunt
who lived in Santa Isabel and had better carriages now and
always received her friends on Tuesdays. But she was suffering
from something bad, in the liver or the lungs or somewhere. She
was still very elegant and very serious, a terrible paragon of
prudery. He, Gouvarinho, was the same excessive talker, scrib-
bler, second-rate politician, inflated fellow as before, twice
minister and covered with orders of this and that.

'You haven't seen him in Paris lately?'

'No. When I knew he was there I went and left my card
but they had already gone on to Vichy.'

The door opened and a hoarse cry rang out: 'At last, my boy!'

'Oh, Alencar!' cried Carlos, flinging down his cigar. They
clasped each other in delight and there was back-slapping and a
noisy paternal kiss from Alencar who trembled with emotion. Ega
pulled up a chair and shouted for the waiter.

'What will you have, Tomás? Cognac? Curaçáo? Coffee, anyway. More coffee! And strong, very strong, for Senhor Alencar
here!'

The poet was meanwhile lost in contemplating Carlos, and he
clasped his hands with a broad smile which revealed the decaying
teeth. He thought Carlos looked magnificent, a superb male, an
honour to the race. Ah! Paris, with its spirit and ardour, preserved people –

'While Lisbon pulls one down!' concluded Ega. 'I've already

said the same thing. Come, sit down, here's your coffee, and
your drink!'

It was Carlos's turn now to study Alencar. And he found him
handsomer, more poetic, with his inspired mop of unruly white
hair and the deep furrows in the brown face, which looked like
the marks left by the tumultuous passage of the emotions.

'You look *typical*, Alencar! You'd make the perfect model for
an engraving or a statue!'

The poet smiled, passing his fingers complacently over his
long, romantic whiskers which age was whitening and cigarettes
turning yellow. What the deuce, old age ought to have a few
compensations. Anyway his stomach was not too bad and he still
had a bit of feeling in his heart, chaps!

'That doesn't alter the fact that things get worse every day
here, Carlos, my lad! Still, that's enough of that. People always
grumble about their country, it's human nature. Horace even
complained about his. And you, my friends, with your superior
intelligence, know quite well that in the time of Augustus . . .
Not to mention, of course, the fall of the Republic, the collapse
of all the old institutions . . . Still, let's leave the Romans! What
have we got in this bottle? Chablis . . . I don't dislike a drop of
Chablis in the autumn with oysters . . . Let's try it. Here's to
your arrival, Carlos my boy! And yours, João, and may God
grant you all the glories you deserve, my lads!'

He drank. And muttered: 'Nice Chablis, fine bouquet.' And
finally he sat himself down noisily, shaking back his white mane.

'Ah, Tomás!' cried Ega, placing a hand affectionately on his
shoulder. 'There's no one like him, he's unique! The good Lord
made him in a day of great verve, and then broke the mould.'

Ah, flattery! answered the poet, beaming. There were many
others as good as he. All Humanity was made from the same clay, as
the Bible said – or came from the same monkey, as Darwin declared.

'All these ideas of evolution and origin of the species, development of the cell and so on, as far as I'm concerned . . . Darwin,
Lamarck, Spencer, Claudio Bernard, Littré and the rest of them
are first-class fellows. But let's face it! For quite a few million
years now man has proved he has a soul, and most sublimely
has he proved it!'

'Drink your coffee, Tomás!' advised Ega, pushing his cup towards him. 'Drink your coffee!'

'Thank you. Ah, that reminds me, João, I gave your doll to the little one. She started rocking it and kissing it straight away with that mothering instinct, that divine something . . . It's a little niece of mine, Carlos. She's lost her mother, poor little soul, and I've got her, trying to make a little lady of her. You must come and see her. You must both come and have dinner with me one day, and try my partridges *à l'espagnole*. Are you staying long, Carlos?'

'Just a week or two, to take a good deep breath of the air of my native land.'

'And you're right, my boy!' exclaimed the poet, pulling the brandy bottle towards him. 'It's not so bad as they say . . . Just look at all this, at this sky out here, at the river!'

'It's charming, it's true!'

The three of them stared for a moment in wonder at the incomparable beauty of the river, vast, gleaming, serene, as blue as the splendidly sunlit sky.

'And what about poetry?' asked Carlos, turning to the poet. 'Have you forsaken the divine language?'

Alencar gave a despondent shrug. Who appreciated the divine language nowadays? The new generation in Portugal understood only the language of money, of cash! Everything was syndicates now, my boy!

'Still every now and again something wakes inside here, and the old man stirs . . . Haven't you seen in the papers? Oh, of course you don't read this rubbish they call gazettes . . . Well, anyway, there's a little something in one of them dedicated to João here. Let's see if I can remember it . . .'

He ran a hand over the lean pale face, and uttered the verse like a lament:

> 'Light of hope and light of love,
> What wild wind cast thee down?
> For the soul which seeks to find thee
> Never more can find thee now.'

Carlos murmured, 'Beautiful!' Ega murmured, 'Delightful!' And the poet warmed to the praise and continued with a flourish:

> 'My soul in former days
> As the moon rose pale,

Began at once to sing
Like the wakening nightingale.

For thoughts then were flowers,
Which the slow breeze of May . . .'

'Senhor Cruges!' announced the waiter, opening the door.

Carlos held out his arms. And the maestro, all buttoned up in a light overcoat, abandoned himself to Carlos's effusive welcome and stammered: 'I only heard yesterday. I wanted to come to meet you, but they didn't wake me . . .'

'So the same disorder reigns?' laughed Carlos. 'They never wake you?'

Cruges shrugged his shoulders, very red and shy after that long separation. But Carlos made him sit beside him, full of affection for the old maestro, as lean as ever, his nose a little sharper, the mop of hair falling in tighter curls over his coat collar.

'And let me offer you my congratulations! I read about your success, the delightful comic opera, the *Flower of Seville* – '

' – *Of Granada!*' corrected the Maestro. 'Yes, not a bad little thing, quite well received.'

'Beautiful!' shouted Alencar, refilling his brandy glass. 'Music full of sun and light, smelling of orange-blossom. But how many times have I told him, "Leave operettas alone, my boy, and aim higher, compose a great historic symphony!" I gave him an idea only the other day: the departure of Don Sebastian for Africa. Sailors' songs and kettle-drums, the weeping of the people, the crashing of the waves . . . Sublime! And then he plays around with castanets! Still, that's that, he's got plenty of talent, and he's like a son to me, for he's dirtied my trousers many a time!'

But the maestro, running his fingers through his abundant hair, looked uneasy, and finally confessed to Carlos that he could not stay, he had an appointment.

'With a lady?'

'No, it's Barradas, who's painting my portrait.'

'With a lyre in your hand?'

'No,' answered the maestro quite seriously. 'With a baton. And I've got full dress on.'

And he unbuttoned his coat and showed himself in all his splendour with two coral buttons on the shirt-front and the ivory baton tucked into the waistcoat.

'You look splendid!' cried Carlos. 'Then if you can't stay, have dinner with us. Alencar, you will too, won't you? I want to hear these verses of yours calmly . . . Six o'clock on the dot, without fail. I've got a nice little Portuguese dinner for you which I ordered this morning – stew and baked rice and chick-peas, and so forth, to get rid of my nostalgia.'

Alencar made a deep show of disdain. The Bragança's chef, wretched little Frenchman that he was, would never be capable of creating these noble Portuguese dishes. Still, it couldn't be helped now. He'd be there punctually at six, to drink Carlos's health.

'Are you going out, boys?'

Carlos and Ega were going to Ramalhete to visit the old house.

This the poet considered a sacred pilgrimage. He'd be off then with the maestro. His path lay in the same direction as Barradas' studio . . . A talented young fellow, that Barradas! His paintings were a bit on the dark side, nothing well-defined, all somewhat vague, but a gifted lad.

'And he had an aunt, boys, Leonor Barradas! What eyes she had, and what a body! And it wasn't only her body! It was her fine spirit, the poetry, the sacrifice . . . ! Ah, there's none of that now, that's all gone and finished. Still, enough of that. See you at six!'

'Six on the dot, don't forget!'

Alencar and the maestro left after furnishing themselves with cigars. And shortly after, Carlos and Ega also set off along Rua do Tesouro Velho, walking slowly arm in arm.

They talked about Paris, about the fellows and women Ega had known four years ago when he had spent such a gay winter there in Carlos's apartment. And what shocked Ega, as each name was recalled, was to discover how short-lived had been the splendour, how abrupt had been the end of all these carefree young people. Lucy Gray was dead. The Conrad woman dead. And Maria Blond? Fat and bourgeoise, married to a manufacturer of tallow candles. And what about the Pole, the fair fellow? He'd disappeared. M. de Menant, the Don Juan? Assistant prefect of the department of Doubs. And that Belgian boy who lived next door? Ruined in the Stock Exchange. And there were others dead, lost, buried in the mud of Paris!

'Well, if you reckon it all up my friend,' considered Ega, 'our little life here in Lisbon, simple and peaceful and uneventful, is infinitely preferable.'

They had reached the Loreto, and Carlos stopped to look round and recapture the intimacy of the old heart of Lisbon. Nothing had changed. The same sleepy sentry walked round the melancholy statue of Camões. The same old curtains with ecclesiastical arms hung at the doors of the two churches. The Hotel Aliança retained its same silent and deserted air. A golden sun warmed the stone slabs; coach-drivers, hats awry, whipped their nags; three fishwives, with their flat baskets on their heads, walked along in the bright sunlight, swaying their large supple hips. At one corner a group of shabbily-dressed loafers stood smoking and in the opposite corner, at the Havanesa, another group of loafers smoked – but these wore frock-coats and discussed politics.

'It's horrible, when you come back from abroad!' cried Carlos. 'It's not the city, it's the people. They're so ugly and grubby and lazy and shabby, all yellowish and bandy-legged . . .'

'Still, Lisbon has changed,' declared Ega in a serious tone. 'Oh, it's changed a lot! You ought to see the Avenue. Let's have a walk up the Avenue before going to Ramalhete.'

They made their way down the Chiado. On the other side the shop-awnings cast a dark, jagged shade upon the pavement. And Carlos recognized, leaning against the same doors, characters he had left there ten years before, leaning there in just the same way, just as miserable-looking. They had wrinkles now, and grey hair. But there they stood the same as ever, dull and faded, propping up the same door-posts but with up-to-date collars on. A little farther on, outside the Bertrand bookshop, Ega laughed and touched Carlos's arm.

'Look who's over there, at the door of the Baltresqui!'

It was Damaso – a sleek, heavier Damaso with a flower in his buttonhole and a paunch, chewing a large cigar and gaping with the besotted air of a well-fed, contented ruminant. At the sight of his two old friends, he made as if to slip away and hide in the confectioner's. But irresistibly, unconsciously almost, he found himself before Carlos, with a hand outstretched and a smile on his burning face.

'Hello there! You here again! What a fine surprise!'

Carlos offered a slack hand, and an indifferent smile.

'That's right, Damaso . . . How are things?'

'The same awful bore . . . Are you staying long?'

'A week or two.'

'Are you at Ramalhete?'

'No, in the Bragança. But don't bother yourself, I'm usually out.'

'Well, well, well . . . You know, I was in Paris three months ago, in the Continental.'

'Were you? Well, nice to have met you. Be seeing you.'

'Good-bye, lads. You're looking fine, Carlos, in excellent health!'

'You flatter me, Damaso.'

And the admiration of old seemed to light up in his eyes as he stared after Carlos, studying his frock-coat and hat and manner of walking, just as in the old days when Maia had been for him the example *par exellence* of his beloved *chic*, 'one of those things you only see abroad.'

'D'you know our Damaso's got himself married?' asked Ega, as they walked on and he slipped his arm through Carlos's again.

Carlos was amazed. What! Our Damaso! Married?!

Yes, married to a daughter of the Count of Agueda, an impoverished family with a crowd of daughters. They had got rid of the youngest on to him. And our excellent Damaso, a real stroke of luck for that distinguished family, was now paying for the elder sisters' dresses.

'Is she pretty?'

'Yes, quite pretty . . . enough to make a nice young fellow called Barros happy anyway.'

'What, you mean Damaso's got horns?'

'Oh yes, horns indeed, enormous ones . . . But as you see, he's immensely contented, unfaithfulness has even fattened him!'

Carlos had stopped and was looking in astonishment at the extraordinary balconies of a first floor which were hung, as if it were a procession day, with bright red draperies embroidered with monograms. And he was about to inquire about them when, from out of a group standing in the doorway of this festive building, burst a gawky youth with a beardless, pimple-covered face; he hurried across the road to shout to Ega, choking with laughter:

'If you hurry, you'll catch her down the road! Run!'

'Who?'

'Adosinda! She's got a blue dress on and white feathers in her hat . . . But quick . . . João Eliseu poked his cane between her legs and made her come a cropper! What a scene! But move, man!'

Back he marched on his long lanky legs to his friends who, with the curiosity of a group of provincials, stood silently watching that exceedingly elegant man who accompanied Ega and whom none knew. Ega in the meantime was explaining the balconies and the group to Carlos.

'They're boys from the Turf. It's a new club, what used to be the old Jockey da Travesa da Palha. They play cards and so on for very low stakes; they're a nice crowd. And you see they're always prepared, with the hangings and everything, in case Our Lord of the Passion should pass by.'

Then as they walked towards Rua Nova do Almada, he told Carlos the story of Adosinda. He was at the Silva, some two weeks ago, having supper with friends after the Opera, when this incredible woman appeared, dressed all in red, and madly rolling out r's in all her words, asking after the *Virrcount* . . . Which *Virrcount*? She wasn't sure. *He was a Virrcount she had encountered in the Croliseum* . . . She took a seat and they offered her champagne, and Dona Adosinda began to prove herself a truly exceptional creature. They spoke of politics, of the ministry and the deficit. Dona Adosinda declared she knew *deficit* very well – he was a charming boy – laughs all round at that! Dona Adosinda took offence, and insisted she had been to Cintra with him, he was a perfect gentleman and worked in the English Bank . . . *Deficit* working in the English Bank – there were howls of laughter at that! And this went on till five in the morning when they'd raffled her and Teles had won! A whale of a night!

Carlos laughed. 'It sounds an orgy on the grand scale; one of Heliogabalus and the Comte d'Orsay.'

Ega then defended his orgy. Where could you imagine a better one in Europe or, indeed, in any civilization? He'd just like to know if you could spend a gayer night in Paris, in the wretched banality of the Grand-Treize, or in London, in the so correct and tiresome Bristol! The only thing which made life tolerable was a good laugh now and again. In Europe nowadays the sophisticated man did not laugh – he just gave a pale icy smile. Only they in Portugal, in that uncivilized corner of the world, still retained that supreme gift, that blessed and comforting thing – good hearty laughter!

'What the deuce are you looking at?'

It was Carlos's former consulting-rooms – now, according to the name-plate, a dressmaker's workshop. The two friends slipped back into the past. How many hours had Carlos stupidly dragged out there with the *Revista dos Dois Mundos* waiting in vain for patients and still believing in the joys of work! And there was that morning Ega had turned up in the splendid pelisse, ready to transform old stick-in-the-mud Portugal in one brief winter!

'All for nothing!'

'All for nothing! But we had a good laugh! D'you remember the night the Marquis wanted to take Paca to the consulting-room to try out that divan which he considered would have been more fitting in a harem?'

Carlos gave a sigh for the past. Poor Marquis! That was one of the things which had affected him most those last few years – the death of the Marquis, learnt by chance from the newspaper one day while he was lunching. And as they strolled across the Rossio, they remembered others who had since disappeared – Dona Maria da Cunha, poor thing, who had died of dropsy, and Dom Diogo who had married his cook; good Sequeira who had died one night in a cab . . .

'And by the way,' went on Ega, 'did you see Craft in London?'

'Yes,' answered Carlos. 'He's found himself a delightful house near Richmond. But he's aged a lot, and complains of liver trouble. And he's grown too fond of alcohol too, unfortunately. A shame!'

Carlos asked after Taveira. That fine young man, Ega informed him, had spent another ten years in office and up and down the Chiado. He was going grey now, but always very elegant and always attached to some Spanish girl and laying down the law in the San Carlos, and claiming every afternoon in the Havanesa, with a calm, content air; 'This country's finished!' All in all a good example of the sophisticated Lisboan.

'And our stupid Steinbroken?'

'Minister in Athens,' answered Carlos, 'among the classical ruins.'

This idea of Steinbroken in ancient Greece amused them exceedingly. Ega imagined good Steinbroken, stiff in his high starched collars, stating prudently regarding Socrates: *'Oh, il est très fort, il est excessivement fort!'* Or, grunting hesitantly, fearful of committing himself about the Battle of Thermopylae: *'C'est très grave, c'est excessivement grave!'* It would be worth going to Greece just to see!

Ega stopped.

'Well, here's the Avenue! What d'you think of it – eh? Not so bad nowadays.'

There in an open space, where Carlos had left a serene leafy Public Walk, an obelisk, with bronze plates on the pedestal, rose up sugar-coloured in the shimmering winter sunlight, and the large globes of the street-lamps which surrounded it, shone in transparent brilliance like great soap-bubbles suspended in mid-air. On both sides stretched solemn buildings of various heights, elegant, freshly-painted buildings with flower-pots on the cornices and stone patios with black and white tiled floors where door-keepers stood sucking on cigarettes. Those two rigid rows of smart houses reminded Carlos of the families who in former times had lined the road on either side of the walk after one o'clock mass, listening to the band in their Sunday finery – black cashmere and silk. The stone slabs shone as if freshly white-washed. Here and there the pale meagre foliage of a bush trembled in the breeze. And at the far end of the Avenue the green hill dotted with trees and the plots of land of Vale de Pereiro brought to a rustic close that short arrogant strip of cheap luxury, which was intended to transform the old city but had stopped short amid piles of gravel.

But there was clean fresh air circulating and the sun bathed the rubble in gold; the divinely serene, spotless blue covered and softened everything. The two friends sat on a bench near a grassy patch which bordered a pool of still, greenish water.

In the shade youths strolled slowly in pairs, flowers in their lapels, elegant trousers, pale gloves stitched in black. They were a new generation that Carlos did not know. Occasionally Ega said: *'Hello!'* or waved his cane. And back and forth they walked with a timid, constrained air as if they were unaccustomed to the space, to so much light, to their own *chic* even . . . Carlos stared in amazement. What were these melancholy youths in their slim

620

trousers doing there during working-hours? There were no women around, apart from a sickly-looking creature sitting on a bench taking the sun and wrapped in shawl and headscarf; and two matrons with sequinned lace-trimmed capes – landladies of boarding-houses no doubt – who were airing a shaggy little dog. What was it that brought those pale youths there? And what shocked him above all were those gentlemen's boots – disproportionately long boots peeping out of the tight-fitting trousers, with sharp upturned points like the prows of fishing-boats.

'This is fantastic, Ega!'

Ega rubbed his hands together. Yes, but it was revealing. Because this simple shape of boot explained the whole of contemporary Portugal. You could see how things were by looking at these boots. Having cast off her old character, the wretched country had decided to turn modern; but having no originality or energy or ability to create a character of its own, it had ordered models from abroad – models of ideas and trousers and customs laws, art, culinary and otherwise . . . The only thing was that as it lacked all sense of proportion, and at the same time was full of impatience to appear modern and civilized, it exaggerated the original, deformed it, carried it to the length of caricature. The original boot from abroad was only slightly narrowed at the point; the dandy straightway stretched it and sharpened it until it was needle sharp. In the same way the writer reads a page of Goncourt or Verlaine in a chiselled, precious style, and immediately he twists it and tangles it, pulls the poor phrase to pieces until it falls into the ridiculous and burlesque. Again the legislator hears that they are raising the level of education abroad and at once puts metaphysics, astronomy, philology, egyptology, chromatics, comparative religion and numerous other terrors into the primary school curriculum. And it's the same in every field, in every class and profession, from the orator to the photographer, from the jurist to the sportsman . . . That is what happened to the Negroes, already corrupted by St Thomas, who see the Europeans wearing glasses and therefore imagine that that is what it means to be a civilized being and a white man. So what do they do? In their ardent desire for progress and whiteness they stick three or four pairs of glasses on their nose – glasses of plain glass and smoked glass and even coloured glass. And they stumble through the cities, noses in the air, trying desperately to balance all these glasses – in order to be extremely civilized and white . . .

Carlos laughed.

'So you mean things are getting worse.'

'It's dreadful! Shabby and artificial! Artificial especially! There's not a thing that's really genuine any more in this wretched country, not even the bread we eat!'

Carlos, leaning back on the bench, slowly stretched out his cane, pointing with it.

'That's still genuine!'

And he nodded towards the upper parts of the city, the old hills of Graça and Penha, with their houses slipping down the dry sun-parched sides. The convents and the church sat heavily on the heights alongside squat ecclesiastical buildings, reminding one of fat sluggish friars, devout and veiled old maids, holy processions, the coloured garments of religious confraternities filling the courtyards, street-vendors shouting their wares, and fireworks in praise of Jesus. Higher still, its ugly wall outlined against the radiant blue of the sky, was the castle, a rude, sordid building, whence in former times white-uniformed troops came down to a bassoon accompaniment to issue a pronunciamento. And in the shelter of the castle, in the dark quarter of St Vincent and the Cathedral, the decrepit mansions with nostalgic views out to sea and enormous coats of arms on the cracked walls, where the old Lisboan aristocracy, cachetic and catarrhal, drag out their last days amid scandal and devotions and playing-cards.

Ega stood for a moment pensive.

'Perhaps it's more genuine. But it's so stupid and shabby! Really, one doesn't know where to turn. And if we turn towards ourselves, it's worse still!'

Then suddenly he clapped Carlos on the knee, his face alight: 'Look who's coming along!'

It was a trim, well-kept victoria, advancing slowly and stylishly at the leisurely trot of two English mares. But it was a disappointment. All it contained was a very fair young man with a complexion like a camellia and down on his chin, leaning languorously back in his seat. He waved to Ega with a maidenly smile. The victoria passed.

'Don't you know who that was?'

Carlos searched his memory.

'A former patient of yours! Charlie!'

Carlos clapped his hands. Charlie! His little Charlie! How he'd grown! And how pretty he was!

'Yes, very pretty. He's very friendly with an old man, always around with him. But he must have come with his mother today, and I expect she's walking round here somewhere. Shall we go and see?'

They walked up to the Avenue looking for her. But whom they in fact saw was Eusèbiozinho. He looked gloomier, more consumptive, and walked arm in arm with a very stout, very red lady who wore a hazel-coloured silk dress. They strolled along slowly in the sun. But Eusèbiozinho did not see them as he plodded along, his dark glasses fixed on his shadow.

'That freak is his wife,' said Ega. 'After various affairs in brothels, our Eusèbiozinho fell in love with this one. The creature's father, owner of a pawnshop, caught him one night on the stairs filching pleasures from the lady. There was a devil of a fuss and they made him marry her. He disappeared completely and this is the first time I've seen him since. They say his wife beats him about.'

'Heaven preserve him!'

'Amen!'

Then Carlos, remembering the hiding he had given Eusèbio and the *Trumpet* affair, wanted to know what had happened to Palma *Cavalão*. Was that worthy gentleman still sullying the universe with his existence? He was, indeed, said Ega. Only he had left literature and become the factotum of Carneiro, one-time minister; he took Carneiro's Spanish girl to the theatre on his arm and was an influential intercessor with him in any political matter.

'He'll be a deputy yet,' went on Ega. 'And the way things are going, he'll be a minister before very long . . . But it's getting late, Carlinhos. Shall we take this cab to Ramalhete?'

It was four o'clock and the brief winter sun was already growing pale.

They took the cab. In the Rossio, Alencar saw them and waved gaily as they passed. Then Carlos remembered the surprise he had felt that morning in the Bragança.

'Oh, Ega! You seem on intimate terms with Alencar now! How did that come about?'

Ega confessed that he really did appreciate Alencar immensely now. In the first place, amid all the falseness of Lisbon, Alencar was the only Portuguese who remained genuine. And again he resisted with profound honesty the terribly contagious meanness and trickery. And there was such generosity and loyalty and goodness in the man. His behaviour with his niece was touching. He had far more courtesy and better manners than the younger generation. A little too much drink at times did not disagree with his lyrical temperament. And finally, in the state into which literature had fallen, Alencar's mediocre verses stood out for their correctness and simplicity and touch of true emotion. All in all he was a highly estimable bard.

'So you see what we've come to, Carlinhos! There's nothing which expresses better the fearful decline of Portugal in the last thirty years than this fact: character and talent have sunk so low that our old Tomás, the author of "Flower of Martyrdom", Alencar of Alenquer, suddenly appears with the proportions of a genius, and a righteous one too!'

They were still discussing Portugal and her ills when the cab stopped. The severe façade of Ramalhete affected Carlos deeply, and the windows sheltering under the edge of the roof, and the great bunch of sunflowers in place of a coat of arms! Hearing the carriage, Vilaça came to the door, pulling on a pair of yellow gloves. He was fatter now and everything about his person, from the new hat to the silver-topped cane, emphasized his importance as administrator – almost proprietor during Carlos's long absence – of the Maias' vast property. He introduced the gardener, an old man who lived there with his wife and son, looking after the great empty house. Vilaça expressed pleasure at seeing the two friends together again, then added, patting Carlos on the back with the freedom and affection of an old friend:

'After leaving you at Santa Apolónia I went and had a bath at the Central and didn't even have to have a nap. Those sleeping-cars are really useful! Ah, there's no doubt about it – our Portugal doesn't lag behind in matters of progress! Will you be needing me?'

'No thanks, Vilaça. We're just going to have a walk round the rooms. Have dinner with us. Six o'clock! But six o'clock sharp, mind, for there are special dishes on the menu.'

They crossed the entrance hall with its old feudal carved-oak benches, solemn as the choir-stalls of a cathedral. Above, however, the antechamber had a new sorry look, for it had been stripped and not a piece of furniture nor drapery remained, and the cracked whitewash of the walls shone bare. Oriental tapestries which had hung as in a tent, Moorish plates with copper lights, the statue of Friorenta laughing and shivering in her marble nakedness as she dipped her toe in the water – all these things now decorated Carlos's rooms in Paris; and other boxes were piled in a corner ready to leave, full of the best china from Hideaway. Then in the wide carpetless corridor their steps echoed like in a deserted cloister. The dim light on the religious pictures there picked out in darker hue a bony hermit's shoulder or the pale splash of a skull. There was an icy chill in the air. Ega pulled up his coat collar.

In the big drawing-room the furniture covered in moss-coloured brocade was now enshrouded in cotton sheets and emitting a smell of turpentine and camphor. And on the floor, in the Constable portrait leaning against the wall, the Countess of Runa lifted her scarlet riding-cosume and seemed about to step from the gilt frame to leave the house as well and complete the dispersal of her family.

'Let's go!' cried Ega. 'This is lugubrious!'

But Carlos, pale and silent, opened the door of the billiards-room. There, in what had been the largest room of Ramalhete, had recently been accumulated haphazardly, in all their various styles and centuries, as in the back room of an antique shop, all the valuable pieces from Hideaway. At the far end, covering up the fireplace, rose the famous cabinet of the times of the Hanseatic League, with its armed figures of Mars, the carved doors, the four Evangelists preaching at the corners clothed in those violently agitated robes which seemed swept by a prophetic wind. Carlos noticed some damage to the cornice, in the two fauns which were challenging each other on the flute amid agricultural symbols. One faun had broken its goat's foot; the other had lost its bucolic flute.

'The clumsy brutes!' he cried furiously, his love of works of art sorely wounded. 'To damage a beautiful thing like this!'

He climbed on a chair to examine the damage. Ega in the meantime wandered about among the other furniture, bridal chests, Spanish escritoires, Italian Renaissance sideboards – remembering the happy house in Olivais that they had once furnished, the delightful nights passed in conversation, the dinners there and the fireworks let off in honour of Leonidas. How everything had passed! But his foot knocked against a hatbox; it had no lid and was full of old things – a veil, odd gloves, a silk stocking, ribbons, artificial flowers. They were obects belonging to Maria, picked up in some corner of Hideaway where they had been cast when she was leaving the house. And by some unfortunate chance, mixed up among these remains of her, as in the promiscuity of a rubbish dump, was a velvet slipper embroidered in self colour – an old slipper of Afonso da Maia's! Ega hurriedly hid the box under a loose piece of tapestry. Then as Carlos jumped down from the chair, brushing his hands and still indignant, Ega decided to bring this pilgrimage, which was spoiling his day, to an end.

'Let's go to the terrace! We'll have a quick look over the garden and then leave the place!'

But they still had to pass the saddest memory of all – Afonso's study. The lock was stuck. And Carlos's hand shook as he struggled to open it. Ega, also moved, could see the room as it used to be – the Carcel lamps casting their rose light, the crackling fire, Bonifácio on the bear-skin rug, and Afonso in his velvet jacket seated in his old easy-chair knocking out the ash from his pipe against the palm of his hand. The lock gave at last – and all their emotion was suddenly lost in the absurd, grotesque surprise of finding themselves both desperately sneezing, suffocated by the acrid smell of some powder which stung their eyes and disturbed the senses. Vilaça it was who, following the recommendation of an old almanac, had had handfuls of white pepper distributed over the furniture and the sheets covering it. Choking and unable to see through the tears in their eyes, the two friends, weak from sneezing, made their way across the room.

Carlos at last managed to open wide the two doors of the window. A dying ray of sunlight fell across the terrace. Recovering somewhat in the fresh air, they stood there in silence, giving a belated occasional sneeze and wiping their eyes.

'What an infernal idea!' cried Carlos indignantly.

Ega, hurrying across the room with his handkerchief over his face, had stumbled against a sofa and knocked his shin.

'A stupid thing to do! A nice crack I gave my leg!'

He turned back to survey the room where all the furniture had disappeared in its white shrouds. And he realized he had tripped over the velvet cushion of old Bonifácio. Bonifácio! What had become of him?

Carlos, who had taken a seat on the low terrace parapet, among the flowerless vases, described the end of Bonifácio. He had died in Santa Olávia, resigned to his lot and so obese that he could no longer move. And Vilaça had the poetic idea, the only one he'd ever had in all his years as steward, of having a gravestone made for him, a simple slab of white marble under a rose-bush below the windows of Afonso's room.

Ega also sat down on the parapet, and both fell into silence. The garden below, sandy and clean and cold in its winter nakedness, wore the melancholy of a forgotten retreat which is no longer loved and visited: a green mould from the damp covered Venus of Cythera's large limbs; the cypress and the cedar were growing old together like two friends in a hermitage; and more slowly than ever sung the fountain as it fell drop by drop into the marble basin. Then in the background, like a seascape framed by the ashlars of two tall buildings, Ramalhete's view – a piece of the Tagus and hill beyond – took on a pensive sorrowful air in the late afternoon: on a stretch of river a closed-up packet boat, prepared for the billows beyond, was slipping downstream and disappearing as if devoured by the uncertain sea; high on the hill the windmill had stopped, chilled by the cold breeze; and in the windows of houses on the water's edge, a ray of sunlight died, slowly fading, wiped out by the first grey of twilight, like a last ray of hope on a troubled face.

Then, in that silence of solitude and abandon, Ega, looking into the distance, murmured slowly:

'But hadn't you any idea of this marriage, not the least suspicion?'

'None at all. I learnt about it suddenly in Seville from her letter.'

This was the important news Carlos had written about – the news he had told to Ega straightway at dawn, after their first greetings in Santa Apolónia. Maria Eduarda was going to be married.

She had informed Carlos herself in a letter he had received

at the Vila-Medina house. She was going to marry. And it did not seem to be a decision taken suddenly, under the heart's influence, but a carefully considered proposal. She gave this idea by speaking in her letter of 'having reflected long, having thought about it a great deal'. The bridegroom, moreover, must be nearly fifty. Carlos therefore saw in this decision the union of two persons disillusioned with life, ill-treated by it, and who, wearied or alarmed by their loneliness and sensing in each other a serious heart and spirit, had resolved to put together their remaining warmth and happiness and courage, the better to face old age.

'How old's she?'

Carlos thought she must be about forty-one or forty-two. She had said in her letter: 'I am only six years and three months younger than my fiancé.' He was called M. de Trelain, and was evidently a broad-minded man, free from prejudice and outstandingly generous, for he loved Maria although he knew her errors.

'Does he know everything?' asked Ega, jumping off the parapet.

'Not everything. She says M. de Trelain knew of her past "all those errors into which she had fallen unconsciously." That means that she hasn't told them everything . . . Let's go, it's getting late, and I still want to see my rooms.'

They went down to the garden. For a moment they walked in silence the path where Afonso's roses had grown in former days. The cork bench still stood under the two redbuds; Maria had sat there when she had visited Ramalhete, to tie up a spray of flowers she was going to take with her as a memento. As he passed, Ega picked one of the little marguerites which flowered in solitude.

'She's still living in Orléans, isn't she?'

Yes, said Carlos, she lived in the country near Orléans in a house she had bought there called Les Rosières. Her fiancé must have some small château near. She called him 'my neighbour'. And naturally he was a *gentilhomme campagnard*, from some distinguished, well-off family.

'She only has what you give her, of course.'

'I believe I wrote and told you all that,' answered Carlos. 'She refused any part of the inheritance. And Vilaça arranged things through an endowment I made her, equivalent to an income of twelve contos.'

'Very nice. Does she mention Rosa in her letter?'

'Yes, she just said she was well. She must be a young woman now.'

'And pretty, I bet!'

They were climbing the wrought-iron stairway which led from the garden to Carlos's rooms. Ega stopped with a hand on the glass door, yielding to one last burst of curiosity:

'What effect did this have on you?'

Carlos lit a cigar; and then, throwing the match over the creeper-entwined rail, answered:

'The effect of conclusion, of absolute termination. It's as if she'd died, and all the past had died with her, and now she has been reborn a different person. She's not Maria Eduarda any longer. She's Madame Trelain, a French lady. With this name all that was is now gone, buried a hundred fathoms deep, finished for ever, without even leaving a memory. That's the effect it had on me.'

'You never met Senhor Guimarães in Paris?'

'Never. I presume he's dead.'

They went into the bedroom. Vilaça, supposing Carlos would be staying in Ramalhete, had had his rooms made ready and everything looked icy – the marble tops of the chests of drawers were freshly dusted and bare, a new candle stood in a single candlestick, the fustian counterpane, showing the creases where it had been stored away, covered the curtainless bed. Carlos put down his hat and cane on his old work-desk. Then, as if bringing things to a conclusion, he said:

'Well, Ega, there's life for you! In this room, for long nights, I suffered the certainty that life was finished for me. I thought of killing myself. I thought of becoming a Trappist. And all this I considered in cold blood, considering it a logical conclusion. But ten years have passed and here I am again.'

He stopped before the tall mirror suspended between its two columns of carved oak, stroked his moustache and concluded with a melancholy smile:

'A little fatter!'

Ega too cast a pensive look around the room.

'D'you remember when I turned up one night in perfect agony, dressed as Mephistopheles?'

Carlos gave a shout: Rachel! That's right! What had happened to Rachel, their Israelite lily?

Ega shrugged his shoulders.

'She's around somewhere, quite faded . . .'

'Poor soul!' muttered Carlos. And that was all that was said about the great romantic passion of Ega's life.

Carlos went to examine a painting standing on the floor, propped face to the wall near the window. It was the portrait of his father, Pedro da Maia, with his suède gloves in his hand, and the large Arab eyes in the sad pale face which time was turning yellower. He stood it on the chest of drawers. And flicking off the dust with his handkerchief, he remarked: 'There's nothing grieves me more than not having a portrait of grandfather! I'll take this with me to Paris, anyway.'

Ega inquired from the depths of the sofa he had sunk into whether Carlos had never had the idea, the vague desire, of returning to Portugal.

Carlos considered Ega for a moment in amazement. Whatever for? To drag his sorry steps back and forth from the Casa Havanesa to the Grémio? Certainly not! Paris was the only place on earth congenial to the type of man he had decided he was: 'a rich man who lives well'. A ride through the Bois; lunch in the Bignon; a drive round the boulevard; an hour at the club with the papers; a spot of exercise in the fencing-room; at night the Comédie Française or a soirée, Trouville during the summer; a few shots at hares during the winter; and throughout the year women and races, some interest still in science and antiques, and a little *blague*. Nothing could be more inoffensive, empty, and agreeable.

'And here you have a man's existence! In ten years nothing at all has happened to me, except when my phaeton fell to pieces on the road to St-Cloud. I was in the *Figaro*.'

Ega got up with a disconsolate gesture.

'We've failed in life, my friend!'

'I believe so . . . But so do most people. That is, they fail in so far as they never attain the life they planned in the imagination. They say: "I'm going to be like this, because it's beautiful to be like this." But it never turns out like this, but invariably like that: occasionally better, but always different.'

Ega agreed with a wordless sigh, and began to pull on his gloves.

The room was growing dark in the cold melancholy winter

twilight. Carlos put his hat on, and they went down the stairway lined in cerise velvet, where the panoply of ancient armour still hung, somewhat tarnished and rusty. Once in the street, Carlos stopped and glanced back at the sombre old house which seemed, in the first shadows of night, to acquire a more ponderous air, like that of an ecclesiastical residence, with its severe walls, its grilles over the ground-floor windows holding darkness within – a silent house, no longer inhabited and already acquiring a ruinous air.

His soul was stirred and he murmured to Ega, slipping an arm through his: 'It's strange! I only lived two years in this house, yet I seem to have lived my whole life here.'

Ega was not surprised. It was there, in Ramalhete, that he had really lived that which gives flavour and depth to life – there he had experienced passion.

'There are many other things which give value to life . . . This is one of your old romantic ideas, Ega!'

'And what else are we then?' cried Ega. 'What have we been ever since college, ever since the Latin exams? Romantics: that is, inferior beings who allow their lives to be ruled by sentiment rather than reason.'

But Carlos wanted to know if those who acted according to reason were at heart any happier, by never wavering from the path of reason, torturing themselves to keep its inflexible line, dry, stiff, logical beings, emotionless to the very end.

'I don't think so,' said Ega. 'On the outside they appear most inconsolatory, and within they're inconsolable. Which goes to prove that in this charming world of ours one must be either insensate or insipid . . .'

'To conclude: life's not worth living . . .'

'That depends entirely upon the stomach!' replied Ega.

They both laughed. Then Carlos, serious once more, explained his philosophy of life – the definitive philosophy which he had built out of his own experience and which now ruled his actions. It was the Moslem fatalism: to fear nothing and to desire nothing . . . Never to abandon oneself to a hope – or to a disappointment. To accept everything, whatever comes, whatever eludes you, with the tranquillity with which one accepts the natural changes of weather, the stormy days and the calm ones. And in this state of placidity, to let the scrap of material we call the ego gradually deteriorate and decompose until it re-enters and loses itself in the infinite Universe. Above all, have no appetites. And more even than that, no vexations.

Ega agreed on the whole. What he had chiefly become convinced of in these lean years of life was the uselessness of effort. It was not worth taking one step to reach anything on this earth – because everything resolved itself, as the wise man in Ecclesiastes had already taught, in dust and disillusion.

'If I was told that a Rothschild's fortune or the imperial crown of Charles V awaited me down the road here if I ran, I wouldn't quicken my pace. No! I wouldn't change this slow, prudent, safe and steady step which is the only one you should have in life.'

'Nor I!' agreed Carlos, with conviction.

And both of them slowed down as they walked down Santos Ramp, as if that were the path of life, at whose end they were sure to find dust and disillusion, and along which they should therefore advance with due deliberation and disdain. They could see the Aterro and its long row of lamps. Suddenly Carlos stopped with a gesture of annoyance.

'Confound it! I've come all the way from Paris as hungry as a hunter and I've forgotten to order a dish of Parma ham and peas for the dinner tonight.'

It was too late now, said Ega. Then Carlos, who up till that moment had been lost in the past and in a synthesis of existence, was suddenly aware of the night which had fallen, of the lighted lamps. Under a gas-lamp he looked at his watch. It was a quarter past six!

'Oh, deuce take it! And there was I telling Vilaça and the boys to be at the Bragança punctually at six! There's never a cab round here!'

'Wait!' cried Ega. 'Here's a tram coming. We'll catch it if we hurry!'

'We'll make it!'

The two friends set off at a brisker pace. And Carlos, who had flung aside his cigar, was saying in the keen cold breeze which stung their faces: 'How infuriating, forgetting the Parma ham! Still, that's that. At least we've decided once and for all on a philosophy for life. As you say, it's not worth making any effort, or chasing anxiously after anything whatsoever . . .'

Ega, at his side, added, a little breathless, striding along on his lean legs. 'Not for love, nor glory, nor money, nor power . . .'

The red light of the tram, shining in the dark, stopped some way behind. And once more Carlos and João da Ega felt a hope and would make an effort.

'We'll make it!'

'We'll make it!'

The red lantern began to move. And to catch the tram the two friends had to run desperately down the hill and along the Aterro under the light of the rising moon.

83
85